Witch World:
Swords & Spells

Other Books by Andre Norton

The *Witch World* Series

WITCH WORLD
WEB OF THE WITCH WORLD
YEAR OF THE UNICORN
THREE AGAINST THE WITCH WORLD
WARLOCK OF THE WITCH WORLD
SORCERESS OF THE WITCH WORLD
SPELL OF THE WITCH WORLD
THE CRYSTAL GRYPHON
THE JARGOON PARD
ZARSTHOR'S BANE
LORE OF THE WITCH WORLD
GRYPHON IN GLORY
HORN CROWN
GRYPHON'S EYRIE (with A. C. Crispin)
WITCH WORLD: THE TURNING: STORMS OF VICTORY (with P. M. Griffin)
WITCH WORLD: THE TURNING: FLIGHT OF VENGEANCE (with P. M. Griffin)

The *Solar Queen* Series

SARGASSO OF SPACE
PLAGUE SHIP
VOODOO PLANET
STAR HUNTER
POSTMARKED THE STARS

The *Forerunner* Series

STORM OVER WARLOCK
ORDEAL IN OTHERWHERE
FORERUNNER FORAY
FORERUNNER
FORERUNNER: THE SECOND VENTURE

The *Ross Murdock* Series

THE TIME TRADERS
GALACTIC DERELICT
THE DEFIANT AGENTS
KEY OUT OF TIME

Other Titles

THE CROSSROADS OF TIME
DRAGON MAGIC
EXILES OF THE STARS
HIGH SORCERY
ICE CROWN
IRON CAGE
MOON OF THREE RINGS
RED HART MAGIC
STAR BORN
VOORLOPER

Witch World: Swords & Spells

Trey of Swords
'Ware Hawk
The Gate of the Cat

ANDRE NORTON

FANTASY

Witch World:
Swords & Spells

Contents

TREY OF SWORDS

Contents

I
Sword of Ice

1

My mother was of the Old Race, those hunted out of Karsten when Duke Yivan put to the Outlaws' Horn all of a blood far more ancient than his, upstart mercenary that he was, dabbler in forbidden things, one who companied with the unspeakable Kolders.

Of a heritage older than Karsten's naming, all my mother brought into Estcarp when she fled death was herself and a tail of three fighting men from her father's lordship. Those she sent to join the Borderers who served under the Outworlder Lord Simon Tregarth, to hold back the evil which had come upon our world. She herself took refuge with a distant kinswoman, the Lady Chriswitha. And later she wed, not with a man of her own people, but with a Sulcarman, thus divorcing herself abruptly from her kind.

But he was slain in one of the forays against the southern ports. And, since she felt no home-love among his people, she returned to her own kin, bearing in her body a child conceived during her short wed-time. Also within her the need for life dimmed, so that when I was born ahead of the proper day, she went out from this life as goes a candle blown by an impatient breath.

The Lady Chriswitha took me, even keeping me though she had married another lord fled from the south, Hervon. His family had vanished during the horning, but he was a man of war learning and wrought well along the Border, rising to his own command. And he had two daughters and a son, Imhar. This Imhar was my senior in age by two years; a strong, healthy boy who took readily to the uncertain world of alarms and war in which we were bred.

With me it was not so. From my birthing I was a weakling and needed much care, given to many small illnesses so that I was ever a concern and a source of impatience to all but my lady, this impatience being made plain to me as soon as I was old enough to be aware of those about me. Though I strove to match Imhar, there was never any chance during our boyhood that I might. A sword fitted into his hand as if he were born carrying that blade, and he used it as if it were an extension of himself, with a skill precise and beautiful to watch.

He rode fearlessly, and was out on patrol before he could count barely the years of his youthful training. And Lord Hervon took pride rightfully in his heir, a youth who had all the attributes necessary to make his way in perilous times.

I trained with sword and with dart gun—the weight of the war ax was ever too much for my arm. Among the dark Old Race, I was a stranger in more than my lack of physical strength, for I had the fair skin, the light hair of the Sulcars—but unfortunately, neither the height nor the fine strong body of that people.

Though I tried so hard to match Imhar, in my heart I longed for something else. Not the sea of my father's people, which might have been natural enough, but rather learning—the forgotten learning which had once been a part of our past.

It is true that no male could possess the Power, or so the Wise Women, those Witches who ruled in Estcarp, proclaimed. But there were old legends, fragments of which I heard from time to time and treasured in my memory, that this was not always so. That once men had also walked that road, and to some purpose.

I could read well enough, and I hunted out all I could that pertained to this age-dimmed past. Though I never spoke of such to those about me— for they would have deemed me stricken in wits, perhaps even a danger to the household should the Witches learn of my heresy.

In the year I belted on my own sword and took to riding with the Border Guard, Karsten loosed against us the greatest threat of all. The Kolders were gone, Lord Simon and his lady having ventured overseas and closed the World Gate through which that horror had come. Yivan, lord in the south, had been a part of the Kolder menace and had died of it. Then, for some time, there had been chaos across all of Karsten, as lord fought against lord for the leadership.

At last Ragan of Cleen triumphed. And, to unite his people, proclaimed a crusade against the Witches. For it is always in such straits a shrewd move to find an enemy outside the borders against which all may march, taking their minds away from wounds and losses nearer home.

So there came a great hosting, but not of our swords, rather of the Power. For the Witches united for a single night and day, summoning such strength as they could call. And then they aimed this southward and the land itself obeyed their commands. Mountains moved, the very earth twisted and rent this way and that. Accordingly they themselves paid a great price, for many of their number perished, being used to channel that Power until it burned out their lives.

Lest chaos fall upon us as it had on Karsten when Yivan was slain, Koris of Gorm took command in the land and the rule passed then from the Council to him.

Lord Simon and the Lady Jaelithe had been lost long since in a quest to the northern seas, and there was no other war leader great enough to command the respect and loyalty of Estcarp.

But there came a strange tale, passing from manor to holding, holding to manor, that the children of the House of Tregarth had fled the land under the great anger of the Witches and that they were now outlawed, to be given no aid by any, lest those be condemned also into the state where all men's hands were lawfully raised to pull them down.

It was whispered that the known "Power" which Lord Simon had had and used was in his sons also. And that they had conspired, against all rightful custom, to aid their sister out of the House of the Witches where she trained. There was a very strange thing about them, unknown elsewhere in the world; the three had been born at one birthing! Thus, they were very close.

I speak of these three because they caused the changing of my life, and the lives of all who dwelt in Lord Hervon's household. And I, myself, was eager to hear all I could of the young lords who, as their father before them, differed from our kind.

Karsten being no longer to be feared, Lord Hervon had set about realizing his own dream for the future. During his riding up and down the land in his hosting, he had found a place which seemed to him a fair setting for a manor. And none would gainsay his claim as it lay well to the east, in a section of the country which had long been forsaken and half forgotten.

Thus, we set out for this place to build anew in a peace which still seemed strange and which we still doubted, so men went armed and we kept sentries about. There were fifty of us, mainly men—though the Lady Chriswitha had five women in her household and she had also her daughters, her sisters, and their husbands, as well as a child born two years after me to her younger sister, who died thereafter.

Now I must speak of Crytha—yet that is difficult. For from the time I looked down into her cradle on the hearth-side, there was something which tied me to her, in spite of all reason. No kin-tie lay between us, nor could any. For by the ancient custom of our people, she must wed Imhar when the time was right, thus unifying the lordship Hervon was determined to found.

She was truly of the Old Race, dark and slender. And to my eyes, there was always something a little remote about her, as if she sometimes said, or heard, that which was not shared by those about her.

Because of my weakly boyhood, I was closer in companionship with Crytha than Imhar, and she began to turn to me in little things, asking that I aid her in nursing a wing-broken bird and the like. For it was apparent from her earliest years that she had a gift of healcraft.

That her talents went farther than that I learned when I was near the age to ride with the Borderers (having gained strength to the point that I could call myself a fighter, if not an outstanding one). I had come upon her unawares by the brook which ran near the farm-garth which, at that time, the Lady Chriswitha called home.

Crytha sat very still in the grass, which there grew nearly as high as the top of her head. Her eyes were closed as if she slept, but she moved her hands gently back and forth. I watched her, puzzled, and then saw, with sick horror rising in me, there coiled in the grass a snake perhaps as long as my sword arm. Its head was raised and swayed, following the command of Crytha's hand. I would have drawn steel and slain the thing, but I found I could not move.

At length she clapped her hands and opened her eyes. The snake dropped its head to the ground, disappearing into the grass as if it had been a hallucination.

"No fear, Yonan." She did not turn her head to look at me, yet she knew that I was there. And as she spoke, that compulsion on me vanished, as had the snake. I took two strides to her side, my anger rising to match the fear that had held me.

"What do you do?" I demanded.

She looked up at me. "Come sit." She beckoned. "Should I explain myself to a mountain whose eyes I cannot meet without a crick in my poor neck?"

I gingerly surveyed the grass, longing to rake through it with my sword that I might not drop upon her late companion—with dire results for both of us. And then I settled down.

"It is a part of healcraft—I think." But her voice sounded a little puzzled. "They do not fear me, the winged ones, the furred ones, and today I have proved that even the scaled ones can be reached. I think we close our minds too often, or fasten them on such as this"—she leaned forward a little to touch a single finger tip to my sheathed sword—"so that we cannot hear much of what lies about us—the good of the wide world."

I drew a deep breath, the anger seeping from me. For some inner sense told me that Crytha knew what she was doing, even as I knew the swing of steel.

"Yonan, remember the old tales you used to tell me?"

For it was with Crytha alone that I had shared my scraps of legend and ancient song.

"In that world, man had Powers—"

"There are Powers in Estcarp," I pointed out. And then a new fear rose in me. The Witches were avid recruits to their number. So far they had not drawn upon the refugees from Karsten, unless some girl child showed unusual skills. Crytha—Crytha must not vanish behind their gray walls, lay aside all that life made good in return for power.

"I am no Witch," she said softly. "And, Yonan, with you alone I share what I know. Because you understand that freedom is more than Power. Of that one can become too fond."

I caught her wrist in a firm grip and held it, also drawing her gaze squarely to meet my own eyes.

"Swear not to try that again—not with any scaled one!"

She smiled. "I do not swear any oaths, Yonan; that is not my way. This much I shall promise you, that I will take no risks."

With that I had to be content, though I was seldom content in my mind when I thought of what she might be tempted to do. And we did not speak of this again. For shortly after, I joined the Borderers and we saw each other very seldom indeed.

But when we went to the east and set up the new Manor hall, it was different. Crytha was of hand-fasting age. It would not be long until Imhar could claim her. And the thought of that was a dark draft of sorrow for me. So I tried not to be in her company, for already I knew my own emotions, which must be rigidly schooled and locked away.

It was before we had the hall complete that the stranger came.

He walked in from the hills, one of our sentries at his back, and he gave to Lord Hervon the proper guesting greeting. Yet there was about him a strangeness we all felt.

Young he was, and plainly of the Old Race. Yet his eyes were dark blue, not gray. And he held himself proudly as one who had the right to greet named warriors on an equal ground.

He said he was a man under a geas. But later he revealed that he was an outlaw—one of the Tregarth sons—and that he came recruiting into the lowlands from the long-lost land to the east—Escore—from which, he said, our race had sprung in the very early beginnings.

Lord Hervon saw danger in him, and to this point of view he was urged by Godgar, his marshal. So it was judged he be delivered up to the Council's guard, lest we be deemed outlaws in turn.

But after he rode away with Godgar, there grew unrest and uneasiness among us. I dreamed and so did others, for they spoke aloud of those dreams. And we went no more to cut wood for the building, but paced restlessly about, looking toward the mountains which rose eastward. In us there was a pulling, a need. . . .

Then Godgar returned with his men and he told a story hardly to be believed, yet we knew in this haunted land many strange things came to pass. There had been a vast company of birds and beasts which had gathered, stopping their journey to the west. And, guarded by those furred and feathered ones, Kyllan Tregarth had started back to the mountains. But that company had let Godgar and his men also return to us unharmed.

It was then that the Lady Chriswitha arose and spoke to all our company.

"It is laid upon us to believe this message. Can anyone beneath this hall roof deny that in him or her now there does lie the desire to ride? I spoke apart with Kyllan Tregarth—in him there was truth. I think we are summoned to his journey and it is one we cannot gainsay."

As she so put it into words, my uneasiness was gone; rather there arose in me an eagerness to be on the way, as if before me lay some great and splendid adventure. And glancing about I saw signs on the faces of the others that in this we were agreed.

Thus, gathering what gear we should need for such a journey, not knowing into what we rode, we went forth from the Manor we had thought to make our home, heading into a wilderness in which might lurk worse danger than ever came out of Karsten or Kolder.

2

Thus, we came into Escore, a land long ago wracked by the magic of those adepts who had believed themselves above the laws of man and nature. In an uneasy peace, it had lain for generations keeping a trembling balance between the forces of Light and those of the Dark. The adepts were gone—some had perished in wild quarrels with their fellows which had left the land blasted and shadowed. Others had wrought gates into other times and worlds and, possessed by curiosity—or greed for power—had departed through those.

Behind, the vanished Great Ones had left a residue of all their trafficking in forbidden things. They had created, by mutation, life forms different from humankind. Some of these were close enough to man to allow kinship of a sort. Others were of the Dark and harried the country at their will.

Before the Old Race had claimed such power, there had been another people in the land; not human, but appearing so. These had a deeper tie with the earth itself than any man could have, for they did not strive to rend or alter it as is the custom of my kind; rather did they live with it, yielding to the rhythms of the seasons, the life which the soil nourished and sustained.

These were the People of Green Silences. When the doom wrought by the adepts came upon the land, they withdrew to a waste yet farther east, taking with them or drawing to them certain of the creatures which the adepts had bred. And there they dwelt, holding well aloof from all others.

But there were remnants of the Old Race who were not seekers after forbidden knowledge. And those had journeyed westward, preyed upon by things of the Shadow, until they reached Estcarp and Karsten. There, even as the Witches had done to defeat Ragan, those among them possessing the Power had wrought a mighty earthshaking, walling out their ancient homeland. So strong was the geas they then laid upon men that we could not even think of the east—it dropped from our memories. Until the lords of the House of Tregarth and their sister, being of half blood and so immune to this veiling, dared return.

Our journey was not an easy one. The land itself put many barriers in our way. And also, though we were met by those Kyllan had aroused to wish us well, we were dogged by creatures of the Dark, so that we won to the Green Valley as pursued as we had been in the flight from Karsten a generation earlier.

But the Valley was a haven of safety—having at its entrance special deep-set runes and signs carved. And none that were not free of any dealing with the Shadow could pass those and live.

The houses of the Green People were strange and yet very pleasing to the eye, for they were not wrought by man from wood and stone, but rather grown, tree and bushes twined together to form walls as deep as those of any Border keep. And their roofing was of the brilliant green feathers shed in season by those birds which obeyed the Lady Dahaun.

She was of our most ancient legend—the forest woman who could call upon a plant to flower or fruit, and it would straightaway do as she desired. Yet, as all her people, she was alien. For she was never the same in men's eyes, changing ever from one moment to the next. So that she might at one breath have the ruddy, sun-tipped hair of a Sulcarwoman, and the next the black locks and ivory skin of the Old Race.

Her co-ruler here was Ethutur, and all which remained steady about him also were the small ivory horns which arose from the curls of hair above his forehead. Yet his shifts of feature and color were not as startling as those of Dahuan.

Under Lord Hervon's orders, we pitched tents in the Valley for our own abode. For, though it might be chill and coming into winter without the rock walls of this stronghold, within lay the mellowness of late summer.

It would seem that here legends came to life, for we saw flying, pacing, sporting, strange creatures which had long been thought by us to be out of imagination—wrought by ancient songsmiths. There were the Flannan—very small, yet formed enough like men to seem some far-off kinsman. They were winged and sometimes danced in the air for seeming sheer delight that they lived. And there were also the Renthan—large as horses, but far different, for they had tails like brushes of fluff clapped tight to their haunches; on their foreheads, single horns curved in gleaming red arcs.

These had borne us from the mountains, but they were not in any way ruled by their riders, being proudly intelligent and allies, not servants, for the Valley.

There were also the Lizard people—and of those I learned much. For I made my first friend among their number. That came about because of my own private heartache.

Crytha had come into paradise, or so she thought. She blossomed from a thin, quiet half-child, half-maid into a person strange to me. And she ever followed Dahaun, eager to learn what the lady would teach.

Imhar was constantly at the councils of the warriors, not always on the fringe as was fitting for one of his youth. He lapped up all the knowledge of war as a house mog-cat will lap at fresh milk.

For we had come into a Valley which was peace, but which was only a small cupping of that. Around us Escore boiled and seethed. Ethutur himself rode out as war herald with the Lord Kemoc Tregarth to visit the Krogan, who were water dwellers. And other heralds went forth to arouse what help would come at the rising of the banner.

There was a shaping of arms at the forge, a testing of mail, and all that stir which had been so long our portion in Estcarp. Save that now we were pitted not against men but against an unholy life totally alien to ours.

Fight I would when the time came, but in me there was a feeling of loneliness. For in all company, I had not one I could call rightly shield brother or cup mate. And Crytha was seldom in sight.

It was the day of the storm which began the true tale of Yonan, as if up to that time I had been a thing only half finished, rough-hewn, and only partly useful.

I had gone with a detachment of Lord Hervon's swordsmen, with one of the Green People as a guide, climbing up into the rocky walls which were our defense, that we might look out beyond and see what lay there, also select for the future those places from which we could best meet any attack. It had been a bright day when we began that climb, but now there were gathering clouds, and Yagath, who was our leader, eyed those with concern, saying we must return before the worst of the wind broke upon us.

The clouds (or were they of the Shadow and no true work of nature?) rolled in so fast that we hurried indeed. But it chanced I was the last in line, and, as the wind came down upon us with a roar to drown any other sound, my foot slipped. Before I could regain my balance, I slid forward, my nails breaking, my finger tips scraped raw by rock I fought to hold.

Now the dark and the wind dropped a curtain to cut me away from everything but the rock pocket into which the force of my descent had jammed my body. My mail had not served to save me from painful bruising; perhaps it had but added to that. And water poured down upon me, as if someone on the surface of the cliff above emptied one pail after another into my cramped resting place.

I pushed with all my strength and so got farther back into this temporary prison, where a rock poised above took some of the wind and rain off me. Later, I thought, I could climb, but dared not try it yet in that rush which was becoming a stream cascading down the wall to my right.

There were fierce slashes of lightning across the small portion of the sky which I could see, reminding me of the most effective weapons of the Green People—their force whips. Then came a fearful and deafening crash close by, a queer smell which made me think that lightning had indeed struck, and not too far away.

The rush of water carried with it small stones, and it did not drain fast from the crevice I occupied, though that had an open end facing outward from the Valley. So the flood lapped about my knees, and then touched my thighs. I squirmed, trying to reach a higher portion in which to crouch, but there was none.

While the drumming of the rain, the heavy boom of thunder never ended.

I was aware now, as I turned and strove to find a better shelter, that my right ankle gave out sharp thrusts of pain, enough once or twice to make me giddy. So I subsided at last, imprisoned until the storm might pass.

It was during one of those vivid flashes of lightning that I first saw an answering glint of light from the wall to my right. For a moment or two, that meant nothing, save there must be something there which reflected the flashes. Then I wriggled a little, to free my shoulder better, so I might feel along the wall.

My abraded finger tips flinched from the rough stone, then they slid onto something smooth; not only smooth, but in a way oddly cool and pleasant. In the dark, I explored my find. It seemed to be a rod of some sort, extending outward perhaps the length of my thumb and only a little larger than that digit in size. I tried to pull at it, and it seemed that it was a little loose but did not yield to the small amount of strength I could exert in my cramped position.

Yet there was something about my unseen find which kept my fingers seeking it out, touching it. That it was part of the natural rock, I doubted. It was too smooth, more like a piece of metal or crystal which had been purposefully worked. Yet the way it protruded from the native rock, with no break in that to hold it (as I was able to discover by touch), argued it could not be man-made.

The fury of the storm continued. From my constrained perch I looked out at the world beyond the valley, but the darkness kept me from seeing anything. Save here and there some glow close to ground, marking, I was sure from all I had heard, a place where a remnant of the Power force still burned. For these we had seen in our journey from the mountains, such being called to our attention. If the glow was blue that signified a point of safety where a man might shelter. But a sickly dull white, or a green, or worst of all a red shot with black—those signaled traps for our kind.

The storm cleared after what seemed to me a very long time. Now the water drained from the crevice. And the lightning no longer was laid whipwise over the hills. I edged forward from under the rock ledge which had been my shelter and tried to straighten up. My wet limbs, my wracked ankle, made such movement painful. I could feel rough outcrops to climb, but could I put enough weight on my ankle to try that?

Then I froze. There was a sound, not of rain nor thunder—more like a skittering across the rock above me. Could one of the Dark creatures have found its way up during the cover of the flood, was it now waiting to attack me?

There came a light, a glow. By it I saw the pointed, tooth-rimmed snout of one of the Lizard folk. And then his forefeet, so much like slender, fingered hands, came into view. The light descended slowly toward me so I saw that it issued from a stone held in a mesh of delicate wire fastened on a slender cord.

The Lizard folk, like the other nonhumans, communicated by thought. But I had none of the mind touch which Crytha had so nurtured. I reached my hand and caught the caged stone. By that I could see my ankle. The boot was very tight and the leg above it swollen. I had given it a bad twist and it was plain I dare not put any weight on that.

With gestures, I tried to make my dilemma plain to my rescuer. He stared at me with jewel-bright eyes, then in a breath he was gone. For help, I hoped. Though I now began to dread that, too. My ineptness had long been a matter of rough badinage among Hervon's men. Here, on my first wall patrol, I had managed to make the worst possible showing.

With the Lizard gone, curiosity led me to duck back under the ledge and survey what I had found in the wall. When I advanced my dull light, there awoke a brilliant fire which was dazzling.

The thing was a rod right enough, fashioned of some kind of crystal which drew light. And it glowed with a bluish sheen. Yes, it projected directly out of the rock itself, but there was no mistaking that it was the product of some intelligence. Even though to find it so encased in solid rock was surprising.

I closed my other hand around it and tugged with all my might. The rod gave only a fraction. It was plain that to free it entirely, one must break the rock in which it hung. But that I would do! I must do! As the geas which had been laid on us all to bring us into Escore, I knew now that some force outside my own imagining was driving me to do this. That my find was important—that I would have sworn oath to.

Now I turned quickly—there was a further noise overhead and the Lizard man came clambering down the wall with ease. To him, this stone was an open stairway. He carried a rope coiled about one shoulder, and when he reached the bottom he made signs that I was to tie one end about me.

Thus, I found in the storm both my destiny in this long-shadowed land, and a friend—for Tsali was indeed a friend such as one could trust his life and more than his life upon.

3

So I was pent in the Valley for a time. But the Lady Dahaun had shared her knowledge with Crytha, who brought to me a basin of bubbling red mud. This she used to make a casing for my ankle once my boot was cut away. And as its heat enclosed my flesh, the pain faded and I slept.

My dreams had never been real, nor of the kind one might name true sendings of the Power—such as favored ones of our Race have from time to time had as warnings. But this time I strode through a land which was as real as if I were waking. And in my hand I carried a sword—one fitted into my palm as firmly as if it were an extension of my own body, so that in my dream I could not imagine my life without that to hand.

Yet there was on me a great sorrow and fear, not for myself but for others. And as I went, I wept silently for a loss I could not remember and yet which was very great, weighing upon me heavier than any scout's pack. I saw that the mail I wore was broken in places and rusted by stains. While my left hand was pressed against my side, the fingers bloodied. Pain gnawed under that pressure, a pain I fought against. For there was that my body must aid me to do before I yielded to death.

Immutably death drove me; I knew that for the truth. All behind me was lost to the Shadow, save what I carried. In my dreaming mind, I knew that this sword must not fall to those who now sniffed my trail.

But I wavered, the burden of pain nigh bearing me to the ground. While that which lay before me shimmered in my sight. Time raced for me, with it my life, oozing in sluggish drops from my side. Yet my will did not yield to either time or my failing body.

The ground under my stumbling feet rose steadily, so that for all my determination, my pace slowed. Still I kept onward. Now there arose a mist before me. My lips shaped words I could not understand. Yet I knew that once I had known such and they had been to me weapons near as potent as the sword.

Perhaps it was the Power of the words which carried me past the limit of human endurance. My breath came in gasps; I could no longer master the pain eating at me, but my will still held.

I faltered at last to a halt, teetering on the lip of a drop. The mists rose from below, and I knew, in a part of my fast-dulling mind, that these were born out of what lay below—raw rock churned and set to a boil as if it were water, molten. Into this I hurled the sword. With it went out of me that strength which had kept me on my feet, brought me from the stricken field where the Shadow had triumphed.

As I crumpled to earth, knowing that now I could meet death, and did it willingly enough, I awoke. I was sweating and my hand was fast pressed to my side. I looked down, expecting still to see the blood dripping down the shattered mail. But instead my skin was smooth, unbroken. And I knew it had been a dream.

I had not been Yonan then—no. Nor could I have put name to the man I had been in that time. But I carried with me from that dream of death one thought—that which I had found embedded in the rock on the heights was of the sword. To my hand had it once well fitted; so would it again.

However there was also in me a need to keep this secret; the reason for that I did not know. I endured Imhar's jeering at my ineptness. But, when Crytha came to inspect the casing on my ankle, I asked her concerning the Lizard man who had found me.

It was she who told me his name—Tsali—and that he was one of the scouts of the heights. I envied her her gift of communication with those other life forms and asked her to give him my thanks. But I was surprised when later that day he padded into the small shelter where I lay and squatted down beside me, watching me with his jewel-like eyes.

He stood perhaps near my shoulder in height, being large for his species. And as he squatted now on hind limbs, limber tail outthrust as a balance behind, he slipped from one wrist a cord on which white and red earth-colored beads were interstrung, counting these through his slender fingers as if he gathered something from the touch alone. I had seen his people do this before and heard some remark about it among our men— that so the Lizard folk apparently kept records among themselves.

I stared at his crested head and longed to speak—though I knew that the words I would mouth, even in the old tongue, would have no meaning. Only those of the Green People could speak mind to mind with all who shared the Light with them, against the Shadow.

Suddenly, Tsali wrapped his beads once more about his wrist and, from a pouch at the belt (which was the only thing he wore over his rainbow scaled body), he brought a piece of thin, smoothed stone about the size of my flattened palm. On this were carved lines of runes, the first interfilled with flakes of gold so that they were clearly visible, the second row with red, the last with ominous black.

I had seen such before. These were for foretelling and were used by Wise Women who had not enough of the Power to become full Witches. Yet, as Tsali held this up before my eyes, I believed that these runes were different in part.

With the plaque still in one hand, the Lizard man reached out his other to catch at my right wrist before I knew what he would do. Holding my hand with his, he raised it until my fingers slipped over the smoothness of the stone, felt the twists and turns of the deeply graven markings. Oddly enough, the stone was not cold as I thought it would be; rather warm, as if it had rested near a fire for a space.

Under my flesh the symbols brightened and grew more distinct. First, the gold, then the red, and at length, the black. Yet my flesh shrank from the last of those rows, for I well knew, even little learned in the Power that I was, that these last were signs of ill omen and despair.

Tsali had watched as the runes came to life and faded in turn, and there was about his scaled body growing tension. For it seemed that if I could not read what I brought to brighter sparking there, he could. When at length I had pointed out the last of those symbols he took the plaque and once more stowed it away. Yet he did not leave me.

Rather he leaned forward, his eyes focused on me in such a steady stare as compelled a like answer from me. Slowly, very slowly there came a faint stirring in my mind. At first that started me into flinching away from him, my astonishment so great that I could not believe that this was more than my imagination.

It was not clear mind speech between us, I was too lacking in skill to handle such as that. Rather, I could sense only a query of sorts. And that had to do with something from the far past—

But there was nothing in my past which was of note, which would send Tsali so delving into my mind. I was, perhaps, the least of the House of Hervon, and not even of the full blood of the Old Race. Or—what was I?

For one giddy moment, I seemed to whirl back into that dream when I walked to my death in order to preserve something (or destroy it); something greater than myself, yet which had been mine. And I found that even waking I remembered now in detail that climb to the lip of the cup, the loss of the sword which had been so wholly a part of me.

But that was only a dream—not of the here and now. I was not that stranger, death-stricken from an unknown battle. I was Yonan, the half-blood, the weakling—

I was—both!

How I knew this now—that I could not explain. I had heard of beliefs held by some Outlanders that, though an adept can live many lifetimes in length during his space allowed in this world, other and lesser men return, to be born again, if some task they have been set is ill done, so that they may once more choose and act. It is hoped this time for the better.

Was the inner me such a one? Had the dream been not fantasy but a far-off truth? Who could prove it yes or no? Only my dying walk was as real to me now as if I had indeed been a part of it—yesterday—or last night when I had thought I wandered in a dream.

Now I knew that I must prove that to myself. For that proof there was only one action—I must return to the cliff top, seek out that which was prisoned in the stone, and bring it forth. If I saw it, if I held it once more in my hand, then—then perhaps that knowledge that it had been mine, was meant to be mine, would come again.

There sounded a hissing from Tsali. Slight as it was, it broke my concentration. He was still watching me, but not with that compelling intensity. Now he nodded, his crest head moving gravely up and down. And I knew that, if I could not read his thought, save in the faintest degree, mine had been far more clear to him.

I spoke, though I did not know if his alien ears could pick up and sort out the sounds I made into an intelligible pattern.

"I must go back—"

It would seem that he understood. For once more he nodded solemnly. And that nod had something of a promise in it, as if he intended that I must do just what I desired.

Now I was impatient for the healing of my ankle and pestered Crytha to be loose from the heavy cast of mud. Until she at last broke that and freed me. I could feel no pain, there was no swelling, no mark. And when I got to my feet, I felt nothing save what was normal.

But time to do what I wished, that was a different thing. I could not walk away from the drilling, the constant honing of our small force into a weapon for defense. Oddly enough, I had in me the strong belief that I must not share with any—save Tsali—the story of my find. So that it was after three full days of frustration and impatience that I slipped away at dawn, to once more climb the cliffs. But before I reached the first handholds, the Lizard warrior appeared out of nowhere, flashing past me up the rough stone with an agility no man possessed.

It was good that Tsali had joined me. For once aloft, I could pick out no landmark; I did not know in which direction to begin my search for the crevice into which I had so unexpectedly fallen. But it was plain Tsali did, for looking up to me and then bearing right, he made clear that he could guide me.

In the day, with no storm clouds about, the rugged heights of the Valley were very visible. There were many crevices in these peaks and they looked much alike. However, Tsali had come to a halt by one, and with a full swing of his arm, beckoned me on.

I got to my knees, peered down into the gash in the rock. From here I could see nothing. My find must lie farther back, under the half-shadow of the roof rock. To my belt I had fastened a small hammer which I had selected secretly from among the smith's tools, with it a sharp-bladed chisel. Though both were metal, I did not know how they would cut this rock.

With care I crawled down into the cut, Tsali lying belly down now on the lip of the crevice watching me with steadfast eyes. I might have missed what I sought, for it was near the color of the rock which held it. But the fact that it protruded was my aid.

Though the rod had the feel of crystal, it was opaque, gray—like any jutting knob about. How then had the lightning revealed it with a glimmer? I fitted my finger to it. Yes, it moved, but a very little. I could see, peering close, that there was a line separating it a little from the rock which enclosed it.

Delicately as I could, for I feared to break it, I began to work with chisel and hammer, tapping slowly, with care. Parts of the rock dropped away in very small and hard-won chips.

But I schooled my patience and worked with a care I have never used in any act before. It was needful that I do this—that filled my mind, possessed me fully. I was not aware of the sun which blazed down, to make the crevice a caldron of glowing heat so that I doffed first mail shirt, then underjerkin of padded leather, and worked with my skin reddening in the force of that beam.

My hands began to shake and I leaned back against the wall of the crevice, suddenly afraid that, with some off-center blow, I might shatter what I sought. There was a hissing from above. I looked up and Tsali held down to me a bottle fashioned of the tough valley gourds.

Working out the stopper, I drank thankfully. My shoulders ached—but when I looked at the stone where I worked, my spirit was as renewed as my throat from that drink. It was indeed a sword hilt I had so painfully uncovered. I had it free now down to the cross hilt. But it would take hours more to manage the blade—if I ever could. How had any metal lasted through the heat generated by the molten rock into which my dream self had hurled this?

I put out my hand, curved my fingers, and grasped the hilt. That which I had felt in the dream once more flooded into me. This was *mine!* Never before had I felt so strong an impression of ownership, as if some object had been fashioned only for my own handling, to be held jealously from all others.

My grasp tightened. Without being truly aware of what I did, I pulled the hilt toward me. There was a moment of resistance, and then it came loose with such a snap that I overbalanced and fell back against the other wall of the crevice.

But—what I held was only the hilt. No blade projected, strong and keen-edged, beyond it!

My disappointment was so vast that for a second or two I could have wailed as might any child. It was mine—but what it had been was gone, lost in time and boiling rock, even as I had feared.

Still, I could not toss it from me. My fingers curled and held as if now their will was apart from mine, or else they were commanded by a part of me I did not know nor understand.

I held my find farther into the sun. Perhaps one of the valleysmiths could reset it to a blade. It was not a treasure in itself that I could see. In color, the crystal of the pommel was gray, yet in the sun I caught a faint rippling of inner light. It had been worked with a carving like a scrawl of runes, perhaps to keep it from turning in the hand. However, those were so worn they were now but a pitted pattern of unreadable lines. The crossbar was of the same crystal-like material. Yet I was sure this was no crystal nor quartz of which I had knowledge.

I sighed. When I shrugged on my jerkin again, I stowed my find against my skin. A useless thing—still—there was something—

Was it a scrap of before memory which stirred deep, deep in my mind? I could not catch it. I only knew that what I held had once been as needful as life to me and that it had come once more into my hand for a purpose.

4

In the days which followed I was tempted often to take the hilt to the smith and see if it could be fitted to any blade he had worked. Yet each time that thought came to me, I found that I could not do this. No, there had been only one blade which would fit. And time had taken that. So my find must remain useless.

But I discovered that when I slept, for some reason, I brought the hilt out (always in the dark and in secret) to hold in my hand. Did I wish to use it as a key to unlock the past? Perhaps. Though another part of me did not desire that either. Still I kept it ever with me.

Perhaps it carried with it some good fortune for a warrior. Or else growing older, and living under the sky of the Green Valley and its healing, brought about a slow change in me. I became more apt as a swordsman— once even disarming Imhar in practice. And that not by chance, for it was ever his way to make me seem awkward and without skill.

Sometimes I believed that had my secret been whole I could have confronted any man in our company and not come out the worse, battle-trained veterans as most of them were.

We of Hervon's House were not the only people to be drawn over-mountain into Escore. Others followed in time. Then we, with the Green People, went forth (for the Lady Dahaun had always knowledge, carried by her messenger birds, of those winning across the mountains.)

This land was awake, and evil paced it, save those few places guarded by remnants of the Power. Thus were we ever on guard when we ventured on an assay. It was during one such, at night, though our people encamped by a place of Light, that the Thas attacked us.

These live underground, seldom seeking the upper world, then only at night or on days well clouded. Though they had not first been reckoned among the followers of the Shadow, in these hours they listened to the call of the Dark Ones, thus becoming our enemies. During the night attack they were defeated only by an outgush of water which was brought about by Lord Kemoc and Godgar of our own troop. However, Lord Kemoc was grievously wounded and, on our riding, he was swept from us in a flood of the same water which had earlier saved us.

His loss was counted a sore one. For, though a man, he has studied the ancient records at Lormt. And it was a fact that he had called forth a summons and had been *answered* by one of the Great Old Ones, even though those had all been deemed gone from Escore. His sister, the Witch Kaththea, withdrew to a place of mysteries, striving there to find some answer as to whether he lived or died. For she believed that he had not departed on the Last Road as yet.

Thus, Crytha became a closer companion to the Lady Dahaun, though she was not trained in witchcraft as had been the Lady Kaththea. So I saw even less of her. This was not a season for wedding, at least that thought heartened me. For Inhar could not claim her at a time when war raged around us.

Twice we had driven off attacks of the Dark Ones. Monstrous forms had circled the valley walls, striven to climb and bring death to all. Those Gray Ones, who are neither man nor wolf, but the worst part of both, came to harry us; other, even more alien things with them. In the sky above wheeled and battled the great Vorgs who answered the summoning of our hosts. But what sometimes fought with them were such creatures even nightmares could not spawn.

I found that Tsali took to accompanying whatever patrol on the heights I was assigned to. It followed that my companionship without words with the Lizard man became more a part of my life. When we were alone (though such times were few) he often let me know by gestures, in very dim impressions I could pick up from his thoughts, that he wanted to look upon the sword hilt. I would bring it forth (it always felt then a part of me), and he would stare at it intently.

Perhaps, I guessed, he knew more of its history, buried in the rock though it had been, than I did. How I longed to speak mind to mind and ask this. Men have their legends—perhaps the Lizard folk also had their tales from an ancient past. Maybe even one about that dying man who had not been Yonan—

I tried very hard to reach out with my thoughts, but it would seem that the talent was denied me. Yet in otherwise I was changing, as I was sure. And what might have happened had not another fate taken hand in my life I cannot fathom.

It was Crytha who brought the end to one part of my life, the beginning of another. For there came a morning when she was missing from her couch in the Lady Dahaun's hall. And the Lady of Green Silences came to Hervon's cluster of tents with a sober face. She held out her hand, on the palm of which lay an image roughly fashioned from clay. Strands of hair had been embedded in its head, a scrap of scarf Crytha favored wrapped about it in a crude robing.

The Lady Chriswitha, looking upon that thing, grew white. Her hands trembled as she reached forth a finger to touch, and yet did not dare. Then there arose such a wrath as I had never seen in her. She spat out:

"We were told that this was a safe land!"

"So was it," the Lady Dahaun returned. "This abomination was not fashioned here. I do not know how it was put within the bed place of your kin-child. I have learned that she went forth at first dawning, telling my people she would seek a bed of Illbane to be harvested as the dew still lay upon it, making it twice as potent for healings. She appeared as always, under no compulsion; though it seems that in this she was certainly moved by another's will."

The Lady Chriswitha looked about us, as if with the eye she could see Crytha's trail. Her lips came firm together as I have seen them upon occasion, as now her fear was under deep control.

"You can follow?"

"We have followed," the Lady Dahaun replied. "But there is an end to her trail up there." She gestured toward the heights which walled in the valley.

"Why—why Crytha? And from whence came that—?" my foster mother then demanded, "She—she must be found!"

"Why Crytha? Because she is who she is—one of budding Power, as yet untrained—at an age when that Power can be used by—others. From whence it came, it has about it the stench of Thas. They possess certain talents which it now seems they are developing to a degree we have not known. As to the finding, I have tried the scrying—there is a wall against the far sight—"

I thought of the Thas I had seen during our battle with them, when they had attacked and been driven off by the gush of water. They were of the earth, smaller than men, dusky bodies covered with a growth which was tough and rootlike. As if they had indeed grown and not been born. To our eyes they were repulsive—like the legendary demons. And to think of Crytha taken by such!

In that moment I forgot I was liegeman to my lord, that I was a warrior under orders. I moved without thinking to snatch that crude image from the Lady Dahaun.

"Yonan!" The Lady Chriswitha stared at me as if I had suddenly myself taken on the guise of one of those deep earth dwellers. "What would you—?"

But I was no longer the Yonan she had fostered, the weakling who owed life to her care. In that moment, as my fist clenched around the image, I felt deep within me a stir which I had known only in my dream. I was someone else struggling for freedom, someone with more certainty of purpose than Yonan had ever possessed. I think that I was no longer a youth of little promise. Instead, two halves of me came together to make me the stronger in that uniting. I did not even answer the Lady Chriswitha, for there was a need tearing at me which I could not control.

"Where on the heights did they lose the trail?" I turned to the Lady of Green Silences, speaking to her as I would to an equal.

I saw her eyes widen as she gazed back at me. For a moment, she hesitated. As she did, the Lady Chriswitha broke in:

"Yonan—you cannot—"

I whirled about, forgetting all courtesy. "This I will do. Either I bring Crytha back or else I die!"

It was her turn to show an astonishment which overrode even her anger and fear.

"But you—"

I made a gesture of silence as I looked again to the Lady Dahaun.

"Where?" I repeated sharply.

Her eyes searched my face for what seemed to me far too long a time. Then she answered:

"No man can hunt safely through the burrows of the Thas. The earth is theirs; for them, it fights."

"So? I do not believe this, Lady." My left hand lay on my mail-clad breast and I could feel (and I knew I was not dreaming this time) a kind of throb against my body sent forth by the ancient sword hilt.

She bit upon her lower lip. Her right hand arose and in the air she traced some symbol. There was a faint light following that tracing, gone again in an instant. But now Dahaun nodded.

"The risk is yours, warrior. We dare not raid into the Thas' burrows without greater protection than we have now. This act of theirs may be intended not only to gain control of a beginning talent which they hope to warp, but also to drain us of warriors needed for defense."

"One man may go without weakening your defense by much, Lady. With or without your leave will I do this thing."

"It is your choice," she returned gravely. "But this much will I warn you: if the Thas are now governed by one with the Dark Power, there is little a man can do against such. You know nothing of what you may face."

"True. But who knows when he lies down at night what the rising sun will bring tomorrow?" I countered with words which seemed to flow into my mouth by the will of that shadowy other which the touch of the hilt had awakened in me.

There was a hissing, startling us both. Tsali reared up to my left. His bright eyes met mine for a single instant before he looked on to the Lady Dahaun. I knew that between them now passed that communication I could not understand. In my hand, I squeezed tight that ugly thing of clay, hair, and ragged cloth. I knew enough of the way of Power that this dare not be destroyed. For such a destruction might harm the one I would protect. However, it was a tie with her. Just as the sword hilt, now warm against my breast, was a tie with that other, greater self I could only dimly sense as yet.

"Tsali will go with you."

It was my turn to be surprised. Though the Lizard men were of the earth, even as those of the Green Valley, still they are not like the Thas, who hate the sun and are not at ease save in their deep burrows.

"He can be eyes for you, such as no man possesses," Dahaun continued. "And it is his free choice to do this."

Perhaps I should have refused to draw another with me into an unknown governed by the Shadow. But at that moment the part of Yonan which was still uncertain, lacking in confidence, felt a surge of relief at that promise. Alone among the Valley People, Tsali shared my secret. It did not matter that his skin was scaled, mine was smooth; that we could not speak to each other. For he could project, and I could receive, a feeling of rightness about what I must now do.

I shouldered a bag of rations and two water gourds filled to their stopper levels, those stoppers being well pounded in. For arms, I had my sword. I would not take the dart gun, for these had very little ammunition left, and what remained must be for the defense of the Valley. The Lady Dahaun brought me a pouch which I could clip to my belt, holding some of her salves for wounds. But it was with the Lady Chriswitha, Lord Hervon still being absent on a patrol, that I had my final word before I left to face the unknown.

"She is already hand-fasted, Yonan." My foster mother spoke quickly, as if what she had to say made her uneasy and she would have this over.

"That I know."

"If Imhar were here now—"

"He would do as I am doing. But he is not, and I am."

Then she acted as she had not since I was a sickly little lad. She put her hands, one on either side of my face. The throat veil of fine mail which depended from my helm hung loose so that I could feel her touch warm on my cheeks.

"Yonan, Yonan—" She repeated my name as if she must. "What you try—may the Great Flame abide about you, hedge you in. Forgive me my blindness. She is of my own blood, even though there is in her that which is not of my spirit. For she is like the maidens of the other years, having that part in her which we thought had flickered and died, save in Estcarp. There will be always that in her which no other can possess, nor perhaps even understand. She is my kin, however—"

"And hand-fasted to Imhar," I replied grimly. "My honor is not totally lost, even though I am not of pure blood, my Lady. She will come back, or else I will be dead. But after, I shall make no claims on her. This I swear."

There were tears in her eyes now, though she was not one who wept easily. And all she answered then was my name—

"Yonan!" But into that one word she put all she could summon to hearten me.

5

I kept the image, tucking it into my belt and making it fast there with a thrice-knotted loop. For such things, even if they are used in the working of evil, are connected with the victims they are used against. It might be that in this rough thing of clay, rag, and hair I could find a guide.

Near midday we climbed the cliffs, following the path of those who had traced Crytha earlier. Tsali took the lead, as ever, his clawed hands and feet far more apt at this business than mine. But I had caught up to him as he paused by a deep cleft in the rock, one into which the sun, burning brightly as it did, could not far penetrate.

I lay belly down on the rock which lipped this, striving to see what lay down below. But there lay a thickness of shadow there through which only part of the rough walls was visible.

While the closer I put my face to the opening, the more I was aware of an odor, fetid and heavy, after the cool clean air of the valley. This carried the half-rotted scent of wood, fast being reduced to slimy sponge by age and water, and with that, hints of other nastiness.

I checked my pack, my weapon, before I swung over that lip, searching for hand and toe holds. The descent was rough enough to offer those in plenty. As I went that smell grew stronger. Tsali had followed me, but more slowly than usual. He wore a cord about his neck, a pouch of netting in which was a jumble of stones. As we went farther into the shadows of that ominous cutting those took fire, to give off a glow of subdued light.

The descent was a long one, far longer than I had judged, and had speculated. And, for all my care, I made what I thought was far too much noise, my boots scraping on the stone as I forced the toes into holds. Time and again I froze, flattened against the wall, listening. Yet never was there anything, save my own breathing, for Tsali made no sound at all.

However there hung about us a subtle warning of danger, the knowledge that we were indeed intruding into enemy territory. So I strove to alert all my senses, bringing to service all that I had learned of scouting.

At last I reached a level surface. With care, I edged around on that, thinking I had merely found a ledge. But Tsali landed lightly on the same perch to my left, and held out his bag of luminous stones. By that dim light we could see that we were indeed at the bottom of a giant slash. A narrow way led both right and left, but Tsali gestured left.

Judging that he must know more of such burrows than I, that then was our choice. Though this was no smooth road, for we scrambled over loose rocks, squeezed by outjutting of the walls. What had been a crevice became a cave. When I stretched back my head to look aloft there was no longer a ribbon of sky to be seen.

Tsali pounced, using his claws to free something from a sharp rock, then held out to me a pinch of fiberlike stuff. From it arose strongly the noxious odor. I touched his find gingerly. The stuff was coarser than any hair I had ever fingered, more like fine roots. I could understand that this marked the passage of one of the Thas who had so scraped free a small portion of his body covering.

Tsali hissed and hurled the discovery from him, his gesture plainly one of scorn. I had not known before his personal feelings concerning the Thas. But with that gesture he made them plain enough. Again I longed for the power to communicate with him.

The roofing of this way dropped abruptly. Water beaded the walls around us, trickled down the stone, to puddle between the loose stones, making hazards. Luckily soon this changed and we crept along, only moisture-sleeked level rock underfoot.

Tsali's light was very limited. We could scarcely see more than a foot or so beyond us, though he held the pouch well out. Then we had to get down to our hands and knees to crawl. I put off my pack, pushing it before me. Still my shoulders brushed the roof of this passage from time to time.

Save for the smell and that tuft of hair, we came across no further signs that this was a way used by the enemy. Perhaps it had recently been opened or explored, in testing for some underground entrance to the Valley. But any such would fail, since the Green People had long ago set about their stronghold such signs of Power as none of those serving the Shadow might cross.

How long we crawled I do not know, but at length that hole gave way to a cavern, one far beyond our reckoning as to size depending upon the feeble light we had. Rows of stalagmites arose like savage fangs, to be matched by stalactites as sharp above. Tsali squatted, his head turning from side to side.

Even my senses, which were far less than his, caught the thick scent which was lying here. The Lizard man closed both hands over his pouch of light stones, shutting off even that small source of illumination. I knew that he so signaled the need for extreme caution.

I listened—so intently that it would seem all the strength of every sense I had was now channeled into one. And there was sound. Part of it I identified as a steady dripping—perhaps from some steady, but small, fall of water.

However from farther away, much muted, came a rhythmic rise and fall of what was neither distinguishable words nor song, but which, I was sure, was not of the cave, rather of those who used it.

There was a very faint gleam to my left, Tsali had dropped one hand from the net bag. Now I felt his clawed fingers close around my wrist. With that hold he gave me a small, meaningful jerk. He wanted us to advance on out into the great blackness of the unknown.

I heard it said that the Lizard people could see above and below the range of men, able to pierce what might be to us full darkness. It would seem that I must now allow my companion to prove the right of that.

Slinging my pack back into place, I arose, Tsali beside me. Step by cautious step, we ventured on. Our path was not straight, for Tsali zig-zagged, apparently to avoid the rock formations which would make this a giant maze-trap for anyone as nightblind as I. As we went that other sound grew stronger, taking on the rise and fall of a chant. But if those we hunted were within the bounds of vision they had no light to betray them.

Tsali took another sharp turn to the left. Now I could see a glow, faint, greenish, but still a break in the thick dark of the cavern. Against this the formations made misshapen rods like a grill, sometimes thick enough to veil the gleam altogether.

The chanting continued, growing ever louder—but in no tongue I knew. Somehow that sound made the skin on my body prickle with that warning which my species feel when they go up against the Shadow. Tsali crept now, dropping his hold on me, since we had the guide of that distant light. And I strove in turn to move as noiselessly as possible.

The unwholesome radiance flourished as we crouched close together to look into a second and smaller cavern. There hunched Thas, unmistakable in their ugliness. I counted at least a dozen. But rising above their misshapen forms was Crytha.

They had half-encircled her, but their low-slung heads were not turned in her direction as if they watched her. Rather they all faced toward a tall standing pillar which glistened in the light cast by stalks of lumpy growths half of the Thas held before them, as might worshippers hold candles at some shrines.

The pillar had a sleek, smooth surface facing Crytha. Now I could see that her eyes were tightly closed. Yet her face was serene, not as someone forced into action by her enemies, rather as one who moved in a dream.

Dimly I could sight something beneath that surface, as if the pillar held a captive or a treasure. The Thas wore no visible weapons. Slowly and carefully I eased my sword from its scabbard, loosed my pack to set that aside. The odds were very high, but it was Crytha who stood there, whom they had somehow claimed to do their bidding. For that she was now engaged in some sorcery demanded by the Shadow I had no doubt at all. I surveyed the stretch of cave between me and that foul company, wondering if a surprise attack might be the answer. The Thas appeared to feel so safe in this hole of theirs that we had found no sentry. And feeling thus secure would not an attack bewilder them for just long enough?

Such odds were very slim indeed, but I could at that moment see no other action to take.

Crytha raised her hands. Though she did not touch the surface of the pillar before which she stood, she made sweeping motions, first up and down, and then back and forth. While those squatting about her continued to chant in their unknown tongue. I readied myself for a leap which I hoped would take me to the girl's side. If I could then break whatever spell they had laid upon her—

Tsali hissed. Something brushed my shoulder. I whirled. Out of the darkness behind us streamed long cords like misshapen roots. Before I understood our peril, one coiled about my ankles, to give a vicious jerk and throw me to the ground. I raised my sword in a slash meant to free myself from that bond.

The metal struck true enough, only to rebound from a surface on which no cut was visible. Even as I tried to swing again, another of those root cords snapped tight about my wrist in spite of my struggles.

Within a space of a few breaths I was both disarmed and helpless. But Tsali was still on his feet. It appeared that the cords disliked those gleaming stones which provided us with light. They feinted and tried to strike, but the Lizard man's lightning-fast weaving of the pouch kept them at bay. At length he made a leap far to the left and was gone, leaving me a prisoner.

There had been no halt in the chanting behind me. Nor, to my complete surprise, did any Thas now advance out of the dark to make sure of me. Only the cords still tightened on my body until I was totally immobile. Now I could see both ends of those, as if they had not been used as weapons, but were in some way living entities acting on their own. Yet all I saw or felt were like long unbreakable roots.

They also had an evil smell, which arose about me stiflingly. I choked and coughed, my eyes filled with tears as do those caught in acrid smoke. So the Thas had their sentries after all, such as I had never heard of. I hoped that Tsali had escaped. On him alone could I depend for help. Or would I die, smothered by this horrible stench? My head whirled dizzily as I slipped into blackness.

There were no real dreams. Rather somewhere—a long way off—a name was called. It was not a name that I knew, yet it belonged to me. And the call became more insistent.

I stirred; that calling would not be stilled. Now I opened my eyes. There was a smell of rottenness, but not strong enough to choke me senseless as before. To my right showed a faint light. I tried to turn toward that. Something about me resisted and then broke; another puff of foul odor struck into my face like a blow, so I gasped and nearly lapsed once more into unconsciousness.

The light was above me. I swung my head farther. I lay at the foot of a pillar of—ice! The cold issuing from it was biting. But the front of the column was smooth as glass. And within—within that stood a body!

It was man-shaped, man-sized as far as I could judge. Only the face was hidden in a strange way by three diamond-shaped pieces of a gleaming metal fastened together by chains of the same substance. Two covered the eyes, the third masked the mouth, leaving only the nose and a bit of cheek on either side visible.

The head was crowned by an elaborate war helm from which a crest in the form of a jewel-eyed dragon looked down at me. And the body wore mail. While the hands were clasped on the haft of a great double-sided ax.

I levered myself up, more puffs of stench answering every moment. When I gazed down along my own body I saw that black and rotted cords were falling away. Apparently the rootlike sentries of the Thas had not too long lives. Also they had dragged me within their shrine, for I was sure this was the pillar before which they had chanted. Therefore—how soon would they return? Or had they believed me dead and so laid me here as an offering for the pillared one?

Action, not guessing, was what I needed. I pushed back from the freezing chill of the pillar and got stiffly to my feet. Perhaps I could break off part of one of the stony growths in the outer cavern, use that for a weapon. I looked longingly at the ax embedded in the ice. That was of no use to him who now held it, and perhaps far too heavy for me even if I had it to hand, but it was the only arm in sight.

I saw now that the column was not the only ice formed in this chamber. Beyond the pillar, to my right, long icicles, thicker than my wrist, depended from the roof. Some of them had sharp enough points—for weapons? I almost laughed at that idea, certainly that of a crazed man. Those would shatter at a touch—

"Tolar!"

I turned my head. Who had called that name? It was the same as had sounded through the darkness to draw me back to life again. I—I was Yonan! Yet something in me responded.

Hardly knowing what I did, I loosened the lacing of my mail shirt until I could grope beneath it, close my hand about the sword hilt, bring it forth. Here in the darkness—it glowed! The gray-white of the dull crystal came to life as strong inner fires blazed within it.

If I only had a blade!

A blade—!

My eyes went, I did not know why, save as if something so compelled them, to those long icicles which hung from the roof. And to them I went, though I knew this did not make sense. Still I selected one of those sharp points of ice, the length of a sword blade. Then I exerted force enough to break it free.

The ice snapped off cleanly as if cut. Still moving under a command I did not understand, I fitted the hilt to it. There was a burst of light which blinded me for a moment.

I might still be dreaming, or I might be indeed mad, but that which I held now was no thing of metal or ice, but a sword, perfect and balanced. It had now been called out of time itself to exist again for the sake of the Light.

6

Now I returned to that prisoner in the block of ice. Surely he was a dead man. Still an uneasiness lingered in me as I studied him, as if, should I walk away and leave him so pent there, I would indeed be deserting a battle comrade.

I approached closer to the pillar, kicking aside the shriveled remains of the root bonds which were rotting away. There was a deep silence around me. Except in my own mind, where, very faint and faraway, sounded once more that name:

"Tolar!"

In my hand the new-knit sword did not cease to radiate light, though not with the full brilliance it had given off when I joined ice to metal. But enough to provide a torch far more effective than those stones of Tsali's, and I wondered if its gleam could betray me. Yet I could not put it aside in this place of dark mystery.

Crytha—Tsali—where were they? How could I track them through this maze? With no mind touch I would be lost as any talentless beast, unless I could gain some clue.

The smell of the Thas remained, but I could see no tracks. For underfoot was bare rock holding no print.

And my eyes were continually drawn back to that inert figure in the pillar, as if some deep compulsion tied me here—to it—rather than releasing me to the quest for the freeing of Crytha. Against my will I advanced toward the chill of that frozen column. Cold radiated from it, even as the light did from my strangely forged weapon. Yet the grip of that in my hand was warm, reassuring.

Who was this prisoner? How had he come to stand so in Thas territory? Plainly, from what I could see, he had no physical kinship with the squat, ill-formed earth people. Was he their god? Or some ancient prisoner they had so set to mock and gloat over at intervals? Why had they brought Crytha here to perform so oddly?

Questions for which I had no answers. But, almost without conscious thought, I reached with sword point, to touch the surface of the frozen prison. As I did that, I was seized as tightly as the root things had bound me. No longer was it my will which moved me. No, another force overrode all which was Yonan.

I raised the sword, to bring it down against that pillar. One unyielding surface met another, jarring muscles along my side and shoulder. Yet I could not stop myself aiming such another blow, and a third; without any effect on either blade or pillar which I could perceive. I could not move away, held as a man in a geas, pledged to beat away at this column of ice, fruitlessly, while my body ached in answer each time the sword thudded home against the unbreakable.

Or was it breakable?

I could not be sure. Had a small network of cracks begun to spread outward from that point I had been crashing my blade against? This was the height of folly, to so fight to uncover the body of the long dead. My brain might know that well, but what moved my arm did not accept such logic.

Nine times I struck at the ice pillar. Then my arm fell to my side, so wearied by that useless labor that I could not summon strength for another blow. But—

The cracks I thought I had imagined—were there! Even as I stared, they widened, reached farther across the surface, deeper, farther—a piece of ice as large as my sweating hand flaked away, to hit the rock below with a sharp tinkle. Then another and another joined that!

I could no longer see the man within, for the cracks were so many that they starred and concealed all beyond the surface. More and more bits of ice fell out. With them came a rush of air so cold I might have faced the worst breath of the Ice Dragon. I stumbled back, enough wit and control left in me to flee the range of that blast.

Now the shattered ice flaked quickly, fell in jagged lumps. There was nothing between me and the body. While always the sword blade pulsed with light showing the stranger.

"Tolar—so long—so long—"

I would have cried out, but my tongue, my lips, my throat, could shape no real sound. Those words had not been spoken aloud, rather they broke into my mind as a great cry holding a note of triumph.

"Tolar—aid—"

There was no longer a greeting, rather a plea. And I knew whence it had come, from that body which had been locked in ice. I moved jerkily, again as if another mind and will, roused from some unknown depth within me, was ordering my limbs—pushing that identity which was Yonan into some side pocket where its desires could not interfere.

I stooped stiffly, laid my ice sword upon the rock, and then I went forward. No longer to meet a freezing blast (perhaps that had been dissipated upon the opening of the crypt) but to reach for the shoulders of the body within.

His mail was ice-cold, the flesh beneath it seemed rocklike. But I tugged and pulled, until the masked man fell forward, near bearing me down also by the weight of his body. He was utterly stiff, as if completely frozen as the ice which had encased him.

I tugged and pulled until I had him stretched on his back, his hands still tight gripping his battle ax, his hidden face turned upward. Then I knelt beside him, wondering what I must do now. It seemed to me that no natural man could have survived that cold. But there had been adepts and men of Power in plenty in Escore in the old days. And it could have been that such as they were able to stave off death in ways we ourselves had lost record of during the years of our exile.

To warm his flesh—I had no fire here and I did not see how I could get him to the surface. Or if I wanted to! For we had been warned often by the Green People that many of those who remained outside their own Valley were more apt to be of the Shadow than of the Light. Perhaps this was some Dark lord who had fallen afoul of one of his own kind and ended so because his knowledge of the Power was less than that of his enemy. If so—we wanted none like him loosed, and what I had already done, under that strange compulsion, was to aid evil.

I peered down at him, holding out the sword, that its light, close to his body, might give me a clearer view. He was human in form as far as I could see. Which meant little enough, as the adepts had once been human, and there were also evil things which could weave hallucinations to cloud their true forms.

The helm and the mail he wore were different from any I had seen. And the ax, with its keen-edged double head, was no weapon I knew. While those odd diamond pieces veiled his face too closely for me to judge what might lie beneath.

Now that command of my will which had brought me to free him ceased. No voice cried "Tolar" in my mind. I was again Yonan, myself. And any decision would be mine alone.

Above all I wanted to leave him here—to go out hunting Crytha. Still—

Among fighting men there are certain laws of honor by which we are bound, whether we desire it or not. If this captive was alive, if he was of the Light—then I could not leave him to the Thas again. But what was he—friend or bitter foe?

I laid down the sword, not again on the rock, but across his breast, so that the metal of its new blade rested partly on his ax. My fingers went to those chains which held in place his mask. For it seemed to me that I must look upon his real face before I made my choice.

The chains looked frail enough, until I took them into my fingers, lifting them a little from the icy flesh against which they lay. I tugged at those which lay across the temples beneath the shadow of that dragon-crowned helm. Suddenly they gave so I was able to pull them up and away from the cold face. A second pull loosened that of the chin fastening, and I threw the whole from me.

I had so bared a human face with no distortion of evil I could detect. But then such evil can lie inwardly, too. He seemed ageless, as are all the Old Race after they reach maturity until just before their long lives come to an end, unless they fall by accident or battle.

Then—

The eyes opened!

Their stare caught and held me, my hand half out for the hilt of my sword. A very faint frown of puzzlement drew between the dark brows of that face.

"Tolar?"

Once more that name. Only now it was shaped by those lips slowly losing the blue of cold.

"I am Yonan!" I returned fiercely. No more tricks would this one play with me. I was who I was. Not a dying man in a dream—a body answering to a spirit it did not know.

His frown deepened. I felt then, and cried out, at a swift stab into my mind. He read me ruthlessly as I writhed, unable to look away. He was—

"Uruk—" He supplied a name. Then waited, his eyes searching mine, as if he expected some answer out of my memory.

I snatched the sword, drew away from him. It seemed to me at that moment that I had indeed brought to life one of the enemy. Yet I could not kill him, helpless as he was now.

"I am not—of the Shadow." His voice was husky, hoarse, like metal rusted from long disuse. "I am Uruk of the Ax. Has it been so long then that even my name is now forgot?"

"It is," I returned flatly. "I found you there." I gestured with my left hand to the pillar, keeping the sword ready in my right. "With the Thas yammering before you—"

"The Thas!" He strove to lift his head, the upper part of his body, but he struggled like a beetle thrown upon its back, unable to right itself again. "And what of the Banners of Erk, the Force of Klingheld, the battle—yes, the battle!"

I continued to shake my head at each name. "You have been long here, you who call yourself Uruk. I know of no Erk, nor Klingheld. Though we fight the Dark Ones who move freely in this Escore. We are allied with the People of Green Silences and others—with more than half the country at our throats—if they can be reached!"

There was a skittering sound, bringing me instantly around, my sword ready. And it appeared that my wariness gave that weapon power, for its blade blazed the higher. But he who spun into the open in a great leap was Tsali, hugging his net of stones still to his scaled breast.

He looked to me and then to Uruk. And it was upon Uruk he advanced. Though his mouth was open and I saw the play of his ribbon tongue, he did not hiss.

While Uruk rose now so that he supported himself on his elbows, though that action followed visible effort. Now he watched the Lizard man with the same searching stare which he had first used on me. I believed that they were in that silent communication and I was again angry that I lacked the talent. My boots crunched on the splinters of ice which had fallen from the pillar as I shifted closer to them.

Uruk broke that communion of gaze. "I understand—in part. It has been very long, and the world I know has gone. But—" The frown of puzzlement still ridged his forehead. "Tolar—Tolar I reached. Only he could wield the ice sword. Yet I see it in your hand and you say you are not Tolar?" He made a question rather than a statement.

"I am not Tolar," I returned firmly. "The hilt of the sword I found set in a rock; by chance alone I found it. Here the Thas had taken my weapon. After, by some sorcery, I was moved to break off one of those icicles. And when I set it against the hilt—it became a full sword. I have none of the Talent, nor do I understand why this thing happened."

"That blade would not have come to your hand, nor would you have had the power to mend it," he answered slowly, "if some of that which was Tolar's Power had not passed to you. That is Ice Tongue—it serves but one man and it comes to him of its own choice. Also, it is said to carry with it some small memory of him who held it last. Or perhaps the speculations of the White Brethren may hold a germ of truth in them—that a man who has not completed his task in this world is reborn that he may do so. If it came to you—then you are the one meant to bear it in this life, no matter who you are."

Tsali had laid aside his bag of light stones, was snapping open a second pouch he had at his belt. From this he took another round object.

Holding that between two claws, he began passing it down Uruk's body from the dragon helm on the man's head to the boots on his feet. From the new stone there diffused a pinkish mist to settle down upon the body he treated, sinking into the other's white, chilled flesh.

Now Uruk sat up.

"You spoke of the Thas," he said to me, and the grating hoarseness was gone from his voice. "Thas I would meet again. And I believe that you also have a purpose in hunting them—"

Crytha!

I took even tighter hold on the blade this man from the past had called Ice Tongue.

"I do," I said quietly, but with a purpose enough to make those two words both promise and threat.

7

Our new companion moved jerkily at first, as if the long period since he last strode by his own will had near locked his joints. But, as we went, he stepped out more nimbly. And I saw that he turned his head from side to side, his eyes under that dragon-crowned helm alert to the dark which so pressed in upon us. Only the bared blade of Ice Tongue and the stones Tsali carried fought against that.

Once more I must trust the Lizard man as a guide, for he beckoned to us and then wove a pattern back and forth among those fangs of stalag-mites, seeming entirely sure of where he went. I hoped that, having escaped the menace of the root bindings, he had followed Crytha and the party which held her when they had left me in the ice cave.

Uruk did not speak, nor did I, for I thought perhaps any sound might carry here, alerting those we sought. But I saw as I went that he began to swing the ax, first with his right hand and then the left, as if with that weapon he was equally dexterous in each hand.

The great ax of Volt which had come to Koris of Gorm—or rather he had taken it without harm from the body of Volt himself; a body which had vanished into dust once the ax was in Koris' hold—that was the only war ax I had knowledge of. It was not a weapon favored by either the Sul-carmen or the Old Race—at least within memorable time. But there was such utter confidence in this Uruk as he exercised that I was sure it had been for him the prime arm, more so than any sword or dart gun.

Questions seethed inside me. Who was Uruk, how came he to be encased in his ice prison? What part had he played during the final days of the chaos which had engulfed Escore after the adepts had enacted their irresponsible and savage games with the Power? He might be an adept

himself, yet somehow I thought not. Though that he had something of the
Power within him I did not doubt.

We came out of the great cavern into another one of the runs which
formed the runs of the Thas. Here the smell of them was heavy. I saw the
ax in my companion's hand rise, his survey of what lay about us grow
even more intense.

Tsali beckoned again, bringing us into the passage. Luckily this was
not one in which we had to crawl. But it was confined enough so that only
one at a time could walk it. The Lizard man went first and then Uruk gave
me a nod as might a commander in the field do to a subordinate officer.
With a gesture at my still-shining blade, he indicated that its light made
my position in the van necessary.

The passage took several sharp turns. Where we might at present be
in relation to the upper world, I could no longer even begin to guess.
Once we had to edge across a finger of stone laid to bridge a dark crevice.
Then I believe I could hear, far below, the gurgle of water.

Suddenly Tsali stopped. While Uruk's hand fell upon my shoulder in
noiseless warning. But, dull as my hearing might be in comparison to that
of the Lizard man, I could catch the sound, just as I could see a grayness.
As if the passage we now followed opened into a larger and lighted
space—though that light must be a very dim one indeed.

Tsali gestured once more. From here we must advance with the greatest of caution. He himself dropped to all fours, as the Lizard men seldom
traveled while in the presence of humans, to scuttle on. I gripped the
blade of Ice Tongue between my teeth and crept on hands and knees
toward that light.

Moments later we reached the entrance to the tunnel. What lay
beyond us must have once been a cave large beyond any measure I knew.
But long ago there had come a break in the roof which arched over our
heads, a wide crack far above any hope of reaching. And it was that break,
very small in comparison with the roof itself, which emitted a light born
of an exceedingly cloudy day, or of beginning twilight. So that it did very
little to illumine what lay below.

This was a city—or at least a town—laid out by precise patterning.
Narrow lanes running between crude buildings made by fitting rocks
together into misshapen walls. These were perhaps as high as a tall man
might reach, were he to stand on tiptoe. And the structures had no roofs
nor windows, only a single door opening at floor level.

The Thas were here—in their boxes of houses, scattered through the
narrow streets. There appeared to be a great deal of activity, centering on
a round-walled building near the center of that collection of roofless huts.
I heard a sharp, indrawn breath beside me and turned my head a fraction.

Uruk, stretched nearly flat, but with both hands clasped about the haft of his ax, stared down into the teeming life of the Thas village, and his expression was certainly not one of curiosity nor of peace, but of a cold and determined resolve.

"They will have the girl," he said in the faintest of whispers, "in the chief's tower. Whether we can reach her or not—"

The chief's tower must be that edifice centrally placed. Though in the outside world I would not have named it "tower," since it stood perhaps only a little above my own height. I was more interested at the moment in those dwellings closer to where we lay.

Stones had been piled to erect those walls, yes. But I could see, by straining my sight to the uppermost, that even though those rocks had not been mortised into place by any form of binder, they seemed to stand secure. And I remembered far back in my childhood watching a master mason lay such a dry stone wall, choosing with an almost uncanny skill just the right stone to lie next and next.

Those "streets" which wound so untidily through the settlement offered numerous possibilities for ambush. To fight on the level of the Thas, when perhaps they had more surprises such as the root ropes, would be complete folly.

Instead, I began to mark a way from one wall to another in as straight a line as I could to where Crytha must be. To climb the first wall (which was rough enough to allow hand and foot holds in plenty) and then, using all one's care, to leap to the next and the next was possible. There was only one place where that leap would force a man to extend himself, and that lay at the open space surrounding the "tower" itself.

The Thas were smaller than men. Perhaps their tallest warrior might barely top my own shoulder. But they were numerous enough to drag a man down—unless he could travel from one house wall top to another across their hidden city. And when a man is desperate, there sometimes comes a confidence which he never before believed he had.

Swiftly, I explained what I believed might be done. I spoke directly to Uruk, since I was sure that he could mind-contact Tsali far better than my clumsy gestures. The Lizard man hissed. But he made fast about his neck his bag of light stones.

I hated to leave Ice Tongue out of my hand, but I would need both of those to make such a try. So I sheathed the sword. Much of the radiance was shut off. But the hilt still showed inner, rolling stripes of alive color.

Uruk fastened his ax in such a way (he tried it twice to make sure it was positioned just right for emergencies) so that he could seize it from over one shoulder from where it rested upon his back. Having made such preparation we wriggled down the slope, going to earth time and time again, until we were behind the first of the box houses I had marked.

I could hear the guttural speech of the Thas, but not near to hand. And, although I had come to grief on the heights of the Valley during the storm, I believed that this I had to do. I pushed all thought of failure out of my mind.

The climb was as easy as I guessed and, only moments later, I reached the top of the wall. Luckily that was wide enough to give me good foot room. Tsali flashed up and past me, rounding a corner, leaping with the grace and ease of his heritage to the next wall. There was no one in the single room below, but that did not mean that we would be so lucky a second or a third time. It needed only one Thas to look aloft and spy us and then—

Resolutely, I shut such mischance out of my mind, followed Tsali. My leap was not easy or graceful as his but I landed true, to hurry in the wake of the Lizard man. Nor did I look behind to see if Uruk had followed, though once or twice I heard him expel his breath in a short grunt.

We were three-fourths of our way toward the goal of the "tower" when we were spotted at last by one of the dwellers in a house we used so unceremoniously as a steppingstone. A shrill cry made me flinch, but I had not really believed we could win across the town without a sighting. And I thought we continued to have a chance—unless the enemy was equipped with more of those noxious roots.

Tsali had already made the next leap; I again followed. But the discovery must have shaken me more than I knew, for I teetered on the stone and had to drop and hold on lest I fall into the room below.

Now I heard cries echoed along the streets, and those I must close my ears to, concentrating only on winning to where Crytha might be. I had reached the last house. Before me was the space which I was not sure I could cross aloft. I saw Tsali sail out, alight on the tower wall, but such a leap was beyond my powers.

As I hesitated, Uruk drew up beside me. "Too far," he echoed my own thoughts aloud.

Below the Thas poured from every crooked way, massing about the doorway to the tower. There was nothing left but to fight our way through. I drew Ice Tongue. And, as if the strange blade recognized our peril and would hearten us to face it, the sword length blazed brilliantly.

From the Thas, there arose a wailing. I did not wait to see what weapon awaited me now. Instead, I leaped directly into the crowded space. At least one body was borne down by my weight, but I kept my footing. Now I waved overhead the blazing sword. It made a humming sound, nor did the light of its blade dim.

Thas cowered away from me, crying out, raising hands to shade their eyes. Then Uruk drew level with me, ax ready in hand. His appearance was a greater blow for the earth men. They fought, yes. Some died, by sword, by ax, but it would seem that the sight of our two weapons, or perhaps us also, had weakened their morale. I heard Uruk chanting as he swung the ax, though the words I could not understand. In that moment, another flash came out of that dream-life. Surely we had fought so before. And Ice Tongue, that was born of water, could tear away the earth.

We pushed our way to the door of the tower. As we reached it, Tsali edged forth from its interior, walking backward. His eyes were fixed on Crytha behind. He drew her as he might lead a horse forced to obey by pressure on the reins.

Her face was without expression, her eyes were still closed as if she slept. Uruk edged beside her. Before I could move or protest, his arm encircled her slight form; he raised her across his shoulder, leaving his right arm free to wield the ax, while the girl lay as limp as the dead in his grasp.

Now Tsali joined the battle. From his belt pouch, he scooped handfuls of powder which he hurled into the faces of those Thas who ringed us around. They cried out, then hands dropped clubs and spears, to cover their eyes as if blinded.

We could not take to the wall tops again, and the largest body of the Thas stood between us and that passage by which we had come. Uruk assumed command now.

"This way." His order was confident, as if he knew exactly what he did. Because I could offer nothing better, I had to go with him.

We retreated, doggedly, not down a lane—but into the tower itself, which to me was arrogant folly. But Uruk, still holding Crytha and the ax, while Tsali and I stood ready to defend the door, looked about him as might a man who knew very well what he should do.

"At least *this* has not changed," he said. "Hold the door, Tolar—I do not think they have found the below way after all."

He laid Crytha on the rock floor, to give a mighty shove with his shoulder against a low table which occupied the middle of the room. When that did not move, he raised his ax, to bring it down with a force I could almost feel. Under the blade, the table split, cracked into pieces, which he kicked aside impatiently.

Then I heard hissing from Tsali and swung around to bare the sword at gathering Thas. They had brought pieces of rock which they held like shields to hide their eyes while behind those they advanced grimly.

"Come!" Tsali remained to throw a last handful of his potent dust into the air. That formed a small cloud, moved out over the Thas, and sifted down. By so we gained a short breathing space. Where the table had stood there was revealed a rectangle of dark. Uruk, with Crytha once more over his shoulder, dropped waist-deep into it.

"Hurry!"

I sped with Tsali to that opening and we crowded through, though my feet must have been very close to Uruk's fingers. The descent was not long. Our stones and the sword gave us light enough to see that we stood in another way leading into the dark.

"Take her—" I had barely time enough to catch Crytha, steady her against me. Uruk reclimbed that stair to jerk down the trap door. I heard the pounding of his ax and saw that he was jamming into place bars I thought nothing might break.

"So—" I heard him laugh through the gloom. "It would seem that a man never really forgets what he needs to know. Now, Tolar who is Yonan." He descended the ladder again. "We walk ways which were old before the Thas came to play vermin in these hills. And I believe we can walk them safely. Shall we go?"

Though Crytha remained in her trancelike state, Tsali could control her in part. So, as we threaded through very ancient corridors which time itself must have forgotten, she walked on her own two feet. Also, the longer we journeyed so, the more she came back to life. When, at last, we came to the end of a final, long passage and Uruk pressed his hands here and there on the wall, she was near awake, knowing me and Tsali, though she seemed uneasy with Uruk.

The stone which barred our way slipped aside with a harsh grating, letting us out into the world above. I looked around, searching for a familiar landmark. And sighted one such directly above. We were again on the mountain wall of the Green Valley. Once back there, the Lady Dahaun could surely bring about the complete healing of Crytha.

Uruk tossed his ax into the air, caught it by the haft.

"It is good to be alive—again," he said.

My fingers caressed the hilt of Ice Tongue. "It is good to be alive," I agreed. I still did not know what kind of ally I had unwittingly brought into our ranks, but that he was a friend I no longer doubted. No more than I doubted that I could face battle as readily as any of my kin. And with such a sword—what might a man live to do? A confidence I had never before known swelled within me.

II
Sword of Lost Battles

1

In the morning light there seemed no shadow able to threaten this land. Below, the cup of the Green Valley lay alive under the touch of the sun with something akin to the glint of a great jewel. While for the four of us on the heights—or at least to three of our company—this held all the promise of welcome and safety we believe possible in this badly riven and disturbed country.

I reached out to Crytha, forgetting at that moment I had no right to claim more of her than common comradeship, or at the most, such affection as she might hold in her heart for a brother. For she was already promised to Imhar, son to my foster lord, Hervon. I was only Yonan, near the least of his household liegemen; though at my birth his lady had opened her heart and arms to me.

But Crytha's arms hung at her side. She did not look toward me. Rather she stood with her teeth set upon her lower lip, blinking her eyes slowly, as might one awakening after a puzzling dream. That she had been completely ensorceled by the Thas, who had stolen her for purposes of their own because she possessed in part some of the Talent of the Power, that I had known from the moment I had seen her with those deep-earth dwellers in my quest for her freedom. In my belt pouch I could, if I would, still find that lumpy figure of clay, hair, and rag which had lain secretly in her bed to draw her to their purposes.

It was Tsali, the Lizard man, who had used the mind touch to control her as we fought our way clear of the Thas. But during the last part of our journey it had appeared she was regaining her full senses. Though to us so far she had not spoken.

Now I dared to break the silence between us:

"Crytha?"

Very slowly her head turned, allowing her eyes to meet mine. But her stare awakened fear in me, there being no depths in that gaze. She still looked inward, I guessed, not outward, and that by her free choice.

"Crytha!" I repeated with an urgency which I hoped would reach her ear as I could not myself reach her by thought.

Now something did stir deep in her eyes. The frown of a puzzled child ridged her forehead. She shook her head as if to banish so the sound of her name as I had uttered it. Then she spoke, hardly above a whisper:

"Tolar—"

"No!" I flung up my sword hand between us. That name haunted me, come out of a dead dream, out of the past. Just as I had felt a stranger move within my mind, take command of my body, when I had brought to being again the uncanny sword which now rode on my hip, seemingly whether I willed it so or no. Such a strange sword, newly forged by some Power from a hilt once bound in a rock centuries old, and a length of ice I had broken free from a cave wall. Yet it fitted my hand as if it had been fashioned only for me.

"I am *Yonan!*" I near shouted that.

She gave a whimper, and shrank back from me. Tsali, in one of his flickers of speed, pushed between us, hissing at me. The fourth of our company spoke first.

He had lagged behind as we came to the inner rim of the Valley wall, as if reluctant to take our path, and yet, because he knew no other, he was drawn to us.

Uruk—and who was Uruk? He had been a prisoner of the Thas, set for what must have been generations of time (as we mortals knew it) within the heart of an ice pillar in one of their innermost caverns. It was my strange sword, which he himself had named "Ice Tongue," that had freed him when that stranger battling for recognition within me had forced my attack against the pillar with the blade. And he had also called me "Tolar."

He stood now, studying me from beneath the shadow of his helm on which hunched the jewel-eyed dragon of his crest, his great ax resting head down upon the rock, but still gripped by both his hands. My uneasiness again awoke as I stared defiantly back. He must have been an ancient enemy of the Thas, yes. But that did not necessarily mean, in these days of war, that the enemy of an enemy was a friend or an ally. And of Uruk, in truth, I knew very little.

"She has been far under the Shadow," he said. "Perhaps she so gained a clearer sight than most—

"I am Yonan," I said grimly. Now I jerked Ice Tongue from my scabbard, and I would have hurled the blade from me. But I could not.

"You hold Ice Tongue," Uruk said. "Having been born again, it carries its own geas. And that has been transferred to you—whoever you may be or how you name yourself. It is one of the Four Great Weapons, and so it chooses its own master."

With my other hand I fought to unflex my fingers, break the hold they kept upon the crystal hilt, which was no longer clouded, as it had been when first I found it, but rather shone with that sparkling of light which had fired up in it when the blade had been once more fitted to the grip. But I knew within me that there was no use in what I tried; I was not the master, but rather the servant of what I carried. And, unless I could learn the mastery I lacked, then I would—

I saw Uruk nodding and knew that he could read my thoughts, as could any wielder of the Power.

"Time is a serpent, coiled and recoiled upon itself many times over. It can be that a man may, by some chance or geas, slip from that one coil which is his own, into another. If this happens he can only accept—for there is no return."

"Tolar out of HaHarc—" Crytha was nodding too, as if she had the answer to some puzzle at last.

HaHarc? That was a tumbled ruin which lay beyond the Valley, a place so eroded by time (and perhaps beaten by the Shadow) that no living man could make sure which was house, which was road, if he passed among its shattered blocks.

Men said that the hills themselves had danced when it fell; but that they danced to a piping out of the dark. Even the legend concerning it now was a very tattered one.

"I am Yonan!" I slammed Ice Tongue back into my sheath. "HaHarc is long dead, and those who lived there are forgotten by man and monster alike."

"So HaHarc is gone," Uruk spoke musingly. He no longer watched me so closely; rather he looked into the Valley lying below us. "And this is your stronghold, Tolar-turned-Yonan?"

"It is the stronghold of the People of Green Silences, their allies, and we who come over-mountain."

"Those are they who now come then?" He freed one hand from the hilt of his ax, to make a slight gesture downward. And I saw that a party was indeed climbing the rock wall toward us.

Crytha gave a sudden little sigh and sat down, as if her legs could bear her no farther. And Tsali flashed away, down to meet those climbers. When I would have moved to follow him that I might speed help for Crytha, I discovered I could not go any nearer to the drop than where I still stood.

In me there was a rise of fear. The valley was guarded, not only by the valor of those within its walls, but by most ancient and strongest signs of the Power. If any carried on him the brand of the Shadow, he dared not cross its lip, unless he was an adept of the Dark.

Which I was not—not of the Shadow! Unless—I looked at Uruk and my lips flattened against my teeth. I had freed this man against my will, but I had done so. Was he of the Dark, such an act would have besmirched me also.

"You—!"

He did not give me time to add to that threat, or accusation. In answer he strode past me, lowering himself a little over the rock rim, only to return and bend over Crytha, lifting her gently to lean against him, where I was helpless to move.

Fear and rage warred in me. It was plain then that the danger to those of the Valley lay not in Uruk—but somehow in me—or in the sword! Yet the hilt of that I had dug out of the very rock of its walls, and that had companied me down into the heart of our defense, meeting then with no barrier. Save that I had dreamed thereafter, horribly, of how it had come to an end and me—or someone who had once been me—with it.

Now I set, with trembling fingers, to the unlatching of the buckle of my sword belt. I could try once more to rid me of this encumbrance, this threat to the Yonan who was. Perhaps if I did not touch the sword itself I could succeed.

And it would seem that in that speculation I was right, for when sword and belt fell from me, I could step over them to the same cliff edge as Uruk had done. But I heard his voice from behind me:

"No man can so easily set aside the fate laid upon him!"

"So," I snarled like a snow cat, my anger blazing high as I had seldom felt it before. "We shall see!"

I would kick this sword, send it flying back, away from this place. The rock broke in many crevices; let it fall into one such and be buried, even as the hilt had been hidden before.

But, before I could move, those from below reached us. The Lady Dahaun moved quickly, nearly as swiftly as Tsali, and she was the first to reach us. Behind her came Lord Kyllan and with him, Imhar, and three others—two of the Green People, one of our own men.

Crytha pulled away from Uruk with a weak cry of joy, such as I would have given the pain of a wound to hear had it been uttered for me. She fled into the open arms of the Lady Dahaun; there she wept with sobs which tore at her young body.

The Lady Dahaun whispered gently and that sobbing ceased. But Lord Kyllan, with Imhar at his shoulder, moved forward to face Uruk and me. And it was to my companion that they looked the first, their glances flitting quickly by me.

Uruk was smiling, a small smile which lifted lips alone and did not reach his watchful eyes. I saw that Lord Kyllan was as much on guard in his own way. But Imhar scowled. However, neither was the first to break silence—it was as if they were not quite sure which words to choose at this moment.

It was Uruk who spoke, and not to them, but directly to the Lady Dahaun.

He swung up his ax, holding its double blade at the level of his breast in what was plainly a salute.

"Hail, Lady of the Green Silences—Merhart that was!"

Still holding Crytha close to her, she raised her head to stare at him as if she would reach his every thought.

"It has been long since *that* name passed the lips of any being—"

"So I have guessed, Lady. But it has been long since I was able to walk this earth. Whether you be in truth she who bore that name, or one come later of her bloodline, still you must know me."

She nodded gravely. "Uruk of the Ax. But the years fled past have been very many."

He shrugged. "To me they were a dream. I was captive to Targi—one of his choicer jests, or so he thought it. I have even been a god—to the Thas—if one can conceive of the Thas wishing a god to bow to. But I would guess that even this long toll of years you speak of has not yet resolved our warring."

"That is so. For a while we dwelt in the waste, to allow the Shadow to grow dim, rent by its own many furies. Most of the Great Ones are gone. But what some of them left spots the land now as diseased fungi will spot once solid wood. And the war sword has gone forth to raise us again."

Uruk laughed. "Then it would seem that I have been roused in time. Uruk of the Ax never refused battle."

Lord Kyllan broke in then, and I believed he still looked at Uruk with small favor and more suspicion.

"This man is truly of our belief, Dahaun?"

"He is a legend," she replied. "And legends grow—"

"Out of proportion in truth," Uruk broke in to end her answer. "Yes, Lord, I am not of the Shadow. Once I was master of a city; I led a province of this land into battle. What I am now is a single pair of arms, a head with some old skills of war hidden among my thoughts, and this." He lifted the ax a fraction higher. "It is one of the Four Weapons. And," now he swung a fraction, pointing with his chin at me, "there stands he who can hold another—Ice Tongue has been reborn in his hands!"

I heard the Lady Dahaun draw a swift breath. She looked from me to the sword and belt I had shed, and then back to me again. There was a little wonder in her eyes, which speedily became measurement.

"The Sword of Lost Battles—" she said.

"Yes. And this young lord has just discovered the first of its secrets—that it cannot pass your protection runes."

"I will not have it!" I cried out and would have kicked it far from me as I had planned to do. But the Lady Dahaun shook her head slowly.

"You can leave it here," she said, "yet it will not leave you. Each of the Four Weapons chooses but one owner, in time to become one with that man. But this one has an ill geas on it. It was meant to serve the Light, but there was a flaw in its forging. It brings ill to him who carries it—to the cause in which it is carried. Yet it is not of the Shadow as we know and hates all of the Dark."

"Yes," Uruk added, "until it be returned to its source it is ill-fated. But who says that the time of return may not come now?"

I shook my head and moved away from the sword determinedly. "Let it lie then. We need no ill luck. And I am no time master to meddle with the Power or the past. Let it lie and rust into nothingness where it is."

And I thrust my right hand into my armpit and held it there, for at that moment my very flesh rebelled against me and my fingers would go forth against my will to pick up once more that ill-omened blade.

2

The fire danced high, its light touching now on this face among our company, now that. For there had been a gathering of all those of authority, both small and large, within the Valley. The Lady Dahaun and Lord Ethutur of the Green People, Lord Kyllan and Lord Hervon from over-mountain, he who led the Renthans, and Verlong, the winged, also the chief of the Lizard men. And together with them had come their chief warriors, spreading fanwise back into a dark where the flame light did not reach. Among the first rank sat Uruk, his ax across his knees, with never one hand nor the other far from it.

Between her fingers, the Lady Dahaun held that figure of clay and hair and rag which had drawn Crytha from our protection to the Thas. And the eyes in that company fastened on what she held.

"It would seem," Ethutur broke the small silence which had lain for a space on us, "that our protection is not as secure as we believed it. For such a thing could not have come into this place otherwise."

I clasped my hands tightly before me. My right palm itched; the fingers kept cramping as if they would hold something. In me a hunger gnawed, a hunger I must fight with all my strength. For I had done as I had sworn. Ice Tongue lay where I had dropped it on the heights above and I would have no regrets—no regrets!

"This," the Lady Dahaun balanced the ugly talisman on one palm, "was not fashioned beyond our walls, but within them."

At that saying, our uneasy glances swept from face to face around our circle. Would she tell us now that among us was a traitor? Yet how could that be? Who had enough strength of the Dark Power to pass the barriers so often renewed and set to our defense?

"The clay," she continued, "is of the brookside; this hair is from the head of Crytha, as is this also hers." She flicked with one finger tip the rag twisted around the image.

"Who—" Lord Kyllan's hand was on his sword hilt. His face, young-seeming as it was, was grim and set as if he looked ahead to some battle wherein he might go down to defeat.

"Crytha." Her answer came so quietly that it took me two or three breaths of time to understand. And then I would have protested, but before me was Lord Hervon.

"Why, Lady, would she fashion a trap in which to entangle herself? This is not sense, but folly!"

"*She* did not fashion it, my lord, not knowingly. But this maiden of your house has more talent within her than we realized. Untrained, the Power can harm as well as aid. She had drawn upon what lies within her eagerly, as a man drinks at a pool of clear water when thirst torments him, foreseeing no evil in her acts since all she desired was for good. She is a born healer of great promise. But no talent is single in one, and where Power opens the door and there are no safeguards, then there can creep in that which we fear most.

"Those safeguards we have set to make invulnerable this Valley work against physical invasion. But some subtle brain has devised a way of reaching out along a level of mind which is not guarded, which cannot be detected, except by the training which those of the Talent use as their shields.

"Such a questing thought will not trouble us who are so shielded. But it can influence—and without their knowledge or understanding—those who have not such shields. Fear not, now that this evil has so revealed itself it cannot use her again as a tool in its hand. Uruk"—she spoke directly to him—"who holds the Thas within his hand?"

He did not answer at once. And when he did, he spoke musingly as if he himself faced some riddle.

"Lady, you say I am but legend in this new world of yours. I lived in another time and a different Escore. My enemy there was Targi. The Thas paid him some liegeship—enough to let him use their burrows for my prison. But Targi—" He shook his head slowly now. "I have not sniffed out any of his mischief since I was freed. If he lives—" He slapped his hand flat down upon the head of the ax. "I would know it! We are too bound in enmity for me not to do so."

"Targi was slain in Emnin." The words came from my lips, but they were not mine. I saw all those in the company turn their eyes, startled, toward me. "It was the Lost Battle." That which was not Yonan continued. "Lost for the Banners of Eft, for the Fellowship of HaHarc. Yet the Shadow was also driven back; no side could claim victory on that day."

My sword hand flew to my lips, covering them. I was shaken by this sudden arousal of that *other*. And was well aware that those on either side of me withdrew a little as if I were revealed as an unclean enemy. Yet I had thrown away Ice Tongue—I was *Yonan!*

I saw that Ethutur regarded me with a frown. His lips moved as if he would speak, but the Lady Dahaun checked him with a gesture. Then she raised her hand and traced in the air certain symbols. As green fire they blazed, and then the green became blue. While it seemed to me that I whirled giddily across the fire between us, that all which was me hung in midair, naked and defenseless before those signs of her witchery.

"Who are you?" I saw her lips move to shape the words, but they sounded very faint and far away. Some mighty chasm now stretched between us.

I struggled. Yonan—I was Yonan! But I heard my own voice answer in the same thin and faded tone of far distance.

"Tolar—Tolar of Ice Tongue."

"And what would you here, Tolar?" came her second question.

"The past must be erased, the evil geas broken."

"And this is your will, Tolar?"

"I have no will in this. It is a geas which has been laid upon me, that my failure be redressed and time rewoven."

I—or that substance which was part of me—no longer hung before the Lady of Green Silences. Rather I was back once more in my own body. But I no longer sat among the people of Hervon. Rather, I had moved into the open, so that the breath of the flame nearly scorched my boots. I knew, bitterly, that he whom I had fought so hard to destroy was now fully awake within me. I had no longer a place here, but must be about some strange and terrifying quest which held little contact with the world I had always known.

"I must return." My lips felt stiff. In spite of the heat of the fire I was chilled, as I had been when I had hacked open the ice pillar of the Thas to free Uruk. And in me at that moment there arose the conviction that I went to death itself, yet I could not prevail otherwise against the compulsion which moved me.

Uruk arose. "This hosting is mine, also. For though the craft of Targi prevented my fighting aforetime, it shall not now. Lady"—once more he saluted Dahaun with the ax—"we go into the dark; think of us with fair wishing, for our path will be very strange and the dangers along it such as few men have ever experienced."

"Boy—" I was aware Lord Hervon was beside me, his hand grasping my sword arm. There was a growing pain in my right hand, a pain which would never leave me until once more I clasped Ice Tongue and carried through what that uncanny sword, and this stranger within me, wished. "Yonan—what will you do?"

I sensed concern in his tone. And that part of me which was still the youth he knew gathered a measure of courage from his thought of me. But so small a part of my person was now Yonan it might have been that a stranger spoke those words.

"My Lord." I gave him full courtesy; to me he now seemed as far away as our voices had earlier sounded. "I go where I must go, do what must be done. For I am what Ice Tongue has made me, and it I shall serve until once more comes the end. Perhaps this time"—small hope struggled within me—"the end will be a better one." Yet memory overclouded that hope, as I knew again the sharp pains of my wounded body as I had dragged myself to that place into which I might fling the sword, lest evil find it and turn it to a still greater danger.

His hand fell from my arm. While that company moved out and back, leaving a path into the dark, away from the cheer of the fire. Down that steadily darkening way I walked, and shoulder to shoulder with me, Uruk. While within me something was stricken and began to die. When it was truly dead I would be a man without hope, with only the geas left to move me on.

Though it was dark my hands and feet seemed to find for themselves the way to climb the cliffs. And I went upward with greater speed and ease than I had ever gone before. Dimly I heard the movements of Uruk to my right. I felt no comfort in his company, he was too much a part of this thing which held me prisoner—which was killing Yonan as surely as if it tore open his breast to slit his heart.

When we reached the top of that way I saw the light and it drew me. The sword I had discarded had a torchlike hilt. I stooped and picked up the belt, buckling it once more about me. Then I fingered the grip, to find it warm, not chill as normal crystal.

For the first time since we had left the fire, Uruk spoke. He did not make a question of that word, it was rather as if he affirmed a resolve.

"HaHarc."

"HaHarc," I echoed in agreement. As yet that stranger (he whom they called Tolar) was not in full control of my mind, only of my will and body. I did not have his memories—except in fleeting, time-broken pictures. But when Uruk had uttered that name, then I knew it for our goal.

But we were not to reach those near-forgotten ruins unchallenged. For, as we made our way down the opposite wall of the mountain encirclement, my skin seemed to prickle between my shoulders; I found myself sniffing the air, listening. Evil was abroad in the night—and the menace it exuded was strong enough to awake every instinct of caution. I could not throw away my life, rather must I live for the veiled purpose to be demanded of me.

It seemed that my hearing was keener, that I had other and new senses which brought me strong intimations of danger waiting below. And in the moment there flashed into my mind words—a thought not my own—

"Those of the Shadow move—"

But I had none of the Talent; how could I have caught this warning? No, *Yonan* had no Talent, but what did I know of the gifts and strengths of Tolar?

A rising puff of wind carried to us a thick stench. Not Thas, no— Gray Ones. Those runners on evil roads who were neither man nor beast, but the worst of each wedded into one. I paused in my descent to listen.

A faint scratching at the rock—not directly below but farther to my right. I peered down into a well of blackness. Then I saw the pallid blink of eyes which had a vile radiance of their own as they were raised to mine.

"Move to the left." Once more that mental message came clearly. "There is a ledge. I already stand upon it."

The Gray Ones made no sound. I set myself to exploring handholds to my left. There were enough to give me easy passage. Only moments later my feet found a firm surface and I could let go of those holds, turn to face outward.

"They are not silent hunters usually," my companion continued his soundless communication. "There are but five." He mentioned that as if five of the Gray Ones meant nothing at all to armed men. At that I wondered, fleetingly.

I saw the betraying eyes below. They moved steadily along what must be the base of the cliff, perhaps the height of a man—a little more—until they were again beneath us. I drew Ice Tongue.

It was as if I had suddenly produced a torch, limited though that illumination was. And in my hand, the sword itself gave forth a sound so strange that had not my fingers clung to it willessly I might have dropped it.

The songsmiths who tell and retell our legends, keeping alive so much which is long since gone otherwise from the world of men, speak at times of "singing swords," marvelous blades which give forth a shrill song when they are battle-ready. But Ice Tongue—snarled! There was no other word to describe the sound it made.

And its snarl was echoed from below. A dark bulk sprang up toward us. Not a Gray One, for it showed no lighted eye discs.

Uruk moved and, in the light of my blade, I saw his ax descend into that black mass, heard a horrible howling as the creature, whatever it might be, fell back and away. Now the Gray Ones leaped up, as if maddened into stupidity by the wounding of their battle comrade. For our position above them gave us a superiority which no sane creature would have ignored.

Again Ice Tongue snarled as I cut down at a misshapen head, felt flesh give, bone shatter. They leaped to reach us as if they were frenzied, compelled to attack in spite of the fact that we could so well deal with them from where we stood.

Thus in the dark we slew and slew again. Screams and whimpers arose from below us. But we twain voiced no war cries. Nor did Ice Tongue "speak" by my will or training, but as if it, itself, had such a hatred for those below that it must vent that in force.

At length, Uruk's thought came to me, "Enough. They are dead."

I leaned on the bared sword, searching for any telltale flash of luminous eye, listening for any sound. But the night was now both black and still. I felt myself weary, drained, as if Ice Tongue had drawn upon my very spirit.

"We must move," Uruk added. And in me, too, a feeling of urgency warred with that weariness. "Those here have their masters, who will soon know that they are dead."

We followed the ledge on for a little and found at length that it narrowed so that we must descend once more. And, when, at last, the ground was under our feet, Uruk turned sharply away from the scene of our struggle.

"HaHarc—" he said. "We are not yet masters of time."

What he meant I did not yet guess, but I wiped Ice Tongue on a rough clump of grass and followed him, though I kept that blade bare and ready as I tramped along.

3

Though there was no moon and the stars were very far away, affording no light at all, yet we two strode through the night even as we had left the fire in the Valley, shoulder to shoulder. We might well be following some torch-illumined path. In me there was a certainty as if my mind saw instead of my eyes. Yet another part of me was ever on sentry duty against what might slink behind on our trail.

I had been tired when we had returned from the venture in the burrows of the Thas. My rest had been but a short one before we had been summoned to that council. Yet now I had no feeling of fatigue, only a burning desire to get ahead with what must be done. Though the nature of that act, whatever it might be, was still hidden from me.

Uruk did not break the silence between us, with either thought or speech. The Lady Dahaun had called him legend, but she had accepted him at once, which meant he was not of the Shadow. And he had known Tolar—yet I was afraid to try to recall any early tie between us. Yonan still flickered faintly within me, his fear enough to impose this last desperate restraint.

If evil did sniff behind us that night, it kept its distance well. Perhaps the slaughter we had wrought at the base of the cliff made the enemy wary. Or maybe they would entice us on in our folly well away from the Valley so that we would be easy meat for them. Dully, I wondered which of these guesses was nearest to the truth as I went, ever on guard.

That wan light of gray which is the first awakening of the morning rendered visible a wild, churned land. Some chaotic movement of the earth had had its way here. Uruk slowed. I saw his helmed head move right to left and back again, as if he sought a sign which was missing.

Now we must weave a path through a choking of brush and shrub which grew up about tumbles of dark blocks of stone. Still, when I surveyed this with half-closed, measuring eyes, I could see patterns—as if buildings of mist and fog spiraled upward from those battered remains, and roads opened for us.

Uruk paused. When I looked at him I saw his face set, his mouth grim-lipped. He searched the ruins ahead with a fierce, compelling stare as if he would tear out of them by the force of his will alone some mighty secret.

"HaHarc—" He did not use the mind touch, rather spoke aloud as if he could not quite believe in what he saw. Then he swung the ax, and there was rage in that swing as he brought the weapon down, to decapitate a thin bush. He might have been striking out against all the past with that useless blow.

For a long moment he stood, the withered leaves and branches he had cut still lying on the ground, the blade which had severed them pressing their wreckage into a drift of soil. Then he shook his head. Once more he stared about him intently and I sensed that he sought some landmark which was very needful for whatever he was to do here. But my battle with that other within me had begun once again, and I felt suddenly drained of strength, of any care concerning what might lie ahead.

Uruk moved forward, but hesitantly, not with the swift purpose he had shown before. It could be that, fronted by these ruins, he had lost some landmark which he needed. Still we wove a way among blocks, pushing through the growth, though now I followed behind him.

The valley which had held HaHarc was narrow at its entrance. I could mark in the growing light that it had been closed here by a wall or fortification running from one side of the heights to the other. Though the stones of that building were so cast about that it would appear the land itself had shaken off that bondage, as indeed it must have done.

Past that point, the way before us widened and those structures which had been divorced from the walls showed taller, less tumbled. The stone was darkly weathered. Still here and there, even in the gray of early dawn, I could sight remnants of carving. Sometimes I had to close my eyes for a breath or two because I could also see the mist curdle, raise, bring back ghostly shadows of what must have been.

We stumbled upon a street, still paved, though drifted with soil which had given rootage to grass, some small bushes. This ran straight into the heart of the destroyed fortress city. For I knew without being told that before its destruction HaHarc had indeed been both. Like the Green Valley, in its day it had stood as a stout oasis of safety against the Shadow.

On Uruk tramped, now facing straight ahead, as if he had at last found the landmark he sought. Thus we came at length upon an open space where the ruins walled in a circling of stone blocks, tilted and fissured now. At regular intervals about this had been set up, on the inner side of that circle, monoliths, carved with runes, headed by time-eroded heads; some of men and some of beasts, strange, and yet menacing—but in their way no more menacing than those creatures of intelligence who comraded the People of Green Silences.

Some had fallen outward, to shatter on the pavement. But others leaned this way or that, still on their bases. And two or three stood firmly upright. Within the guardianship of these there was another building, which, in spite of its now much broken and fallen walls, I think had been tower-tall. And the stone of its making was different from that I had seen elsewhere in the ruins—for it was that dull blue which marked those islands of safety throughout Escore, the blue we had been taught to watch for during any foraying as a possible place of defense.

Once more Uruk stopped, this time facing a gateway in the tower. Had there ever been any barrier of a door there, that was long since gone. I could see through the opening into a dim chamber, wherein blocks fallen from the higher stories were piled untidily.

"Tower of Iuchar—" Again he spoke aloud and his voice, though he had not raised it, echoed oddly back. "Iuchar, Iuchar."

My other memory struggled for freedom. Iuchar—I had known—

A man—tall as Uruk—yet not one I had seen in the body, no. Rather he was—what? A ghost which could be summoned at will to hearten people, who in the later days of HaHarc needed strongly some such symbol to reassure them in a war they sensed was already near lost? Iuchar of HaHarc. Once he had lived—for very long had he been dead—dead! I denied Iuchar, for all his tower. Uruk, leaning a little on his ax, turned his head toward me. I saw his eyes beneath the rim of his dragon-crested helm. They held a somber anger.

"Iuchar—" he repeated the name once more, to be echoed. He might so have been uttering a warning to me.

Then he raised the ax in formal salute to that travesty of a tower. And I found myself willed by that other to draw Ice Tongue also, and give with it a gesture toward the open doorway.

Uruk went forward, and I followed. We passed beneath that wide portal. And I saw on the walls without the traces of flame, as if Iuchar's tower had once been the heart of some great conflagration. But within—

I halted just beyond the portal. In my hands Ice Tongue blazed, and there was an answering fire running along the double blades of Uruk's ax. There was an energy in this place, a flow of some kind of Power which made the skin tingle, the mind wince and try to escape its probing. However badly time and disaster had treated HaHarc, in this, its very heart, the Light held, fiercely demanding. Bringing with it a fear which was not born of the Shadow, but rather a foretaste of some great demand upon courage and spirit, from which he who was merely human must flinch.

But there was no evading that demand. My hands shook and Ice Tongue quivered from that shaking. But I did not drop the sword, that I could not have done. Uruk had moved on until he stood in the very center of that circular chamber, and now he turned and beckoned to me.

Unhappily, but realizing that I could not resist what had lain here so long waiting, I took three or four long strides to join him. No earth had drifted here, the stone under our boots was clean; for those rocks which had fallen from above lay close to the walls. It might have been that the force which clung here determined to keep the core of its hold clear. Now I saw that the pavement was crossed and recrossed by lines, into which some dust had shifted, so that the pattern they fashioned was not to be too clearly defined.

Uruk took his ax, and, going down on one knee, he used one of the blades with infinite care, scraping away that shifting of ancient dust, to make plain that we stood within a star. While again moved by the stirring of that other will which had become an inner part of me, I used the tip of Ice Tongue in a like manner, bringing into clarity certain runes and symbols, all different, which had been wrought near each of the points of that star. Two I recognized; those the Valley used for its safeguarding; the others—I could have opened Tolar's memory perhaps, but stubbornly I resisted.

While always about us, pressing in upon mind and will, was that sense of waiting Power. Had any of it drained during the ages of HaHarc's loss? It did not seem so to me. Rather I thought that it had stored energy, waiting impatiently for the release we were bringing, if unwillingly on my part.

His task done, Uruk arose and gestured again to me.

"The fires—"

I knew what he meant, though the logic of Yonan denied that this could be done—even while the sword of Tolar moved to do it.

I passed slowly around within the star, reaching out with Ice Tongue. And with that ice-turned-uncanny-metal I touched the tip of each point of the star set in the rock. From that touch sprouted fire—a fire unfed by any lamp, or even any fuel, burning upward unnaturally out of the blue rock itself.

Then Uruk raised the ax high and his voice boomed as might the gong in one of the shrines tended by the Witches. I did not understand the words he intoned, I do not think perhaps that even that long-ago Tolar would have known them. To each adept his own mystery, and I was certain that Tolar had never been one of the Great Ones of Escore.

If Uruk was (but somehow that I doubted also), at least he had given no other sign of such. But that he could summon *something* here I had no doubt.

From those points of flame my own sword had awakened into being there now spread a haze—sideways—though the flames of blue still arose pillarwise toward the broken roof above us. And that haze thickened.

As Uruk's voice rose, fell, rose again, the wall of mist grew thicker. I sensed that out of our sight, hidden behind that, presences were assembling—coming and going—uniting in some action which Uruk demanded of them. I kept Ice Tongue bared and ready in my hand, though the Tolar part of me felt secure. Excitement was hot along my veins, quickened my breathing.

The mist had risen to fill the chamber save within the star where we stood. My head felt giddy. I had to tense my body to remain standing; for I had an odd idea that outside the mist the whole world wheeled about and about in a mad dance no human would dare to see, or seeing, believe in.

Uruk's chanting grew softer once again. He dropped the ax, head down, against the floor, leaned on its haft as if he needed some support. His whole body suggested such strain, a draining of energy, that, without thinking, I took a step which brought me to his side, so that I could set my left arm around his shoulders. And he suffered my aid as if he needed it at that moment.

His words came in a hoarse, strained voice, and finally they died away to silence. I saw that his eyes were closed. Sweat ran in runnels down his cheeks to drip from his jaw line. He wavered, so I exerted more strength to keep him on his feet, sensing that this must be done.

The fires on the star points flickered lower, drawing in that mist, in some way consuming it. There were tatters in the fog now, holes through which a man could see. But I did not sight the fallen blocks, the same chamber in which we had entered. Now the floor was clear, and there was other light beyond our flames, flowing from lamps set in niches. Between those lamps strips of tapestry hung, the colors muted perhaps, but still visible enough, blue, green, a metallic golden yellow, with a glitter, as if the real precious metal had been drawn out into thread to be so woven.

Then the star fires flashed out as if a giant's breath had blown them altogether. We were left in the glow of the lamps, while beyond the open doorway shone the brightness of the sun. I saw near that door a table and on it a flagon and goblets.

Steadying Uruk, who walked as if he were nearly spent, I brought him to that table. Laying Ice Tongue on its surface, I used my free hand to pour pale liquid from the flagon into one of the cups, then held that to my companion's lips. His face was drawn, his eyes were closed. But he gulped at what I offered as if he needed that to retain life within him.

And as he drank I heard sounds—voices, the hum of a town. I looked over Uruk's shoulder. As the room had changed, so had HaHarc. My hands shook as I realized what must have happened. We were—*back!*

No!

Tolar memory no longer warred with Yonan, but with its own self. I could not—I could not live this again! The pain from my first dream shot through my body as I remembered, only too vividly, what the past had held then, and now it had returned to face me—*no!*

4

There was no brightness in this day. Dusky clouds covered in part the sky, while from the ground mist curled like smoke from uncountable camp-fires. Thick and evil was that mist, eye could not pierce its billows, nor could any mind send exploring thought through it. Thus we knew it was born of wizardry and what it held was truly the enemy.

I stood with Uruk, with others who wore battle mail and helms fantastically crowned by this and that legendary creature. To most of them the self I once was could give names, yet we did not speak one with the other. Our silence was as thick as the mist below on the plain.

Uruk shifted his weight. I could guess what was in his mind, for memory had returned to me full force—Tolar memory. But that was also a memory which stretched into the future. This was the Lost Battle. Though I could not see them, I could count over in that memory the names—and species—who gathered within the mist below.

What task lay upon Uruk and me now was something which I believed no man, nor adept, had tried before. Could we, knowing what we did, alter the past? Or would we be slaves to it—marched on to face once more the same fates which had overtaken the men of HaHarc in the long ago?

Though I had searched my small gleaming of legendary lore, I had never chanced upon any tale of time travel, of the ability to so alter what had been. And if we were so fortunate—what would be the result? Would HaHarc later fall to some other Power from the Dark?

Time—what was time? A measurement we ourselves forced upon the world, counting first by light and dark, then perhaps by the building of cities, the reigns of notable lords. Time now stood still as we drew our battle line and watched the forward creep of the fog.

"Be ready." Uruk's half-whisper reached my ears only because we stood shoulder to shoulder. It was coming—my skin crawled, my body tensed—the first of our chances to fight memory reached out to us. My mouth seemed overfull with saliva. I swallowed and swallowed again.

If we were not the puppets of time—then—

There was a sudden swirl in the mist. A dark figure strode through its curtain. Manlike, it stood erect. But it was not human.

"Targi's familiar—" Uruk's ax lifted slowly, very slowly.

Memory supplied what was going to happen now. In the before Uruk had met that creature, slain it—and then the fog had taken him. I watched, waiting for the pattern to grip him now. I saw him sway, as if some force pulled at him strongly.

"*No!*" His voice was as loud as a battle cry. "I play not this game the second time!"

I heard the men about us stir, mutter, and knew that stares of astonishment were aimed at him. For them there was no coil in time; this happened in the here and now, not in the distant past.

The thing which was Targi's servant was fully in the open. It was thick-bodied, wearing no mail, covered only by a wiry pelt of coarse, tangled hair. Its head was both feline and apeish in contour, and it snarled, its lips curling back to show tusks. Its great paws were clawed, and in one it carried a short spear with long, serrated metal for a head.

Those with us still looked to Uruk. We could all catch the challenge now. The thing below did not issue that. It was only a vessel which carried Targi's hate. Its legs were bowed as if by the great weight of the barrel of its body, and it rocked a little from side to side as it came.

No, the challenge shot into our minds, as a burning fury of battle lust and red hate. I saw men surge forward, ready to break our line on the heights, drawn by that defiance in a way they could not control. So had it happened before—

But Uruk did not stir. He must be using all his own Power—for still he wavered forward a step or two jerkily. On him was that challenge centering. Once he had answered it, not realizing then what it meant.

"No!" The word broke again from between his teeth. His eyes were aflame by the rage aroused in him, rage which perhaps (even knowing to what fate it would deliver him) he could not long continue to control.

If Uruk went to meet that thing it would die—but we would also lose our small advantage bought of memory. This was the first test set the twain of us.

And if Uruk did not go? Two men were already running downslope, heading to answer that overwhelming challenge. While those about and behind us were muttering, watching Uruk with unbelieving eyes. They might all break, dash forward into that mist. Only Uruk could hold them from such folly. But—

I was running. Without taking any straight thought, I headed for the beast, whose ears went flat like those of an angry cat. Spittle flecked about its fangs. Ice Tongue swung free in my hand, and again I heard the snarl which was its own battle cry. As I neared Targi's servant, fear was a weight on me. The hairy thing towered well above me in height; that weapon it was swinging up might shatter the sword I held if blade met blade—of that I was sure.

There were more dark forms breaking through the curtain of the mist. I heard a human voice scream, but I dared not look save at the monster before me. Tolar had not done this before. In so little might I indeed disjoint the flow of the past.

I did not think, it was rather that something outside myself commanded my body. The thing lumbered on, its awkward-seeming pace much swifter than I had guessed. I dropped to one knee. Ice Tongue slipped through my hand even as the full force of that hate which moved the enemy switched from Uruk at last, to beat at me, an unseen weapon worse than any forged steel.

Did I cry out my horror and fear when that mind thrust struck me? This is one memory I cannot search and find. But I used my sword, not as I would have in decent and honorable open battle. Instead I hurled it as one might a throwing knife.

It was not balanced for such work, yet the impetus of my throw carried it true to target. I saw the point of the flaming blade strike into the creature's swaying paunch, not biting deep enough perhaps to count, but cutting skin and flesh.

The shaggy thing paused, staring down at the sword piercing into its body. Its left hand caught at the blade. Then it threw back its head and howled, its red eyes coals of sullen fire. I felt its pain—but my own spirit leaped. It could not bear to touch that blade. The Power which had wrought Ice Tongue was utterly enemy to any of the Shadow.

Now the monster swung its weapon, not to reach me as yet, but to batter at the sword. One of those serrated edges caught at the hilt and jerked it free from the thing's body. Ice Tongue whirled away to my left.

I threw myself, with such force that my body skidded along the ground, the tough grass sleeked by tendrils of escaping mist aiding me. But just as I reached the blade, put out my hand to close about the hilt, a great clawed foot stamped down upon my wrist. The weight of the beast towering over me, the stench of its body, near laid me open to panic. So— if I did not die in one way from the Lost Battle, I would in another. We might not alter that final reckoning, even if we turned back time.

Straining to turn my head, I endeavored to make myself face death as it came by the hands of Targi's servant. There was shouting around us, yet I was not aware of any other caught in that struggle. My world had narrowed to the hulking shape hunched over me. Blood dribbled from the gaping wound in its belly. It tossed away its weapon. One hand strove to close that wound; the other, claws ready to pierce me, mail and flesh alike, descended to tear me apart. I fought madly against that pressing weight on my wrist. Then some saving sense took command. Instead of struggling I went down limp, as if easy meat for this nightmare.

Only my left hand caught at Ice Tongue. I had time for a single act. In my fingers the blade cut at my palm; still I had no choice. I pushed up a little to stab at that descending paw.

Perhaps the force of the blow the creature aimed at me added to the success of my desperate defense. For the point impaled the paw even as it had cut the paunch.

The thing squawked, jerked up its paw, drawing by so the cutting edge of the sword grievously cut my palm. I could not hold on. So I had to watch helplessly as, with a shake of the fist, it again freed itself from Ice Tongue, sending the sword flying out of my sight.

Now it raised its other great foot, the one it balanced upon grinding my wrist into the ground so that the pain made me dizzy. I knew what the thing planned to do. One mighty stamp with that other foot and I would be as smashed as an insect under a boot sole.

I had no defense. I could not even see well, since the pain from my pinned wrist and lower arm drew a red haze between me and that very certain death. Yet the smashing blow I expected did not fall. Instead the beast reeled away, back from me. I heard it give a grunting howl and its body crashed not too far away, blood pumping from a huge wound in its throat. For its deformed head had been almost, but not quite, severed from its neck.

"No!" In spite of the wave of pain from my wrist and the other hand which streamed blood, I held on to consciousness. There was no mistaking the swing of that ax. To save my life (or perhaps because the ancient compulsion had indeed been greater than he could withstand) Uruk had followed the pattern of the past—he had killed Targi's servant.

I saw him go into a half crouch, his ax once more at ready. Somehow I levered myself up on the elbow of my injured forearm, though each movement was like a stab into my shrinking flesh. Ice Tongue—?

Then I saw something else—something which whirled out of the mist. I found voice enough to warn:

"Behind you!"

Uruk whirled with a skill born from long hours of training. His ax was up as he turned. Something dark, ropelike, hit the blade of that, dropped limply away again, severed. But it was only the first of such attacks. He ducked and struck, ducked and struck again and again. Then, in backward stumble to elude a larger one of those flying cords, he tripped against the body of Targi's servant. Before he could right himself one of the cords snapped home about his arms, drawing them together though he fought in vain to get ax blade against them.

I knew those living ropes—Thas' work! Now I got to my knees, holding my broken wrist tight against my body. My other hand was sticky with my own blood—to move it or my fingers was torment. But—

Just beyond where Uruk struggled and fought for liberty, I saw something else. Ice Tongue was standing, point into the ground. Its hilt was a light to guide me. Somehow I tottered to my feet, skirted the severed root which still wriggled, reached the sword. I could not close either hand about its hilt. Giddy, I went once more to my knees, leaned closer to the shining blade. My mouth gaped wide. I bent my head sideways and caught the hilt between my jaws.

It took effort to work it free of the soil. Then I had it. Uruk—I turned around. He was now completely prisoner; even the severed ends of roots crept to weave their lengths about him though he struggled and heaved.

I did not have strength to get to my feet again. Rather, on my knees, I crossed the space between us.

"Your hands—" I aimed the thought at him.

I saw his eyes go wide as they found me. He lay still as I moved toward him. The mist had not parted, but we could hear shouts, screams, and the sound of weapon against weapon. In spite of all our plans and hopes, the men of HaHarc *had* been drawn into Targi's chosen battlefield. Uruk free might make the difference; his orders they would follow.

I reached his side. The hilt of Ice Tongue wavered in my mouth. Any blow I could deliver with it would have little force. I now possessed only one small hope. Targi's creature had not been able to touch it; might it then have the same effect on the living ropes?

Bending my head, I pressed the point of the blade into the root which had so ensnared Uruk's arms. I had no strength, the point would not penetrate—my gamble had no hope—

But—

The root under the point of the sword wiggled, strove to elude that touch, light as it was. I fought grimly to bring all the pressure I could bear on it at that point. Suddenly, as if the metal had sawn through tough hide to reach a core no tougher than mud, the point sank in.

Like the living thing I more than half believed it was, the root snapped loose from its hold on Uruk's wrist to strike upward at my shoulder and caught. I could no longer hold Ice Tongue. The sword fell from my mouth. In its falling it clanged against the head of Uruk's ax. Now the ax blazed under that touch as the sword had upon occasion.

As I slumped forward, the roots writhed away from that blaze, reaching instead for me, clinging and squeezing, where they clung, with a kind of vindictive anger. But I saw Uruk swing the ax once more, slicing through what was left of his bonds.

Just as he won to his feet, had half turned toward me, the fog gave up another form and with it smaller things I knew of old. Thas! While he about whom those clustered—

I heard Uruk's cry:

"Targi!"

As his dead servant, this Lord of the Dark towered above the smaller Thas. He was a figure brought out of some tomb—his dark mail dull, bedewed by the condensing mist. But his head was bare, and he carried no weapon save a slender black rod, topped by the bleached-bone skull of some small animal. His skin was a pallid white, showing the more so because of the darkness of his mail. And his hair, which grew in a brush like the mane of a Renthan, was brilliantly red. Tongues of fire might so appear to rise from his long skull, for that hair bristled erect.

Nor was his face entirely human. It bore no expression now—only the eyes were alive. And in them boiled such a fury as no man could show. Uruk was on his feet, his ax ablaze as I had seen Ice Tongue. That blade lay on the ground. I saw a Thas dart to seize it, leap backward again with a guttural cry. I held on to consciousness with all my strength.

"Well met." Uruk's voice did not soar to a shout, yet it carried even through the din of the mist-shrouded valley. "This match of ours is long overdue, Targi."

There was no answer from the sorcerer, nor did the deadness of his bleached face show life. But he paused and I saw his eyes go from Uruk to the ax.

"You are a dead man." The words burst in my mind, coldly, shaped without emotion behind them, formed with such a vast self-confidence as struck at the beginning hope which had sprung in me. For by this much had we altered the past—Uruk was not prisoner to the commander of the Thas.

I then saw Uruk laugh, though I could not hear the sound of his laughter. The two of them had forgotten me. Hugging still my broken wrist against me, I strove to pull myself up. There was a flick across my body. One of the root cords looped there. I plucked at it feebly with my wounded hand. Then the Thas closed in, though they did not drag me from the field. Rather stood about me, watching their master and Uruk.

One of them gave a coughing grunt and fell. I saw the end of a dart between his shoulders. Then the others scattered, or threw themselves to the ground, striving thus to present the smallest of targets. I saw a Gray One lope from the mist. He stood watching for a moment, his tongue lolling from his fanged jaws. Then he sheered away. It would seem that Targi was to be left to his own actions.

The black wand wove a pattern in the air between the Dark One and Uruk. But the latter raised his ax and slashed down, his target not yet the man, nor even the wand. Rather that weapon was used to cut through the air whereon reddish symbols shone. As the ax passed, they did break into wisps of mist, blood-dyed in color.

I could have cried out at what filled my mind—syllables roared there. It was as if my thoughts were shattered before I could shape them, dashed and broken. Targi—what man could stand so to the spells Targi could command?

There was one—Tolar was of this time, he had been shaped by the knowledge of such as Targi. But—Yonan had not. And—

I was Yonan!

Deep I reached, fighting against the pain of both body and mind, seeking that other who knew not Targi, nor HaHarc, nor this world. Yonan who had none of the talent—could I hide behind his very lack, that lack which I had half resented all my life, at this moment?

My head was a battlefield. The will of the sorcerer might be aimed principally at Uruk, but some of his compulsion spilled into my mind, churned and obscured my thoughts. I concentrated, first on pain, summoning the pain of my hand, my wrist, to dwell upon it, surrender to it. While behind my embrace of that pain of body, I sought for Yonan.

He was buried—as near death as any personality might approach before the final flickering out of identity. I *was* Yonan! And over Yonan men long dead had no dominion, no matter how potent their talent might be. I was Yonan!

My pain I cherished, used it as a barrier while I sought to nourish into life that small spark from the far future. "Yonan!" So did I call upon my other self.

Targi raised his wand, pointed it at Uruk. In spite of my own efforts I could sense, through every nerve in my battered body, even through the mind I sought to fortify against his sorcery, how he was drawing Power to him. It was almost visible to the eye, that Power.

Still Uruk swung the ax back and forth before him, touching nothing tangible. It might be that in that ceaseless swing he erected some barrier against the other's attack. And, slowly, he moved forward.

I felt Thas' crooked hands on me, drawing my bound body to one side, as they kept well away from the space between those two. The forces there might well be lethal to lesser beings. I was Yonan—momentarily I had been diverted from my own quest within. No, I dared not relax my poor protection again. Waves of that force had lapped against me, bringing a black despair so great that, had I been free and Ice Tongue within my reach, I would have turned its blade upon myself. Who can stand against such as Targi's assured thought? Master of Power that he was, who else could put himself forward as an enemy?

The very body in the dull black mail seemed to swell, to grow. The eyes of Targi were twin flaming suns under the still-clouded sky. And this man who would front him—who was he to challenge the strength of Targi! That demand burst redly in my mind.

"Who am I, Targi? I am what you yourself made me." Uruk spoke aloud, as if he would not touch minds with the sorcerer. In that way instinct told me danger did indeed lie. "To each evil, Targi, there is an answer. It would seem that we are so paired." Once more his ax swung.

Now the Dark One no longer painted his blood runes on the open air. He drew the wand between the fingers of his left hand. And I saw, yes, in truth I saw it—unless it was some ensorcelment which touched and held my mind—that the skull which crowned it opened its fleshless jaws and from that issued a shrill keening.

The pain I had called upon for my defense became at that moment my bane. It arose in a red agony, pulsing in answer to the keening of the skull. And I saw the Thas cower on the ground, their gnarled hands, which looked so much like twisted twigs, tight held over their ears.

Did Uruk's swing of ax slow? I could not be sure. Now Targi balanced the wand as a man balances a light throwing spear. Even the Tolar part of me did not know what would happen should that weapon of the Shadow strike Uruk. But that it would be more potent than any steel—that I could guess.

Ice Tongue—I glanced at the sword, which lay with its glittering blade belying the grayness of the day and the fog. It was far from me now as if it did indeed abide in another age.

Ice Tongue obeyed but one master—had not Uruk said that once? How well did it obey? Dared I—dared I let Yonan retreat from part mastery within me? I believed that now Targi's awareness was centered on Uruk; I had only to fear the side lash of the power he might use against the axman. Tolar—and Ice Tongue. Oddly enough I had not tried to explore before what that stranger within me knew of his forceful weapon. I did not know—

No, that was false! Tolar leapt into command within my memory. Ice Tongue—one of the Four—it became part of him who took it—but only if he were the one to whom it would answer. There were things about the sword which even Tolar had only heard rumored.

Taking a great chance, I fought against the wall of pain I had so carefully erected as my defense. I opened wide once more the door for Tolar.

Though the Thas squatted about me and I was surely their prisoner, my mind was not bound. I willed my attention only at the sword.

Ice Tongue! Of my desire and need I feverishly wove a cord as strong and supple as the root ropes. I was not even aware at that moment that what I would do was utterly beyond any knowledge of Yonan's, even of Tolar's. In the world where I lay now existed only two things—Ice Tongue and my will.

I had heard much spoken of the disciplines those who wield the Power must set upon themselves, of the years they must work to bring into their hands the reins of illusion and ensorcelment. Yet they were then able, by pouring energy into the right channel, to make the earth itself obey them—even though they might die, burned out, in the doing of it.

Ice Tongue—

Was indeed that blade blazing brighter, glowing like a narrow stream of fire in the grass trampled down by our struggle? I closed off all surmises, everything but my driving will. It was like shutting all the doors along a corridor, so that one's mind dwelt only upon what lay at the far end.

Ice Tongue—

In my sight the sword appeared to grow, no longer fitting the hand of any true man—rather such a weapon as only a giant might swing. And it began to move—

For a moment a small tinge of triumph broke my concentration; I was quick to wall that off. All which lay within me, which I called "will," "desire," "determination," must be focused on what I would do.

Ice Tongue! I put into that silent call the full strength I could summon, sending forth that order silently but still as strong with any Talent Tolar might possess.

The blade slid forward, as if indeed my thought was a cord or one of the root ropes looped about its hilt.

It came between Uruk and Targi. The Dark One still balanced his wand as a spear, but he had not yet thrown it. Or did he need to throw it; was he rather aiming its full energy? Uruk was forced back one step and then a second.

Ice Tongue!

I put into my unvoiced command the last distillation of all I had called upon, that faculty I had not even known I possessed until I put it to this final test.

The sword gave a kind of jerk, its point rising though the glowing crystal of the hilt still rested on the ground. It arose so—and fell again as the energy drained out of me far too swiftly. But it fell toward Targi, striking across his foot.

There was a bolt of force no one could see, but which struck straight into the mind my efforts had left wide open. I had a single instant to think that this was death—then there was nothing at all.

But if death were nothingness it did not claim me. For pain sought me out first, and I could not set that aside. It filled me with a deep torment. Then I became aware of a touch on my forehead between my eyes. At first that touch, light as it was (though it was firm enough), added to my pain, which throbbed and beat, making of me a cringing animal who had no hiding place.

Then, from that touch, there spread a coolness, a dampening of the fires of my agony. Little by little pain subsided, though it left me apprehensive even as it went for fear that raging torment would be unleashed again. But the coolness which came now was like rain on long-dried soil, soaking in, strengthening me.

I opened my eyes.

Above me was a sky still drably gray. But hanging over me was a face which my dulled, exhausted mind could remember.

"Uruk?"

I must have shaped his name with my stiff lips, but he read it, and some of the frown which the rim of his helm nearly hid smoothed out.

Memory came limping back. I shaped a second name:

"Targi?" Only to see the frown once more return.

"We were cheated in so much—he lives," he said aloud, as if mind touch was somehow not to be used. I thought I could guess why—my brain felt bruised, shaken. Perhaps it was as wounded as my body had been and to have entered it would have driven me mad.

"Where—?"

"He wrought an illusion in the end and escaped in it. But there is no safety with Targi free."

"The Lost Battle—?" Memory again stirred and somehow hurt, so I winced.

"We changed that. When Targi fled, those who followed him did also."

"But before he did die." My memories were mixed. When I tried to think clearly, to sort one from the other, the process made me giddy and ill.

"Not this time. In so much we altered time, comrade. But whether for the better after all"—Uruk shrugged—"how can we tell? This much I know, Targi must be our meat."

"Why—?" I found it too hard to voice my question. But he must have read it even in the chaos which now mixed memory with memory.

"Why did he go? That was your doing, Tolar. Your sword upon his foot disturbed his spell casting. The Power reflected back on him, as it will when any ensorceling is incomplete. He fled the death he would have drawn on us. But he is master enough to win some time and build therein his own spell. We can only now be hounds on his trail."

I closed my eyes. At that moment I could command neither my body nor my shrinking mind. I wanted only darkness once again, and some mercy gave it to me.

6

My wrist was stiff-set, with a splint to keep it so; my other hand had been treated with the healing mud to which both man and animal turned when there was need. Ice Tongue was sheathed at my side. But we were still in the past, the Valley of HaHarc behind us—the open countryside before. And if the clouds were gone, and the sun shone there, yet it still seemed that there was a shadow between us and its warmth and encouragement.

Tolar had no more memory to lend me now. For we had changed the course of action—I had *not* lurched, deathsmitten, from that fog of Targi's brewing to destroy my blade and die hopeless and helpless among the rocks. Nor could I now have much in Yonan to call upon either. Though I had tried with all my determination to learn the ways of war, yet here and now I was like a green youth who had never ridden on his first hosting.

A little apart stood Uruk, leaning on his ax. And though he stared straight into the day, I thought that he saw nothing of what lay before us; rather his mind moved in another fashion—questing—

There had been those of HaHarc who had volunteered to back us; still that Uruk utterly refused. It would seem that the hunting of Targi lay upon the twain of us alone.

"He will go to the Thas." Uruk spoke for the first time, that unseeing stare not breaking. "He will seek his heart—"

"His heart?" I echoed. For in these moments of supreme effort when I had commanded Ice Tongue I believed I had burned out of me most of Tolar memory—even as the Witches of Estcarp burned away their controls when they set the southern mountains to shivering down on Karsten invaders.

Uruk blinked, the masklike brooding left his features. "His heart—

that part of him which is his talisman and the core of his strength. He would not risk that in battle, not even with us, whom he deemed so much the lesser. But if he would replenish his Power, then he must seek it to re-energize what he has exhausted."

"To the Thas? We seek them underground?"

Uruk blinked for the third time. "Where else? And we march into a trap if we do so. He will expect our coming, lay his own ambushes, and dispose of his forces to defeat us. Already he has spun a maze through which no thought can penetrate for our sure guide. And he will strive to take us—by body, or by that part of us he wishes the most to control—our minds. This is a wager of high Forces, comrade. The result may fall as easily against us as in our favor—perhaps even the former is more likely.

"Before when his body died," Uruk mused, "his inner essence was helplessly pent where he had concealed it. I remember." The ax shifted a little in his hands. "Why think you he had me kept living in that pillar? He needed a body—but somehow the Thas failed him in that ploy. Perhaps that was why they took your Valley maid, sensing in her some hint of talent which might accomplish what they themselves could not do."

I recalled vividly that scene Tsali and I had witnessed in the cave where Crytha, completely under some spell, had confronted the pillar which had imprisoned Uruk. That—had *that* been a part of the attempt at transference Uruk now spoke of frankly?

Now, too, I thought of those roots which were obedient to the men of deep earth, of the darkness of their burrows, of the fact that we possessed no guide. On the other side of the scale lay even heavier my conviction that Uruk was entirely right—we must destroy this Targi in one time or the other. And it would seem that fate itself had decided it would be in the past.

My bandaged wrist—I could still hold Ice Tongue in my newly healed hand, but I was not ambidextrous in battle. And in any sudden attack I would doubtless prove a hindrance. Still the sword itself, as I had had good proof, was potent against the Thas.

"When do we go? And where?" My voice sounded weary in my own ears. Yonan, who knew so little and in his life had lacked so much confidence in himself, asked that.

"We go now," Uruk returned. "And Ice Tongue can sniff out the door to any Thas burrow for us. It is in my mind they core these hills now, perhaps striving to weaken the very walls of the earth beneath in order to bring an end to HaHarc."

There was more than a ring of truth in that. I thought fleetingly of the old legend that someone—or *something*—had piped and HaHarc's walls had tumbled in answer. If there existed a honeycomb of tunnels running beneath those upper walls, such might indeed have come to pass.

So we went forth from the place where the mist had hidden the valley of the battle. The bodies of our own slain had already been gathered, laid on a pyre of honor, and reduced to clean ashes.

The Dark Ones had been also so dealt with—but with no honor paid them. For all men knew that some of the Dark Lords could reanimate the dead, though no spirit returned to bide behind their empty eyes. Rather the raised dead were clumsy tools, difficult to use, for they must be eternally held to any task set them.

Gray Ones, monsters—and some were men, so like those I had known all my life that meeting them I might not have realized they had sold themselves to the Great Dark.

Though the bodies were gone there was a litter of weapons still to be garnered, and a squad of men of HaHarc was about the harvesting of those. Those, as they moved, looked straightly at us, but none questioned where we went nor what we would do.

There were tracks cutting the soil, some left by hooves, others by the clawed, half-human feet of the Gray Ones. Also there were trenches, slimed within, smelling vilely, as if what had impressed those upon the once clean earth had crawled upon their bellies after the fashion of giant slugs.

It was only for a short space that Uruk followed this plain trail of those who had fled the battleground. He was heading, I was sure, for a line of hillocks, very small beside the ranges which protected the valley behind us, yet heaped high enough to form landmarks.

And one, I noted under this weak and wayward sun, had three tall stones planted on it, seeming like the bolls of trees whose branches had long ago been riven away by some storm wind. These were not of that sleek blue stone which marked the "safe" islands. Rather the stone was a strange to the eye, being much pitted and of a rusty red.

I found I had a dislike for those stones, and the closer we advanced to them, the more my uneasiness and distaste grew. Now I swallowed, as does one who strives to conquer nausea. Ice Tongue, which I had drawn and carried awkwardly in my left hand, still gave forth a light discernible even in the sunlight. Now, through my grip on its hilt, there spread in me a kind of warning.

"Where—?" I dared to break the silence between us. But Uruk neither glanced at me nor spoke. His strides were deliberately measured. Yet there was no hesitation as he climbed the hillock toward those ominous pillars.

Ice Tongue moved in my hold. The point dipped as I climbed, trying to keep up with the axman. I have seen the Wise Women locate water, or things of metal long underground, how their rods then turn in their hands without their willing, pointing to the proper spot in the earth.

So it seemed that this sword out of time now acted in a like manner. I would not have had the strength to force it up and away from the earth which lay at the foot of the red pillars. Uruk was right again; in such a way the Sword of Lost Battles was our guide.

I noticed that Uruk passed the first of the pillars with care as if he wished no part of him or his clothing or armor to touch its forbidding surface. By the second stone he stopped. Ice Tongue pointed in my own grip at the ground beneath my boots. I had to struggle with the blade to keep that hold, for it fought as if the metal had a will of its own and would bury its point into that spot of earth.

Uruk's lips curved in more a snarl than a smile. "Did I not say so?" he asked. "We have found what we have sought, the door to a burrow. But I think such doors are not for the wary. It would be best we choose our own entrance to Targi's runways. Do you try to trace if it runs beyond this point."

I fought with the sword, finally forcing it away from that point where it seemed to wish to bury itself. Uruk edged by the first of the three pillars, seeking the opposite downward side of the slope. Now he stepped back to let me take the lead.

The sword continued to point earthward, and Uruk uttered a sound close to a harsh laughter.

"So goes it then." He glanced back, measuring the distance from that last pillar. And then he gave a swift nod, as if answering some question of his own which he had not voiced aloud. Raising the ax, he aimed a blow, one with all the weight of his trained strength behind it, at the slope of the hillock.

The metal edge of one head bit deep, gashing the turf, throwing clods of it broadcast. A second and a third time Uruk sent the ax against the hillside. The fourth time it broke through in a small place, loose earth shifting into the hole he had so uncovered.

It took very little more ax work to clear a space so that I could lie belly down and lower Ice Tongue slowly into that opening. The sun did little to pierce the hole, but the gleam of the blade showed that this was perhaps not a cavern, but rather a tunnel in the earth, large enough for us to force a way through.

With a deep breath, walling swiftly from my mind all the warnings lest I not be able to go at all, I set Ice Tongue between my teeth and wriggled through, landing in a confined space which carried the heavy reek of

Thas in its stale air. Though there was no sign of any lurking earth dweller. Swiftly I moved farther down the passage to give Uruk room enough to follow me.

The passage had been shored up here and there by heavy roots deeply embedded in the earth, and rough-sided bits of stone rammed in to aid that precaution, as if this was a runway which it was important for the earth people to keep open.

"Paugh!" Uruk spat. "This stink is foul."

We found that the passage had not been constructed with such visitors as us in mind. For it was necessary to move ahead stooping, our bowed shoulders now and then rubbing against the roof, bringing down ominous trickles of earth I tried not to think about. Here Uruk took the lead once more as if he knew exactly where we were headed.

As we moved away from the hole our only light came from Ice Tongue. I raised it high so that its wan glitter might shine over my companion's shoulder. The earth under our feet was as tightly packed as any long-used game trail, and always the smell of Thas clung.

Within a very short space we came to where the passage ended in a well-like opening. Uruk knelt and felt beneath its crumbling ruin.

"There are climb holes," he told me in a soft whisper. "Shallow, but I think we can wedge toes and fingers into them." Then he slung the ax over his shoulder and warily lowered himself into the dark opening. I kept Ice Tongue between my teeth as I felt I dared not lose the small light it gave us. But I waited until I heard Uruk's soft whisper before I dared swing over and seek those limited holds.

Down, down, down—my jaws ached first, as I kept that grip on the sword; then the ache spread down my tense body, shoulders, arms, fingers, toes, feet. And still there seemed no end to this descent. I feared I might choke and lose hold on the sword by spewing forth my last meal because of the stench here. But I hung on grimly, limiting my world to two things—keeping Ice Tongue ready and hunting the next and then the next hold.

That descent seemed endless—but perhaps to someone not so tense as we were, it would not have been any great feat. But I was very glad when Uruk's warning reached me and I felt once more a wide and solid surface underfoot.

There was more rock in the walls here, only that rock was crisscrossed with root supports. And the stone on the walls showed signs of having been roughly worked, to the extent of having the worst of the natural protrusions broken away. We no longer had to climb down—but the passage itself sloped more and more, making certain that we were fast going well below the surface of the ground outside.

"Wait!" I had not really needed that command from Uruk. Tolar was not yet totally dead within me, and the sense of an evil presence was so strong that it brought my hand up to hold Ice Tongue at ready for an attack. I saw what glowed ahead—swirling tendrils which reminded me of that other fog which Targi had used to cloak his force. Save that here light was a part of it and the billows shone with a greenish radiance which made me think of long-buried corruption. While an odor even viler than that of the Thas puffed forth at us.

7

Uruk's laugh startled me, for to my mind those arms of mist were indeed ominous. However, there was contempt in the sound he made as he watched them thin, reach out for us like tentacles of some sea monster such as the Sulcarmen knew in the far south. And quick on that laughter he began a soft chant.

I *saw* his words. By what feat of sorcery this happened I could not explain. But the words formed blue sparks in this gloom, issuing from his lips as a stream, yet spreading out beyond to gather in a glittering puff cloud of their own. He moved confidently forward and perforce I followed.

Then that glitter of blue sparks touched upon one of the threatening tendrils of mist. There was a flash. The mist whipped back to join a center core which grew opaque, ever darkening, as more and more of the unnamable material was drawn to it.

Now there was no mist, rather a wavering figure which did not appear certain of what concrete form to take. From it issued a feeling of menace, building so quickly that it was like a blow. But if whatever that thing was thought to find us open to such counterattack, it learned quickly that we were not. For though it flung itself to the rocky way under our feet and strove to crawl at us, the blue mist dropped in turn.

"Ha, Targi!" Uruk no longer chanted; now he called as a man will shout a personal challenge to the enemy. "Do you then think me already your plaything? Helm-biter"—for the first time he gave his weapon a name—"is no steel of any man's forging. You should know that."

The mist winked out.

Uruk nodded. "He must be greatly shaken," he said musingly. "Targi is not of the Great Ones, no more than am I. But I would have thought he fancied his hold on the Dark Power stronger." Now his voice sharpened and he demanded of me: "How did he die—in that time we know?"

I dredged up Tolar memory. Targi—had Tolar seen him die? Or only heard it reported before his own grievous wound had driven him from the field? Then the words came to me haltingly, for the pictures in my mind were very dim and far away.

"He died by an ax. They raised an outcry when they found his body—that I remember."

"By an ax," Uruk repeated. "Then—"

I knew what troubled him. If it had been his Helm-biter that had so dealt with Targi, to slay him again might avail us nothing. Unless we could also reach the inner core wherein Targi or what was of the real Targi might find secure refuge.

"He will strive to repeat the pattern," Uruk said, this time as if to himself. "So—"

The way before us was dark. That evil coiling thing of little real substance had vanished. However, we had not lost our wariness, which was well. For now out of the dark again came snaking, some actually crawling upon the rock to better entangle our feet, those root ropes. The ax swung—I need not use the proper hand on Ice Tongue to prick at those reptilian, wriggling lines of dark.

It was butchery there in the half-dark. Neither Thas nor rope could truly face our weapons when we set our backs to the wall of the passage and swung the bright metal to bring death. The sword snarl was that of a wolf eager to be at the throat of its prey. And, while Helm-biter did not give tongue in a like manner, yet the very passage of the double-bladed head through the air made a kind of singing. While the Thas squealed and grunted.

Uruk raised his voice above their clamor. "Make an end now!" he ordered. "Targi used these to buy him time—the time he must not have. He thinks he will be safe in that place he has devised, so we must reach him before he sets a lock to guard his safety."

We came away from the wall in a charge. Uruk roared aloud the old battle cry of HaHarc. The sound of his voice was nearly deafening in that small section, and the blaze of our weapons made them living fire in our hands.

The Thas broke. I knew of old that they were fighters who needed the dark to make them confident. And there were bodies enough, mostly from Uruk's hewing, to discourage them. Whether Targi withdrew the compulsion he had laid upon them to attack we never knew. But at our advance they broke and ran. Some fled ahead down the lefthand section of the passage, some withdrew to the right behind us.

Uruk moved swiftly. He might not trot nor run through this murk, but he made the best pace the cramped quarters and our uncertain footing allowed him. And I kept at his back, though I looked often to make sure that those who had run had not doubled back to follow us.

In my own time, the Thas had envenomed their spears. But those we tramped over, lying still sometimes in hands no longer able to raise them, showed no discoloration of point. In so much were we now favored.

We came to a forking of the passage, then a second, and a third. Each time Uruk turned right or left with no hesitation. I did not ask, but somehow I believed he knew where he went.

Thus we broke from a side way into one of those caves through which Tsali and I had earlier gone—or if not that, one so much like it no man could tell the difference. The stalagmites shone with crystalline sparkling as Ice Tongue's brilliance caught them. I would have been muddled by the number and variety of these age-long mineral growths, but my companion did not pause, nor search. I saw that Helm-biter swung a fraction in his grasp; perhaps that was acting now as one of those needles the Sulcarmen kept locked within bowls to point a path across the sea.

So we reached at last to another opening in the wall, a crevice I might have overlooked, for it required careful squeezing to get by a large lump of rock into it. Another narrow passage awaited beyond, only the walls of this had certainly been hewn smooth, and I saw here and there a pattern of runes I did not know—save from them seemed to reach a coldness to touch the innermost part of a man, awakening in him uneasiness and despair. Only the warm sword hilt in my scarred hand fought that subtle assault upon my courage.

Uruk slowed his pace. His head was well up, for that passage had not been the cramped size beloved by the Thas. Men, or something much like men, had made it.

"Now—" The word was half a breath he expelled. "Now we win or fail, Tolar-that-was, for we have tracked him as he never believed any man born in the Light could do. And at the bay he will throw against us all his strength—"

He had hardly gotten forth the last word when a blow out of nothingness struck against us both. It sent me reeling unsteadily back, toward that half-concealed entrance. This was as if a giant and all-powerful hand had thumped against my chest, leaving me no defense, hurling me away. I lashed out wildly with Ice Tongue, seeing nothing tangible to so attack but feeling that I must do something or be utterly overborne and rendered helpless.

Uruk was forced back also, but only a step or two. His shoulders were hunched a little, his feet planted apart as if he were determined there would be no more retreat. I tried to copy his stance. More than that, I fought to edge forward again to join him.

The pressure continued. I had not been able to win a palm's-length forward; no, instead I had lost two backward. Anger, dour and sullen, filled me, unlike any I had felt before; Tolar's anger, which had in my touch with him been so tattered by despair. Tolar—once more I turned to that hidden other part of me which the sword had brought to birth.

Uruk *was* moving forward, his action resembling that of a man wading through thick mud. Each step he took was short, but he made it. I rubbed shoulder against the wall where my last retreat had borne me. Now I took the sword into my right hand, put out the left. As I had felt for those holds in the deep well, so did I now lock finger tips into the lines of the runes. Very small was the purchase such holds gave me. But I came forward again, slowly, one hindered step against another, just as Uruk moved.

Perhaps his ancient enemy could not divide that force easily, so that he was not able to fend us both off at the same time. Thus we were winning by small lengths. The throat veil of mail of my helm swung loose, I was breathing heavily, concentrating on my battle along the wall.

Uruk fared better—his steps grew longer. Under the threatening dragon of his helm crest his eyes were set, glowing.

Thus, through a time which seemed endless, we worked our way along that passage. And the pressure against us seemed never to relax. I was panting, and the beating of my own heart pounded in my ears. On—On—!

Then, even as quickly as the mist had gone, so did this vanish. I went to one knee, overbalanced by that withdrawal which came between one breath and the next. I saw Uruk stagger, but not more than a step.

Holding the ax still before him, he broke into a jogging run, one I was quick to try and match.

We emerged into a place filled with that green-gray radiance I had long known marked a strong center of the Dark Forces. There were no stalagmites here, rather pillars worked into shapes of horror, each a monster or a man, the latter seemingly locked in some unbelievable torment from which not even the end of time might deliver him.

Down the wide center aisle between those pillars, which, after a first glance, I would not look upon—for even seeing them stirred in me a fear I feared I could not suppress—Uruk went directly to the center core of this place.

It was perhaps a temple. But what god or force had been worshiped here, that had been none born from the adoration of my species. Here the pillars formed a circle, and in the center of that was set, on a half-pillar of rusty red, a crystal skull.

At the foot of the pillar lay, in a lank tangle, the man I had seen on the battlefield—Targi. His eyes were wide, staring unseeingly overhead, and his body was flaccid, that of the newly dead.

But in the brain pan of the skull—!

I could not force my gaze away from that swirl of raw colors, colors which hurt one to look upon. They surged, interwove in patterns, and— they had meaning. I need only look so for a little longer and that meaning would be made clear to me. It was the greatest thing I had ever done—I would be privileged beyond any of my kind—I would rule—rule!

I saw Uruk step over the body, raise his ax. Uruk—he would destroy—he—it was he who was the enemy in this place! Kill—Kill—!

Only the fact that my injured wrist would not obey my will made my blow a feeble one. Ice Tongue grated against the mail covering his shoulder. But that was enough to deflect the fall of the ax. It clanged instead against the pillar.

The skull rocked on its perch, as the colors caught within it moved in an even madder interweaving. I had kept grip on my sword, but only barely. That ill-aimed blow had nearly taken it from my hold.

Uruk—he was danger! As long as he lived—as long as he lived—

He had turned those blazing eyes on me.

"Let me in, comrade—" In my mind a powerful voice cried like a burst of pain. "We can finish him—together—"

Uruk's ax swung aloft again. I was no match for him even with Ice Tongue—

"Thrust low!" that other in my mind urged. "There is a weak spot beneath his arm—thrust for his heart! And then—"

"Yonan!"

I tottered, raising my hand to my head, crying out with the pain which was a torment there. The sword hung heavy in my hold, its point toward the blocks of rock under our feet.

"Yonan!" came that call again.

"Thrust—now!" bade that other commanding presence pouring into my mind. Weakly I knew or guessed what was happening—

I raised the sword and I brought that blade down, largely by the weight of it alone, since there was very little strength left in me. Ice Tongue fell square upon the dome of the skull.

There followed such a torment within my head that I hurled the sword from me, fell to my knees, clasping my head on either side and moaning.

I did not see Uruk raise the ax again. But I heard the clack when one of its edges met the skull, cleaving it, shattering it, as if it were indeed ancient bone. There was a wild clamor in my mind—I would go mad— that thing which had tried to possess me would see to that. Babbling I sank forward, face down on the pavement, while eye-aching light swirled about me, closing me in.

But there had been a small part of Yonan unconquered, a fraction which had retreated into hiding. And now (how long I was under pressure of Targi's will I shall never know), that scrap of the one I had once been came out of hiding, in desperation, I think. I was stiff, cold, yet I was still alive and Targi no longer held me in his bonds. I centered what remained of my own will on moving my hand—to prove mainly that this I could do. Then, aching in every muscle, I struggled up.

Around me was a very gray light, forbidding, though only a faint shadow of the threat I had conceived had earlier hung there. Within reaching distance lay Uruk, while beyond him, where we had seen the discarded body of Targi—

Had those fragments of brittle bone, those ashes, once really been a man or the semblance of one? Of the crystal skull which had dominated this hall, strove to master us, there was not even a broken shard remaining. But there was something else—there lay the hilt of a sword, a bladeless weapon now as dingy gray as the light around.

I crawled to Uruk. His ax had not suffered the same change; no, it lay intact under his hand. I felt for a pulse at the side of his throat. He still lived. Now I fumbled my water bottle loose from my belt, raised his head to rest against my shoulder, and dribbled the liquid between his teeth. At last he swallowed, coughed, and his eyes opened.

For a moment he stared at me as if I were a stranger to him. Then—

"Tolar—?" but he hesitated over that name.

I shook my head. Putting aside the water bottle, I reached for the sword hilt, to hold it into his line of vision.

"I am Yonan—even as you summoned me."

His lips curved very slightly. "And return you did, to our salvation. Targi, great in sorcery as he was, could not control the yet unborn. So Ice Tongue has left you—for good or ill this time, I wonder?"

Somewhere in me laughter bubbled. "For good, so shall I believe. I am done with ill-omened weapons and ancient battles, either lost or won. The future is what *I* shall make it!"

Then I remembered—were we still in the past? I had only the evidence of what remained of Targi to bolster my hope that we were free of time change.

Uruk must have followed the glance I gave to those nearly vanished remains; his mind caught my thought. "I think it is *your* time now, Yonan-who-was-more. Targi, at least, is very dead. And the shattering of his power could well have swept us onward once again. If that is true, Escore still has some use for us. Shall we endeavor to prove that?"

The hilt of Ice Tongue was dead. I sensed that never again would it play any part in the schemes and ploys of men. I laid it down on the wide step which supported the pillar on which the skull had been. Targi had striven to use me; he had failed. It was that intangible trophy which I would bear from this struggle; no man save myself would ever see it. I was not Tolar, yet something of him would always remain within me, honing what I was now into a better self, even as a careful warrior hones his blades. I could not deny that—I did not want to. But I *was* Yonan— and somehow I did not want either to deny that or forget it.

Perhaps time had indeed swept us forward as the sea tide will sweep that which it carries. If so, there would be other swords, other battles, and for me a new life into which I must fit myself carefully and with more self-knowledge than many men are given to understand.

"Time was, time is, time will be—" Uruk said—no he did not say it, the words seeped into my mind. And in me there was a sudden heady spark of joy. Tolar I could thank for this—that I had at last that other sense I had always longed to possess. I got to my feet, reached down a hand to aid Uruk.

Time will be—the words sang in my mind, awakening impatience in me. Ice Tongue no longer held me, and all Escore waited!

III
Sword of Shadow

1

Around me the night was very still, yet it seemed that just beyond the range of my sight, the seeking of my ears, there was movement. I pressed the palms of my hands tightly together, breathed deeply and slowly, summoned not only courage, but that strange part of my mind which I had never understood, but which, even in earliest childhood, I realized dimly was there—something which could change all the world for me if I could harness it properly. Only there was no one to teach me that then; I had only faulty instinct to depend upon.

I looked down at those hands so tightly enfolded. I had seen them sticky with clay and—no, I was not going to think of that. For remembering too deeply might open a door—like the one of the ever-to-be-feared Gates of the Old Ones—to that which I sensed prowling out there.

Yet there were those moving close about me now, each and every one willing to raise protection such as the Shadow fears, to wall me around with their own defenses. It was in me that the flaw lay. And how deep or dangerous that flaw might be haunted me waking, was a part of my dreams sleeping, sometimes strong enough to bring me gasping to full consciousness, to lie shivering—wondering what *I* might have done during that time my waking mind was not in command.

In my race many women are so cursed. Most may consider it rather blessed, but I do not. In Estcarp those with Talent are early detected and taken for training, taught all the safeguards one must have when one deals with the Power—even lightly.

But I was born into a time of chaos, my people fleeing over the mountains from Karsten, the few remaining members of a very ancient race which the ruler of that land had outlawed. And even had we been left alone I might never have developed my unexplainable gift—since there were no Witches in Karsten to seek out and train their kind. While the Wise Women who did dwell among us did not meddle with the greater Powers, but the lesser, which have in them only a portion of the Talent.

I was born to the sister of the Lady Chriswitha, who fostered me when my mother died of an illness I think now she willed upon herself, since she could not face a world in which her lord lay dead. They said that at my birthing she turned her face to the wall and would not even look upon me. For it was the fact that in protecting her escape from a band of Karsten over-the-Border raiders my father had died.

But the Lady Chriswitha had a heart which was big enough to open wide its door for me. And I was not her only fosterling in those turbulent days. She had also Yonan, who was half of the Old Race, half Sulcar, the son of her heart-friend. There were also her own children—Imhar, heir to the House, the Lady Dalhis and the Lady Meegan, both of whom were older and wed young to liegemen of Lord Hervon. But I was different—

At first they thought that I had been given only the healing gift. For I could look upon man or beast and somehow see the ill which encompassed them. And with the animals I had kinship, so that in time I could not easily eat meat or wish any hunter well. Though this I kept secret within me.

When the Witches of Estcarp performed their last and greatest feat of battle, making the hills and mountains themselves move by the power of their united wills, and so walling off Karsten, then it seemed that a new and more peaceful life stretched before us. I could remember nothing but days of war—it seemed very strange to face peace.

And I wondered how those like Imhar would live. For he was born to war and knew nothing else, nor cared for it, I was certain. I knew so little of him, though he was to be my lord, thus uniting the kin more solidly together. But I think that meant little to him, and mostly it made uneasiness for me.

Yonan was more friend than Imhar. He came from two races which were born to hold sword and measure steel with enemies—yet he was seemingly a son to neither in that fashion. Doggedly he practiced sword-play, shot at targets with the dart guns, strove to do all which was expected of a man in those years. Yet with me he talked of other things, old legends and strange stories he had heard. He might have been a song-smith perhaps—save that to his clumsy fingers the lap harp was more unlearnable than was the sword. It was as if within him the cleavage of race had somehow marred or lessened the man he had really meant to be.

What would have become of us had we stayed in Estcarp? Sometimes I have wondered a little concerning that. Would I have come to wed with Imhar and perhaps never have known what lay buried within me? Would

I have been happier for that ignorance? Sometimes my heart answers yes. But there is another part of me which denies that I could have done this.

However, even as we worked to build the Manor for the House, a youth came to us from the east. And his story of a need for us struck so deep into our minds that nearly without thought we found ourselves riding not only into the unknown, but into a war which was more grim and black of purpose than all the struggles we had known before.

Thus we came over-mountain into the Valley. And there I was like some plant which is given the soil it needs for full nourishment, sun, and water. For I met the Lady of Green Silences—she who bears many names in our ancient tales, but who in this cycle answers to that of Dahaun. She and her people are not of our race, perhaps even of our species, but they are human-formed. And with those of the Old Race who had not defiled themselves with dealings with the Shadow they held kin-friendships.

When Dahaun and I saw each other for the first time there was between us instant knowledge that we sought the same road. She took me into her household, where I first learned how much there *was* for me to learn, and how little I had been able to give because I lacked such knowledge. I was like one long athirst in a desert waste who is offered a flagon of cool water. But I knew that also as one who thirsted, this I must take slowly, a sip at a time. For the talent too strongly seized may turn upon one.

The Valley was a beleaguered fortress—of the Power against the Shadow. For in this land of Escore there had been much ancient evil wrought by adepts who had set themselves above the rules of the Talent, feasting their crooked spirits on what they could warp nature into doing. And that ancient evil, though perhaps much weakened by time, was now waking, gathering its strength to rage again.

Within the Valley, we were told, safety lay, for it was guarded by such strong runes of Light that naught which carried the foul mark of the Dark might come. Yet our men (together with those who were not men in form and yet gave liegeship to the Light) patrolled the upper reaches of the heights, beating off attacks that strove to win up sheer rock to come at us.

Then—one morning I awoke and my hands were sticky with clay such as I had seen along the riverbank. And in me there was such an uneasiness that I felt as guilty as one who unbars the door of a keep to let through the enemy. Still also this I could not speak of, not to the Lady Dahaun, nor to my foster mother. But I had that to keep me busy. Yonan had been injured in a fall upon the heights—and might have died save that Tsali of the Lizard folk found him wedged into one of the crevices there.

I was glad that I must tend his ankle, occupy myself in other ways. For, though I had at once washed that clay from my fingers, it seemed to me that I still somehow carried the stain of it on my flesh, and the uneasiness which was part of it lay at the back of my mind where I firmly imprisoned it. Three times I tried to speak, and found that I could not shape the words; and so my unquiet grew, and I used what skills Dahaun had taught me—still there was no suggestion that anything of the Shadow had won through our barriers.

But I was reluctant to sleep that night, wishing even I might be watched by someone—yet this I also found myself unable to ask for.

The dream came as suddenly as if I had passed through a door. And it was as vividly real as awakening, so real that all which lay behind me at this moment seemed more of a dream or vision than where I stood now.

This was a hall—not like those I knew in Estcarp—unless very ancient Es might hold such. The walls appeared so far away on either side that they were hidden by dusk. But the pillars on either side were tall, and their carvings of strange monsters very clear. A light which was not the warmth of sun, nor that of any lamp, but which seeped greenly-yellow from divers of the pillars themselves, gave me full vision.

There was someone waiting here—someone I must meet—

I did not seem to walk normally as I flitted forward down the well-marked aisle; rather it was as if I were drawn through the air, weightless and without the power to resist. Then the aisle ended in a circular space. And on a pillar which was the center core of that, was a skull—life-sized and carved of what seemed the clearest crystal. Still the brain pan was filled with whirling, dancing light of rainbow colors, one shade eternally fading or deepening into another.

And resting one hand lightly on the base where the skull was placed stood a woman. She had some of the same look of Dahaun's people, for she changed color—her hair flaming near to scarlet, then deepening to brown, and at last to black; her skin one moment ivory, the next sun-browned. Yet I knew that she was not of the Valley.

Power radiated from her as if she aimed that directly at me. And, though her coloring changed so from one moment to the next, her features did not lose their own set expression. Her full lips were curved in a small, secret smile, as if she dwelt exultingly upon some knowledge she would share with no one.

Her body was clothed only by whirls of mist which also writhed and moved, revealing now a crimson-nippled breast, again a smooth thigh, the beginning of a slight curve of belly. There was something utterly wanton in that play of clothing which was faintly disturbing, reached perhaps that part of me which was not here in answer to her sorcery.

"Crytha!" She flung out one hand in a parody of friendly welcome. And her voice echoed in my mind, not in my ears. "Well met, little sister—"

There was that in me which cringed at her careless claim of kinship. I was *not* of her blood—I was not! And perhaps my instant revulsion troubled the spell she had set upon me, for I saw her smile disappear, her eyes on me burn with anger.

"You are what and who I will you!" So quick was she with the leash of ownership. "You will do as I say. Come to me—"

I could not fight that compulsion any more than I could have broken chains which might have been forged about my wrists or limbs. To her I went.

"Look you!" She waved a hand toward the skull with its blaze of inner fire. That was now brighter, harsher, alive!

Without my willing it my hands went forth and touched the temples of the skull, one on either side. Into me swept another will, imperious—overriding the last remnants of what I was. I was given my orders; I knew what must be done.

"So!" the woman laughed. "We have chosen well, eh, Targi—" She spoke to the skull as if it were a living being. "Now you"—contemptuously she looked at me—"go you about your task."

Out from the pillars came scuttling shapes. Thas—the underground people, such as had already tried once to betray us. The leader of that band caught at my hand and I could not draw away. Under his urging I turned to the right.

We went through burrows; how many and where they ran, that I could not tell. All which burned within me, with near the same blaze which the skull had shown, was what I was to do. For it came to me that there were limitations on the woman and the skull. What meant so much to them they could not accomplish because these ways were forbidden them. Perhaps the passage ran somewhere under the cliffs of the Valley and, even deep in the earth, the safety runes had a measure of power. If so, such did not now work in my favor. I could pass this way easily enough, but I could not free myself from the tasks laid upon me.

The rest—it became disjointed, more like the broken episodes of a dream wherein one slides from one bit of action to the next without any logical connection. I remember mouthing words which someone else—either the woman or the skull had locked into my brain. And then—

There was something wrong. I could feel the ensorcelment lock even tighter on me. But beneath that prisoning arose baffled rage. I had not completed my task—there had been unseen interference. The Thas surrounded me, pushed and pulled me along their black burrows. What happened after—I could never piece together.

But there came a time when I knew I moved above earth, I saw faces which I should remember, only the hold on my brain would not yet let me. Then—

Then I came fully awake—or alive—once more. I stood in the open air and around me blew sweet wind, the chill of which I did not mind, because it carried the freshness of the world I knew. And there was Yonan, and with him another who wore strange armor and carried a great double-headed ax. There was also Tsali and then—up from the depth before us which must make the Valley—Dahaun came and with her Lord Kyllan, who was hand-fasted to her—others behind.

I cried out—this must be real—not another dream. But only when Dahaun took me into her arms was I sure of that.

2

The barrier against speech no longer held, and I told Dahaun freely what had been my dream. Though dream, it seemed, it was not. I *had* been drawn out of the safety of the Valley—and that by the betrayal of a part of my own wayward mind. For they showed me a figure wrought of clay. And set to its rounded head were hairs from my own; about its form was wrapped a rag which I had once worn. And this I knew without telling was of the Old Evil. So had I been reached and worked upon by a greater force than we had suspected had yet striven to break our boundaries.

When I described the woman who abode with the skull, Dahaun frowned; still, there was puzzlement in her frown. She made me stay within her own quarters, taking care before she left me to use a wand, white and fresh-peeled, to draw around the cushions on which I rested certain tokens confined by a circle. And, before she had done, the need to sleep had so weighted my eyelids that I drifted away. Though I struggled, for I feared above all to lose my will and thought and be drawn into dreams.

Dream again I did, and not happily. I was not now physically a part of that second visit to the hall of pillars and the skull as I had been the first time. Yet I could see—I could hear.

There was a change in her who had woven that earlier spell, for I was as certain as if oath had been taken that it was the woman who had reached out to draw me to her through the runways of the Thas; I so much under her spell I did not know where I went.

She no longer showed the pride and arrogance which had clothed her better than the mist at our last meeting. And her beauty was marred, as if time had served her ill. But still she was one to be feared and I did not forget that. Though at this time she did not look in my direction nor show any sign that she knew of my presence there.

Rather she stood by the base on which the skull rested and her hands caressed the crystal of its fashioning. Those blazing lights had died, or been muted so that only a near-colorless fogging of the inner part remained.

I saw her mouth and lips move, believed that she chanted or spoke to the thing she fingered. There was a kind of passion in her face which was greater than wrath—although that emotion underlaid the other. I could sense the forces she strove to bend, to break, to control by her will—and her frustration and despair that this she could not do.

Then she stooped to set her lips to the fleshless mouth of the crystal. She did that as I believed a woman would greet a lover, the one who was the center of her life. And her arms went around the pillar so that the "face" of that grinning thing pressed tightly against her ruby-tipped breasts. There was something so shameless in that gesture that I felt revulsion. But I could not flee, for that which had drawn me here still held—dream though it was.

She turned her head suddenly, as her eyes sought me. Perhaps she now knew that some portion of me had been drawn once more into her net. I saw exultation blaze high in those eyes.

"So—the spell holds yet, does it, younger sister? I have wrought better than I hoped."

Her hands arose in the air to trace lines I did not understand. Straightaway that which was me was locked fast. Now she came away from the skull, and so vibrant was the Dark Power in her that her hair stirred of itself, arose in a great flaming nebula about her head, more startling than any crown a queen might wear. Her lips were slightly parted, their burning redness like a gathering of blood on her ghostly fair skin.

She came one step and then two; her hands reached out for me, that triumph swelling in her and about her like some robe of ceremony.

"There is yet time—with an able tool—" I think her thought was more her own than sent to me. "Aye, Targi," she glanced back for a breath at the skull, "we are not yet lost!"

But if she had some plan it had failed her. For in that instant the spell broke, the woman and the skull she tended so passionately vanished. I opened my eyes again upon the hall of Dahaun to see the Lady of Green Silences standing at my feet. While over me she shook a handful of near-withered herbs, leaves of which broke off at the vigor of her gestures, shifting down to lie on my body. I sniffed Illbane, that very old cure for the ills of the spirit; with it langlon, the tri-leafed, which clears the senses, recalls a wandering mind.

Only I knew what had happened, and I cowered on my bed of hides and springy dried grasses. Tears which were born both of fear and the sense of my own helplessness filled my eyes, to spill down my cheeks.

Dahaun, though she looked grave enough, reached out and caught my hand even when I would shrink from her, knowing now that some part of me had been attuned to the Shadow and that I was held by all which had and was most evil in this land.

"You dreamed—" she said, and she did not use mind touch but rather spoke as she would to a small child who awakes terrified from a nightmare.

"She—I was drawn again—" I mumbled. "She can draw me to her will—"

"The same woman—?"

"The same woman, the skull, the place of pillars. It was as it was before."

Dahaun leaned forward, her eyes holding mine locked in a gaze I could not break, for all my feeling of guilt and trouble.

"Think, Crytha, was it *exactly* the same?"

There was some reason for her questioning. I dropped my guard and drew upon memory, so that in my mind hers could see also what I had witnessed. Though I began to fear for her, lest some of the taint sleep with the knowledge, to infect her also.

She sat down cross-legged by my bed place. Crushing the last of the Illbane between her hands, she leaned forward, to touch those now deeply scented fingers to my temples.

"Think—see!" she commanded with assurance.

So I relived in memory, as best I could, what I had seen in the dream. When I had done she clasped her hands before her.

"Laidan—" She spoke a single name. "And—Targi—"

"Who is Laidan?" I ventured at last.

"One who mixed—or mixes, since it seems that she must still live in some burrow of hiding—the worst of two races within her. Laidan was of the People by her mother's right—her father—" Dahaun shrugged. "There were many tales in the time of her bid to rule as to whom he might be—though he was not one of us. It is most commonly accepted that she was sired by one of the Hill Lords who accepted the rule of the Shadow— willingly. Laidan—and Targi—" she repeated thoughtfully.

"Well, for that combination there may be an answer. Those who went forth last night (*if* they can do as Uruk believes) perhaps can make sure Targi shall no longer be a factor in any campaign. But Laidan they would not have met in that past—for at the battle time she was elsewhere, very much engaged."

"The battle?" To me she spoke in riddles. After a long measuring look at me she did not answer that half-question. Rather she spoke about what seemed the most urgent to me now.

"It would seem that Laidan, and that which she has so long guarded, have set part seal on you, Crytha. How this may be I cannot understand. But the roots of it all may lie in the far past. However—if she can compel you to come to her—even through dreaming—"

I already knew the answer to that, though my body was so cold with an inner fear that it began to shake in vast shudders I could not control.

"Then—then I am a danger to you—an opener of gates—" I said in a low voice which I could not hold steady. I knew what I must add to that, but my lips and tongue would not shape the words. The fear which had seized on me was now in near control. However, if I would threaten a break in the defenses of the Valley—it was very plain that I had no longer a place here. I stared at her dumbly, unable to do what duty pressed on me to do.

Dahaun shook her head slowly. "We are not totally defenseless in Power. But it may be that you shall have to face that you will be a prisoner, little sister—"

I flinched. "That—that is how she named me!" To hear the same words from Dahaun added to my burden of terror and guilt.

"So?" There was a firm line about Dahaun's lips. "So—she moves in that way? There is this you must understand, Crytha, because you have not had the training in control which should have been yours when the talent first manifested itself; it is true that you are left vulnerable to such as Laidan. I do not know what she may have learned during the dusty seasons between the time of the Lost Battle and this hour. But that there are limits on her is also the truth, and you must believe it. She never commanded the Green Silences—" Now there was a proud self-confidence in Dahaun. "It took too long to learn and she was ever impatient and greedy. Last time she took your body to do her bidding. This time—that being well guarded—" she gestured toward the runes on the floor—"she could only summon up your dream self—which is useless to her, for it is of another plane of existence and cannot operate physically. If Yonan and Uruk succeed—" Then she stopped shortly.

"Yonan—what of Yonan?" I was for the moment startled out of my own self-absorption. "Does—does he go to hunt this Laidan?"

Dahaun shook her head. "No, for she will not be where he would venture." She said no more, and with a sick feeling, I understood why. In sleep I could be milked of such information should Laidan again summon me.

"That she shall not do either," Dahaun picked the thought from my mind. "For there are other precautions we shall take. Believe you this, Crytha. There is no reason to feel guilt because you have been caught in this snare. Adepts even, in the past, have been ensorceled by their enemies. Warned as to the nature of the foe, then we can take precautions."

It was thus I became for a time a prisoner of my own people, of those I would not have harmed and yet who could not trust now what I might be forced to do. I lived apart in a smaller house where one of the Lizard women waited upon me, for those of that species could detect, through some faculty of their own, inborn and not to be influenced, any change in me. Also, I was forbidden to use the talent in any way—even for healing—since such a use might open a path of thought between me and she whom Dahaun called Laidan.

Yonan and Uruk—through the days I wondered where they went and to what purpose they had gone. None dared tell me, nor could I ask. But the Lady Chriswitha came to me with a suggestion which might be an answer to my fears for the future.

It was well known that among the Old Race she who married, or she who was bedded by any man (as had sometimes been deliberately done in the old days to Witches who were captured by the enemy), lost their power and talent. Only one exception in all the passing years had been known—and that was the Lady Jaelithe. But her lord had been an Outlander, of another race. While he himself (against all nature as we conceived of it) possessed a portion of the Talent. However, even after she proved that the Power had not departed from her when she became a wife, still the Witches of Estcarp would not receive her again among their number and she was looked upon askance.

Thus there was a solution to my future. Let me wed and bed with Imhar and I would no longer be any threat to those in the Valley, since I would lose my Talent. And in my despair I almost seized upon this solution.

For Imhar I had no love. But among my people marriages were always arranged for the good of the kin-clan. Though during the years of exile and war some had come about differently—for I knew that the Lady Chriswitha herself had wed by inclination, since there was no clan elder left in her House to arrange such a match for her. Lord Hervon had already lost his family during the massacres in Karsten and had met with her first to bring some news of kin—escorting my mother to her.

Thus her wedding had been of her own choosing. But those of her daughters had come about in the old way, their husbands being now landless lords who had joined with Lord Hervon among the Borderers and so had agreed to add to the solidity of his House rather than start new ones of their own. I had been hand-fasted to Imhar nearly from my birthing; only the constant war had delayed marriage by cup and flame.

Now, though we were still ringed by danger even more perilous, I need only signify my willingness for marriage and take my place as Imhar's lady, putting aside all hope of ever being once more a wielder of Power.

Imhar was well enough. He was comely, a warrior born, and the heir to Hervon. Only—only in spite of my present fear and hurt I could not give consent. I was worn within me by the need for keeping, or striving to keep, that which was my birthright. I could not say the words my foster mother and aunt wanted—they choked in my throat. I thought that my dear lady would be angry with me and I was prepared to add her anger to the rest of the burden I must bear. But she only voiced the suggestion of what I might do and then, after a moment's silence which I could not break, she added:

"No one is born with the same gifts or talents, dear child. Imhar is his father's son, and in him there is a vast energy which since his boyhood has been centered on the making of war. Dalhis and Meegan were content with what life brought them. They wished for nothing else but home hall and children to be born from their bodies. But if something else is given us—" She fell silent and sat for a long moment looking at her hands where they lay upon her knees. "We are in a place and time of wonders, child. And we of another generation have not the right to choose for you as has always been done.

"Imhar—" Again she paused and then shook her head as if at her own thoughts. "He has his own talent, and he is happy to use it as he does. If you wish to bide as you are—there shall be no pressure put upon you for any wedding—"

"But I am hand-fasted—" I was bewildered, hardly able to believe that she meant what she said.

"Wait, Crytha." Her words came fast and with emphasis as if to impress their meaning the more upon me. "Wait until you are sure!"

"But I—as I am I may be a danger to you—all of you—even to the Valley."

"Trust the Lady Dahaun—and wait—" She got to her feet a little heavily and I saw with eyes which were a little clearer that, though she showed no signs of age (for the Old Race do not until very near the end of their lives), her face was very tired, as if sleep might come to her pillow at night but true rest fled.

I caught her hand in mine and held it tight.

"Thank you—"

Gently she withdrew her fingers. "I would not see waste," she said. "Dear as you would be as a daughter in my house, I would not see waste."

And, so saying, she went away, leaving me only the weight of time and the conserving of my patience.

3

Though I feared each night to dream again—and eagerly drank the potion Dahaun sent me that perhaps this might not be—it was that very night that once more our defenses were breeched. Perhaps it had taken Laidan so long to build powers of her sorceries that she had not until this hour been able to reach me again.

Sight came to me and hearing, and it was as if somehow I had been blind and deaf all my life to that moment. For there were subtleties open to my senses now which I had never known before. Whether I stood in body or mind in that open I was not sure.

But I shivered in the chill of the wind, smelled the heavy scent of the trees which it scooped up from the Valley to fling outward with a prodigal force. Overhead hung the moon—an old moon, nearly dead and ready to vanish from the sky in order to be reborn in a new cycle.

I raised my hands, looking down along my body. I wore riding dress and my hands were scratched, nails broken, as if I had pulled myself by main force to this place. Now I wanted to turn, look down upon the Valley behind me, wondering (if I were indeed here in body) how I had won to this height.

Then I realized that I was caught in the trap of a geas which did not permit me even to look back—but only forward. So I wavered across the uneven footing of this place, where there were many treacherous cliffs and slides to trap the unwary. Also, I moved with purpose and certainty, though it might not be my purpose or will which drove me on.

And I could well guess whose will had drawn me out of safety and set me on this journey. Twice I tried to break the hold upon my mind and body, but so great and concentrated was that it was as if I beat with bare and bloodstained fists against a door cast of sword steel.

Then, realizing that in this there was not yet any chance for escape, I surrendered to the will of Laidan. I crossed the fissured rock, my feet bringing me unerringly to a cavity in the side of the height. There I stooped to push within a very narrow entrance which was half choked with fallen rubble.

There was no stench of Thas here. If Laidan held rulership over those burrowers, she did not use them now, perhaps believing that my will was so locked by hers that I would do exactly as I was bid and not strive to escape.

Though I was not Witch-trained, I had the example of those of Est-carp always at the back of my mind. To control and force obedience on another demanded a vast concentration, continued, unrelenting. I did not know how close to an adept Laidan might be—and had not the Lady Dahaun said even the adepts themselves might be ensorceled? Every step I took drained more energy from her who bent me to some task which lay in her desire. I walked haltingly, as slowly as I could, ever seeking, with sharp unexpected darts of mental force, to find some weakness in what held me.

That none had yet been found was no reason for me to embrace despair. Laidan, I believed, had fastened the full of what must be a not inconsiderable talent on me. Sooner or later she would—she *must*—feel the strain of what she did. So I must keep probing, at irregular intervals, ready for any second which might win my freedom.

These underground ways were dark. I was swallowed up by blackness as if the maw of some great beast had engulfed me. But I resolutely held fear at bay. Laidan needed me; she would not waste what she needed. Therefore, even in the dark I did not have yet anything to fear—except the will which held me captive.

Now there was a kind of nibbling at my mind. It did not come, I believed, from what Laidan had laid upon me. She had to hold her manipulation of me too taut to take any such liberties. No, this was like a very vague memory struggling to throw open some door and issue forth.

All of my species have such occurrences of memory we cannot account for—times when we see a stretch of country, a building, when an inner voice swells in instant answer—saying, "This you have seen before." Even when we know that that cannot be possible.

What tugged so persistently at me now must be such a false memory. Or can it be true that we live more than one life, seeking in each to repair the wrongs we have willfully committed earlier? I have heard some of the Old Race discuss this theory upon occasion. But for me heretofore, this life had been enough—the wonder and promise of it filling me always.

But—sometime—somewhere—I had walked these ways. I was so

certain of that I thought, black as it was here, I could be sure of the walls rising on either side. And those walls were not bare stone. No—deep cut in them were symbols. So, to prove myself wrong or right, I put out my right hand, confident that I would find my fingers sliding over such stone. And so I did. And the wall was pitted and slashed with deep cutting. Though I did not strive to trace any of the patterns I *knew* were there.

For those patterns were not of my Talent. Around them hung a taint of evil, lessened perhaps a little by the many years they had been wrought here. My flesh recoiled as if I had touched fire, or burning acid, when I found them.

The pavement under my boots was smooth, with no falls of rock nor crevices to provide any barrier. Then—I was brought to a halt.

I sensed a sighing—a disturbance in the air. That which had taken command of my body turned me to the left until both my outstretched hands once more scraped across engraven stone. And I tapped out with one foot, knowing, as surely as if I could see, that here a pit opened in the floor and the only way around it was a narrow ledge which my tapping toe located.

So I set my shoulders against that wall, my hands braced tightly against it, facing outward to the pit. Step by step I squeezed by the trap I could not see. While from the depths came ever that sighing, and with it a stale smell. My journey seemed to take an hour, though it could only have been minutes before I was once more on a wide and solid surface of a corridor.

Now I saved my strength of purpose, no longer making those attempts to break the power holding me. For that passage shook me greatly, the reason for it lying, I was sure, in the depths of that memory which was not a real memory.

I felt also that the passage now sloped upward—at so gentle a curve that at first I was not aware of it. This became steeper as I went. Finally I knew that my feet unerringly had found a flight of steps and I was climbing. Here the wall to my left was smooth and I ran my hand along it for the sense of support it gave me in the dark.

Up and up—was I inside the heart of some mountain? Though I could not remember any peak of unusual height among those walling in the Valley. No, the true chain mountains lay to the north and the west—those we had come over in our venture into Escore.

My hands arose, at the command of Laidan rather than by my own desire. Flat-palmed, they struck a surface just above my head. And I guessed that I had reached some kind of trap door sealing off this place. I exerted my strength, and not altogether at the bidding of my captor—for I wanted out of this trap.

At first I thought that exit must have been sealed or barred. Then, very slowly and reluctantly, it loosened in its frame. Gray light, thin like the last of any winter twilight, outlined a square on three sides. I arose two more steps that I might set my back to the door and, with a last compelling effort, sent that crashing up and back. Ancient dust puffed into my face, making me cough.

For a moment I hesitated, for what might lie above in waiting I could not guess. Then, because I must, I climbed into the open. There were piles of tumbled stone, even a trace of a wall, as if this hidden way had once issued into the room of a building of size and presence. But if that were so, the way was—

I blinked and blinked again. For a second or two I saw clearly the desolation which had been plain enough still in existence—the fallen blocks like shadows. Then those winked out. Walls arose out of the very earth itself, took on sturdy substance. There was a roof high over my head veiling the sky. The place of the skull—?

No—there were no pillars here and the wall was round. I could have entered the ground floor of some tower. Window slits there were, but those gave little light. Rather that came from torch rods set at intervals on the wall, pulsating with a steady, contained flame.

The opening of the trap door through which I had emerged had pushed aside a tanned, furred rug, into the making of which must have gone more than one snow-cat pelt. And there were stools and benches, much carven, a table nearer to the wall on which sat a bowl of ruddy crystal overflowing with those small red grapes which are the sweetest and the rarest my people knew. Beside that was a flagon of worked metal with the sheen of silver and gold interwoven, which had been fashioned in the form of a traditional dragon—its neck curved upward, its mouth open to emit whatever fluid might fill such a container.

All illusion; my mind gave a quick and, I thought, true answer. Yet when I stooped to touch the wrinkles of the rug, my fingers held the softness of fur. So this illusion could control more than one sense at a time.

I swung around toward the table, determined to test that guess further, but there came a curdling of the air. So strange was that I stared as the atmosphere itself appeared to thicken, form a body. Then I faced Laidan.

She laughed, lifting one hand to brush a strand of flame-bright hair out of her eyes.

"So you are duly surprised, little sister? Well, time can be obedient to the will, even as is space—or the other boundaries men so complacently accept as always unchangeable and fixed. This is Zephar—"

For a moment after she spoke that name her eyes were intent upon me, almost as if she expected I might recognize the word. Then she shrugged.

"It does not greatly matter whether you remember or not. But all this"—she flung her arms wide, the mistlike covering that she had worn before seeming in this setting to be more opaque and more like some normal weaving—"answers readily to my call since I once had the ordering of it. Where memory is the sharpest, there we can beat time itself.

"However, that is of no consequence. You are—"

She seated herself with deliberation on the only true chair in that chamber, one placed at mid-board by the table, its dark high back framing her hair to make those strands appear even brighter.

"Yes, we are in Zephar, younger sister. And in Zephar there is that which even in this crook-coiled time you can do." Now she set her chin upon one fist and planted the elbow of that arm firmly on the table. Though her mouth might still smile easily, her eyes were like bits of ice drawn from the teeth of the Ice Dragon, as from them appeared to spread a chill which grew strong within that tower room.

"You are life-linked with this one you call Yonan—though once he had another name and played the part of a fool—only not well enough. He had his death of his own pretensions, but not in time—"

And the word "time" seemed to echo through the chamber like a gong from a distance, a sound not to be denied.

"Now he would play the fool again," she continued. "But the past must not be reversed, rather it shall be improved upon. You, and through you Yonan (who is nothing but who unfortunately can move to destroy what a lifetime—twenty lifetimes—cannot bring once more into being), must be used. Therefore—younger sister—you shall take a hand and all will be as we wish—"

I found my tongue at last. Perhaps it was the thought that she would make of me a tool to pull Yonan down which brought that croak out of me, rusty-sounding as if I had not given tongue in a score of years.

"As *you* wish—" Had the two of us ever stood and bargained so before? A teasing ghost of memory assaulted me once more. Perhaps not just in this same way, I believed, but we had been opponents long ago. Then I must have known more—much more—

For a second time she laughed. "If you hunt down that very forgotten trail you will not find much at the end of it—save that you failed then even as you will fail now. Believe me"—her eyes were afire or else had put on the diamond brightness ice can sometimes show under the sun—"you will fail. You are even less this time than you were when once before we fronted one another. Yes, you shall give me Yonan and all shall be well. I will make very certain of that. Come!"

She arose, beckoning me. And, as it had been since I had come into consciousness this time among the hills, I was wholly subservient to her will.

She did not even glance back to see if I followed. Rather she went directly to where a stair spiraled around the circular inner wall of this place and climbed quickly, I constrained to follow.

We came so into a second and upper chamber where the ceiling was not so high. Here were shelves and tables holding all manner of basins, beakers, and small boxes. From the ceiling and along the walls dangled bunches of withered vegetation which I thought I recognized as dried herbs. But the center of the chamber had been kept bare of any furniture. And there, set into the floor in various colored stones so that it would ever be permanent and ready to hand, was the pentagram of witchery. On the points of the stars were thick black candles, which had been lighted before, as drippings of evil-looking wax ridged their sides.

Beyond the pentagram was a smaller circle, this bordered by runes which had been drawn on the pavement in black and red. But lying in the middle of that, tightly bound, a gag forced between his wide jaws, was—Tsali! Though how the Lizard man could have been brought here I could not guess.

4

Instinctively my mind reached to touch his. Only my thought send recoiled from an unseen barrier so intricately woven that nothing could pierce it—more of Laidan's sorcery. She had turned her back upon me, and there was contempt in that. She must now have believed me so poor a thing that she no longer even had to exert her power to hold me in control. Rather she was concentrating upon a search along those crowded shelves, taking down here a closed pot of rude workmanship, there a flask in which liquid swirled as if it had life.

I looked into Tsali's eyes and strove, though I could not reach him mind to mind, to make contact. And I saw that he knew me, yet there was that about his gaze which held shock—and—did I read repudiation?

In the beginning I had learned what I knew of my Talent because I could communicate with other life forms—those which are not the lesser (though ignorant men may deem them so because they do not walk, speak, or think after our fashion). The Lizard people, the Renthans, the Vorlungs of the Valley—they had arisen from stock totally unlike our own forefathers, but they were no less than we, only different.

Just as a fish lying in a sun-dappled pool, a pronghorn grazing in a meadow, a snow cat stalking in the upper reaches, have in them all the love of life, a way of thought equal to our own in power even if we cannot understand it.

I have also called to me the scaled ones. And I remembered now, in a small flash, how greatly I had troubled Yonan when he had once found me and a serpent as close-linked as was allowed by our divergent natures.

But all those were clean beasts who had nothing of the rot of the Shadow in them. While here in Escore prowled creatures which to mind-touch would be to open wide a gate through which I, myself, could be

invaded. How much did Laidan use those born as a result of ancient meddling on the part of a people grown so decadent that they would tamper
with nature to amuse themselves—or to provide servants for further evil?

The Lizard man was clearly an enemy. And that she planned worse
for him I did not have to be told. But since she had lifted from me most of
the force of her will, leaving only enough to keep me here, I began tenta-
tively to look about me, seeking any weapon, any ally I might find.

This cradle of sorcery had no windows, and the thick stone walls
were all shelved. Also, the ceiling over my head was much lower than that
of the chamber below. Now I could see that in the corners of that there
hung the soft thickness of years of webs, some so heavy with settled dust
that they seemed small ragged bits of curtains. And in those webs—I sent
out a very small quest of thought.

The mind that I touched was totally alien, the spark of intelligence
frightening in its cold avid hunger. I had never tried to summon any of the
insect world before. But that I had managed to touch at all was a small triumph. And, apparently, Laidan, in her preoccupation, had not been
warned that in so much—or so little—I had begun to evade the geas she
had laid upon me.

I located another creeper consciousness, a third. It was very hard to
hold to them, for their level of consciousness was so different from my
own it was like grasping a cord which was constantly jerked from my fingers, caught again just before it had totally escaped me.

There were huntresses in those dusty webs, cold and deadly. Of our
concerns they knew nor cared nothing at all. But they were there. And
now I made an effort, concentrating on the largest and what might be the
oldest of the webs. Something moved in the hole that was its center. So—
I had drawn its inhabitant thus far into the open! I had no plan at all, nothing but a hope which was very dim at that moment. But I put my own
talent to the test, summoning those who dwelt above. They seemed to
have fared very well, for when they appeared their bodies were bloated
with good living—and that in the largest web was larger than my palm.

These were no ordinary spiders. There was poison in their jaws. They
could immobilize their prey, enclose it in the web for future eating while
it still lived. And their tiny eyes were sparks of evil light.

Laidan had finished her selection of supplies for whatever infamous
sorcery she would do here. Now she moved purposefully around the star,
setting a second candle beside the first, sprinkling the lines uniting them
with powdered herbs—the smell of which was noxious.

I could guess what she intended—that we would be within the barriers she was making very secure, but that Tsali would lie in that wherein

should appear whatever being of personified evil she strove now to sum-mon from Beyond. Tsali was meant to furnish the blood-gift to that—

However, she had to release more of her hold on me to concentrate on what she did. Now she muttered words I did not know, keening spells no true Witch would soil tongue with. These must be very exact—for her life would also be forfeit were she to neglect any of the safeguards she now wove here.

The largest of the web dwellers came scuttling to the edge of her noi-some dwelling, teetered there, her sparks of eyes seeking the prey which I had set in her mind was not too far away. She launched forth into space, spinning as she came the cord linking her to her dwelling. Now she swung back and forth, her fat body an orange and black dot in the air.

I sensed the creature's dislike of the scents rising from the bruised herbs below. She longed to retreat, but the mental picture of rich feasting I forced upon her held her suspended. A second lurking spider dropped from her dust-coated den—then a third.

"Ah." Laidan arose and rubbed her hands together, freeing them of the last fragment of leaf and stem. "We are ready, little sister. There need only go forth the summons—the sacrifice will be accepted—and you shall be welcomed as one of us—"

"And if I choose not?" I no longer watched the spiders lest Laidan look aloft and see them too.

"You have no choice," she told me. "You have no defense against what I shall call, and it will possess you—for a space. When it withdraws, you shall be its, and then"—she gestured with one hand to indicate all which lay within the room—"you shall learn willingly. There is that in you which shall open doors for us. Think you that we could have sum-moned you elsewise? And"—now she eyed me oddly—"I think that you even long for this deep within you. You are of our kind, little sister, one who would mold instead of be molded. And that is a truth you cannot deny."

"I am not of the Shadow," I returned stubbornly.

She shrugged. "What is Shadow, what is Light? You have heard only one story, and that told by our enemies. There is much to be learned. Shall we shut doors and lock them upon that learning merely because of some fear of what lies beyond? There is only one true thing to desire—and that is Power! All else is swallowed up by time, broken and forgotten. Nothing within one lasts as long as the will to Power. You shall see, yes, and you shall rejoice in that—that you are one of those into which such Power may be poured, even as winter wine is poured into a waiting flask."

There was something in her words which did find a part of me receptive. Just as I had doubted myself when the Lady Chriswitha had talked with me, so did that doubt grow now in me. I wanted—I wanted to learn what I might do were I to use my talent to the full! I wanted—Power!

Still—another part of me arose to do battle now. Power—it could twist and mar, it could defeat its user, too. It—

The foremost of the spiders hung now above Tsali. I saw the bright eyes in his Lizard skull had moved from me to that dangling creature, marking too her sisters unreeling their threads to descend.

Laidan had come to stand with me within the star. Now she raised a small black wand she had brought from beneath her mist draperies. She pointed it from one candle to the next, and each started aflame with an oily, scarlet light. While she chanted as she moved.

Within me a sickness arose, so I crouched a little, my hands pressed against my middle. Whatever there was of my species which could be aroused by her sorcery was in such revolt that it tore at my body. And my own resolve strengthened.

Even as Laidan summoned that which she would force to obey her, so did I fix my will upon the spiders from above. I still did not know what I might do with them as weapons, but they were all I had. And I had learned enough from the Lady Dahaun to know that in such sorceries the balance was very delicate and easily disturbed. Laidan had enclosed both the circle and the star in which we stood with her precautions, but she had not thought of what might lie overhead.

The candles gave forth what was to me a disgusting smell. However, I saw Laidan breathing deeply between the words she still mouthed as if, from their scent, she garnered some needful food or energy. Then—

In the circle the air moved. But into that maelstrom there dropped the first spider from aloft. There was a swirling—I saw Laidan start, her chant faltered. A second spider, a third, disappeared into that misty column. Laidan started back—her hand raised to her mouth, for the first time shaken by what she witnessed—or felt—

I might not be as receptive as the sorceress, but I was aware of a vast troubling. Something which had been summoned—it had recoiled; it was angry. And—it was gone!

Laidan gave a cry, her hands arose to her ears as if to shut out some intolerable sound. Though I was aware of nothing, except that withdrawal. Then she, too, vanished—winked out instantly.

The flames of the candles were extinguished, leaving the room in near darkness. I was—free—

In a moment I crossed the star, grabbed from the table a stout-bladed knife and went to Tsali, slashing at his bonds. There was no longer any mental barrier between us. But something else weighed on the spirit in this chamber of the place Laidan had named Zephar.

Tsali stood, his clawed hand closed tightly about my wrist.

"Come—!" He scuttled for the stair, drawing me after him.

There followed a blurring of the walls, of all the things in that room, as if stout stone were melting, flowing away into nothingness. I thought I felt the steps of that stairway crumble and tremble under my weight. And I guess whatever illusion Laidan had set there was now disappearing, and that we might even be either trapped between times or perhaps buried under blocks of stone which the ages between would tumble from their settings.

At last, panting, we stood in the open, with around us only moss-grown and broken stones, a corner of what might once have been an outer wall. Tsali did not relax the hold he had kept on my wrist. His head darted from side to side with a speed my own species could never have equaled as he stood tensely, in such a position of instant alert that I knew that we were far from safe.

"Laidan?" I aimed a single thought at his mind.

"Is not gone—yet—" he confirmed my own fear. "She fled into her own corner of nothingness lest that which she had summoned turn upon her. But there she nurses her hate—which will grow the greater when she learns what has happened elsewhere. And because she has linked with you—then you can furnish her a door through time once more."

"What has happened elsewhere?" I seized upon that part of his warning.

"He whom she would have awakened is at last truly dead. The youth you call Yonan and Uruk of the Ax have wrought their own kind of magic. But in so much will Laidan's hate now be the greater. Though I think she dare not try anything as yet. That recoil of spell drove her too far from us. Only not yet are we finished with her."

He led the way, still keeping hold on me, out of that shell of ancient ruin. Now autumn-withered grass brushed thigh-high about me, near waist-high for him.

"What—why did the spiders—" I began. For though those spinners had done my will and had apparently broken Laidan's sorcery, I did not understand how such a thing could be.

"The balance of all spells," Tsali returned, still more than half of his attention given to what lay about us, even though the last of the tumbled blocks now lay behind, "rests very delicately. What Laidan summoned demanded a blood price—and that she had ready for it." He thought-sent matter-of-factly, as if *he* had not been that same price. "But when other

life came into it, then it was confused, angry—believing that Laidan had
sought to engage its aid with so poor an offering. Those which are truly of
the Shadow trust no one. Some spells they are forced to obey, but if any
bargain is not kept scrupulously, then they are freed from their obedience.
Three spiders did not equal one Tsali—" There was wry humor in that
which brought a smile to my own lips in spite of that lowering feeling of
being naked of defense in a threatening world which had and did burden
me as we went.

"Where are we?" I asked. Was this my own time? And could we win
back to the Valley?

"To each question," my companion picked up those thoughts very
quickly, "I cannot give full answer. But we must go with all caution.
Laidan will have a chance to replenish her powers. When she finds that
Targi is no more"—his scaled head shook from side to side—"then she
will not be appeased except by a full letting of blood. Since she perhaps
cannot get at those who killed that which was Targi, she shall be the more
bitter against us—"

"Yonan—Uruk?" I made a new question of their names.

Tsali's answer came as if now more important matters were in his
mind.

"Their road is their road—they have done well. It is up to us to keep
faith with the Valley. We cannot return while Laidan—" his thought
seemed to flicker there as if he wanted to veil it from me. But, bitterly, I
knew what he would have added and so did so myself:

"While Laidan can lay her spell on me." I made no question of that,
for I knew that it was the truth and one which I must face with all my
strength of body and spirit.

5

We wandered on. Tsali amended his pace somewhat after we had won farther from the ruins. The land was drably brown. Autumn in its last stages had set its imprint here and had emptied the country of all growth, even as frost had drawn subsistence from the grass and weeds, now so dried and sere they rattled faintly in the wind.

There showed the remnants of a road, mainly a block here and there, overcast with drifted soil, or canted upward by the roots of a leafless tree. I stared around, trying to locate some landmark that I could fix on. Though I knew now I could not venture back once more into the Valley—not until I was entirely free of Laidan's influence.

Now I knew hunger and thirst, and I wondered where Tsali would lead us. But I did not ask. Rather I walked as one in a dream, following his urging. Yet inside I sought for what might lie there as a part of my Talent. Against Laidan I had no defense—or so I believed. How long before she dared venture out of hiding, strive to make me again her tool?

Tool?

Somehow my apprehensive thought fastened on that word. Man wrought in two ways, by the vision of his mind (which is not sorcery in itself) and with his hands—or those extensions of his hands which in the dim beginning some thinkers had devised to answer problems they strove to solve.

There were the tools of a landsman—the plow to turn the earth for the receiving of seed, the rake and hoe, the hammer, the saw; others I could not even name. There were, in addition, the tools which I had known—pots one could sling over a fire to withstand heat and cook the food within, the spindle for the making of thread, the needle, the loom—the spoon, if you will, and a short knife, and—

Also, there were other tools—those of war. There was the dart gun—my fingers moved without conscious orders as if to close about one of those weapons, seek its firing button. There were the swords, and lances; men turned more to them in these days when we could no longer fashion the darts. There were shields for defense. And in the Valley, each of the Green People carried at belt one of the force whips which were the children of lightning, tamed and domesticated to their service.

All these were tools—even the mind. But my defeat lay in that I had not been properly taught what might be done with the tool I was born with.

Tsali angled off from the ancient remains of that road, pulling me eastward. I stumbled along at his bidding because I had no other plan to follow.

The day was as ash-gray as the life-sapped grass through which we trod a path. But there were no clouds I could see. Now I caught the sound of running water, and my tongue moved in a mouth which seemed filled with dust. Down an incline which grew even steeper, Tsali pulled me. Only now I was eager in my going for I saw the water, running around rocks and over a stony bed.

I knelt at the stream bank to wash my hands in the flow, which was chill, then made a hollow cup of closely held palms and fingers to raise to my lips. Tsali had gone a little away and crouched to lap with a long tongue. When I had drunk my fill I looked about me with a more conscious gaze. Drink I had had, but there was also the need for food.

Tsali made a sudden lunge with both forelimbs, and arose, water dripping from his scaled skin, a fish wriggling between his claws. He waited until it stilled and flipped it to the ground behind him, then squatted on the bank, his eyes once more intent upon the stream.

Though I had long set my own path of life, that I would not kill a living thing for eating, still now I knew that logic must determine my survival and if Tsali's catch meant life and strength, that I must accept.

But I could not bring myself to touch the dead fish. I could only watch as the Lizard man snaked a second out of its world. He hunted among the drift which bordered the stream, to return with a sharply pointed stick which he used to gut his catch and a stone with which he skinned the bodies.

There was no fire—Tsali would prefer his raw anyway, I knew. I eyed the portion he had set before me with repugnance. But I must live and this was the only food available. I made myself worry loose bits of firm flesh, choke them down. This was no worse than many ordeals a warrior must face. While against Laidan and her world, I had no choice but to go to war.

From overhead came a scream, startling me so I near spit out the last mouthful I had forced between my lips. I looked up to see a bird, its bill opened to voice another such squawk, impudently planing earthward as if to snatch the food from our hands.

In plumage it was almost as dull-gray as the sky. But around its eyes there were circlings of light, blazing red—which gave a momentary impression that it looked upon us through dots of fire. Its like I had not seen before. And, though I immediately alerted my bruised and battered other sense, I found nothing in mind touch save what it appeared to be— a bird of prey, yes, but one which followed its own fierce nature and no order of the Shadow.

Its cries brought another of its kind. However, as they fed upon the offal Tsali had thrown to one side, I experienced once more that far-off stir of what could not be memory (for I would swear I had never seen these birds before), yet—

The flash of their drab feathered wings, the burning scarlet of the mask about their eyes, grew more and more important to me. I found myself on my feet, my hands forming fists pressed tight against my breasts.

"Ninutra—!" I cried that aloud, my voice at that moment rising even above the incessant crying of the birds.

Ninutra? A person—a place—? Under that need to know, I reluctantly opened my mind and sought, deeper, deeper—recklessly. For such delving I had done before only under the control of the Lady Dahaun. And in such a place and time as now I stood, the peril must be very great. But that I brushed aside. I must know!

Ninutra—there was a hazy image forming. I shut my eyes to the sky, the birds, to the world I knew, turned my sight inward. Ninutra—come! I gave order to that fragment of thought—or memory—what was Ninutra?

There was a feeling of giddiness. The mental image sharpened, I felt breathless, filled with an expectancy in which excitement outweighed, at this moment, both fear and prudence.

A figure—about which held a nebula of flame color to match the patches about the eyes of the birds. If I could only brush away that curtain of brilliant radiance—see the clearer!

Ninutra—a *Power*—not a place. Of the Shadow? What had I then evoked?

No, that built-in warning which Dahaun's teachings had strengthened, did not come to life. Only neither did I feel the confidence I believed would flow about me if I summoned that which was turned to the Light. Could there then be a third force in this rent and warring land, one which stood apart from both the Dark and the Light—followed some path incomprehensible to both?

I fought to clear my mental sight of that image—or Power. But the light clothed it too well. However, slowly there came from it, as water circles outward when one throws a stone into a pool, a feeling of energy which was warm, growing hotter—hotter—

Maybe I cried out. I know that I shrank within me, strove now to will away that image, but I could not. Heat licked at me, but with it no feeling of anger. I sensed that what Ninutra might be was curious, that it stirred out of some deep contemplation of its own because my feeble summons had disturbed it. Was this one of the adepts?

If so, all which had been its human heritage was long since gone. It was pure force of a kind I did not understand, so alien—

Then that image receded from the fore of my mind. With it went some of the heat. Now it was rather as if I looked down a long aisle to see at the far end a form standing. The red glow drew back into its body (I say "it" for there was no sense of sex in this Power, there was little left but a pure force).

As I looked upon it so I was certain that once *"I"* (or the inner part of me), now flawed and long buried perhaps by other lives and ages of time, had once had contact with this Force and it had sometimes answered me. But that was long and long ago and the cord between us had frayed into dust—

I opened my eyes upon the dreary world by the stream. The birds were gone. Tsali squatted on the stones, his jewel eyes on me. I found myself whispering still that name:

"Ninutra—" And then I mind-spoke to my companion. "Tsali—what or who is—was *that* Power?"

His head bobbed, not to me, but as if to the image I had evoked so mistily.

"One of the Great Ones—not born of your blood, nor of mine, nor of any race now living. One of the ones who lingered among us for a space—until those who sought the worst of the Dark arose and tried to summon—"

"But why do I now see this thing?"

"I do not know, Witch maid. Save those birds"—he made a gesture at the sky where I saw the distant wheel of wings—"were once, long and long ago, found in the Place Apart where Ninutra chose to dwell or else maintain some small contact with this world. There were also those there who opened their minds and hearts and at times they spoke of what lay in the future so that even the adepts listened when they were the Mouths of Ninutra."

"Tsali—was I ever such a Mouth?"

He shook his head. "Ask me not riddles, Witch maid. Each race and species has its own legends. Do we live again once we have gone to the cleansing fire? And if we so live, can we remember? I do not know."

"I saw—Ninutra—" I answered slowly. "And—" I wrapped my arms about myself. "I was warmed by the Force. I—"

My head came up. Now it was not memory which moved within me, rather a portion of knowledge laid out clear and fresh in my mind, as if there was held in the air before me a scroll fresh from the writing of a keeper of the Deeper Knowledge. I had sought for a long time. And as such a seeker, I had left myself open so that Laidan had been able to enter into that part of me which lay vacant and ready for her sly suggestions. I do not know how my vision had worked upon me in those moments when I had fronted Ninutra, but now some of those empty chambers in my mind were filled.

Tsali stood tall, his crested head erect and swelling in color. I saw those flaps of skin quiver slightly as if his whole body would express emotion.

"Witch maid—what would you now—?"

"I do what must be done," I cut across his half-question, half-protest.

Eyeing the bank of the river under our feet, I found what I sought, a length of stick, drift, brittle and bleached, but as straight as the eye could measure it. This I took up, gripping it steadily. And as if it were a brush to lay on paint in the making of a picture, I drew with it in the air that which lay now in my mind. So it must go, and go, and go—

What I had drawn could be seen there. First only as faint lines. Then the color spreading inward from those lines, to give an opaque solidity. It glowed as a coal on a half-dead night fire might glow. I dropped the stick and stood looking at what hung in the empty air, while from my lips came sounds unlike any words, more resembling the harsh calls of those birds which had once nested in Ninutra's dwelling of force and now had come to scavenge in this much later day the results of Tsali's fishing.

Slowly, I put out my hand. In me was the certainty that once my fingers closed firmly on what hung suspended between the Lizard man and myself, I would have pledged my strength to a struggle I could not understand.

The red of that thing was fading, but its appearance of substance grew sharper and more distinct. Why hesitate? I had really known ever since Ninutra had answered me that this was to be done. I closed my hand upon a hard surface, though that was nearly as dull-gray now as the sky above us. Thus, I resolutely drew from the air what a knowledge I did not yet understand had wrought—a sword, which to the eye still seemed vaguely and mistily edged.

"Thus works the will of Ninutra," I said slowly aloud. "For here is the

Sword of Shadow—not of the Dark, nor yet of the Light, but which can be born by either belief. Only now do I claim it—and for the Light!"

I swung the miracle blade through the air, as a warrior would test the balance of a new weapon. For that is truly what I did in that moment. It was not as heavy as the steel I had known, nor did it possess a slashing edge or even a sharp point for thrusting. Its threat lay in other directions.

Tsali's thought came to me. "It is done—" I read into those words a heaviness of forelooking.

"It is done," I agreed. "It was for this that I was born—I think. I am now what I must have been fashioned to be. And let Laidan think of what hand she had in such fashioning."

6

The strange sword lost substance slowly even as wisps of mist are banished by the strong sun, though there was no sun over us at that moment. Soon I held—nothing. Still there was now in me the right and learning to call it forth again. I drew a long breath of wonder. My mind—if I could only have a space of peace in which to sort out what had poured without any sequence in my mind. Now I had no guide but my own instinct, that and the sure knowledge that battle lay before me; such a battle as I could not imagine, even though brushed by a Power I had been.

I stared down at my empty hand and I knew that, when I summoned it, that weapon forged in the name of Ninutra would return. But Tsali suddenly looked to our back trail. He hissed as the crest on his head blazed near blood-red.

"Hunters—" his thought reached me in warning.

I was sure that those hunters were not from the Valley, nor perhaps of humankind at all. I sent my own mind questing out, to touch for a bare instant of time, traces of the Dark Ones. Though of what species they were, I dared not probe the deeper to discover.

"They hunt us—" Of that much was I sure.

"They quest for scent; as yet they have not found it," Tsali returned. He flexed his claws and hissed once more.

So—we were hunted. Had Laidan returned to betray us to her evil co-forces, or had our trail been picked up only by chance? The reason for their coming did not matter. It would appear I was not to be given the time I needed to marshal this new awaking of a talent I had never known lay within me.

"Can we seek a hiding place?"

Tsali's head had swung around to a degree no human neck would allow. There were hillocks about us—but the mountain heights lay well behind. And also to those I did not dare to go now. I saw no beacon of blue stone set up anywhere, promising a kind of phantom shelter to those who hated the Dark. We had early been advised that such could be islands of safety in a dubious land.

"Water—" My companion made purposefully for the stream, sliding down the bank to wade out into its slow current.

Of course, the old, old truth—evil of many kinds dared not cross clean running water. I scrambled swiftly after him, felt my boots fill as wavelets set up by my strides lapped in over the tops of that footgear. I held my divided skirt as high as I could, but the hem became sodden quickly. While I discovered the uncertain footing of loose stones slowed me whereas Tsali skittered easily ahead.

My questing sense picked up an emanation as foul to my mind as corruption would be to my nostrils. Yet I had not enough yet to name our pursuers. Now I resolutely did not try to touch again—lest that reveal us in our flight.

The bed of the river was wide but, as we went, the stream grew narrower, a curling ribbon of water as its center, stretches of gravel edging it. Which hinted that there were periodic floods to leave the drift along the way, higher water unknown at this season. Also, it was shallow here and quite clear. I could see the flight of fish and armored things which crawled across the bottom we disturbed by our coming. One thing troubled me greatly—Tsali had turned his back upon those heights which might or might not wall the Valley. And now I made a decision, reaching out to meet his mind.

"Tsali, warrior of warriors, I have taken a fate upon me which is not your burden. You can return—"

I got no farther. He looked back over his narrow scaled shoulder to hiss at me. And I felt the anger boiling in his mind.

"We go together, Witch girl. Should one of the Brother-Kin of Reto, whose wisdom held even the Great Snake for the space of two heart beats so that it could be truly slain, turn his back on an ancient enemy and say, 'This is no task of mine'?"

"Your pardon, warrior." I could make no other answer. "But there is this—I have accepted the weight of something I do not understand, which may even play me false at the moment we must face our enemies. I would draw no others into what may be a net of ill fate."

"What creature can claim free choice when the Great Ones stir again? Our legends speak little of your Ninutra—whether he was for the Dark or the Light. But I think he was one of those who turned his back upon both and went to a place which he alone mastered. And—"

What he might have added I shall never know but I heard again the squawking cries and saw that over us winged once more those same birds of gray and flame. They whirled and dipped, screeching. And in those moments I began to believe that they were now allied with the evil which trailed behind, scouts sent to make sure we had no chance of escape.

I tried to shut my ears to their clamor, yet they held my attention so well I stumbled on a slime-coated stone and went to my knees, the water shockingly cold as high as my waist. Tsali stood still, as intent upon those winged pests as I had been. Now I saw him rub a clawed finger along the base of his head comb.

He had the attitude of one who listened intently, as if their incessant squawking made excellent sense. I could understand nothing of it; even though in the past I had always before been able to establish contact with any living thing. For, when I cautiously sought mind touch, there was nothing, not even that residue of instinctive cunning which I had worked upon with the spiders in Laidan's sorcery room.

There were—just blanks! I could not even sense a mind barrier at work. And the very fact that these birds were so protected made me uneasy.

Their flying darts came closer; I ducked my head when one screaming bird seemed about to attack my face, my eyes. And I raised my hands over my face in protection.

"Our guides—" Tsali appeared unmoved as they flew so closely about his head that it would seem their wings would brush his crest or his face.

"Guides to where?" I challenged, cowering a little once more as one aimed straight for me.

"Who knows?" The Lizard man shrugged his narrow shoulders. "But if we follow, they will cease this calling, which must ring well down stream by now."

It was a choice between two evils, I knew. No one had ever said that those of the Dark had no cunning. The racket of the birds must indeed alert anyone within perhaps more distance than I wanted to believe.

Tsali already waded toward the righthand bank. Now the birds circled once above his head, flitting on to pay full attention to me. More slowly, because of my waterlogged skirts, I followed him. Then, when my feet were on the bank, their screaming stopped as if cut off. Instead the birds, though they still dipped and fluttered around, mainly before us, were silent.

We were away from the area of the ruins where I had felt stifled and so ill at ease. Before us sloped a meadow. Though the tall grass was dull and near dry, yet here and there a late lingering flower made a scarlet or rust-yellow patch. However, aside from the birds of Ninutra, the field was empty; an emptiness which spread out before us until there stood afar an edging of woodland.

Across that lengthy field we went. Of course in so doing, we left such a trail behind us as the Dark Ones could sniff out with little trouble. But the grayness of the day now lifted a little. I held up my soaked skirt, sitting down once to draw off and empty my boots, which were beginning to show hard usage.

That way through the open was farther than it first looked; rather as if the distant line of trees, through some power, stealthily retreated at each step we advanced. The birds of Ninutra remained silent, but they wheeled and dipped, their movements certainly following a pattern, urging us forward toward the distant wood.

It was very quiet. And then, so faint it was hardly more than a vibration on the air, I heard a howling. That I knew from my days in the Valley for the call of a Gray One—those creatures of the Dark which are neither man nor wolf, but a blasphemous uniting of both. The sound came from downriver, giving me at last a clue to the nature of the enemy.

I had no long knife in my belt, no sword or dart gun. And Tsali's scabbards for knife and sword hung empty, for his captors had despoiled him when they had taken him. I heard him hiss and lift his hands, extend his claws to the greatest extent.

We pushed forward with the best speed we could muster. The Dark Ones who caught any of us in the open had a potent charm against which no magics known could operate. They need only ring us thrice and we would be helpless to escape, fit meat to be pulled down at their desire. If we could reach those ever-beckoning trees, then such ringing would be far harder to accomplish.

It was here that the birds deserted us. Beating well up into the air, they formed a vee of flight and sped straight on toward the wood. Perhaps whatever strange task had been set them was completed.

My dragging skirt tripped me twice, though I held it as high as I could in my hands. Nor did I waste time looking back. For the hunting howl broke again and manifestly nearer. Tsali, unencumbered by clothing, could have flashed away and been out of sight long before I gained the shelter of those trees. But he did not. Instead he stooped swiftly twice, each time arising with a stone caught fast in his claws. No true defense, for all his courage, against what followed us.

I labored on. Hardly was I aware I had reached the trees, so hard set I was, my breath came in great tearing gasps, until I struck one shoulder against a trunk with bruising force. Then I caught at that bark-clad pillar, holding on with a despairing grip lest I fall and be unable to win once more to my feet.

Tsali's hand caught one of mine; he pried to loosen my convulsive hold.

"On!"

He was right, but I was not sure that I was able. There came a third howl from behind, this full-voiced and close, feeding my panic enough to make me let go, stagger ahead with Tsali tugging at me.

I brushed painfully against other trees; my clothing caught on low-growing thorns, tore when I jerked loose from their grasp. On and yet on. Here was only a small gray glimmer of light. These trees, I began to realize, had not lost their leaves—or rather needles, for the refuse under my slipping and sliding feet was composed of brownish needles near as long as my forearm. There was very little undergrowth—even of the thorns— once we had broken through the outer barrier of the wood.

Now I saw the birds once again, settling on branches, only to flutter farther ahead as we made our laborious way in their wake. And there was no sound—no breeze troubled the needles of the trees. Not one squawk issued from a bird throat. My own panting was loud, and that I was not able to control.

I staggered once and nearly fell—reaching out frantically to my right for a huge stone set on end. Only when my fingers dug into the moss which had covered it did I realize that this was no natural pillar but one once embellished by some intelligence. As I clung to that to catch my breath, I could see that this was the first in a line of such pillars which marched on into the depths of the woods. And the carving my fingers had laid bare was that of a bird, its eyes deep pits into which even the moss had not rooted.

Another fragment of that not-memory gave me a moment or so of vision—of the stones of this way unencumbered by any growth, rather gray and splashed with color where the carving on them had been inlaid with paint. I sought the warn-off of Dark-fashioned things, since these were not blue stone. But—no—neither Dark nor Light held here. And I think I then guessed what lay before us—another realm altogether, one in which what concerned those of my blood was immaterial. Was this the place of Ninutra?

Another howl from very close now—the Gray Ones must be coursing the meadow. I looked about me for some hint of shelter. We could set our backs to this stone, but the outcome would never be in doubt—we would be speedily pulled down—

Or—

Of itself my hand stretched forth into the air, prepared to accept something from the unseen. I opened in my mind the door to that chaotic place into which had been poured all I could not yet understand.

Substance fitted into my palm. I speedily curled my fingers about to hold it firmly. There was the glow—scarlet as if outlined in fresh flowing blood. Once more I had the Shadow Sword.

Now there welled in me something which was not born of my species, which I must fight to hold steady. I looked from the sword to Tsali and spoke what I now knew was the truth.

"This is not yet the place. Let us go!"

From that point, it was I who took the lead along that line of pillars, Ninutra's birds fluttering over my head and a very grisly death, as I well knew, sniffing behind.

7

We fronted a great arch which was a marvel, for I think it had indeed been hewn of a single block of stone so large I did not see how any thereafter could move it to this place or set it upright. This was bare of carving, save at the very top where there was set a face, its eyes well above us to stare down the path we had come. Human in contour it was, but there was a lack of expression, a withdrawal in its gaze, which was not of my kind. Nor could I say whether it was man or woman. Rather the features held elements of both. But what made that image the most notable was, unlike the pillars which had guided us here, it seemed untouched by the years; no marks of erosion lay upon it.

The sword in my hand moved, almost of itself, rising up in formal salute to that carving. I guessed that here was locked part of the essence which had drawn us on.

Behind the arch was only bare earth—or rather sand—silver in color. However, laid out upon that background, in bold patterns, were tracings of other sands to form symbols I did not know. The area was divided into four quarters, each bearing its own range of complicated designs, the division being two narrow paths bisecting it at precise angles.

I went forward down the path which had its opening at the gate. The instant I was passed beneath that portal my flesh tingled, my hair moved as if drawn by energies I had never encountered before. I did not look back to see if Tsali followed; at that moment it was only needful that I reach the exact center of this place.

There was power here surely, such as I had never felt before—even in that chamber where Laidan had woven her abortive spell or in the circles Dahaun used in her own green sorcery.

There are many kinds of magic; the green which is of the earth and growing things and includes in it the healer's craft; the brown which has to do with animals, our younger or unlike brothers we may strive to understand but seldom can; the yellow, the blue, the red, the black. Of most of them I knew a little. But this here was neither of the Dark nor the Light. Its source lay (or had been moved) otherwhere. But what had been left made me feel, as I so moved boldly toward its heart, as if I had flung off all clothing, to bathe myself in a substance neither liquid nor light, possessing elements of each.

I came to the centermost point of that strange sand-covered area, where the four patterns met to form a space only large enough for me to stand and not infringe on any of those squares where lay the symbols. This—this too—I had known!

All my life I had never had a real home—though with the acceptance of my kin I had lived pleasantly and well guarded. Still within me had there always been that longing for somewhere else, something beyond the life I had always known. First I thought I had found it in the Valley when the Lady Dahaun opened my mind to what I might become, should I have the skill and patience to follow the way she pointed.

But this—

I held the sword with both hands, the fingers of one curled about the other. While at that moment I heard—strained to hear—whispers which lay just beyond my distinguishing, so that in my frustration I could have cried aloud in rage and disappointment.

Now I raised my head so that I could look to the sky, that same gray sky which had overhung us from the first. No birds wheeled there, not even a cloud broke its stretch of lowering menace.

And I dared to call aloud—not by the mind touch—

"Great One, I am here!"

It seemed to me that the presence I so eagerly sought could *not* be far away, that any moment I might see before me that form I had mind-visioned so wrapped in mist I could not distinguish its true being. This was the place of Ninutra, of that I was certain. Yet—

There was only silence. Even that murmur of voices, which had so vexed me because I could make nothing of the gabble, ceased. There was some fault in me. If I *had* ever come this way before (and I was sure now that in the far-distant past the *I* who was the inner part of me had done so), then all true memory of that was lost, leaving me now bereft and lessened.

My eyes filled, tears overflowed, to trickle down my cheeks. Because I had somehow been so sure of part of this I had clung to the belief that I knew all—

I dropped my eyes. There would come no answer, no. I was no longer one able to enter into those secrets which drew me so strongly. I glanced at the patterns of the colored sands. Once I had known, now I could push at the buried part in my mind and sense—very faintly—a small part of the meanings of those convolutions and spirals.

In my hand the sword—it was warm, heating. The blade glowed dully red, as if it were indeed steel which had been thrust for a space into flames. More intense grew that heat, yet still I held fast, though I needed to set my teeth fast upon my lower lip to endure. I was only humankind and not for me was the knowledge I knew was locked within this place.

"Ninutra—" Within my mind I shaped that name, shutting from me the pain in my hands. It felt as if the very flesh was frying from my bones—still I held. For this I had commanded the small Talent I possessed and I would not be robbed of even so poor an answer.

Now in my mind a command rang sharp and clear—

"Slay!"

I turned on my small square of path. Tsali had not followed me into this place—no, he lingered just beyond the great arch.

"Slay!"

One step I took and then a second; the pain in my burning hands could only be cooled by blood—blood running down the blade I held. I had only to strike and that blood would burst forth, to quench the fire which so bitterly punished me for my presumption in invading a shrine not now open to me.

"Slay!"

And at that moment Tsali was gone, rather one of the lean flanked Gray Ones crouched in his place, his wolf's muzzle raised as he gave the call for the pack.

"Slay!"

I was being tricked again. This much I realized as I tottered forward. Then I took a last step, but I fought more valiantly for my mind.

"I pay no blood, Ninutra," I said and tasted the salt of my own blood from my bitten lip. "I deal not in death, but in life!"

As if those words had been a key turned gratingly in some lock long since near rusted into immobility, they brought me freedom. I held the sword and saw the blisters of burns arising on my flesh until the torment was more almost than I could bear—but only almost.

"No blood of mind-friend do I shed, Ninutra!"

There was another long moment of utter silence. Was I even able to communicate with that *Power* which had once been strong here? Or had its essence long since withdrawn, leaving only a residue of what might have formed the baser part of it?

Then—I was free of any pressure. In my hands the hilt of the sword cooled. I did not turn my head to look, but I was certain that that shadow-misted thing I had seen in my own vision was watching me, that I was being weighed one way and then another. I sensed even a very faint surprise, the first trace of emotion which had ruffled the spreading pool of oblique communication in which I was caught.

There was no Gray One at the gate—Tsali stood there, looking back the way we had come, his whole body as tense as one who expected to meet the shock of a battle charge the next moment.

Now I could join him. And I believed that I knew what alarmed him—those who had traced us dared to follow even here. Though in spite of that recent order which I had defied, I still did not believe this was any stronghold of a Dark One.

I glanced at my hands. Those welts of blisters had vanished, and with them the pain. But I still held the sword. In this much had the Presence in this shrine left me armed.

We stood together, Lizard man and girl; Tsali with the rocks he had earlier hunted brought forth from his belt pouch and ready to fling, I with Ninutra's sword. And so they came upon us, but not up the path marked by the stele—rather from the wood itself. As they bounded into the open, the birds of Ninutra screeched and dived at their heads. I saw blood run from a wound which just missed the left eye of the foremost of that stinking band.

Tsali let fly with his rocks. One of the Gray Ones flopped earthward, a great hole in his forehead. Another howled and pawed at his shoulder. But I raised the sword. From its tip there shot a lash of fire as brilliant as any laid by an energy whip. And the Gray Ones pushed back.

Their force parted to let through another, two others. One was hooded and masked, carrying in hands with unnaturally long nails a whip which he aimed (the lash skillfully snaking out) to entrap my wrist. But I slashed down with the sword and that thing was sliced cleanly through.

His companion laughed, a sound which seemed to infuriate the Gray Ones, for they snarled at her as might dogs who knew her to be their mistress but also hated her.

"So, Handmaiden of one who has long since withdrawn," Laidan spoke aloud. And I knew that, in using her voice, she sought subtly to insult me, perhaps so trick me into some foolish act. "Did you at last remember and come running—to find the Power you sought gone? Did you not recall more—that the Lady of Fire was the first to open her own gate and go elsewhere—?"

I was a little startled. Somehow I had thought of Ninutra (for no reason I could understand) to be one of the Great Ones, yes, but a sorcerer. Adepts had been both women and men. If the inner *I* had served Ninutra in the far past, I did not remember as much as Laidan thought.

"Ninutra is gone," Laidan repeated. "Too many years has her gate been closed. Do you think *your* thin voice can reach between scattered worlds, and even if it did, she would answer? They said of her then that she walked her own way and had none she cherished greatly."

I did not try to answer her jeers. *Something* had answered, or I would not hold the Shadow Sword. Something had reached me when I had stood within that place of multicolored sands. But whether that was only faint lingering of Ninutra's power still able to, in a little, answer those who knew how to call it—who could say?

And was it that same indefinable something which now put words in my mouth to answer Laidan? I do not know, but I answered without conscious thought.

"You have come seeking me, Laidan. Now you have found me. Let us pledge that this lies between the two of us alone—"

For a moment I thought she would not agree. Still that twisted smile which was a grimace held about her lips.

"*Very* little sister," her voice rang with bitter mockery, "do you presume to challenge *me?*"

"If you wish."

Her smile grew the wider. "Very well." She snapped her fingers and the Gray Ones drew back. But their hot eyes were on us, and I knew well that her hold over them was a thing perhaps I could not count upon continuing for long.

From within her misty clothing she brought forth that black rod she had used in her sorcery, while I took firm grip on the sword. She had never once looked at it, nor seemed to mark that I held any weapon. A small suspicion fluttered in my mind—was it that Laidan actually did *not* see what I had?

She pointed the tip of her weapon at me breast-high. I saw her lips shape words I did not hear but rather felt, vibrating through my whole body as a wrenching pain. I tightened my hold on the sword. Once more that began to warm within my grasp. Slowly I swung it back and forth in the air before me, as if by such a pitiful act I could ward off the maledictions she hurled at me.

It seemed that I could even see those words she did not speak aloud, that they turned into vicious darts seeping through the air to center on my body. Yet the blade of the sword began to glow an even brighter red as once more I must subdue the pain of my flesh where my fingers tightened upon it.

Then I saw Laidan start; her eyes go wide; her gaze follow the swinging of the sword blade, as if for the first time she had seen it.

"No!" She threw her wand as a trained warrior might loose a small spear.

I saw that fly through the air. And, in some odd way, time ceased to exist for a few heartbeats. So that instead of flying at normal speed, it appeared rather to hang transfixed in the air well within my reach. I brought down the blade of the Shadow Sword, fighting the torment that movement caused me, so that it struck full upon the black wand.

Laidan screamed, higher and more terribly than any of the birds of Ninutra. The wand splintered into pieces, shattering into only small needles which hit the ground between us. And from each of these there burst a small black flame and a puff of noxious odor. But Laidan writhed, her body twisting as if she were gripped by great hands which strove to wring her about.

I heard the Gray Ones howl, saw them run madly away. Two blundered into the path marked by the stele and stumbled, falling forward, crawling feebly on, and then lying still.

But Laidan jerked and twisted and screamed—

"Slay!"

Once more came that order, and this time I did not resist it. I threw the sword, even as she had thrown the wand. The misty-edged point entered truly into the hollow of her throat. She crumpled, her body drawing curiously in until—there was nothing.

As the wand had vanished, so was the Shadow Sword now also gone. I stood with empty hands, staring at what I had wrought at that last order. Then Tsali's hand touched my arm gently:

"She is gone—but they," he pointed with his muzzle toward the silent Gray Ones, "may get their courage back—or rather their fellows will. It is best we go also—"

I shook off his hand with the same gentleness he had used. Rather, now I held both my arms wide and straight out from my body. Down from the leaden sky wheeled and darted the birds of Ninutra. They settled on my arms, my shoulders, silently but as if this was right and seemly.

I thought of Imhar. He was just someone very far away whom I had once known and wished well, but with whom I no longer had even kin-tie. And then, Yonan. In me I realized a little sadly that Yonan had wished me better than well, that I could have put out my hand and he would have taken it eagerly. But no longer could I do that.

Perhaps the gate Ninutra had found was closed past all opening. But in me that other *I* which had been stirring was near fully awake. I could not choose now the road which tradition laid before me, as Imhar's lady. Nor could I accept the richness Yonan wished to offer me. I was myself— alone. As yet I did not know just who or what that self was—or could be. But, even as the Sword of Shadow had burned with its power my hands, so now my spirit burned within me, lighting a hardly endurable fire to learn, to know, to be—

I looked at Tsali, my mind working to fit the proper words together. Before I was sure of them, he nodded.

"So it must be then. You have tasted Power; be very sure it is not tainted."

"It is not!" Of that one thing I was confident; I had been since the defeat of Laidan. So much would not have been allowed me had I been beguiled by the Dark. "Tell them that I must learn—and that I am still— no matter what may happen to change me—kin-bound. I swear this on blood I would not shed!"

I watched him go. Then I turned my back upon the huddled forms of the Gray Ones. And, with the birds still about me, I faced inward to Nin-utra's Shrine. Or rather, was it a school for the learning of things not of this time and place? Now it seemed to me that already some of the lines of colored sand were beginning to send forth understandable meanings, even though the Great One who had wrought them was long gone.

'WARE HAWK

For Pauline Griffin, whose encouragement and suggestions brought this tale into being.

Estcarp, the last-held land of the Old Ones in the latter days, was ruled by the Witch Women with the Power that had once been the heritage of all those from whom they had sprung. The land had been caught between two enemies—the new peoples—those of Alizon in the north, and Karsten in the south. To the east lay the mysterious land which, by the Power, was closed to the people of Estcarp, as protection against ancient evil. Then, from the sea in the south, came the Kolder who were rapers of men's minds, who used strange machines to create armies of living dead. Determined to rule the world, they had come through one of the Gates. They hated the Witches mightily, for their minds could not be overborne by the Kolder machines.

They captured Gorm and the city of the Sulcar sea people who had been long allied with Estcarp. In Karsten they made Duke Yvian one of their mind-dead. So they moved upon Estcarp as though it were a nut to crack between two stones.

Then, out of another space and time, came Simon Tregarth who swore liege oath to the Witches. With Koris, exiled from Gorm, and the Witch Jaelithe, as well as Loyse of Verlane (axe-wedded to Duke Yvian whom she had never seen), he moved to mighty action, rousing all the land.

The Kolder were driven back to their Gate, and it was closed by Simon and Jaelithe (who had wed with Simon against all the custom of her people and so lost the Witches' favor but not her own powers). Then, because Duke Yvian was dead without heirs, there was war in Karsten.

Before Yvian's death, by the Kolder orders, he had outlawed—or horned—all of the Old Race who lived within the borders of the Duchy of Karsten. There was red massacre and much horror, but some escaped, to flee north to their distant kin in Estcarp. There they became the Borderers under Simon, and, with the Falconers, held the mountain passes.

Now a "new man," called Pagar, appeared, and he united the quarreling lords of Karsten by giving them a common goal—the invasion of Estcarp. The Estcarp forces were too few to resist. To save Estcarp, the Witches gathered all their might and, in a single night, struck at the land itself, destroying the mountains, turning and twisting rocks and earth into chaos. This came to be known as the Turning. Many of the Witches died in the backwash of the Power and the few left were reft of much of their strength, but Pagar and his forces were annihilated.

Jaelithe Tregarth had borne her lord three children at one birth—a thing hitherto unknown. In their childhood she went seeking her lord who had never returned from a scouting trip. The three young Tregarths held fast to each other, though the sister was torn away to be trained by the Witches. It was on the very night of the Turning that her two brothers brought her out of imprisonment. Together they fled east, for the old barrier did not hold against them who were of half blood. So they came into Escore, the forgotten homeland, and there they warred with evil stirred to new life by their coming. To them, little by little, were drawn many of those who had once been of Karsten and then had defended the border, together with their kin and clans—moving into the same country from which their ancestors had fled.

Karsten, after the death of Pagar and his army in the mountains, was in a chaos of warring lords. The turned and twisted mountains gained an evil reputation and only outlaws sought refuge there. Also, from Escore, now awake and seething with magic, came strange other beings to prowl this new territory.

Estcarp, exhausted by years of war, first with the Kolder, and then with her neighbors, was under the rule of Koris of Gorm. He was joined in time by Jaelithe and Simon Tregarth, returned through the aid of their children and choosing to defend the west and not the east.

Alizon, to the north, having been tricked by the Kolder into invading the western continent where lay the dales of High Hallack, was badly defeated there. Now it held an uneasy peace, though there were frequent raids south to test the defenses of Estcarp, and on that border the forces of Koris centered.

These later years were a time of many perils, of the wandering of masterless men, especially those exiled from Karsten by the Horning. Some settled in Estcarp, though they did not accept that as their true home, others took service wherever they might.

The grim and deadly race of Falconers, forced to flee their Eyrie in the mountains at the Turning, became marines on Sulcar ships or sought employment where they could, their tight organization scattered. Their once-great hold was a pile of stones. So the years sped and there were no firm roots for most men. Estcarp, under a new type of rule, was unsure of the future.

1

The wind blustered through the gray dawn. There was a crash as one of the slates from the inn roof shattered in the courtyard. Once Romsgarth had been a major town where far-traveling merchants met—the last Estcarpian hold before the overmountain way to Karsten. It was very old and worn, with perhaps a third of the stone-walled, ancient buildings falling in, to become weed-grown rubble. The days of those merchants, with their busy going and coming, were nearly two generations ago, banished now into the past. Karsten—who went to Karsten by mountain roads now? There *were* no roads since the turnings for the mountains themselves had set up new barriers unknown to any save outlawed men, skulkers and raiders, drawn from afar to seek refuge in holes and dens.

The pickings hereabout for such outlaws must be scanty. Three years of severe winters would have reduced even the most lawless to a small threat.

The girl standing by the inn window, holding the edge of a shutter against the push of the wind, looked out upon the not-yet stirring town, the tip of her tongue showing between her lips. This nervous habit, of which she was not aware, betrayed her anxiety, though none now were left to care what troubled Tirtha of Hawkholme.

There were many roaming along the broken border who, worn by long years of war, sought aimlessly for some refuge or had some business they held secret, lest it be taken from them, as so much else had been. Questions were not asked of travelers in these broken, dying towns. Such life as had returned to Estcarp now lay in the north—in those rich lands once more to be set under plow in a week or two, and in the ports where Sulcar ships nosed in, those hardy traders already seeking their old sea tracks.

Within this room, where a twisted rag—anchored as a wick in a bowl of oil—gave more smoke than light, hung the sour smell of too many wayfarers, too little pride in the inn, too long a span of years. Time weighed on the cracked walls, made the floor uneven, its thick boards worn by the passing of countless booted feet. Tirtha breathed in deeply of the cleaner air outside, then closed the shutter and slipped the bar into place. She moved swiftly to the uneven-legged table with the lightfootedness of one used to dangerous trails.

There she sought, for the second time since her awakening, the purse carried within her jerkin, part of the belt clasped about her waist beneath layers of drab clothing. Made of serpent skin, it was supple enough—as well as tough—for her to feel its contents without opening it. There was money there—gathered slowly, painfully. She need only to look at her calloused hands, feel the ache rising from a sudden shift of her thin shoulders to remember how most of it had come into her keeping. There was also a small hoard of ten irregular discs of gold—so old that all markings had long vanished from their surfaces—the gift of fortune itself. This she had taken as a sign that what she must do had advanced from wishful dreaming to reality.

She had hacked away a fallen tree to free a path for the plow, thus revealing in the turn of its roots a shattered bowl—and in it—this hidden treasure! Fortune had been with her also that she was alone at its discovery. The surly garthman who had hired her as a harvest hand had seen fit to send her out alone on the roughest job he could find—merely, she believed, to teach her that as a woman she was of little use.

Once more Tirtha's tongue touched her lips. Service at the hearth or with the wash paddle along a streamside was not for her. She wore men's clothing; a sword hung at her belt, though its blade had been so nicked and thinned she feared any use of the weapon might break it. On its pommel was still the tracing she treasured—the head of a hawk, its bill a little open as if voicing a cry of defiance. That was all of her heritage unless . . .

Karsten—Karsten and a dream. Since the Witches of Estcarp had wrought their magic in the Turning, upheaving the mountains and making the land walk and so destroying the invading forces of Pagar, who had risen to rule in the southern duchy of Karsten, no one knew what lay overmountain in these days.

The bits and pieces of knowledge Tirtha had gathered so avidly from any wayfarer (and most carefully, lest curiosity be aroused as to why this sun-browned, hard-featured female was interested in anything beyond the earning of her bread) made clear that the duchy had been split into many small holdings often at war with one another. No lord since Pagar had gained power enough to make the broken duchy whole again.

This present state of Karsten might well serve her purpose in one way, hinder it in another—she had no way yet of knowing. With the discovery of the hoard of gold discs, which she took as an omen, she had come to find out that one did not venture south without a guide. In the rending of the mountains by the Power of the Witches, all landmarks had disappeared and she could not wander alone.

Hence—the hiring fair.

Tirtha buckled on her sword belt and swept up a hooded cloak of stout weaving, lined with hareskin—an extravagance to one slim of purse. Yet the garment was a necessary protection against the weather, like the winds that howled outside now, as well as a sleeping nest for the night. There was her shoulder pack also and her bow and quiver of arrows. She had worked a whole season to learn the making of those, practicing thereafter with dogged patience. She had no dart gun. Those were for the wealthy, heads of households and their guards or for the Lord Marshal's own forces, which kept such law as now ran in Estcarp.

Down in the stable there was a rough-coated but sure-footed mountain mare—used to living off scant grazing—a mount with a rolling eye and a wicked temper. However, that temper was also a good protection against her being stolen. She was as gaunt and ill-looking as her mistress, her rusty black coat matching the short-cropped hair that hung in scallops across Tirtha's forehead.

With calloused fingers Tirtha pinched the wick of the lamp, before moving noiselessly out into a hall where the stink of too-close living made her nose wrinkle as she descended use-hollowed steps into the common room.

Early as it was the innkeeper, a woman with a sagging fat belly beneath a sack apron, sleeves rolled up over arms that were thick enough nearly to match Tirtha's thighs, was at the hearthside, a long-handled iron spoon in one hand, the other rolled into a fist which she had just used to cuff a girl who had been watching the pot. A smell of scorching worked its way through the other odors, and Tirtha guessed at the sin of the younger cook.

Scorched perhaps, but it was food. She had long since learned not to be dainty—if food was hot and filling it would do. Also she had no money to waste by calling for any special dish. She scooped up an empty wooden bowl from the table, picked out a horn spoon, which looked as if it had been at least wiped clean after its last use, and advanced to the scene of conflict.

The serving wench scuttled away on hands and knees, snuffling, seeking a safe distance from her mistress who was stirring the pot with a vigor that sent bits of its contents slopping over the rim. Now her attention switched from what she was doing to Tirtha.

"Porridge—you can have a chop of beef—" Her small eyes had already valued and dismissed this visitor as not being worth urging to eat a more varied meal.

"Porridge," Tirtha agreed, extending the bowl into which the inn-mistress ladled an even six spoonfuls with the ease of very long practice and an eye for profit.

The smell rising from it was not only of scorched meal, but musty as well—the end of the winter grinding. No lumps of chopped bacon, not even a shaving of onion, cut the dusty taste. Still it was food—energy to see her through the morning, and she was not about to add to her reckoning. There were supplies that she must buy. Game did exist in the mountains, yes, and she was adept with a snare—not even wasting an arrow unless she had the fortune to meet a pronghorn. Also, she was country-wise, and with the beginning of the growing season, there were a number of newly green sprouts that could be boiled, not only as food, but for their tonic.

There remained salt and some other things that she must reluctantly lay out money for, and she had the list ready.

The inn-mistress glanced Tirtha's way now and then, as she methodically emptied her bowl, doubtless ready to answer with a quick tongue any complaint. That this woman was wary of her, Tirtha had known from the beginning. She was neither bird nor hare in this land. A woman who rode as a man might, who had no proper place. She was marked, yes, but there were other strangers, some as odd as she was. If they tattled among themselves about her for the space of a day or so, there would arrive some other to make them wonder and surmise. She had nothing to fear this side of the border. On the other side—well, even her face might condemn her there, if the old stories were true, and she was certain that none of their grimness was the matter of a songsmith's imagining. Her own kind—the Old Race—had been thrice-horned, outlawed, hunted, slain—sometimes horribly—when Duke Yvian had ruled, and those days were still unforgotten.

Those who had escaped into Estcarp had formed the Borderers, to ride a blood-stained trail back and forth, providing the first wall of protection for the north. Men and women of the Old Race, who had seen their dead, did not forget. The sword at Tirtha's side had been a part of that time, though the fighting was over when she was but a child not as tall as the table at which she now sat. Still, hatred was bred into her. The Old Race was long lived—unless death cut them down prematurely in war— and their memories were even longer.

Others were stirring in the inn now—tramping down into the common room. There were at least three, who, she decided, were bound for the same place as drew her—the hiring fair held here in the early spring. They were better dressed, fuller of face than she was, as if they did not know the gauntness of late winter. They were garth stewards, perhaps, sent to pick up a herdsman, a dairy maid, even a weaver, if they were lucky.

Her own seeking was different, and only rumor had brought her here. Though many of those who had served in the wars had been granted lands to the east, and others were still attached to lords to whom they had given shield oaths (and some were outlaws because raid and rapine were all they knew), a trained fighting man down on his luck could still be hired. With the better sort, who still had their pride and kept to the old customs, sword oath might be given in return for hire.

She needed a man who knew the mountains, was not an outlaw, yet might be a guide into Karsten. For such she was willing to give a good weight of what now lay snug about the upper curve of her hips.

Tirtha scraped the last unappetizing morsel from her bowl, dropped the licked spoon into it, and rose. The hiring lines would be gathering now where the long-ago guild merchants had had their principal market. With the wind still shrieking, those seeking employment might shelter in the pillared and roofed alcoves, which had held stalls in the old days.

She fastened her cloak throat buckle, jerked the hood well up over her head, and pushed out into the courtyard, to the street beyond. It took only a few moments' quick walk to reach her goal, but the wind cut and pulled, leaving her gasping when the full strength of it hit against her face. There were few to be seen on the street. It was a foul day, and by a new lowering of clouds overhead, like to be fouler. She turned into the square and saw that she was right—those who waited huddled in the alcoves.

Each wore in his hat or her hood the small symbol of the trade offered—a whittled staff for a herdsman, a tuft of wool for a shepherd, a miniature paddle for a dairy maid. Tirtha gave only a quick glance as she strode by. Perhaps she faced disappointment—what she sought might no longer be offered.

It was in the last of the alcoves, as the rain began—carried in fierce lances by the wind—that she saw what she hunted. There was only one. He was alone, as if he were indeed an outlaw—some venturer whom none of these peaceful serving folk wanted a part of, a hawk dropped into a flock of domestic fowl.

Hawk—

Tirtha halted, her hand seeking the half-effaced insignia on the pommel of her sword. This one was as out of place as if he had been painted brilliant crimson and hung about with gem chips.

He leaned against a pillar until he saw her stop. Instantly he straightened, to match her stare for stare—cold-eyed as something that was more of the Dark than the Light. Where she wore leather beneath her cloak, he was mail-shirted, his own cloak cut about at the hem so it came only to his knees, two rents in it badly cobbled together with large stitches. Though he had on a horseman's boots, they were spurless, showing signs of heavy wear. But it was his headgear that left her astounded.

Instead of the plain helm of a Border fighter, he wore a far more ornate one, which masked him half-face. It was badly battered, and there had been a clumsy attempt, even as there had been to repair his cloak, to restore it. Its form was that of a hawk, or a falcon rather, and the right wing had been riveted back into place so that it hung slightly askew.

A Falconer!

This was legend indeed. Had those men, born for no other life than that of fighting, been so reduced through the mischance of chaos? Their Eyrie had stood in the mountains—but Tirtha had heard that the warning, which had brought the Borderers down from the heights before the Turning, had been relayed to them also, and surely they must have survived. Yes, in the months past she had heard of some serving on Sulcar vessels as marines—even as they had done centuries ago when first they had come to Estcarp.

They were not such as to find any favor with the Witches of Estcarp, even when they offered their well-trained force to augment the badly depleted army of Estcarp. Their way of life was too alien. To those all-powerful women, it was also hateful and perverse. For the Falconers were a purely male clan—holding females in contempt and revulsion. They did have their women, they bred their own kind, yes. But those were kept in an isolated village to which selected sires went at ordained times of the year. Also they were ruthless with their own get—killing any child not whole and perfect at birth. To the matriarchy of Estcarp they were totally opposed by custom. Thus they had settled in the mountains, built their great stronghold—the Eyrie of Falconers—and border watch towers and carried on a service of protection—first for the merchants who would travel the roads, and then as a barrier for Estcarp against Karsten in the latter bad days.

The Borderers claimed them, though not as sword brothers, and held them in respect. They served together in good accord. Supplies were sent, first secretly since the Witches forbade it, then more and more openly to both the Eyrie and their village of women. In the last days of all there had been very little barrier between the male fighters of Estcarp and these strangers who had come originally from some disaster overseas.

Not only were they expert at arms, but their prized falcons, fitted with devices that were part of their secret, formed a network of aerial spying, which time and time again had proved to be the deciding factor in many skirmishes and mountain battles.

Now Tirtha instinctively looked for that bird—black with the white vee on its breast, its dangling red jesses—which should be riding on its master's wrist. But there was none. Also there was no hand on the arm that would have offered perch to such a bird. Instead there protruded from the fine mail of the sleeve a thing of brighter metal. The man kept his mail, his dilapidated helm, and doubtless his sword, well polished and honed. This thing he wore was not a hook; rather it split at the end into five narrow prongs, resembling a bird's tearing talons. Tirtha thought that it was a formidable weapon, nor did she doubt that he knew well how to use it.

But a Falconer—and she could not deny her own sex. This was the tool she had been seeking, but whether he would consent to her service might depend upon how desperate he was. She wished she could see more of his face—but the half-masking helm turned it into a mystery. Well— Tirtha squared her shoulders as she faced him, taking two steps forward to be out of the fury of the swiftly rising storm. She raised her voice to outbattle the wind as she asked:

"You are a blank shield?"

Such were for hire, though she had never heard of a Falconer who proclaimed himself so. They were a clannish lot, and, though they hired out their services, it was always as a troop or a squad—their commander making the bargain for them. Nor did they then mingle with those they served.

For a moment she believed that his inborn contempt for her sex would keep him silent, that she would have no chance at all to suggest hire. However, he did break that almost too long moment of silence.

"I am a blank shield." His voice was emotionless. He had not raised it to outvoice the storm, but it carried well.

"I have need of a guide—a mountain guide—and a fighter. . . ." She came directly to the point, shifting her position a little, not liking it that he could stare at her through the eye holes of his helm and yet deny her a similar view of him. As she moved, her cloak loosened, fell a little open, so that her leathern riding dress, that of a Borderer, though she lacked the mail overshirt, was plainly seen.

"I am for hire. . . ." Again that level voice. It was as if she spoke with a man of metal, one lacking all emotion or purpose. Had what brought him here made him only a husk of the fighting man he had once been? She could not waste her small funds on any such. Still, he kept his armor as well as he could. Her glance returned to that claw hand. It was, to her mind, more dangerous every time she saw it.

She looked out into the storm, then back to where he stood so statue-like by the pillar.

"There are better places to talk of this. I lodge at the inn—the common room is not private—but the stables . . ."

He made his first real movement, a nod of his head. Then he turned and stooped to pick up a bundle lashed into a blanket, which he shouldered, steadying it in place with his claw. Thus they returned to the inn stable where she had left the mare. It was by the latter's stall that Tirtha seated herself on a bale of hay, waving her companion to a similar perch.

With this one it was best to be direct, she believed. There was something about him that reassured her instinct, which she had come to rely upon through the past four years. She dealt with a man who had faced the starkness of ill fortune, but not one who had betrayed himself because of that. This one might break, but there was no bend in him—nor perhaps much breaking either. The more critically she surveyed him, the more she was aware that he was a fighting man still to be reckoned with.

"I need to go through the mountains—into Karsten," she said abruptly. There was no reason why she should explain her mission there. "The old paths and trails are gone—there are also masterless men abroad. I am not ignorant of the use of arms nor of living off the land. But I have no desire to be lost and perhaps make an ending before I do what I desire to do."

Again he answered her with a nod.

"I shall pay two weights of gold for a service of twenty days—half in advance. Do you have a mount?"

"There—" He was certainly sparing of speech. He gestured with his claw to another stall two away from where Valda crunched hay.

Another mountain pony, slightly larger and heavier than the mare, was stabled there. Its mane had been clipped and over the edge of the stall hung a riding pad with the forked horn that should have given rest to a falcon. But there was no bird here either.

"Your falcon?" She dared now to ask that.

There was a feeling of chill; she might have walked into some forbidden place of the Power where there was a walling against her and her kind—so it seemed for an instant. She feared a second later that her question had indeed put an end to any bargain that might have been struck between them—natural though the question was under the circumstances.

"I have no falcon. . . ." His voice came a note lower.

Perhaps that lay at the root of his exile from his kind. She knew better than to pursue the subject any farther.

"The terms suit you?" She made her voice as cold as his to the best of her ability.

"Twenty days . . ." He spoke as if he mused upon something in his own mind. "And at the end of that time?"

"We can see what comes." The girl got to her feet and held out her hand for the bargain grip. At first she believed he was going to lay that cold metal claw across her flesh, his arm twitched a little as if that movement came the more natural to him. Then his other true hand clasped hers.

She had reached under the shadow of her cloak during their walk here and loosed a disc of gold from her money belt. Now, as he speedily broke their clasp, she gave it to him. He held it for a moment, as if weighing it against her offer, then nodded for the third time.

"I have supplies to buy," Tirtha told him briskly. "But, in spite of the storm, I would be out of town this day. Do you hold with that?"

"I have taken shield service. . . ." He began and then stopped as a thought seemed to occur to him. "What badge do I now raise?"

The old custom still held, it would seem, with this Falconer. A blank shield taking service put on the new badge of the House employing him. She smiled a little grimly and slid her sword out of its sheath, holding it into the rays of a stable lantern that some groom had lit against the storm dark and left hanging nearby.

Though the device was faint it could still be seen, the head of a screaming hawk, voicing defiance to both man and world.

"The House of Hawkholme, Falconer. It would seem that we share something in common, though Hawkholme has been rubble for more years than I would waste now to tally."

He bent his head well forward, as if to see the better. Then he looked to her.

"Who speaks for the House?"

Again she smiled, and her smile was even more bleak and bitter. "I speak for the House, Falconer. For I *am* the House, and the Blood, and all the kin there is in this world—and no one yet has learned the trick of summoning ghosts to answer any rally. Thus you ride for Hawkholme and I am Hawkholme."

So saying, she turned and left him, to carry out the rest of her bargaining, the beginning of what she had planned for so many hard-lived years.

2

The storm's fury lasted half a day, forcing them to brace their bodies, huddle into their cloaks, and urge their unwilling mounts onto an upward trail that became only a bare trace a half-league out of Romsgarth. From the first, the Falconer took the lead as a matter of course, moving with a self-confidence, which assured his employer that he did indeed know something about the twisted lands of the heights.

However, that faint trail did not hold him long. Within a short time of turning into it, he paused for Tirtha to draw level with him, speaking the first words to break the silence between them since they had ridden out of town.

"It is your will to go with as little notice as possible?"

He had asked no questions concerning their reason for heading south, nor did she intend to supply any. However, now he appeared to guess part of her purpose.

"You know another way?"

She resented once more, with a growing spark of warmth, that he could look plainly upon her and she could not view him unmasked.

"It will not be easy, but I do not think anyone moving along the path I know will be overlooked. There was a hosting hereabouts two months ago. The Marshal's men swept out a nest of raiders and their lookouts."

"Well enough." Tirtha had no mind to ask him how he had become familiar with a raider path. Falconers did not turn outlaw—or so she had always heard. Also, she had her own way of recognizing danger. The Old Race—yes, a measure of their heritage still held, even for such draggle-tailed roamers as herself. She did not claim even a shadowing of true Power, but she had that sense which she could also use with animals in the wild, knowing where lay peril and where was only common hardship, such as she had long faced. This man would be true to his oath; he was no turncoat.

Thus they struck farther west, and the way *was* rough, leading up slopes where it was necessary to dismount, urge their snorting ponies to tread delicately over chancy footing, winding around drifts of season-old avalanches, halting at regular periods to rest their mounts and themselves.

By night they emerged upon a ledge half-roofed by an overhang. This certainly was a former camp, for at the back of the shallow cave was a smoke-blackened half-pit in which were charred ends of wood.

By all the signs, there had been none nighting here for some time. In the windblown ash Tirtha could trace the clear marks of paws. The gorex of the heights—and they were timid creatures—had padded freely about since the last fire. There was room enough at the far end of the cave to shelter the ponies. Pulling off the riding pads, they rubbed down the beasts with twists of coarse rags carried for such purposes. There was no herbage here, but both carried bags holding supplies Tirtha had frugally bargained for—grain out of Esland which she had found in Romsgarth market.

She divided portions scrupulously between the two ponies, though she must scant on what she would give them, since they had passed little grazing during the day's trailing—sighting no valley or slope that gave root to fodder plants. Nor had they found water, so that this also must be rationed.

Having seen to their animals, they returned to hunker down on either side of the fire pit. Tirtha, willing enough to be guided by one she was sure knew this land, looked to her silent companion for a lead. Was it wise to risk lighting some of the small stack of wood? He had said that this portion of the country had been cleared by Estcarp forces. Still, during two months, another band could well have descended upon an empty territory, setting up its own holdship.

The wind, which had pushed and punished them in gusts throughout the day, died down, while the clouds lightened, turning gold and crimson to mark a sun that had been sullenly veiled. There was a clean, fresh taste to the air here. Oddly enough her spirits felt a lift—as if, having taken the first day's journey successfully, she sensed that fortune was smiling. Yet she also knew that same fortune was fickle and had seldom favored her.

Tirtha's fellow traveler fitted wood carefully into the fire pit, using his claw with dexterity now and then to snap some longer piece into place. Thus they had fire, a comfort to the eye, as well as for its limited warmth, as the dusk closed in.

They whittled sticks to spear pieces of the dried meat Tirtha had added to their provisions, toasting them between bites of journey bread, sliding the hot morsels directly from the improvised spits into their mouths.

Having finished, her new shieldman slid off his helm for the first time, so she could see the full face of the man she had taken on trust. He was neither young nor old—she could not have set any age on him. Though there was a gaunt youthfulness about his chin and thin-lipped mouth, there were also lines between his eyes and a great weariness in those eyes themselves.

His hair was as dark as her own, clipped tight to his skull like one of those woven caps the Hold Ladies wore abroad. For the rest, she thought he looked much as any man of the Old Race might—save that his eyes were not the dark, storm-gray of her people, but rather held in their depths a spark of gold—as might those of a bird of prey.

She learned this by quick glances, not wishing to reveal open curiosity. He seemed unaware of any regard from her, smoothing his forehead with his one hand as if to rub away an ache caused by the weight of the helm, his hawk's eyes on the fire between them. He might be reading some message in those flames after the fashion of a Wise Woman, learned in far- or foreseeing.

"You have traveled this path before." Tirtha made of that more a statement than a question.

"Once . . ." he returned absently, his attention all for the flames toward which he now stretched his single hand. "I was scout two years ago when there was some thought of return. . . ." His voice trailed away—still he did not look at her. "There was nothing left."

The finality of those last words came harshly, and for the first time, he raised his eyes to meet hers. In them the yellow sparks might be the fire of long controlled rage.

"We were caught by a mountain fall. These ways are still unsettled. That which the Witch Women stirred into life does not yet sleep. I was to the fore and so—" He made a small gesture with his hand, not enlarging on it but leaving it to her imagination.

"You have ridden alone since then?" Tirtha did not know just why she wanted to force him into some personal disclosure. This was no man of easy words; to pressure him at all might lead even to his withdrawal. All she knew of his race and kind argued that they held strictly aloof from those not of their blood.

"Alone." With a single word he made answer and in such a tone as left Tirtha well aware that she must press no farther. However, there were other questions she could ask now, and those he could not deny answering, for they were no part of his own inner life.

"What do you know of Karsten? Men talk, but I have had only rumors to sift and those can be less than half-truths."

He shrugged, setting the helm beside him on the rock, once more smoothing the band of furrowed skin immediately above the well-marked line of his brows.

"It is a land of battles—or rather petty skirmishes, one lordling against another. Since Pagar, their last overlord, fell, there have arisen none who can impose their wills—or the weight of their swords—enough to bring a binding peace. The Sulcar come, under arms, to deal with some merchants. The iron out of the Yost mines, the silver of Yar—those can pay any captain. But trade is near dead, while there are those who die for lack of food because none dare tend fields which may be at any moment trampled by raiders. The riches that were once here are plundered, hid, scattered to the winds. Thus it is, along the western coast and below the mountains. What lies farther east . . ." He shrugged. "There are not even rumors that seep back from that region. When Duke Yvian horned the Old Race, he began the rot and it spread, until now the whole land is half-dead and the rest forsaken."

Tirtha wet her lip with tongue tip. "The Horning then began it—" Again she did not question, for her thoughts were quick and alive. Did the secret, which had brought her here, have such a root?

He shot her a measuring look, and she thought that, for the first time, she had shaken him out of that deep preoccupation with his own concerns which had held him since their first meeting. A fighting tool and an efficient one he had hired himself out to be, but he had shown no curiosity at all concerning what drew her south.

"The Old Race"—he paused, put out his claw to snap another length of wood and feed it to their fire—"they had their own secrets. Perhaps one of those was keeping a firm peace. It is said that, before Duke Yvian was possessed by the madness of the invading Kolder and turned into one of their mind-dead, men held the Old Race in awe, and their being there—few as they might seem—was a check upon lawlessness. Then the Duke proved that the Old Race could be killed—like any others—when he ordered their Horning, and there were those who had always hated and envied them. They wanted to appease that hatred. Also the Kolder, possessed, rode to push the slayings. But why do I say this—it is your blood that we speak of—is that not so?"

"Yes." She could be as laconic as he. In her mind, Tirtha weighed impulse against prudence, not quite sure as yet which might serve her best. Then she added, "Hawkholme was of Karsten. As you see, I am of the blood Yvian strove to erase from a land where he and his were, to begin with, intruders and invaders."

"You return to no easier a fate than was granted those who were Horned. That still holds. Too many seized and killed and profited by that blooding." He did not seem greatly moved, rather he spoke as if merely pointing out that they were two travelers united only for a limited purpose.

"We have learned something." Tirtha bit off each word as one would bite upon a binding cord. "There is no such thing as trust in Karsten for us. Still, I have that which takes me there."

Further than this she would not go. He had hand-grasped for his allotted time in her service. There was no reason to think that any further quest beyond the mountain-crossing would draw him. Nor, she thought, was he one with whom she would willingly share secrets, being who and what he was.

So Tirtha spread out her cloak and rolled in it, pillowing her head on one of her saddle bags before she resolutely closed her eyes, saying:

"We share night watch. Rouse me at the time the red star shines."

He inclined his bare head, accepting, as she had wondered if he would, that they would share, as if they were comrades, the needful duties of any camp. While she settled herself to sleep, summoning that nothingness of mind as she was able to, he made no move to reach for the rolled blanket that was part of his own gear, only sat beside the fire which glinted red on his claw, alternately revealing and hiding his well-cut features, their emotionless mask as complete as that of the helm he had worn during the day.

Though Tirtha had willed herself to sleep, it was not a dreamless one. What followed was that vision, or series of visions, which had haunted her for years, until each detail remained so engraved even on her waking memory that she could have recited all she saw and something of what those sights meant. She knew that there was true dreaming, which was part of the Farsight. She might not be a Wise Woman, but she was a full daughter of the Old Race, and she never believed that all vestiges of the Power had vanished from any of her blood, even though her kin had not held grimly to such knowledge as had their cousins of Estcarp.

There the Power had made the race thin. For the Witches gloried in gifts that they would not surrender for any man. So, fewer and fewer children had been born, until the race came near an end through their pride. However, since the Witch Women had united in the Turning, their last great battle, and most of them had died of it (their bodies unable to hold and project the forces they summoned and still survive), there had come a change.

He who ruled in Estcarp now—Koris of Corm—was only remotely of the kin. There were also the Tregarths who guarded the marches of the north as once they had held these very mountains where she sheltered this night. Simon Tregarth was an Outlander, not of the kin at all. His Lady was a foresworn Witch who, in her day, had been outcast because of her choice of him, and who, by some quirk of strangeness, had NOT lost her Power when she married him. These three ruled Estcarp, and their influence was felt. So there was no longer any recruiting of Witches, save among those of such manifest talent that they withdrew from life by their own desire. There was more mingling, more wedding and bedding. Those from the Border shared blood with Sulcar and with their kin of Estcarp. There were more children in the holds, and also there was some traffic with the mysterious east—that Escore where the children of Simon Tregarth and his Lady had gone to seek the ancient foundations of their line. There was war there still, but it was with old evil. Had Tirtha not been who and what she was perhaps the east would have drawn her also.

Drawn her! She walked again easily down a hall—wide—only half lighted by dim, wall-set bars of light, the secret of whose ever-burning had been lost long since. There were shadows that moved among shadows, had a sometime life of their own. But what they did, when, or why, had no meaning for her.

Though she had never come this way except in a vision, still it was better known to her than many of the places into which her actual wandering had taken her. This was a part of her as no other place, waking or sleeping, could ever be. She had come here in dreams since childhood, and always it remained the same, save that its hold on her grew stronger and deeper, more real than all else in life.

This was the hall of a hold—a place near as long established as the ancient walls of Estcarp itself. There at the high table were the tall chairs of a lord and lady. Those shades she could not see clearly were tenuous, forming a company around her. Tirtha knew that this was a time of formal meeting, that though she could not hear, yet there was deep meaning in what was being discussed.

Most of her attention was for what stood on the table, midway between the two tall-backed chairs. *That* was real and fully visible! A casket gleamed with a light issuing from it, for the cover had been raised and thrown back. The carvings on it did not seem set or sustained as they should have. Rather they possessed a life or purpose of their own, appearing to change shape, to crawl and move, so that she could not ever be sure of them. Some, she realized in the moments when she could catch them at rest, were words and symbols of Power.

Nor had she ever seen what the casket held, for its lid was raised at an angle which prevented direct sight. Only—this was the very heart and substance of all she witnessed here—it was more alive than those who had cherished it.

Now the dream followed its set pattern. That wisp of half shadow which was the left hand of the lord and the one which was the right hand of his lady moved forward as one. Together they clasped the lid of the casket, closing it.

Tirtha felt the old and familiar rise of cold fear in her. Now was the coming of the evil. She could not escape it—ever—because for some reason it was necessary that she see—see and know—see and remember!

That shadow, which was the lord, held its grip on the lid of the casket for a long moment. The glow of life, which the girl had felt dwelling within it, dimmed. It might be that by some warning a flow of the Power had been alerted, was taking certain steps of its own for needed protection. Reluctantly—Tirtha always sensed that reluctance as sorrow or foreboding—the lord pushed his treasure toward the lady.

A pillar of mist she was, with only a round ball for a head, extensions which were not hands or arms, but served her as such, no more than fragments of fog. Yet she took up what her lord passed to her, arising while that flitting company stirred about the far edges of the wide hall as if hurried, pushed into action—and the lord stepped from his place to join them, moving out of the range of Tirtha's vision.

She never followed him. No, it was the casket that was of importance and that drew her now as the mist woman raised it, pressed it to her unsubstantial form, close to where a human heart might beat. Then she, too, turned and went.

It would seem that Tirtha then also became a specter, a thing without body or form, for she followed that other as if she floated—shadow herself—in this half-and-half world. Down the hall they went to the space behind the high table. And the pace of the lady wraith was swift—she might have been running, time itself her enemy now.

Thus they came to a paneled wall against which the shadow flattened herself oddly—as though releasing a secret lock. A narrow opening was revealed, and she squeezed into a dark place—the power of the thing unseen drawing Tirtha with it.

This was a place where Tirtha felt, even though she possessed no body in her dream, the touch of Power—Power which had built up and lingered—drawn and fed by talent used for years, perhaps centuries, to guard the casket.

There was a stone table in that small windowless chamber; the walls were tapestried by misty hangings. The aura of this hidden chamber was enough to make known to any who came what it was, a place into which only the talent trained might come. Still—even though that be so—Tirtha in the dream was not walled out, forceless and empty-handed though she was.

The shadow lady, still holding the casket against her breast, freed one misty hand and raised it high, making a gesture that seemed to bring the edge of her palm and fingers to strike against the center of the stone table.

That massive block appeared to quiver on the very spot which she had struck. Now the lady looked as if she must free herself of any touch speedily, moving up her hand—or that wisp of mist which served her for such—into the air above. Tirtha, though she had never witnessed otherwhere any such ritual, knew well that this was mastery of an ancient kind in which mind controlled matter and made it obey.

The casket, set in place on the table, quivered as had the rock—rooting itself there, the envisioned girl believed. Still the shadow woman stood and wove her ensorcelments—she might have been locking and bolting unseen doors, making very sure that this place might not be breached.

And—

Tirtha stirred, the silence of her vision—dream broke—she was being touched, and she was again in the flesh, able to feel, even as she was able to hear a whisper very close to her ear where her cloak hood had fallen or been pulled away. There was a faint puff of breath against her cheek. She opened her eyes upon darkness, but she did not move, for a hand kept her pinned where she lay.

"Quiet!" The whisper came again.

She had been shaken so suddenly out of that other place that she was not yet truly aware she had returned to the camp on the ledge. There was no longer any sign of the fire. She roused enough to realize who knelt by her, holding her in place, perhaps even ready to slip his hand across her mouth to muffle any sound she might make, being so summarily aroused.

Tirtha was too well trained a rover to do that. She remained where she was, her ears straining now to pick up sound. He must have known she had been awakened, for his hand left her body speedily, and she had a flash of thought that to touch a woman, even for such a reason, would be difficult for a Falconer. But he did not move away.

One of their ponies stamped and blew. Then the man was gone in a flash of movement. Tirtha realized that he must be on his way to make sure that no sound from their two mounts might betray them. Still she listened.

At last a sound came from a distance, though she could not judge how faraway. There was a scrabbling as if something strove to find a path across none too secure gravel or loose earth. She remembered that not far distant there was one of those mounds of debris left from a slide, such being still only too common in this shaken hill country.

Tirtha sat up, throwing off the enfolding material of the cape. She had her well-worn sword, her bow lay beside her, but night did not favor an archer. Slowly, with caution, she reached out, feeling for a pile of stones she had noted near their fire hole. They were still warm from the heat of the vanished flames as her fingers curled about the top one, which fitted well into her hand. It was heavy, and she had used just such a rough weapon before to good purpose.

The Falconer wore a dart gun at his belt. However, unless he was one of those legendary fighters trained to fire correctly at a sound, that weapon would serve him little better than her bow could aid her. He had a sword also, and she had little doubt that it was now in his hand. There was his claw also, and that—Tirtha could not suppress a small shiver, stupid though she knew any shadow of distaste might be—that was as able a weapon at close quarters as anyone could wish.

The scrabbling had stopped. Yet Tirtha was certain that whatever sniffed about had not gone. No, it had another way of locating its prey.

She did not gasp, she was struck too hard by the new attack to do more than reel back against the rock. The thing hunted with its mind! She had met that blow, which was meant to locate them, with the instant instinctive mind lock that was part of her heritage. But was the Falconer able to counter such a seeking? She knew very little of how his race thought or what defense he could raise against such a questing.

Unfortunately, a mind lock of this kind worked two ways. She dared not relinquish her tight mental cover to seek out the nature of the thing waiting in the dark. That it used mind-send at all meant that they had not been tracked by any outlaw raider, for it was only the Old Race who could seek thus. She herself could handle beasts so, but she had never attempted to trail one of her own kind. That was an abomination which was of the old evil, against which all her blood had stood since they had come into Karsten or into Estcarp.

Now there arose something else, wafted by a rising breeze—a thick animal odor. Not an honest one, such as any beast she had ever known would give forth. This was foul, as if dregs of filth had been stirred or some utter rottenness had breathed a great sigh.

No snow cat, none of the rare verbears rumored to have come into these mountains since the Turning, would so befoul the night air. This was something different. She sent a fraction of her thought to the ponies— surely all their instinct and fears would be speedily roused by that stench. But her would-be soothing thought met a barrier, and she was no longer left to wonder what the Falconer might do. Perhaps the long years in which his kind had schooled and lived with their birds had sharpened a native talent. He was holding a mind wall about their mounts, and to that Tirtha speedily lent her own strength of will.

3

Since that thing below trailed by thought-touch, then the barriers they both had raised must have alerted it to the fact it was discovered. Tirtha arose noiselessly. The thick soles of her boots were soft enough not to crunch as she inched to the lip of the ledge, listening, striving also to see, though the moon was under cloud and starshine could not aid her. She had only nose and ears to serve her.

A second rattle of loose stones sounded. She judged that the stalker had not been able to avoid a misstep. The sound was certainly closer—just as that rank stench was stronger.

Then—

There was a dull yellowish glow—two such on a line. Eyes! And a kind that did not need any reflected light to betray them, possessing within themselves that which was perceptible in the dark.

Perhaps the lurker had better than human sight, an ability to pierce the night for its prey. Still, the eye-gleam betrayed it in turn as it climbed. She could now hear a steady scrabbling, as if claws searched out irregularities in the wall up which it must come to reach them.

Tirtha laid aside her stone, reaching for the pouch on her hip. She had had a chance to renew its contents back in Romsgarth, and she knew well how to use one certain packet among the rest. This might not work against the unknown, but that was not certain until tried. She located it by touch, an envelope of the same supple serpentskin as her belt. Through that skin she felt the grating of grains inside, and with care she shook some into the palm of her other hand.

Those eyes never blinked nor broke a steady stare—they only drew closer. She watched carefully for a second pair—or a sound revealing that the climber was not alone. She was well aware that what strove to reach them was wholly of the Dark—a thing such as the Songsmiths averred dwelt in the halls of Ever-Night. There came the faintest of sounds on her own level. The Falconer had left the two ponies, was coming to stand ready at her side. Tirtha longed to ask if he knew what manner of creature threatened them, but she hesitated to speak while she held the thought barrier.

Her cupped hand ready, she reached through the dark with her other hand until her fingers touched a mail-sleeved arm. She squeezed, hoping that he was astute enough to recognize it as a signal. Then, leaning farther forward, watching those evil, pale discs now raised to hers, sensing that her mind barrier was under assault, Tirtha turned over her palm, releasing the coarse dust it held. There was no breeze to hinder what she would do. Thus she could hope that fortune would move to favor them.

A moment of waiting was followed by a squall such as could not break from the throat of any known animal. The evil eyes blinked and blinked again as the thing hurled itself up at their perch.

The Falconer had jerked out of her hold. Her own worn sword was drawn. Something as large as a pony hooked appendages over the edge of the ledge while it screamed and spattered a foul moisture, which burned her skin as might fire sparks.

Tirtha stabbed outward, felt her blade strike a hide so tough that ancient steel could not penetrate. Beside her sounded the snick of a dart gun. One of the blinking eyes vanished. There was another scream, a last heave of the misshapen body. Then their attacker lost its hold, to fall outward, its cries tearing the night. They heard a heavy sound, which must have marked the striking of a body against some projection on the down slope. A rattling of stones followed, as if the falling creature had started another landslide.

Though the noisome smell remained, plainly the thing was gone, and there were no more cries nor any sound of struggle as a last shift of sliding stones died away. One of the ponies cried out now—in the throes of a great terror. Tirtha was quick to add her talent to that of the Falconer, suggesting to the beasts that all danger was past—and she judged it was, that nothing was left to fear.

As their mounts quieted, Tirtha dared to go and run her hands along the ponies' rough coats, dank with sweat, using touch systematically to convey peace, soothing the distraught animals. Once her hands slipped across her companion's only hand, and she realized that he was aware of this need also.

With their mounts reassured, Tirtha returned to the edge of the ledge. It would appear that the Falconer did not expect another attacker, at least not yet. Still he knew that this was a time for strict watch. The creature they had defeated might be only a scout for more of its kind. She glanced up at the sky, guessed that dawn was not far off. There could be no move until they had more light. Once more her companion joined her, and for the first time, she dared a question: "What was that?"

Tirtha was half surprised at his answer.

"I do not know. There are rumors that things have drifted from the east, that, with the death of Pagar's invaders here, such a great slaughter drew what had not been seen hereabouts before."

"The east," Tirtha repeated. "Out of Escore—the barrier being broke . . ."

She felt cold, but it was not the night air and the absence of her cloak that chilled her. It was the fragmented tales she had heard of that eastern land so long barred—by choice—to her blood, where death walked in the guise of monsters with unknown powers. Many of her kin had since returned there, engaging in a war being fought against the Shadow, it was said. Could that war—or at least some of its evil—be slipping westward? The barrier had been broken in Estcarp with the passing of men into Escore. Might it have been cracked here as well when the Witches of Estcarp had summoned all their Power to rive this country? Perhaps in that act they had also destroyed defenses they had not known existed.

Against men, against animals, Tirtha was willing to take her chances. That was the price of living in these darkened days. Only what could she do if faced with a Dark talent when she had none to raise in turn?

"It was not an animal," she mused aloud, "and certainly not a man—not even Kolder-ridden—if such still exist. Yet it had Power of a sort."

"Yes." His answer was crisp. "The Power—always it is the Power!" There was anger in his voice as if he would deny the talent and yet could not.

They sat side by side, Tirtha drawing her cloak about her, waiting for the light. This had been a harsh warning against her journey, but one she could not heed. Nor had the Falconer said aught about turning back. Once having been given, his sword oath would hold him to the end of what she demanded from him.

The sky grayed, a few stars, showing through ragged rifts in the clouds, faded. She could see the ledge, the ponies, their gear piled by the sunken fire pit. However, Tirtha was more interested in what lay below. At first true light she must see what had crept upon them in the dark, learn the nature of this enemy.

It would appear her companion shared that need for he swung over the lip of the ledge, with her close beside him, down the scar of the attacker's slide. Protruding from the debris was something Tirtha first thought to be a broken branch of a winter-killed tree, then saw it for what it truly was—a hairy limb rising out of the mass of stone and gravel.

Working together they shifted the rocks until they laid bare most of the night hunter's body. Tirtha drew back with an exclamation of disgust. They had uncovered only the head, the upper limbs, and a wide portion of a distended paunch. In color those were near the same gray-white of the stones about them. The skin was matted over by a coarse growth of thick-fibered hair or fur.

From one of the large eyes protruded the end of a dart. The other had wept tears of mucous, oozing down to a mouth that formed the lower part of the face, if it could be termed a "face." In that much her own action had succeeded in their night battle.

Though they did not bare the entire body, Tirtha believed the creature would stand equal in height to her, and she surmised that it had gone erect, two-footed, for the upper appendages ended, not in paws, but in handlike extensions possessing talons as thin and cruel as the Falconer's claw.

Tirtha had never seen or heard of its like before. But if such as this had spilled into the southern mountains, she wondered that even the hardiest or most desperate of outlaws would choose to shelter here.

The muzzle gaped open, but even closed, the fringe of teeth within must have interlocked outside, and those fangs were as long as her middle finger, sharp-pointed, able to tear any body those talon hands could drag down. Her companion knelt, hooking his claw about the butt of the dart he had aimed so well, to pluck it forth, following the sensible action of not wasting any of his small store of weapons. He flipped it away from him to lie in sand, and not touching it with his hand, rubbed it back and forth there to cleanse it.

But he did that mechanically, looking to her the while.

"You also fought," he said abruptly. "How?"

Her hand sought the bag at her belt. "There are herbs of the fields which, when powdered and mixed by those who understand their essence, can blind a creature. I tried such—I think it"—she nodded to the body— "was a night hunter. Blind them and they are as easily brought down as a snagged hare."

"To do that," he commented, "you must be close, closer than a warrior would choose."

She shrugged. "True enough. Yet one learns the use of many weapons within a lifetime. I have trudged the fields—and worked them also—there is much to be learned there. My sword"—she half drew that blade from its sheath to show him the too-often-honed length—"is not such as I would willingly use in battle, though it is mine as Holdruler. I have my bow and arrows." She would not boast, considering her skill. "And I have no credit or favor to purchase a dart gun. Thus I must study other ways."

He said nothing. Since he had resumed his helm, she could not read his expression unless there had been a small tightening of his lips. However, she thought she could guess his reaction, and she resolved not to allow that to anger her. To each his own—let him fight with steel and dart since that was what he was bred to do.

However, she well knew what had schooled and tempered *her* during the past years. She had her own code of honor and dishonor, and as Holdruler (though that was only a name and one she had never claimed) she held to it. Tirtha begged no bread, sought out no fancied kin for roof and shelter. Her two hands earned her that, and if she employed weapons that seemed to him beyond a warrior's code (for perhaps he looked upon her blinding dust as a kind of poison) then she would answer herself for such.

A gift from the earth was free to all. If a discovery was not used in a mean or dark way, then it was as true a defense as any steel forged five times over. If he wished to quarrel with her over that, let him say so now and they would break bargain.

Apparently he was not moved to do so. For, having run his befouled dart into the sandy ground several times over, he brought out a rag and wrapped it about, setting it into a loop of his shoulder belt. A scuttling noise aroused them both.

Tirtha saw a small brownish creature—it might have been scaled, certainly it moved on several pairs of legs. She guessed it to be a scavenger eager for such bounty as was seldom found in this barren land. They left the night hunter behind with no more words between them, climbing up to the ledge again, where they gave their ponies another limited measure of feed, watered them sparingly, ate their own cold rations, and moved on. Her companion was again to the fore, leading his mount, tracing a path where it took all her sharpness of eye to mark any trail at all.

They reached a ridge top by sun-up, and here there was indeed a narrow way, scored by old hoof prints, as well as the slot tracks of what must be the smaller species of pronghorn which had withdrawn centuries ago to the heights. Those were wary game, but Tirtha kept her bow to hand, hoping to bring one down to replenish their stores.

The trail dropped from the heights before midmorning, ushering them into a cupped valley where greenery grew about a stream trickling from a spring. Snorting, the ponies made for the water, and Tirtha was content to linger there a space to give the beasts forage and thus conserve their supplies.

There were signs here, too, that they were not the first to find this campsite. A lean-to of piled rocks, roofed by poles overlaid with thick branches (their lengths and dried leaves weighted down with stones), stood there. Before its door, a fire pit had been dug. Tirtha hunted for wood, sweeping up any dried branches she could find. She was exploring what appeared to be the wreck of a mighty storm, for dead trees lay in a crisscross maze, when she chanced upon more recent evidence that they might not be alone.

Here a patch of soft earth held the impression of a boot—recent enough that the rain two days earlier had not washed it away. She squatted down to brush aside dried leaves, examining it carefully.

She herself wore the soft-soled, calf-high, travel gear known in the border land—supple, with many layers of sole, the bottom one of which was made of sac-lizard hide, which wore as well as or even better than any thicker covering known in northern lands. They could grip and anchor on shifting ground, and in her pack she carried extra strips of the sole-hide for repairs.

This was plainly a northern boot and one, she thought, in excellent repair, which certainly meant that its wearer had not tramped for long among the rough mountain trails. She was still studying it when the Falconer joined her.

He stretched out his hand above the impression, being careful not to touch the earth.

"Man—perhaps a soldier—or a raider who has had some luck with loot. Perhaps yesterday morning . . ."

Tirtha looked back at the shelter, thought of her plans for resting the ponies. With such plain proof that they were not alone here, would it be wise to linger? She was beginning to weigh that when he spoke again. "He rode with trouble."

She saw that his nostrils were expanded showing wider below the half-mask of his helm. Now he gestured to where a mass of half-buried bush leaned crookedly. She saw the flash of wings. Here again were scavengers—bloated flies that sought filth even in the lowlands. They clustered and fought over gouts of blackened blood that bespattered the withered leaves of the bush and formed an irregular splotch on the ground.

On his feet, dart gun in hand, the Falconer moved forward with that soundless border tread. Tirtha was in two minds over following him. Manifestly, someone wounded had come this way—an outlaw forced to lie up because of some weakening hurt might well shoot from ambush any who searched him out. Thus she wondered at her companion's instant attempt to trail. Or could he believe that this stranger might be one of his own kind, lost and needing aid?

Standing in the shadow of a larger mass of brush, Tirtha deliberately opened her mind. She had done this before on the road, seeking to make sure that she was not walking into danger, and it seemed to her that each time she used her small talent so, it grew stronger.

Only now she met with nothing.

She returned to where they had left the ponies hobbled and grazing. Swiftly she brought in the reluctant animals, resaddled them, and looped their reins well within hand reach. When that was done she studied the valley in which they had found this campsite. The water was hardly more than a small brook, spouting out of the ground between two rocks and then pouring along ice cold—perhaps snow-born—to run into a screen of green brush. The spring season touched here early.

There was a colored scattering of small flowers under the shelter of outstanding bushes, and she saw bees at work among them. This valley was a cup of renewed life amid the desolation of rock walls. She put aside her cloak to give freedom to her arms, strung her bow, and held her head high as might a pronghorn buck on herd sentry, listening.

The rippling of the water, the hum of bees, the crunching of the ponies who now pulled leaves from the bushes to satisfy their hunger— that was all her ears picked up. If the Falconer made any sound along the path he had taken, it was too slight to reach her ears. Nor did her other senses find anything to alert or warn.

Her companion appeared again abruptly. He still had his dart gun in hand, and what she could see of his weather-browned face was set and cold. She was beginning to know him perhaps as well as she ever could one of his race, and there radiated from him a chill anger such as she had not felt before.

"You have found . . . ?" She determined that he was not to consider her the less as was the manner of his kind toward women. What they shared here in this debatable country must be equally faced.

"Come—if you will then!" She believed there was still a tinge of contempt and suspicion in his voice, as if he thought that she was of no consequence, save that he needs must serve her whims for a space. Bow in hand, arrow to string, follow she did.

There were other patches of blood, about which the carrion flies crawled. Then they reached the other side of the brush wall. Before them spread a wider strip of meadowlike open land. At the far side of that was a horse, bridled and saddled, with such trappings as she had seen lowlanders use. This was no mountain pony, but instead a Torgian—one of those beprized mounts that might cost a holdkeeper near a year's crop in price. They were not large or imposing as to looks, but their staunchness, their speed and endurance, made them the choice of any who could raise such payment.

It stood above a body lying in the trampled grass, and when they came into view the horse drew back its lips, baring wicked teeth as it moved from side to side as if planning to charge. Some of its breed, Tirtha had heard, were battle-trained, specially shod on forefeet to cut down a dismounted enemy.

She strove to beam toward it such soothing as she would have used with the less intelligent ponies she knew and believed that the Falconer also was trying to so reach the uneasy and angry beast. For there was anger in it, more than fear—the radiation of that emotion was easily detected.

It lowered his head twice to nose at the body in the grass. Then, with a lightning swift swerve about that limp bundle, it made to charge. That she had not reached it mentally surprised and alarmed Tirtha. The mount might have been truly enraged past sanity. She did not want to shoot the horse—and she was sure that her companion had no idea of loosing a dart to bring it down.

Into her attempt to touch the beast's mind Tirtha poured all her strength. The Torgian swerved again, not stampeding directly at them, rather turning to run back and forth across their path, keeping them from the fallen rider. They stood where they were, concentrating, striving to project that they meant no harm, either to it or the one it defended.

Its run became a pacing, then it stood, snorting, a ragged lock of its mane falling forward to half cover white-rimmed eyes, while with one forefoot it pawed up chunks of turf that flew into the air.

Though neither spoke to the other, it would seem that Tirtha and the Falconer could communicate after all, for at the same moment they walked toward the aroused horse, shoulder to shoulder. The Falconer's arm had dropped, his dart gun pointed barrel to the ground. She did not put aside her bow, but neither did she tighten the cord.

The Torgian snorted again, beginning to back away. Its anger was becoming uncertainty. They had passed the crucial moment when it might charge them blindly.

Step by step, always striving to keep to the fore of their minds their good will, the two advanced while the horse retreated. It moved to one side at last, letting them reach the man who lay face down in blood-soaked grass. He wore the riding leather of a lowlander and over it a mail shirt, which had been mended by slightly larger rings, but was still plainly better than most one could find in any market these days. His head was bare, for his helm had rolled to one side. Still they could not see his face, only the tangle of his black hair, for he had fallen belly down.

There was a crush of blood along one leg, and more had flowed from his neck across the shoulder. The Falconer knelt and turned him over, and the body obeyed in one stiff movement as if frozen.

The face was that of youth—as the Old Race knew it—and it was pain-twisted from what must have been the agony of death. Only it was what was fastened heart-high on the breast of that mail shirt which caught Tirtha—stopped her and brought a gasp from her lips. The dead man did not surprise her. She had viewed death often and in more than one ugly guise—many worse than this.

But none of those bodies had worn a metal badge fashioned like a device from a coat of high ceremony. She was looking down at the open-beaked hawk which was her own single hold on the past. Hawkholme—*she* was Hawkholme! Who was this stranger who dared sport a badge that was all she had to claim in the way of heritage?

She leaned forward to study it, hoping to note some small difference. But the Hold badges were the proud and cherished possessions of each clan, and to copy or wear one that was not blood-sealed was so unheard of as to be an impossibility past all reckoning.

"Your kin?" The Falconer's tone was cold, measuring.

Tirtha shook her head. There was no denying that badge. Could it be that some refugee out of Karsten had brought it, then had it stolen, looted, had even given it away? A Hold badge with the hawk's head never would be given away! That was not to be even thought of!

"I have no kin," she returned, and she hoped that her voice was as cool and level as that of her companion. "I do not know this man, nor why he should wear what he has no right to. That is no kinsman's mark—it is a holdmaster's." She was sure of that. "And though there is no hold now in Karsten, yet I alone am of the Blood!"

She lifted her eyes from that unexplainable symbol and stared straight into the yellow-sparked ones of the Falconer. Perhaps he and his fellows believed all women liars and worse. She might not be able to prove the truth of what she said. Let him go then. But *she* was Hawkholme, and she *could* prove it when the time came.

4

They had searched the dead man. There was nothing about him that could not have been worn or carried by any blank shield riding out of Estcarp on some private errand. His wounds, the Falconer declared, were not from steel or edged weapons but were caused by tooth and talon. To Tirtha's surprise, the dead man had no weapons. There was a sword belt, to be sure, but the scabbard it supported was empty, as were all dart clip loops. He certainly had not ventured into this high, dangerous land bare-handed. Had he been stripped after death? If so, how had the looter passed the Torgian? And what enemy had traveled with a fanged and clawed hunter?

The mount snorted and pawed the turf at intervals, even though it kept its distance. Attached to its light saddle hung a pair of travel bags. It was to those Tirtha turned her attention next. If the Torgian would allow her to free them, they might just learn more of the dead.

He had lain there for some time, the Falconer averred, judging from the post-death stiffness of the corpse. Oddly enough, except for the clouds of flies, he had not been preyed upon by any scavengers, such as gathered elsewhere, no doubt because of the Torgian.

Since they had no tools, the Falconer used his sword to hack at the turf, loosening clods which Tirtha broke away and piled to one side. The grave they so dug was a shallow one, but they did the best they could. When they laid him in it, the girl brought forth a square scarf, such as she used in bad weather to cover her head under the folding of her hood, to lay over his face. She helped repile the clods of turf, then brought stones from the brook edge to add cover. When they had done, she arose from her knees, regarding broodingly the mound they had raised.

Tongue tip swept across her lower lip as she found words. They were not those formal ones she had heard said many times when she was not yet woman grown, but they were the best she could summon at this hour:

"May your sleep be sweet, stranger, may your path beyond be smooth, may you come to your desiring and it give you peace." She stooped, picked up one white stone that was nearly round, fashioned so, she thought, by water's rolling, and which she had laid aside for this purpose. As if she were indeed kin-blood and close kin, she placed this above the hidden head of the dead man. It bore no symbol of the old Power, nor could she breathe into it any spell of releasing. But through the last hard years, Tirtha had come to believe that such formalities were intended to lighten a little the grief of kin left behind rather than touch one who had already taken the Long Road and who, perhaps, had already forgotten this world, impatient for what lay beyond.

She knew nothing of what the Falconers believed concerning this life or what lay beyond it, but now she saw her companion take his sword, holding it by the blade, its hilt high. Then he turned the length of steel so that the hilt, as he moved his arm, traveled down the length of the grave while he chanted, in a voice hardly above a harsh whisper, words that held no meaning for her.

Afterward they looked to the horse. It would seem that the sealing of its master into the earth had, in an odd way, broken the anger that had made it so wary and wild. It had wandered away, and was now cropping grass awkwardly, the bit in its mouth manifestly bothering it. Slowly, with care, Tirtha approached, stopping short when it lifted its head to stare at her.

There was no longer any emanation of fear or hatred. She went ahead coolly, lifted the two saddle bags from their place while the Falconer busied himself with the horse itself, stripping off saddle and bridle, rubbing down the rough coat on which there were matted splotches of dried blood.

Within the bags were a packet of trail bread, another of dried meat, both very meager, a twist of coarse woven stuff which contained a mass of dried huk-berries squeezed into an uneven ball. Below those was a flask, battered, with its intricate plating scratched and dented. Tirtha forced the stopper out and sniffed the odor of the fiery corn spirit which could not only inwardly warm a man in the cold, but was equally useful for treating wounds so that they did not mortify.

Turning the flask around, she studied the style of ornamentation. It was Old Race work plain enough, and indeed out of Karsten, from the aged look of it. However, there was no particular part of its patterning which made it unique—no crest on this anyway.

The other bag yielded a shirt, which had been poorly washed and then rough dried, creased into as small a roll as possible. There was a honing stone and a small amount of oil for the tending of any edged weapons, though the dead man had not managed to keep his. But, last of all, there was a tight-capped cylinder about the length of her palm—also old metal—with only faint traces of some engraving to be detected along its sides. Such she had seen once or twice. They were fashioned to protect parchments, which were precious things—records to which hold-lords and songsmiths clung.

Each had a trick to the opening of the cap. It could not be forced lest it and perhaps its contents be destroyed. She turned it around now, its smooth surface slipping in her grasp as if oiled. This might be the answer to their mystery—to her mystery. But as yet she was in no hurry to pursue it. Tirtha sat back on her heels as the Falconer loomed over her, looking down at the result of her rummaging. She knew that his attention centered on the thing she held, so she made no attempt to belittle her discovery. "It is a record holder—very old."

He could see that much for himself. Though she did not in the least want to let the thing out of her hands, Tirtha held it out to him as if her own curiosity was only nominal. Since the sighting of that badge-crest she well knew that he must believe she kept more than one secret, and she had no wish to add to his suspicions.

"Open it!"

That was an order and she stiffened. She was right, his suspicions *were* aroused. Had he some idea that she had come into these mountains perhaps to meet with the dead man? But she owed him no explanations. When he took sword oath for a stated time, he must serve her in every-thing save that which would dim his own honor as a warrior. What stood between them now was the aversion of his race toward any female, their refusal to accept that a woman had truth in her. She had heard enough of the Falconers in Estcarp to be aware of their belief and what it had cost them.

"If you know anything of these"—she gestured to the rod he now held—"you also know that they are sealed secretly and that only those who carry such and perhaps their close kin—or a sword brother, a shield mate—know the trick of the fastening. This man was no kin to me—I cannot loose his secrets."

It might become necessary to try, at some point, Tirtha thought, even if it meant destroying the container. Though again that could well threaten any contents. She wanted very much to know who the stranger was, why he rode these mountains. Had he also been headed for Karsten? Would it advance her case with this other, whose distrust now appeared so tangible that she could feel it, if she were to tell more of her story? She shrank from such a self-betrayal. Her quest was hers alone, a precious thing to be doubly guarded because, if she told the story properly, he might well consider it either part of an hallucination spun for some dark purpose or think it the dreaming of a stupid woman, such as he was already certain she must be.

He was inspecting the faint line of cleavage at the top of the rod closely. Certainly there was no lock or fastening here. Now his eyes sought hers again through the helm slits.

"You call yourself Hawkholme—perhaps so did that one." He used the rod itself as a pointer to indicate the mound they had built. "Yet you say he was a stranger. I know the Old Race well. They are closely kin-tied as a part of their heritage."

Tirtha shook her head slowly. "Yes, we are kintied—just as securely as you are tied to your sword-brothers. Still I found you alone in Romsgarth and you answered to Blank Shield—is that not the truth? Where then are those you shared comradeship with?"

Those yellow sparks in his eyes blazed. She saw his lips move as if he wished to lash out at her with words of hot abuse. What *had* brought him without his bird—in such a sorry state—into Romsgarth? She had never heard that it was in any Falconer born to leave his company, to drift alone. It was as if they held a wall against the whole world and could not see past that barrier into any other way of life.

Tirtha had no wish to force an answer from him. What lay behind him was his own concern. But he must grant to her the same dignity of no questions. However, she could yield a little, without laying bare all that had driven her through the years.

"We were Horned in Karsten, hunted without warning, as the farmers sometimes hunt hares in the spring—beating the fields to bring them into a circle where they can be clubbed and killed. So was the Old Race hunted. Though we"—she raised her head proudly, meeting him stare for stare—"fought and did not cower and scream beneath the clubs. It was death and blood from the hunting packs for us or any who dared to give warning.

"Some of us got into Estcarp. The Borderers were Karsten warriors. You must know that—your own people rode with them. But there was a breakage of kin lines. Some holds were overrun, none of their folk escaping. From others a handful might flee safely. I . . ." Her hand sought that well-worn sword, brought it out of its scabbard into the light. "I am of the Blood of two who fled so. Hawkholme went down, but the younger brother of the Lord and his newly wedded wife were not within its walls. They had gone to a guesting with her kin and so were closer to the border—to freedom. There was a farseeing—for in my mother there was some of the talent—and she saw death. I am the last of Hawkholme." She slammed the sword back into its scabbard. "Who this stranger was—that I cannot tell you. For farseeing does not lie and it was plain—Hawkholme went into the fire and with it all those of the Blood."

"Farseeing . . ." he repeated and paused.

She nodded. "Witches' trick—would you call it that, Falconer? To each race its own secrets. You have talents, even if they are not of a Wise Woman's summoning. How else could you have trained your birds, kept so well the watch in these mountains before they were moved? I do not disdain what you have of your own; see that you do not try to lessen what my people possess either. I have not the real talent, but I have seen it work, and well, many times over! Now," she reached forward, and before he could prevent it, she had plucked the record rod out of his fingers. "What do you say that we move on? You have said that the dead died of . . ."

Something glinted behind his shoulder. She caught sight of it and stiffened. He must have read her expression, for he slewed about, sword ready. Only what he saw was not moving, certainly had not yet presented any threat. It was visible on the valley wall above this strip of meadow, and no living thing could perch on that perpendicular height.

The angle of the sunlight now brought a definite pattern into sharp visibility. Without conscious volition Tirtha moved forward, brushing past the Falconer, her full attention claimed, as if she were indeed ensorceled by those shiny lines which spiraled, outward, becoming more and more distinct.

As Tirtha pushed through a last screen of brush, unheeding when it caught at her garments, laid scratches across her hands, she saw that the whole face of the cliff must have been shorn away during the troubling of the mountains. But if that were so, then what was so plainly visible now must have been hidden deep before. For what purpose?

What she read was a sign she had seen only once before, when she had wintered in Lormt, that greatly revered and nearly deserted repository of truly forgotten knowledge. She had made herself useful in a barn-like barracks once dedicated to the use of scholars and legend-keepers, now inhabited by a handful of the very old, some still delving into rolls and records, others content to doze away the latter days of their lives—a haven for those withdrawing from the cold winds of the world as it was.

That symbol had been on a scroll unrolled on a table where one of the most forgetful of those Tirtha had come to look upon as her charges had left it. She had researched during scraps of free time, striving to learn anything that could be of service in the future task which she had set herself. So she had asked concerning that symbol, to be told that it was indeed very old, once a defense against any encroachment of evil where it had been pictured or inlaid or engraved after proper ritual. Now it shone out here, apparently set into the stone.

But why? Tirtha swung around to view the pocket of valley. What lay here, to be protected in days beyond modern reckoning? Or had it been intended for this valley at all? The churning of the mountains must have brought it into sight. What had it once guarded in hiding?

"What is it?" The Falconer came to stand shoulder to shoulder with her. He had not returned his blade to its sheath. Now, with his claw, he pulled off his helm as if he could so see those marks the clearer.

"That is a strong defense against the Dark—one used in very ancient times to hold safe a portion of the land as no wall or steel could—more witchery, warrior," she added, a fraction of mockery in her tone. "I wonder . . ."

That thing they had slain in the night—it was certainly not of Estcarp, nor Karsten either. There was that war which still raged to the eastward between the Shadow and the Light. Had such a conflict once touched *this* land? Mystery upon mystery. Yet below that mark on the wall, unless all she had ever learned was false, there lay safety.

Had the dead man fought to reach this valley because of it? Not wounded by dart or steel, but by claws and fangs. Had he suffered those wounds some distance away and headed for this small island of safety—reached it too badly injured to live?

"This is wild land." Now the Falconer sheathed his weapon, his helm swung in his claw. "Who would put such a safeguard here?"

"This is an old land, very old," she returned. "It hides years upon years of secrets. Perhaps the mountains, when they leaped at the Call of the Council, merely moved into a pattern once known before. At any rate, this is a protected place." She brought up her hand, stretching the fingers to form a sign of recognition. "Here we can be safe. He might have been," she glanced over her shoulder at the mound, "had he reached it unwounded. We cannot tell what may be abroad now. Would you still move on, or shall we give our beasts a chance of rest and good forage?"

He still studied the sign on the cliff side. "You speak of years—and I think those may have piled up beyond counting. Does any ensorcelment last so long?"

"By the legends it may. Let us see . . ." She pushed on until she could touch the stone of the cliff wall. The symbol was well above her head. Looking about, Tirtha caught up a branch half embedded in the earth, jerked it free. From her pouch she took the record rod they had found. There could be yet another reason why the dead man had fought so valiantly to reach this place, if he knew of the symbol and had not come here by mere chance or the wandering of the Torgian bearing a near-conscious rider.

In her belt pouch was a looping of leather for the mending of her boots, and she selected one strand to bind the record rod to the branch end.

"These holders," she explained as she worked, the Falconer watching her closely but plainly without understanding what she would do, "are made charged with certain powers. They cannot be fashioned in these days for their secret has been lost. But I was at Lormt two winters since, and one can learn *how* things may work, if not why—that being forgotten. The symbol there is wrought of charged metal—worked by smiths who had talent, who knew their witchery, as you would say. It is a very old knowledge that like answers to like. If the power still lies in these two workings, the cliff and the rod, different as they may seem, then we shall have proof of it. Now!"

Having tested her lashing, Tirtha stood to tiptoe, one hand braced against the cliff side, the other raising the branch as far as she could, so that the record rod did, indeed, reach the bottommost looping of that inlay. She nearly cried out.

Feeding downward, even through the dead wood she held, came a surge of power, while both symbol and rod gave forth a thin bluish light. She jerked the stick away, afraid that perhaps such an awakening might consume the rod itself. But she had been right! Blue was the color of protective Power always. There were many accounts at Lormt concerning places of refuge which could be so identified, though those must lie in Escore since Estcarp boasted none that she knew of. And if the rod had also blazed blue, then what it contained held Power, was not just some simple message!

Her hand stung as a queer prickling ran along her fingers. Quickly taking the branch into her left fist, Tirtha flexed and bent those fingers. An exclamation from her companion brought her attention away from her own reaction, from knowing that she meddled with what she did not understand and had probably been too reckless in trying.

He had seized upon the branch above her own hold and nearly shook it free of her grasp in his excitement. Then she saw, also. The hair-thin line which had marked the sealing place on the rod was not only wider, but it was ringed by a slim blue line of fire, as if energy ate the old metal.

"Don't touch it—not yet!" Her cry came swiftly, as he was about to free it from its lashing. "Not unless you want, perhaps, to lose another hand!"

He loosed his hold to stare at her, suspicion again in his face. Tirtha laid the branch and rod carefully at the gravelly foot of the cliff and watched. It was true! There was an ever-increasing opening. She looked at her hands, at her sword. If that blue light did not continue, she might try to force it more. However, the reaction that had reached her even through the length of dead wood was a warning. They must wait until whatever had begun worked itself out.

She glanced up. There was nothing to be read now by the lines on the rockface. Their shining was as it had been at her first sighting. The influence, whatever it might be, had passed into the rod. Now that was failing also. At least the blue strip about the one end was losing brightness. As it failed she could see a dark space, and she was sure that the sealing had been sprung. That she had succeeded in such an act was as surprising to her as it must be to the Falconer, who watched the cylinder of metal intently, even as he might look into the eyes of an enemy, with the same wariness and readiness for battle.

It had been only experimentation, a wild guess on her part. That it worked . . . ! *Had* this been the reason to draw the dead man here with his last failing strength—that he might read a record as important to him as life itself?

The blue light vanished. Tirtha knelt, stretched out her hand, very cautiously, toward the lashing of the rod. She could sense no heat, nothing of that energy which had touched her before. The gap in the rod remained apparent.

Very carefully she worked at the knotted thong, moving gingerly when she had to touch the rod itself. When there followed no pricking, she took confidence, twisted it free. Gripping the cap in her fingers, she gave a sharp pull. There was resistance, but only slight. Then the small round of metal came free, the rod remaining in her other hand. She dropped the cap, upended the rod to shake it above her left palm. Nothing was forthcoming. When Tirtha inspected it more closely she could see a roll inside, tight against the wall of the small cylinder. That had to be worked out very carefully. If this scrap was old, it might well vanish into dust under rough handling.

She held a roll of what could only be several layers of the same reptile skin as formed her money belt, glued one to another to make a sheet akin to parchment, but infinitely more durable. She spread it wide to view a jumble of symbols that made no sense at all.

Her disappointment was so keen, she gave a little cry of disbelief. A thing of power this doubtless was, but as locked against any use by her as if she had never freed it from the rod! None of the symbols on it were familiar. Not even at Lormt had she come across such meandering lines, such swirls, as were inscribed here in red paint or ink. They did not even form lines as if they were some enciphered message—rather sprawled here and there, some large, some small, in no reasonable pattern.

"Perhaps it is a map."

Almost, Tirtha had forgotten the Falconer. He moved beside her again to stare at what she held, his slanting brows drawn together in a half-frown.

"A map!" Tirtha had reason to consult such in the past. Though nothing had been done since the writhing of the mountains to lay out guides for travelers into the borderlands, she herself had contrived to fit together bits of information which she believed would guide her to her future goal. She had set down, memorized, and destroyed them methodically. Nothing she had ever seen or heard of matched this peculiar scrawl. Yet it had not been done roughly, she could perceive that the longer she studied it. The pictured symbols must have definite meaning, yet it was a meaning that eluded her.

"Not of this." With a wave of his hand her companion dismissed the countryside around them. "I think it is a different kind of map—perhaps of a place, a hold even, rather than the countryside."

"But there are no lines for walls, no. . . ." she began her protest.

His frown had lightened. "I think everything that might have been used in that fashion was deliberately omitted. So that the place could not be identified. This is a seeker's guide, one pointed at a special place, perhaps a treasure."

She did not miss that quick glance he had given her, before his eyes went back to the paper again.

"Also," he continued, "it is a part of that witchery." He raised his head toward the symbol on the cliff face. "It could well be that there is sorcery in what is written here, and only one endowed with your talents—you of the Old Race—can make much of it. He—this man you speak of as a stranger—was of your blood. He carried this, and it meant much to him. Could he have been seeking out just such an aid as that hanging up there to make it plain to him?"

So he shared that guess with her. Well, there was a good chance he was right. However, that dead seeker must have known much more than she did. That presented a new fragment of mystery. In Estcarp only the Witches pretended to any use of the Power. It was not given to any man to read such a puzzle as she held—nor would a Witch believe that in a man's hands the rod could ever have given up its secret.

Therefore the rider must have been instructed what to search for. Tirtha drew a long breath and rerolled the layered skin, pushed it back in its container. Stooping, she picked up the cap, but she did not restore it to the top of the rod. There might just be a chance that time and fortune would give her a means of penetrating the secret of what she had found, and she had no intention of sealing it away. Another time there might not be a way of forcing it open.

She stored it in her belt pouch, and they returned to the meadow. But as she went, Tirtha was busy with scrambled thoughts. The Falconer's guess—which could only be a guess, of course. Was this really some clue to the inner parts of—say—a hold hall such a one as she had envisioned? *Had* the dead stranger and she both been drawn by a stroke of fortune or troubling of Power past their understanding to make this journey at the same time and in search of the same thing? It was a disturbing thought, but she could not force it out of mind.

5

They chose to camp in the protected valley, returning to the crude shelter they had earlier discovered, turning their ponies loose, though hobbled, to share the meadow with the Torgian. Because of that symbol on the rock wall Tirtha dared a fire. Also, at the coming of dusk, the intricate design there began to glow blue, even as a portion had done at her testing. Whatever virtue it possessed was still locked in it, and Tirtha believed that this was indeed a pocket of safety where they need fear no monstrous prowler of the night.

The rations they carried were so limited she made a very careful division of what she had brought out of Romsgarth. However, the Falconer ventured down stream to return, swinging from a reed thong, a brace of plump water hens, which he rolled in mud and pushed well down into the coals of the fire. So they fared better than she would have thought, the feathered skin peeling away from this feast with the mud.

They did not choose to lie within that half-shelter. The night was not cold and somehow Tirtha wanted not to be pent in. It seemed the Falconer shared her desire for freedom. However, she agreed readily that, in spite of the glowing symbol on the rocks, it was well to keep watch turn by turn. This night it fell to her to stand sentry first.

Once the Falconer had rolled into his blanket, she did not remain long by the fire. Hearing the even breathing of the sleeper, she got to her feet, followed the faint path meadowwards. The three beasts grazing there paid her no heed. All the defiance and fear, she sensed, had gone out of the Torgian. He was perhaps ready to accept a change in traveling companions, and certainly he would be a welcome addition—a horse of his stamina and speed might well mean, in Karsten, the difference between success and failure.

Of course, the Falconer could bespeak an equal claim on that mount, but Tirtha believed she might buy him off by an offer of extra gold. Perhaps she might even add her mare whose worth was high in the border country. Now she turned her back on the grazing trio and stood, hands on her hips, looking up at the symbol on the cliff.

What it had been intended to guard was a mystery to both intrigue and disturb her. If it had been hidden until the quakes had revealed it so, then what lay or had lain under the land hereabouts? There were certainly no holds this deep in the highlands—only the Eyrie which the Falconers had built and which had been destroyed. Nor was this Falcon "witchery."

Never more than at this moment, she longed for the talent. One who possessed farsight—or even the smaller gift of water-seeking with a peeled wand—might have unlocked a little of the ancient puzzle. In spite of her winter at Lormt, Tirtha had been too lacking in early training to absorb more than the knowledge of what might exist—with no chance of making the smallest usage of what someone else could have put to the test.

What did she possess, in truth? Only her dream and the conviction that it drew her, that there lay before her something that must be done—the reason for her existence. It was that which had carried her through these years, worked upon her body and spirit as a smith works upon the metal he handles to fashion a cunning tool, a stout weapon. A tool, a weapon—to be used by whom and for what? She had asked herself that also, knowing that there would be no answer out of the heavens to make all plain.

There was the Power, and it did lie in all things that had life. However, it was comprised of many different energies, some of which served those trained in use, some of which could harm—and another, a larger part, that was beyond even the greatest adept to understand or know. Out of Power came birth and life—to it, after death, returned that which was the spark of all inner essence. Once there had been ritual and ceremony where kin gathered to warm their hearts at a summoned manifestation.

That was long ago. Tirtha could only stand and stare at lines upon a rock wall and wonder who had wrought them so carefully. Had the Power drawn her here? The Falconer had chosen the trail leading to this valley, but she was certain he had not known that it lay under such protection; if so he might well have sought another road. For his kind were not, they had often declared, to be caught in any spell laid by the Old Race.

Again, almost shyly since she was alone and had no need to impress anyone with the fact that she faced something of her own people, Tirtha raised a hand to sketch in the air the sign of peace and acceptance. Then she turned back to sit by the fire, feeding it stick by stick, listening to the sound of the running stream.

She realized that, save for the carrion flies, there had been no stirring of life in this valley. Though the Falconer had caught water hens, she had heard no calling of such fowl or sighted spoor of any beast. Yet in this wilderness of stone, the water, the meadow should surely have attracted some wilderness life. It was too quiet here. The girl moved restlessly, arose again, once more pacing into the meadow where the ponies seemed undisturbed. She listened for the wing-sound of any night bird. During all her roaming she had slept out many times, and she knew only too well the cries of the great hunting owls which were common in the lower border lands.

A quiet night . . .

There was a thin sliver of new moon showing, as well as stars. Moon Magic also—she had a fraction of it herself. It was special to the Wise Women—if not to the Witches—woman's magic. . . .

Magic—it was all magic! Tirtha's fingers balled into a fist that she pounded against the earth as she hunkered down again. She deliberately fastened her mind upon what she must do once they were cross-mountain, even though all would depend upon what they found there. Would she be wise to try to keep the Falconer past the time they had bargained, even if she must, in turn, then share something of her secret? There were no decisions she could make now—only try to think a little ahead so that she knew what decisions might await her.

The silence, the sight of that symbol, made her restless, ill at ease. She tested with seek-thought for any slinker, any life form that might dare the valley in spite of the guardianship. She caught the life essence, which came from the sleeping man; and farther away, that of the three mounts; also some smaller sparks—without anything about them of Dark threat— which she guessed might be wild life. Then . . .

Pain and despair—horror—need . . .

Tirtha was on her feet, running her sword out.

She came to the cairn, stood staring wide-eyed at the mounded turf, the stones they had chosen and fitted above them.

Need—need! Such a wave of it struck at her that she was unaware of falling to her knees beside the mound, watching it in pure horror, which gripped and froze her whole body with waves of unknown force.

Need!

No! Death was a final gate through which all life essence passed. There was no imprisoning of self in rotting flesh that had been discarded. They had buried a dead man. He could not summon—demand—assault

her with this desperate cry for help! She dropped the sword, put her
hands to her head when the demand she could neither explain nor deny
struck at her, set her swaying back and forth as if blows were being rained
upon her.

The sword had clattered across the stones. Its Hawk-signed pommel
touched the white stone she had added for the very old ritual of her people. Hawk!

Kin-blood—kin-blood to take up a burden, accept the need!

Kin-blood? There was none. She denied that fiercely. Dimly, out of
the stories she had heard in childhood, Tirtha knew what sought to
ensnare her now. There was the kin oath-laying, which could pass from
dead to living and which could not be denied. But that was a true kin
thing, accepted by the chosen as a duty coming before all else in life! She
was not blood-tied to this stranger. What lingered here could *not* set its
mark on her!

"Peace . . ." She got out that word with great effort, as if she must
speak past a constriction in her throat. "Peace to you, stranger. I am not
kin-blood. Go you on into the Power's way. We choose not our endings;
we choose only the manner with which we meet such. Your task may have
ended, but it was the body that failed you, not. . . ."

Tirtha gasped. The sword and the stone—above them where they
touched forming something that might well have issued from her abiding
and commanding dream—save she was not asleep. There, in a faintly
blue mist, was the casket even as she had seen it carried into hiding by
that hold lady whose face she had never viewed. *There* was what she must
seek and find—and it grew sharper, more distinct.

Need . . .

Fainter now, as if the last vestiges of whatever had summoned her
were fast fading, as if the call she heard came only from a distance, growing ever more immeasurable.

And that need—it was hers also! Stranger—no! In some way past her
understanding, this one *had* been kin-born. However, the dead did not
have to bend her to his fading will—that geas was already a part of her.

"Hawkholme—!" Tirtha said. "I go there, yes. And what lies within
that"—the casket was merely a wisp of vapor again—"is to come forth. I
knew you not, kin-blood. But your need is already mine."

The haze vanished—also that other—that remnant of will which had
outlasted death itself. She was bound, but no more tightly than she had
been before she entered this valley. Save that it seemed, in that moment,
that when she took up the sword again from where it had fallen, there
passed into the hand gripping it a new kind of energy, a strength she had
not hitherto known.

Tirtha was still trembling, fighting down the raw fear that had touched her, as she returned to their camp. The night had swung by. She roused her companion, wrapped herself in her own cloak. Almost, she was afraid to surrender to sleep. Would the dream enfold her now, or would something else—a last lingering trace of that demand—strike at her? She closed her eyes with determination and willed herself to rest.

No dream came this night, nor did she confront, as she had more than half feared, that other presence. Instead, her sleep must have been very deep and heavy, for when she was awakened in the morning, she felt a reluctance to move, as if weakened.

They discovered the Torgian now biddable enough, standing quietly so that he might be saddled with the riding gear from which the Falconer had scrubbed the blood stains. But neither of them wished to mount in the place of his dead master; rather they put him on a leading rein and kept to their own sure-footed ponies.

Tirtha hunched her shoulders a little as she passed both mound and symbol, glancing at neither. In the brightness of this new day she could almost believe that illusion had enfolded her last night, and she kept her hand well away from sword hilt as she rode. Let the dead lie in peace— and might she ride so. She owned no debt to anyone—carried nothing but the purpose that had brought her here.

There was a thin trace on the far side of the meadow, a shadow trail such as only the very sure-footed mountain ponies could follow, and one they must have taken unencumbered. Both riders dismounted to lead their beasts, the Falconer hooking the Torgian's halter rope to the empty perch on his own saddle pad, thus securing the horse in line.

The climb was one to be taken slowly and with care. When they at length reached a split in the valley wall, Tirtha stared eagerly ahead, hoping that they were not to be faced by another such ordeal. She was heartened to see that the trail beyond widened and when it did descend, the angle was far less sharp. Also there was greenery to be sighted in pockets ahead, as if they had now passed through the sharp rock desert which had been the outer forbidding part of the mountain ways.

Shortly before midday she brought down a pronghorn—a young buck—and they stopped to skin and butcher the kill. When they broke their fast at nooning, it was with good meat, fire-roasted. Nor was there any lack of life to be seen hereabouts. The fresh slot tracks of other pronghorns, the calls of birds, even a lazy scattering of well-fed quarewings out of a patch of fresh standing law-leaves—the crops of the birds so stuffed that they seemed too weighted to take to the air—all testified to that.

This was good hunting land, and Tirtha wondered if it might be well to try smoking some of the meat, halting for a day or so to add to their supplies. Oddly enough, along this particular trail, where she would have thought it more natural to find snow still lingering, spring growth was more advanced than in the lower valleys from which they had come. There were flowers in pockets of earth, wild fruit trees in bloom, so that the perfume blended on the air, bringing back memories of those farm garths where she had labored.

They were two days crossing this gentle land, and there was no trace in it of any evil. Sometimes Tirtha felt a freedom of spirit, in short flashes, as if nothing pushed at her. To live here in peace and quiet, depending upon the bounty of the earth alone, troubled by no dreams, no need—she wondered dimly now and then what such a life might mean.

If her companion had such thoughts, he never voiced them, any more than she revealed hers. They traveled mainly in silence, and she believed that he was intent upon accomplishing their journey as swiftly and with as little danger as possible. They still kept night watches in turn, and he rode ever, she noted, with the attention of a scout invading unknown territory.

Strangely enough, she no longer dreamed. That visit in her dreams to the ghostly hold had been for so long a part of her nights that Tirtha felt disturbed when it was not repeated. Several times she had drawn out during their camping that "map," as the Falconer would call it, studying the symbols set on it to no better purpose than she had done the first time she had looked upon it. Was it a map at all? There were patterns for calling of Power; hastily she pushed that dangerous idea out of her mind.

On the afternoon of the fourth day after they had ridden out of the protected valley, the vegetation grew sparser, their path once more led into a barren country as it climbed. Just before nightfall they sighted a fall of stone. The Falconer halted, staring ahead—not as one who faced some to-be-expected barrier, but rather in bemusement, which showed openly on his usually expressionless face, for that day he had ridden bareheaded—a strange choice for one who had always kept to his mask.

Tirtha could see no reason for this sudden halt, but here the path was so narrow that she could not push ahead, but must wait on him to move. When he did not, she broke what had nearly been a full day of silence.

"There is no way beyond?"

For a long moment she believed that he was so lost in what thoughts filled his mind that he had not even heard her. Then, haltingly, his claw swung out, gestured at the river of broken stone.

"The Eyrie . . ."

Some trick of his voice, its pitch, awoke an echo from the rocks around them.

Eyrie. That was like the wail of a mourner at a Sulcar burn burial.

Tirtha stared. There was certainly little to show that this had been the site of the centuries' old dwelling place of his race—at least nothing she could distinguish. She had heard that the Eyrie had been so well designed that it had the appearance of a hollowed-out mountain, and that very few, if any, outsiders (and those only the Borderers and males) had ever crossed its one-time drawbridge.

Here was nothing but river stone resembling any other slide they had skirted or crossed during their travels. Her companion held his head well back on his shoulders, gazing up the line of that heap of rocks, as if he hunted desperately for something that should still exist. In turn, she imagined a mist out of the past come to cloak that slide, to show for a heartbeat or two the fortress that had been. Yet she could truly not trace anything at all.

He called, the words she did not know spiraling up, then running into a single sound that might be the scream of a hawk. Three times he uttered that cry. Then he was answered!

Tirtha clutched her reins tighter, her mount shifted foot to send some small stones rattling. The answer was thin, not full-throated—yet she could not deny that she had heard it. Ghosts—the vanished dead who should be peacefully at rest—was she not yet done with them? Had *his* kin a call for blood vengeance and was that demand strong enough that it could manifest itself in the full light of day? The Falconers had been well warned; surely they had taken refuge down in Estcarp before the churning of the heights. Certainly also her companion could not be old enough in years to have been sword-oathed to one who had lived here before the end of the Eyrie.

The Falconer shouted—for a ringing shout was what he uttered this time, echoing and reechoing—something in the pitch of sound making the ponies snort, the Torgian whinny, and her own ears hurt.

Once more an answer. Then she caught sight of a speck in the sky overhead. Down it struck, as if it would bear with it from the air some intruding prey. She watched with some awe the swiftness of that descent out of the heavens. The flyer passed from sunlight into the more shadowed air of the half-choked cleft into which they had headed.

Now the strike eased, wings flapped, a black body circled, and circling, came closer and closer until it passed above them. A falcon settled on an edge of rock, its wings still a little spread, as if it would take to the heavens again once its curiosity was satisfied.

Black of feather, with the white V marking on the breast, a falcon of the Eyrie—or else the descendant of such a one—wildliving, for it did not wear the scarlet jesses that marked the partnership between man and bird. Bright eyes regarded the unhelmed man. From his lips came a series of birdlike notes, scaling up and down. The falcon answered with a scream, mantling, appearing ready to lift again, be away from this creature of another species who strove to communicate with it.

Still the Falconer forced out sounds, which Tirtha would not have believed any human throat or lips could have shaped. He made no move toward the uneasy bird, simply spoke to it, Tirtha was now convinced, in its own language.

There was no scream; rather the sound the bird uttered in return was not far different from those made by the man. Its head was slightly to one side. Tirtha could believe that it was considering some proposal or striving to come to a decision of its own.

Then, with one more cry, it took to the air. Not to approach the waiting man but to rise steadily with all the force of its wings into the heights from which it had come. There was no disappointment on the weathered features of the man, he simply sat and watched it go.

It was only when it winged to the west and was fully gone from their sight that he seemed to remember he was not alone and looked back at Tirtha.

"This is no road, not now." His voice was steady, as cool as it had always been. "We must go back and take a northward turning, and that before the dark closes in."

Tirtha asked no questions, for there was that about him which said he was entirely certain of what he was about, and she had learned to trust his sense of mountain ways. Turn north they did, and in the end found a basin that was clearly the work of men, into which ran a runnel of water, falling out of a pipe made to handle thrice the amount that now trickled through. There was forage of a sort—tough clumps of grass growing along the overflow from the basin—at least enough graze for overnight.

They had no fire. Though there were sticks enough among the stones of the stream's banks for the feeding of one, the Falconer shook his head when Tirtha would have gathered them.

"This is a place of watchers."

"Falcons?" she asked. "But fire would not rouse them."

He shook his head again emphatically. "Others have come into this country."

His exchange of sounds with that bird—what had he so learned? She felt she had a right to demand such information, when he continued: "Such are not outlaws—nor those from Karsten. They are others from the east."

From the east! That snout-nosed monster out of the dark! Things on the move from Escore over-mountain! With that in mind Tirtha glanced quickly about their camp. It was as well protected by its situation as any place she might have picked, she thought. As soon as the mounts had had some grazing, before the dark closed in, they could bring them up here and tether them, satisfy them with handsful of the grain together with a strewing of salt across the gritty stuff. To reach here any attacker would have to approach along a very narrow way that either one of them could defend alone. It was not the stoutest fortress in the world, but it would have to serve tonight.

They ate sparingly, then brought in the ponies and the Torgian. It was Tirtha's turn for the first rest period of the night, but she was not ready yet to try for sleep. Instead she found herself casting out thought loops, as a cattle herder of the plains might spin his catch rope, striving to pick up any trace of a Dark mind which might be lurking even now to spy upon them.

Dead by tooth and claw—that was what he had said of the stranger. Perhaps that unfortunate invader of these haunted hills had been trailed, preyed upon, by just such a night-running creature as they had faced with greater fortune. Tirtha searched in her pouch for the small packet of herb dust that had served so well during the attack, bringing it out to hand. Twilight was already gray within their refuge. The ponies stamped and whickered, straining a little at their halters, so now she went to share out the handsful of grain with the trace of salt to keep them quiet.

She realized that to sit staring into the growing dark would avail her nothing. The Falconer was on watch and upon his skill she depended with unbroken trust. These were his homelands after all, and he knew best what need be feared.

Tirtha sought to empty her mind and sleep. For a space the dreamless rest that had recently been hers settled down upon her.

When she awoke it was to the summons to take her place on watch. He answered her question before she asked it.

"Nothing."

Nothing but the night, and the memory that picked at her, of what had crept upon them in the dark before, and of that other night when she had been caught by the cry from the dead, shown something which she thought was hers alone. She sat cross-legged, moving now and then to the animals to smooth her hands across their rough-coated hides, sending soothing thoughts into their minds. For she did not believe that it was hunger alone that kept them restless.

Far keener than the senses of her own kind were those of the beasts. They could measure danger at a greater distance than even her thought-sweep might reach. She no longer wished to try that—knowing that any creature of the Dark could seize upon it as a guide and so be drawn to them.

Yes, out there somewhere, things moved that were not of the world she had known. Legend and the chronicles of Lormt—neither had made such real. One had to confront them for one's self, sniff the foul stench of evil, see it—then one accepted and understood.

The falcon—what had it seen prowling about these ruined heights? It must be a descendant of those that had once been the pride of the Eyrie. Perhaps such birds, too, had their own legends of another time—one in which they had been companions to men and ridden out to war on a saddle perch. A legend that today had drawn the winged scout to give its warning.

Tirtha wondered if the Falconer had longed for that free flyer to join with him. Or was it only once in the lifetime of each that bird and man united into a fighting, living whole, and when one died there was no second such coupling? There was so much Tirtha did not know and could not ask. For she was certain her companion would count it an intrusion such as might even be strong enough to break his sword oath. His secrets were his, just as hers were hers.

6

IF evil did run that night, it did not seek their camp. Nor did the mounts show any increasing uneasiness. However, Tirtha was not in any way lulled into believing that her fellow traveler's warning had been exaggerated or false. With the morning light she roused from an uneasy sleep to see him carefully checking his dart gun, slipping his small supply of its loadings in and out of their loops on his shoulder belt, as if he would make certain they were ready to hand at a moment's demand. There were only a limited number of them, and Tirtha realized very well that they would be used, if it were necessary, most sparingly and with all the skill he could summon.

She sat up, shrugged aside the folds of her cloak, to thought-listen. There was the essence of life forces which marked man, ponies, Torgian. Nothing else abode here. Caution limited her to a very narrow sweep, but even so fleeting a touch had alerted the Falconer, for his yellow-fired eyes were sharply on her as he turned helmed head in her direction.

"That is folly." He spoke with cold precision. If they had fallen into slightly easier ways with one another during the days past—very slightly easier—that had changed. Perhaps sight of the ruins of his people's hold had fastened on him the bonds of their long training. She was not of the kin, and she was that distrusted, even hated thing—a woman.

Tirtha refused to be irritated by such change in attitude. All knew the Falconers and their ways—what else could she expect?

"There was nothing during your second watch?" She made only a half-question of that, knowing well that, had there been invasion of the camp territory during her rest, he would have aroused her, even as he had on that other night.

He finished with his examination of his ammunition. Now he drew sword to inspect its edge, his attention seeming more for the steel than for her.

"It is out there, perhaps watching, spying."

"You know because your falcon would have it so?"

Again he swung a cold and quelling gaze at her. "I have no falcon." The words were like icy pellets hurled across the small space between them. "The free one and his brood have scouted afar. There are movements through these heights. One needs not touch to know."

She must not provoke him. Instead Tirtha nodded. "Yes," she agreed and went to wash her face in the chill water gathered in the basin. The sting of it, like a swift slap, awaked her fully.

They allowed the mounts another short period of graze while they broke their own fast, eating most frugally. Having filled the water bottles, watered their horses, and saddled up, they moved on, the Falconer riding ahead, Tirtha bringing up the rear.

It did not take them long to get beyond the stream and the ragged growth about it, picking a careful way around rock falls. As far as Tirtha could determine they now headed southward. She had no way by which she could calculate how much longer this mountain travel would take. All roads and known trails had been destroyed with the army that had marched along them, on the day the mountains had been moved.

They had been on their twisting trail, having to backtrack sometimes to seek another route (for hereabouts the ravages of the overthrow were far worse and more apparent to the eye), for a period of time well into the morning when they came across the first signs of that drastic wiping out of the invaders a generation ago.

Their discovery was signaled by one of those harsh cries that Tirtha associated with the Falconer, though the sound had not issued from the lips of her companion—rather it echoed from some point ahead. There was a division of possible ways here, and at that sound, the Falconer turned unhesitatingly into the one from which that cry had come.

Ahead, after they had wound their way around another slide of jagged and cruelly broken rock, was a space nearly choked with a fall, even as had been the site of the Eyrie. On a boulder that overtopped Tirtha's head as she rode, perched a bird—like the one that had answered her companion's call the night before.

The sun struck gleams from metal caught in and among that tumble of cracked and broken stone. There were red stains of rust streaming down from some of these twisted and crushed weapons. Other scraps had remained oddly untouched by the years and the weather, as if they had lain ensorceled during the time since the disaster. A roundish yellowed stone, when touched glancingly by the mare's hoof, rolled over to show that it was a skull.

The falcon screamed again, and the man he appeared to summon slid from his mount, leaving reins dangling. He went to climb that crumbling hill toward the waiting bird. Tirtha watched them narrowly. There was certainly no open path across this battlefield between men and the unleashed Power—why then had they come here?

She saw him reach a rock that brought his head on a level with the waiting predator. Then his hand shot forward as he jerked at one of those bright bits of metal, its surface showing no rust. There was resistance, which his strength bested. What he drew into the open was a hilted blade—not the length of a full sword—nor yet that of a long dagger, but somewhere between the two.

The bird was watching him intently, its head forward as it looked down. Now, as the man pulled forth that weapon, it again uttered a cry— a scream that might be one of fierce triumph—and rose into the air a fraction with a beat of wings. The Falconer held out his arm straight and still, still, and the feathered hunter came to perch on his wrist. It settled there as if it had chosen a resting place it liked well. So it remained for a long moment while the eyes behind the mask-helm and those within the feathered skull met and held a gaze Tirtha knew was silent communication of a kind unknown to her race.

Once more the bird took to the air, this time descending to the pony which the Falconer had ridden. The mount jerked up its head sharply, but the bird came to rest on the empty saddle perch. It folded its wings, and the sound it now made was soft, such as Tirtha thought could never have come from the throat of such a fierce hunter and fighter of the skies.

The Falconer climbed down the rocks, taking the last step as a single leap, for stones began to shift, the knife-sword swinging in his hand, his claw out for balance. Then he looked, not to the waiting bird, but at her.

Something momentous had happened. Tirtha believed that as if it were part of the life-sensing that could reach her at times. There was a change in the man that was not physical, but lay within. Now for a moment he gazed down along the blade he held and then again to her, holding out the find to which the falcon had drawn him.

"A thing of Power . . ." he said slowly.

Tirtha did not attempt to touch it, but she leaned well forward to study it as well as she might. The blade was not smooth, as it had seemed from a distance. Rather it was deeply engraved with a pattern. She saw thereon such symbols as she knew were of the long forgotten elder knowledge, and where the blade widened near the hilt there was also the image of a beast inserted in another metal—blue like the symbol on the valley wall. This was a creature such as she had never seen, though it might not be even a living entity, but rather a dream vision of some adept, used as a chosen mark for his blood and house.

The hilt, which was revealed through the loose clasp of her companion's fingers, was of the same blue metal as that inlay, ending in a bulbous globe of murky substance like a huge dull gem, smoothed but unfaceted. Tirtha put out her hand slowly, not to touch it, no. The tingling in her fingers was enough. This was indeed a thing of Power, perhaps never meant to be a slaying weapon at all, rather a focus used by someone who would command forces. Yet who in Karsten would have dabbled, or dared, to meddle with *the* Power?

Those who had hated and hunted her people professed to believe that any such contact was evil, that they might be blasted out of life by it. They had done all they could to stamp out any contact with it. All with talent had been slain—or else, as in the case of witches, rendered helpless. Witches did not lie with men, but if a man took one by force, then her talent was drained and lost.

Tirtha drew back her fingers. "It is alive—there is Power," she agreed. "But from *Karsten*?" There was no denying that what they had come on must have aided the destruction of the invading force. Who among *them* would have dared carry a weapon charged with Power into a country where that force ruled?

"From Karsten . . ." He spoke musingly, glancing around at the tumble of stones that must hide many dead. "Yes—who and why?"

"And how did the falcon know?" Tirtha dared then to ask.

"The feathered brothers have their own ways," he answered almost absently. "This would attract such a one."

He drew the long hunting knife out of his belt sheath, leaned over to slip it into the top of his riding boot. Then he slid his find into its place. It seemed to go easily, though a part of it projected above the edge of the sheath.

"A thing of Power . . ." Tirtha repeated his words. She had no desire to handle it. The energy that had reached her even though her flesh had not touched it was enough to warn her off. Yet if the Falconer had felt that same surge, it did not appear to turn him against a thing that his own people had feared as much as those newcomers in Karsten who were not to the Elder Race.

"It came to me." He said that evenly, and Tirtha remembered another tale—that story of the Axe of Volt and how it had come into the hands of Koris of Gorm, from the hold of Volt himself, long dead and entombed.

Volt's Axe had chosen. Was this once more a case whereby a weapon charged with unknown life had chosen to fit into the hand of a new owner?

"Volt's Axe," she blurted out, caught in amazement that such a thing might happen a second time. Yet this blade had no such history, no name, and he who had taken it was of a race without the talent.

His head in the bird helm moved as if he had taken a blow.

"It came to me," he said slowly again. "There will be a cause and that shall also be revealed in time."

Then he swung upon the pony and pulled at the reins, bringing the mount around so that once again they retraced a way, out of that rubble- and death-choked valley into the second passage. Tirtha found her atten- tion turning often to the blue knob of gemstone where it rode at his belt, shifting a fraction now and then, since it did not fit the sheath. She could not believe that chance had led him to it. Now she, too, moved uneasily on her riding pad from time to time, discovering a desire to watch their back trail or the walls of the mountains about them. Still her companion displayed no uneasiness, nor had he appeared to question the fact that the falcon now occupied what had been the empty perch on his saddle. It was as if he accepted all that had happened as a necessary part of what was meant to be.

That night they advanced into a more open section of a valley that sloped upwards at the far end in the direction of what Tirtha believed must be a pass. The jagged peaks guarding either side looked as if sec- tions of the earth had been slashed out by sword strokes, turned edge upward against the sky. There was a brutal savagery about this entrance to the land ahead that posted a warning against further advance. She fought down such thoughts with a firm hand. Perhaps it was the ravaged look of this country that added strength to her feeling that they were always under observation.

Twice more during that day they passed evidences of the slaughter that had ended the army of Pagar and pushed the southern land back into barbarism. There was rusted metal, once the pole of a standard, planted upright among stones, the width of its banner now only a few threads windwhipped and knotted about the pole. There were bleached bones. They were well content to skirt such traces of the carnage that must have filled these ways.

However, they could not attempt the pass until morning, so they made a dry camp beneath heights where the wind howled and whistled until one could almost believe that it echoed cries of the dead. Their supply of water was so limited that they wiped out the mouths of their mounts with wet cloths and allowed each only a small cupping of water in one of the eating bowls from Tirtha's saddlebags. They scanted themselves even more, and it was very hard to choke down the now crumbling journey cakes which stuck in the throat.

The falcon had taken to the air as they had come to camp and perhaps found some forage in the heights above. It did not return until the dusk neared night, and then it communicated again with the man it had chosen to accompany in the same series of notes they had used at their first meeting.

As the bird settled down on its saddle perch the Falconer spoke. "We are within perhaps a day's journey of the foothills. I have served more than a quarter of my oathed time. What would you have of me when we are down from the heights?"

It was a fair question. She had set his service as twenty days simply because she had wanted to make sure of his guidance and company through the mountains. Did she now want him to accompany her further? Tirtha was faced at last with a decision that she must make, and then abide by the results of the making.

Hawkholme lay to the east. She had—her hand went into the front of her jerkin seeking to finger the money belt. In one compartment of it she had a map, the only one she had kept, though it could hardly be an accurate one, drawn as it was from bits and pieces of information she had managed to assemble.

Her simple plan as far as she had made it, not knowing the country except by repute, had been to angle along the foothills themselves, not venturing far down into the open country, until she believed she could strike fairly straight across to the hold, or what remained of it. It was certainly not a plan that carried any certainty. Now she was silent a long moment.

Well, she had very little to lose, she decided. Perhaps she had answered the question without being conscious of having done so during these days of journeying. The Falconer would be no more welcome in Karsten than she herself, having harried the borders with his own kind.

To whom could he betray her? And what did he have to betray, save that one of the Old Race sought to return to the land that had once been held by those of her blood? She herself could not tell him exactly what she sought there, or why she was driven into that seeking. Let her tell him what was most of the truth, then let the decision be his whether he asked oath release or not.

It was dark in the valley, and they had lit no fire. He was only a blacker dot of shadow against the wall of rock behind him. It made little difference as even in the light of day she was not able to read anything from his expression. Let him use his voice to answer her aye or nay.

"I seek Hawkholme," she began. "It is the land anciently bound to my blood, and I have waited for long to go there. I have thought to travel east through the foothills and then strike over land."

"You know the road you must go?" he asked, as she paused.

Tirtha closed her eyes. In a way, yes, she knew—or felt within her that she would know when the time came. The dream—whatever had sent that—it would guide her. How could she speak of dreams to this one? Or—she considered that point. Since his finding and taking of the odd sword-knife, she had somewhat revised her first opinion of the Falconer. Reputed as he and his kind were to be bitter enemies of all her own people prized and revered, why then had he put that weapon in his belt? He should by rights have hurled it from him, if he set hand to it at all!

"I know it," she returned now firmly. There was, she decided, no reason for her to explain how tenuous was her foundation for that assertion. "But I do not know the length of such a journey. It may run far longer than your bind-oath. I asked for guidance through the mountains. When we reach the foothills, you will have fulfilled your part of that bargain. If the days are not accomplished, the purpose is."

When he made no answer through the dark, she licked her lips. Why was she disturbed? She had never intended, had she, that he should accompany her on the whole of her mission. Why was she waiting now, with an eagerness she did not understand, for his reply?

"I am oath-bound for twenty days." His voice held its usual cool and steady note. "For twenty days I ride, whether it be through mountains, foothills, or Karsten."

Tirtha could not understand her feeling of relief. What had she to do with this man? Their own lives were alien to one another. Yet had he chosen otherwise, she knew, it would have been a disappointment. This was so new and strange a thing for her who had built her life upon her own silence and aloneness that she pushed it from her foremind, telling herself that there might well be trouble in the foothills, and two fighters were better than one if that came. Also the falcon seemed to have taken up service with her companion, and the scouting ability of those birds was legendary.

"So be it," she returned, and thought that her voice sounded overly sharp. Still, she had no intention of allowing him to believe that she had nursed a strange hope he would answer exactly as he had.

In the morning they climbed to the pass. The way upward was longer than it had looked from below, for the footing was rough, and they dismounted several times to lead their beasts. The falcon took to the sky early, returning periodically to perch on some higher portion of the trail and await them, always then exchanging sounds with the man.

It was past midday when they stood in the notch of the pass itself to look down upon the outward sweep of the over-mountain country, which was no longer one land but a number of quarreling fiefs in which war and pillage had ruled for years.

The foothills were tree-crowned—it would seem that the fury of the Power had not reached here to uproot and crush. Tirtha, looking upon them, was pleased, for it seemed to her that this was the type of country that would best serve those who needed cover. She turned a little to gaze eastward and saw that there were the dark lines of what could only be woodland in that direction.

In the old days, the plains of Karsten had been most fertile and open to the west. There had been the garths of the farmers and the landowners among those younger, newer people who had spread inward from the sea. The cities and the holds of some pretense of importance had all lain there.

The Old Race, her own people, had withdrawn gradually from those settlers who had come overseas in days now shadowed into legend. They had established their own holdings to the eastward. In some places the advancing newcomers had proved hostile, and there had been no inter-course at all between the old blood and the settlers. In other sections there was friendliness and sometimes a trading of skills, neighbor aiding neighbor. So it had come about that some of those neighbors had suffered death and worse in the day of Yvian's Horning because of aiding the escape of her own kind.

It would be mainly in the plains, where the land was rich and there were cities, that any struggle centered now. Farther south lay other provinces (from one of which Pagar himself had come) where the new people were even more firmly established and occupied the whole of the area.

However, these foothills, just like those on the other side of the border, might give refuge to outlaws and masterless men who had become pillagers and raiders. It was the kind of country to attract such.

Tirtha mentioned this, and the Falconer nodded. He swung out with his claw. The sun glinted on metal as he pointed.

"It is true there are others here."

She saw it now—a column of smoke rising from between two of those hills. It was far too thick a pillar to be born from a campfire. Something of greater consequence, perhaps even the buildings of a farm, burned there. Though what farmer would choose such a setting for his holding? Or did that mark an outlaw post raided by whoever stood for law and order here—even as the Marshal's men strove to clean out such vultures' nests to the north?

In any case that billowing smoke was warning enough that they must travel as secretly as they could. There was no reason to throw away all she had struggled for these past years by being too bold now.

An afternoon of descent brought them into wooded land. Then the lead pony snorted and quickened pace, the Torgian pushing up beside, the mare quick to follow. It was plain that the animals scented water. They found it in a stream that ran fast and clear at an angling path from the north, where it must have been born among the mountains, toward the west and south, perhaps to join the river on which Kars stood.

There was cover in plenty—a copse of trees growing closely—composed of that mountain pine which flourished in these upward lands. The falcon returned twice, each time with a young hare in its talons. Tirtha set about a craft she had learned on the trail long since, rolling up stones under one of the trees to form a wall about a fire pit, the branches of the tree to break up any trail of smoke that might arise. She grubbed under the trees while the Falconer hunted the stream side, each bringing the driest sticks they could find for a fire large enough to broil the meat, which they ate eagerly. Then they allowed the flames to die down.

Tirtha went to the stream and along to a thicket. It was still light enough to see as she stripped off her trail-worn clothing, waded resolutely into cold water, which brought a gasp from her, and bathed, putting on fresh shirt and under-pants from her small supply, washing out those she had taken off, wringing them as dry as she could and returning to hang them not far from the warm stones of the fire's back wall. The Falconer watched her, then took up his own saddle bags, disappearing in turn to do likewise, she guessed.

It was good to feel clean of trail sweat and dust, and she had rubbed her body with the dried leaves of a scent herb—an affectation she seldom allowed herself, but which she had done now as a small celebration of triumph that they had actually done what she had been told so often could never be accomplished—come safely across the accursed mountains.

Wrapped in her cloak, she found herself once more listening. There were sounds here as there had not been in the twisted lands through which they had just passed. She could pick up life sparks of woods creatures about their night business. The falcon stirred on its perch, eyeing her with the same feral fires as appeared in the man's eyes upon occasion. She made no effort to touch its mind in her own imperfect fashion.

The bird was surely wholly his, one of the things which Tirtha and he could never share. Eat the same food they could, feel discomfort (though they did not reveal that to each other), perhaps share some of the same fears and dislikes, if not for the same reasons. But a barrier existed and always would.

Tirtha leaned forward and on impulse dropped into the very small flame before her a pinch of one of her herb packets. There was a puff of whitish smoke and then scent. She inhaled as deeply as she could, striving to draw it into the full expansion of her lungs. Tonight she must dream!

But she must not allow herself to be pulled into the same old vision. Rather now, while she was still desired and needed—a guide to the road ahead.

This lore she had had as a child from a Wise Woman, though she had never dared to use it before, in spite of the promises she had been given concerning its effectiveness. Because she must remain always in command of herself, she feared such aids to farseeing, if farseeing could be so summoned. Then, too, she had been alone and she had not known how long the visionary state would last or whether it would affect her in some other way. Tonight she had to discover what she could while she was not solitary. She inhaled a second time, feeling an odd lightness rising within her. This was not power—no, she could only hope that what summoned the vision could be induced to work in another way.

Tirtha enfolded herself in her cloak, having refused any more food, since what she desired was better accomplished fasting. Had she followed the proper ritual, she would have fasted for a full day while clearing her surface mind of all thought. Now she must take the Falconer into her confidence—what she practiced was the "witchery" he distrusted, but there was a need for it. Tirtha used flat and decisive words to settle the matter. After all he was an oathed shield man; thus what she did, unless it threatened them both, was beyond his questioning.

Already Tirtha floated in and out, half aware of their bare camp, half into gray nothingness. Then she slid entirely into the gray, like a feather or leaf tossed by air, without substance and with no control, though she tried firmly to keep her purpose to the fore of her mind.

No Hawkholme lay before her this time, though she emerged from nothingness into sharpening clarity. Before her, smoke trailed upward in rank, standing amid trampled earth beds of heat-withered or broken plants. She recognized some of those as sources of balms she well knew. Whoever had dwelt here had cultivated the gifts of earth.

The rankness of spilled blood was foul through the acrid stench of fire. There was another odor also—a sickening one. For a moment or two she thought perhaps this was Hawkholme after all, that she viewed it after the vengeance of Yvian's attack.

Only this was surely much smaller, even though she had never been granted a complete vision of Hawkholme in its full pride. No, this was not the remains of any great hall or lord's hold, rather more the garth of a small landholder.

A hound sprawled on the crushed herbs. A ragged wound had ripped its side to bare the white arch of its rib cage. Beyond the dead beast lay another body, small, crumpled together, as if flung contemptuously aside. Because Tirtha knew that she was being shown all this for a reason of importance, she willed herself to approach the dead.

A child lay face down, her unbound dark hair swirled, mercifully hiding her features, but there was no mistaking the brutal usage which had been given that fragile broken body—discarded in death as a worthless bit of refuse. In Tirtha awoke a flame of deadly anger. She had seen much in past years of pain, death, and hardship; she had believed herself immune to easily-aroused feeling. Now some part of her, long hidden and buried, was aroused to life.

This dead child, she knew—perhaps by virtue of the drug that had awakened her talent to its utmost—had not been the only one slain. Within the fired building lay others, as hardly treated, as ruthlessly used and slain. There had been those here who had played with their victims, relishing the cruelty they employed—who might call themselves men but were no different within (save perhaps less strong and powerful) than the beast thing she and the Falconer had killed in the mountains.

Why vision had summoned her here, Tirtha could not tell. She strove to master her anger, to loose herself, that she might be guided into learning what meaning this held for her. For she did not believe that the single purpose was to warn her. There was another and far more powerful reason to summon her for a viewing of murder and ravishment.

She moved, not by her own volition, but as if she rode a mount she could not control. Past the burned-out house that compulsion carried her, on into a stone-walled field where a stand of young grain lay beaten into pulp in ragged paths as if riders had crossed and recrossed it. Riders—*hunters*!

That impression of a deadly hunt struck her full on. She could view those tracks and visualize the action that had taken place here. What prey had they ridden down?

The need that drew her, now drove her toward a pile of stones at one corner. A break in the wall about to be mended—those stones were piled ready to hand. Behind them, crouched in so narrow a space that Tirtha would not believe any body could exist there, was another child. Dead?

No! This one lived—with a mind filled by overwhelming horror and terror. The one in hiding had been driven near to the point of complete withdrawal and denial of life by what had happened, but there was still a faint spark of identity remaining.

Tirtha had asked guidance for her own purposes. It would seem that the knowledge she had sought was not of importance to whatever force she had so hazily called upon—but this was. She had been summoned, she was being used, and to the demand there could be no denial.

She opened her eyes upon the night, their handcup of fire, the Falconer seated cross-legged beside it. In his hands was the dagger-sword, its pommel beaming with a fierce, demanding light, his head downbent as he stared at the now living gem, bemused.

Out of her vision, she had brought urgency.

"We must go!"

His head jerked as if she had startled him out of a vision of his own. Tirtha was already on her feet, hurrying toward the picketed ponies. A full moon above provided brilliance stronger than she had ever seen, the better for the task that must be done.

"What is it?" Her companion was at her heels, his weapon in sheath.

Tirtha pivoted slowly, struggling to pick up the trace which must exist. Time might be against her. No! This duty was a part of her, as compelling as that other search had been through all the years, only much more immediate.

Fire! That smoke they had witnessed from the pass! That must be the place! She was suddenly certain.

"A garth they burned." She spoke out of her vision, not caring if he could not follow her thoughts. "It is there!"

Swiftly she loosed the mare, girthed on saddle pad. He did not question her, only followed her example, and the falcon on the saddle perch, mantled, raising wings, then took to the air, up and out into the dark. Perhaps the man had dispatched it without audible command.

They angled toward the west, yet farther south. Where the land opened, they went to a fast trot. As they rode, Tirtha gave a terse account of what she had envisioned. The Falconer listened without question; when she had done he made comment. "Raiders or some lordling's men who had reason to loot. This is a riven land." There was harsh distaste in his voice. For all their somber reclusiveness and their well-tested fighting ability, those of his race did not kill wantonly, nor ever amuse themselves with such nastiness as she knew had blasted the garth. Falconers dealt clean death when and if that were necessary, risking always their own lives in the doing. But for the rest, no man could ever declare that they were merciless barbarians, no matter how much the Witches of Estcarp disliked their private customs.

Down from the night sky spiraled the falcon, alighting on the saddle perch to face the man. Tirtha heard what sounded like sharp clicks of its beak. The Falconer turned his head.

"It is as you saw—the burning, the dead. There is no one there."

She shook her head determinedly. "Not at the house, in the field. They hunted but they did not find. There is still life. If there is not"—she hesitated—"then I think it would be given me to know that there was no reason for us to go on."

He said nothing. Perhaps he thought that as a shield man there was no reason for him to contradict her. Still she believed that he thought her wrong—that only the dead awaited them.

It was graying for dawn when they picked up the odor of the burning and that sweet stench of death which was a part of it. Then they came to the edge of open land, and she saw before her a wall of logs deep set to make a barrier. This had not been a part of her vision; but just ahead of them a gate swung loose as if, for all their guard, those who dwelt here had relaxed vigilance for some reason, allowing entrance to the very wolves they prepared to defy.

Tirtha's mare snorted and shook her head vigorously, not liking the smell. But she did not resist when Tirtha urged her on, and with the Torgian trailing behind them on a lead rope, the two rode into this once guarded place.

Facing her stood the smoke-blackened ruins she had seen, the trampled garden. The fire had burned itself out. She could sight the dead hound, the other pitiful body beyond. The dead did not need them now; the living did.

Tirtha pulled rein, sending the mare circling to the left, away from the destroyed house. Yes, there was the stone wall—high here, built as part of that protection which had proved so futile. Another gate stood open as she pressed on into the field where signs of the chase were so deep printed.

Straight across pounded the mare at a harder pace than Tirtha had pushed her before. While they were still some distance from that neat pile of rocks, Tirtha pulled up, slid from her riding pad, and ran, throwing her cloak back across her shoulders lest it impede her speed.

As she went she mind-sought. Life essence—yes! They were still in time! She reached the neat pile of stones, looked around it. There was nothing wedged there! Tirtha swayed, so dismayed by the evidence of her eyes that she could almost believe she was again not here in body, but rather caught up still in sleep-vision.

Once more she sought mind touch. There *was* life essence, faint, wavering as if almost drained away—yet still here! Only she *saw* emptiness. Tirtha pulled away some of the stones—letting them thud outward into the field. Then she knelt to stretch forth both hands. Where her eyes could see nothing her hands felt what her vision had told her was there— a small body huddled into such confined space it would seem that there was no room for breath to enter the lungs of the compressed form she could feel.

She spoke over her shoulder to the Falconer as he joined her.

"Can you see . . . ?" she began.

His bird helm, easy to mark in this growing half-light, turned from side to side in denial.

"Then come here." She reached out, caught his hand, pulled it and him closer, dragging him down so that his fingers might tell him the truth. He jerked back, freeing himself from her grasp, and she could tell that he was aware of the same mystery.

"There—it is there, though we cannot see it!" She was triumphant.

"Witchery!" She heard the word as a half-whisper. Still he loosened stones with his claw, hurling them afar with his hand. Now the falcon perched on the wall to watch them, leaning forward to peer into the small space they uncovered, much as it had looked upon the knife-sword it had led her companion to find.

Slowly, carefully, Tirtha ran her hands along that body they were freeing though they could not see it. This was another thing she had read of in Lormt—the strength of a hallucination whereby one could hide safe from danger, though in the accounts she knew, such had consisted mainly of form-changing. To achieve complete invisibility was another matter of which she had not heard. Still, anything was possible with the Power. Who had hidden the child here so successfully?

By those marks in the field the hunters had pursued prey back and forth, played with a victim after a brutal and beastly fashion, prolonging the terrible fear of the one who had fled. A woman carrying a child—who had had something of the Talent brought perhaps to the highest level because of her fear for her own blood, who had managed to so conceal son or daughter and then had herself fallen prey to ravishers and murderers?

All Tirtha knew of such matters had firmly stated that any building of illusion was a weighty exercise, for which one needed time and knowledge of complicated ritual. Certainly there had been no such time granted the hunted here.

Cautiously, with the utmost care, because she could only use her hands to aid, Tirtha drew out the small body, held it against her so she felt the weight of an invisible head against her shoulder. The flesh she touched was very cold, and she quickly drew the edge of her cloak around it, the bulging of the material proving that indeed she held substance, not shadow. With fingertips she sought to examine the face, feeling against her own flesh a faint surge of breath, just as a faltering rhythm of heartbeat could be distinguished. How they might aid a child who remained invisible, she had no idea.

There was a sound from the falcon. The man's head whipped around, his helm tilted as he looked up at the bird and listened to the sounds uttered by the feathered scout. Then he turned to Tirtha, where she still knelt, cradling the child.

"The Brother can see it," he said quietly. "What witchery holds for us does not curtain his eyes. He says that it is not wounded, but in deep hiding within itself, that there is great fear in it."

Tirtha remembered other lore. Deep fear, terror could strike so into a mind that there would come afterwards no reawakening of intelligence. Had this small one retreated so far that they could not draw it back? She had some healing knowledge, that was so, but nothing to handle such a problem. In Estcarp this victim could be taken to one of the hospices set up by the Wise Women to be treated by those specially trained to seek out the inner essence of the mind, draw it carefully back once more. Even those trained to do so had failures when a case was too severe. She had nothing save the belief that she would not have envisioned the plight of the one she held unless that vision meant she could aid.

They could not remain here. The raiders had gone, yes, but that did not mean that their own small party might not be sighted. There was nowhere she might deliver what she held into safety; she must take the fear-bound child with her. For all her cultivated hardness, Tirtha recognized that truth.

The Falconer dropped his hand to the butt of his dart gun. Now the bird took off in the sky. Tirtha's uneasiness at remaining was obviously shared.

"There is no place for . . ." She indicated what she held. "We must take it with us."

She half expected a protest. Falconers knew nothing of children. They did not even own those they fathered. In their villages of women, men impregnated selected females, perhaps several of them, within a stated time, but they were never true fathers. When they were six, the male children went into the Eyrie, or they had in the old days—to be housed apart, trained by selected fighters who were old or maimed and unable to serve in the field. They had no true childhood, and it would seem that the custom served their way of life adequately. To be saddled not only with a child, but one invisible and perhaps catatonic, would be an experience none of his kind had faced before.

Yet he made no comment, only went for Tirtha's mare, bringing the pony to her. She loosed the throat latch of her cloak, wrapped its folds about the limp body of the child. She passed the bundle to the Falconer, mounted to accept it back. Then, with nearly the same speed with which they had come, they recrossed the field to pass by the ruins. To bury the dead—she nearly checked her horse by that other small body, then realized that her first charge was the child she carried and that their own safety might depend upon a swift withdrawal.

Back they rode into the forested hills; again the Falconer led. They went more slowly, while he took the precautions of the hunted, dismounting at times to draw a leafed branch over ground where they had left too plainly marked a trail, winding a way that took every advantage of the nature of the country and any cover offered.

The falcon made periodic flights, reporting back at intervals. Though the man did not translate for her any messages it brought, Tirtha guessed that they were in no immediate danger from any other travelers in this land.

In her hold the child lay unmoving, inert. She tried at intervals to break through the mind barrier terror had set, longing fiercely to know more, have the ability to help. There was, she feared, a very good chance that if the conscious mind was lost forever, the will to live might follow. Death would then ensue. Such an end might be merciful, but she knew she would fight for this life with all her strength.

They reached a place before noon that the Falconer appeared to believe spelled safety for a while, and there they halted. There was no water, but a tough growth of grass satisfied the ponies and the Torgian. There was a half-shelter formed by some rocks to conceal them from any but the most intent search.

Tirtha sat, holding the child across her knees. The small body, still invisible, which had felt so cold when she had first taken it up, was now warm—too warm. Her cautious hand brushed aside fine, sweat-dampened hair to rest on a forehead where fever heat burned. She located a small mouth, which hung a little open, was able to dribble into it some water from her saddle bottle. There came a faint gulping noise, the first hopeful sign she had received, and she eagerly gave her charge another drink.

At the same time her mind was busy. To break an ensorcelment as strong as this—no, she had not the power. On the other hand there were spells of the shape-changing kind that possessed their own time limit. She gritted her teeth against hot, hard words she had learned in her tramping, which could be a release for her frustration and anger.

Having done what he could to establish their camp, the Falconer returned to squat on his heels beside her, pulling off his helm as if he felt his sight too limited by its half-mask.

"What holds it so?" he asked.

"Illusion, I think." She could be sure of nothing. "It could have been carried there for hiding—you saw the tracks in the field—they were hunting someone. A mother might have possessed some talent. If she feared enough, she could have cast a spell to cover a child, hidden it away, even allowed herself to be taken. . . ."

"Those now of Karsten have no witchery," he pointed out. "And the Old Race . . ."

". . . were long since damned and doomed here, yes. But that is not to say that some of the old stock could not have remained in hiding. Also, we can wed with others and prove fruitful. Some of us have mated with the Sulcars who have no witchery in them, their power lying in their sea knowledge only. There is also Simon Tregarth, the outlander. He bedded with one of the Wise Council. They outlawed her for it, saying she was none of them but a traitor to their beliefs. Yet it is true that he had something of the talent, and neither did she lose hers for being wedded as they had sworn she would.

"Three children she had at one birthing, which was never known before. And all three have the Power—still have—for it is they who, they say, now lead the war in Escore and have opened that land again to the Old Race.

"Thus it could be that one of my blood bred half kin here, who had talent. If that lies within one, then it can be summoned when the need is great. Still . . ." She paused.

"Still—?" he persisted.

"Even Lormt held no such secret as this. No"—she shook her head vigorously—"I am of the Old Race, but I have very little talent. I am a healer of sorts, and I can use the vision-seeing. That is the best of my learning. As you know, I can sense life essence and communicate with animals after a limited fashion. But all that I know or have heard of illusion is that it must be summoned by ritual, and that is not done swiftly or with ease. I do not see how one pursued, as those tracks showed, could have so wrought to hide this child in that way."

"Then how else—?"

She had considered that all morning, striving to fit this and that answer to the same question. What was left was only a suspicion and one that seemed near impossible to believe, though she had long ago learned that the world was full of strange and awe-filling things.

"The child itself," Tirtha replied slowly. "In Estcarp, girl children were tested early—sometimes when they were no more than five or six. The power can be recognized even at so small a score of years. Here in Karsten there would be no such recognition. Suppose a child of the full old blood—even of mixed blood—was born with full power. Such a one might see the world differently from the way we view it, and that early enough so that it would learn to hide what it was and what power was in it or be taught to so hide it by one close to it. There would be no formal training, but if danger—fear—were great enough, that fear in itself might open a door to the full talent, such as comes usually only after a long training.

"Uncontrolled, frightened by great terror, then a child's instinct for survival might react as a protection, overriding the need for ritual that a trained Witch or Wise One would have as a barrier to betrayal through their own emotions."

He nodded. "What you have reasoned sounds sensible. I know little of witchery. But fear which is strong enough can give a man physical strength past his own potential; this I have seen. The will, which is the inner core of a man, if it is determined, can lead him to accomplish more than his fellows would believe possible. Given this talent you speak of and fear great enough—yes—it might be so. But if that is the truth, how can we then help? Is this one so lost within itself that it cannot be summoned forth again?"

"I do not know." Tirtha looked about her. If she were only sure they were safe here—perhaps the same drug that had sent her into the vision . . . But she could not herself seek within the child. That was an art far beyond her. "I know so little!" she burst out, her frustration banking down the anger that had been in her since she had gazed upon the work of those worse than brutes, making her voice rough and hard. "Mind healing or touching is a chancy thing."

"I wonder . . ." He rubbed one of the prongs of his claw along the side of his thin cheek as he might draw a finger. "The Brother in Feathers can see where we cannot; can he reach farther than we may hope to?"

"The falcon!" Tirtha stared at him in open amazement. "A bird . . ."

He frowned. "The Brothers in Feathers are more than birds. There is much they know that we do not. Some of their senses are far clearer and keener than ours. Remember, he saw the child, the illusion did not hold for him. Therefore, if the outward illusion does not blind him, perhaps the inner one might not either. Would it be harmful to try?"

Such a thought had not crossed her mind. However, with his intent stare on her now, she was forced to consider what he said. Such an attempt could cause no harm she could see. And perhaps—just perhaps—it might provide the key to unlock a stubborn door. Slowly she made answer, though her arms tightened involuntarily around the child as she did so. "I see no harm."

His lips twisted into a ghost of a smile. "But still little good? Well, let us see."

His claw flashed in the sun as he made a small gesture. The falcon took wing, flying from its perch to light on one of the rocks overshadowing Tirtha and her burden.

8

Tirtha sensed the flow of energy issuing from the bird. She would not have believed that from such a small body, and that of a species to which most of her kind assigned neither intelligence nor purpose, this summons—for summons it was—could come. Amazed, she stared at the falcon until she became aware of a second strain of energy joined with that which the black winged flyer controlled. Even as a man might draw upon one of his fellows for strength and aid, so now did the falcon draw upon the Falconer.

She felt movement before she saw what her companion did; he was bringing forth his weapon of power. Holding it by the blade, he stretched out his hand so that the pommel knob hung steady above the child she held cradled in her arms. The dull gem took on life, within its heart a spark of fire glowed and grew. This was even more impressive and awesome than the light awakened from the rock wall in the valley. She felt now not only a tingle within hand and arm, but through her whole body.

Deliberately Tirtha calmed her mind, set herself to furthering, strengthening, if she could, what the bird summoned. She sensed energy speeding like a dart into flesh, striving to reach to the heart. It sought the very essence of the unseen child whose head rested against her breast.

In and in! The body in her arms twisted in a quick convulsion, so she must tighten her hold to a near bruising grip in order to keep the entranced one steady. There came a thin cry! Of pain? Terror? Perhaps both.

Still the bird raised power, the Falconer fed, the gem blazed.

They sought—surely they could go no deeper lest they carry death with them, while the one who was so sealed away fled their seeking!

Again the small body arched in Tirtha's arms. An invisible fist thud-

ded against her breast, as the mewling cry grew stronger, so that she tried
to feel for the mouth in a head that turned back and forth on her arm, to
press her hand over it, to stifle any sound that might carry in these dangerous hills.

The gem pommel became so brilliant a ball that Tirtha dared not look
directly at it. To whom had that belonged and what sorcery had gone into
the forging of such a blade?

Then the falcon gave a croaking cry. Tirtha sensed that it was fast
nearing the end of its strength. The body she held continued to struggle.
She was able to sense now not just life, which had been near to the bor-
derline of extinction, but overwhelming and terrible fear like a black
cloud streaming upward about her to bemuse and stifle her own mind.

There was . . .

In her arms she held a child she could see. Its face was twisted,
wrought into an ugly mask of terror so intense that perhaps sanity was
lost. Tirtha drew on her healer's comfort, strove to pour down and in the
quiet confidence which was a large part of that talent. She made herself
picture a wide meadow, bright and open under the sun, a sky untroubled
by even the smallest cloud. And through that open land, where fear was
unknown, the child she held—yes, now that she could see it she could
mind-picture it—ran in happy delight.

Tirtha fought to hold, refine that vision, let it fill her mind and flow
outward.

"Nothing to fear." It was a growing rhythm, an unvoiced chant within
her. "Safe—safe—no fear—safe."

She was no longer aware of either bird or man, only of the pitiful
creature she so held and tried to comfort.

"Safe—no fear—safe."

The open meadow, the flowers she visioned growing to charm the eye
with their color, to catch and hold even a most fleeting attention, the
cloudless sky . . .

"Free—no fear."

The child's body, which had been stiff, taut, rigid in her hold, began
to relax. Was this the relaxation of an outer covering of flesh that had
been tried too far and too long—a withdrawal of life essence shocked out
of its chosen hiding place? She could not tell.

"Safe—safe . . ." Tirtha strove to increase her flow of assurance, even
as she would have with some injured animal, as she had times in the past
tried so to heal or comfort.

Those eyes, which had been screwed so tightly shut, slowly opened.
Dark gray they were, and with that in them which she recognized. This
was blood of her people—the child was one of the Old Race.

The mouth, which had so shortly before shaped those woeful cries, opened a little. There came from between bitten lips, where flecks of dried blood had gathered in the corners to mark the small chin with a dribbled stain, a sigh.

Tirtha dared now to try to reach the child's mind directly. It was free and it was still sane! She had hardly dared hope for that!

With a joyful cry of her own, she embraced her charge closely, crooning a wordless murmur of relief and thanksgiving. Then there shot into her own mind, so sharp and clear it might have been spoken aloud by the child, a touch her fumbling attempts could never have produced.

"Gerik!" Fear flamed with that name as a fire might rise when fresh wood is laid onto its blaze.

"There is no Gerik here." She summoned words. To answer mind to mind was no skill of hers. "I am Tirtha and this . . ." For the first time she looked to the Falconer a little at a loss. She had never asked his name, knowing well that they did not yield such to those outside their own kind.

"I am Nirel, little brother," he answered for himself, speaking to the child. There were runnels of sweat down his face, gathering in large drops to drip from his chin. He had sometime during that battle swept off his helm, so the child who turned his head could see him plainly.

Little brother? Yes, it was a boy she held, which surprised her. For so legendary was it that such power of illusion could only be summoned by a woman, Tirtha had been certain she had carried out of that carnage a small girl. He was young, but perhaps older than his size would suggest, and his body, hardly covered by a short, tattered shiftlike garment, was brown and wiry. The dark hair of the Old Race had a slight wave where one longer lock fell across his forehead, near touching his level brows. What looked out of his eyes, though, was nothing of a young child.

"I am Alon." He spoke clearly. "I . . ." The shadow was back on his face, and his hands reached for the front of Tirtha's jerkin, clasped it so tightly that his nails cut into the soft leather.

"Where—?" He had turned his head against her, hiding his face so that his words came muffled.

Tirtha chose to ignore what might be the true meaning of that question.

"We are in the hills," she replied calmly.

His shoulders hunched a little as he gave one convulsive sob. He held to her for a long moment and then turned to look at both of them once more.

"They are all dead." It was no question but a statement of fact, and Tirtha found that she could answer only with truth.

"We believe so."

"They said they came from Lord Honnor; they showed his seal rod to Lamer, and so the gate was opened. Then *he* laughed and . . ."

Again that body convulsed and Tirtha answered with a tighter grip. But it was the Falconer who leaned forward and spoke.

"Little Brother, there will come a time for blood payment. Until then, look to the days ahead, not the hours behind." Such words he might speak to one of his own kind and his own age. Tirtha felt a rising indignation. Did he believe that a small child could be so comforted, if comfort was what he intended by that somber advice.

Only it would appear that he was right, for Alon met him eye to eye. His small face wore an intent, serious look and there was almost the same communication between the two of them as existed between bird and man—one Tirtha could not even sense.

"You are a bird man," the boy said slowly. "And he—?"

He loosed his hold on Tirtha, raised a thin arm to point to the falcon who now looked as if it wished to sleep, its yellow eyes half closed, its wings tight held to its body.

"In his own tongue he is called Wind Warrior. He is a flock chief and . . ."

"One of the Learning," Alon said softly. He spoke directly to the bird. "Brother in Feathers, you are a great fighter."

The falcon unlidded its eyes, gazed down, uttered a single small and very soft sound deep in its throat.

Now Alon turned his head once more to look directly up into Tirtha's face.

"You are—are like Yachne, no?" Again a shadow frown crossed his small face. "She has the Calling in her; you—you are different. But you are of the Blood."

Tirtha nodded. "Of the Blood, but one born in another place, kin-brother. I am from overmountain."

He had moved, not to free himself entirely from her hold, but rather to sit higher in it. She helped him so he could be more comfortable.

"Overmountain," he repeated. "But there is evil . . ." He glanced up, then stared at her. "No—the Dark ones—one can *feel* those. You are not of the Dark, kin-sister. Are you from the east where there is the clouding? Yachne has tried to read the throwing stones many times, but always there is the Dark between. There are the prowlers who come down from the hills, but they are not like Gerik"—his lips met tightly together for an instant—"for Gerik is a man, and he has chosen to serve the Dark of his free will!"

"Overmountain from Estcarp. There is little evil there in the way you know, kin-brother," Tirtha answered as gravely and with the same tone the Falconer had used. "But my kin were once of this land, and now I return for a purpose."

He nodded. His growing composure was far from childlike. She wondered if this was natural to him, or whether it had been born of the release of power that had sent him into hiding and so changed his mind, perhaps enlarging a talent. He seemed twice as old as he looked.

"There are such as Gerik patroling." He hitched himself even higher in her hold. "They will be watching, and they hate all of the Old Blood. We kept mine secret, yet somehow they knew."

The Falconer resheathed his strange weapon and put on his helm.

"Then it would seem that we must find a shelter better than this." He got to his feet, held out the wrist of his claw, and the falcon moved onto it.

Alon pushed out of Tirtha's hold, though she kept one hand on his shoulder to steady him. It was difficult to believe that the child who had been so limp and helpless when she had borne him here could now show such vigor. He wavered for a moment, then stood as tall and straight as his small body would allow, though he did not shake off her hand as the Falconer went to bring up their mounts.

Alon looked at the Torgian round-eyed and hesitatingly lifted his right hand. The beast snorted, moved toward the boy one step at a time as if puzzled and wary, the man loosing the leading rein to let it go free. The shaggy head of the horse dipped, it sniffed at the boy's palm, pawed at the ground, and then blew.

"He—he is different." Alon's gaze swung from horse to ponies, then back again.

"Yes. In Estcarp," Tirtha answered, "his kind are horses of war, and they are highly prized."

"He is alone." It was almost as if Alon had either not heard her or else that what she said meant little to him. "The one whom he served is dead; since then his days have been empty. But he will take me!" There was a sharp change in the boy's face. A smile, as bright as the sun Tirtha had imagined when she was pulling him out of his inner darkness lighted it. There was an eagerness in his voice as both his hands tugged at the flowing forelock of the horse. "He accepts me!" It was as if something near too wondrous to believe had changed his world.

For the first time since she had traveled with him, Tirtha saw the Falconer smile and gained a dim idea of how different he might appear among his own kind. He caught Alon around the waist and swung the boy up to settle him in the empty saddle of the dead man's horse.

"Ride him well, little brother. As the Lady has said, his kind is not easily found."

Alon leaned forward to draw his hand down the curve of the Tor-gian's neck, and the horse tossed its head, whickering, taking one or two small steps sidewise as if he were very pleased with both himself and his rider.

With them all to horse and the falcon settled on saddle perch, they headed back into the foothills. Tirtha watched the boy anxiously. Though she claimed hardness of spirit for herself and even in childhood had cultivated a shell to protect both her inner self and the feeling that some important destiny lay before her, she could not believe that so young a child might so quickly lose the remembrance of the raid and of how he had escaped from it.

Perhaps her first suspicion was right—the use of his power had released within him also an ability to accept things as they were. So, as the Falconer suggested, Alon was able to look forward and not back—yet another protective measure which the talent brought to him without even his conscious willing.

They halted for nooning at a spring, for these foothills were well watered. The boy shared the last of their rations of crumbling journey cake, as they had not tried to hunt along the way. By questioning, they discovered that Alon's knowledge of the land eastward was limited to stories that had come through infrequent contact with either a single small market town to the south or from such travelers as the master of the holding had trusted enough to shelter overnight.

There was a Lord Honnor who claimed rule over part of the land, but, by all Alon's accounts, his hold was a precarious one, his title often in dispute, though he was a man of some honesty—for Karsten—and did his best for those loyal to him. The master of the garth had been one Parlan, not of the Old Race but with a dislike for the perilous life of the more fertile plains where there was almost constant warfare. He had brought his family clan into this foothill region trying to escape the constant raiding he had encountered during the past dozen years or more.

It was when he had been taken sick two tens of days back that the mastership of the garth itself had fallen on his nephew Dion. Parlan was old enough to have served in Pagar's force, being one of the garrison left behind when the fateful invasion of Estcarp had been ordered. A seasoned fighting man, he had suffered a crippling wound in the chaos that had followed the turning of the mountains, and had then taken a wife and the land his lord commander had offered, only to change his mind and move into the foothills when that lord commander himself was treacherously slain and his forces badly routed.

Alon's own relationship with Parlan and his family was apparently not a close one. He had been added to the household when they had left the plains, as a very young baby, and he had been told that he was the only child of a kinsman who had been killed with the lord commander, his mother slain in a resulting raid.

"It was Yachne who fostered me," he told them. "She—they were all somewhat afraid of her, I think." He frowned a little. "And she was not of their blood either. But she was a healer and she knew many things—she taught the maidens weaving and the making of dyes. So Parlan got fine prices for their work in the market. Also . . ." He shook his head. "I do not know why, but he often came to her when he was in trouble and she would sleep, or seem to. Then when she wakened again, she would tell him things. But always she sent me away when she did this, saying this must not be told or understood by men. And when I asked her questions, she grew angry, though I cannot understand why."

"Because she dealt in witchery," returned the Falconer.

"And perhaps because she believed, as most do"—Tirtha herself had only today revised her own beliefs in that direction—"that the talent is only a gift for women."

"The talent?" Alon repeated. "When I was frightened, then—what did I do? They said that they would have a hunt and that this was a fair way to bring down their hare." He shivered. "Gerik's shield man tossed me out into the field and I ran, and then . . . then . . ." He looked questioningly to Tirtha. "I do not know what happened. There was a dark place, but it was not of the evil, that I know—rather it was like a house, strong-walled to hold me safe. Somehow I found that and hid until I was called, and that calling I could not stand against."

Tirtha found it ever more difficult to think of him as the child he looked. Now she asked abruptly:

"How old are you, Alon?"

Again he frowned. "I do not know, for Yachne would not tell me. I know"—he glanced disparagingly down at his own small body—"that I am too small. Frith, who seemed close to me in age when we were little, grew; he was near half a head the taller. They called me 'babe in arms' when they wished to tease me. It seems that I do not look like the others. Even Sala who was only ten stood above me. I think I can count for myself near twelve years since we came from the plains."

Twelve years—perhaps more! Tirtha, startled, looked to the Falconer and read a trace of the same amazement on his face. The small body she had carried was certainly that of a child who looked hardly half that toll of years. Perhaps there was more than the blood of her own race in this one. There were stories of strange matings to be read at Lormt. A long-lived elder race might well produce a child whose development was very slow and whose seeming childhood much prolonged. The Old Race was long-lived, and they retained a semblance of late youth into scores of years, in fact until they were near death. But this very prolonged childhood was new to her.

Over the mountains from Escore—if the servants of the Dark had thus wandered, perhaps other blood had come also. It could be that Alon had less human blood in him than appearances warranted. If that were true, his self-caused retreat, even from sight, could well be a natural thing.

By evening they found a good camping place. There was a moss-and-turf-covered ledge projecting from a rise of ground, sided in part by an indentation that was close to a cave. Tirtha, seeing on the down side a covey of hares, loosed three arrows in close order and descended to pick up the bodies, while Alon, for the first time since he had mounted the Torgian, displayed fatigue, sitting on one of the saddles the Falconer had stripped from their beasts, hunching his shoulders against the rising evening wind. His scanty clothing certainly gave him little protection against it.

They pulled stones together and lighted a fire at the back of the half cave, broiling the joints of meat over it, to avidly eat dripping bits to which Tirtha added some of her powdered herbs. Comfortable warmth radiated from the back wall of stone. The Falconer rummaged in his saddle bags and brought out a pair of under-trousers which were far too large until they were tied around Alon's waist with a doubled cord, the legs turned up and laced tight. There were no boots to pull over them, but at least they kept the saddle pad from chafing the boy's inner thighs, which were already red. Tirtha covered the marks with salve before he drew on the improvised leggings.

He sat by the fire eating hungrily, wiping the grease from his fingers with a tuft of grass before he turned to the Falconer.

"Lord Nirel . . ."

"I am no lord, Little Brother," countered the other. "We do not use the lowland titles, we of the Eyrie." Then he paused, for he must be remembering, Tirtha knew with a flash of insight, that the Eyrie and its brotherhood had long since vanished.

"I think then," said Alon, with his head a little on one side, "that I shall call you Swordmaster Nirel, for you are surely one who is that. But you wear more than one sword at your belt . . ." He pointed to the strange weapon. "And I have never seen the like of that one. Though Master Parlan had old comrades come now and then to visit with him, and many of them carried weapons which they cherished and in which they had great pride. What is that?"

The Falconer drew the dagger-sword. Now the gem in the pommel was darkly opaque—even the firelight could raise no gleams from its inner part. It might have been as dead as any lump of metal.

"I do not know, in truth, Little Brother. It is a gift from Wind Warrior, and it holds within it that which I do not understand." He extended it closer into the firelight so that the flame lit the inlays on its blade. "I think that it is not only very old, but that it is a thing of Power, perhaps even like the Axe of Volt."

It was apparent that Alon had never heard of that fabulous weapon. But now he held out a finger not to touch, but to sketch in the air just a little above, the symbols on the blade as he passed each one in a sweep from hilt to point.

"This picture"—he paused above one near the end of that line—"is like unto a thing which Yachne wore beneath her robe on a chain about her neck. It was a secret thing, I think. I only saw it the once, and she quickly hid it again. Did this come from overmountain, or is it falcon power?"

"The Falconers do not deal with any power," came a somewhat repressive answer. "Nor is this out of Estcarp, as far as I know. It must have been borne by one of Estcarp's enemies, for we found it where a mountain fall had trapped and killed those who were the invaders. Though why one of Karsten would have carried a thing they would have deemed cursed—that is also strange and hard to believe."

"Yes, it must be very old." Alon swept his hand up the length of the blade, this time toward the hilt, as if he could, by the very gesture, read something of what it was and for what purpose it must serve its possessor. "But it is not for the letting of blood—none has ever stained it."

He spoke with an authority that made them both stare. Then he gave a little self-conscious laugh. "If Yachne were here, I would have a clout across the mouth for speaking so. She did not like me to say what I knew, even when I knew it. But it is true. There is a feel to a thing that has killed; it clings to aught which has let blood. I do not sense it here. Yet in its way this is a weapon."

"Rather," Tirtha interrupted, "I would call it a key of sorts. For it was through this the Falconer brought you—or he and his falcon—brought you back to this world. It is a power thing, and it answers to them, whether they claim the talent or not."

Alon blinked. "In time it may do even more. I should have Yachne's learning, then perhaps I could take it in my hands and see. It is strange, but inside me now I feel very different, as if there is something before me that is all new, standing ready for me to discover it. I . . . I am no longer Alon, the always-babe, but another—one I do not yet know, and yet whom I must speedily learn."

9

For three days they drifted westward. There were no trails in the foothills, though once or twice they chanced upon indications that they did not travel through a deserted country. There were signs of old campfires, unhidden, and hoof prints of horses stitched soft earth. Still the falcon, scouting aloft, reported only native animals.

The last of the supplies they had brought over-mountain were gone. Tirtha's bow kept them in meat. There must have been little hunting hereabouts for years, since the pronghorns and the hares were easy to bring down. Alon also possessed knowledge of the wild. He triumphantly dug up fat roots which, when roasted in the fire, broke apart to be tasty and filling.

More and more the older two came to accept Alon as an equal in spite of his childish appearance. Tirtha's careful questioning produced more of his relationship with Yachne—plainly a Wise Woman of such talent as would have placed her high in Estcarp.

"She was"—Alon frowned slightly as he tended the fire on their third night of encampment—"not of the kin Parlan claimed, nor was she, I am sure, even of the blood they knew. She had been many years with his household, for she came with his mother when she was a girl first hand-fasted to his father. She was old, yet always she looked the same without change. And it was she who went alone to find me when I was left kinless, bringing me back to the household. Also"—his eyes darkened oddly, as if to hide part of his thoughts—"she was not there when Gerik came. She had gone seeking a rare herb which she thought would draw Parlan out of his fever, or so she said. Had she been within the walls I do not think Gerik could have entered. Yachne"—he nodded, as if to underline the importance of what he said—"could read the Dark Ones. Twice she told

Parlan to send away men who came to him seeking shelter, and one of them was a long-time comrade he would have trusted."

"And this garth master always listened to her advice?" the Falconer asked.

Alon nodded once more. "Always. I think he was even a little afraid of her. Not that she would do him or his any harm, but because she knew things that he did not understand. Men always seem to fear what they cannot find a direct reason for." Again it was as if someone far older sat there, licking grease from his fingers, wearing the outward appearance of a child who must be protected from the rigors of the world. If Tirtha closed her eyes and listened only to his speech, she built up in her mind a far different Alon, always to be slightly startled when she looked directly at the boy again.

"She was—is a Wise Woman," Tirtha said now. "Such are always to be found among our people. But if she returns and finds the garth as it now is, will she follow us?"

One possessing the Power could well use the trance (as she herself had attempted) and trail them as easily as if they had left all manner of open markings behind. She saw the Falconer stir. His frown was twice as heavy as Alon's had been. This man could accept her, Tirtha, since she had dealt with him after the established custom, claimed his services by open bargain. But that he might ride with a true Wise Woman whom his kind held close to hatred—no. Nor would she herself welcome such a one who might read her and her mission as easily as one would understand a fair-written scroll.

For a long moment Alon apparently considered her question, his head a little atilt in the same fashion as the bird would hold *his* feathered crest when appealed to. Then, slowly, he shifted his gaze, past Tirtha, past the fire, out into the dark.

"I do not feel her," he said simply. "When I try, there is nothingness. Yet I do not think she is dead. Perhaps, knowing that the garth is gone, she has followed some plan of her own. She is a secret person." Now he looked back to Tirtha. "I could tell many things about other of Parlan's people. I knew when they feared, or were happy over some matter, or when they were about to sicken. But with Yachne you did not know. There was always a barred door past which you did not go. I think that she aided Parlan not because she held any liking within her for his clan, but rather as if there rested between them a debt she was paying. Perhaps it was so with me also. Though I also believe that she found in me some future use . . ." He appeared now to be thinking aloud rather than trying to answer any of Tirtha's yet unspoken questions, turning over ideas which had long puzzled him.

"You would know if she were near?" The Falconer asked that sharply, in a tone that was meant to arouse, bring a quick answer.

"Yes. Even if I could not find her directly, I would mind-touch her inner wall."

"Good enough. I think"—the man regarded the boy measuringly, those old yellow sparks plain in his eyes—"that you will tell us if you sense such." He might have meant that for a question, but it came forth more as an order.

"Yes." Alon's answer was brief. Tirtha, at that moment, was in two minds whether they could rely upon it or not. She knew that there was nothing of the Dark in this child. Still, that did not mean that he would consider himself committed to their own quest. They might claim a debt for saving his life but she had no wish to do so. Those who weighed and balanced such acts were tarnished by the doing. One gave aid freely when it was necessary. There was to be no payment returned, save by the desire of the debtor. In so much, in spite of all the hardness of her life, she held to the ways into which she had been born. Nor did she believe that the Falconer would argue differently. The sword-oath he had taken made his road hers as long as their bargain held.

She shifted restlessly. To head on guideless, as they had been doing, was folly; she must know more concerning the direction in which their goal lay. In order to do that, she must dream or else evoke another trance. Only such dreams had eluded her now for days. Her sleep was deep and heavy at night. If she had walked in strange ways, she carried no memories back into waking. To try once more the herb-induced trance, with perhaps this Yachne somewhere about . . . The entranced one was always vulnerable. She had been reckless when she had attempted it before and certainly she had not been in command, for she had not been led to Hawkholme—rather to Alon.

Tirtha had come to suspect that it had been the force of the power Alon had employed without willing it that had drawn her own talent and that led them to the garth. Any gift so much greater than her own small one could bend her to another's will when she was in the disembodied state. Also, Alon had spoken of the Dark spreading eastward. To be caught by a strong evil will . . .

Yet to continue to wander aimlessly—that achieved nothing. She looked to the boy across the fire now, her eyes narrowed a little. There was one way—yet she shrank from discussing it, from even considering it. All her life she had fought for her independence, for the ability to order her own existence as much as any living creature might in an uncertain world. To surrender in even this need came very hard. She looked down at her calloused brown hands, clutched so tightly on a fold of her cloak that her knuckles stood in sharp relief. Will fought need within her until at last that same common sense which she had clung to during all her plans triumphed.

"I must use the trance." She spoke as sharply as the Falconer had done in his questioning of Alon. "That need may not be delayed any longer. I seek guides, and those I can only gain in that fashion. But one entranced, without protection, is in danger. My—my talent is limited. Therefore, when I go seeking, there could well be those of greater power to take and bind me to their will."

The Falconer's frown was dark, his mouth a straight slash across his face. Tirtha knew that with every word she uttered, she aroused opposition in him, brought to the fore all the dislike he had for such as she was. Only his oath bound him, but in that she had a foundation. Alon was watching her with a similar intent stare, but with none of the resentment that the Falconer radiated. His attitude was one of excitement and interest, such as any ordinary boy might show before a feat of action.

"I need your help." Those were the hardest four words she remembered uttering in years.

The Falconer made a quick gesture of repudiation, using his claw as if, with that symbol of grim loss, such a negation of what she had asked was thereby made the stronger. Alon, however, nodded briskly.

Now she looked directly to the man. "This is a thing you wish no part of, that I know. It is not bound without your oath." In that much she would yield to him. "But I have seen what you and your bird brother can do, and so I ask of you, not aid in my going forth, but another kind of help—protection against what might well net me while I am in that other state."

It was Alon who answered her and not the Falconer, and he did not speak to her but to the man.

"Swordmaster, this Lady asks of you protection. She says that you are not oath-bound to give it after the fashion in which she must now have it. Perhaps that is so. I know of sword oaths and shield men only what I have heard in tales and accounts of the old wars and troubles. Perhaps it is against your own beliefs that you do such a thing, but this is not of the Dark. Therefore a man does not break his innermost allegiance if he follows a path that helps, not harms. I do not know how great an aide I can be in such a matter." He now addressed Tirtha directly. "I think there is much, very much, that I must learn concerning myself. But what I have now"—he held out his hands as if he were offering her something as invisible as he himself had been when they first found him—"is at your service." Once more his eyes swung to the Falconer as if he waited.

The man had drawn from its sheath the weapon of power, then rammed it back with savage force. His rage, controlled with an icy strength, was visible to them both. He spoke as if he would bite each word drawn from him and answered harshly.

"I hold not with witchery. But also I am indeed oath-bound, though you"—he looked flame-eyed at Tirtha—"have said that in this that is not so. However, the boy is right—one does not give half oaths if one is of the blood. What would you have of me?"

She felt no elation. To have him believe that she had in a manner forced this might even endanger what she would do. For their wills must be united lest there be an opening for the Dark to twist one against the other. Tirtha leaned forward to pinch up dust, as much as she could hold between her thumb and forefinger, her eyes on him rather than on what she did. She saw his gaze narrow.

"Twenty days we agreed. However, if I will it and say I am now satisfied, then our bargain is dissolved even as . . ." Her hand raised, about to toss what she held into the air.

He moved the swifter. His fingers imprisoned her wrist in a hard grip, holding her hand fast so that she might not loose the dust and so break their bargain. She did not believe that it was altogether the firelight that made his face seem flushed. Surely his eyes were fully alive with anger.

"Twenty days I said, and in all ways I do my duty—on shield oath."

"It must be done willingly." She disliked this inner struggle between them, wanting none of it. Let him ride off and be rid of her and all witchery. "For one to hold back even in thought will open doors. I do not know what may threaten, only this is a dangerous land. What I would do is as perilous as if I rode disarmed into an outlaw camp. Help—must—be—given—willingly."

He dropped his hold on her, settled back. "You know best your needs," he returned tonelessly. "I shall endeavor to aid as you wish. What is it you desire of us?"

"I must go again out of my body," Tirtha said deliberately and slowly. "Perhaps that power, which you and the feathered brother share and which Alon has a portion of, can in a manner follow me and so protect my return road so that none else, or no alien will, can make of me a tool or a weapon."

"Very well." He turned his head a fraction, gave one of those small chirruping calls which summoned the falcon. The bird perched on his claw wrist where it rested on his knee.

"I cannot tell you against what or how you shall stand guard," she continued. "Nor do I know if this thing is even possible. But fasten your minds upon the wish that I may succeed in what I strive to do. I hunt a guide to Hawkholme that we may head overland to where it once stood. Keep in your minds that name and the wish that I, in vision, may travel swift and sure over the countryside between where we are and that place. This"—she lifted her hands a little—"is all I can ask, for I do not know how else to bind us together."

"Go, we shall follow." It was not the Falconer who had given that firm promise, rather the boy.

Tirtha took from her belt pouch the potent herb and tossed it into the fire. She saw the Falconer again draw his weapon of power, drive the point of the blade into the earth before him. She leaned forward and inhaled deeply the smoke which brought with it a strong smell of spice and other goodly odors.

There was no going into dark this time. Rather she was enveloped by a blaze of blue light so strong that she nearly retreated, then warmth and strength reached out to surround her. She moved as firmly and with such purpose as she might have walked on a road in Estcarp.

The light accompanied her. She looked up to see a globe of blue (the blazing pommel of the weapon?) spinning with her into the place of otherness. Then that light began to fade as she moved on into a grayness.

Though Tirtha had no impression of foot touching ground, there was land about her, solid looking and as real as any they had covered in their passage through the foothills. The darkness of trees, massed together, arose on one hand, while to the right stood a bare escarpment of rock across which ran a notable vein of black. This was one of the marks to remember, that much Tirtha understood.

The veined wall began to sink lower and lower into the earth as she left the heights behind. Now that distinguishing sable marking disappeared; it was only a ridge of rock she followed.

Hawkholme—even as she had told the others to do, so did she now hold that name firmly in mind. Her one fear was that she might be whirled into the repetition of her old dream and not learn the way, only arrive within that hold, to relive once more the final action.

Tirtha was out of the hills. Open country lay beyond and to her right. To her left the wood thickened into a forest, a growth so tangled that she did not believe anyone could force a pathway through. When she turned her head slightly to view it, she saw a flickering movement that was stealthy and yet continuous. Within that screen of entwined limbs and vines and brush, something paced at her own speed, spied upon her.

She caught glimpses now and then of a pallid grayness but with no distinct form, which slid easily in and out, the thickness of the wood offering it no opposition. Tirtha would have kept to the open, yet what she had summoned up by her will drew her toward the wood in spite of misgivings.

Always that which paced there watched. Tirtha sensed a malignant threat, but she determined not to try to learn more. All her concentration must be centered on reaching Hawkholme.

Even as she set her will so determinedly, Tirtha turned a fraction to head straight for the wood. Here the underbrush appeared less inter-woven. There were faint indications that there had once been an opening, that perhaps a long overgrown road had run in this direction. The lurker was still there, yet it did not manifest itself to meet her, rather it followed the same procedure, heading into the undergrowth parallel to her own path.

At intervals the old road was more open. She sighted once or twice a tall stone set on end, as if to mark her path. There were other objects far-ther back, emitting a pale and ghostly light. She sensed essences there of things that were totally alien, rooted or imprisoned where they stood. Against these the girl hurriedly raised mind barriers, for she felt the touch of a demanding desire reaching for her.

This wood was a place of menace. Even were she here in body and not just in essence, she would have found it so, that she knew. Yet what she sought lay beyond it, and there was no escaping the journey.

How long it would take to traverse the sinister forest, she had no way of knowing. Tirtha had the impression that such a journey was no short span.

However, there came at last an end, where the overgrowth trail opened again on meadow land. Here were fields which had once been walled, those stone barriers crumbling now, yet their lines plain to read. Through them curled a stream nearly of a size to be proclaimed a river. On the other side of that . . .

A vast surge of emotion, which she could not define, gathered within her, such as she had never felt before. Even from afar she could see that the defenses the builders of this hold had planned had failed in the end. Strong walled towers, a mighty keep had been raised upon a mound, at the foot of which washed a side channel of the river which had been diverted to ring around the hold. There were the splintered remains of a bridge— now only broken timbers—across a stretch of water to the gap that formed the entrance.

In all, this was a larger and more formidable hold than she had thought, although the huge hall of her dreams had argued it was part of a major building. The clan that had wrought it must have been a strong and well numbered one—and one with enemies, for the whole scene before her suggested that defense had been highly important.

Tirtha had found her goal. Now she deliberately set about relaxing her will—that will which was still bearing her onward toward the ruin. There was no need to travel farther.

The blow came like a blast of winter's wind against an unclad body. Deep and numbing cold cut at her. Tirtha had not believed pain could be felt by one in her present state. How wrong this thing out of nowhere was proving her! She fought, strove to free herself from that agonizing icy horror which battled to keep her prisoner. Now, her will cried out, now— if you can hear me, sense me, aid me—bring what power you have to draw me back!

Had the other two indeed followed her, did they know that she had been so taken? If she had no aid, she was lost, for that cold ate into her will, tearing it apart as a wild wind shreds a cloud.

"Come!"

She could not cry that aloud, but her whole self shaped itself into that plea. Was she being driven back into the same limbo that had held Alon when they found him?

Warmth—a faint glow of warmth. The cold pressed, but there was warmth, and somehow she could draw it to her little by little, hoard it within to keep cold and death at bay. The strand of warmth gave an upward surge, grew stronger.

The cold had reached for her, had sought to compel her onward toward the ruin just when she had striven to break the compulsion she had used to bring her here. It wanted her inside. Now she wavered—if an essence could waver. The drag forward, the chilling against the warmth being fed into her. Her will awoke from the effects of that first, numbing, near-fatal blow. Back—she fastened not on Hawkholme, rather on her memory of their camp.

Think of Alon—the warmth grew! The Falconer—a thread more of freedom gave her strength; the Falconer—it was his face that filled her thoughts now—a face bearing a terrible set concentration like a mask laid over the man she had grown to accept as a trail comrade. Within his eyes those yellow fires flared high. She could see only those eyes and the fires in them—warmth against the cold—the OTHER who willed her to Hawkholme in a state which it could use. Yes, warmth!

Fire rose about her; tongues of blue flame formed a defense wall. Abruptly the assault of the cold ceased. The fires lingered for a moment, died, and she was in the dark.

Rain—she lay out in the rain—water ran down her face, into her open mouth. She heard hurried breathing, fast, shallow, such as a near-spent runner might have. She opened her eyes—there was a blaze of half light around her head, so that she quickly closed them again, feeling that somehow she had been cut adrift and caught up in something that she could never hope to either escape or control.

"Tirtha, Tirtha!" A call, faint at first and then very strong. She was once more aware of her body, of stiffness and pain. The warmth that had aided her return to life slowly traveled from her head down her entire length.

"Tirtha!"

She dared to open her eyes once again. There was Alon's face, one side of it strangely blue. His eyes held fear; then it faded and he smiled—laughed—as if a burden had been lifted from him.

Tirtha saw that other form kneeling by her, in his hands the sword, tight gripped, its pommel ablaze and the blue light bathing her from head to foot. Increasing strength followed the warmth, flowing into an emptiness she had not realized was there until it was refilled. Cautiously she lifted her head. Almost instantly an arm was thrust beneath her shoulders, bracing her higher. She felt the small, chill touch of that claw against her cheek for just an instant.

Alon squatted on his heels directly before her, his expression one of eagerness. The Falconer, because he supported her, she could not clearly see. He had laid aside the sword. Its output of energy had faded; there was only the faintest glow from it now.

"I—am—back." Her lips, as they shaped those words, were stiff. In her own ears her voice sounded hardly more than a whisper. "You brought me back."

For it was from the two of them—no, the three (she must not forget the feathered brother she had sensed as part of her rescue)—had come the warmth, generated within themselves to combat what had lain in wait for her at Hawkholme.

Lain in wait? Tirtha for the first time thought clearly. She had not only the ruin to find, but there was an unknown terror there—one determined to have what? That which she sought herself and still could not name? Logic told her that that might well be the truth. So . . .

She moved her head, her shoulders a little, though she did not try as yet to pull free from the Falconer's support. Perhaps she needed that strong arm behind her to strengthen her—even to remind her—of what she must say to these two, of the decision that was hers to make and about which there could be no choice, for the very honor of the Hawk.

"You found the way?" Before she could speak, Alon's question came.

"I found the way."

"Then we can go." He glanced over his shoulder as if he were ready to saddle and ride at once.

"Not 'we'." Tirtha had herself in hand now. "This is my quest only." She looked directly to the Falconer. "I release you—take Alon. There are those over-mountain who will give him shelter—the Tregarths—for they know that power does not always run in the same channels. From here I ride alone."

He regarded her with that same level and angry glance he had worn before when she would have broken their bond in full ceremony.

"There are twenty days—no less."

Tirtha sat upright, and he moved away from her quietly. The falcon gave one of its soft cries and fluttered to his claw wrist.

"I lead no one into that. . . ." she declared sharply in return, determined this time to have *her* will in the matter.

10

Yet strong as she thought herself to be, Tirtha did not have her way. The Falconer was stubborn, determined to fulfill his bargain. Though she ordered him twice to use that sense of duty by taking Alon over-mountain, swearing that she would be satisfied, that this would set the balance straight between them, he refused. Tirtha wondered if she must slip away from her companions, only she could not be sure whether the stubborn man would not attempt to track her. It was Alon who confirmed that suspicion when they were alone the next morning, the Falconer having taken the water bottles down to the stream.

"He is single-minded and that rides hard with him," Alon observed. "These bird men are trained to what they believe is their duty. Thus he would pursue it and you to the end. You cannot shake us off, Lady." He smiled and gave a small laugh.

Tirtha was not to be beguiled from her own sense of right. "There is danger waiting at Hawkholme. Did that not already strike at me?"

"And did you not then beat it?" he interrupted. "Yes, it waits, but *you* do not draw back because of it. Neither shall this Swordmaster allow any foreboding to lessen his intent. Nor"—he paused for a second or two before he continued—"shall I. There is in me"—his hands went to heart level at his breast, touching the wrinkled smock Tirtha had washed in a stream—"that I must learn to master and live with. Yachne would not teach me. Did she," his face screwed up into a frown, "*fear* me?" He asked that not of Tirtha but of himself, as the girl was well aware. "Yet there was much of the power in her—one could feel it always. And I am not Wise. I am not—what then *am* I?" Again he spoke to Tirtha. "Have you seen my like before? They tell me many tales of Estcarp—that the old knowledge was treasured there, not lost, forgotten by the Old Race as it was here."

Tirtha made fast the latching of her saddlebag. "I have not seen any male before who has commanded the Power. The Witches who rule in the north say such a thing is unnatural, and therefore perhaps of the Dark."

Alon was on his feet in one supple movement, to stand staring at her, wide-eyed.

"I am not . . ." His protest came sharp and quick.

"Do you think that I do not know that? The Dark Ones cannot hide what they are to any of our blood. Also there is one man, Simon Tregarth, who has something of the talent. However, he is not of our blood, but an outlander who came through one of the Gates. It is also true that his two sons command strange forces, and they carried them and their Witch sister westward into Escore so that they broke the old curse to open that land to all of our race again.

"Though perhaps to no peaceful purpose, for there were many evils loose there, and now they war. Those of the Old Race, who followed the Tregarth calling to the east, fight against many Dark perils. There have been scores of stories during the past few years, perhaps twisted in the telling as such often are. Still we hear of battles won and lost, a country rent by the will of things unlike human kind. It could be that Escore blood has ventured westward here." She sat with her hands clasped together studying Alon measuringly.

"You said that you were son to one this Parlan knew," she continued.

"I said"—he was quick to correct her—"that that was what was told me. The truth is that Yachne brought me to Parlan's clan and told such a tale. So I was accepted, for the man she named as my father was blood-brother by sword oath to Parlan—and it was true he was dead, his lady having vanished also after the battle, and was thought to be slain during the retreat that followed. That was Yachne's story, but"—he drew a deep, long breath—"can one believe it? There are the Gates. Those I have heard of—even of Tregarth's coming—and of that which the Kolders used when they entered this world and strove to make it theirs. Could it be that I am also such an outlander?"

His eyes were large, wide open, and there was that same eagerness in his face which he had shown the night before when she had asked of them their aid in farseeing.

"You have the look of the Old Race outwardly," Tirtha observed. "Yet you have also power—and the measurement of how much is something I cannot make. I have only a scrap of the talent. I can heal a little; I can farsee when entranced; and I can dream. I am not your Yachne. Also perhaps I am now one who is walking straight into such danger as cannot be reckoned."

"Still you must go to the Hawkholme," he said slowly, and she did not need the ability to read minds to guess that he longed to ask her the reason for this journey.

Odder still was the feeling within her that, for the first time, she wished to share her secret. As if this small boy, with his oddly mature speech and apparent understanding, had a full right to know what had driven her for so long. However, there was no time for such a sharing, even if she had been willing to break the cautious silence of years, for the Falconer returned at a pace quick enough to set the bottles he carried swinging from his claw, his hand on the butt of his dart gun.

"We ride." He swung past them to where the ponies and the Torgian were picketed, making it plain that he meant a hasty departure. Tirtha and Alon asked no questions, rather hastened to saddle their mounts. When the Falconer took the lead, he swung north, leaving the stream, holding his pony to a trot that was the best pace for such rough country.

Tirtha pulled level with him. "What have you seen?"

"We may have escaped notice." He had resumed his helm and now the falcon took wing, ascending into the sky in ever widening circles. "But there were fresh tracks on the other side of the stream."

She thought furiously. What she had done the night before, drawing the other two into it also? If there were any hereabouts with the faintest trace of talent, they would have been alerted as quickly as if she had purposefully marked a plain back trail or set a signal fire. Perhaps her action had been foolhardy, wildly reckless.

"Outlaws?" she asked. Most drifting through this country would certainly be men from the plains, not those generally receptive to whispers of the Power. Their passing would be by chance only.

He shrugged. "What can one read from tracks in the mud? There were two shod horses of a larger breed—the rest were ponies. A party of six I would say. They headed south and east."

South and east—that was the direction they themselves must take. Tirtha had sensed in her trance journey that what she sought was not too far distant. Perhaps that ridge with its black veining might be only a day's journey on. However, if they had to detour, it would add to the leagues of travel while their supplies were very low, and they might not have time to hunt or garner any fresh spring plants.

"How long since, do you believe?" she asked.

"Since sunrise."

His curt answer offered a little relief. Dared she believe that what she had wrought last night had nothing to do with this near meeting? The evidence could point to another camp not too far away—or maybe pursuit! This Gerik—what motive could drive him to follow them? Tirtha could think of one lure—Alon. If the outlaw had guessed that one of the Old Race with unusual powers had slipped through his fingers at the massacre—would that be prod enough to set him following? Gerik—who was he? Was he an outlaw? Or shield man of some ambitious noble now raiding and fighting over the remnants of Karsten? She waved to Alon, bringing him forward until the three of them rode abreast.

"Who is Gerik? Does some other stand behind him?" She shot the questions quickly, saw the Falconer turn his head as if he understood the line her thoughts had taken.

"He is a raider," Alon answered slowly, "who has come only in the past year into this country. His men—they are . . ." The boy's face was pale, he moistened his lips with tongue tip. Tirtha knew well that she was forcing him back to memories that he had been setting firmly behind him. Still they must know all they could.

"His men . . ." Alon straightened a little in the large saddle. One of his hands rested against the Torgian's neck as if he drew strength and courage from contact with the animal. "They are . . ." He turned his head farther to look directly at Tirtha and the Falconer. "I know it now." There was a quick lift in his voice. "I thought that they were only what Parlan called the scum—those blank shields no lord would allow to ride under his banner, murderers and worse as some of them were. Only now I understand—there was a real Dark One among them!"

Tirtha's hold on the reins tightened, and her mare near came to a halt. The Falconer's hand, which had hovered near his dart gun ever since they had ridden forth, closed upon its butt.

"And Gerik—he was the one?" Somehow Tirtha kept her voice steady.

Alon shook his head. "I am not sure. Only that he is evil, but . . . No, I do not think that he is anything but a man, a true man, though there was in him . . ." His puzzlement was becoming distress. "When they hunted me, I was too afraid. Now that I am here and know more, I realize that I feared not death alone—though that was a part of it—but something beyond, which was worse."

"Could they have learned"—the Falconer's mind followed the same path Tirtha's had chanced upon—"that you held control over Power?"

"I do not know, but then I did not know it myself. It was the fear of them that, I think, broke some barrier in me."

"There were times in the past when barriers against power could be and were induced in children." Again Tirtha recalled her researching at

Lormt, which had sometimes wandered into side lanes away from the main search she had gone there to make. "Perhaps it was so with you, Alon."

His distress was open to read. "Then could it have been *me* Gerik sought? Did I then bring the death—the . . ."

"No." Only the Falconer's mouth could be seen below the half mask of his helm. It was set and stern. "Do not think that is so, Little Brother. This Gerik was a raider, and by the looks of it, that garth was worth plundering. Also he may have had some old quarrel with the clan master."

Alon's face cleared a little. "He had with him a man whom Parlan had warned off two moons ago, Yachne telling him that the man was dangerous, even though he had come with a message from Lord Honnor, and that was a true message as we learned later. The stranger had been with my lord for a full twelve moons and served him well. It was after that Parlan felt ill, and Yachne went forth to hunt what would relieve him. But the same man rode with Gerik, I saw his face clearly. He was not of the Dark, the full Dark."

"But you have said at least another was," Tirtha persisted. "What manner of man was he?"

Again Alon's face was haunted. "I cannot tell. I do not remember, truly I do not. I only know that there were some who would hunt me in the meadow and that they wanted to . . ." His voice broke, and he dropped the reins, raising his hands to cover his face.

Tirtha was quick to understand. "Put it from your mind. If it is meant that you should remember, then it will come to you at the proper time. Do not seek it now."

He dropped his hands again. Once more that shadow of an age beyond his stature and his outward appearance crossed his face.

"I shall not seek such inner hiding again." That came as a promise and a firm one. "But I do not have full memory either. Perhaps, as you say, that shall come to me."

Tirtha looked to the Falconer. "Gerik seeks us, do you think?"

His head tilted back a little on his shoulders, and he did not answer her. The bird was winging in, settling on its perch. Once more she listened to the twittering exchange between the two of them. Then the man turned from the feathered scout to speak to them both.

"There is a party moving slowly southward. There are six, and one of them is strange." He hesitated. "My brother cannot explain in what manner save that, though this one wears the appearance of a man, within the body's shell, he is not as we are. Still neither is he Kolder nor one of the dead-controlled who once served Kolder. For that breed is well known to us of the Eyrie that was. This is something else, and it is wrong."

"Out of Escore?" Ever since their encounter with the thing in the night, Tirtha had been alert for any other evidence that the monsters said to run with evil in the west were patroling into this country. The wildness of this torn land, the chaos into which its people had been plunged, both reasons might well draw evil. The Dark reveled in such circumstances by all the old accounts.

Or—suddenly another thought crossed her mind—what of that which she had encountered, the presence manifesting itself as freezing cold, at Hawkholme. Could that also summon? If so, she must not lead her companions there. Though she did not realize it at that moment, Tirtha was glancing hurriedly from side to side as might a hunted one seeking some path of escape.

"There is something. . . ." Alon's hesitant voice barely broke through her preoccupation with her own alarm, but his next words did. "Lady, you carry a sword and on it there is a symbol. . . ."

She must have centered her gaze on him so suddenly and sharply that she disconcerted him a little, for he faltered, and it was the Falconer who cut in with a question before she could speak.

"What is this about a symbol, Little Brother? The Lady is Head of Hawkholme, the last of her blood. What she carries is the House sword. What do you know of that?"

"You are a Falconer, Swordmaster, and your bird rides with you," Alon replied. "But the bird which is like unto that on this Lady's sword, that I have also seen—and before our meeting."

"Where?" Tirtha demanded. On some piece of loot taken at the fall of the hold, tossed about from one thief to another through the years?

"There was another man who came just before the Moon of the Ice Dragon, when the thick snows fell and closed all the mountain ways. He guested with Parlan for ten days, exchanged his mount for another. On his left hand he wore a ring of metal, which was not gold nor silver, but rather it had a reddish look, and it bore a carving like that on your sword hilt. He had the habit of playing with it as he talked, turning it around and around on his finger, and so one noted it."

"What was his name?" Tirtha demanded.

"He gave it as Ettin and said that he was a blank shield from past service with the Borderers, one who thought of returning to Karsten. He . . ." Alon's puzzled look was back. "I do not think he was of the Old Race, for he was fair of hair and had blue eyes."

At the sound of that name, Tirtha had drawn so sharp a breath that she realized she had caught the attention of the Falconer. The dead man they had found who had worn the hawk crest—he had been a stranger, but this one . . . So many years, could it be true?

"You know this man who wears a lord's ring?" Suspicion was certainly back in the Falconer's voice.

"There was a child, years ago. The Old Race weds sometimes with the Sulcars. And there were Sulcar-men who rode with the Borderers, though their first allegiance is always to the sea."

"And the lord's ring?" Once more he was challenging her. Tirtha sat the straighter in the saddle, met his gaze level-eyed.

"There could be no such true ring. Hawkholme's lord wore one of its like on his hand when he met death within his own walls. His younger brother, who was apart when the attack came, never possessed it. Perhaps it was loot fallen into Ettin's hands. He might claim it, but its wearing was never for any half blood." Her chin was high, and she spoke with force. "Of the true House, I am the last—nor would I have come into Karsten had it been otherwise."

With his helm on, his face so masked, she felt, as always, at a disadvantage—even though the Falconer's expression was never easy to read. He could believe her or not. If he chose to brand her liar (and did not his kind think in their innermost minds that all her sex were?), then she could declare their bargain broken and so be rid of the burden of leading him and Alon into dire disaster. For surely he would take the boy with him to save him from further contamination by one who was tainted like her.

However, what he faced her with now was a question that had undoubtedly been eating at him from the very start of this venture.

"What has Hawkholme to offer anyone?"

In other words, Tirtha knew he meant—what did it have to offer a lone woman who ventured into an act of sheer folly in seeking out a ruined and despoiled hold where perhaps no one had gone for more than the length of her own lifetime.

This was it—the moment when she must share part of her confidence or be defeated before she began. How much would he believe—that she had indeed been compelled by dreams to seek out a heritage, the nature of which she herself did not know, save that it was of the utmost importance and that it must be found?

"There lies in Hawkholme that which I must find." Tirtha chose her words carefully, with no talk of dreams that had pressed so heavily upon her that all her life had led to this journey. "I *must* seek it out. Only it would seem that there are others who would have it also. I do not know why I must do this," she felt constrained to add, though perhaps it was self defeating with such a listener. "It is laid upon me. Have you of the Eyrie never heard of a geas?"

Almost she thought that she saw his lips begin once again to shape the word "witchery" as they had done so often before. Yet he did not say it when he spoke after a short moment of silence.

"There was told to us the tale of Ortal. . . ." He might be drawing something from deep memory. "Yes, I have heard of a geas—and of how such may be laid upon one, allowing no freedom until the deed is accomplished. Ortal took ship in the days of Arkel, who was the sixth Master in the Eyrie, because he offended one with the Power, and it was set upon him to obey, and no ransom offer from the Master could break it. It is a hard thing that you do then, Lady."

That he would accept so readily her explanation of what brought her south was a relief.

"Then you know why I must ride. But again I will say to you, Falconer, and to Alon, this binding is not for you, and you should not follow me. I do not know what lies now in or about Hawkholme, but it is no pleasant or easy thing that I must do."

He gestured with his claw as if to silence her. "Perhaps this Gerik is a part of what would prevent your accomplishing your task. We ride . . ." Without another word he pulled ahead a little, and she thought it better not to trouble him with any new protest at this time. That he was a strongly stubborn man she had known from their first meeting. It could well be that he now believed his honor was engaged, which would seal their companionship tighter than any bargain formally struck.

"This Ettin"—she turned to Alon, for he continued to ride beside her as the Falconer drew a little apart—"he was a young man?"

"He looked so. He did not talk much, but he had guesting manners, and Parlan took a liking to him. He tried to tell the stranger that to ride alone to the south was a danger for any man, but his answer was always that he did as he must do. He had a fine mail shirt and a plain helm such as the Borderers wore, and his sword was a good one. But he had no dart gun nor any bow such as you carry. He was a good man, I think."

She remembered a slender, fair-haired boy who had grown so fast, who had ridden with a small border company of patrolers when he was not far out of childhood—for there were few children along the fringe land. They learned early lessons which carried them into playing the parts of men and women. She and he had met twice under the roof that had been her first home, or the roof that had sheltered her from birth, but they had not known each other well. Kin of part blood they were.

How had the Hawk ring come to Ettin, and what had led him to attempt this lone journey ahead of her? Was he also dream-led? Was there a power playing with them and perhaps with others also, such as that stranger whose mail had borne the Hawk emblem and who had died of wounds in the wilderness? Him she had never seen, nor had she heard of

any of her House elsewhere in Estcarp. The Houses and Clans of the Old
Race were tight knit, holding together the stronger because all else had
been torn from them. If there had been other survivors of Hawkholme,
then through the years—as refugees poured over the mountains and thereafter joined the Border legions—such would have drawn together, for
there had been much passing of names and messages among all who had
fled and were seeking the fate of kinsfolk.

The gravel-paved valley sloped upwards, and the Falconer waved
back a signal to dismount, so that they advanced on foot at a slow pace,
leading their animals, the bird taking once more to the air. At last, leaving
the three beasts to be rein-held by Alon, the girl and the man crawled on
their bellies to look down a far slope.

Nearly beyond eye distance traveled a party of riders, seemingly with
no desire to hide their presence. To the east Tirtha sighted the landmark
that had been so plain in her trance—the cliff with its black bands. She
pointed to it.

"That is the first of my trailmarkings."

"How do they ride?" He lifted the claw in a slight gesture toward the
knot of men proceeding easily at a distance-eating trot.

She considered, then had to speak the unhappy truth. "They ride in
the same direction as we must go."

In her own mind she no longer doubted that their destination must be
the same as hers—Hawkholme. Was Ettin one of them? No, if he had
been among the riders at the garth, Alon would have known him. Nor
could she believe that he, being who he was, had been drawn into any service of the Dark.

The Falconer studied the ground before them, in particular the fringe
of trees to the east.

"With those for cover, and warnings from the Brother-in-Feathers,"
he said slowly, "we follow."

Tirtha thought of the sinister wood that would form the second stage
of their journey. It was fitted perfectly for ambush, so she spoke of it
while the Falconer listened. He glanced at the sky. The sun was well west,
near time for a night camp, though it must be a dry one, and they might go
hungry.

"They do not ride as if they believed any watched them. Men do not
go openly through such a land as this unless they have reason to think
themselves beyond pursuit."

"Or else," she commented dryly, "they set themselves as bait to draw
those they wish to take."

"Yes, there is that. But what Wind Warrior can do, he will, and in this
open country he can see if they are joined or if they have any contact with

others. You are right concerning the danger of the wood ahead. There even his sight cannot serve us, so we shall have to go with full caution. But for now, let us try for those trees and there take cover until morning. Or perhaps even wait out the coming day and move on at night."

Night was when the Dark held its greatest power, and Tirtha did not forget that, with those ahead, there rode a servant of evil. On the other hand, perhaps the others believed that any such travelers as this party of hers would not dare a journey in darkness. There were so many different things to think on. Suddenly she was tired, as worn as if she had tramped for days along an endless highway. She wanted rest, freedom from this burden, this geas, which had been thrust upon her and which she must continue to bear because of the blood that had been hers from birth.

11

They took cover in a fringe of trees, traveling slowly, while the falcon, in short flights, kept an eye on the party ahead. Those others continued to move in the open as if they had nothing to fear and a definite goal awaiting them.

It was the falcon, also, that brought from two of its ventures small hares, lean at this season, but still food, though they must eat the flesh raw, chewing at strips shaved from the carcasses. Tirtha, long since having learned that one could not be dainty during hard travel, accepted thankfully, even though her stomach was queasy.

They camped that night where the black-veined ledge descended into the earth. Ahead they could sight the forest, dark and threatening to the east, displaying even at this distance the thick weaving of its outer wall, a warning threat.

The party ahead did not attempt an entrance into the forest, though they had changed course to camp on land edging it. Nor did they hide their camp, for the wink of their fire was bright.

Making a last ascent into the dusk-curtained sky, the falcon circled toward it. When the bird returned, it eagerly reported to the man. He listened, though he himself was now only a blot of darkness Tirtha was hardly able to distinguish.

"One of their party is gone," he reported, when the bird was done. "Wind Warrior believes he has entered the wood. That holds danger. Perhaps he goes to treat with what dwells there for a safe passage."

Something which *they* could not do, Tirtha thought bitterly. Or else the rider had been sent to set up the ambush that she suspicioned might await them. Her shoulders drooped. There was no question that she must go on, but why must she take these two with her, to add to her trials?

It was Alon who broke the silence, following upon the Falconer's translation of the report.

"You said"—he spoke to Tirtha—"that there were the remains of a road leading through the wood to your Hawkholme land. Then once men must have ridden it safely. Did not the Old Race have their own guards, not all of them men?"

"Guards—if those ever existed—" she answered out of a dull sense that she faced the impossible and could not hope for better, "who were of no service on the Day of the Homing. Hawkholme fell then, and that was many years ago. Any guards of my clan are dead or long since swept away."

To her surprise the Falconer said slowly, "There is this—only the mountains' fall brought down the Eyrie. For we in turn had safeguards that were greater than men with sword and dart. Still . . ." His outline moved; she thought that he was putting out his arm, and she heard a small rustle of sound. Perhaps Wind Warrior was settling on his favorite perch, that metal claw. "Some of what we had remains there. Otherwise the Brother-in-Feathers would not have come to me. His kin remembered across the years. Do not dismiss too quickly what our little brother suggests. There might yet be something that will answer to your blood even as Wind Warrior came to me."

She gave a bitter bark of laughter. "There is nothing to aid and everything to stand against me. I say *me*—for I will not have the two of you on my conscience, knowing that I may lead you into what may be worse than any death by steel. Alon has already tasted of what this Gerik can turn against one. None of us has any knowledge of shield-building by ritual or appeal to Power. That forest is bad. What waits beyond is worse."

Unseen, her fingers moved in age-old signs, warding off evil fate. Some signs she had always known, some she had learned with difficulty, but these gestures carried with them no authority at all. If she were like Yachne, perhaps, Tirtha could stand against the Dark; but she was not a Wise Woman, certainly no Witch.

"To think of defeat is to summon it." Out of the dark Alon's voice was that of a man, save for its higher pitch. "You would not have been called unless there was a chance."

"What if," she retorted between her teeth, "I was brought hither to satisfy some purpose of the Dark—a sacrifice? How can I swear that this is not so? There were forces in Karsten that always hated and feared my kind. In the past some of them linked with Kolder. Perhaps now they strike bargains with another power."

Her depression was like a thick cloud. She had never so mistrusted the future. Before, the need for the quest had upborne her through much trouble, nor had she been visited by such feelings of despair and helplessness.

Fingers caught at her moving hands, wrapped about them tightly, holding with a fierce grip.

"Swordmaster"—Alon's voice sounded as sharply as one summoning another to battle—"your sword! There is a shadow striving to engulf her."

Tirtha struggled to free her hands from the boy's hold. He—they must go, leave her now! There welled up inside her such a wave of darkness as she had never known. This was not the icy evil that had struck at her during that farseeing. Rather it appeared to be a part of herself, born out of her own fears and doubts, out of every disappointment, hardship, and past danger she had fought. It welled up, filled her, was sour in her mouth, invaded and routed coherent thought. She wanted nothing but to be free of it—of this other self—to find peace, peace forever and ever, all struggle gone.

She felt, through that dreadful fog, pain that was not this new and frightening pain of body and inner essence, but physical pain. Tirtha struggled to win free—to be herself.

"Hold her—the sword—take it . . ." A voice thin, far away, meaning nothing.

Let her be free—at peace! She could not think; she was filled with fear and despair that clawed within her, tearing down, crushing.

"Hold her! She is invaded!" Again that voice. The words were meaningless. There was nothing left for her. Dark—into the Dark—let her go into the Dark. There lay peace, rest, a refuge.

She saw nothing but threatening shadow arising from a depth in her she had not realized existed. Therein crawled all the harshness of her life, all the self-denials that she had made. Now she was alone with the worst that dwelt within her. To face it was breaking her so that only—only death . . . Death—if that would come at a call! Tirtha felt an ache in her throat as if she shouted aloud to summon the end. What she was now was as monstrous as anything that could come crawling out of Escore to run through these hills. *She* was the monster, the evil, she polluted the world—she. . . .

Within that shadow she writhed in a torment worse than any torment of body, for torture of one's body could end in death. For her there would be no death, no peace, no. . . .

"Tirtha—Tirtha!" The voice was very, very far away—so thin that she could hardly hear it. Nor did she want to. There could be no one else in this evil world she had made for herself. She had fashioned this horror, unknowingly perhaps. Still it had grown out of *her*—let it not engulf anyone else.

She could not drive the murk from her mind, still she was dimly aware of other warmth.

"Tirtha!" A voice not so faint, possessing more depth, stronger, even more demanding than that other one. She strove to turn, twist, to outrace the voice.

But she was held. Her body lay against another's, immobilized. For a second or two—the length of perhaps a heartbeat—that realization pierced through the emergence of the *thing* to which her inner spirit had given birth.

Tirtha strangled on a cry, begging for release, lest this other presence be tainted, befouled, lest he suffer because of her.

"No." So emphatic was the denial that it broke through to her. "No, this is not of you, you are not so . . ."

She thought that she whimpered as her strength fast drained away. The shadow was winning; it was possessing the last remnants of her, devouring all she had believed once that she was or could be. That belief was built on rot within her.

"Tirtha!" Again that summons.

Then like a sun rising into the cloudless sky on a fair day of spring when the renewing of life could be believed in, the heart know a stir of joy and well-being, a spark of light rayed through the fog of evil about her. Larger, stronger grew that pinpoint. She was aware of another strength that pushed into the murk of her own failure.

Slowly, steadily it pushed. There came a sharp innermost thrust that pierced directly to the heart of what she now was. Death? If so, welcome.

Once more there whirled through her mind all that she had done, all that she had made of herself until this hour. However, the light followed, fought against sick self-contempt, her deep debasement of spirit. That portion of her confidence, which had been defeated, beaten into the ground, stirred. Slowly, oh, so slowly, a part of her answered the light, was nourished by it. Her thoughts no longer drew pictures of all that had gone wrong in the past—the least of those actions weighing against the good in her.

Again Tirtha strove to ask for help as she had done once before, only this was for help against her own being, a prayer that she be strengthened to face what she was and accept all her faults. The warmth which held her fed that need for comfort and strength of will, even as did the light.

She sighed, and the shadow no longer pressed in so tightly. Yes, this she had done and that, she had been harsh and cold and wrapped within herself, but she was no longer so utterly alone. There was a presence with her lifting her up and out, and out. . . .

Tirtha saw the blur of a face close to hers, another beyond. She lay within a firm hold, while both her hands were imprisoned in another grasp, so tightly that her flesh was pinched and cramped. There was dark about the three of them. However, not that terrible inner darkness that had captured her without warning; this was the natural dark of the night. The Falconer held her, supported her, as he had when she emerged from the trance, while Alon knelt, her hands in his.

"I . . ." She tried to speak, to tell them. It was the Falconer who laid his sword-calloused hand across her lips.

In his claw, as it came about her shoulder, rammed well into the grasp of that cold metal, was the weapon of power. Light shone from it—lighter in color, not blue, but a golden-white—to illuminate all their faces. He had thrown off his helm, was unmasked, and as she looked up into his face, it was no longer impassive. Tirtha could not have said what the strange expression she saw there meant, save that he was more moved by some emotion than she had ever seen him. The flames in his eyes were steady while he watched her searchingly as if she were a land—a gate—that must be defended from all comers.

His bird, which she believed would never leave him, perched on Alon's shoulder as the boy knelt before her. The avian eyes flamed with a fierce light, and the head turned at an angle to survey her with a predator's steady, unblinking gaze.

Alon's small face was nearly ashen in spite of the warmth of the color from the weapon's glow. His lips were pinched between his teeth, and there was such strain in his face as she believed he might have shown had he once more confronted Gerik's men.

"I . . ." She turned her head, slipped the Falconer's hold from off her lips. "I was . . ."

"In the Dark." The man answered her somberly. "This attack . . ."

Alon interrupted him. "You met that which only the Full Dark can summon."

It was her turn to protest. "Not from without." It was difficult to find the proper words. Her mind felt benumbed, beaten and sore, as might her body had she come through, survived only by inches, some battle. "It was inside—inside me."

Alon shifted a little, settling back on his heels. "You even tried to use your sword—against yourself." He had dropped his hold on her hands; now he motioned to what lay between them—that old, worn blade that was her talisman. "What possessed you would have made you self-slain."

"Possessed . . ." Tirtha repeated his words. She had heard, had read of possession. That had been the worst and greatest weapon of the Kolder. Was this how they had possessed men's bodies—turned them into their dead-alive servants? No, that had been done in another way—by the machines that had been destroyed in Gorm, so completely broken that no living man could hope to puzzle out their dread secrets. Yet now she said the only word that had once fitted such a state. "Kolder."

The Falconer shook his head. The expression she had not been able to read had vanished. His features were again set in the somber mold they had always worn. "Kolder is gone. This is another matter."

Tirtha roused herself, feeling that she must explain, must make them understand for their own sakes what she had learned within that shadow—that she carried in her the seeds of dire things, and the longer they companioned her, the more danger for them. All the truths and memories that shadow had used to weigh her down into despair still lay in her mind. This last crime she would not have added to the score to be balanced against her.

"It showed me to myself—what I have been, what I am. I beg you— go, if you have any compassion for me, you have no reason to do more than wish me well and ride. Grant me this much: that you will not be drawn into darkness because you think it your duty to follow where I must travel. Let me go alone; so take such an added burden from me."

Alon's lips parted as if he would speak, but it was the Falconer who answered first.

"Would you play *its* game then? I think, Lady, that you have too much courage to allow yourself to be so misled. Look you to what has happened. We are yet afar from Hawkholme, and yet something which has great witchery seeks to separate us. Therefore it fears. For only against what we fear, do we begin battle or launch a surprise attack. We do not know even the nature of this enemy. However, it would seem to me that when we unite, as we have done twice now, we provide it with a problem: strength it fears to face.

"In Karsten in the long ago the Kolder worked so; deep was their intriguing, their possession of Yvian and others near him, which led him to drive forth your people. And the reason for that was that Kolder could not take over one of the Old Race. The Old Race had to die because they could not be bent to another's will. To seek to divide when there are allies united in strength is a very ancient move of strategy. If we ride hence, and you go on alone, then *it* has won. Do you wish such a victory, Lady? I think not, that is not in you. This enemy seeks to strike through your sense of duty, would set upon you the illusion that you already serve evil and so will lead you to open a door for it."

Tirtha watched his face, intent upon his words, and she knew that he spoke in all sincerity. That part of her which had been awakened through his efforts, through Alon's—the belief in herself, was now strengthened. She was as one recovering from an illness who feels the touch of return-

ing health. There was good council in what he said. Suppose she had succeeded, and these two left her at her demand?

It might not matter that she went on to oblivion save that, though she
in herself did not count, what she must do had strong reason and purpose.
As Tirtha faced that thought, another clear flow of energy surged into her,
bringing with it the will to banish the last of the shadow.

Also, breaking their bonds with her now might not save the Falconer
and Alon. Alon was the one to point that out.

"They will search for us, even if you send us from you, Lady Tirtha.
We have been one. If they take you, then maybe they can still compel us
to them—or it—because of that very fact. We have made a choice. . . ."

The girl shook her head a fraction. "I have forced one on you," she
corrected.

"Not so," was the Falconer's quick denial. "I have long thought that
perhaps we are all under a geas—that you came to me in Romsgarth not by
chance but by purpose. I was minded to ride that very morning for the coast.
My comrades were dead; I felt but half a man. There was nothing to hold me
to the hills. Yet against my own planning, I returned again to the market
because"—for the first time real puzzlement crossed his face—"I cannot
tell you why. And see, already I am more of a man, once more a warrior with
a feathered brother, such as I had never hoped to be again. That, too, was not
chance. Wind Warrior was waiting for one he believed would come."

"And I would have died," Alon said softly. "I think you yourself this
night touched on the same death that would have taken me. But you and
the Swordmaster and Wind Warrior, you brought me to life and awakened
in me that which I had never understood, so that I had only a half life
before. Can you say all of this was by chance alone?"

Tirtha moistened her lips with tongue tip, staring first at the Falconer
in whose arms she still rested, then at the boy, who was certainly more
than he seemed to the outer eye—at last to the bird on his shoulder. The
wall she had built around her for years had cracked.

"I do not know what must be sought at Hawkholme," she said, "but it
is of importance to more than me. I have come to believe that my clan
were guardians of something of great value, which must be found. They
say that very ancient powers are awake and move in Escore from which
our blood first came. Did those of my House bring with them some
weighty symbol of force, some treasure, which is needed now in the war
that rages there between the Dark and the Light? If only I had more of the
talent . . ." Her old regret was heavy in her voice. "Perhaps had I been
trained and not had to forage for myself, garnering bits and pieces I have
not the wit to use, I could foresee as well as farsee. I am not a Wise
Woman."

"You do not know yet what you are," the Falconer interrupted her. "Make no statement that you are not this or that. But this I know." He looked straight into her eyes. "Our bargain has changed, Lady. There are no twenty days of service. No, what lies between us now shall continue to the end, whether you will it or no. That is the way that things must be."

He used her with a gentleness she did not expect, had not known that one of his schooling could summon, wrapping her in her cloak, settling her with one of the limp saddlebags for a pillow. Then he held the power sword in the air. Its light had faded to the smallest glimmering, hardly more than the flash of a night-flying insect. But by it she could still see the blur of his face and believed that he was staring upon what he held.

"This came into my hand, even though those of my blood trust not in things that are of witchery. Yet it slipped into my hold as if it were made for no other man in this world. That is another sign that I am one in this quest. I, too, have a geas laid upon me to bear this where it must go, wield it as it must be used. I do not know, but perhaps he who was Nirel has died, and I am someone else. If that is so, then I must learn who. Now, Lady, I set it on you to sleep, for you have come through such a fight as would exhaust any warrior. And the feathered brother, though he hunts by day, is an excellent sentinel, so we need not keep watch and watch. Tomorrow we face perhaps other trials, but those are for the morning and one does not look ahead for the evil that may lie in wait."

She was indeed tired. His voice had softened, lost that harsh bite it so often carried. Now it seemed a flow of reason, carrying her easily with it, sliding into rest, which was not the dark peace she had sought, the nothingness of non-being, but rather that which renewed both body and spirit.

Alon, the blanket that had been rolled behind the Torgian's saddle wrapped around him, settled down so that she need not even reach forth a hand more than a palm's width away to touch him. And she heard movements through the dark that told her the Falconer was also seeking rest. What had happened tonight, Tirtha still did not understand. But she was too weary to seek an answer; there would be time with morning light for that.

There was warmth on her face when she opened her eyes again; a patch of sun lay across her cheek, having found entrance between two overhead branches. It required determination and will for her to pull herself up and allow the cloak to fall away. For a single moment of surprise and confusion, she thought that for all their talk the other two had obeyed her and gone their own way, for there was no one in sight. Then the evidence of the saddles to one side, their bags lying beside them, was proof that they had not left. Near her was a broad leaf on which rested two long white roots so recently washed free of earth that stray drops of water lay upon them. Beside them a water bottle sat upright.

She recognized the roots as ones Alon dug now and then. Eaten raw, they were crisp and slightly biting to the tongue but palatable. So she ate and drank, finding that she was near famished, and then wobbled to her feet, leaning back against the trunk of the tree under which she had lain. There was a swishing in the brush as Alon pushed through, his face lighting as he saw her.

He came across the small open space into which they had edged their camp to catch one of her hands, holding it in both of his.

"Tirtha, it is well with you?" His eyes sought hers and satisfaction grew in his expression. "You slept—ah, how you slept."

She looked at the sun and suddenly felt guilty. "How long?"

"It is midday. But it does not matter. In fact, the Swordmaster said that it was a good thing. For he thought us best here until those others are well into the wood. Wind Warrior has gone to settle on one of the trees at the edge of it and watch what they do, look for any guards that may be on the prowl there. Swordmaster is hunting—he put down snares and caught two meadow hens. Also he believes that we dare light a fire if we keep it under cover here."

Alon made a small face. "I do not like raw hare; this is better." He loosed his hold on her and briskly set to work with the bundle of sticks he had dropped when he first sighted her, laying them with care, choosing only the driest, those least liable to give forth smoke.

When the Falconer returned, he had two plump birds swinging from his belt. Also he told her he had found a small side dell in which the ponies and the Torgian had been put on picket lines and were grazing well.

"We are a day late," she said, as he plucked the birds skillfully and impaled them on sticks, to be set to broil at the pocket of fire Alon tended.

"Time not wasted," he reassured her. "It is best to have those well ahead. We shall take the trail tonight. I would not cross the open in the day. And there may be something of a storm later to give us cover." To her eyes, he seemed his old self, impersonal and intent on what he conceived his duties. She was well content to have it so. Her own shell of independence seemed to her at this moment a cloak she did not want to discard.

12

The night was moonless, cloaked by clouds from which fell a drizzle, searching out every opening in their clothing. Tirtha had insisted on mounting the Torgian, bringing Alon with her under what protection her cloak could afford. They kept as much as they could to ways that trees overhung, giving them whatever shelter possible. Wind Warrior reported at dusk that those they trailed had taken to the woods and that they had left no sentry or spy behind.

The three still had no assurance that they were not seen, or sensed, and what lay ahead might not lead to an ambush. Thus they moved slowly, the Falconer as scout. He fell quickly into a pattern that Tirtha was sure he had long ago often followed.

It must have been well past the mid-hour of the night when they at last approached the bush-veiled entrance into the old wood road. In this dark the forest was even more overpowering with its thick shadows, and for the past hour or so, Tirtha had kept doubly alert, striving to pick up any sense of being under observation, such as she had known when her vision had laid open this passage. She dared not, of course, probe too deeply, lest she rouse that which might, so far, have been unaware of their coming. It could well be an entity able to detect a farseer.

The boy in her hold had ridden passively enough, making no sound, during those hours when they had traveled so slowly and cautiously toward their goal. But as the Falconer headed his pony into that near-masked opening of the forest road, Alon stirred, his voice came as a whisper, hardly more than a breath.

"This is a place that lives. . . ." He spoke as one who did not quite understand or, if knowing, could not find proper words to make plain his warning.

Tirtha bent her head so that her lips could not be far from Alon's nearest ear:

"Are we watched?" Her whisper was as low as she could make it.

"I . . . I think not . . . not yet," he returned.

Her own eyes swept from one side of the trail to the other, seeking that wisp of thing that had entwined itself among the trees during her vision of this place. That, she was certain, had been of the Dark, also of a nature far removed from a common existence with those who called themselves human. Let *that* come upon them in its own place and—she disciplined her thoughts, refused to allow fear to rise the higher.

Ahead, the Falconer was hardly to be seen. His bird had joined him at the wood's edge to ride now on the saddle perch. However, if Tirtha could not follow them directly with her own sight, it appeared that her present mount had no difficulty in keeping up with the lead pony, just as her own mare crowded in behind. The three beasts drew as close as they might in such a narrow way without being urged.

There was a glimmer of pallid, faint light on her right. Tirtha's heart beat faster for a succession of thumps until she located the source as one of those stones that marked the road they must travel, as her vision had shown her. She did not like that glow; it carried some of the pallid obscenity of the night fires given off by certain fungi she had seen— loathsome, evil-smelling growths, by tradition nourished by the bodies of unburied dead.

At least the rain was partially kept from them by the overhanging branches of the trees, so she could push back the hood of her cloak, affording her a clearer sight of the way. Then Alon moved in her hold. His hand closed about one of her arms tightly, before his grasp relaxed a trifle. She took that as a warning.

Yes!

What she had thought to face ever since they had headed into this shadowed forest was coming. As yet perhaps it had no more than vaguely sensed them, or maybe it was only making sentry rounds. But Tirtha's skin crawled as she felt the deadly cold spreading before it. Like that monstrous thing which had sought mindlessly to get at her and the Falconer back in the mountains, so was this not of her world. The impact of it was like an open-handed blow.

Whether the Falconer had picked it up also, she could not tell. Yet here the trail widened out a fraction so that the Torgian, without her urging, matched pace with the pony. Thus she dared to loose part of her hold on Alon and put out her hand in turn to touch the man's arm.

He did not return her touch. Still Tirtha sensed, as she had never done before, that he realized what message she would send to alert him and that he was already aware of the prowler. They might still retreat, get out of this place overwhelmed by the shadow. Yet that would solve nothing, for the geas held fast for her, and this was the only road to what she sought.

Their mounts plodded ahead. There were more of those glimmering stones, some set sentrywise along the trail, others to be glimpsed back in the woods. Tirtha, tense in the saddle, sought with what skill was hers to pick up the skulker in that place of utter blackness.

It was like seeing a distant flicker, visible for one second, gone the next, only to show again. This did not register in her eyes, rather in her mind. Whatever creature skulked here was far removed from man or animal. She heard Alon draw a deep breath, a fraction later his whisper reached her again.

"Think of light—of good . . ." His words trailed away, leaving Tirtha for a second uncomprehending. Then she understood. Fear was so often the first weapon of Dark Ones. Perhaps the three of them could indeed draw a curtain between themselves and this thing by bringing to the fore of their minds all that was right and natural, good and clean, within their own world.

She strove to build up a mind picture of the fields of Estcarp where she had labored only last harvesttime, swinging a sickle with the skill she had learned, gathering to her armloads of sun-warmed, fragrant grain. Here were the brilliant eyes of the field flowers making splotches of color—scarlet, yellow, against the gold. Sun lay warm on her shoulders, and there was still the taste upon her lips of apple squeezings which a serving maid had brought in leathern bottles to satisfy the thirst of the reapers.

Sun, color, the gold of grain ripe and ready for the harvest. There was the piper who sat cross-legged on the wall toward which the harvesters were working their way, and the trilling of his instrument roused hearty voices into song. She could feel the sun, taste the apple juice, hear the pipe song even here in the dark. Nor dared she break the web she so strove to weave, though the temptation to do so pressed ever on her.

The trail that had been so narrow at the entrance widened out. Now and then a hoofbeat raised an echo of sound, as if, under the blanket of last season's leaves, there lay an ancient pavement.

So they came into what was a clearing, though ragged-walled, with an outgrowth of brush seeking to reclaim it. Those unhealthy stones were hereabouts in thick company, a number of them set on end to the north to form a rude barrier. But it was what lay in the very center of that way which held them where they were on the edge of this opening.

Lying crosswise on a patch of bared stone were two staffs or wands—

wood that had been stripped of bark and shone bone white. Between them, positioned with care to form two sides of four squares, were skulls. These were old, greenish, as if overgrown in part by some vile lichen, and each had been braced to lie face up, the eyepits, the gaping jaws turned toward the sky.

Skulls, yes, but of no normal living thing Tirtha knew. The general shape *was* human in part, save there were heavy ridges of bone above the eye sockets. It was the jaws and lower sections that were the strangest— long cruel teeth sprouted still from the bone there, teeth that must have protruded far out and down from the flesh that had once lipped the mouths. Also there was a forethrust of the jaw line itself which hinted at a muzzle.

Like the thing on the mountain. Tirtha's memory flashed the picture of it as she looked upon this carefully wrought warning, if warning it was.

She was aware of movement to her right. The Falconer was no longer sitting quiet in his saddle. A flash of light through the air . . . Into that display of wood and bone whirled something that came to life in the night with a flare like that of a torch hurled into dry brush.

Point down it struck, straight into the crossing of the staffs, metal biting into the wood. From that point of contact there burst a true flame which ran out along the lengths of the staffs, bringing light to bathe them all.

Was it only a sorcerous illusion, or did those greened skulls open yet wider their fanged jaws as the flames reached out eagerly to lick across each they passed? Had she heard a wailing afar in the distance, or if not in earthly distance in another place? Had that fire, which looked to be here and now, touched also into a world that lay beyond one of the fabled gates? Tirtha only knew that she felt—heard, sensed, she was not sure which—a moment of torment, and then a wink out of a life or lives which had no being in this time and place.

The skulls took fire, each exploding with a burst of sound that she heard. Already the staffs were but lines of ash laid upon the ground. The Falconer urged his pony on, leaned from the saddle to hook his claw about the hilt of the dagger knife which he had so thrown, drawing it out of the ashes that the hooves of his mount had stirred into nothingness.

"Well done." Alon's voice came, not in the faint whisper he had used since they had entered the wood, but as if there was nothing to fear now.

"How"—Tirtha ran her tongue across her lower lip—"how did you know?"

This was witchery, and he had always turned from it, shunned it as she would a manifestation of the Dark. Yet she had seen him now take on the practice of a Warlock.

Alon came to sudden life in her arms, plunging against her lax hold and so leaping forward to the ground.

"'Ware!" The alarm came out of him in a child's voice. Still there was a man's urgency in that cry.

Tirtha swept back the folds of her cloak. The Torgian had moved up beside the Falconer's pony, and the mare crowded in against the two of them. Alon reached up and caught a handful of the coarse mane of that smaller beast, drew himself up on the riding pad. The falcon mantled, screamed a challenge.

She drew her worn sword. They had somehow gotten into a defense position, the three of them facing outward, the rumps of their mounts pressed together, each fronting a separate portion of the wood about them. Was the destruction of the warning—or the spell—leading to outright attack?

They came out from the strange stones afoot, shadows flitting from shadows. Smaller than men, yes, and carrying with them a stench that Tirtha had come to associate with creatures of the Dark. She saw flames of eyes turned toward her, yet it would appear that, though they now ringed in the three, they were not ready for an outright attack. Instead they fell into a shuffling circle around about the riders, staying out of range of steel.

The Falconer had his dart gun. Tirtha wondered why he did not put it to use, pick off some of those moving creatures. The targets they provided were not so difficult that his aim could not have removed them as they passed him in that circling.

Her sword was little enough defense, yet she slipped from her belt sheath her hunting knife, reached out to press it into Alon's hand. It was all she had in the way of an extra weapon.

From her left there was a glow. The weapon of power which the Falconer had retrieved before the emergence of these night crawlers was ablaze. She could not see that he had armed himself otherwise. Perhaps he had come to depend upon this strange arm more than he did on the weapons he had always known.

Their shaggy attackers—if attackers these were indeed—made no sound save by the shuffling of their feet as they kept their circle moving. Though they stood upright and had only four limbs, they were certainly not of her race, nor of any that approached the human blood. They wore no clothing. The glow from the weapon revealed, as they passed, squat bodies covered with a thick growth of such coarse hair or bristles that they might have had fine roots instead of natural strands sprouting forth. The round heads were marked by no visible features, save eyes that were pits of red fire, and were set directly on their wide shoulders. Their overlong upper limbs dangled so that their claws nearly brushed the ground, though they held themselves upright as they scuttled about.

The circle which they wove was not an even one. They pressed closer toward Tirtha and Alon, kept a farther distance from the Falconer. In him they might believe that they had a more formidable opponent. Why they did not launch their attack puzzled Tirtha. She began to believe they were only a delaying device, and the real strength of those who held the wood as their domain had yet to show itself.

For the second time, the falcon screamed. Those of the haired things nearest it at the time wavered. It would appear that they liked that sound no better than the sight of the sword-knife which blazed ever higher with its own light.

Just as silently and swiftly as the beast things had appeared from the stones there emerged another. This was no hair-coated shuffler. Instead he strode into the foreground, the shamblers breaking their circle to let him enter, before resetting their ring.

Tirtha surveyed him steadily. He was truly human in the size and pro-portion of his limbs and body, and he wore mail, leggings and boots, and a helm. At first glance he could have been any border rover or perhaps an outlaw more cunning and with better luck at looting than most.

Unlike the Falconer's helm, this one's helmet did not hide the fea-tures of the wearer, nor did he have looped about his throat twin veils of silken-fine chain mail which afforded battle protection for the men of Estcarp.

His features were well cut, regular, and of the cast of the Old Race, though the eyes by which he regarded the three were not normal. Rather they held a tinge of red like those of the shambling creatures he com-manded. Though he wore a sword, as well as a dagger, he advanced empty-handed, the long fingers of his hands oddly pale in the half-light. There was no badge on the breast of his mail coat. However, on the center ridge of his helm was fastened a carefully wrought, hideous creature which might be a snake with stumpy legs, or a lizard of misshapen form. This had specks of gems for eyes—sparks that caught the light strongly to reflect it with unusual power.

He did not speak, rather examined one after another. When that level and measuring gaze traveled over Tirtha she was hard put to hold herself steady. Accompanying it was a lapping, a pulling at her mind, an attempt to empty her of all she thought or was or would be and do. She resisted, expe-riencing a recoil of surprise as if he had not thought to feel any resistance.

For the third time, the falcon screamed. The man stood halfway between Tirtha and the Falconer, his attention having passed on to the lat-ter. What would he meet there? Was the Falconer also inwardly armed, or did he lack her own protections? Yet the weapon was his, and no one of a lesser breed could have it fit his hand so well.

Still silent, the man from the forest took another stride to the left until he fronted Alon with his compelling gaze. Tirtha twisted about in the Torgian's saddle to witness that meeting. There had been no change of expression on the stranger's face, in fact no expression at all. For all his partaking of any of the emotions of the living, he might well have been one of the infamous dead-alive from which the Kolder had fashioned their armies. Yet this one was very much of a power, and what dwelt within that outer covering of mankind was to be distrusted, perhaps even rightly feared.

He gave the boy only one long, searching stare. Then once more his attention shifted to Tirtha herself, and for the first time he spoke:

"Welcome, Lady, to that which is rightfully yours." His voice was surprisingly gentle and courteous in tone. He might have been greeting a guest at the door of a holding, the plate with bread, salt and water held ready for the sealing of the guesting bond.

She found her own voice, glad for the breaking of the silence that had covered much.

"I make no claims on this land," she returned. "This is no rule hold of mine."

"It is of the Hawk that was," he returned. "Though the years have dealt hardly with it of late. And do you not"—he made a light gesture with one hand to the sword she had bared—"carry the Hawk's weapon by right of blood?"

How he knew this (had he picked it out of her mind though she thought she was closed to his probe?) was a blow, but Tirtha believed that she had not allowed him to guess he scored against her.

"Hawkholme lies beyond. I make no claims, wood lord. If the years have wrought a difference, then let it so abide. Rule you as you will."

To her amazement he bowed gracefully with the ease of one who had been born to sit in a hall's high seat.

"You are gracious, Lady, and generous," though if she was not mistaken there was clearly a note of mockery in that. "To give freely what cannot be held might seem to some to be a superfluity. I do not believe you deal in such. You seek Hawkholme, but you are not alone in that. I think"—for the first time there was a curve of his well-cut lips as if he smiled—"that it might be amusing to see how you will deal with *them*."

"And who are *they*?" the Falconer demanded.

The stranger's smile grew a fraction wider. He shook his head.

"Such a valiant company." His mockery was at last open and it had that in it which stung, though Tirtha had long ago schooled herself against any serious acceptance of her quest. "Such a very valiant company! And who can say whether the Greater Powers may not be amused enough to allow you, in your time, some advantage. I think I shall step aside, since you, Lady, have been so gracious as to invest me in my ruler-ship, and allow this game to be played to the end without me. It"—now he glanced at Alon and his smile faded a fraction—"might have certain aspects that do not appear openly at present. So . . ." he swept her a second bow, then gestured. The haired things broke their circle, opening a way before Tirtha, who faced that gap in the wood where the path led on again. "Pass, Lady. And when you come into your full inheritance, remember that what you have surrendered was by your choice, and you have made a bargain. . . ."

"I have not!" she caught him up. "There is no oath-swearing between us, forest lord. No oath-taking nor giving. I have said only I do not want what you have claimed. What I seek lies elsewhere. But you are not sworn to me, nor am I turf-enfiefed to you!"

He nodded. "Cautious, yes. As well might you be, Lady. I will concede that we are not oath-bound. I owe no shield service and come not before your high seat."

"Be it so." She said the old words denying fiefship with emphasis. No pact with the Dark. Perhaps in even accepting this much from him, she was making a mistake. But it was true—even if all Hawkholme hailed her as liege lady, which she did not expect—she wanted no rulership over this dire wood.

"Yet"—the Falconer urged his pony a step or so closer to the stranger. He had not sheathed the weapon of power, and in what appeared a half-involuntary motion, the man from the forest raised his hand as if to shield his eyes from the shine of the weapon. "Yet, still you have not answered me. Who are they with whom we shall deal?"

The forest stranger shrugged. "To you I owe no answer, Swordsman. You have chosen your own road. Ride it or leave it as you will. What you find on it is none of my affair."

"Still," Alon's childish voice broke through the antagonism that Tirtha could almost see forming between the two of them as a darker and even more ominous shadow. For there was something in the Falconer that answered to this other as one drawn sword rises to meet another when the battle is enjoined. "Still, since you have told us some, do you deny us the rest?"

He sat quietly on the mare, a child looking thoughtfully at the man. Tirtha watched the two of them. With every hour they rode together, she was surer that Alon was more than she could understand, that he was no son of the Old Race, but something different and perhaps far older and longer tied to the Power.

The features of the forest dweller lost their imperviousness. He registered cold anger now. Still it was anger strictly curbed, one that might consume but could not be released.

"Seek you also . . ." His voice had dropped, it held almost the hiss of the scaled ones in a slight slurring of the words. "You are not yet a commander of the Great Lords! Nor do you command *me!*" With that he turned and was gone, as if his will alone had wafted him from their sight. The haired ones scuttled back into the shadows, leaving the three alone.

Tirtha made no comment, falling in with the Torgian behind the two ponies, which now paced abreast down the wider trail leading out of the clearing. She was disturbed more than she wanted to admit, still she made herself face the fact that those she rode with were certainly not what they outwardly seemed. Alon, she had accepted from the first as a mystery, for his introduction into their company had come through such a feat of the Power as she had never known. However, the Falconer, whom secretly she had dismissed as a dour fighter with perhaps pain of body and mind behind him, but one so narrow of belief that he would or could have no part in any life save that he had been bred to—what indeed was this Falconer who had named himself and still was a man divided? One who strove inside him (of this she was somehow sure) to unite two vastly different ways of thought. He carried his weapon of power, and he had used it this night as one trained in at least the lesser mysteries. Yet he clung to his role of fighting man, and he had fronted the man of the wood openly to demand an accounting as would any blank shield on escort duty.

No, she was faced with many puzzles and perhaps two of them, which might yield difficulties in times to come, were the innermost natures of those who companioned her.

Why should she now question them when she must also honestly question herself? She was no longer sure either of Tirtha or what Tirtha might do or become. All she was certain of was that she must reach Hawkholme. What would chance thereafter? Her dream had never led her any farther than that single room somewhere within the ruined pile in which had been hidden that casket. She did not even guess what it held and what she would do with it thereafter. She was sure that the forest man had been right in his mockery. They were riding on blindly into perils that could be far greater than any this wood held.

It would seem that they had passed the worst the forest could offer. The withdrawal of the forest lord and his crew—the granting of an open road to them—ended her foreboding, the need for listening which held her since they entered on this forgotten road. He had released them—for what? Trials which he undoubtedly thought much worse and which would give him a perverse pleasure (even as he had admitted) to see them meet. She had no doubt that he firmly expected a sure and final defeat for them from such a meeting. Knowing that, her old stubbornness arose, and for all her realization that there was little in the way of preparation she could make against the unknown, Tirtha rode on with a straight back and high-held head, sword still in hand, threading among more thinly spaced trees and the shaggy brush that marked the other side of the wood—morning and Hawkholme lying before them.

13

Sun banners overspread the east when they left the wood. The Falconer halted behind a last screen of brush between them and open lands stretching to Hawkholme. The hold stood as Tirtha had visioned, stark amid desolate fields from which there had been no harvest for many years, though there was a straggle of blighted greenery rising raggedly now to greet the spring. No breaks showed in the walls of the hold, though the moat drawbridge had been destroyed.

The Falconer dismounted at the same moment his feathered scout winged out into the morning, rising so high that its black body was but a dot against the heavens.

"We are here, Lady. Is this not your Hawkholme?"

"It is the place of my vision, of the dreams." For the first time she mentioned them. Since he had chosen to ride the full way, then perhaps the time had come to be frank with him. She nodded toward the distant hold which had the appearance of a grim fortress. Those who had built it must have had good reason to believe that a time of trial would come.

"Within that lies what I must claim. I do not know why, but it is set upon me to do this."

His eyes, through the slits of his mask helm, were full upon her, measuring. However, it was Alon who spoke.

"There is that which waits." The boy shivered as his face turned toward the fortress.

Instantly, he gained the Falconer's attention.

"Gerik?" the man demanded, as if he believed that Alon's sight was as keen as that of his questing bird, could even pierce those fire-stained walls.

Again Alon shuddered. That horror and terror, which had before thrust him into deep inner hiding, might once more have reached out to touch him.

"Him, and the other, the Dark One. They wait. Also, they have that . . ." He shook his head from side to side, raised one hand to his forehead. "I cannot see . . ." There was a touch of fear in his voice. "Do not ask me."

"Close your mind!" Tirtha ordered. Here was the same problem that had existed in the night-haunted wood. Any use of a talent might well draw upon them attention they did not want. She turned to the Falconer.

"If there is an ambush within . . ." She need not carry that further; he nodded in turn.

"Yes." His head swung from right to left, as he surveyed the land before them for possible concealment. Then he gestured to the left and, remounting, led off, still within a fringe of wood, keeping it between them and the open. Tirtha had already sighted what must be his goal. The river, which watered the land before them and which, in part, had been diverted to fill the moat as one of the defenses of Hawkholme, had been bridged not too far from where they had emerged from the forest. A small ruined building stood on their side of that now-broken span. Tirtha was reminded that in Estcarp's far past shrines to unknown and long-forgotten powers had been so erected.

Certainly the tumbled walls of the small building gave forth no warning of any evil. Its stones were not of that loathsome gray-white such as stood in the wood. She longed to test by thought-probe, but knew she dared not. The Falconer held the point of his sword-dagger toward that possible shelter, and his attention swung between the stone rubble and the hilt of his weapon. He must have come to depend upon its efficiency for ferreting out traces of evil. However, the pommel remained opaque and lifeless.

They were favored in that the river here made a northern curve so that the ruined shrine stood not too far from their present screen. A river running from the east—Tirtha considered that. Where lay its source? There was the dim line of bluish heights across the eastern sky, the sun now above them. Beyond that barrier—Escore. A river born in those heights or even running through them from beyond—what might it carry out of that wild and Power-ridden land?

Why had her kin settled so close in the early days? Had their ties with the east been stronger than those generally nursed by others come to settle in the west, those who deliberately willed out of memory all thought of Escore? She knew the formal history of Karsten well enough—that the Old Race had settled the land, living quietly and without incident until the coming from the south of the invaders, those of a younger race with whom their predecessors had no ties, and from whose company they had withdrawn, farther back into the interior of the duchy. There had followed no intermingling of blood with the newcomers. And as their own numbers had never been many and they had kept aloof, they had gone without strife until Yvian and the Kolder had turned the country blood-mad against them. Was Hawkholme one of the very earliest holds in Karsten? Had its lords kept alive ties with Escore, the ancient homeland?

Tirtha was startled out of her musing when Alon pushed the mare to a quicker trot, sidled past the Falconer, and reaching the edge of brush, slipped from the pony, to drop to hands and knees in last year's brittle weeds. Then he went belly-flat, crawling so into the open, heading for the pile of rocks that marked the end of the broken bridge. A moment later she understood.

To ride into the open would certainly be to court notice from Hawkholme. They could not believe it was without sentries on watch. Wind Warrior was aloft, but who knew what eyes those inside might possess, just as keen and farsighted.

They could tether their animals here; there was rough grazing to keep them satisfied. Tirtha dismounted, stripped the Torgian of his gear, looping the straps of her nearly flat saddle bags over one shoulder, seeing that the Falconer was doing the same.

Once they had the three beasts on lines—the fastening of which the Falconer tested well—they, too, crawled to where Alon squatted behind a breastwork of fallen rocks, staring at the fortress. The protection was not much; the roof of the small building had vanished, but at least they had the best cover possible hereabouts.

Though Tirtha studied the distant ruin of the holding with strict attention, she caught no sign of movement there. She had half expected to experience again the cold attack that had struck at her in vision. Perhaps it attacked only in vision, and the next assault would come in bodily form. She knew so little, could only guess at what might lie ahead.

Alon did not move or look around as they joined him. He was as frozen in his place as he had been enwrapped in the catatonic state in which they had first found him. Except that he had not retreated into invisibility. Now Tirtha crept up cautiously, dared to put an arm about his thin shoulders. His utterly silent watchfulness she found disturbing.

"What do you see?" she asked, determined to break through this abnormal absorption.

"I see. . . ." He shook his head. "It is not see, Lady, it is feel—here!" He raised a small, grubby hand to plant its thumb between his eyes. "There is trouble, anger, someone is very angry. That is the one who, if he were not so angry, would be searching for us. But now he thinks only of this thing which feeds his rage. He . . ." That long set stare with which he regarded the fortress ahead broke as he turned his head a fraction to glance at Tirtha. "He causes pain to another, seeking to learn a secret, one that other does not know. Aieee—" Suddenly the boy clapped both hands to his ears as if shutting out dire sounds neither of his companions could hear. His face screwed into a mask of mingled fear and pain. "It is evil what he does—evil!"

The Falconer reached out his single hand, and with a gesture Tirtha would not have believed his breed capable of showing, he touched Alon very gently at the nape of his small thin neck, rubbing the flesh almost caressingly, as one might soothe a small trembling animal. The boy turned, drew out of Tirtha's loose hold, to fling himself into the man's arms, hiding his face against the tattered cloak across the Falconer's mailed breast.

"Little Brother"—the Falconer spoke in a voice that Tirtha had never thought to hear—"break that tie, do it swiftly! Yes, there is evil, but it does not touch you."

Alon raised his head. His eyes were closed; from under their lids, tears streaked down through the dust and grime on his thin cheeks. "It does, it does!" Now his hands became fists, and he no longer clung to the Falconer, rather pummeled him vigorously. "It is pain for all of us when evil strikes at the Light!"

"Well enough," the Falconer answered. "But we do not spend our own strength heedlessly. There is evil there, and without a doubt, we must face it sooner or later. Do not let it fore-weaken you, Little Brother. You have that within you which is ready for the battle when it comes, only it must not be wasted."

Alon stared up into the half-masked face, then smeared one hand across his own. "You are right," he said slowly, once more that odd note of seeming maturity back in his voice. "What strength one has must be saved for a time when it is most needed. I . . . I will not . . ." He fell silent as if whatever promise he would make was to himself. Then he detached himself from the Falconer and looked again to Tirtha.

"They have not thought of us. I think that they are sure we could never have won through the wood. They believe themselves—for now—safe!"

"They are indeed singularly lax," the Falconer observed slowly. "Why have we seen no sentry? And if they expected the forest to stop us, then why did we so easily win through?"

"Perhaps because of what you carry." Tirtha indicated the weapon once more within that inadequate sheath at his belt.

"Or perhaps"—there was a lightly sharper note in his voice— "because you made pact with that forest runner."

Anger such as she had not felt for days flared in her. "I made no pact. I have not come here to reclaim any lordship. If he wishes that ill-omened wood to rule, then it is his. You heard me deny all fiefdom over it! Also, from what he said, he has no close ties with those ahead. I think it would suit him very well if we finished each other off without any meddling from him."

"A safe and trusty plan for *him*," admitted the Falconer dryly. "It remains that, if we are not expected, this is the time when we should move."

"Across the open fields, crawling over the remains of the bridge, fording the moat." Tirtha reckoned up the utter folly of such action. To her the problem facing them was a nearly insurmountable barrier.

"In the open day, perhaps not," the Falconer conceded. "We have the night; also we must not go into action without rest. Alon," he addressed the boy now, "Wind Warrior can tell us only what he sees. Can you perhaps let us know if there is any hidden move toward seeking us out?"

The boy did not reply at once, nor did he any longer look at the two of them, rather down at the dirty hands locked together about his knees. He appeared so small, so childish, that Tirtha wanted to protest. Talent—Power—he might possess that beyond many Wise Ones, but drive him too far, and he could once more escape into that other existence. And perhaps a second time they could not draw him back.

He raised his head at last, and still not looking around, he answered in a low voice, "I dare not hold on them—on what they do there. I can—cannot! But if they seek us through any ensorcelment, yes, that I shall know—of a certainty I shall know!"

"We ask no more than that. Also, we shall watch by turn. You, Little Brother, and you, Lady, must rest first. I await Wind Warrior, for to me only can he deliver his report."

Tirtha shared her cloak with the boy, and they curled up together, her head pillowed on the saddle bags, his on her shoulder. She carefully kept in mind that she would not dream, for it could be that even dreams might alert whoever ruled in Hawkholme now.

She roused out of what turned out to be but a light doze often broken, though Alon seemed sunk far into the depths of a heavy sleep. Her shoulder was numb under the weight of his head. There came again the soft sound that had disturbed her. The Falconer and his bird, their heads close together, were exchanging twitters. Then the bird quieted down, to settle on one of the stones, apparently done with its tour of duty. The man took off his helm and wiped his forehead with the back of his hand, leaving a smudge of stone dust there. He seemed to sense that he was being watched, for he turned his head quickly, and his eyes met hers.

Cautiously Tirtha slid away from Alon. The boy sighed, turned on his side, and curled up. She left the cloak huddled over him and pulled herself up to join the man.

"Well?"

"Not so well. There are broken roofs yonder, so Wind Warrior was able to see more than we had hoped. The party—those we followed—are there. But they met with others who had a prisoner. The boy"—he glanced at Alon and then quickly away—"was right. They have been using their captive foully. Perhaps they believe him the one they have been seeking."

Tirtha's teeth closed on her lower lip. He need add no details. She had seen and heard much of how outlaws handled those they amused themselves with or would pry information from for their own purposes. What they had looked upon at the garth as this Gerik's doing had made very plain what tricks he thought worth the trying. But there was something else in the Falconer's words.

"The one they have been seeking," she repeated. "You believe then they have been waiting for me?"

"For you or another with the Hawk blood. There was the dead man, and he whom Alon told me of, the one who wore the Lord's own ring and you said was half-blood. Why should you all be drawn here?"

Why indeed? She considered that. In her pride she had believed herself to be the only one of the kin so summoned. There might well have been others; even a half-blood would answer if a geas call came strong enough. It might be that someone, or something, had indeed summoned any who had enough of Hawk blood to answer, and that these had all been burdened by the same command. If so, the one this Gerik amused himself with now was kin, and his blood debt would fall on her.

"Yes," she said softly. "Though it was my belief that I was the last of the true blood—the full blood—yet it could be so."

"What do you know of that pile over there?" A jerk of his head indicated the ruined holding.

"I have seen part of it in dreams." The time had come when she must be utterly frank with him. "The great hall and a secret place beyond it. Therein what I seek is hidden or was hidden. I do not know"—her frankness swept her on as days earlier she would never have believed possible—"*what* I so seek, only that it must be found. That is the geas laid upon me."

"Little enough." His tone was flat. "You have no other knowledge—none of its doors or how it might be entered?"

She was forced to shake her head, resenting that she must seem so stupid in his eyes. Why had her dreams *not* given her more? To her this ignorance seemed so utterly defeating that she knew again some of the soul-darkness that had struck her on the way.

"There is that which you found with the dead."

Tirtha started, her hand went quickly to her belt pouch. She had forgotten that bit of over-written skin. Now she pulled it out with desperate eagerness, smoothing the scrap upon the nearest flat surface.

Together they bent over it, but still the lines there made no sense. If it possessed a secret, Tirtha could not connect it with the ruined hold. There was no indication of a wall or passage, anything that looked to be a guide.

"Ritual perhaps," she said at last. Nor did he deny her identification.

"Yet it had a meaning for the dead."

"Which perhaps died with him." She rerolled the page, set it once more within its container. No, there was no easy way for them. This venture depended upon their wits and strength alone. She slipped the container back into her belt pouch.

"Wind Warrior sees with other eyes," The Falconer spoke musingly. "He is of the old stock, one keen-witted beyond the others remaining of his lost folk, or he would not have come to me. However, he was never battle-trained, and he cannot supply us now with such information as would point out any weaknesses in what defenses they may have."

"Since he has returned," Tirtha said, "why do you not rest, leaving the watch to me? You cannot take all sentry duty upon yourself."

He did not refuse. Though she knew well that his sort made no complaint, his body was human, and she could guess that he needed sleep— even desired it—that he might be better prepared for what lay ahead. When he had settled himself, discarding his helm and drawing his worn cloak about him, Tirtha moved into a position where she could stare directly at Hawkholme, wishing that she dared use a trance to reconnoiter, though she realized the fateful folly of that.

The sun was warm. She tugged a little at the fastenings of her jerkin. A breeze lingered over the river, and the constant murmur of the water could be lulling. Tirtha sat up the straighter, strove to plan. The curling of the flood about the remains of the bridge piers attracted her attention from time to time. Where the stones had fallen from the broken span, there were pile-ups of captured drift. Not long ago the water level must have been higher, fed by spring storms wild and strong enough to tear small trees, as well as brush, from collapsing banks, sweeping such along. There remained enough force to tug loose pieces of that wreckage which caught on the broken piers, sending them tumbling on. In fact, Tirtha began to watch the rush of water with more care. The current was apparently still to be reckoned with.

The river curved below the bridge, where rocks broke the surface, standing foam ringed, with more drift jammed among them. Beyond that the water ran between banks where bushes were still half buried in its swollen abundance. Well within the range of her sight was the artificial cut made to feed water into the moat.

Surely, with such a force of running water at hand, there must have been drains from the fortress into that cutoff. And even as Tirtha studied the rippling of the current, she could see some of the debris caught among the rocks being pulled loose from time to time, to be whirled or bobbing and tossing in the water. This could just be their way. . . .

By the time dusk arrived and she had awakened the Falconer, allowing Alon to sleep on, she had a plan, a shaky one and risky enough, but was not their whole venture risky? He listened to her suggestion, and half to her surprise and feeding her pride, he agreed.

"To enter below the rocks"—he studied the scene carefully as she had been doing all afternoon—"yes, it is possible. Also it would appear the only way one might gain that place without being sighted. Masked by drift, it is possible."

"You can swim?" She knew that while she was no mistress of water ways, she could handle herself well enough, using floating branches as a screen to make the attempt.

"We have served as marines on the Sulcar ships," he replied. "None go to sea with those warriors unless they are able to take care of themselves mid wind and wave. The mounts we must leave behind. To attempt to tow them through the water, no."

"Falgon will go. . . ." Alon's voice startled them both. They turned as one to look at the boy.

"Falgon?" questioned Tirtha.

"Him whom you call the Torgian—he has made bond with me," Alon returned simply. "And if he goes, then so will the ponies, for he is strong, and they will follow where he leads."

Tirtha was not surprised. The Torgians were noted for choosing masters whom they served until death. "It might not work," she cautioned. "We seek a way into the hold, perhaps through a drain, some small passageway, which a horse could not follow."

"Yes," Alon returned. "But he will wait nearby, the ponies with him. We shall need them later."

"And you shall wait with them." Tirtha was inspired. She had no wish to take Alon into what might well be a trap. It was hard enough to bear the burden of leading the Falconer into battle. This boy-child—no, let him remain with the horses and relieve her mind that much.

"No, you shall need me." He spoke with authority, an odd compelling authority, which stifled any protest she might have raised.

So, when at dusk they made their way down past the rocky stretch of river, Alon, as well as the three mounts, were of the company. They squatted by the water's edge, working as quickly as they could in the dark, fashioning narrow rafts of drift on which they piled most of their gear, including their clothing. The falcon had taken off, heading toward the main tower of the waiting ruin, as they stepped into water cold enough to wring gasps from them all. Then, having waded out a few steps, they abandoned themselves to the steady pull of the current, their shoulders supported by the rafts, kicking their feet to steer them straight.

Thus they reached the entrance to the moat. Here a fall of stone had nearly dammed the entrance, but they scrambled over it. On the other side the Falconer tested the depth where the water washed directly against the walls and found it no more than knee-deep, though stagnant and evil-smelling, so they redressed hurriedly. Alon stood and set his hands on either side of the Torgian's head. Then he released the animal, which turned to climb the nearest bank, the ponies following. The beasts were gone before Tirtha could send Alon with them. Luckily it was a dark night, with the beginning of rain, and the animals, with near-human intelligence, picked as silent a way as they could.

Above, the building showed no lights, nor had they, during all their drifting with the current, sighted any signs of life. Did those now holding the place believe that, in the prisoner they had taken, they had the one they had waited for? Tirtha found the lack of any sentries suspicious, but there was nothing they could do except go on. With the Falconer moving in the lead, they began a search along the wall for an entrance into the hold from the moatside.

They were dwarfed by the rise of the walls above, and the stench of the mud they stirred up by their passing made Tirtha sick, though she had had only one scant meal that day. To all outward evidence they rounded a deserted building, and Tirtha kept a tight hold on her thoughts, did not try in any way to sense out what might be above. She saw the dark shadow that was the Falconer stop short, set both his hands against the slimed wall, his head at an angle. She, too, looked up.

There, just above them, was what they had been seeking, a rounded opening. Alon pressed close to the man.

"Up! Let me see."

The Falconer caught the boy about the waist, lifted him until Alon's feet were on his shoulders and Alon's arms and chest above the lower rim of the opening. Alon stretched out his hands. By straining her sight, Tirtha could see them against the opening, moving back and forth.

14

Alon set one hand against the edge of the opening; with the other he thrust inward. Tirtha heard a rattle and was alarmed lest the sound carry. It was plain that Alon worked to loosen something within the shadow of the opening. The Falconer braced his body closer to the slimed wall, holding steady. There came another sharp *ping* from above. Alon swung down a dark bar that Tirtha hastened to catch.

It was metal, foul smelling, flaking off rusted bits in her hands. She let it slide on down into the sludge about her feet where turgid water swallowed it up without sound. Alon was at work again, and it was not too long before a second bar, torn from its setting, was freed, dropped, and likewise disappeared.

They might be striving to force entrance into a totally deserted building, and the very fact that they heard nothing, saw no sign of any guards, was to Tirtha a source of continued uneasiness. Those within might know very well that their prey was coming to them, resting at ease, needing only to wait. Yet what other recourse had she and her companions?

A third bar was freed. Then Alon dropped down from his perch to report in the thinnest of whispers:

"There is now a full opening, and I felt within. It is a foul place, but it is clear. There are even hand holds on the walls. Perhaps the lord here once planned a way of escape for a bad time."

"That could be true," murmured the Falconer. Tirtha could also understand the logic. Had this moat not been half dammed off from the river by the fallen wall and if, instead, the water in it had been up over the old markings they had felt as they had come, the opening would have been below the surface, completely masked. A determined or desperate in-dweller could well use it secretly. However, she eyed this particular door to Hawkholme with little favor. This opening was narrow, it was good that they had gone short of rations recently, and that she had always been thin, with few curves to plump out her jerkin or leggings. She wondered if the Falconer could force entrance, but, like all his breed, he was wiry, not thick of body.

"I go first," Tirtha declared firmly. "But how will *you* reach it?" She looked to the Falconer; he could give her a hand up as he had Alon, but who could do the same for him?

"There will be a way." He spoke with such confidence that Tirtha knew he was sure of his own ability. He caught her quickly under the arms to lift her, steadying her body against the wall until she thrust her hands into the mouth of the drain. One arm scraped across a broken space from which Alon had loosed a bar. She groped frantically within, seeking those holds Alon said existed. Then one hand, digging deep into noisome, crusty filth, hooked into what was manifestly a loop. A moment later she discovered its twin on the opposite side.

Tirtha was grateful for past hard work in the fields. What she had learned on Estcarp farms gave her the strength needed. Had she not had those years of hard physical work behind her, she could never have fought her way up that hidden ladder where the stench near choked her, her hair and garments rendered sodden and thick with foulness. Her cloak she had left bound to her saddle, and she was glad of that, for its folds would never have allowed her passage. As it was she felt the harsh rasp of stone against her leather garments, with now and then a painful scrape on her skin.

Luckily the way was not straight up but slanted. And Tirtha discovered, once inside the hole, she could feel ahead for each hold, drawing herself along more easily than she would have believed possible, though it was a worm's progress. The nastiness of the foul encrustation choked her, so that she could only hope that the exit lay not too far ahead.

In the dark she could move only by touch. Also the stench grew even thicker, though this drain had been abandoned for many years. Finally, her hand hit against a solid barrier and she could have cried out in her dismay. Holding on with one hand, she clawed along that surface. The drain took an abrupt turn here.

The long slant, up which she had worked her way, ended in a right-angled space. Above that there seemed to be nothing but solid roof. She refused to let herself panic. She ran first one hand and then the other back and forth across the barrier. Her third such try brought success. She knocked loose a solid cake of encrustation, enough so that once more her fingers hooked into a space that felt carved to receive just such a grip.

First she bore down, dragging with all her might, to no purpose. Must she believe that, if there had ever been an opening here, it was now impossible to move? A last desperate try made her shove instead of pull. There was a grating sound. So heartened, Tirtha changed hands again quickly and put all the effort she could into a full sidewise push. Stationed so awkwardly, able to work only with one hand, she fought stubbornly. There was a give, the barrier moved, though with a louder grating that winged her heart to a faster beat. She held on for a wild moment, five fingers gripped on the sliding panel, the other hand flailing out into an open space. Then she was able to hook that hand over an edge and pull herself up with a wrench that took what seemed the last flare of her strength. Her head and shoulders rose into clean air as she flopped across the edge of a stone bench onto the floor of a narrow chamber in the heart of the wall itself.

A cool rush of night air struck at her as Tirtha pulled herself around to face the fissure in the wall through which that welcome breeze came. This must be the upper floor of the main dwelling chambers wherein the family had once had their private apartments. She scrambled to her feet, feeling about her. Her outflung hand broke a remnant of charred wood, as she stumbled into a narrow hall. The far end of it showed faint light, radiating from far below. Sighting this, Tirtha crouched, trying to still the gasps of air she had been drawing into her lungs, as if such sounds might betray her to any keeping vigil by that distant gleam of light.

Sounds from the wall chamber marked Alon's arrival in turn. The boy moved out to clutch at Tirtha's shoulder. They leaned against the wall together, intent upon the far end of the hall, until the Falconer joined them. With him came light, dim and wan yet visible. The pommel of the power weapon was awakening.

Again Tirtha left the other two, to slip along that wall. She passed yawning caverns on her right where more burnt wood marked doors to chambers, but those were not important. She had to reach the Great Hall. Only from there could she trace the steps to be taken for conclusion of her mission. And surely the Great Hall would be the one place where their enemies within would be.

Corridor's end gave upon a staircase circling about a center core, winding steeply downward, the steps narrow edges of stone. There was a groove cut in the wall about this formidable coil of descent, perhaps to provide a hand hold.

At the foot of the spiral was a lamp in a niche, a basin of stone with a wick fed into it through a hole in the loose lid. The light it gave was limited, but that any here had seen fit to light this stair at all was a warning, one that Tirtha thought it well to heed. She hesitated at the top of that well-like way. Only one person at a time could descend, and if a guard waited below, out of sight . . .

She became aware of a soft rustle and glanced back. By the eerie light of the Falconer's weapon, she saw that the bird which accompanied him was again perched on the man's shoulder. Its head was extended well forward as it also stared down.

The presence of the lamp bothered Tirtha. Since they had come into the upper hall, the place had been utterly silent. Though these walls were thick, much of the interior had clearly been destroyed by fire and sounds should carry. Such quiet only meant to her that the three of them were, in spite of Alon's earlier reassurance, not only expected but that a trap awaited them. She edged away from the stairway, then wondered if that was exactly how she was expected to reason—that the lamp below was set so as to make them take another path.

A hand caught hers, startling her, pulling her down so that she was on a level with the boy.

"*He*—he is here. . . ." There was fear in his voice.

His grasp on Tirtha tightened, held with frantic force, pinning her to the fire-stained wall. If he should lapse now into that state of withdrawal . . . Terror was building up in him to such an extent as to awake panic in Tirtha herself. By his very touch he fed it to her. She caught at him, strove to shut out of her mind any dread of her own, to return only what strength of spirit she had to offer.

Somehow their alarm must have spread in turn to the Falconer, perhaps through the medium of the bird on his shoulder, for he swung up between them. The dim glow of his sword rested on both woman and boy, its pommel pulsating with the light that was both a warning and a solace against the spread of the Dark.

Alon's involuntary shudders shook Tirtha. She could see his face, a vague blur turned up to hers. Then the light swept over him. He had closed his eyes tightly, his mouth was twisted as if to utter a noiseless scream. However, as the thin glow of the gemstone touched him, that expression of witless terror receded, even as she, also, felt a warmth rising within her body.

They had more than one weapon, these enemies who made their den in Hawkholme, and perhaps the strongest could not be seen or heard. They who invaded must seek action, for to remain cowering here was to open gates to this other, more deadly form of attack.

If she had only had better preparation! Those dreams—they seemed now to her to have been more deceptive than helpful. There must be a way through this ruined stronghold, yet she could only blunder and hope and perhaps fail.

No! Again that insidious thing which attacked through mind and emotion had struck at Alon through one kind of fear, at her with another. What of the Falconer—what did it strive to reach in him? For the impression grew in Tirtha that the thing lairing here with its servants might indeed need to reach them by devious means, that it shrank from physical attack. Why? The Sword—yes, it could be that weapon of power which had spun about them its small light. Perhaps, because it had come into the Falconer's hand from the first, he was now the best armored of the three.

She heard again a rustle of wing as she deliberately pushed closer to the man so that her shoulder rubbed against his.

"I must," she said in the lowest whisper she could manage, "reach the Great Hall. It is only from there that I know my path."

He did not answer at once, but neither did he draw back from that contact between their bodies as she thought he might. As she had tried with Alon, perhaps in the same way he sought now to reassure her. Even as she thought that, there was in her, this time, no answering surge of rebellion. The three of them *were* locked into action which they must share; upon each other they must depend until the very end.

Again came a rustling of feathers. Tirtha could see by this faintest of lights that the falcon was mantling, bobbing its head, stretching its neck forward, not toward the stairwell from which they had retreated, but toward the other end of this hall. The Falconer swung in that direction, holding the sword in his claw, for he had drawn his dart gun in one sure movement, and had as usual taken the lead, walking with a scout's care that Tirtha tried with all her might to equal, drawing Alon along with her. The reflection of the powered gem appeared to exert a soothing effect on Alon for though he clamped fingers tightly in Tirtha's belt as an anchorage, he opened his eyes, pacing beside her in the wake of the man.

What they came to was the ruin of another staircase. Its core was stone, but that had once been covered with wood, and paneled walls must have once enclosed it—now burnt away. So again the descent would be a perilous one. Still, there was no lamp below, while the roof stretched high above their heads, for they had issued out of the mouth of a hallway which was on one level of what must have been a towering chamber.

The falcon winged out into this open space of which they could see so little. Now the Falconer began to descend the stairs, one step at a time, his helmed head turning slowly from side to side, as if he sought to hear the more clearly since he could not see. There was no change in the quality or strength of the light given off by the sword. Oddly enough, as Tirtha and Alon began their own halting descent some two steps behind the Falconer, the boy appeared to have fully shaken free of his fear. In his small face his eyes looked larger than before, as if his sight could pierce the dark.

Thus they came into a vast space surrounding the foot of that ruined stair. For the first time Tirtha believed she recognized the necessary path. She turned to the left, bringing Alon, by his continued hold on her, along, the Falconer falling in at her side. Through the darkness, lit only by the small glow the sword gem spun about them, she guessed what lay before her, as if her dream had once more enclosed her.

This *was* the Great Hall. In Tirtha arose an excitement that fear could not touch. Because she had won this far, what had drawn her here was strengthening, taking over within her. She strode, not crept, confident of where she went.

The dais with the chairs of honor had stood there. She could not see them; doubtless they had been swallowed up in the fire or hacked wantonly to pieces by those who had overrun the hold. Now she must turn this way, behind a screen. . . .

So sure was she that a screen stood there that she put up her hand lest she run into it. Yet there was nothing but a wall. The Falconer, as if anticipating her request, held the sword up and forward. What she sought lay beyond, of that she was certain. Almost roughly she loosed Alon's hold, ran to that wall, swept her grimy hands back and forth across it. Her fingers left trailmarks in the dust and ash, but she had no luck this time. There was no possible hold she could discover that would open for her like the door in the drain.

It lay here! She knew it. Tirtha strove to command her impatience. She closed her eyes—this might be the most dangerous thing she could do, but she must throw open the gate of memory to the dream, command it, as in the past it had commanded her. Only so could she come at what she must take into her hands.

The great hall—piece by piece she labored to draw it out of the nothingness and ruin about her. Just so had the lord sat, and his lady, between the two of them on that table the casket. Then had come the alarm. The more Tirtha pulled and drew, the clearer the picture became. She could feel those others she had not seen clearly in her dreams, their rise of emotion, fear and excitement, determination, dread, above all a flare of courage that was like a lighted torch in the dead dark.

The lady—Tirtha did not know it now but her own hands were up breast high before her, cradling the invisible at the level of her heart. Behind the carven screen—now the wall—a wall once paneled in wood carving, fancifully wrought, painted and gilded here and there. Only it was not the wall that was so important. She did not raise a hand now to its surface. Instead she advanced the toe of one worn boot, planted it firmly on a pavement fashioned of many small colored stones in strange and angular pictures. So by instinct she sought out one of those fitted stones slightly larger than the others, and upon it she bore down firmly, with as much weight as she could bring to bear on such a small surface.

There was resistance. She tried again, the need for speed lashing at her. Once, twice, three times. Surely it would not refuse her entrance now that she had come so far!

The wall moved. With a thin screech of sound as if metal crossed metal long ungreased and near-rusted in place, a passage opened. From that shone light—blue, faint, but still light!

Tirtha threw herself forward. With the opening of the door the dream vanished. Still the summoned vision had served her well. This was the secret place, and before her must lie what was being guarded—which those of her line were pledged ever to protect until they were released from a very ancient bond.

Beyond lay a small room, and though time had wrought some ruin within, the wrath of men had not reached here. There were tapestries on the walls. At the stir of air which entered at her coming, they moved. From them fell patches of paper—thin fabric, like dead and dried autumn leaves. What she had come for stood as it had been left—on a narrow table of stone jutting forward from a wall of which it was a part. The top of the table was deeply incised with symbols, which had once been brightly painted but were now dulled and dusty. They were words of Power so old that no one among those who served what rested here could any longer understand them. Tirtha, looking upon them, knew that these were Names here that, were they spoken, could destroy the walls about her, change perhaps even the running of time as men knew it.

Within a concentric circle of those Names stood the casket. It was of the same silver metal as the sword that had come to the Falconer, and from its surface arose the diffused light filling the room. Tirtha put out both hands. With widespread fingers she drew in the air above that waiting treasure signs issuing from buried knowledge as old as the land on which Hawkholme stood. Then, between her two palms she felt the weight of the casket as she lifted it, to hold against her, even as the lady had borne it hither in her dream. Lifted it and turned . . .

The scream was that of a war cry, given to waken and alarm. Over her head swooped the falcon, out from the dark behind them. One of the bird's feet was now a stump from which curled a thread of noxious smoke. At the same moment Alon and the Falconer were both hurtled inward toward her. They did not bear her to the floor, as perhaps they might have done had there been more room. Rather, they threw her backward so that her spine hit hard against the shelf table, bringing a pain so sharp and terrible that Tirtha lost control over her body and sank to the floor, folding over the casket which she still held.

There followed a crash, and she heard another scream—not from a bird's throat this time, but from Alon she was sure. The pain that filled her brought darkness, and she sank into it as an exhausted swimmer sinks into a sea he can no longer battle.

"Tirtha! Lady!" Moisture on her face, a burning within her lips. She strove to see who called, but all was a haze that swam back and forth, making her ill so that she quickly shut her eyes. Pain filled her. When she strove to move, to crawl away from the fire which she felt as if about to consume her utterly, there was no life in her body. Her hands—no, she must not loose—loose what? She could not remember. But, save for the pain that burned, her body was as the dead.

"Tirtha!" Again that call. She sought to escape it, to find a way to flee both the pain and the demanding voice. Only there was something that compelled her to open her eyes once more.

The haze this time separated itself into two parts, one large, one much smaller. Tirtha frowned and squinted, trying to see the better. Faces—yes, Alon—slowly she fitted a name to the nearest—and Nirel— yes, that was his true name—Nirel. She thought she repeated both, but perhaps she did not, for she could not hear her own voice. It was such a struggle to try to hold on to this contact that she would rather they allowed her to slip back into that place of darkness, of peace.

"Holla!"

The force in that call was as terrible in her ears as the scream of the injured falcon. It offered no rest and it held her there.

"Hawk's brood!" A second time words rang through the very air of this place, a torment added to all the rest she bore.

"Give unto the Dark Lord what is his and all shall be well."

Yet that was no true promise or bargain. Even through the waves of pain that beset her, Tirtha knew that much.

"By Harith and Haron, and the Blood of the Hawk Brood"—Tirtha did not know from whence came the strength to draw intelligible words out of her, making her voice firm for that moment—"only to the Appointed One do we resign our guardianship. The hour is nigh. . . ."

"The hour is nigh in truth," roared the voice out of the air. "Treachery begets treachery. What is of the Dark shall return there, be it bound as might be. To all sorceries there comes an end, just as there is an end to time itself. Render up what was never of the Light."

Deep in her something else stirred. He who was without, he could not enter, he dared not take, save by the permission of the true blood. And she—*she* was the true blood. This must not end in Hawk defeat—only in death. And against death who may fight?

Her mouth worked. Tirtha strove to fight the dryness that filled it so she could shape words once more.

"This I hold—I of the Hawk—and if death is the portion of that holding, then let it be so."

"Aaaaghhh . . ." That came as a wordless howl of fury, dying away in an echo, as if he who had voiced it had withdrawn to a far distance.

Tirtha looked again to the two with her. She lay flat upon the floor in the heat of her pain, and she believed that her body was so broken she could not long be contained within it. Perhaps that purpose which had drawn her here would strive to hold her so, even in this agony. Now she gazed first at Alon and then at Nirel who held close to his breast the injured falcon. The bird's eyes were dim, and its head sagged forward. It was dying—more blessed than she might be, Tirtha thought fleetingly.

"I ask pardon of you," she said, first to the Falconer, for he had truly been outside this dire pattern before she had deliberately drawn him in, and he had lost much already. "This is an end my dream did not foretell, but there are many times unexpected changes in life's weaving. Give me a comrade's passing farewell even though I am what you deem the least— a woman." She did not wait for any answer. In fact she shrank from gazing longer at him, since she did not want to read refusal in his eyes. Instead she spoke now to the boy.

"Your pardon, also, Alon. Though I did not willfully draw *you* into this venture. Perhaps that, too, was another fault in the weaving for us. I have failed, and by my nature, you both are caught and with you the brave bird. If there is any truth in the old stories, perhaps lives so oddly bonded here shall be later led to understand the why of such geas-setting. I think we shall not issue forth from this place alive. The secret I hold is not for those without. For that I must thank the Power which I never could summon."

Her words came slower and lower as pain lapped her round. She looked once more to the Falconer. His face was again only a blur.

"Leave in my hands," she said, "what I have taken up. That I must guard as best I can until the end."

15

Alon reached across her, his hands out, not to her but to the Falconer. Into that hold the man relinquished the limp bird, which the boy drew as protectingly to him as Tirtha kept the casket. The Falconer arose from where he knelt, and she saw him, through the pain that held her, turn slowly, gazing about, sweeping off his bird helm to see the better, while he still clasped the sword within his claw. From it issued a wan light to vie with that from the casket.

Tirtha closed her eyes, ready to surrender, yet death did not reach for her as she hoped. The Last Road might lie before her, but something held her back from that journey. Alon murmured to the stricken bird.

Bird?

Tirtha blinked. Now her injury built illusions. There had been a falcon in Alon's hold. Now a shimmer covered that huddle of black feathers, as if one misty picture were fitted over another. What Alon nursed was not the same—rather a strange thing with gray-feathered body and large open eyes banded round with scarlet feathers. This other bird raised its head high, though behind its shadowy form she could see still the drooping crest of the falcon. Its bill opened as if voicing a challenge or cry of anger.

Alon's eyes had closed. Now they flickered open, appearing large in his thin face. He stared down at what he held as if he, too, was aware of change.

The Falconer, seemingly alerted by what he sensed rather than heard, swung swiftly around, to stare at boy and bird. That doubled misty outline faded in and out, sometimes blotting out the falcon, at other times losing the gray bird. There might be a struggle between the two, one life force striving to impress itself upon a weaker one.

Alon shifted the bird, leaned closer still to Tirtha. She gained a measure of strength to dispute pain, to clear her mind. For that this had important meaning, she was sure. Perhaps some act might follow which, even if it could not save her, would carry to an end what the geas demanded of her. Guardianship was not enough, though it had been faithfully held to the last of the Blood to whom the task had been given. There was more, and if events were out of her control, yet all was still not swallowed by Dark mastery. Did the Falconer nurse some suspicion of unknown danger? His sword swung into place above Tirtha's body from the other side, its point aimed at the bird that struggled from one form to the other.

The gem in the pommel flashed, emitting waves of light to encircle the bird. The bird became whole, complete, not dead but vibrantly alive, a species unknown to Tirtha. When its beak opened once again, its cry could be heard, as fierce as the call of the falcon it had replaced, yet with a different, even wilder note. Its head darted forward on a longer neck than the falcon had owned, a sharp bill struck at Alon's fingers—struck but did not break skin. Instead the head jerked back, to slew about at a nearly impossible angle to view the boy.

It did not threaten such attack again, but it beat its wings, and Alon loosed his hold, so that it fluttered forward and down, coming to perch on the casket still resting between Tirtha's numb hands. There it again elongated its neck, its be-ringed eyes approaching her own.

The bird spoke—this was no cry or twitter, but a recognizable word. She had heard of birds trained to mimic human speech. Yet this was no mimic. Whereas the falcon had communicated by its own twitterings, which only the man could understand, this one, arisen out of the other's death, uttered what they could all distinguish.

"Ninutra . . ."

In the sway of Tirtha's mind, where pain and the need for holding strove against one another, there flickered the faintest memory. Out of Lormt, out of some legend she had picked up in her wanderings? No, this was another thing, perhaps a blood memory, descending to her from the line of those who had worn the Hawk and kept faith with something greater, not of man and woman at all.

The pain became a raging fire enveloping her, and she recognized that the fire was not entirely of the body, but a sign of Power alien to anything she had dreamed might exist. They said there had been Great Old Ones who had left humanity far behind, made of themselves that which in later days had little touch with mankind. This fire—and within it a face of carven beauty—was utterly remote. Yet the face bore eyes that still lived, looked into this place, considered the three of them, weighed them, before making judgment. The old accounts spoke of adepts who were neither of the Light nor the Dark, who withdrew from quarrels and strivings for power among their kind to seek only new and stranger knowledge. Tirtha did not feel the Dark in this one, nor did she sense any surge of strength the Light might have granted her. Still in her mind remained that face, until Tirtha was sure that she would carry it with her even into the death that must come. To such a one as this, no plea she might offer could reach.

Or . . .

The geas! Had this one laid *that* upon her? Had there been ancient dealings between this One of High Power and those of the Hawk? If so, then she could surely claim, if not for herself, then for the two with her, some aid. Tirtha strove to form that appeal, a last demand that a faithful servant be so repaid.

There was no change in the face she saw, only intelligence and measurement. Tirtha felt more pain—the numbness in her hands and arms was receding—though the rest of her body was only a vehicle for torment, dead to all else.

Her fingers fumbled with the casket, feebly running about its sides, hunting clasp or lock. There was none she could find by touch alone, and her sight was dim. Nor could she lift her head to look closer at what she clung to. It must not be given into the hands of another. The bird still squatted upon it—wings outstretched as if to hide it from view. Tirtha suddenly realized she could not even feel the touch of feathers. Illusion? Yet Alon no longer held the dying falcon—it was gone.

"Ninutra!" The bird raised its neck and head to form a single line, the open beak pointing at the shadowed roof above them. It summoned— surely it summoned! Still, who could reach them here save what prowled without, lacking the secret of the door?

From the four corners of the ceiling in that hidden chamber burst scarlet flame. Between those fiery tongues the air moved, as if all the dust the years had deposited here was drawn in, whirled about, kneaded into mass and substance. Over Tirtha that whirlwind centered and took form. There was a sword—a long-bladed, plain-hilted weapon of a misty- gray—a thing pulled from shadows not of a human world.

The point was above the casket and the bird. Tirtha understood. What lay within the guardian's hold was to remain secret. Yet it was also a focus for the power that had been summoned. There was nothing they could do but watch and wait, for they were only a very small part of another's plan. Perhaps in the end they would be discarded. One did not strike bargains, make pleas to such as this.

There was something about the shadow sword. Even as the Falconer's weapon bore unreadable symbols along its length, so did similar markings appear here. And those in part she recognized. Some of these were written on the dead man's scroll! She marveled at that for a long moment.

Alon, no longer holding the bird, had dropped his hands to lie limp on his knees where he sat cross-legged. His eyes, taking on a kind of luminance, not from those flames lashing over his head, but rather from the Falconer's weapon, were fixed upon that shadow sword, and there was that in his face which no child could know nor feel. He was gathering what he had not yet learned properly to garner, fighting a private battle of his own.

The Falconer stood as might a defender, waiting for a last fatal charge meant to bring down all he would protect. His weapon of power was held point up as if to engage that shadow weapon should it strike.

"Nirel." Into that Tirtha put what strength she had left. "Take the scroll, for it is a part of this, though I know not how."

The Falconer did not move, but Alon, as if he were well aware of what she carried and recognized its value, opened her pouch and pulled forth the metal rod thrusting it upward into one of the empty dart loops on the man's shoulder belt.

Within her mind the face of carven beauty withdrew as by a click of fingers, though Tirtha was sure that what it represented had not yet put them out of mind. Instead she felt, through the stone on which she lay, adding to her torment, a quivering of the rock, a tremor. Again she found voice, this time to cry a warning.

"Away from the walls!" She was not sure in what direction what was coming might strike, and they might all be buried. In that fashion, what she still held would be made safe.

The Falconer threw himself forward. With his clawed arm he swept the boy flat to the floor, thrusting him against Tirtha, while she cringed from the pain the contact caused her. Then the man was on his knees, arching his own body over the two of them. His mailed chest nearly flattened the bird as he tried to protect them.

A second tremor moved the floor. The flames flared out fiercely, still there was no heat in them. Now the shadow sword tilted in the air, though perhaps Tirtha, lying face up as she did, was the only witness. No longer did it hang point down; rather it stretched horizontal, and it grew longer, wider, casting over the three of them a shadow.

The ragged tapestries on the walls swung as they might have had a tempest caught them. Pieces of cobweb-thin fabric tore loose, to settle on the three so entwined.

There came a crash. Behind a fall of the rotting fabric, a widening break in the wall showed, stones loosened, fell outward and away. In the dark beyond, a second wall came into sight. That, also cracked, swayed out, to crash. The light of day flooded in—a day of sullen skies and great bursts of lightning, which sent force whips lashing across the sky. Thunder was war drums beating up an army.

Tirtha saw that opening. They could go, these two, the way was open. In so much had the Power which had brought her here answered her plea. She tried to break her hold on the casket with one hand, thrust the Falconer up and away from her so that he could see that door to freedom and take it—he and Alon. Yet she could no longer detach her flesh from the box. There was movement; the bird swept across her face, though she felt no brush of feather. It passed out from under the hanging sword, turning in the air, sped like a well-thrown lance out into the midst of the storm where its gray body became one with the half-light, gone from their sight.

"Go . . ." Tirtha tried to raise her voice above the violence of the thunder. There came another crash, another portion of that outer wall disappeared. Now there was a strange smell in the air, though it held none of the noisome stench of the Dark. She was sure that lightning had struck very close, perhaps somewhere on the building.

The Falconer levered himself up. The flames that had played about their heads had been snuffed out; the outline of the shadow sword was gone. It would appear that all manifestations of that other Power had been withdrawn. There was an open door to freedom, yes, but one she could not take.

Tirtha was enough of a healer to be sure that her back had been broken and that, even if they moved her (which she believed they could not do), it would only prolong the end for her, in turn putting them into greater danger. Better she had been buried under collapsing walls, taking with her what she was born to guard.

The Falconer was on his feet, pulling at remnants of the tapestry. There were lengths here and there, which, when he dragged them free of the broken walls, seemed stouter. These he smoothed out on the floor, Alon scrambling up to help.

They had at length a padding of four or five thicknesses, as long as Tirtha was tall. She could understand their purpose and knew it would fail. But also she realized now they would not go forth and leave her. Perhaps death would come swiftly when they attempted to move her; she could wish for nothing more than that.

They were done at last. Now Nirel stooped above her. Tirtha bit her lip until she tasted blood. She gathered all her last strength to make certain that she would not give tongue to her agony. He knelt, and she felt his hands slip slowly under her shoulders. There followed such a wave of torment as made all her earlier suffering seem as nothing.

"My . . . belt . . . pouch . . ." She mouthed the words, and Alon must again have heard them first, for she saw his hands swift in their movement. "The . . . bag . . . with"—she had to swallow before pushing the last words out—"the dragon sign . . . put all . . . in . . . my . . . mouth. . . ." This was the last mercy she hoped for. So powerful was this drug one used it with great care. To swallow all she carried was inviting the end. Let it come fast and free the two of them.

Alon had the smaller bag open. He held the mouth of it to her lips, shook free dried leaves that struck her tongue like a spoonful of dust. Tirtha choked, swallowed, choked, and fought to get the full portion down. Rightly, it should be taken as a brew. Swallowed dry in this fashion, she did not know how long it might need to work—she could only hope. Since the portion was far more than had ever been advised for use, she trusted it would serve.

Pain again, but through its piercing agony she continued to fight the dusty mouthful into her throat, swallowing convulsively. Then the world went scarlet with another protest from her broken body, and from that she passed into blessed nothingness.

She became aware not of her body, but of the self that had only before ventured forth in dreams and farseeing. The relief of being free of pain was so great that she exulted in nothing else for a period of time. This, then, was what came afterwards—what mankind had so long speculated might lie at the end of the Long Road—freedom indeed.

Only she was not free. Dimly, through her relief, she felt the tug of some tie. At once she opposed it. Might a geas last past the very fact of death? How could she still be entrapped? Tirtha knew fear and then rage, and her rage was a fire blazing up about that inner self. No! She would answer to no one, to nothing!

Nothing, not even that call.

Call? Yes, from a far distance there was a call, a demand, an urgent command.

Then she knew that she was indeed not free, that her body still encased her. It was immobile, that body of hers—dead—while within it she was hopelessly imprisoned. There was no longer any pain, only the deadness. She was looking up into the sky from which rain fell in great sheets, though on her dead body she could not even feel its beat. It filled her eyes, and so she could only see as through a heavy mist.

Yet she saw and she heard.

"Take it, fool—it is what we have sought!"

"Take it and die, is that the way of it, Lord? You saw what happened to Rudik . . ."

"She is dead. Have you not proof of that by the bite of your own sword?"

"I have also seen Rudik. I do not seek what happened to him, Lord. This is of your desire—do you then take it."

"Fool! Have I not said many times over, to each his own Powers? This is not of my knitting, and should I reach for it, it will be destroyed and none of us thereafter shall have the good of it. There are laws of the Talents and those may not be broken."

"It was perhaps wrong to shoot down the bird-lover. We might have used him then . . ."

"Not so—you saw his weapon. It was well that your dart struck first, for that was a thing bound to him, and thus the same rule would have held."

"Then use the boy. He has no weapon and he . . ."

There came an angry laugh. "Why must I be plagued ever by the service of fools? The boy—he is perhaps near as great a catch as this trinket box you so fear to meddle with. There will be pleasure for the Great One in meeting him! No—take up that box and now! I have held my hand because I know that you are short-gifted in wits and courage—you ravagers of an undone and ruined land—but need I compel you?"

"Lord, remember you are still only one among us, for all your talk of mighty forces that will come riding at your call. And Rudik is dead, in such a way as none of us here has any desire to follow. There is that other . . ."

A moment of silence and then, "Perhaps you are not so great a fool as you would seem, Gerik. Yes, he is still alive, even after your kind attentions and earnest discussions. I think he has enough of a hand left to do our bidding. He may not be a true Hawk, but there is a part of the proper blood within him, unless that was all spilled during our time of reasoning. So he may be able to achieve what must be done. Get him forth and try! I do not like this storm, there is the smell of Power here, such as is no friend to the Great One."

Tirtha lay within her shell of death and tried to understand. The bird man—Nirel—dead? It would seem so. For a moment she felt a thrust of strange pain, though not from her dead flesh and splintered bones but rather from another part of her. And the boy—that was Alon—him this "Lord" would take as captive to present to some greater doer of Evil. But it would seem that the casket was still hers, or at least within the guardianship of her dead body—and it had already caused death to one who would take it from her. That was true—the guardianship might pass only by right and by free gift, she knew, perhaps had always known in some hidden part of her.

So—one of the Blood? One to take from her even in death if it could be . . . And she had not the power—no longer any command. Again she knew the swelling fire of anger—a rage that filled her world. She could not be foresworn—she was the Hawk and in her hold this . . . !

Still the rain blinded her eyes which she could not close or blink; but she could hear, even as she heard voices now, whimpering sobs of pain, the cries of one broken and vanquished. She saw approaching her three shapes half hidden by the storm, two dragging a third between them. The two, who carried rather than led that helpless one, hurled him to the ground beside her, so he fell out of her range of sight. Then one of his captors stooped and caught a fistful of hair, drawing him up into her murky vision once again.

She saw a face bearing such scars and mutilations as made it a mask of horror, yet that part of her imprisoned in death felt emotion only vaguely, as if it were such a distance from her now that it was one with the helplessness of her own body. The other guard grabbed at the limp and helpless man, seizing an arm down the scorched and beaten flesh of which water runneled. There were fingers on a hand that was fire-shriveled. All but two of them were bent at impossible angles, but the hand was dragged forward above Tirtha, and though she could see only a fraction of movement, she realized that it was being made to reach for the casket, which must still lie upon her breast, perhaps tight in the hold of her dead hands.

The guard dropped that hand. She heard a scream such as could be torn only from one suffering the deepest agony that the Dark might devise. His body arched into her sight, nearly won to its feet in that last terrible torment, then fell back and away. There was silence, save for the battering of the rain and the distant beat of the thunder.

"You see, Lord, even your half-blood could not do it."

There was a sound in answer that was no word, rather a hissing of sheer rage. Then he who had been so addressed apparently mastered his flaming anger.

"Well enough. The puzzle remains. We shall take the dead with us, since no one seems like to master her. Sling her over a pack pony and let us be gone. There are those who can be summoned by the very smell of Power, and we are in debatable land."

"You ride for Escore, Lord?"

"Where else? Get your men together, Gerik, and let us be about our business. As for the cub—I shall see to him. She, at least, will need no guards."

"Lord, my sword-oath serves only this side of the border. We do not ride crosswise into what lies eastward."

Again that snarl. "You will discover, if you try otherwise, Gerik, that your oath is more than you deemed it at its taking. When I speak, you ride where and when it is my desire that you do so."

Once more a length of silence. Tirtha discovered that while she might no longer sense by physical means or judge by what she saw, still she was keenly aware of all about her. That Gerik was cowed was untrue. He was in a little awe of the one he addressed as "lord," but already a wily and subtle mind, well melded with cruelty and ruthlessness, was twisting and turning to find a way free. Murder was the least, perhaps, and the most forthright of the thoughts now in the outlaw's head.

However, for the time being, he was willing to adopt an outward show of being completely under the other's domination. She heard stamping of hooves on stone. Moments later she was lifted, and inwardly waited for the pain to strike—no, she must have been right. Her body had died, and it did not matter how roughly slack flesh and broken bone was handled. She felt nothing save that she was indeed lying across a pony's back and that she had been lashed in place there.

Alon had made no sound. She wondered then if once more he had fled back into that hiding place he had found during the attack on the garth. But he had certainly not become invisible, for they spoke of him as booty to be carried off.

They rode under the fall of the rain, eastward bound. Behind them they must be leaving the dead. She had no idea what might have happened to the unfortunate Rudik, but that the Falconer had found the end of his journey and that the tortured rag of humanity they had brought to rob her had been finished, Tirtha did not doubt.

She hung in her bonds unfeeling, and at length she was able once more to flee imprisonment from the shell of her inert self, sink back into the darkness. Still she was not free. Even in death the casket rode with her, and she came to believe that she would be bound in essence of spirit as long as it existed and was not returned to the one who could claim it by full right.

Was that the woman figure she had seen in her mind—the one the bird had called upon as Ninutra? If the bird had flown free from the keep to summon help, help had not come. Tirtha wondered about what had happened when Nirel and Alon had gotten her out of the destroyed secret chamber. But all that was very far away and had no more meaning for her. She need only wait and hope that that wait would not be long, until the final meeting wherein it would be decided once and for all whether a blood-oath might hold past death and how strong such a tie would be against the Dark.

Tirtha thought once more of the woman—not to make any plea— that was no longer in her power. If this Ninutra was the prime mover who had set the geas into action, then it must be her time and place and power that would bring the end into view. Surely there would be freedom thereafter, but perhaps even yet—though she no longer had a body worth the struggle—a final battle lay ahead.

16

Perhaps time and death had no meeting place; or perhaps it was that, even though dead, she was still held to the world she knew. Tirtha drifted between a place where she knew nothing and was at rest and being remotely conscious of what lay about her. There was the rain and storm, winds that buffeted the land, vicious strikes of lightning, though the fury of the unleashed weather led the commander of this party to make no concessions. They rode through the worst of it as if there were clear sky above.

Tirtha's vague touches of the outer world caught strange, floating fragments of thoughts that were not her own. She did not try to gather or consider them, yet she knew that those who rode were certainly not united. There were fears here, anger, dour resentment, weariness, but above all fear. That emotion gathered force, aimed in one direction, toward the leader under whose orders they journeyed.

During one of her feeble contacts with the world she was transfixed, caught. Not by any confused emanation from those whose prisoner she now was, but by a far more vigorous and demanding force.

"Tirtha!" That came like an arousing shout uttered in her very ear, drawing her into far keener awareness than she had had since they had fought that battle for the casket across her body. "Tirtha!"

The call, having found her, fed energy to awaken and strengthen her.

"You live . . ." That was no question, rather a demand. "You live!"

Which was folly. Still that bit of her which was able to respond could not say this was not true. She wondered if the fact that she still must fulfill a guardianship, that she had not been absolved of the geas, kept that small ember of life aglow in her.

What sought her—this was not the Great One who had rent open their prison. Nor was it the Dark Lord who commanded here. The Falconer was dead. Alon?

As if she had asked that aloud, there came an instant strong reply—wordless, yet unmistakable. The boy lived, nor had he retreated so far into his inner hiding place that he could not reach her.

"Where . . ." She found it exhausting to bring out even the beginning of a question. Let the dead, or the almost-dead rest; she resented being bound by any will.

"East . . ." It would seem that she need not form a full thought, that Alon could pluck meaning from what was vague even to her. "There is a Dark One—he believes me in his hold. But I have seen the bird twice!"

The bird that had flown into the storm? What had the bird to do with them? Oh, just let her go! Tirtha strove to will herself back into peaceful nothingness.

"Messenger . . . They come!"

She did not care. The fleeting strength that touch had brought was not enough to hold her. She slipped once more into the dark.

Then it was dark and yet not truly dark. Rain no longer beat on her face. Somewhere, not too far away, there must be a fire, for there was a ruddy glow, though she could not turn her head to find its source. She stared unblinkingly upward at rough stone. They must have taken refuge in a cave.

This could have been one of many such camps as far as her slight hold upon the living world could tell. Tirtha lay looking up at that rock. Perhaps the dying, or the dead, dream of life, and this was such a dream. She was content that the pain was gone and that there seemed to be a barrier between her and any contact with the real world or the unreal one.

"Tirtha!" Once again she was being summoned back, she thought, sluggishly and resentfully. "You are awake—I know it!" There was some heat of anger. Alon might have been hammering at a door that had refused to open to him.

"The bird—it is out there in the night! I have heard it call twice. They are coming! This Dark One—he knows it, he will try me!"

There was nothing left in Tirtha to raise an answer. What moved Alon had no meaning for her. A shadow appeared between her and the fire as a tall shape loomed above her. The shadow leaned forward, so her moving eyes saw a helmed head, a face in partial darkness. A second shadow was now beside the first, someone dragged to her side even as that miserable prisoner had been brought to her to steal the casket—a smaller, thinner shape.

"He's scared into an idiot, Lord. Look at the face on him."

"Yes, look at him, Gerik! This waif you would have hunted for your pleasure has more strength in the smallest finger of his hand than you can summon to swing that sword of yours! Idiot? Ah, far from that. He is hiding—hiding! But there is a trick or two that will peel him out, even as you peel a fos-crab out of its shell after a good steaming."

Hands hard and heavy on its shoulders crushed that smaller shadow to its knees beside her.

"I thought as how he was so very precious, Lord, that none of us was to lay finger on him. Yet you want to risk him . . ."

"There always is a time, Gerik, when one plays for high stakes. I do not think that this one will be risked. He is of another heritage. Among such, like does not prey upon like. It may diminish him somewhat. However, that can be risked for what we shall gain. To transport this other carrion only slows us, and time has become our enemy. We are not the only seekers, and I will tell you, Gerik, you would find some who come searching such as you would not care to face." Laughter, low and heavy in contempt, came out of that shadow. "Now!"

She did not know what he did to the boy he held prisoner. There came no cry out of Alon, nor was there any longer any touch from him to her. He must have retreated into his own refuge.

"Seems like he isn't too quick to answer, Lord!" Gerik said after a long moment. "We could try a trick or two . . ."

"Silence!" The word was sharp enough to stop even Gerik in his covert rebellion.

The two beside her seemed linked unmovingly. Tirtha sensed, very far, the faintest touch against her near-buried self, a lapping of power that perhaps might well have blasted one who accepted or was forced to accept it fully. The smaller shadow moved a fraction, its arms hanging limply from the shoulders and prisoned in its captor's grip raised, the hands extending toward Tirtha's body. That lapping power arose the stronger—exultation fed it.

Then there came a tearing cry, so wild and strange that it might have been a shout a man charging into battle would voice, his nature drowned in a lust for blood and death. Another shadow appeared, over the shoulder of the standing man. She saw it clearly. The bird that had been born from the body of the falcon!

The man at her side stumbled back a step. One of his hands fell away from Alon's shoulder, while the boy sagged forward as one whose full strength had drained away. Now he lay across her, his rain-wet hair drifting over the lower part of her face, as motionless as she herself. Though Tirtha did not believe that he was dead—or dead-alive as she was sentenced to remain.

The bird now perched on Alon's shoulder, twisting forward its long neck so that its eyes were very close to her own as it gazed steadily at her. No, no bird! This was again that head, that face she had seen in her pain back in Hawkholme.

Only for a moment did the bird stare into her eyes, or the face thus look upon her. Then it swung about to confront the man shadow, and from it came once more that sound which was a name, "Ninutra!"

From the man it so confronted, there sounded an answering cry. Or was it a summons for help—a backing for himself in some struggle he now feared unequal?

"Rane!"

He might have laid a goad to the bird. The thing hissed viciously. It fairly leaped from Alon's body straight for the man who had been trying to jerk the boy up again. The blow it delivered was out of range of Tirtha's sight, but she heard a cry of pain, then an oath. He was no longer between her and the fire, and she could hear other cries, not all in the same voice. It would seem that the bird was waging battle with more than one.

Alon remained where he was. She could not feel his weight upon her, his voice reached her in the faintest of whispers, which the cries and sounds from beyond covered.

"They fight. The bird has drawn blood. But the Lord summoned, and there will be more than one come to us. Also there is one who follows. Time is drawing in. Oh, Tirtha, hold—hold, for the end is far from decided."

She guessed that he had used speech lest that which had been summoned, or the lord, having extended his own power to that summoning, might pick up their touch by mind. But she could make no answer. Nor did she desire to do so. This was no longer her battle. It was rather a trap wherein she was held, from which she longed to be free.

The clamor lessened, and then a shadow strode once more between the light of the fire and her body.

"What's to be done with the boy now, lord?"

"See he's well bound and stow him safe." The reply was sullen. "There is too much abroad now to try again."

Alon was lifted off her, taken from her sight, lying limp in his guard's hands. Once more Tirtha was allowed to drift into her blessed nothingness.

What came to arouse her next was pain—a memory of it, or so it would seem, not a part of her. Still she carried it with her as one carries an annoying burden one is ordered to bear. She looked out upon the world, losing her hold on nothingness with reluctance. There was sky above her again—dull and gray, but from it no rain flowed. Her head jerked to and fro so that she caught glimpses now and then of mounted men, mainly one who rode beside her, leading the pony on which she was lashed. She gathered she had been bound to that mount in a strange fashion, face up, probably because of the casket that must still be frozen into position on her breast, making this the only way she could be transported.

More than her surroundings, the girl grew aware of what was awakening inside her. Not only the pain, but also her thoughts were coming alive once more. She had not this time answered to Alon's call, rather to something else—a reaching out from . . .

Warmth—the casket! What she bore was alive? No, that could not be true. It was metal, unless it cradled more than she could have guessed— some sentient power? One could believe anything of the Great Ones and that what she bore was of their earlier possessing, Tirtha no longer doubted. There was feeling within that thing, which rested not far from her heart, to the covering of which her hands were still frozen. Her head bobbed again to give her a quick glance down the length of her body.

Yes! She held the casket as firmly as she had since she had taken it up from its resting place at Hawkholme. The rope, which helped to bind her to the pony, also was looped carefully about her hands as if those who transported her had doubts about her being dead and had thought that she might rouse, to throw the treasure from her, perhaps into some place from which they could not fetch it forth again.

Dead? For the first time her less sluggish thinking began to doubt this. The drug Alon had fed into her at her urging had been a huge dose of what was meant to give healing sleep. Perhaps it had paralyzed her body, taken the pain but left her living. The thought of being forever so enchained was much worse than any physical pain, striking her as hard and swiftly as a sword thrust.

The sky appeared to be lightening a little. Now with the bobbing of her head she sighted a patch of blue. Since she faced the tail of the horse, back the way they had come, she caught sight of what must be the rear guard, a single man who rode as one who was uneasy, turning watchful eyes on the back track. There was no mark of any roadway. This was all open moorland with a round mound or hill here and there. The spring growth was already high and green. She saw a hawk wheel into the upper air, a flock of smaller birds turn sharply, forming a fan pattern against the enlarging patch of blue.

As Tirtha became more and more alert mentally, breaking through layers of shadows that had wrapped her around as a moth might lie encased in its cocoon, she watched the rear guard with greater care. Twice he pulled to a halt, sat looking back over his shoulder. Yet the land behind was so open one could view it for an ever-lengthening distance. Even she—who had no control over her eyes and had to watch those portions the movements of the pony allowed her—saw nothing move there.

Again her interest awoke so that she longed to reach out. Alon? No, she dared not attempt to touch the boy; she did not know how deeply he was kept captive, not only physically, but by the talent of the Dark Lord. Surely that Lord could sense, since he must be very alert to any manifestation of the talent, any attempt on her part to contact her fellow prisoner. So feeble a gift as hers would lie as open to his reading as one of the record rolls of Lormt.

Still—were they pursued? She remembered Alon's whisper of one who followed. The raided garth where Gerik had caused red ruin—could that have set on their trail some band of a lord's following determined on vengeance? Tirtha believed not. Hawkholme lay too far inland. No one would have followed the raiders with such single-minded fury unless it was their own homestead that had been so despoiled, and Gerik had left only death behind him at the garth that had been Alon's home.

There remained Alon and that Wise Woman Yachne who had taken him into the homestead. Why had Yachne tried to protect and hide one who was manifestly not of her race or kind? Had she perhaps foreseen a future in which Alon could be forged into a tool or a weapon of her own? The Power had always been a danger to those who could summon it even slightly—in itself it was a peril. He or she who could accomplish a little began to yearn to be able to control more. If that inner desire became great enough, it corrupted. Such corruption was of the Dark.

Yes, Tirtha believed that one who valued, who craved Power above all else, might trail behind and seek, single-minded, to regain what had been lost. Even though the odds against any success were very, very high. Yachne had been said to be a Wise Woman, a healer of sorts, which meant one limited in talent. However, that did not also mean that the face she presented to the world was more than a mask. She could well have come out of Escore on some business of her own, adopting a lesser role in Karsten than she would play among those with whom she was bred. Alon had been her charge or her possession.

Tirtha had not realized how much her mind had cleared until that faint pain began to increase. Her body, which had been so dead, was coming awake. She cringed inwardly, realizing the torment that lay ahead, carried as she was, if the action of the herb began to fail. The end could be that she would face such pain as that poor remnant of a man from Hawkholme must have felt before the last act his captor had forced him to had released him forever. Tirtha knew some of the disciplines of pain-containing—had used them during her journeys to combat the ordinary small trials of any tramping of the roads, but they had never been meant to cope with such an ordeal as would be hers now. There was no one to aid her, unless she could provoke the lord of this party to finish her off as they had done the Falconer. Perhaps it would come to that, if she could persuade him that the casket would be his after such a merciful stroke.

Only, what she held could not be so easily surrendered. That knowledge was deep in her. Tirtha was still guardian, dead or alive, until released from her bond. A provoked sword thrust would not be the answer.

The rear rider had reined in his mount once more, facing the back trail. He was a brutal looking fellow, clad in rusted and badly mended mail, a pot helm a little too large. Its ill fit appeared to bother him, for he put up a hand now and then to tug it more firmly in place. All the rest of their party that she could not see plodded on, drawing her, in turn, farther and farther away from the rear guard who still sat where he was, his horse's head hanging as if it had been ridden too far and too long.

This was a quiet group. There was no conversation among them, only a snuffle of bit, the whiffling snort of mount now and then to break the silence. Pressing in on Tirtha came their combined feelings of uneasiness, fear. She remembered more clearly Gerik's protests about crossing the border. There were hills between fabled Escore and Karsten, though not the stark mountainous country that formed the Eastern barrier back in Estcarp. Even so, crossing into such debatable land was nothing to be taken lightly. Those of lowland blood, with their hatred and fear of what the Falconer termed witchery, would have little desire to push on.

The Falconer . . . Shot down . . . she had a dim memory of hearing that. He must have brought her out of the crumbling fortress-hall with Alon's help, only to meet death. What had become of his power sword? She was somehow sure that none in this company would dare to claim it. It had come to him, and there were many old tales of weapons that chose their masters—or mistresses—serving no others. Now her memory grew vivid for an instant or two, and she remembered his body arching over her and Alon, keeping from them, or ready to do so, the tumbling walls. A blank shield served his employer to the death—that was the code. Yet it was Tirtha's thought that in the end the Falconer had not lived only by the code, that, woman though she was, he might have forgotten her sex in that moment and viewed her as a shield-mate cut down in battle. She remembered his dark, hollow-cheeked face and what lay always in the depths of his eyes—that strange yellowish fire that could be heightened by anger or perhaps by hidden thoughts she had never understood. He had found peace, which was all she could wish for him.

His falcon, which had so oddly taken on that other-seeming when death finished it—what had been its real end? And who or what was Ninutra?

Even thinking that name opened a new inner path of thought. This time Tirtha did not see a woman's face, rather she felt a warmth through-out her whole body—inward surely, not in her drugged and deadened flesh. While . . .

The air twisted, turned. Could *air* twist and turn? In spite of the bob-bing of her head, that constant motion which was disruptive to clear sight, Tirtha detected movement overhead, and it *was* in the air! A gathering of fog—whence came a single patch of fog on so clear a day? Some small cloud might have been dispatched to hang directly over them, traveling steadily with them. Was she the only one who saw it? She heard nothing from those riding about her.

Fog? No, shadow! Only one should not be able to see an airborne shadow at midday! It twirled, lengthened, solidified. The same sword that had hung above the three of them back at Hawkholme was now visible, growing in both breadth and length. They traveled under it, and there was a threat in it.

Not for her; Tirtha had already decided that. This was a manifesta-tion of the same power that had aided them at Hawkholme. Like the gray bird, it was representative of a warning, a challenge. She half expected to hear the scream of the bird, perhaps that name uttered out of the air overhead.

What she did hear was a loud cry that must have issued from the man leading the pony to which she was bound. He had reined in and jerked the pony in turn to a halt. Her head had fallen a little to one side so that she could see his arm stretched upward as he pointed to what hung above them. There were other exclamations. Then came the voice of the one she had not yet directly seen—that Dark Lord who commanded Gerik in spite of the outlaw's will.

"It is a vision only. Are you such as to be frightened by shadows?"

"There are shadows and shadows." Again Gerik spoke, his impudence hardly controlled. "If it is a vision, Lord, then whose? And it has an uncanny look to it. I do not think *that* and your cup-brother would deal well together. You have said that there will be those in Escore to hail us with 'well done' since we bring that dead thing over there with its hell box, and this youngling whom you drag along in spite of the death-coming look to him also. Well, are we not in Escore, or so you have told us? Where then are your friends? Does it not seem that it is those with little liking for you who have found us first? I say"—his voice came a little louder now as if he were approaching the pony upon which Tirtha was tied—"that we have fulfilled our part of the bargain, Lord. This dealing with Powers—

leave witchery to them who know it better than we. There are good enough pickings in the Duchy; why should we go hunting trouble?"

It would seem that the only man Tirtha held in sight agreed with that. For he who had led the pony dropped the rope and backed his mount away from the smaller beast. A moment later he was joined by another, who looked much like him and was surely close akin to the one she had seen stop behind them on the trail.

Above them all now the sword had taken on such firm substance that it looked—at least to her—to be a very solid object suspended in the air and of a length that only a man near the height of a foothill could have put hand to, had it indeed been a weapon to be used.

The Dark Lord laughed.

"It is too late, Gerik. As I told you once—though perhaps you did not believe me—those who take service with my lord (and by pledging your aid to me in certain matters, you did just that) are not released at their will. No, not until he has had his full usage of them! Try to retreat—if you can!"

The two men within Tirtha's range of vision looked a little pale beneath the dirt and the wind-browning of their faces. Both turned as one and used the spur. Their small horses bounded forward down the back trail. However, they had only gone a length or two before they slowed and cried out, as beasts do, in an extremity of terror.

Crouched in the grass confronting them was such a creature as Tirtha had never seen, though the thing she had faced in the mountains had been strange and evil enough. This was in its way worse, for it had nothing about it of any sane animal. Rather it was insectile, as if one of the harmless spiders, which wove morning webs in the meadows, had grown nearly pony size in an instant. The thing was furred with coarse, bright scarlet hair, thickening about the joints of its huge limbs into vast masses. Across its head was a row of pitless dark eyes above mandibles that clicked, while a thick green slime oozed from those threatening crunchers.

The riders were fighting their horses as the mounts whirled, dashed back past Tirtha, carrying their riders with them, away from that creature, which squatted and eyed the party with an intent glare.

"Yahhhhh!" It must have been Gerik himself, the man who had refused to be totally cowed by his employer, who bounded up. He had a heavy spear in his hand, holding it with the ease of one who had victoriously gone into battle many times before, and he must have had iron control over his wild-eyed and now screaming horse, for he was forcing it to carry him straight forward, the spear aiming directly at the monster crouching to close the back trail.

17

The spider creature did not await Gerik's charge. Rather it leaped, apparently willing enough to spike its hairy body on a spear in order to reach its enemy. It was Gerik's horse that reared or dodged. The pony's mad fear gave it an agility never meant for such a stocky body. Losing footing the beast crashed sidewise, carrying the man down with it, but not before the spear pierced the thick abdomen of the monster.

Perhaps it was his example showing that the monster could be attacked or the compelling personality of the man who had led them, which now brought those who had first fled back into combat. They returned into Tirtha's line of vision, spurring toward that mass of animal, monster, and man interlocked on the ground, their swords out, flailing at the heaving red-haired form, slashing at any part of it they could touch.

The downed pony screamed as only an animal in dire pain and fear can do. There had been no cry from its rider. Perhaps the shock of that spill had made Gerik an easy prey to the creature. But the thing itself was in dire straits. Twice it strove to draw itself together for another leap. The dribble of poisonous stuff from its mouth parts ran in a thick green stream. It had lost two legs, hacked off by the frenzy of those who attacked it.

A sword thrust, well aimed, cut into one of those intelligent, malice-filled eyes. He who had been so lucky in that stroke tried again. A stream of the evil green slime sprayed outward, sending him back screaming, dropping his blade, tearing with both hands at the skin of his lower face. He began to run in circles, howling like an animal in its death throes.

Part blinded, lacking two limbs as it did, the spear driven far into its paunch, the thing managed to raise itself from the now silent yet still twitching body of the pony and swung to face its second attacker. One foreleg, armed with a vicious looking claw nearly as long as Tirtha's forearm, stabbed out at the fighter who backed, then stood his ground, aiming shearing strokes at the creature. His steel met the claw and rebounded. It would seem that this part was not so vulnerable. Once more that envenomed spray arched through the air from the monster's mouth.

The man leaped back, more lucky than his comrade, as the creature made a jerky move to follow. Then a head and arm, the upper portion of a body, arose from where the thing had squatted over its first prey. Gerik was on his knees. His two hands gripped the hilt of a sword, and he stabbed into the round body now half turned from him. If the claw had been armored well enough to turn away steel, the body of the thing was not so protected. That sword, driven by all the strength the man could summon, sank into the wide back, hilt-deep. There came a fountain gush of black liquid spurting up and over Gerik, who fell, hidden again from sight.

However, the monster did not swing about to savage him. It struggled still to reach the man who had struck it from the front—he retreating hastily. Until at last he broke, turned and ran, while the thing still attempted to leap after him.

At last it toppled, such limbs as remained intact no longer able to support its thick body. Still it was not defeated, for it continued to spray into the air that green slime. Where that fell on the ground, small tendrils of steam or smoke arose, while the air was filled with a vile odor.

It was then that the reins of the pony on which Tirtha was bound were seized, the animal pulled into jolting trot. They were on their way from that battlefield, giving no aid to the man who crawled upon the ground, his ruined face a mask of horror as his screaming became a thick bubbling in his throat. Nor was there sight again of Gerik. The other man who had fought the creature was running, crying out, following behind them. Yet the pony and he who led it gained more ground drawing away from the survivor.

Because of the jolting of the pony, Tirtha could no longer see the battlefield clearly. Nor did she know how many of their party were left. The Dark Lord in command certainly—perhaps he was the one who led her pony—and with him Alon, but were there more? The fact that their captors' numbers had shrunk so drastically might have meant a chance for escape, had she not been in this dead body. However, Alon had perhaps a chance. She longed to contact him.

Pain awakened stronger in her. Perhaps that pain would overtake and hold her a prisoner in another way. Now, however, her mind cleared.

Tirtha seemed to be pushed into thinking, to be far more aware of what lay about them, above them. Above them!

She strove to settle her bobbing head for a fraction of time to glance overhead. Yes, the sword was there. Perhaps that was what had kept the pony steady, kept it from running wildly from the monster. Had the blade also protected them from attack, or had that been the result of Gerik's recklessly brave charge?

Tirtha fought hard to keep the gray length within sight. Yes, she had not been mistaken. There were symbols on the blade of that overshadowing weapon. Many of them appeared on the skin roll the dead man had carried. She recalled Alon thrusting it into the empty dart loop on the Falconer's shoulder belt. If they had not despoiled the dead, these carrion hunters, then there it still remained. Even were it now within her hand, Tirtha would not have known how to make use of it.

They were passing from the open rolling lands now. She caught glimpses of hillocks rising like steps to greater heights on either side. There appeared no road, but she believed that they were following a trail well known to him in command.

Since she dared not try to reach Alon, and she must, as long as she could, remain master of her body (in which the pain was waking more and more with every swing that the swifter pace of the pony brought about), Tirtha set her mind on the shadow sword continuing to hang above them.

She was sure that this manifestation was not of the Dark, that it answered, in a manner not given to her to understand, the thing she carried. Was the sword a weapon of that woman who had come to view them in the hidden chamber?

Ninutra—though Tirtha did not shape that name with her lips or utter it aloud, yet she formed it slowly, letter by letter, in her mind with all the concentration of one following the intricate weaving of a spell. There were words that went with healing; many of them she knew and had used. Such words in themselves had no power, it was the intonation that counted, the fact that the same phrases had been thus employed for countless generations to build a channel for the healing to pass through, even as a mason built a hallway, choosing the best and strongest of the stones available for his task.

Names were power. There were the Great Names, which no one, without strong safeguards, dared to utter. If this was such a one—well, what had she to lose? Life meant very little now. If what she bore, beyond any will or desire of her own, was tied to one of those ominous names, that gave her a small fraction of right to attempt a summoning.

She closed her eyes. Tirtha's heart jumped, and that she also felt. In so much had she gained control of her body. She could lift and lower two eyelids, sense the beating of her own heart!

Closing her eyes firmly again, she turned her sight determinedly inward and for the second time strove to build that name into something she could visualize.

First there were flames, like those that had burst from the corners of the hidden room. They flared in fierce warning. Warning! What did that matter to one like her, already doomed?

Ninutra!

Her will had wakened. If there abode somewhere a power that could be so summoned, then let it come! She was perhaps a plaything, a tool of forces she did not understand. Yet she was the Hawk—and there existed a bargain out of the past. Tirtha had a queer feeling, as if an inner part of her had swung then, quick as a flash of light, across a wide gulf measuring years of time, only to return again.

Ninutra!

It was not the impersonal woman's face that formed or was borne through those flames which died, leaving a mind-picture, indistinct, yet still discernible. This was the countenance of someone not unlike herself— young, a woman, one of the Old Race. Still there was in her great strength, even though she might be but a voice, a channel, for a greater one.

Ninutra!

Behind the woman hung the outline of the shadow sword. Tirtha saw a hand appear also out of the haziness about that face. Fingers closed upon the sword hilt, brought the weapon to swing outward, so that its point was aimed as if ready for combat. There were two other figures moving, one advancing on either side, to stand with that woman. But of those Tirtha could see so little they were like pillars of smoke and mist.

This much she had learned—there were indeed those who could claim the shadow sword. Perhaps they might be, in their own way, favorably disposed toward her. Yet what lay ahead was of more importance than a single woman of the Old Race who had stood by the word of her blood to the end. For that end, when it came, was not concerned with Tirtha herself, but with greater matters.

The three in the mist vanished; not so the sword. It continued to fill Tirtha's mind with its presence. Those symbols along its blade blazed with angry fire. From it she was drawing something—this much had been granted her—strength to hold firm against the pain of her body, that dead body which could no longer serve her. She would be sustained, for there was yet a need for her, and that she would have to accept.

Thus she lay within her vision, holding to it with all her will, striving to force out of it a barrier against her pain. She was never to know how long that vigil of hers lasted.

The sword began to fade, the symbols were gone, sinking into its more and more tenuous length. Tirtha looked upon empty darkness before she opened her eyes upon the outer world again.

She had indeed been deeply sunk inside herself, for she was no longer upon a pony. Instead she lay upon a flat, unmoving surface, a hard surface, as her body returning to half-life told her. There was light here, thin streamers reached like the flames of giant candles up into the sky. Also with that light was a chill, the miasma of evil. This place was of the Dark, no matter what light played on it and within it.

Beyond the upriding columns of light was a night sky. Tirtha saw the far wink of stars, yet between her and their glitter there was a wavering curtain, as if even clean starlight must be so veiled in this evil place. With a determination that drew upon every portion of the strength she hoped still abode within her, Tirtha strove to turn her head.

Pain answered, but pain was not important; she was mistress of her body, of its pain. She threw pain from her as she would throw some evil thing that unwittingly crawled upon her. Then Tirtha discovered that indeed she could shift her head a fraction, see a little of what lay to her left, enough to know she was not alone.

The light came from pillars of what might have been ice, congealed through centuries of freezing. Deep within them lurked shadow cores. Between her and the deadly cold of the nearest pillar was Alon.

He sat, his legs stretched before him, a loop of rope about his ankles. His arms had been drawn cruelly together behind his back and there lashed. With upheld head he stared straight ahead, wearing the blind look of one so overcome by fate that nothing mattered any longer.

"Alon!"

He did not look to her, the trance which held him did not break. Had he retreated into nothingness? No, something assured her that was not so.

"Alon!" The effort to get out that single word for the second time was almost more than Tirtha could rise to.

There was a flicker of expression across his face. Yet he remained so caught in misery he could not be reached. For a long moment she watched him, unable to summon again such strength as those two attempts to reach him had demanded.

"He is gone, he has left us—with the Dark . . ." Those words came from between lips that hardly moved. But in her was a quickening of spirit. Alon wore only the outer mask of shock and despair—within he was still alert!

"This is a place of Dark. He believed us safe-caged here. . . ." Alon was continuing. "Do not summon. The one who rules here will know it."

Do not summon? Had Alon somehow been aware of her earlier struggle? No, do not even think of that within this place! Caution flashed
instantly across Tirtha's mind. There was a Power that made of this a
prison—she had no knowledge of its range—but apparently he who had
brought them here trusted in its strength of guardianship.

Alon still stared into nothingness, but now Tirtha saw that, for all the
cruel straining put upon his arms where they were so lashed behind him,
his hands were moving. His fingers did not try to reach the knotting of
those cords—that would be physically impossible, bound as he was.
Rather, to her wonder, he was smoothing the coils as he might have
smoothed or patted the hide of an animal. What he so played with was not
woven rope, she noted, her full attention drawn by Alon's actions, but a
long strip of braided hide.

What the boy sought to do Tirtha could not understand, but his
motions were purposeful, so she did not try again to distract his attention,
only watched his struggle to pat, stroke, and fondle what bound him,
always giving otherwise the appearance of one completely cowed.

Realizing suddenly that her very attention on the boy might attract
whatever held grim rulership here, she strove to lock it out of her mind
and was about to follow a second line of defense by closing her eyes so
she could be sure she would not turn her head again. Then came a sudden
flicker at the joining of those punishing cords.

Tirtha watched what she thought at first must indeed be an illusion,
deceptive, meant to tantalize, to bring false hope. If it were illusion, it was
a remarkably exact one. The hide loops, which Alon had rubbed and
caressed with his fingertips, moved of themselves. They might have been
sleek creatures of the serpent family that had curled into awkward (for
them) tangles and were now loosening themselves at their own whim.

Tirtha saw the constricting knots unfasten, allowing the rest of the
cords to slide at apparently no other will than a desire within their own
blind lengths. They wriggled across the boy's body, slipped away. His
arms, ridged by brutal welts, fell forward. Tirtha could well imagine the
torment the sudden release of such binding brought him. Yet one hand
lying half across his thigh was twitching, and he leaned forward, to bring
its fingertips against the second drawing of cords about his ankles.

Once more he began that rubbing, that caressing; Tirtha watched his
face intently. He retained his unrevealing mask. One glancing at him
would say he was under such complete control as vicious handling and
fear could force on a young child. There was no movement of his lips—
he could *not* be reciting any spell or words of power.

Yet again he succeeded, as the second loop slackened, drew itself out
of the tightly drawn knots, and he was free. He made no further move as

yet, simply sat loose of bonds. Then she saw his chest arch in a deep breath and his hands come together, as he deliberately rubbed ridged wrists and the grooves on his arms with a dogged determination.

Was there other restraint laid on the boy besides the cords from which he had just released himself? Or could Alon now get beyond these lighted pillars? She could do, say nothing, only watch and wait.

However, it would seem that whatever talent the boy had brought to his freeing had not been exhausted. He continued to sit rubbing his wrists, staring ahead. Save that now there was a quality in that stare which was not one of resignation or retreat. Tirtha's own senses heightened little by little. That she lay in a place which was wholly inimical to her and all her kind, which generated within it a chill she could feel faintly as her body slowly awoke, she had accepted. Yet there was something else beyond. . . .

Alon changed position for the first time, drawing his feet under him, so that he now squatted on his heels. He made no move toward Tirtha, appearing to be still locked in that stare. Yet there was a subtle change, a kind of alertness, as might be sensed in one awaiting a signal.

Tirtha longed to be able to change the position of her own head enough to follow the direction of the boy's continued line of gaze. Only she could not. Alon had stopped rubbing his bruised wrists and arms; now he put out his hands and drew to him those lengths of cords he had in some manner made his servants. He stretched them out side by side. At her present angle, Tirtha could not see what he was doing; she could only speculate.

Once more his hands moved. He was again using his fingers, presumably passing them along the cords. These movements were more emphatic, swifter. She watched as best she might, and at the same time she grew to sense, more and more, that outside the ghastly candle pillars of this cage there was another entity at watch. The miasma of evil which encased this place was like a wall. If a would-be rescuer prowled there, the girl could not know, nor dared she strive to learn.

Alon raised a hand slowly, the fingers moving as if he beckoned. A dark shape obeyed his summons, lifting to follow. Serpent? No, the thing was too thin, it lacked any swell of head she could see, having only a questing tip. The cord! It was taking on a form of pseudo-life, or else Alon had wrought from it an hallucination!

As the boy spread both hands outward in a vast sweep, the cord end remained aloft, stretching up near as high as his own head from the pavement. It swayed back and forth. His hands met palm to palm and then pushed apart. The tip of the cord swung away from him, flung itself toward the line of pillars, then fell completely out of Tirtha's line of vision. Alon's hands continued to move. Not in the wide sweeps he had first used, rather up and down in small motions, as if, though they were flattened out palm down, still he had grasp of an invisible line that fed along the ground. He had risen to his knees, his back straight, so concentrating on what he did that the aura of his intense effort reached her.

All Alon's strength was centered on this. She remembered how once she had asked of him and of Nirel that they lend their energy to support her in farseeing. Could she, in some manner, now back Alon in a like fashion? There was the pain ever pushing against what barriers she had set her inner will to hold. Were she to release that will, strive to add its force to what the boy needed, those barriers could well fall entirely.

Tirtha closed her eyes for a moment, faced firmly what might be the result of such action on her part. Alon was risking much, using full energy on what he strove to do. She could only believe that he was battling their enemy. While Alon himself—she had come to accept that the boy understood more than she could even guess.

She chose. Will could be aimed, and in that moment before she could shrink from the results of such a breaching of her own defenses, Tirtha did just that. She kept her eyes fast closed, but held Alon clear in her mind, as she summoned up a picture of a touching between them, not for any communication that might arouse a guardian here—rather a picture of her own hand reaching out to clasp the boy's squared shoulder and, down that arm and hand, flooding the strength of her own will.

The fire of pain leapt in upon her. Tirtha was wrapped in it. Still she fought to keep mental hold on her vision. Might even pain itself be a source of power? That flashed across her mind and she seized upon it, held it, strove to add the force, not of the torment, but of the power that generated it, to what she had to give.

This was a descent into such agony as she would not have believed anyone could bear. Nor could she even be sure that what she was trying to do met with any success. Had her offering reached Alon—could she spur, energize him further in his strange ordering of the very bonds that had held him prisoner?

Agony filled her, as if her flesh swelled outward, unable to contain the full force of this. There was a burst of fire in her head. Alon was gone, and then everything . . .

"Tirtha!" Then again, "Tirtha."

Into the great nothingness rang that name. Something answered against its will, fighting, and yet unable to withstand the drawing of that voice.

"Tirtha!"

Three was a number of power—an ancient bit of knowledge. Thrice summoned, one could not remain apart. She was drawn—all that remained of her.

Searing pain came, then it was gone. For another had cut it from her even as one might cut away a tattered body covering. Tirtha was sealed against what her body might strive to raise for her punishment. Also that awakening which had begun in the place of the Dark had carried forward. She knew that she breathed, if in shallow gasps, that she heard with her ears, and now she saw with her eyes, for she opened them.

Around her there stood no tall pillars of corpse candles. The scent and strength of the Dark was gone. There was light, yes, but it was the true coloring of the sky at sunrise, while over her blew a gentle wind carrying the scent of flowers. Only more important to her, was the face of the one who knelt beside her. Hands a little browned by the sun—long-fingered, slender hands—were outstretched above Tirtha's breast, and she knew that it was those hands that barred the pain from overwhelming her.

This was the girl she had seen in her mind vision—she who had held the shadow sword. She was not the Great One who had looked upon them with detachment and no hint of pity, rather this one was a Voice, a priestess. In her the human still abode and was alive in her face and in her voice as she spoke.

"Welcome, Hawk Blood, who kept well the faith. The conclusion of the guardianship is near upon us. We come to an end—and perhaps a beginning—if the Power reckons it so."

"Who . . . ?" Tirtha found a weak word.

"I am Crytha," the other answered readily. It would seem that there was indeed to be a naming of names. "I serve Her whom you have knowledge of, even though that came to you only dimly. She of the Shadow Sword, the Lady Ninutra."

As she spoke that name, it was echoed. In the air over her downbent head appeared the bird that had been born from the dying falcon, or else one so like that there could not be feather's difference between them. It opened its beak to scream. Crytha looked away from Tirtha, her eyes viewing something or someone beyond.

"Yes, it is truly time," she said. "Our ingathering begins."

18

Though pain had been walled away, Tirtha had no strength or power to shift her helpless body. She could only see what advanced into a narrow range of vision. Crytha still knelt beside her, but two others now moved forward to stand, one on either side of the priestess, each in his own way memorable to look upon. One was tall, broad of shoulder, thick of body, as befits an axeman. For the weapon he bore two-handed before him was a double-bladed axe. His helm mounted a marvelously wrought dragon from beneath which he looked upon Tirtha with compassion. Yet his eyes moved from side to side at times, as if they were in a place where constant close watch must be kept.

His companion was younger, more slender, fair of skin, and he held a sword such as was common enough among those who had ridden along the border. He might not be wholly of the Old Race, yet he was plainly human born. It was he who spoke now.

"There comes a rider. . . ."

Crytha made a small gesture. "Yes. But there is more than that one. Rane walks . . ."

The wielder of the axe shifted his weapon as if making sure of its balance. His features lost all softness, his upper lip lifted the way a hunting cat would snarl.

"We are too close to *his* source," he said. "Best we . . ."

Crytha interrupted him. "She cannot be moved." Her gesture was to Tirtha. "This must remain our field of battle whether it appears a fitting one or not. For she also has a part still to play." Crytha got easily and gracefully to her feet. The three of them, Tirtha saw, looked beyond in another direction.

With infinite care she brought her small strength to bear, willed her head to shift. It lay a little raised, as if there were support beneath. Thus she discovered she could see farther, even look upon what still rested on her breast, her hands frozen so tightly to it they might have become a part of it. The casket was still hers.

She raised her eyes from it, to follow the others' line of gaze. So she caught sight of Alon. He was not standing as they did, awaiting what came, rather he raced forward. She heard the high neigh of a Torgian, a cry of triumph from an equine throat.

There were many rocks about. She still felt a chill issuing from behind. Though they may have, through some trick of power, won free of that Dark cage, yet the newcomers had not transported her too far from it. From the amount of debris lying about, she could be amidst ruins of either a temple or perhaps a hold or a village. Between two still-standing heaps of time-eaten stone, marking nearly destroyed walls, Alon dashed. Moments later he returned, fingers laced into the mane of a horse, to the riding pad of which clung a man, his body drooping, his dark-haired head bare, half his face masked by a brown crust of dried blood. Yet no mask could ever again conceal him from Tirtha's recognition.

Within her prison-body, her heart gave a great leap, as if to break all bonds of bone and flesh. She was half—three-quarters dead, yes. But here she saw another dead arise to ride.

The mount followed Alon, rather than being directed by its rider. Though his eyes were open, Tirtha wondered how much he really saw of what lay about him. The Torgian came to a halt, its head down, as Alon smoothed its rough forelock, murmuring to the horse the while. Now the rider stirred, strove to straighten. A measure of intelligence came into his eyes, piercing whatever daze he had fallen into. It was plain he both saw and knew Tirtha. Then his gaze traveled to those three who stood by her. She saw his claw waver toward his belt. He wore no sword now, there was no dart gun in its holster, but the glowing pommel of the weapon of power was still within his reach.

He dismounted, perhaps would have fallen had he not caught at the mane of the Torgian to steady himself. Crytha took a step or two ahead of her companions.

"Long awaited, come at last . . ." It was as if she recited part of a ritual. "Brother of the winged ones, you to whom the weapon, Basir's Tongue, has cleaved and made choice, we give you welcome, even though it be not to your rest but perhaps your bane and ours."

The Falconer stared at her. Now he loosed his hold upon the horse's coarse upspringing hair, raised hand toward his head in an uncertain gesture.

"You—are—the—night—walker. . . ." He spoke hoarsely, as if against his will. "You came to draw me back from death."

"From death?" Crytha said, as his last pause lengthened. "No, you were not dead, Falconer. They left you for such, but while you serve the Great Ones, then death comes not so easily."

"I serve the Lady." There was a tightness about his mouth. Flecks of dried blood fell from his jaw as he spoke. His hair, as Tirtha could see in the ever brightening day, was matted with dust and blood along his skull over the left ear. "This lady . . ."

His claw pointed to Tirtha where she lay. "What would you do with her? Does your Great One claim her, too?"

"She does," Crytha answered promptly. "And you, also, for what you carry."

It was her turn to point, and her fingers did not indicate the sword whose light gleamed bright enough to contrast even with the day, but rather the dart-looped belt about his shoulder. He looked down, following the line of her finger. Then he reached up slowly and clasped what he had carried out of Hawkholme—that rod with its concealed roll of the unreadable.

"How . . ." He looked totally bemused, as if this were the last thing he expected to find.

"By the wit of your lady," Crytha told him briskly. She crossed to stand before him, holding out her hand. He fumbled, freeing the dead man's legacy, then gave it to her.

The younger man who had joined her had half turned his head, looked over his shoulder to where Tirtha believed might be the site of the cage from which she had been brought.

"There is a stirring . . ." he cautioned sharply.

He of the axe laughed, giving a small flourish of his ponderous weapon. "When is there not, Yonan? Let it stir. It must come to terms sooner or later—its or ours. And I will wager the weight of this"—again he gave a short dip and lift of his weapon—"that the result will not be altogether to the Dark's liking, if at all."

"He who comes is Rane." Holding the tube of parchment, Crytha had moved back toward them.

"Meaning, Lady of the Shadow Sword, that I am too hopeful? Ah, when has it ever bettered a man to foresee an ill end? Such foreboding will sap strength before the contest even begins. And this is a foreseen meeting—what of your Great One?"

Crytha frowned. "You are bold, Uruk. One of the Four Great Weapons may be yours, but that fact does not open all gates for you."

The man, still smiling, made her a half salute. "Lady Crytha, as a twice-living man I have seen much, heard much, done much. There is lit-tle left of any awe in me. I have been a god to the Thas, those under-ground dwellers of the Dark Rule, and I have twice been a war captain. We are facing now a battle, so I ask you frankly, what may we expect in the way of allies?"

It was not the priestess but Alon who answered him. The boy had advanced a little, the Torgian following him, and Nirel, one hand again on the mount's neck for support, pacing along.

"You have us . . ."

Uruk turned his face toward the boy, and his smile grew the wider.

"Well said, youngling. Having seen how you broke from Rane's cage and drew this lady with you, I give you good credit as one to stand beside in line of battle. And"—his gaze swept on to the Falconer who met it head up, back straight, with a lifted chin—"any man who carries one of the Four is a shield to the arm, a stout wall to one's back. Welcome, you to whom Basir's Tongue gives willing service. And"—now his eyes dropped to Tirtha—"Lady, you are of the Old Blood, and it is plain that this was a meeting planned out of the time we know and bow to. I know not what your weapon may be—is it left to you to be able to wield it?"

She looked down at the casket between her locked hands. "I do not know"—she spoke for the first time—"whether what I bear is weapon or prize. I only know that of it I am the set guardian, and this geas has not been lifted from me. I think that if you depend upon me for any weaponry you must plan again. This body is dead and I remain in it still only through a power I do not understand."

She heard a breath quickly drawn and saw the Falconer's claw swing forward and then back again against his body. Just the claw, she did not look higher to his face.

"Rane!" The younger man appeared to pay but little attention to the rest of them, his concentration was on what lay behind, which she could not see.

There came a crackling in the air about them, a feeling of Power gath-ering, sweeping. Not yet at them, rather for him, or *that*, which sum-moned. Uruk glanced once in the same direction his companion watched, and then he spoke to Crytha. His smile had vanished; there was a sharp-ness in his voice.

"I have asked—what of your Great One?"

"She shall do as she desires." The girl was abrupt in her reply. She was angered, Tirtha thought, by his question or his insistence upon an answer to it.

Uruk shrugged. "It is true that the Great Ones make it a habit to con-ceal their plans from their servants. Well enough. If this is to be our force, then make you ready." His sweep of eye passed over them all. "Rane, I do not know in person. In the telling any story grows the greater with each repeating of it. He is a Dark One who has his own strengths. It would appear we are about to test them."

The short sword to which Crytha and Uruk had given a name was free in the Falconer's hand. He stood away from the horse, came to Tirtha after the proper fashion of a shield man serving his employer. She looked up the length of his lean body. The tattered cloak had disappeared, along with his battered helm, his long sword, and dart gun. Now he worked his arm through the useless dart belt, tossing it from him. His hand showed blue as if the light of the sword pommel pierced his flesh.

Tirtha felt a new warmth. Her hands that had been so useless and dead—were they coming alive again? Between them, the casket blazed. Alon had come up on her other side. Even as the other three appeared to draw together into a unit, so were they also forming a common bond. The boy made a summoning wave with one hand. From the ground where Tirtha had not noticed it lying, there arose, swaying back and forth serpent-fashion once again, one of those coils of leather rope. The end of it swooped forward into Alon's grasp. He twisted a goodly length of it about his bruised and blood-stained wrist as if to give it stout anchorage, and then he raised the loose-hanging portion to swing it back and forth.

Uruk's axe was in plain sight, Yonan had drawn his sword, touched its point to earth, grasping its hilt in both hands. But Crytha seemed not to note all those battle preparations. Instead she had drawn the skin of symbols forth from its carrier, letting the rod fall free, and was studying it with care. Tirtha saw her lips move as if she shaped sounds, but there was also a frown of puzzlement between her eyes. Then, with a quick step, she was at Tirtha's side, had stooped and laid the roll of skin on the lid of the casket. Once more back among her companions, the priestess then held out her empty hand.

Mist whirled, gathered, intensified. What she held was the Shadow Sword, save that Tirtha would now swear that blade had real substance and was of the same strong steel as she had seen in many a warrior's scabbard. Along it runes glowed brightly, faded, then glowed again, as they might if they winked in and out of another time and space.

This Great One who might be moved to join with them or not—Tirtha's thought went to her. It would seem that perhaps her active help was not to be counted on. Surely they had come out of the sealed room at Hawkholme with her aid, only then to fall straightway into the hands of the enemy. Or had that been all a part of a plan? Perhaps they were of no value for what they were, only for the services they rendered. Perhaps she and Alon had been deliberately given into captivity that they might be brought to this place at this hour. Tirtha was sure she could not depend on any concern for her as a person, she was but the means of controlling what was frozen into her grasp.

Controlling? Why had that particular word come into her mind? She had no control over the box or what it might contain. Hers was only the guardianship. Yet in her dreams the Lord and Lady of Hawkholme had known . . .

Tirtha looked to the casket. Warmth—the warmth had grown. The scroll fashioned of ancient skin hung across the lid, touched her two hands, for Crytha had left it unrolled when she had put it there. Tirtha struggled to grasp some wisp of thought hovering at the very edge of her consciousness, the importance of which—yes! It was important! Hawk was the guardian—she was Hawk!

But the Great One was not here, unless some portion of her dwelt within Crytha, now armed with the Shadow Sword. Certainly she was *not* in Tirtha. What could be done, must be done—that would be of Tirtha's doing. She began her own moves, though her broken body lay inert. To use power only a little—that added to one's talent. To be a guardian of Power—one did not remain unchanged! She was left only her thoughts.

She envisioned the casket as it had been in her dream, standing on the high table, open, an equal distance from both lord and lady. What lay within—what must be guarded? An open casket—perhaps now she was fatally loosing what should be bound—but she *would* be a part of this battle, not an inanimate prize for them to fight over.

Two of them—lord, lady . . . Did it then take two, a man and woman, to complete the full pattern? Balance was ever a law of nature, perhaps of witchery also. Witchery—the Falconer had called it that, her own small dabblings in the unknown. Yet he carried now what this axe man out of Escore called a "named weapon," one of four of power.

Two to summon—Alon?

Tirtha did not raise her eyes to the boy where he stood beside her. She tried to shut from her mind, from *her*, the outer world beyond. If they moved into battle, there was nothing at all she could do now to aid and perhaps she could hinder. Therefore let her try this.

It was like feeling one's way along a passage in deep dark, through unknown halls and runways, never sure of taking the right turning. Two and an open casket . . .

"Nirel . . ." Names, true names were of importance. He had given his into Alon's keeping; yet she had been present when that was done. Therefore, whether he had intended it or not, it was also hers, though he might not have gifted it directly. "Nirel . . . Nirel . . ." Three times called—the power lay in such calling.

She did not look to him either. Had she even called aloud so that he could hear?

"Give me"—now she spoke deliberately, with the full power of her thought behind what she would say—"your sword hand."

The metal claw—that was not the man. She must have flesh to flesh, even as it had been in Hawkholme with those others of whose blood she was.

Did he hear? Would he answer? Tirtha centered her thoughts, concentrated with all the force she could raise. Those dark corridors—yes! She had chosen a way that was open, though to where it might lead she did not know, and there was danger in this. But what could stand as true danger to one who was already dead-alive? Danger to him also, but at this moment they were all in peril, and who could balance one against the other as the worst?

Tirtha still watched the casket. However, she was aware of movement at her right. A shadow fell across the upper part of her body. There was the claw, wedged into it the sword, but stretching out to her breast and the casket was a true hand of browned skin, grimed with trail dust, bruised and blood-stained.

The casket—when they had tried to take the casket from her in the outer part of Hawkholme men had died. To take, yes, against her will, in opposition to the guardianship. This she invited, and she believed that she now held that right. If she were wrong, Nirel would die horribly. Yet if he had any such fear, the steadiness of his hand did not betray it.

His palm fell over her hands where she kept her locked grip. She could not feel the warmth of it against her own deadness or perhaps she could not because of the fire rising in the box.

"Raise!" Her voice rang out commandingly. "Lord of the Hawk, help me to raise!"

She saw his hand tighten over hers. A sweep of his fingers flipped away that roll of pictured skin. As if some breeze which could not be felt caught it, it fluttered up. But her inert hand so tightly clasped in his was moving—yes!

At that very moment there came a roar of sound so blasting they might have been struck deaf. Instantly, a vast wave of darkness followed, washing out from behind where Tirtha lay. Things moved in that darkness. She heard cries, saw quick flames that might have come from axe blades, from swords, even from the lashing of a cord whip.

No, this other task was for her, for Nirel. If he followed his warrior's instinct now and arose to fight whatever had spread from the trap, they were lost! He must not!

The blue light from the sword in his claw still hung over her, joining the glow from the box. And his hand remained on hers! He was slowly raising that lid, even as she had asked of him. Still she could not see what lay within, for the box was so placed that the opening was on the other side.

The lid arose until it was straight up, and the glow from within burned bright and even. His hand remained firmly on hers, holding them so.

Now Tirtha cried aloud: "The time is served, Ninutra—Hawk bond is given."

What loomed out of the dark before her, standing at the foot of her supine body—this was not the woman of the impressive face nor her priestess. This was another. Nor was he . . .

Human in his outward form, or did he wear that as he would wear clothing when he treated with her kind? He was weaponless, nor did he wear mail—rather a tight half garment, which seemed made of reptile skin clinging tightly to his lower limbs, reaching to his waist. It was black, but the edges of the scales glinted with the scarlet of new shed blood. Above it the dusky skin of his torso was smooth, his face awesomely handsome, his head capped with a tight-fitting covering of the same jet and scarlet scaled skin, enclosed at the brow edge by a broad band of scarlet gems. He raised his hands slowly, and Tirtha could see webs of skin as he spread wide his fingers.

He straightened them out flat as if waiting for something to be laid upon them. Nor needed he to voice his demand; he desired what Nirel and she together had uncovered.

"Time is served." His lips did not move, but words rang into silence. For though that black cloud still swirled about, there was no longer any flash of weapons through it, no sound of a struggle.

"I . . . am . . . the . . . Hawk. . . ." It was as if a heavy weight rested on Tirtha so that she had to force out those words with a pause for breath between each of them.

"You die. . . ." he returned, with that same indifference she had sensed in Ninutra. "Your death can be swift and in ease. It can be otherwise. . . ."

"I . . . am . . . Hawk. Lord and Lady—theirs the guardianship . . ."

"Lord?" There was mockery in that. "I see no lord, only a discredited beggar of a masterless fighting man."

"He is what I choose by my own right. . . ."

For a moment Rane made her no answer. He was looking, she knew, to Nirel. And as if she had seen it written on the air between the two of them, she knew what Rane would do, was doing now. He was calling upon age-old beliefs, all the prejudice of Nirel's people, drawing upon their disgust for women which abode within the mind and memory of the man beside her, striving to use such to end this alliance. She could not fight this portion of the battle—it was Nirel's alone. Perhaps it was already lost.

Yet still his hand remained on hers, and the claw-held sword was steady to light that joining.

What *did* Rane raise in Nirel? Tirtha could not guess. Nor could she reach out, she discovered, to aid the other in his fight. Would the fact of sword-oath, as great a bond as that was among his kind, be any armor against such an assault as this?

"Fool, die then!"

Rane's palms turned down. He no longer waited for a gift. His fingers crooked. Through her ran pain—red pain—a fire eating away her body inch by inch. She struggled to keep back her screams, wondering how long she could. Let Nirel release this common hold, and that other—the victory would be *his*!

The fragment of skin with its scrawl of pictured symbols, which had been fluttering in the air above the box, though it could not be wind-borne, suddenly began to twist upon itself. Even through the haze of her pain, Tirtha saw it change. The twisting substance took on a bird shape—not that of the gray bird which was Ninutra's messenger. This one was darker, black of feather as the clouds about them.

It . . . it lacked a foot, its head drooped, its wings beat with such a manifest effort that it could barely keep aloft. But it flew straight toward Rane. Then, with a last desperate burst of speed, it sped into his face as if determined to pluck out an eye, as Tirtha had heard the war falcons had once been battle-trained to do.

The Dark Great One threw up an arm to beat the flyer away. As he did, that claw, so close to her own body, moved also. The sword of power that had been found in a place of death hurtled through the air, crossing over the casket from which, in its passing, it appeared to draw more light—went on—aimed at the dark-skinned breast of him who threatened.

There came a blast of red, of black, if both could be the color of flames. Tirtha was blinded by that vast surge of energy, that upward flare. She felt the pressure laid on a hand coming to life—alive to agony. Nirel's flesh against hers, so tormented and torn, was forcing down the lid of the casket, to seal it again. She twisted under a final upsurge of agony, and at last she screamed in a way that tore at the very lining of her throat.

Dreamy content, a feeling of rightness in the world—what world? Where? She was dead. Could one dead feel the beating of a heart, draw deep breaths of scented wind? There was no pain, there was only . . .

Slowly Tirtha opened her eyes. Sunlight beamed over her head—the sun of early summer. She was stronger, more alive than she had ever felt before in her whole pinched, grim existence, as if she had been truly dead before and only now awakened into life. Her body was whole. Instinctively she used a healer's sense without thinking to assure herself of that. In fact, it was as if she somehow stood above and beyond that body and could see into it. There were no broken bones, no harm. She was healed!

She lay in a strange place—a round hollow filled with red mud that gave off an odor akin to certain herbs she knew. There came a tapping. She looked down. Mud had been mounded over her body, had hardened into a crust that covered her. A bird now perched upon the smaller hump above her upturned feet, and with its bill, it was chipping away at the covering which fell in flakes. A bird? No, a falcon, black and strong and standing on *two* feet!

There was a stir by her side. Quickly she turned her head. Nirel knelt there, even as he had done when they had united to open the casket. There was no encrusted blood matting his dark hair, no sign of any wound. His fine-drawn body was bare, unscarred. He, too, was picking at that which covered her, picking with *two* hands. The cruel claw was gone, he had ten fingers busy at his task.

She gasped and he smiled—such a smile as she thought could never have touched the somber face she had learned to know so well. Then he raised his restored hand, spread, retracted, spread again, those fingers.

"It . . ." The wonder of that or of her own healing encompassed her, and her voice was lost in it.

"It is witchery," he said with such a light gaiety that she wondered if this could be someone else wearing Nirel's body. Then she looked into his falcon eyes and knew that could not be so. "The witchery of Escore. We have been here long, my lady, but it has served us well."

She remembered. "The casket!"

"There is no more geas for the Hawk," he told her, as he pulled away with his new-found fingers a long strip of dried clay. "That witchery has been reclaimed by the one who set it, having once sent forth the casket into safety with those of your clan who swore to guard it when the Shadow fell here in the long ago. It was returned that it might serve now as a weapon in the right hands."

"Ninutra?"

He nodded as he pulled off more of the clay, then clasped her hand, drawing her up toward him. She looked from those entwined hands to him.

"I am still a woman." She forgot Great Ones and their dealings.

"As I am a man."

"And a Falconer?" She could not yet accept this change in him. Dim in her mind was that dream vision, Lord and Lady under the Hawk, closed in a bond she had never known or thought to know, but which might possibly exist again.

He turned his head and chirped. The bird arose from the crumbled clay, gave a cry, alighted on his shoulder.

"In so much as this"—he lifted his free hand and caressed the feathered head which bent to his touch—"do I hold with the old. But now I am a Hawk—did not you yourself name me so, my lady?"

Was there a shade of anxiety in that? Could it be that he looked to *her* for reassurance?

"A Hawk," she returned firmly, and allowed him to steady her on her feet. More than their bodies had been cleansed and healed here. There might lie before them much that was of the Dark—more pain, more needed strength, but neither of them would walk alone again.

"Alon?" For the first time she remembered the third one of their comradeship.

"He too seeks a destiny—that which is truly his."

Tirtha nodded. Yes, that would also follow. Alon in his own way was now free.

"A Hawk," she repeated softly. "And let them 'ware all hawks henceforth, my lord, Nirel."

His arm was about her shoulders where the weight felt right, a part of a life to be. The falcon took wing and spiralled heavenward as together they walked away from what was past and could be forgotten at will.

THE GATE OF THE CAT

*With gratitude for Ingrid without whose help
this book would never have come to be.*

1

The long evening twilight pulled pools of shadows from small bushes. Kelsie shivered though she was warm enough in the quilted coat and the thick slacks above boots which seemed to sink a little more at every step she took over the reach of peaty soil which lay between her and the rise of the mist-crowned hills beyond. It was to her an unreal, even threatening landscape, yet she was far from turning back. She set her teeth and tightened her grip on the small basket she carried. Maybe tonight she would succeed; she refused to give up and accept all their stories.

At the present she saw nothing beautiful or imposing in the land about her, for all the gushing of the travel brochures on which she had first built her ideas of what was to be found and seen in these far northern Scottish highlands. Instead, she had the feeling of tramping over a deserted land in which some invisible menace lay in wait. One could well believe in Black Dogs and Daft Ponies out of Hell, of the meddling of otherworld things hereabout. Goodness knew there were stories enough— and she had listened to them eagerly when they had been told about the fireside. Only this was not the safety of a room lit and undercover.

She listened apprehensively to the noises of the night. There was the bark of a vixen, a distant answering howl from some farm dog. In answer to that stark loneliness, which those cries only accentuated, she hummed under her breath. It was the wordless up and down of notes that she always used when she confronted injured or frightened animals. Injured— She felt again the white hot stab of rage which had filled her two days ago when she had seen that torturous trap and, caught in it, ragged, bloodstained toe pads—two pads of a cat's paw gnawed purposefully to give the captured freedom.

Good for nothing they said—to be hunted down before the next lambing season if possible. That Neil McAdams had been very sure of himself about that!

Only she had seen the predator. It was a female, close to kittening. This past day under better light she had traced it up into the wilderness of the hillside. The grouse were thick and she had started up a whole covey, which was doubtless against the strange laws of this place also—

Kelsie set her lips obstinately together as she remembered the parts of fireside talk which she had not relished. The hunting down of a five point stag— Culling (as they called it—why not say what it really was— murder of the innocent) of the deer herd last year. The hunting drives to send birds into the air to be shot for sport—sport!

At least she knew in time she would never fit in here. She would put the house up for sale and—

Up ahead a tall shadow dislodged itself from a clump of brush and moved purposefully in the same direction she was going. There was no mistaking either the nature of the elongated part of that shadow—a man with a gun. And what he hunted here would be—

Kelsie began to run forward. This was still her land and certainly she would have the privilege to say who would come on it, and a right to distrust the motives of any skulker.

She saw ahead the standing stones—they called them that though all but three had been overthrown by the church in the old days. As a lesson to those who clung to the old times and ways, a warning later for those who might meddle in the forbidden. The three which still stood forming a rough arch, one mighty stone of crudely hewn rock balanced on two of its fellows. It was toward that that the intruder was walking.

She was nearly abreast of him now.

Of course it was Neil. Somehow she had known that from the first. The trap had failed so now he would hunt down a wounded animal and use that gun— On her land, never!

There was a wailing sound from beyond. Pain in it as well as feral hatred and determination to be free. The man raised his gun and Kelsie threw herself forward, but tripped. It was only her upflung arm which jarred against his so that when he shot the charge went wild.

"What do you do!" There was hot anger in his voice but Kelsie's attention was beyond—the squat shape drawn in upon itself, huddled in the very center of that archway. The wildcat—perhaps too injured to run, facing them both with hatred and the determination to fight to the death.

"Stop it!" Kelsie was breathless as she regained her feet. "Leave the poor thing alone! Haven't you tormented it enough by now?"

"Stop it, girl!" he snarled angrily back. "Yon beast is vermin. It will savage lambs in the spring—"

He was raising the rifle again just as the moon broke through one of the twilight clouds full upon the arch and the cat crouched in it. This time Kelsie was more surely footed. She dropped her basket and snatched for the gun with both hands. He fended her off and her foot turned on some stone deep buried in the turf. As his fist cracked against the side of her face she spun out and around, voicing a cry of protest and anger, and then fell into the arch from which the injured cat sprang but a second before. As her head hit against the stone Kelsie rolled forward through the same opening into the place of the fallen rocks.

Kelsie was first aware of the warmth. Without opening her eyes she twisted a little so that her face felt the full heat. That small movement sent pain shooting through her head and she cried out. There was movement beside her shoulder, a rough surface rasped across her cheek. At last she opened her eyes and then blinked rapidly as a full force of sun beamed down upon her.

She had a confused memory of falling and then darkness. But surely this was not night in the Scottish foothills—this was day! Had she been hurt and just lain there? And Neil! She propped herself up on one elbow and looked around.

This—how had she come here? Those stones, which had been age buried when she had fallen in among them, were now set up guardian straight. A warmth radiated from the nearest against which she had lain. The stand of grass within that circle was not the stubby, coarse growth she had known, but was even closer to the earth and patched with what seemed to be moss. What did spring higher was spangled with flowers of a cream white, cupped like tulips, except they were not like any tulips she had ever seen. Among them fluttered insects with bright wings.

"Rrrrrowww—" Again she turned her head, so suddenly that pain brought another cry from her. The wildcat crouched there, licking its torn foot, but looking now and again to her as if it perfectly understood that she could help it.

Her basket lay a foot or so away and she stretched out an arm to grasp it, each movement bringing that sickening pain in her head. With one hand she gingerly explored her own skin and hair on that side. There was the ooze of liquid and she brought away fingers painted the bright red of blood. She could only explore by the lightest of touches but she believed that the cut was a small one, more of a rasping and bruising of skin than the larger wound she had expected.

Fumbling with the contents of her basket she brought out the antibiotic salve and the cotton swabs she had carried on her mission of mercy. These she shared equally with the cat who only growled warningly as she handled its foot and smeared on the same protective jelly as she had used on her own left temple.

It was still difficult to move. Any sudden change in the position of her head not only brought a stab of pain but a feeling of nausea. So, when she had done with her battlefield surgery for them both, she leaned her back against one of those standing stones, which had so unbelievably raised itself from the ground, to look about her with more intent interest. The cat crouched some distance away again, licking its torn paw but showing no desire to withdraw further.

Now that she had time to observe—to think of more than her immediate plight, she studied what lay before her with eyes narrowed against the glare of the sun. She had already shed her coat because of the unnatural heat and now wished she could slip out of her heavy turtleneck sweater into the bargain.

Surely this was not even the brightest of summer days such as she had heretofore known on Ben Blair. Nor were the flowers, rippling gently under the teasing fingers of a light breeze, any she had seen before. And the stones—how had they come to be set upright?

Of course this might be all illusion and she still lay back in the night twilight with her battered head against the stone which had so roughly met her fall. Yet—it seemed so real!

The wildcat stopped her licking and made a small sound deep in her throat. She limped over to the coat Kelsie had abandoned and pawed at it intently as if searching the padded surface for something of her own.

Kelsie did not try to fight the vast fatigue which had settled on her when she had finished the last of her nurse-care. She closed her eyes and then opened them suddenly twice, as if she tried to catch the landscape before her in the midst of some change. However, it remained always the same—the standing bluish stones, the patches of flowers, the unnatural heat. She began to feel thirsty.

Now if she were indeed on the slope of Ben Blair there should be a spring not many paces away from the place of stones. The very thought of water curling out of the ground made her run her tongue over lips suddenly even more dry. Water—

She did not try to stand up, even creeping on her hands and knees made her feel qualms of nausea. However, she forced herself across a quarter of the circle, out between the stones, in the general direction where that spring must lie.

Only there was no spring, at least none where she sought. She slipped down again to lie full length in the midst of a patch of the wild flowers, the perfume of which was so strong as to add to her illness.

Water—with every moment she craved a drink more. Now it seemed she could actually hear it. Perhaps she had not been headed in the right direction. Muzzily she somehow once more got to her hands and knees heading south. Moments later she was indeed looking at water—down into water, for here was a steep falling away of the land above a pool which mothered a small rill trickling away among moss grown rocks.

In spite of falling painfully once, Kelsie reached the edge of that pool and cupped her hands to drink liquid as chill as if it had just been imprisoned by ice. Still the chill cleared her head a little and she slapped more of it on her face, avoiding the edge of the cut. Until, for the first time since she had awakened, she felt wholly herself again.

There was no such pool on Ben Blair, just as the standing stones had been lying once there. Where was she? Still wandering in the depths of some hallucination produced by the blow on her head? She must not panic, and panic came from just such thoughts and questions without answers. For the moment she seemed to be herself even if the rest of the world had changed.

She pulled out the shirt she had worn under her sweater and soaked it in the cold water, wringing it as dry as she could before tying it around her head. For the first time she became aware of a twittering and flitting at the other side of the pool. There was a bush there bending under a burden of dark red berries and birds were feasting, showing no interest in her at all.

Not grouse, nor any others she had seen before. There was one species with a golden breast and wings of a muted rose color, another a vivid green-blue, such plumage as she had seen before only on the throats of peacocks.

Berries—food—

Just as the need for water had risen in her so now came the need to appease a hunger. She edged around the water. The birds fluttered a little away but did not rise on the wing as she had expected them to do. She drew a hand down one dangling branch and harvested a full palm's load of the berries. They were sweet, yet had a lingering tartness which somehow added to their flavor, and, having tasted, she straightway set about gathering and cramming into her mouth all she could reach and snatch from the same branches where some birds were still boldly feeding.

Two or three of those with the metallic blue feathers had withdrawn a little and were watching her—not as if they feared any move at attack on her part, but rather as if she herself provided some kind of puzzle they must solve. At length one of them took off, soaring up into the sky, the sun making a rich glory of its wings.

The cat— Kelsie looked at the birds, some of whom were eating fearlessly only a hand's distance from her. She wondered if the creature was

worse injured than she had thought, and she turned to make her way back
to that inexplicable circle of stone pillars. The upward slope she took
cautiously, now back on her feet to feel the ground swaying under her.
Then she reached the top of that rise and looked ahead. There was the
yellowish-black patch of her discarded coat and she stumbled her way
back to it, concentrating on the garment rather than what stood around it.

There came a tiny mewling cry as her shadow fell across the edge of
the coat and an instant answering growl. Then she saw the kittens—two
of them, small, blind shapes which the cat had just finished washing.

She knew better than to approach too closely, that growl had sunk to
a low sound in the mother's throat but that she would allow an interference with her family Kelsie doubted. She spoke softly, using the same
words that she had used many times over at Dr. Atless's when she had
been the attendant in his veterinary hospital.

"Good girl, clever girl—" she squatted down, with her back to one of
the stones, to survey the small family. "You have pretty kittens—good
girl—"

She was startled then by a cry which certainly had not come from the
cat or her new family. It might have been the howling of a tormented dog,
only Kelsie's knowledge of dogs said no to that. Twice it sounded. The
cat's ears flattened to her skull, her eyes became warning slits. Kelsie
shivered even under the strong beams of that sun. She faced outward from
the circle toward the heights which lay beyond. For the third time that cry
sounded and it was certainly nearer and sharper, as if a hunter were hot
upon a trail. The girl looked about her for a weapon, some hope of
defense. At last she tugged at the coat on which the cat had bedded down,
loosing the belt and drawing it out. With no stick nor stone here that was
her only possible choice.

At the fourth howl the creature who had so given tongue came into
sight—first only a black blot padding out of a stand of brush. And then, as
it came closer, Kelsie had difficulty in stifling a cry. A dog?

No, no hound that she had ever heard of or seen resembled this! It
was almost skeleton thin, the ridges of its ribs plainly visible beneath its
shiny skin. A mouth which appeared to split two thirds of its skull
dropped open and a scarlet tongue lolled out, saliva and whitish foam
dripping from it. The long legs seemed only bones with skin stretched
tightly over them as it padded forward, not with a rush but steadily as if it
had marked its prey and had no idea of losing it now.

Kelsie pulled herself up, one shoulder against the pillar, the buckle
end of her belt dangling loose, the other end wrapped tightly about her
hand lest she lose her hold on it. She heard a growl and glanced for a
moment at the cat. The kittens were half hidden under her body where fur

bristled up in challenge. Though she visibly leaned her weight mostly on her uninjured paw, it was plain she was prepared to do battle.

The hound did not leap forward as Kelsie expected. Instead it stopped while still several feet away from the pillared circle. Throwing back its narrow head the beast gave vent once more to its chilling bay as if summoning some companion of the hunt. Though she and the cat were weak enough, Kelsie thought with fiercely beating heart, to give but token defense.

There was an answer to that last bay, a cry which was not a similar howl but rather more like a call in words she could not understand. Then out of the same knot of brush which had concealed the dog creature came a horse and rider. The girl drew a startled, shaken breath.

The horse, or whatever that beast was, showed as much a walking rack of bones as the hound. In its skull the eyes were pits of whirling greenish-yellow flame. While the rider was cloaked, so enveloped in a muffling covering that could not say what manner of thing it might really be. But it was plain that this newcomer had eyes for and interest in her. One begloved hand raised a rod and swung it in her direction with the same calm assurance which McAdams had shown toward shooting the cat.

Kelsie did not even have time to put the stone between her and that crooked dash of flame which sprang from the rod. Only it did not strike her. To her overwhelming surprise it was as if that meant-to-be flash of fire struck an impenetrable wall a little before the stone—sprayed out in a red burst and was gone, leaving a trail of oily smoke to rise in the clear sky.

· The hound howled and began to run, not straight for the girl, but circling about the stones as if it sought some door or opening which would let it at its would-be victims. For a moment or two the rider was motionless. Then he used reins and swung the head of his mount to the left joining the hound in that circling of what might be a fortress the twain of them could not best.

Kelsie held tight with one hand to the stone beside her but also turned her head and then her body to watch the encirclement. She had had no trouble leaving the circle nor returning to it, but these two beyond now appeared totally walled away.

In her mind bewilderment fast became panic and fear. Where was she? She could not be anywhere but in some hospital racked with wild hallucinations because of the blow on her head. But this was so real—!

The hound gave tongue continually, almost querulously, as if it could not understand what kept it away from the two inside the circle.

However, the rider remained where he was, his mount now and then nervously pawing the earth but held firmly in check. That rod was handled negligently, its tip pointed earthward. It would seem that they were under siege, perhaps being held for the coming of some even greater menace. Yet when the next stroke arrived it was not Kelsie who was aroused to front the danger but the snarling wildcat.

Within the circle of the rock a moss covered patch of earth heaved upward and burst into separate sods as if from some explosion below. Out of the cascading earth pushed what looked like a bird's beak, a sickly yellow-gray, and from beside Kelsie the wildcat sprang into action.

Her leap carried her farther on so that she was behind that questing beak and in spite of her injured foot she used both forepaws to land them together on a thing struggling up from the burrow it had made.

There was a whirl of furred body and a slapping length of what looked mostly like a land-going lobster. Then the cat's teeth met with a crunch just behind the end of the beak, and, though the many-legged thing went on flopping, it was clearly out of the battle. The cat settled down over it, tearing loose clawed limbs and worrying at the thing's underbelly until she passed its chitinous armor to the flesh beneath, which she ate as if famished. However, Kelsie, so warned by its appearance from the earth made the rounds of the circle, searching the ground intently for any other suspicious tumbling of the soil.

She came upon one such near across the circle from the still-feasting cat and made ready with her belt. The narrow tip of that beak or nose which quested for the upper world thrust through a clump of the flowers and she lashed her belt at it. More by luck than any skill the loop of the buckle did fall about that tip and she gave a vicious jerk, putting into that all her power of arm.

As a fish that had swallowed a hook the thing came out of the ground flopping over on its back, sharply clawed feet waving in the air. But the rising had also freed a long, jointed tail which ended in what could only be a sting. That snapped back and forth evilly while the creature's head, flipping from side to side freed it from the buckle, it arose again, seeming to turn in midair to land on its feet. For a moment only it hesitated and then it leaped, springing at least three feet from the torn flowers to aim straight at Kelsie.

She swung the belt a second time, managing again to strike and so ward off attack. But, as she also retreated, she came sharply back against one of the blue pillars and was caught up in something else, a sharp tingling of her body such as one might receive from a minor electrical shock.

Her left hand clawed at the stone which was not cold, as she had expected, but rather held a warmth which appeared to be growing. In doing so she rasped her fingers upon a protrusion of the rock which broke away into her hand.

There was one chance now. She could not even have told from whence came that saving idea but she pulled in her belt and worked the stone into the buckle, wedging it so with all her might, her attention all for the many-legged creature out of the earth and her fingers working by touch alone.

It was the cat who gave her the few precious seconds out of time to do that. Having finished with the carcass of the first of their attackers it was now creeping up behind the other. Then Kelsie struck, this time with careful aim and intent purpose.

The weighted buckle met the creature in midair for it had sprung again even as she had swung. There was a flash of brilliant light and a puff of smoke, a nauseating odor which made her retch. The thing struck the ground charred and black. It might have been tossed through a blazing fire. Kelsie was so heartened by the success of her desperate hope that she turned to claw again at the pillar behind her, striving to free more such useful bits of rock. But it would seem that luck or chance had loosened only that one for her aid.

Snarling, the cat drew back from the charred curl of body and leaped now for Kelsie's coat where it settled down, drawing close to its body, with a sweep of foreleg, the two squeaking kittens.

Neither the hound nor the rider had made any move during that odd battle and now they showed no dismay that it had not succeeded—if the earth dwellers were allies of theirs after all. It appeared that they were willing to wait—either for their prey to be somehow shaken out as a nut is shaken out of a broken shell, or for more efficient reinforcements.

Time, Kelsie thought, did not favor her or the cat. There would be another attack of sorts—or she would wake from this dream which was so real that the fear of it nearly paralyzed her if she allowed herself to consider it.

She continued to absently rub one hand along the rough surface of the stone, her attention going from hound to rider and back again—waiting for what would happen next.

There came a clear trilling call out of the air overhead. The hound was on its feet, snarling, leaping now and then. Kelsie saw winging back and forth over the animal was one of those blue birds which had watched her eat by the berry bushes.

From her left there came a harsh grating sound which to her ears bore no resemblance to speech. The rider had brought around his skeleton mount and now he lifted his rod and tried to aim at the darting birds, but the shooting flames were ever far behind their swift turns, fast swoops, and soarings.

2

The cat's head was up, it was staring south to another roll of hills. Now the rider, so hood muffled that Kelsie had never seen his face, turned halfway in the saddle to face the same direction. The birds uttered sharp high cries and began a flight pattern which encircled the stones. With a sharp jerk the rider pulled at the reins and his mount plunged forward as if to bring it and its rider down upon Kelsie. But it did not complete that charge. Instead the mount reared and the rider seemed for a moment to be fighting—his will against his mount's. The hound crouched closer to the ground, near creeping on its belly back the way it had come. Though Kelsie watched carefully there was nothing else in sight save the wheeling birds.

The rider no longer fought his horse (if such a creature could be termed a horse). He allowed it to swing around to the direction from which they had come. Then, though he did not seem to be urging it, the creature first broke into a trot and raised that to a gallop as it disappeared in a cut between two of the hills, the hound now running beside it.

Kelsie waited. The birds broke off their circling to fly east. She and the cat were alone in the circle of pillars which had indeed proved a sanctuary.

The girl slipped to the ground, sitting cross-legged near her coat where the kittens now nursed—the cat having relaxed enough to allow them to her.

For the first time since she had awakened, Kelsie had a chance to think clearly, to look more slowly about her, to weigh one strange thing against its neighbor. She had been struggling with Neil McAdams in the long summer twilight of the Scottish highlands. But it was plain that where she now was bore no relation to that. She raised her fingertips to smooth the damp shirt she had tied over her head wound. It was all so real—

Slowly she pulled herself once more to her feet and began to make a complete circuit of the circle, looking outward for a point of reference which would assure her that she was still in the world she knew or at least recognized a little. She was not even of highland blood—even if she bore the name and had the heritage from Great-Aunt Ellen she had never been here before. She belonged back in Evart, Indiana, ready to start for the animal clinic, to dream her own private dream of somehow raising the money to get a veterinarian's degree. That was the world of people and things she understood. This was not. She swung the stone-weighted belt and tried to arrange her thoughts in a logical pattern. One minute she had been struggling with Neil to keep him from shooting the already injured wildcat and then she had awakened here—

She wanted to run, to scream out her denial, to awaken from this nightmare. It went on and on and it was indeed so real. She could not remember ever having eaten and drunk in any dream before but the stains of the berries still were on her hands and she could taste their sweetness when she ran her tongue over her teeth. She looked to the cat who lay nursing the two kittens. The animal was believable. But the hound, the rider, and all that had happened since she had been besieged here—those were out of some fantasy.

None of the distant, mist veiled mountains looked familiar. Also who had raised the fallen pillars to make this fortress to what it must once have been, a circle of protection?

The cat arose, shook off her two clinging offspring and came to stand before Kelsie, regarding her straightly as somehow she had never seen an animal eye her before. It was as if an intelligence which was equal, or at least close, to her own looked out of those eyes and that some desire for communication moved the animal.

Kelsie knelt and held out one hand to the cat.

"Where are we, old girl?" she asked and then wished she had not, for her words sounded queerly here as if they had been picked up by one stone and echoed to the next and the next, coming back to her, not clearly, but in a hoarse whisper.

The cat extended a tongue tip and touched it to the girl's thumb. And she knew a glow of triumph. So a wildcat could not be tamed—so much for all they had told her when she had spoken up for the animal last night. Last night? She shook her head and then wished that she had not, for the pain which flashed outward. She was suddenly tired. Better to lie down here on the moss and just rest a little. If she slept so much the better, she might then awaken in her own place and time.

Only there was to be no rest. The wildcat suddenly yowled and Kelsie wondered, even as she clapped her hands over both of her ears, if the animal had sensed the same dislocation as she did now. This was a different kind of pain than that which had driven her since her awaking here. It was like a cry for help so intense and demanding that the girl was on her feet, stumbling back through that gate to answer it.

Back through the gate but not to her own place. The land about her remained the same. Her shuffle became a run as she was drawn on. She was aware of the furry shape which followed in her shadow, also pulled perhaps by that demanding cry which she knew now, but could not understand how, rang within her head not outside through her ears.

Together cat and girl rounded a heap of moss-grown stones which might have been the remains of some very ancient ruin not treated as well by time as the pillars behind. Kelsie skidded down the dale, the belt swinging in her hand ready to use. What they came upon were the signs of tragedy. Three forms lay there, a soaking of blood curling from between their shoulders where upstanding feathered shafts proclaimed arrows. Arrows!

The girl's startlement at that was gone in an instant when she saw the fourth member of the small party. A woman, both her gray clothing, and her flesh beneath rent, and soaking flowing blood, lay half rested against a stone. Before her crouched either the black hound which had not too long ago menaced them, or else its twin. There were blood flecks in the foam about its jaws yet it did not spring as it was crouched to do. The woman held in a shaking, near falling hand, something from which swung a chain and was glistening with light. Yet for all her struggle she could not continue to hold that steady.

For the moment, forgetting her own horror of that beast, Kelsie stormed in swinging the belt. The stone heavy buckle thudded neatly home on the hound's bony side. It sprang, not at the woman but back, giving tongue in a fearsome cry. Kelsie swung again and this time the very edge of the rock contacted with the side of one forepaw. Again that cry and now the beast turned and fled though it did not go out of sight but ran back and forth as if awaiting reinforcements.

Kelsie backed away, toward the woman.

"Sister—"

The word rang in her head and she dared, for a moment, to look away from the hound to the bleeding survivor of that stricken party. The woman's hand had fallen across her body, but her eyes were still open and fixed on Kelsie with such appeal that the girl dropped down on one knee. As she did that the wildcat moved in closer, ducked its head so that the woman's limp hand lay but a fraction away. To Kelsie's amazement the mouth in that white, pain stricken face drew into the shadow of a smile.

"Sister—in—fur—also—" The words were in her mind. Kelsie shot a look at the snarling hound, but that had not advanced again.

"I—the—last—gate—" the words formed for her with pause between. Though she did not loose her belt weapon she tried to reach to the body before her. That steady streaming of blood—she *must* do something. As if she had in her turn spoken aloud she saw the woman's head turn the slightest from side to side.

"The—last—gate—" came the mind word which Kelsie had to accept sprang from that limp body. "The jewel—" it was as if the woman had a last spurt of strength, "do—not—let them take it!" With infinite effort she again raised her hand.

It was the cat who darted head forward through the loop of the dangling chain. Straightway the woman loosed her grip on what she held so that a sparkling ovoid fell free to dangle against the cat's brindle fur.

"We must get help—" Kelsie for a moment looked wildly around as if she could produce by will alone medical assistance which did not exist.

The smile had not faded.

"Sister—I—am Roylane—" There seemed to be some great significance in that. Then the lean body shuddered and the smile faded. "The—gate—" She who was wounded looked beyond Kelsie at something which the girl, quick to turn, could not see. Then the woman sighed and her head dropped upon one shoulder. Though Kelsie had seldom seen death of her own kind before—just once and that was long ago—she knew that this stranger who spoke without the need for words was gone.

She held the belt between her teeth and straightened out the slight body, shrinking in spite of herself from the blood on her hands. Then she looked at the other bodies. Though the hound paced back and forth before two of them, the third lay closer and one outthrust arm pointed straight toward her still clasping a sword. With one eye ever for the hound Kelsie crossed quickly and freed that weapon from the flaccid fingers, finding it so heavy compared to the fencing foils she had known that she nearly dropped it. But clumsy as she might be with it she took courage from the very heft of that blade—a weapon much better than her belt-and-stone defense.

There was a croaking from beyond. The hound took heart from that, throwing back its head to voice another of the direful howls. At that sound the cat took off in great bounds and was gone back to the safety of the stones. Kelsie hesitated by the body of the woman. But there was nothing she could do for her now and apparently the reinforcements the hound expected were on the way. So she followed, but partially backing that so the evil thing could not jump her, swinging the belt warningly, lifting the sword in her other hand.

It made no move to lengthen its stride as it ran back and forth, nor to come at her. Only it howled and that noise tore at her. Finally she broke and ran.

"The gate—" the dead woman had said. Had she and those others with her been heading for the only gate Kelsie knew, that of the circle beyond? It might have been their gate of safety but somehow she knew that the "last" gate was not made of coarse stones and stood waiting here. No, beyond that lay what no living thing might guess.

She saw that gem the cat now carried so awkwardly about its throat give off glints which might be the sparks of a real fire. Already the animal had joined its family on the coat. Kelsie put on a second burst of speed to join it. Throwing herself down on the sod, the sword falling out of her hold, and gasping for breath, she looked back the way she had come. So far no lean black hound, no rider on a skeleton mount appeared.

Only that this was a land haunted with peril she was firmly convinced. She took up the heavy sword for a second time and examined it. The blade tapered from hilt to point, but not with the thin grace of a rapier. The hilt was plain, with a stiff wire wound around and around it to secure the grip. There was no ornamentation on it at all. She got slowly to her feet and tried a thrust and parry, but this was not a point weapon, she decided, rather one meant to be used with the edge of the blade for the blow and of that kind of fighting she knew nothing at all. Fighting? What did she know of that?

For the second time she turned slowly as if she stood on a pivot surveying all which lay beyond the circle. Had the murdered party beyond that down slope been trying to reach this place when they had been overwhelmed? But—where was *here*? What *had* happened to her? Somehow she could no longer hold onto the tattered story she had been telling herself that this was all hallucination. The "last gate"—did "last" signify that there were other gates which the dying woman had known of? She was facing a gate now—two unworked slabs of stone standing well above her height with a third laid across them. That was a gate—yes, and the one on Ben Blair's flank back there—had that been a gate, too?

Kelsie shivered. There were tales enough told in the Scottish mountains—of people who had gone away and then returned—seemingly having been gone by their own measurement of time for but a night or so, but really for years!

Tales—

She got to her feet and walked toward that gate. There was nothing beyond but stretches of mossed rock, stands of the white bell flowers and the rise of stones which was a screen between them and the dead. If she tried could she go *through*?

She closed her eyes and tried to concentrate on the tumble of stones she had seen for such a short time before she arrived here. They had been in the long summer twilight with the moon hardly giving any help. One had lain so—she remembered that, for the cat had leaped it even as she had struck up Neil's shotgun. And there had been—she held to a badly faded mind picture and took two steps more. She opened her eyes.

Yes, she had ventured out of the shadow of the gate but she was still in the unknown. Behind her came a warning cry from the cat and she saw the snaky form of the lean hound among the rocks. Kelsie leaped backward into what she had come to consider the only safety in this place of many alarms and death.

The cat snarled. Somehow she had managed to get her neck out of the chain of the jewelry. Now she stood once more before her kits one paw planted flat upon that fiery stone. Kelsie waited alertly for the appearance of a rider, since the first hound had come so attended.

Instead there was a crawling man, striving on hands and knees to come toward her, wavering back and forth. Kelsie's first thought was to run to his aid. But she expected the hound to turn and rend him as he passed and the beast made no such move. It was that which held her in her place.

"Ahhheeee—" surely that cry had come from the crawler. And it was followed by another. If he spoke words there were none that she knew. On impulse she went down on one knee by the cat and reached for the chain but now the cat snarled at her and struck out with its injured paw as if it would flay the skin from her fingers.

"Aaaaahaaaa—" there was no mistaking now that the wounded man crawling toward the circle had thrown back his head and was screaming.

The hound crossed over behind him and was apparently driving him toward the very shelter that he sought. Perhaps the creature had by this some way to force the barrier which had defeated its fellow accompanying the masked rider. If so Kelsie had no mind to see how it would work.

She strode toward the gate with some vague idea of defense in her mind. Thrusting the sword point into the center of a bed of moss so that it stood up close to her hand she stood dangling the once tried and to her more effective measure of the weighted belt.

Now the crawling man was mouthing sounds like frantic words— though they meant nothing to her. Once he crouched, leaning heavily on one arm as he held out his other hand beseechingly in her direction. And, she noted, the hound did nothing to harass him. The creature wanted him in and anything which would serve that one's purpose was to be avoided.

Now he was lower to the ground, drawing himself painfully along by grasping the turf. Between his shoulders an arrow shaft nodded back and forth. Still the hound held off, even withdrew a pace or so.

There came a keening call, Kelsie ducked as a shadow swept over her, looking up at a large black bird, its wing sweep stretched near as far as she was tall. She ducked, thinking that it was seeking her. But it shot up as quickly as it had swooped. Not before she saw that its overlarge eyes were, like those of the rider's mount, pits of swirling, greenish-yellow flame.

Once more it planed down at her. She swung the belt wildly and snatched for the waiting sword, but it stayed just beyond her reach. She heard above the whimpering noise which was now coming from the crawling man, the yowling of the cat, crouched above its helpless kittens.

Whether the purpose of the bird thing would ever have succeeded and driven her out of the circle Kelsie was never to know for there shot through the air a flash of blue light followed by the cracking sound of a whip.

Kelsie, her back now firmly against the rock which helped to support the gate on one side, looked toward that slope down which she had gone to hunt water.

There were two of them, riders. But not like the muffled black one who had tried to reach her before. Their mounts were not horses but shining coated red-cream beasts, each with a horn on its forehead. And the riders—Kelsie blinked and blinked again. Surely now her eyes were playing tricks on her.

When they had first burst into view certainly they had been dark of hair, almost dusky of skin, but now that they were in the full sunlight they showed hair as gilt as true gold and cream skin which their vividly green clothing made all the more fair. There were no reins in their hands, they might have been allowing their striking mounts to range freely. But each bore what looked like the stock of a whip, and, even as she watched, Kelsie saw the woman draw back her arm and snap out what seemed a line of pure fire, not as visible as a real lash, at the flying thing above.

It squawked raucously and soared well above that flash while the hound gave forth another of its coughing howls. But the crawling man lay supine and unmoving now. Around the circle of the stones pounded the newcomers. The woman leaned over and looked at the body bearing the arrow but she did not dismount nor strive to give any aid.

Her companion wheeled on the hound and it was not as lucky as the flying creature in escape, for the flicking tip of the burning lash the rider wielded struck on its flank and there was a puff of oily smoke. To be followed an instant later by a bursting noise and then the hound was gone, leaving only an oily black deposit on the stones among which it had tried to hide.

The woman's mount paused before the gate and she called aloud, her words unintelligible but clearly aimed at Kelsie, who made a helpless gesture with her free hand, still keeping grip upon her belt weapon.

"I do not understand you," she called back. These riders did not bring with them the miasma of evil which had hung above the other creatures and the black rider. That they meant her no harm she was halfway satisfied. But they were clearly of this world which had changed so much and so—could they really be trusted?

The woman stared at her for a space and now she was joined by the other rider. As his mount came to a halt beside hers Kelsie witnessed again that weird change in the two of them. Their hair changed to a red and there was a golden glint of freckles now across the woman's high-bridged nose. It was as if instead of two riders she faced a number, all contained in a single person. Now the woman no longer spoke, rather she stared straight into Kelsie's eyes, a look of concentration making hers intent and searching.

"Who—" the word was faint and if anything more had been added to that mind touch Kelsie did not receive it. But it was plain that she had been questioned.

"I am Kelsie McBlair," she spoke slowly, sure that the rider could not understand. Then, with a great effort, she tried something else—pictures out of her memory—of the fallen stones, her struggle with McAdams and her awaking here. She was aware of a yowl from behind her and knew that the wildcat was also answering in its own fashion.

"—gate!" Again Kelsie was sure that she had missed all but one word of something which might be of importance to her.

She nodded, taking the chance that the other meant somehow the archway in which she now stood. The woman rested the stock of her light whip across her mount and with both hands made a series of passes in the air. Where her fingers moved there were left traces of bluish light, not unlike that emitted by the whips, in a complicated design. Seeing that seemed to reassure the spinner of those symbols for she nodded and spoke to the man at her side.

His mount moved back and then he was riding along the trail of blood which had been left by the creeper who lay so flat and silent now. In a moment he had disappeared beyond the rocks toward that scene of death which Kelsie had found earlier.

However, the woman, whose hair had again darkened to near black as there swept a cloud across the sun, slipped from the saddleless back of her mount and approached the girl at the gate. Kelsie kept her tight hold on the belt. She found nothing terrifying about this newcomer but what did she know of anything in this strange and frightening place?

Fur brushed against her leg. The wildcat had come out of the nest she had been so ready to defend. In her mouth gleamed the jewel she had taken from the dying woman, its chain dragging along the ground behind, catching here and there on the flower leaves as she came.

She went forward, out of the stone circle, to drop what she carried at the feet of the woman, who went to one knee caressing the cat with fearless fingers before she caught at the chain and held up the jewel. She did not touch the stone, keeping instead her hold only on the chain. But there was wonderment and then a flicker of anxiety in her expression. Now she looked to Kelsie again.

"Who—" stronger this time, that mind question, yet still but a single word.

"Roylane—" she answered aloud, guessing again at what the full question might have been. And this time she saw the woman's eyes go wide, her mobile features picturing shock.

"Who—?" the mind word came again and now the hand holding that chain swung it so that the gem gleamed in the sun.

"Kelsie—" the girl repeated.

"Kel-Say," this time the woman shaped the word with her lips not her thought— "Kel-Say."

3

"——with——"

Again the woman gestured, this time summoningly. Her mount moved up beside her and stood waiting. The eyes it fastened on Kelsie were not burning circles of evilly colored fire as she had seen in the hounds' heads and in that of the skeletonlike steed of the black rider— rather a warm brown and—surely there was intelligence in them!

Kelsie guessed once more at what they wished of her—to accompany them. The circle meant safety from what she had seen threatening in this land—that she knew. Dared she obey that invitation—or was it an order? She could not stand against the flame whips of these two were they to drive her.

To gain time she pointed to the body on the ground.

"What about him?" she asked, spacing her words carefully, trying to think her question at the same time.

The answer came sharp and clear.

"Dead!"

She heard the cat mew and looked down. Already the mother's jaws had closed upon the nape of one of the squirming kittens. Lifting her child high the cat advanced toward the gate, plainly ready to go with this stranger even if Kelsie delayed. That made up the girl's mind for her. She went to gather up her coat, the other mewling infant in it, and returned, stooping, offering the bundle to the wildcat. The mother allowed her burden to drop in with its sibling, winding about Kelsie's legs as she went through the gate at last.

Up the slope came the other rider. He carried before him the body of Roylane and passed them, taking his burden on into the circle. No opposition arose to keep him out, but, as he entered, the blue standing stones flared up like candles and a drifting haze spread from one to another of them. He dismounted and lifted down the body which in his hold seemed small and spare. Then he laid it on the ground, choosing, Kelsie was sure, not just by chance, a bed of the white flowers to receive it. From his belt he produced two brilliantly blue feathers, gleaming like those which formed the tails of those birds she had seen earlier. He pushed one into the ground at the head and the other at the feet of the dead woman, standing up and back at last to raise his two hands to his forehead in what appeared to be a salute, while from his companion there came a sing-songed flow of speech which might have been of farewell or invocation.

As he turned to leave, the trails of mist from the stones rolled out into the center of the circle, settling about that small broken body until only their one rippling substance could be seen.

"——Go——"

Again Kelsie was summoned, and since there was little other choice she went. She sat awkwardly on the back of the woman's mount, her arms full of the coat in which squirmed the kittens. The woman caught up the cat in turn and slipped her into the folds Kelsie held. Then, to the girl's surprise, she also put in the jewel. The cat pawed it beneath her own body as she settled with her family, looking up at Kelsie with a hint of a growl as if warning the girl to take care.

They skirted the gully where the stream flowed and the animal under her fell into a swift pace, joined immediately by its companion. They headed southwest, as well as Kelsie could tell from the sun.

As they went it became more and more certain to the girl that wherever she might be it was no country she had ever seen or heard of. Strange vegetation arose around them and there were things moving in the tall grass of open glades which had no relationship to any animal she knew.

She noted as they went that the man kept behind and sometimes his mount dropped to a slower pace—he might have been a rear guard. Yet they heard no more of the yowling howls from the hounds, nor any other sounds save the calls of the bright winged birds which swung about them as they rode.

Across open land they traveled. Now and then their mounts trotted by long overgrown fields guarded by the tumbled stones of what were once dividing walls. This had the look of a land long deserted.

At last they came to a way which was marked by a scarring of hoof and footprints and undoubtedly was a road, if one might call such a dusty trail a road. The land began to rise on either side and Kelsie could see that they were entering the throat of a valley between two rises which, a little beyond, assumed the height of real mountains.

On the rock walls they passed were carved a series of signs or what might even have been words of an unknown tongue. The woman with whom Kelsie shared this mount pointed with her flame whip as they passed each of these symbol-graven rocks.

There was a scuttling around a large rock where, settled in a squatting position on the crown, was a shape as bizarre as that of the hound and the monstrous beast the black rider had bestridden.

Shorter than a man, this sentinel, for so she would deem him with its spear held up in salute to the riders, was a giant lizard, green-gold of scaled skin. It had a domed head which was nearly human in shape, though the lipless mouth which stretched a third of the way back into the skull and the red tongue which quivered in the air (as if testing a breeze which was not at that moment blowing) were grotesque copies of human features. The woman responded to his salute with a raised hand.

Kelsie was sure that they must have passed other guards during their journey, but that was the only one she had seen. Then at last they reached the mouth of a gully road at the border of a land which made her draw a deep breath.

She had seen strangeness and horror since her first awaking here— wherever *here* might be. Now she looked upon true beauty. The land ahead was brilliantly green with lush growth starred here and there with flowers jewel-like in radiant color. She saw to one side a small herd of animals like the one she now bestrode grazing peacefully. There were also people before and beyond, though none of them appeared to show any interest in the emergence of their own small party.

Down they went—the road now vanished and the hillside covered with velvety grass. Then, for the first time, Kelsie saw houses—the brightness of their roofs betraying them to the eye, for their walls were masses of flowering vine. Had the feathers been plucked from countless flocks of the birds such as escorted them and woven into a thatch it would look like that!

For the first time the inhabitants of the valley looked up. Some gathered in a small group of welcome. A few of them shared the peculiarity of those two who had found her, their color of skin and hair changing as they moved. But the others were closer to the woman she had found dying. They were tall and slender and their hair remained very dark, their skin sun browned yet fair.

Four of those who so waited were men, wearing coats of fine mail which, when they moved, appeared to be as supple as cloth. There were two women, one of whom wore green garments which were no different from those of the one whose beast Kelsie shared. But the other had a long straight robe of gray which brushed the grass with its hem and had a circle of tarnished silver girding it. Her dark hair was drawn severely back and bound into a net also of silver, while her pallid face reminded Kelsie strongly of the woman who had died from the savaging of the hound.

It was she who started forward as they drew up, but her attention was all for the gem half hidden by one of the cat's paws. Her lips moved, breaking the statue-like stillness of her face, and she stared first at the woman in green and then at Kelsie. It seemed to the latter that there was both suspicion and threat in that long moment of straight regard.

She herself slipped from the back of the sleek mount, her coat with the kittens still held close. But the cat had leaped lightly to the earth the minute they had come to a halt and was now weaving a pattern brushing against the long gray skirt, the chain of the jewel gripped between its teeth.

The woman stooped and drew her fingers across that bushy head and then looked again to Kelsie, speaking in that lilting language. Regretfully the girl shook her head.

"I do not understand—"

Several of those waiting looked startled and the woman in gray frowned. Then in her aching head Kelsie felt once more that troubling sensation:

"—who/—what/—"

For the second time she pictured the scene on the side of Ben Blair, trying to remember every small item. If these people could read minds surely they must be able to pick out an answer from what she spread before them. But the frown on the woman's face only grew sharper and there was a murmur of near whispers speeding from one listener to another.

"——gate——" That had come from the woman who had found her. She now touched Kelsie's arm to attract her full attention and pointed to herself:

"Dahaun." She shaped that name with exaggerated movements of her lips, and once again Kelsie answered:

"Kelsie."

"Kel-Say—" Dahaun nodded, pointed to the woman in green, and said a word which again Kelsie faithfully repeated. Thus those others were made known to her.

After two tries the girl managed:

"Crytha, Yonan (who looked to be the youngest of the men), Kemoc, Kyllan." And for the one who towered above the rest "Uruk."

The cat reared on its hind legs and clawed at Kelsie demandingly. When she put down the coat with its family the mother went to them at once, licking them all over as if she distrusted what might have happened to them during that ride. Kelsie herself was urged on into the nearest of the strange living houses and into an inner part of that where behind curtains there bubbled a shallow pool of water. Dahaun made motions to suggest that she shed her clothing and make use of such refreshment. She began to point hither and thither and give words which Kelsie said after her, striving to use the proper intonation.

By the time she was through with her bath and had toweled herself dry on a square of stuff she had a vocabulary of perhaps twenty-five words which she continued to say over to impress them on her mind.

She ate from a tray loaded down with fruit, nuts, and small cakes, feeling strangely free in the garments Dahaun had provided. There was an under smock of pale green and trousers not unlike rather tight jeans. Then came a long-sleeved jerkin which was laced up the front with cords of silver and belted with links of that same metal embossed and engraved into intricate patterns. On her feet were soft boots, calf high, which fitted fairly well. She was offered a comb to set her short cut locks into order, still being lessoned all the while in the language.

There was a stir outside which even small rustling of the leaves set in the wall above could not hush. At a call from Dahaun a tall man, mail clad, tramped in. He carried his helmet on his hip, showing himself bareheaded and full faced. His was a face to attract interest. The skin was weathered brown as if he had been much in the open, and there were silver streaks in the very dark hair at his temples. His eyes were gray and he looked at Kelsie searchingly almost as if he would open her head if he could, and have out of her answers to questions she did not even know existed.

"You are from the gate—"

Startled, she stared at him openmouthed. He was speaking her own language!

"Gate?" she floundered. "There was no gate—just the stones. Neil knocked me down when I tried to keep him from shooting the cat. I had every right," the almost forgotten heat of her temper was again a trace of warmth in her. "I had posted the land—up to the Lying Stones and beyond. Where . . . where is this?"

She made a small gesture to indicate what lay about them, house, strangers—this land itself.

"You are in the Green Valley," he told her, "in Escore. And you came through one of the Gates— May the Lady turn her favor to you now."

"Who are you?" she came directly to the point, "and what are the gates?"

"For the first, I am Simon Tregarth. And for the second—it would take an adept to make that clear to you—if he or she could."

"How do I get back?" She asked the most important question of all.

He shook his head. "You do not. We have only one adept now and your gate is not his. Even Hilarion cannot send you back."

The woman in gray had entered behind him. Now she pushed to the front though she kept a space between them as if she had some aversion to the man. She addressed him abruptly and he shrugged before he turned again to Kelsie. It was plain that there was little liking between the two of them.

"She who is Wittle would know how you came by that jewel. Surely you did not bring it with you."

"She had it—the woman who died—Roylane."

There was complete silence and they were all staring at her as if she had uttered some word or words which had dire meaning.

"She gave you her name?" countered the man who had called himself Tregarth.

Kelsie's chin went up, she sensed disbelief in that question.

"When she was dying," she returned shortly.

Tregarth turned to the woman in gray and spoke quickly. Though she might be listening to him she never looked away from Kelsie. Something in that unending stare made the girl more and more uneasy, as if in each blink of an eye she was being accused of the death of the traveler and her companions.

However, Tregarth had once more turned his attention full upon the girl.

"Did you also take her jewel, and by her word?"

Kelsie shook her head emphatically, her denial aimed more at that woman in gray than to him. "The cat took it," she said. Let them believe or not it was the truth. And she added to her first statement by describing just how the animal had taken the gem from its owner. Once more she was aware of a brush of thick fur against her and looked down to see the wild-cat come to a stop before her, seating itself with tail tip covering both its good foot and the mangled one together, as if it was the two of them against this world.

The woman in gray was plainly startled by the appearance of the cat. The ornament still lay around the animal's neck. The cat dipped its head to catch the gem between its jaws once again.

Though she had started forward a step and uttered a sound as if deny-ing the cat its trophy, the gray woman now stood, plainly completely astounded by the creature's actions.

"This is as it was before?" Tregarth asked.

"Yes. Only the cat took that—" Kelsie thought it wise to make that point as soon as possible. She had no desire to be thought of as one who had robbed the helpless dead. Though why she would want such a bauble she had no idea.

"And the cat entered the gate before you or with you." He did not make a question of that statement. But she saw fit to answer:

"Yes."

Now it was Dahaun who broke in with a fast burst of speech in which Kelsie heard her own name and the word "gate" mentioned several times. First Tregarth and then the gray woman nodded, the latter reluctantly, Kelsie believed. She watched the other bring a small bag out of some hidden pocket in her robe and pull at its drawstring until the pouch lay flat on the mat covered floor. Going down on one knee she spread out the bit of cloth yet more and then turned to the cat, meeting it eye to eye though she uttered no sound.

If she was asking it to give up guardianship of the stone she was unsuccessful. For the cat drew back, though still facing her, until there was more space between them. A line showed between the woman's eyes which looked so pale under her dark brows. She spoke now, something with a certain rhythm which could have been part of a ritual. But the cat did not move. At length she picked up the bag and as she did so shot another keen and threatening look at Kelsie, speaking as one with authority.

Tregarth heard her out and then translated for Kelsie's benefit.

"You are bidden to make your familiar let the power go—"

"Bidden?" snapped Kelsie. "I have no control over the cat. Familiar—" a scrap of old knowledge came suddenly to the fore of her mind, "that's what they used to say about witches—that they had animals to help them. Well, I do not know where your Green Valley is, nor Escore, nor any of this country! I am not a witch—such things do not exist."

For the first time there was a quirk of smile about his lips. "Oh, but here they do, Kelsie McBlair. This is the very home and root of what you might call witchcraft in your own place."

She laughed uncertainly. "This *is* a dream—" she said more to herself than him.

"No dream," his voice was entirely serious and, Kelsie thought, he was looking at her with something close to pity. "The gate is behind you and there is no going back—"

She threw up her hands. "What is all this talk of gates?" she demanded. "I'm probably back in a hospital somewhere and this is all coming from that bump on the head—" But, even as she tried to hearten herself with that thought and speech, she knew that it was not the truth. Something far past her ability to answer with anything believable had happened.

The woman in gray advanced another step, now her hand came out palm up to Kelsie and her frown grew the darker. She exploded into a burst of words which ran up the scale of sound near to a command shout.

"She is the witch!" Kelsie counterattacked.

"Yes," Tregarth answered calmly and with a certainty which made it the truth. "Have you any control over the cat?"

Kelsie shook her head vigorously. "I told you she took the thing from that woman—that Roylane, when she was dying and the woman let her. It was not given to me. Let this—this *witch* beg it from the cat."

Tregarth was already studying the animal, now he turned to the one who had brought Kelsie here. He asked her a question in that other tongue which sounded almost like the twittering of excited birds. It was Dahaun's turn to face the cat, taking the disputed stone away from the self-proclaimed witch and moving it nearer her own hand.

For a long breath or two they all stood waiting, Kelsie was plagued by the thought that the cat understood all that had passed and was content now to tease them. Then at last the animal dropped her head to spit the stone straight before her into the center of a piece of shimmery cloth which the woman of the riders had produced. The witch moved but Dahaun waved her back. It was she who drew the cords to make a bag and then held that by the drawstring.

"For the shrine—" Tregarth spoke to Kelsie. "Its power has died with she who held it." Then Dahaun arose, leaving the bag on the ground where the cat caught it up by the string, and spoke to the witch whose pallid face was a little flushed now and whose mouth was a straight line of severity. She turned quickly, her gray robe spinning out at her momentum and went, all those gathered there allowing her wide room.

Tregarth watched her go and now it was his turn to frown. Once more he spoke to Kelsie.

"She is not in agreement with this. Stay away from her until she accepts the fact that her sister-in-power really did as you and Swiftfoot have said," he gestured to the cat. "They have ruled too long, those of Estcarp, to take easily being thwarted, even in small things. And she had counted much on the coming of her sister-in-power. That one died—how?"

The "how" came with a snap of a whiplash. Kelsie told of the arrows she had seen which had cut down the guards and the hound which had attacked the woman.

"There was little to be seen, though," she said and he was as quick to seize upon that:

"Rider?"

She told of him who had besieged her in the circle and Tregarth's hand went to the hilt of the sword he wore, his lips drawn tight in a grimace which was far from a smile.

"Sarn! Sarn riders—and so close—" his words changed to the chirping speech of the Valley people and she caught one now and then which she understood—such as "near," "stone," and "gate."

Dahaun suddenly reached out and took Kelsie's hands before the girl could move or draw back. She nodded abruptly to one of her own people, who produced a dagger in the hilt of which was set a piece of glittering blue metal, akin in color to the stones behind which the girl had sheltered. He passed it across Kelsie's upturned palms, not touching her flesh but close enough so that she felt warmth as the metal seemed to blaze up for an instant. Then, with her eyes still on Kelsie, Dahaun's face became a mask of concentration.

Some of the old pain awoke in the girl's head. But there was more too—not words but thoughts—thoughts not of her own.

"You are—summoned one. Foretold—"

She was not getting the whole message, she knew, but those words made her blink. Summoned—she had been brought here, yes, but not called—unless their quick bearing of her away from the circle could be termed that. Foretold—more of this witchcraft business, that was what that seemed to mean. She spoke to Tregarth:

"I was not summoned—and how—"

Now she was sure there was a note of sympathy in his voice as he answered her.

"The gates open by powers we do not understand. That you came through one unused for generations is enough to single you out as one of importance. This is a land torn by war—Light against the Dark. It is easy to believe for those of us who have faced much which is outside ordinary experience to say that you were summoned. And it was foretold in the last scrying that one would come—"

"I don't know what you mean! I don't care! If there IS a gate let me go back—" she cried out then.

He shook his head. "The gates open but once, except when an adept lays a geas upon them. There is no going back."

Kelsie stared at him and within her a chill spread outward from the very center of who and what she was.

4

There had passed two nights and this was the third day. Kelsie climbed from the green bowl of the Valley into its guardian heights and crouched in a huddle between two rocks facing that stretch of the unknown. She had to force herself to accept what Simon Tregarth had told her, that she and the wildcat had come through some mysterious gate in time and space to another world—and, as far as Simon knew, there was no going back. She was not ready to accept the rest of it—that she had been somehow summoned or kidnapped and brought by the Gate to answer some need here. It was far easier to accept that chance had entrapped her.

If there was no going back then it was best that she prepare herself for this country. She worked hard at the lilting tongue of the Green Silences people, even picked up words from the other race who shared this outpost of safety, for such Tregarth assured her that the Valley was. It was only because she had been able to pass by certain symbols when they brought her here that she was judged to be worthy of the refuge at all. Even then she had been closely questioned concerning both the black rider and the dying witch several times over.

That other witch—the cold gray pillar frightened her more than anyone she had met—even the Rider and his hound. Mainly, Kelsie thought, it was because the woman was here on equal terms and could influence minds against her if she so chose. That was a chance she would be likely to take on the first sign of any weakening on the part of Dahaun and her people. Kelsie avoided her with determination though she believed that twice at least that other had made an effort to approach her.

Thoughts—or were they threats in the form of thought?—had crawled along the edges of her mind and she had fought them fiercely. She had discovered that fixing her attention full upon some object and concentrating intently seemed to baffle that crawling, creeping invasion of her mind. Twice she had been driven to inner battle to defend herself, both times when Dahaun and Tregarth were not there, nor even the gray woman so far as she could tell—only that pressure in her mind. Both times she had been able to banish such a ravishment of her inner self by thinking of the dying witch, by saying the name which had passed between them as a kind of talisman of protection.

Each time she had detected that pressure she sensed that the impotent anger grew colder and more menacing. At least the other had not obtained the jewel which seemed her great desire. For the wildcat had taken it to the small lair Dahaun had caused to be made for her and her kittens, and she had not brought the gem into the light again.

Resolutely now Kelsie began again to turn over and examine the facts she had learned. Not all within this place of safety were even of human form—yet they all appeared to share intelligence and a common purpose.

There were those who went armed like Tregarth and others of his kind, both men and women. There were the people of Dahaun whose ever-changing color seemed to draw strength from the belts and arm bands they wore. These were made of bright blue-green gems which might have life—of a kind.

There were the lizard folk, golden-green with crested heads and eyes as hard as gems, who skittered in and out among the rest or sat at ease playing games with small brilliantly colored pebbles. With them were the Renthans—those tireless beasts, one of whom she had ridden hither. And there were airborne creatures even more strange.

Those she had learned to call the flamen—tiny humanoid bodies supported by dazzling iridescent wings. To watch them dance in the air brought more astonishment than many of the other wonders. Then there were giant birds, or creatures which had the appearance of birds, who cruised the air in regular flights as if they would keep off some danger aimed from the heights. For, for all its assured safety, this Valley and those it held were under siege.

Twice she had seen parties of sentries depart from or go up into the heights and once there had been a wounded man among those returning. Each night there was a great fire in the open space beside the river which was a loose coil of silver ribbon in the land. And into that Dahaun's people tossed in solemn ritual certain bundles of leaves and faggots of sticks so that the light smoke which arose was scented with spicy odors.

"Kel-say—"

She started. Under one of the soft boots she wore a stone loosened and rolled.

Not Dahaun, nor Tregarth, but she whom Kelsie had taken the greatest pains to avoid—the gray woman. Now she seated herself composedly on a well-chosen rock where Kelsie could not get away without actually brushing past her.

"You are very brave—or very foolish—" The woman might have been as at home in speaking the language as Tregarth—or else by some power she had opened knowledge for the girl she faced, "to give your name so openly. Do you not believe then in your own place that a name is the proper label of a being? Or are you so well protected that you need have no fears? What craft do you practice there, Kel-Say?"

There was a mocking note in her voice and Kelsie was quick to define it. Her resentment for that moment was greater than the uneasiness and wary fear this one always aroused in her.

"I practice no craft," she returned sullenly. "I do not know why I am here and your gate—" she drew a deep breath.

The witch shook her head. "Not *my* gate—we meddle not in such matters—though once," she sat very straight and there was a shadow of pride on her face, "we could do much which perhaps rivaled the secrets of the gates. But—" did her square shoulders slump a little now under the heavy folds of her gray overmantle? "that time is past. Tell me, girl—Kel-Say," again she drawled out that name, mouthing it as if she said something momentous, "who rules the craft in your place and time?"

"If you mean witches," Kelsie flashed hotly in return, "there are none—really. It is all just stories— Oh, some people dabble with old beliefs and talk about the moon, have ceremonies which they swear have come down from the old times—but it is all just their imaginations!"

There was silence between them and again Kelsie felt that probing within her head as if the other tested her for some shield.

"You believe what you have just said." The woman's stare changed from challenge to wonder. "You believe! How did matters go awry then in your time that the true knowledge was so lost? Yet Tregarth," it seemed to Kelsie that she spoke that name with a lip twist of disgust, "has a measure of the power and he says that he is from your world—by another gate."

Kelsie pulled herself up to sit on a rock so that they were face to face, the woman not looking down at her.

"I do not know what you mean by power—" But was that the truth? There had been the besieging of the circle and certainly the Rider had used no normal weapon to try to get at her, nor had he been able to force his mount into that circle of stones, yet she could pass easily out and back.

"See? You do—at least power as it is here and now." The other might well have reached within and read her thoughts. "The scrying said one would come and it would mean portentous things. And Roylane," again her mouth twisted as if she found it very difficult to say that name, "yielded up her jewel—"

"Not to me," Kelsie pointed out.

"Ah, yes. The cat. And what is the meaning of that, Kel-Say? Answer me now with the truth." She raised one hand and snapped her fingers. A flash of blue light sped toward the girl and Kelsie ducked. Not soon enough—the spark touched her temple and it was as if a ball of fire had broken apart inside her head. She screamed and swayed.

"*Arkwraka!*"

Kelsie, still swaying, saw another lash of fire come apparently from the sky, cutting between her and the witch. A man, one of Dahaun's people, raised his arm again and a second lash of fire, for she could feel the very heat of it, passed before her but not aimed at either her or the witch.

He who had used the flame whip advanced another step or so and Kelsie recognized him as Ethutur, the co-ruler with Dahaun of this place of peace, while at his shoulder, keeping step with him, though he carried no bared weapon, was the young man Kelsie had had named to her as Yonan, one of the scouts who went beyond the limits of the Valley and dared the evil at its blackest.

"You call on no such tricks here," Ethutur spoke directly to the witch and her previously calm face now was drawn up into a snarl.

Her lips moved as if she would spit like an enraged cat. But when she answered her voice was even enough.

"This one is no kin of yours—"

"Nor of your blood either," he returned. "If she gives anything she will give it openly and by her own consent. This is a place of freedom— there is no mistress, no servant here—"

"You are all servants!" flared the witch.

"To a greater Power than you or anyone else within this Valley can call upon!"

"The Dark has penetrated many places where the Light says or once said that it holds rule. Even your oath-bound Lady does not know for sure what she has welcomed into the heart of her safe land. Those who come through the gates have gifts, talents, compulsions that none of us can name. I would learn more from this one—that she not be the key by which the Dark can open *your* gate!"

"Your rule runs over mountain—or it did, Wise One. But it would seem that you cannot now summon any quorum of your sisters to do much more than the Wisewomen who follow the Lady can. You came to us of Escore for aid for your losses and now you go your own bold way and do not abide by the bounds laid upon power here. You know well that the use of one power always awakens the Dark and in a way strengthens it by that arousing. I say to you now—go your own way or that shall not run with ours!"

"You are a man!" Now there were flecks of spittle shot forth from her lips, an unusual flush painted her sharp cheekbones. "What do you know of Power save through such toys as that!" she gestured to the whipstock he still held. "The higher power—"

"Is for any who can hold it—man or woman," he said. "We follow not your ways of Estcarp here. There are those to be named who wrought mightily in the old days and who were also men. Boast not too loudly of your sistership, seeing to what it has been reduced."

"To save our world!" Her flush was fading but her eyes were wells of anger and Kelsie could feel that emotion, or believed she could, issuing forth from that spare, gray-cloaked body.

"To save your world," he nodded. "Well you wrought for your people. But again I say your ways are not ours and under our sky remember that."

He spoke with none of the emphasis which anger had given her words but she was still wrapped in a red rage as she turned and walked away from them. And Ethutur did not turn to see her go, as if she had already been put out of mind. He spoke now to Kelsie:

"You would do well to avoid that one. She brings with her all the narrowness of the west and I think that she will be a long time giving way to another way of life. It is true that the witches of Estcarp wrought mightily to defend their land against two different evils, but in their last battle they not only exhausted their realm of power but they also lost many of their number, drained of life itself. Now they come questing here for a renewal of what they lost—not only power for those still alive within their citadel but also for those with talent whom they may take and train in their own ways of life. And I do not think, Lady, that you would find what they have to offer good—"

"She came to me," protested Kelsie, "not I to her. I want nothing more from her. And this power of which so much has been said, I do not know or want it."

Ethutur shook his head slowly. "In life it is not what we want which balances our scales—rather it is what the Greater Ones have seen fit to give us at our birth hour. There can be that locked within a man—or a woman—which such do not know that they bear and which comes forth at a time of stress unsummoned. Once awakened that can be trained as any weapon is mastered by one who wishes to wield it." Now he smiled and pointed to the young man still a pace or so behind him. "Ask of Yonan what he found to be his portion."

But Yonan did not match that smile. Instead his face remained in somber lines as if he saw little that was lighthearted in his world.

"Unasked for," he said as Ethutur paused, "To so gain anything one walks a hard road. But—" he shrugged, "we come to you, Lady, to ask where walks that furred one who came with you through your gate."

"I don't know," Kelsie was surprised at his change of subject and the young man must have read that in her expression for he added:

"There is reason." Yonan had been carrying one arm close to his chest, the bulk of a cloth wrapped loosely around it. Now he held it out to her and there sounded a thin mewling cry. The movement disturbed the wrapping of the cloth and she saw a small white furred head upheld, blind eyes fast shut, and a mouth open for another cry.

"The gray ones," Yonan's voice was harsh, "cornered a snow cat and had their pleasure with her and one cub. This one Tsali found and rescued. It will die if it cannot be fed."

"But it is so big," Kelsie was already reaching out for the well-wrapped cub. "It must be as big as both of the kittens—and the wildcat—"

"Swiftfoot," he corrected her and she looked at him amazed.

"Have you already named her then?"

"She named herself to the Lady of Green Silences. All which run, fly or swim, and are not of the shadows, are friends to the Lady. But the cubling will die—"

"No!" The weaving of that blindly seeking head, the small wail of hunger and loneliness brought Kelsie out of the preoccupation with herself and the anger of the witch to the here and now. "She took her kittens to a place of her own yesterday. I have not seen her save when she came to feed."

As he relinquished the weight of the cub into her arms she knew that she must indeed find her fellow wayfarer and see if Swiftfoot would accept a fosterling. Some cats did so readily as she well knew.

Surely the wildcat had found a lair somewhere along the gashed cliffs which sheltered the Valley. Their many shallow caves and cracks would attract her—and it could not be too far from the living houses as the cat had easily come morning and evening for her own nourishment.

Kelsie gathered the bundled creature to her and then looked to Yonan. "What is this?"

"Snow cat," he repeated shortly. "The mother must have been hunted well out of the mountains to come so far afield. The gray ones are roaming afar when they fasten on such prey."

The cub was nuzzling her fingers, sucking hungrily, halting now and then to whimper its need. Resolutely Kelsie turned her back on the gathering of houses and the tents of the people who were not Valley born and headed for the cliff side. As she went she began to call—not the "kitty-kitty" of her own time and place but with her mind. Before that moment she had not thought of trying to do that. It was easy enough to picture the wildcat and her kittens, to hold to that picture and keep on summoning, in a way she could not have put words to, that unsought companion in her adventure.

She was aware that Yonan followed her, but some distance behind as if he feared in some way to confuse her searching. They scrambled over several falls of rock and past one stream which bored through the hills to find its path to the river. Then Kelsie stopped short.

It was as if a new sense had been added to the five she had carried so far through life. This was not scent, sight, nor hearing, but it was touch of a different kind. As she concentrated upon it the wildcat came into sight around the side of a large boulder, one of those on which ancient carvings had been so weathered that only traces of their pattern could be sighted. Kelsie took a step toward her and Swiftfoot's lips drew back in a warning snarl. Though the girl had carried both the cat and her kittens on their journey to the Valley, Swiftfoot was announcing that this had been only a temporary measure and she would allow no more such liberties. What had they said back beyond the Gate, that no one could tame a true wild-cat? It would seem that such warnings were right.

Kelsie went no farther. Instead she juggled the wrapped cub to one hip and braced herself against the ancient work to come to her knees at its foot. Then she settled the cloth on the ground before her and pulled away its folds so that the hungry and now continually wailing cub was wholly revealed.

She carefully kept her thoughts to herself. Even if she could think Swiftfoot into coming to examine this newcomer she would not dare to try. She knew too little about this new force she had tapped to try to use it further.

The cub continued to wail. Swiftfoot snarled and then her slitted eyes turned toward the youngling. Slowly, only an inch at a time as she might have advanced upon some prey, she came forward, belly low to the gravel, stopping now and again to eye Kelsie who held herself stiffly quiet, waiting.

Perhaps the cub scented something of its near kin for now its head swung toward the cat, though its eyes could not see, and its wail reached a higher pitch. The cat sprang and Kelsie flung out one arm fearing that death rather than life for the cub was the result of her experiment.

Swiftfoot crouched over the cub which was perhaps a fourth of her own size. Her tongue flicked forward and licked the blind head. Then she sought to grip the loose rolls of skin at its neck, to carry it as she might one of her own kittens. It was almost too great a task for her. The cub bumped along the ground, still wailing, as they disappeared from sight behind the rock. Kelsie turned and saw Yonan some distance from her watching intently.

"She will accept it, I think," the girl said. "But whether it can survive—that no one can promise."

For the first time she saw a shadow on his serious face—a shadow which might serve for a smile.

"It will be well," he seemed very sure. "This is a place of life, not death."

Kelsie thought of all she did not know about the Valley, about these people, of all which she must learn. Must learn? Again that thought thudded home. All Tregarth's talk of gates and how one passed by a single way through them, how much was true? Perhaps all the asking in the world would not tell her that. But what she could learn—that she would.

"You are not of the Valley people," she stated that as a fact not a question. There were truly two humanoid peoples within the Valley—to say nothing of those who were winged, pawed, hoofed, or scaled.

"No," he dropped down facing her, sitting cross-legged, the rumpled cloth in which he had carried the cub lying in a heap between them. "I am of Karsten kin—also of the Sulcar—"

He must have seen from her expression that neither word meant anything to her for he launched into more speech than she had heard since Simon Tregarth had ridden out a day earlier.

"We are of the Old Blood—from the south—or my mother was. And when they drove us out because we were what we were we came into the mountain borderlands and took service against the Kolder and those who put our kinsmen to the death. Then when the witches turned the mountain—"

"Turned the mountains!" Kelsie broke in. Maybe she could accept some things but the turning of mountains was not among them.

"All those who ruled in Estcarp," he continued, "they gathered their power so it was as if it were wielded by one alone, and that they threw against the earth itself, so that the mountains tumbled and arose anew, and no man could recognize the border thereafter."

It was perfectly plain that he believed every word he was saying no matter how impossible the feat he described.

"Then," he was continuing, "we sought land of our own and Kyllan Tregarth came to lead us into the older homeland, even this Escore. But there was ancient evil here and it awoke at the coming of the Tregarths for their sister Kaththea is a notable witch, though she wears no jewel, and, what she did in ignorance troubled the land. So once more we war and against a host of Darkness which is more than men such as we faced before. Strange indeed are some of our battles—" He glanced down at his own hand where it rested upon the hilt of his sword. She remembered then that these men who went mail clad were different from the change- able people and seemed often to have hand close to some weapon or another as if they expected nothing but war and alarms as a way of life.

"Who is Simon Tregarth—you speak of Kyllan—"

"Simon is one who came through a gate—even as you, Lady. He was great in the councils of Estcarp when they went against the Kolder and has but recently returned from another venture which took him beyond the accounting of men. He is wed to the Once-Witch Jaelithe and sired Kyllan, Kemoc and Kaththea all at one birth. That was a marvel unknown before—the warrior, the warlock, and the witch—and all have done great things in this land.

"But there is still much to be accomplished here. Also there are many things which a man cannot understand—" he was frowning again and running his fingers around the hilt of his sword, even drawing it a fraction once and then slapping it back into the scabbard.

"And some such have happened to you," Kelsie encouraged him when he fell silent, wishing to store away in her memory as much as she could of this place and all there was to do with it. That she was caught here at least for now she could no longer deny. So the more she knew the better it would be for her in days to come. Though what part she could play in such affairs she could not see, nor did she wish to speculate.

"Such happened to me," Yonan agreed. "For a space we have believed that we have beaten back the shadow and that it sulks in its own fast- nesses. But you have told us of a Sarn Rider who has dared to come this near to the Valley and deal death to one who should have been mightier than he—"

"Roylane?"

It seemed to Kelsie that he winced as she repeated that name.

"A witch has no name. To give one's name among them gives them power over another. Yet she said her name to you and her stone came with the cat. Thus another change—"

Now she looked at him squarely, catching his eyes and holding them in a way she had never tried with anyone before—as if she could compel him to answer even against his will.

"What do you think I am?"

It was a matter of four or five slow breaths before he answered and then he said:

"You were summoned—the Lady Dahaun had the foreseeing of that. And none can come so unless there is a geas laid upon them—"

"A geas?" she demanded.

"A fated journey or deed against which nothing nor no one can stand. Yes, we knew that one would come—and perhaps *they* did also or a Sarn Rider would not have dared the inner hills. What your geas is—that you will discover for yourself, Lady—"

"You are right about that," she returned grimly, forced against her will into at least half belief.

5

Kelsie arose abruptly, turning to the rock in which those weird spirals and indentations were plain as the sun moved.

"I know nothing of this . . . this geas—"

He shrugged. "Sometimes that is so and you will find that it leads you only after many days— But where it points, there you shall go."

"You speak as if you know something of such things beside just idle tales."

Yonan again looked at her with the shadow smile. "Now that is also the truth. It once fell upon me—this need for doing an action which I did not plan and—"

Whatever he might have added came to nothing, for one of the lizard folk flashed into sight among the rocks. Yonan was instantly on his feet, staring upward at that green-gold scaled body as it descended the Valley wall with a speed which made Kelsie gasp so near was it to a downward plunge. The girl saw that while using all four limbs for his quick drop the sentry carried in addition something in his mouth, an untidy bunch much the same as the cloth in which Yonan had brought the cub and she wondered if another was to be added to Swiftfoot's family.

Once the lizard reached relatively level ground where the two stood he spat forth what he carried and it slammed against the stone of the carving. There came a tingling sound and then a puff of black smoke accompanied by a foul odor. Yonan exclaimed, drew sword while the lizard man stood, panting to one side, his golden, black slitted eyes on the man.

The tip of the sword caught in the covering of that untidy package, flipped part of the covering up and back. The smoke had disappeared but the odor was stronger, seeming to poison the very air about them.

Under the flap of the material Yonan had lifted there lay a short rod, perhaps the length of one of the lizard man's long-fingered hands. It was a murky grayish color and there was a knob at either end. Plainly it was hollow and a smoky substance within appeared to swirl and billow as if it fought for freedom.

Moving with what appeared exaggerated care Yonan rolled it out of the cloth. By the expression on his face he was as puzzled as the girl as to what this might be. Though she knew from her instant reaction to it that she would not have laid her bare hand upon that artifact, even had she been offered free passage back through the gate. Her quick, nauseated reaction puzzled as well as alarmed her.

There was something like a far off fluttering of speech within her head and then the lizard was gone, running at top speed toward the houses closer to the river, leaving his find under the sword point of Yonan.

"Tsali goes for help—" the young man said. "He must have found this in the rocks above on the very rim of the Valley."

"Look!" Kelsie may not have wanted to touch the stone but she clutched in her growing uneasiness at Yonan's arm.

For that thing on the ground was moving!

Not from any stirring of the sword point. In fact it looked as if it were somehow veering left to escape touch with the steel. As if it were a sentient creature with a will to escape—escape or attack?

This was near to the same anger she had felt when the Witch Woman had turned against her. There was a will here, somehow clipped within, or acting from a distance without, upon that rod. It had turned enough now to be wholly clear of the cloth and she saw that the knob end coming around to face them was fashioned in the likeness of a head—a grotesque travesty of a human head in which eye slits boiled with the same evil yellow fire she had seen in pits of the hounds' narrow skulls.

To her surprise Yonan reversed his sword in one swift movement and held toward that rolling thing the hilt instead of the point. There came a blaze of blue haze from the pommel of the weapon. It touched the rolling rod and—

That solid looking thing quivered as if it were indeed endowed with life. Also it would appear that Yonan's quick action baffled it though it raised the head end a fraction and wavered for an instant back and forth.

"What is it?" demanded Kelsie. "Is it alive?"

"I have never seen its like before," returned her companion. "But it is of the Dark—the Deepest Shadow perhaps."

Before the words were barely out of his mouth there came a yowl of rage. One she had certainly heard before. Around the rock padded the cat, dragging behind it something which flashed with fiery light. The chain of the witch's jewel dripped from between those cruel fangs and the gem itself boiled and throbbed as if it, too, had a new kind of life within. The cat made a wide circle about that which still quivered and fought for its freedom where Yonan held it in balk.

Padding straight to Kelsie, Swiftfoot dropped the chain of the jewel over the toe of her soft boot and, looking up into the girl's face, gave a second demanding yowl.

The girl bent and scrabbled for the chain which had fallen into the gravel and arose with the sparkling gem twirled only inches from her hand, nearly crying out from the heat the thing was generating.

Now the rod went into a frenzy, rolling back and forth, but Yonan was watchful and his sword hilt blocked any swing right or left which might take it even temporarily out of the ward that weapon kept upon it.

"Fool!"

It was the Witch Woman's biting voice which led Kelsie to glance back over her shoulder. Her skirt caught up with both hands, the woman out of Estcarp was actually running, outpacing in this instant Dahaun and behind her two others, one in the mail of the Old Race, the other, whip-stock steady, a girl of the Valley. But before the three of them came Tsali with a whir of speed.

"Fool!" The witch was panting a little but she arrived first and had strength enough left to swipe outward at Kelsie's hand, as if she would wrest the jewel stone from her then and there. "Would you burn out the last of life—"

"Or the first," Dahaun's voice was much more collected. "What mischief has Tsali discovered within our borders?" She came closer to that trembling, fighting rod, dropping down to view the thing the closer. They were all silent now waiting for her to judge. But at last she shook her head.

"Never has the Valley had its ancient safeguards broken. Yet Tsali found this rolling between rocks and about to fall into the spring, perhaps to let the water hide and bring it down. It is not of the Sarn, nor the gray ones, and certainly not of the Thas—or if so it is something they have never turned against us before. This is very old—and—"

"And," for the first time the man in mail spoke. Kelsie thought at first he was Simon returned. But the face half seen below the helm's nose guard was that of a much younger man. "And, what does that argue, Lady? That those of the Dark have broached some place of ancient weaponry?" He held no sword, rather what seemed a flimsy stick peeled of its bark and with half of its length colored the green-blue of the bird feathers which roofed the Valley houses.

"Well enough," he said to Yonan, "let us see what the Valley can raise against this."

Obediently Yonan stepped away and withdrew his sword hilt from the weaving pattern before the strange thing.

The other man spoke. The single word he uttered held no meaning for Kelsie but once more, as she had shrunk from the powers the witch had called upon her, so again her head was instantly filled with a roaring sound as if the very air about them had been ruptured, letting in she knew not what.

The green half of the wand the man held burst into real flame and with an exclamation, he threw it from him at that rod. It fell into the tangle of cloth and smoldered, beginning a fire which seemed to excite the rod for it rolled deliberately toward that piece of scorching fabric and thrust the head end into the small flame. It might have been feeding greedily on the fast dying spark.

"Ha," the Witch Woman flung back her head and actually uttered a bark of laughter. "See what you would do, Kemoc halfling? This is not for such as you no matter what knowledge you dabbled in in Lormt. Get you off before you make bad matters worse. See—it feeds upon that very thing you would use to quiet it!"

The swirling within the rod part of the lizard man's find did indeed appear to gather strength, and the murkiness was, Kelsie thought, taking on a glow. There was a sudden sharp pain in her hand and she looked to see that the gem was also awhirl at the end of its chain and the links of the chain were sawing at her flesh.

"By Reith and Nieve—" was that her own voice? Whence had come those names? From her lips right enough, but they had not been generated by any thought of hers!

The twirling stone was throwing off sparks, though none reached as far as the object on the ground. She discovered she could not stop the motion of her wrist which controlled that passage through the air.

"No!" Again the Witch Woman gave tongue and she aimed a blow straight at Kelsie's arm. Only Yonan's left hand intercepted that and she was forced a little backward by his abrupt rebuttal to the stroke she tried to deliver.

"She is no witch!" The voice reached a screech. "She dare not use the power. Would you have that which waits fall upon us all? Stop her!" The Witch Woman looked to Dahaun who had made no move either at the destruction of the wand or at the witch's foiled attack on Kelsie. But now she spoke.

"We do not give names—those are given to us. She was given a name and perhaps more by one of your own kin—"

"Who is dead!" That sounded as if the witch thought such an ending might have been well deserved.

"Who is dead," Dahaun agreed. "But in dying she may have passed—"

"There is no likelihood of that," cried the witch. "She has no right— she could not have done so. This one comes from where? She is not of the blood, she has no training, she is nothing except a danger to all of us. Give me the jewel!" Her demand was aimed at Kelsie who had just made a discovery of her own.

Just as she could not stop the twirling of her wrist which kept the gem in motion, so she could not now loose her grip upon it. Instead she was pulled forward as if someone tugged at her with greater strength than she could sustain. The witch gem swung faster, though its circle was wider until it seemed to rest upon the air itself a distance beyond the circumference of that rod.

All the while the rod flapped up and down, strove to roll and could not, as if it did indeed hold life within it. The whir of the jewel grew faster until Kelsie's wrist seemed to be the center of a brilliant disc and the sparks it flung off now shot at the thing on the half-burned cloth.

Again Kelsie's lips shaped words she did not understand:

"Reith—Reith—by the Fire of Reith—by the will of Nieve may this be rendered harmless!"

Wider and more accurate became the rain of sparks. Now they centered straight upon the rod. Then there was a burst of glaring light, first an angry threatening crimson, then blue above and nothing below save a twisted piece of what looked like half-melted metal.

Kelsie's arm fell to her side without her willing it. It was numb as if she had lifted some great weight and held it out for a time past her own strength. The glitter from the jewel had vanished—it was an ashy gray, like a piece from the fire which had burned itself out.

Dahaun broke the silence first. "It is gone—the evil of it."

"Back to the sender," the witch's harsh voice sounded no relief. "And what message will it carry so? That we have come seeking and are ready to stand with you—"

"Seeking you did come," Kemoc reminded her. "But it was not to cast your lot and power with us—you thought to take, not to share."

"Be silent, halfling who should never have been born," her harshness close to hoarseness as if she would scream at him but did not have the power.

"Halfling I may be," he told her, "but that half blood has wrought well for Escore. And before that for Estcarp—"

"Man!" she spat at him. "It is against all nature that a man has the power. Because your sire brought that with him through the gate—what has happened?"

"Yes, what has happened," he returned. "The Kolders are no more, the way to Escore lies open—"

"Which is no blessing," she interrupted. "Things from the foul Dark roam the mountains now and venture down upon the land. You and those two who share birthday with you have stirred into being a mighty stew of war, disaster and death. And now—" she pointed straight to Kelsie who was trying to rub life back into her numb arm, "there comes this one who took from one of the sisters—stole—what she does not know how to handle and so—"

"And so," Dahaun's voice cut clear and cold through that tirade, "and so this thing whose like we have not seen before has been rendered harmless." She spoke to Kemoc and the girl of her own people. "Let it be buried where it lies and then do you," she motioned to the stone in which the ancient carvings were still to be half seen, "set this upon it. Reith and Nieve," she went to Kelsie and laid her hand protectively on that numbed arm. From her touch came a surge of warmth and the girl discovered she could flex her fingers. "Long and very long has it been since those names were called upon—though they were mighty weapons in their day. Do you still have a touch with them?" she asked the witch.

The latter looked around at the rest of them with both anger and contempt in her face, stronger yet in her voice as she answered:

"Such things are not for talking on—they are secrets—"

Dahaun shook her head. "The time for secrets is long past. When the Dark arises, then the Light must stand united and all knowledge be shared from one to another."

The witch answered her with what sounded like an exclamation of contempt. However, if she would have denied Dahaun's suggestion she did not do so more openly. Instead she gestured toward the now dead looking stone which still dangled from the chain wound about Kelsie's fingers.

"That is of our magic not of yours. It should have been left to rest with her who first gained it. Not given to one who has none of the proper training. How do we know what she is, in truth?"

There was no mistaking the anger which still bubbled in her whenever she glanced at Kelsie. The girl was swift to reply. With the fingers of her left hand she plucked at the chain until it did unwrap from that tight hold and she offered to give it to the witch, only too glad to be free of it, but the woman in gray made a gesture repulsing it, seeming almost to shrink as it came near her.

"Take it," Kelsie urged. "I do not want it—"

"You have no right—" began the witch making no move to accept the stone.

"She has the right of death-gift," Dahaun said. "Did not she who died give also of her name to Kel-Say? And with the name might have gone her power."

"She also had no right!"

"Then call her up and ask her of—"

The flush was high on the angular face of the woman in gray. "That is foulness which you suggest! We have no dealings with such darkness."

"If that is so, why question what your sister has done?" Dahaun asked. "One can pass the power willingly and she did—"

"To a cat!" sputtered the witch. "It was that beast who carried the seeing stone."

"And in a time of need passed it again to one it judged would use it—"

Kelsie was tired of this wrangling over what she might have done or what she might be. She tossed the jewel from her, though she had to use all her willpower to achieve that. For it seemed that her body was a traitor to her mind and would not let it go. It arched through the air, struck upon one of the tall rocks and then slid down into the coarse grass clump at the foot of the stone.

"Take it!" Kelsie had never heard such a note in Dahaun's voice before. Thus in spite of all her defiance and desire to be free of their quarrels she found herself moving forward, her fingers reaching down to a loop of the chain caught about a stiff blade of grass. Once more she held the stone. It was still opaque, showing a muddy gray, and she began to believe that it had burned itself out of whatever mysterious "power" it had shown while confronting the rod. She swung it a little as one might swing a smoldering branch to brighten fire again, but there was no answer from that lump of crystal.

"Give her the covering," now Dahaun had turned that demand upon the witch, who, her anger plain to read in every stiff gesture, brought out that patch of cloth which could be drawn into a bag and smoothed it out on top of one of the stones.

Thankfully Kelsie loosed the chain and let the jewel fall onto that circle releasing her hold. The witch had drawn the drawstrings the minute she placed it so and stepped away, leaving the knobby bag on the rock's crown.

"Take it—" Dahaun ordered.

Kelsie dared to shake her head. "I do not want it—"

"Such things of power choose you, not you them. This has doubly come to you, from the hand of she who earned it and from your use of it. Take it up—its use may be over. But I think not."

Yonan had used sword and knife points to dig a pit, and he pushed the twisted, blackened rod into the earth. But as he did so he uttered an exclamation. For on the stone against which that thing had burnt there was now a boldly black picture— There grinned up at them a face which was more closely human than the one Kelsie had noted on the rod, yet so foully evil that she could not believe any such thing could exist. During its destruction it had painted its likeness on the stone, into the stone, for when Yonan strove to pick away at it with the point of his sword he could not scratch a single fragment of the sooty black free.

Dahaun strode around the rock and came back in a moment her hands cupped, holding water which dripped down from her curled fingers. She bent her head and breathed on what she held, reciting words—perhaps names. Then she turned to the witch who, plainly against her will, yet moved by a belief strong in her, dabbed one finger in the fast disappearing water and muttered some incantation of her own.

Next it went to Kemoc who passed his hand above the clasped ones of the Valley dweller and spoke his own prayer or ritual. Thereafter Dahaun went to the black mask on the stone and allowed the water to cascade down upon the burnt picture of the demonic head. Kelsie was sure she saw the lips of that writhe as if it would call out. But the image blurred, thinned, and was gone.

With her foot Dahaun prodded that stone into the hole after the remnants of the rod, then from her belt pouch took some withered leaves and allowed them to flutter down on top of that defiled bit of rock. Yonan struck with his sword. A cascade of gravel poured down, to utterly hide the buried. But it took them all—except the witch who made no move to help—to loosen and push over that burial of evil the stone with the carvings. Dahaun was the last to withdraw her hand, rather smoothing with her fingers those long eroded signs and symbols carven thereon.

"What manner of weapon was that?" Kemoc asked when they were done.

Dahaun shrugged. "Its like I have not seen. But in the days when this land was rent, adept fighting adept and no safety to be found save here in this Valley, there were many weapons which have been long forgotten. Who animated this— We have had a measure of uneasy peace since we fought the battle of the cliffs. I think that that is now at an end—or nearly so. The very fact that this could be planted above, perhaps to open a road to the Dark, is a threat I never thought we would see. The Sarn and the gray ones are up and out. If they stir so must the Thas and all the rest of the Dark. We must be ready to see perhaps something more than what lies here."

Kelsie held the bag with the Witch Jewel. She felt battered and bruised inside. There had been too much too soon. She knew that this was no dream. She had to believe Simon Tregarth, that by some chance she had come into an entirely new world where other natural laws held sway. Yet it was only with difficulty that she could make herself accept that. If she went back to the circle of the gate with the jewel she now held—if she passed between those standing stones—could she not win back to a life which was real—

Oh, this was real enough but it was not her reality. Simon Tregarth seemed to have accepted it without question. But she—

"Keep you that—safe!" the harsh croak of the witch disturbed her thoughts then as the woman's angular form stepped close to Kelsie. One long pale finger stabbed the air in the direction of the packet she held.

"I am no witch," Kelsie returned, her dislike for the woman overriding all her caution at that moment.

The other laughed but there was only sneering amusement in that guttural sound. "Well may you say that, girl. But it seems that this Escore can turn upside down truths we know in Estcarp. Men hold power—" she favored both Yonan and Kemoc with a savage frown, "and those of no training wield the weapons of Light. But that has obeyed you once—"

"I gave no order!" Kelsie was quick to answer.

"If you did not—whence came the names you called upon? Out of the air which holds us all? What were you in your own time and place, girl? You have some power or that would not work for you. And an unknown power—" she shook her head, "who knows how it may hold when the times comes to face the Dark?"

Dahaun's hand fell again on Kelsie's arm, drawing her away from the witch toward the light trail descending into the heart of the Valley. "We have seen its work this day. I would say that you—and it—wrought mightily," she said to the girl. "Be not fearful—or only so much as to make you cautious. You bear now that which will be half protection, half weapon. Kaththea sent us word three tens of days ago that there was to come one who would be a balance for us in new struggles to come. It would seem that she was very right—"

"The babblings of a half witch—a traitor who fled from the place of learning before she was knit to the sisterhood," the witch was not to be overborne by Dahaun. Her sour mouth dropped the words like acid.

"She chose her own road," Dahaun said. "And now she is Lady to Hilarion. Do you set even the combined forces of Estcarp against him, Wise Woman?"

"An adept? Who knows? In the old days it was those of his kind who rent the land."

"And in these days he helps to heal it!" countered Dahaun. "Enough, Wise Woman. You say you come to us for aid and yet you do nothing but question what is done. Perhaps Escore and Estcarp have grown too far apart in these days to be allies."

Her tone was very cool as she drew Kelsie with her, and they passed the witch on their way down into the Valley.

6

Kelsie lay on the narrow sleeping mat. She had pushed aside the covering of net and feathers. Now she put one hand slowly, against her will, underneath the higher end of the mat which served as a pillow.

Yes, it was still there—the wad of bag which held the Witch Jewel. She had tried to give it to Dahaun and now she remembered what had happened then with a shiver which did not spring from the night air about her.

It had moved—like some sluggish turtle or other living creature—the bag and its contents had moved—not through any doing of her own nor, she felt sure, through the action of Dahaun. Returning to lie again within close touch of her own hand. Willing or not it had been made plain that it meant to stay with her. Though how could one accord conscious feelings to a piece of crystal, no matter how finely wrought?

She rubbed her aching head. The pain which had come from the blow she had suffered when she fell through the "gate" had vanished at least two days ago. This was something which had come into being since she had taken up the crystal. It was as if within her head something stirred, struck against walls, bulging out to occupy more and more space.

Without truly knowing why she did so, Kelsie raised one hand, and, with outstretched forefinger, she drew a sign in the dark as one might paint upon a stretch of canvas. And—

The stone flared into life—showing through the cloth blue and bright for just an instant. How and why—those had begun to mean more now than "where" in the great hoard of questions which she wanted to have answered. Only those she had already asked had either received a flat denial of information or, as she suspected, a devious sidestepping from a clear reply.

"Who am—No, I am Kelsie McBlair!" she whispered aloud. Once

more her thought followed that firmly beaten path. She had reached forward to stop McAdams' shot. He had struck her, sending her sprawling forward, and she had awakened in the circle of stones with the wildcat. Did the cat feel as strange as she? Or had Swiftfoot, now with her expected family, adjusted to this new territory without those raking questions which gave the girl so many sleepless hours in the night?

Gates—there were portals here and there in this ensorceled country which opened or shut, through which might come by design or chance castaways such as herself. Tregarth had told her there was no return. She forced herself to lie flat again, and, with her eyes squinted shut, she attempted by force of will to be again within the safe and well-known past.

Only that was difficult also. Why—Kelsie sat bolt upright again once more shivering.

Where had she been for those sharp instants out of time? Not back in the Scottish highlands. No! There had been a hall with many seats and at one end four chairs with tall backs and thronelike appearance set up on a dais before her. Not all the seats in that hall had been occupied—only two of the dais thrones. There had been a stirring about her—a feeling of expectancy and of the need for action—hurried action.

She rubbed her eyes with both hands as if she could reach through them into her head and so rub out that scene and the feeling it left in her, as if she were only a part of a great whole—that there was a need to be—what?

Now she reached beneath the pillow mat to seize the wrapped jewel and heave it away from her, as far away as she could send it. She went on her knees to the curtains which enforced the privacy of this sleeping quarter and drawing those aside she hurled the witch thing out and away. Then with a sigh of relief she settled back to sleep—or else to think her way out of this land and all the pitfalls it held for the stranger.

She twisted and turned, trying to hold in mind McAdams' angry face, the toppled stones behind him. That was what was true—the rest—

But it was the hall which closed about her. She was sitting in her proper seat, the one which had been assigned to her upon her taking the jewel oath, which would be hers through many, many years to come. To her left was an empty place—to her right, she was sure she heard the fluttering come and go of breath from Sister Wodelily. She could even smell clearly the scent of that flower which seemed to cling to the old woman's robes—it drowned out the spicy scent of the incense burning in braziers at either end of the dais.

They were supposed to be in meditation but her own thoughts skittered about. There was the lamb which had been found this morning beside its dead dam and which had been given to her to raise, there were the three gazia orphans she had found just a little while ago—surely the Second Lady would let her bring them into her own workroom to cherish. Were they not all oathbound to save life no matter how lowly on the scale? There was also the brewing of the tisane which so helped the pain of lower limbs in winter that they even bespoke commendation for her in the general assembly. She herself, Sister Makeease——Roylane——No! Never that name, even in her straying thoughts she must bury it so deeply that it could never be said again.

All thought of lambs, of herbs, or the quiet and gentle life she loved were driven from her by the words of the woman in the middle seat of the dais.

"Let the lots be drawn then."

A little before her was a wide-topped jar of time-aged silver and to this she was pointing with a rod which had appeared from the folds of her wide-skirted robe.

Within the bowl there was a fluttering, a rise of small bits of white as if someone had dumped there scraps of paper. They arose, their swirl forming a cloud as high as the head of the seated woman who had so commanded them, and now they traveled, swifter than any cloud, from above the dais out over the seats, those which were empty, alas, and those which still had occupants. Over each of the latter they made a quick revolution and they journeyed on. Then—one bit fell from that swarming cloud, fluttered down into the lap of a woman who sat five rows away from Sister Makeease. It was the dour-faced Sister Wittle that it so chose.

Sister Wittle! She wondered at the decision of the choice. Surely that was not influenced in any way. She had seen it in operation too many times and often enough it had fallen on some one of the sisterhood who seemed the least likely to be the proper one to handle the problem involved and still the end result had been success. Yet Sister Wittle to be sent as an emissary of the depleted Council—that was one of the oddest chances she had seen in many a year.

The cloud having loosed its first surprising choice was flitting on. Over one row it sped and then another. Now it was coming toward her. There was a sudden small cold feeling within her breast—the cloud was fast nearing the last of the number of the sisterhood who were eligible for any choice.

Above her head at last—and that white mote shifting down to lie upon her tightly clasped hands. No! But there was no appeal. She must leave the warmth, the sisterhood—she must travel out into the world which she had left what now seemed so long ago. It was a wild land as yet bearing the scars of war, one in which the sisterhood was not still held in esteem. But there was no questioning the choice of the lots—the bit of white rested on her like a burden which grew heavier by the moment and from which there was no escape.

She arose and the bit of white melted from her as might a flake of snow. Sister Wittle was standing also and together they moved forward to the foot of the dais looking up into the face of All Mother, her features set in the mask of perfect composure with which she faced each and every change in the quiet passing of their days here.

"The lots have been cast and have chosen," she said in a neutral voice. For a moment of forbidden questioning Makeease wondered if All Mother was not as surprised at those two choices as the rest—or most— had been. "The Lord Warden has promised an escort through the mountains. The third day by the scry-cup is the most fortunate one. You will find that which our far mothers knew, and draw from it what we must have."

No question that they might fail in their task, she was as firm with her words as if she had been sending them to the storehouse to draw everyday supplies. But Makeease wanted to cry out that she was no rightful one for this sending—that she was weak in power and what she had was for the easing of hurts not for the taking of something which might be well guarded—by what she could not begin to guess. Only here in the Refuge itself there had been tales in plenty of things now wandering over mountain to plague the land. They must go by their vows into the very heart of the black unknown and take there what no one would rightfully and freely give—the very strength of power!

"It is done," Sister Wittle spoke aloud but Sister Makeease could not even shape the words with her stiff lips.

No—

Kelsie was sitting up once more on her sleeping mat. She was *not* that one. Her outflung hand bore down to steady herself and there was something under it. She held so the very stone in its bag which she had hurled away earlier. But she was herself—not that other one—truly it was so. She shut her eyes and snatched her hand from its grip upon the shrouded jewel, concentrating upon her own memories. She had been working in the kennels with the puppy when the telegram had come.

Someone she had heard of only as a kind of tale—Old Jessie McBlair, the aunt of her long dead father, was gone—leaving her a house and what was left of a once large estate. She must claim it herself said the will, the lawyer explained.

So she had gone to Scotland with high hopes of a home of her own at last—only to be faced by a ruin in which only one wing was barely habitable and that fast falling in upon itself into the bargain. There had been sullen and surly faces to front her and no liking for the place or the people had been born in her during the few days she had been there—before this had happened. She was no daughter of power—

She huddled together, her knees against her chest, her arms laced to hold them so. The hand which in her sleep had somehow summoned the jewel bag was tingling and she believed that she could see a faint bluish light about the pouch until she kicked an edge of the covering over it.

There was movement in the dusk of the small, curtain-walled cubicle and she smelled the musky scent of the wildcat. The yellow eyes viewed her from near floor level.

"Go home to your kittens!" Kelsie whispered. "Have you not made enough trouble for me when you brought that—that thing into the Valley?"

She did not expect any answer from the cat, certainly not this sudden thrust of compulsion—that she must be alert—that there was that which needed her attention. The girl fought it with all the willpower in her. Perhaps it was that other one she had seen in her dream—been in her dream—who took command now. For against her will Kelsie loosed that tight grip upon herself, took up the bag and put it into the front of her laced shirt where it lay warm and pulsating as if it held sentient life of its own. She had carried small animals so in past days and felt the same glow of life against her skin.

Still under the order she could not break, she arose and took up the hooded cloak they had given her, sat again to pull on the soft half boots, fastened tightly her belt. Swiftfoot was moving back and forth impatiently before her though she did not offer any cry. Now she stretched forth her blunt muzzle and caught, with sharp teeth, the corner of that cloak, giving a pull toward the direction of the door.

Kelsie obeyed—both that and the force which had settled on her own will muffling her fear and her stubborn need for freedom—moving silently into the night. There was a moon riding high but yet giving a full light to the small gathering of buildings. Still pulling at the cloak edge the cat steered her toward the cliffs. One foot before the other, fighting that drive all the way Kelsie covered much of the same way she had taken in the day.

Twice she passed sentries and both times it was as if they did not see her. There was no challenge, no notice of her going and her own voice would not answer her command to call out. Fear grew in her, blotting out a little of the order which had set her moving. She strove to turn but there was no such thing possible.

Already they had reached the rock which by Dahaun's order had been moved to stand upon the place where the artifact of evil had been buried. There the cat paused and dropped its hold upon her cloak edge, snarled and pawed at a small stone sending it whirling against the large rock. But it was not to view this battlefield of sorts that Kelsie had been moved here. For the cat was going on, climbing another rock. And where Swiftfoot went Kelsie seemed bound to follow.

There was a narrow break in the wall of the heights and from it came a mewling sound. Swiftfoot sprang forward and the girl stumbled after. She had to duck to avoid the heavy rock overhead. There was a narrow passage and then, dark as it was, she felt space about her. From somewhere came a wind carrying with it a foul odor. She heard the cat snarl and then the sound of a struggle and she wavered back against the wall too blinded by the darkness to try to reach the scene of battle.

A body thrust against her in that dark and her skin was rasped by coarse hair or fur while something caught at her hand and tried to jerk her toward the sounds of the struggle. She used her other hand to catch at the bag and pull out of it the Witch Jewel.

The burst of light was eye dazzling to her but apparently painfully blinding to the thing which had attacked her. She saw a mound of what looked like tangled roots flatten itself as far as it could to the ground. While the wave of light swept on to encounter and hold another dire sight, Swiftfoot before the three kittens, the cubling being at least half her size, facing with bared teeth and claws two more of the evil smelling creatures of the dark.

Thas! Though Kelsie could not remember having more than heard the name in passing, now her mind instantly identified these lurkers in the dark. She swung out the jewel by its chain and there were guttural cries from the trio in the cave. The one at her feet was crawling as might a giant insect after the other two, still standing backed away, their crooked fingered hands over the matted stuff covering the upper parts of their faces, hiding their eyes.

Back they edged and now Kelsie came away from the wall against which she had taken shelter and continued to swing out the jewel its light growing ever brighter. She was aware of a draining down her arm, through her fingers and into the chain, as if she herself was the energy which had revitalized the thing and brought about this awakening.

The attackers fled while Swiftfoot licked her litter, still raising her head to snarl now and again. What the trio sought was a tumble of earth and stone at the back of this slitlike cave, apparently the burrow through which they had made entrance here. The first of them reached that and threw itself forward as one might enter surf pounding on the shore of a sea. There was a frenzied scrabbling and an upward shower of earth and small stones. Taking heart at the very visible fear of the noisome invaders Kelsie resolutely drove the other two after the first. She faced now a hole through which she would have to creep in order to advance and she had no intention of doing that. However, she continued to stand and wave the jewel back and forth until her arm tired and fell heavily by her side, as weary as if she had been carrying some great weight.

Nor was it only her arm which was limp with fatigue, her whole body was suddenly struck by a feeling of great lassitude so that she sank to her knees before that evil smelling opening, the light of the jewel fading to a dim glow.

Thas—the underground workers of evil. The very name in her mind appeared to open a door of knowledge. How dared they come into the Valley? There were age old guardians here and those the People of Green Peace believed could not be broached. Yet had the Thas not chanced into the cave Swiftfoot had chosen as her den what might they have done?

"Much!" That answer to her thought was spoken aloud and she nearly sprawled on her face as she strove to swing around to confront the speaker.

Wittle stood there. The gray of her robe faded into the shadow so only her bone-white face and her hands, cupping her own jewel where it swung about her throat, could be clearly seen. For the first time since she had first met her Kelsie saw no animosity in the witch's expression. Instead Wittle was studying Kelsie with an intensity which had something of astonishment in it.

"You are—" her voice was hardly above a whisper.

"Kelsie McBlair!" The girl flashed back. For all her dreaming this night she would hold to that with every bit of strength she could summon.

"She—she chose you then—it is the truth. She exercised the choice!"

"I am not Makeease—" Kelsie denied.

"You have that of her in you now whether you will it or not!"

Wittle's hands dropped away from cupping about her own jewel and it broke into a clear blue light. The stink of the Thas seemed to disappear and Kelsie's strength began to return so that she was able to stand without feeling that her legs were ready to give way under her.

"This must be closed," Wittle was past her in two strides to face the hole. Swinging her jewel by its chain, even as Kelsie had earlier swung the one she carried, she began to recite a cadence of words, words which called upon the very earth itself to provide a stopper to evil. The air between her jewel and the opened earth was filled with ever changing symbols which curled in and out and at times seemed to catch upon one another and cling. Until there was formed a kind of net which floated on until it crashed between the pile of excavated earth and the wall behind it.

"Be it so!" The three words crackled like a flash of lightning across a storm rolled sky. Instantly stone and rock moved, were tossed, pounded, driven back into a firm wall once again. Still glowing therein were flecks of blue as if the net still held. The witch had already turned her back on what she had wrought and was again measuring Kelsie with narrow eyes.

"The Sisterhood grows smaller each year," she said, as if she were reminding herself of something. "Perhaps it is to the gates we must look—and Makeease at her dying saw the truth. You are of us whether you won your jewel by lessoning or by gift—"

"I am not!" Kelsie dared to deny that. Wittle had always been her enemy, why now was she changing, subtly calling upon Kelsie to join forces with her?

"I do—" Again it was as if the other read her thoughts. "We were sent and we have not yet obeyed that sending—"

"I am not a witch." Somewhat to the girl's surprise the witch inclined her head in answer to that.

"By our laws you are not. Yet Makeease knew it. Though perhaps it was because she was on the edge of death that it was made clear to her. You cannot deny what lies in you now—"

"There is nothing in me!"

Kelsie backed away, even as she had during the night dark attack of the Thas, until her shoulders were against the rough, cold stone. Perhaps she would have run— But she could not! That same compulsion which had brought her here had swooped back, to seize upon her once again. She could have screamed in her rage and fear. That she was not master of her own body was the most frightening thing of all. Yet she could not take the single step which would carry her past the witch and on her way out of here.

The girl said in a voice she fought to keep from trembling. "Stop playing your tricks on me and let me go."

Wittle swept both arms outward in a gesture which offered Kelsie full freedom. "I play no tricks. Look within yourself to see what lies there now."

Look inward? Kelsie tried, not sure of what the witch might mean. She discovered that, without knowing it, she had set the chain of the jewel about her own neck and it, pulsating, rested on her breast even as Wittle wore hers.

She gasped a ragged breath.

"What would you have me do?" she asked in a small voice. The drain she experienced was not yet repaired, she felt as if, should she stand away from the wall, she might fall.

"Breathe so—" Wittle was drawing deep, slow breaths. "Think of your body, of the feet, the legs which support you—of the blood which runs through them nourishing, cleansing. Your body has served you well, think kindly of it, slow—ah, slow, sister. Think of having slept through the night sweetly with no dreams to disturb your rest. It is morning and you awaken renewed, filled, mistress of yourself, sister to your jewel which will serve you now even if you try to send it away. Come—"

Without waiting to see if Kelsie obeyed her or not, Wittle bent her tall form and left the cave and indeed the girl discovered that she was drawn after. There was still silver moonlight among the rocks and the witch sought out a place where the beams were full. She stood there, her arms upraised and out, as if she desired to indeed draw the moon down into her hold. Hesitatingly Kelsie followed suit.

Her jewel was glowing again. Not with the forceful blue it had shone when it had stood against the Thas, but with a pure white light. It warmed and the warmth spread through her also, so that the last of that backaching fatigue was banished. She felt rather as if indeed she had awakened into a good day and had bathed cleanly at the pool in the Valley, that all was well within her and that she had already accomplished much that she had been set to do.

How long they stood there Kelsie could not reckon, but at length Wittle lowered her arms as a shadow of stone crept to them and there appeared a cloud touching the moon shield overhead.

"Good—" Her voice held a sigh. "So it is with the power when one uses it. It draws, ah, how it can draw," there was remembered pain in her voice then, "but there is always the renewing. How is it with you now, Makeease—" then she hesitated, "No, for one there is one name, for another another. You have received no name in company—"

"I am Kelsie!" Some of her old antagonism flared.

"Do you not understand," she had never expected Wittle to show such patience, "to use your birthing name so boldly is to invite the ill to enter. It will offer a key to that which we must fear the more. The body can be ill used by the Dark Ones, yes. But it is the worse when the inner part is touched. Perhaps it is different with you and the naming of names is not a danger."

"Sometimes perhaps," Kelsie had a sudden memory of times which a name might bring a person into danger even in her own time and place—perhaps not the same kind of danger, but peril as her world knew it. "Yet we do not change them—" No, that was not so either. People did change their names, their very kinds of life—what of witnesses and spies? Still she was neither and her name was a part of herself she was not prepared to surrender, for by doing so she might well join herself even tighter to wild adventure.

7

The witch reached behind one of the rocks and drew forth a backpack, and then another which she slung over to fall at Kelsie's feet. The girl edged back and away from it.

"What are you doing?" she demanded.

"We go," Wittle returned calmly. "What we were sent to do lies still before us. If we wait upon the favor of these of the Valley we may never reach it. They war when attacked or when the Shadow draws too near, they do not invade its own places."

"I won't!" Kelsie watched Wittle draw her arms through the lashings of her own pack, settling it on her shoulders with a shrug.

"You cannot now do otherwise. You have used the jewel—it is yours and you are its."

Kelsie would have fled away from this mad woman, taken the trail down back to the Valley. But once more her body rebelled against her will. With warmth from the stone flooding through her, she discovered she must also stoop, pick up that burden and prepare to carry it.

"Do not fight it, girl," the witch's voice held its old superior and contemptuous ring. "You are of the sisterhood whether or no and this is the geas laid upon you."

Thus against all her desires she began to climb, following Wittle farther and farther up the steep slopes using toes and fingers, striving to compensate for the backward pull of her burden. They reached the top of that barrier which nature, or those who dealt so close to nature that they could summon her services on demand, had set about the Valley. Beyond was a country which seemed to draw more shadow than light from the moon, to be truly a place of peril. That Wittle was calmly descending into that, taking Kelsie with her, the girl could not retreat.

If there were sentries and watchers on duty in those heights (Kelsie was sure that there were) the witch had her own method of passing unseen and was able also to encompass Kelsie. For there arose no one to bid them halt or inquire what they would do.

There was a usable trail which zigzagged down the opposite side of the heights and they did not take it swiftly, Wittle making methodically sure of her footing while Kelsie followed close behind her.

Once a winged blot of darkness flew swiftly over them and the witch stood still, Kelsie freezing into a similar halt. But the thing did not return, and, after a time in which Kelsie drew short shallow breaths, Wittle once more started on. Again she froze into immobility, startling Kelsie so that she nearly ran into the pack the other wore when there sounded a single ear-grating howl from the lowlands toward which they were going. This time Wittle hissed an order to the girl:

"A gray one. Put your jewel into hiding! They have eyes which can comb the darkest shadow." She was fumbling with her own jewel, holding open the neck opening of her own robe and dropping her glowing gem within the inner folds. Kelsie followed and nearly yelped aloud. For the heat that the stone now emitted was such as if she had slipped a live coal against the skin of her breast.

Wittle appeared to believe that this was the only precaution they need take, for she was striding on again. Kelsie, perforce, still drawn by that overriding other will, must follow.

They came to the stream which burrowed a way through the mountains to feed the Valley river and here the witch kilted up her long robe so that her thin white legs were bare to her knees, motioning for Kelsie to shuck her soft boots even as the witch abandoned her sandals.

Free of foot Wittle stepped into the shallows of the stream and marched confidently forward Kelsie again behind. Perhaps it was because she had a need for establishing her superiority again that the witch whispered:

"Running water is disaster to some of the Dark Ones. It is best to hold to it while one can."

Trying to keep her own voice low Kelsie demanded with what small power she could summon:

"Where are we going?" That she was following one she did not trust was the stark truth, but if she could summon the strength of the jewel again perhaps she could break free of Wittle should the other release any of the control she had established. Meanwhile to humor her might be best.

"Where we are led," was the very unsatisfactory answer she was given. "As you know—no," the witch corrected herself. "You who are one of us and yet not one—perhaps the knowing was not given with the jewel. We seek the source of the ancient power—that which formed our sisterhood in the beginning and where we must stand again to gather to us that which will raise up anew all that we were once. That it lies to the east is all that we know. Sister Makeease was questing for it—"

"And she died!" The cold of her own frightened self fought the warmth of the jewel she wore. "What promise have you that your purpose can be served—"

"She went with guards—she rode openly though the warning was clear. But she would not listen to those of the Valley," Wittle's tone was once more cold and sharp. "This is not a search which can be done by a trampling force of clumsy men. She was wrong and so she paid for it. We shall search by night and this—" she cupped her hand over the wan glow shining through her robe, "shall be our guide. For we brought the jewels out of this land in the ancient days and they will be drawn to that which gave them their first life. This much we can be sure of. If we watch them carefully by their waxing and their waning shall we be guided."

"What if," Kelsie moistened her lower lip with her tongue tip before she continued, "this source you seek is now held by the Dark?"

"It may be besieged by the Dark well enough," Wittle agreed, "but taken it has not been or our stones would die. The Light and the Dark cannot lie together."

"Shadows and moonlight do," Kelsie was finding apter words of protest than she had known existed in her mind.

"The Moon is at full, as long as it remains so we can draw sustenance from it. When it begins to wane," the witch hesitated, "then we tread even more carefully."

It was clear that she had a vast confidence in herself and Kelsie, as wary as she was, was cowed by that as they went forward through the night, keeping to the stream as their roadway. When the first shafts of gray dawn appeared along the horizon the witch pointed ahead to where a sandbar projected well into the stream. On three sides it was surrounded by water, which flowed with a swifter current in midstream. The fourth was connected to the land by a narrow neck on which drift had caught in a tangle as if there had been some recent storm which had brought such debris out of the land before them.

The witch waded out on this neck of land and Kelsie gratefully followed, though she had to tread over gravel as well as the sand. Then they were ashore and Wittle shed her pack, Kelsie following her example, her shoulders aching from the strain put upon them. But if she were tired from their night's tramp, Wittle was not. Already the witch had approached the drift and was pulling at pieces of it, working crooked branches around to form a barrier across the narrow scrap of land which connected them with the shore. She was plainly building a barricade, though what such a defense might save them from Kelsie had no idea. That Wittle appeared to think this important set her working beside the witch.

It was not until they had a breast-high barrier there that Wittle seemed satisfied and went back to her pack, worrying open the strap around its midsection to bring out a packet of wilted leaves fast lashed about. She freed those also and Kelsie saw that she had a flat cake of some darkish substance from which she broke a small piece and began to nibble around its edge.

"Eat," she sputtered through a full mouth and gestured toward Kelsie's own discarded pack. The girl found a leaf-wrapped parcel within containing the same rations, and tasted a bite gingerly. Though its looks were not encouraging the flavor was better and she got it down, washed by several palmfuls of water from the stream.

However, here on this patch of sand, though barricaded as it now was from the land, she had no sense of security. Thus as she watched Wittle settle herself on her bundle for sleep in the early morning Kelsie wondered at the unconcern of the witch. Was she so very sure that they were in complete safety?

"Trust your jewel, girl—" Wittle's eyes were closed but it was as if that allowed her to discern Kelsie's thoughts better. "The Dark hunts mainly by night—"

"Then why do we—?" began Kelsie bewildered.

"Travel by dark?" Wittle finished for her. "Because as long as the full moon is overhead we can cast for the better that trail we must discover. Where the Dark masses—there we may discover the seed we seek."

Wittle might be very sure of herself and her methods of hunting but Kelsie did not agree. The witch was breathing evenly asleep while the girl still sat looking around her with a wariness which was an ever present part of her now.

The stream ran across the plain until it reached the hills over which they had come during the night. She could sight some moving humps in the distance ahead to the east which she thought might be animals browsing. The sky was very clear, with not even a trace of cloud, and once in a while again to the east some shape flapped lazily across it.

There was life in the stream also. Now and then a fish broke the surface of the water chasing one of the gauzy winged insects which near filled the air only a few inches above the river, engaged in some complicated dance or maneuvers of their own. Then there crawled out on the sandbank a lizardlike creature as long as her forearm which paid no attention to the two already occupying that stretch of territory but wheeled about, its head pointing waterwards, and apparently went to sleep in the rapidly warming sun.

Though the plain stretched well to the east there were also the irregular lines of hills or mountains to be sighted beyond and here and there were dark clumps of trees gathered in thick copses as if they had been deliberately planted so. There were also tumbles of stone perhaps a half mile farther on which to Kelsie suggested ruins of a very ancient and now unidentifiable building. While the tall grass of the meadowland, already beginning to brown under the sun's searing heat, was troubled now and again, not by any wind (for the dawn breeze had died away and there was no movement of air at all). Those waving fronds and blades must mark the comings and goings of small life.

The sun was hot and she found her head nodding, her eyes shutting of themselves. At length she chose a place closer to the barrier they had woven from the drift and, in spite of her wariness, fell asleep.

What nightmare awoke her, shaking and sweating, she could not piece together once her eyes were fully open. Perhaps it was just as well that her waking mind repudiated that memory for the fear carried over and she huddled shivering by the mass of drift.

Wittle lay exactly as she had when Kelsie had gone to sleep. Almost she could believe that the witch had died save that her breast rose and fell with long deep breaths. The creature from the stream was gone again and—

Kelsie looked about her for a weapon. There was a water smoothed root bigger at one end than the other. She worried that loose, winning so a crude club. She must have slept half the day or more away—the sun was to the westward. But though the land looked as peaceful as it had before, she was sharply aware that there was something moving toward them through the tall grass.

Very slowly she pivoted where she still knelt, giving each section she could see a questioning survey. Those moving stands of grass which she had earlier believed marked the coming and going of the inhabitants of this land were no longer in evidence. There was a stillness over the whole of the land which instinct told her was not natural. Then she heard the splash of water and turned instantly to front the screen of willows downstream.

A figure pushed through them, treading as she and Wittle had done barefooted in the water, his boots slung by their lacing cords about his neck. He was fully armed and the metallic links of light mail which formed a veiling about the helm he wore showed only a very small portion of his face. Yet she knew him.

"Yonan," her word was but a whisper but it appeared to carry to him for he threw up one hand, whether in salute or warning she did not know—in this time and place she took it for the latter.

She was on her feet, though she still grasped the club, and her own wave was a vigorous one, beckoning him on. Had he been sent to take them back? She would indeed welcome such a summons, if this strange compulsion she was caught up in would allow her.

As she and Wittle he wore a small backpack, and, seeing that, she was not so sure that his coming meant the end of their journeying. There was an angry exclamation from behind her as Wittle moved forward, to stand nearly at the water's edge watching that newcomer.

"What do you here?" demanded the witch while he was still some distance from them, her voice low but carrying over the splashing he made as he moved.

"What I am sent to do," he returned. One of the veil strips of his helm swung free, and Kelsie could see by the set of his firm chin a suggestion that he was angered.

"We do not need you—" Wittle's voice was that of Swift-foot's hissing growl.

"Perhaps that is so," he replied, now near enough to wade out of the stream, by his very coming forcing the witch back a step or two. "This is a troubled land, we will not have it troubled further—Return to the Valley lest you be taken. There are mighty forces on the move."

"Who has been a-scrying and read that in her bowl?" Wittle's contempt once more ruled her voice. "Certainly this is a troubled land. Perhaps we move to put an end to some of that troubling. Let us reach the force and—"

"And be blasted by your own folly? Well enough, if that means that only you will suffer. But each bit of the power is precious and to risk it in the midst of enemies—"

Kelsie saw Wittle's hands snap upward to jerk at the jewel chain and bring her gem out of hiding. Even in the daylight its blue fire was not diminished. She took it in one hand and pointed it toward Yonan.

He laughed and swung his sword out of its sheath, holding the blade and raising the blue stone grip between them. There was a flash from the jewel, a similar answer from the stone, and those two met, pushing each other until there was nothing left but a wisp of smoke.

"You—you—" for the first time Kelsie saw Wittle truly at a loss for words, her usual arrogance gone.

"Yes, I am not for your guiding, Lady Witch," he said. "We have discovered other bits of power ourselves. Quan iron, in the hand of he who dares to carry it, lives. Now that we have settled that you are not to be so easily rid of me," he allowed his pack to fall from his shoulders, "let us discuss the matter. The Lady Dahaun has sent a message to Hilarion. Do you also think that you have the power to stand against an adept? He feels strongly about this land and will not allow tricks to be played which will bring in the shadow forces past our control."

"What would you do?" Wittle asked sullenly.

"Go with you. Do you not realize that we are as eager to mark sources of power as you are? That we must know what lies hidden whenever we can that the Dark does not reach it first?"

"This is no affair for men—"

"This is an affair for any who dare it!" he countered. "As a scout, and one who has dared before, it is my choice to come on this quest. You head for the Sleepers—"

Wittle's head jerked as if he had struck her across the mouth. "How know you that?" she demanded and for once there was flaming heat instead of the cold in her voice.

Yonan shrugged. "Think you that you can keep such purpose hidden in the Valley? We have known all the time you waited for your sister what it was that you would do."

She glared at him and her hand tightened on her jewel as if she would again strive to try strength against strength with him. But he had already turned to Kelsie.

"You do this of your free will?" he asked.

"No, but not because of her urging," she replied. "There is something in the jewel which has claimed me."

"Take it off!" That was more an order than a request and her hands moved to obey—moved only a fraction. The stone blazed hot beneath her jerkin as if in warning.

"I can't," she was forced to admit.

What she could see of his face was a frown. "Touch—" He held forth his sword by the blade and the blue band in the hilt had a subdued fire of its own. Kelsie reached for the hilt and then dropped her hand with a small cry of surprise. Her fingers were numb and that deadness was creeping across her palm and up her arm. "I can't—"

He nodded as if he had expected that very answer from her. "You are under a geas."

"A what?"

"An order from some Old One or adept. Perhaps it lies in the heart of that stone you wear. That you must obey now that it is set upon you."

Wittle laughed unpleasantly. "Think you that you can wear a stone of power and escape the payment it calls from its wearer? You are set upon this path now whether you will or not."

It seemed to Kelsie then that this whole venture had been imposed on her even before the jewel of the dying witch had come into her life.

"I'm not one of you," she protested. "Why must I be drawn into this?" It was a question that she might have asked hours earlier but it was not until the coming of Yonan that some bit of reality had broken into that drive which had held her.

"You have no choice," Wittle turned and walked a step or so away to settle once more on the sand, her back to them, plainly preparing to return to the sleep from which Yonan had awakened her. Kelsie looked to the young man.

"I do not choose—" she began when he shook his head.

"Lady, in this land our choices are limited. I, myself, have walked strange ways because I was caught up in something which was stronger than any will of mine. This is a haunted place and what haunts it are bits and pieces of old struggles and old commands, which, once voiced, still hold. We have held against the Dark for many seasons now but there have always been rumors that inland," he pointed with his chin upriver as he still held his sword in his two hands, "there are pockets of ancient power which are allied neither with the Dark nor with the Light. If such can be found, and what you wear is indeed a key to it or them, then there is purpose in what we do here."

"Purpose but not choice!" she said bitterly. Her failure to touch the sword had given her a shock which had somehow awakened her out of the bemused state which she now recognized must have encompassed her since they left the Valley.

"Purpose but no choice," he agreed quietly. "Now, will you rest, Lady, this is the last night of the full moon and after that we shall move by day. And how far we travel, who can tell?"

Feeling was returning to her hand as she rubbed it vigorously. She wanted to argue but his complete acceptance of what seemed to have happened to her made her believe there would be no profit in that. She sought out her own bed in the sand and pillowing her head on her pack allowed herself to relax. She had not really expected sleep but it came and quickly.

She roused when an ungentle hand was laid on her shoulder and it was to look up into a sky with scudding clouds and the first drops of rain coming with the evening. Wittle stood over her, pack already on her shoulders, a piece of the dried journey cake in her hand.

"Time to go—" the witch said after she swallowed. Her shoes were once more in her belt and she waved toward the water. Yonan stood on the edge of the stream itself, the water curling up as far as his knees.

"We cannot take to this too long," he commented as Kelsie found her own provisions and chewed at the dry bits which rasped her tongue and gums. "There may have been a hard rain upstream—the water is rising."

But they did begin the night's trek splashing through the water. While the few drops which had fallen became part of a downpour to soak through Kelsie's clothing and set her shivering—though neither of her companions seemed to take any notice of the storm.

The night came fast though the clouds were illuminated now and then by flashes of lightning and there was the drumbeat of thunder to follow. The waves of the stream washed Kelsie up to mid-thigh now and she could feel the pull of the current. Once her foot connected painfully with a rock and she might have fallen had not Yonan's hand caught and held her up.

At length they were driven to the shore and huddled under the wide spreading branches of a willow to put on their foot gear. In the dark of the night and the storm her two companions were only half-seen blots and she wondered how they could keep together and whether it might not do well to stay in the flimsy shelter they had found until the storm passed.

She felt Yonan stir first and then came his low-pitched voice through the clamor of the rain and the stream.

"Do you smell it?"

She obediently sniffed, but all she was aware of was a musty, earthy scent which she vaguely associated with the wet ground. Yonan got to his feet and started away from the water. By the lightning flash she saw the gleam of his sword, drawn and ready in his hand. At the same time the flesh of her upper arm was bruised by a harsh grip of the witch seeming intent on holding her where she was.

There was a sound like a shout cut in half and Yonan disappeared into the ground. Kelsie broke away from the witch and ran forward only to have her feet swept from under her and feel herself falling. She thought she screamed and the jewel at her breast burst into a strong light as she landed, knocking Yonan face down into wet earth which was all about them. There was truly a stench here, one she had smelled before.

Thas! They had fallen into one of the underground ways of those dark dwellers. Wittle made no such mistake as Kelsie's and she did not join them in their tangle of arms and legs. By the time they had regained their feet in the hole one whole side of mudlike, noisome sludge fell in upon them, sending them to their knees again and nearly burying them.

Kelsie strove to escape when, out of the deeper dark which marked that part of the tunnel which had survived the cave-in there snaked a thick length of what seemed a root and it settled about her drawing tight enough to make her gasp as it pinned her arms to her body.

8

Another coarse-skinned line struck about her hips and in a moment all her struggling could not move her, except as her bonds wished, and she was being drawn straight to the shadowed side of the pit where there was an opening. By the floundering noises which she heard, Yonan was faring little, if any, better.

On her breast the jewel glowed, and she caught a faint glimmer ahead which might mark the power inset on Yonan's sword hilt. By the light she herself carried she could see now that what held her in bondage looked to be two thick roots. Yet they had the mobility of serpents and by these she was being pulled roughly along, bumped from wall to wall, down a passage intended for creatures smaller than herself. Dank earth smeared her all over and she was spitting to clear it from her mouth.

Also the scent which thickened the air was stomach churning and Kelsie had to battle the nausea which arose to choke her throat. She judged from sounds that Yonan was being forced along behind her as she heard exclamations of disgust and anger.

It seemed to her that that passage lasted at least an hour or more—though it could not have in truth. Then she was jerked like a cork out of a bottle into a place where there was a ghastly phosphorescent light, such as might come from something rotten, proceeding from the tops of crooked stakes set up in a square. Into this trap the ropes snapped her and a moment later she was bowled over by Yonan landing hard against her as her bonds withdrew and his followed.

There was a crunching sound. A rock taller and wider than her own body had fallen to close the gap in the cold fire of the palings around them. Yonan was already on his feet and facing that doorway.

The tops of the palings, where that weird light gleamed, were well above her head as she got to her feet. There the light gathered into an unwholesome mist which hid from sight what might lie directly over them. She crossed her arms, rubbing the bruises near her shoulders where the ropes had cut the hardest. There seemed to be scratches there which smarted under her touch as if the rough surface of the rope had rubbed the skin bare. Yonan, because of his mail, must have fared much better.

He had given but a short inspection to the stone which served as a door and was now prowling along the side of the square, sword out and ready as if he expected some instant move against them. At length he aimed at a crack between two of the palings and levered but the steel made no impression on the giant fence.

"Your jewel," he said abruptly, "can it cut our way clear?"

The gem still blazed, but it seemed to Kelsie that the light was less, as if the waning beams from the paling smothered it. However, obediently she stepped closer to the nearest fetid smelling pillar and held up the stone so that a lesser beam of the blue light focused directly.

To her eyes the wood, root, or stone, whatever that fencing might be, did writhe under the prod of the light. However, when Yonan, with an exclamation, pushed beside her to add his sword tip to the spot of light there was nothing but an adamant surface there.

"Where are we?" Kelsie tried to tamp down her rising fear by asking in the most normal voice she could produce.

He shrugged. "In Thas hands. Where? We can be anywhere, as far as the outer world is concerned."

"Wittle—"

"I do not think she was caught."

"These Thas—"

"Serve the Dark," he interrupted. "They hunt in packs and so can better pull us down. And their root ropes are harsh holding."

"What do they want?"

"Beyond just evil mischief? I would say that jewel of yours. Probably not for themselves, they are servants of more mighty masters and have probably gone to report to those now. Soon we shall see what manner of the Dark they serve."

"My jewel—" She slipped the chain over her head, allowing it now to dangle from her fingers and began to swing it back and forth. In her mind she concentrated upon it, bedazzled by the pulsation of its light as if she had never seen it so before. That waxing and waning followed a beat which began slowly but arose to draw faster and faster flashes from the stone.

Her own heart was beating quickly, in time with the stone? Of that she could not be sure. Nor did it matter. What did was that she must hold the jewel in her sight, concentrate on it completely, forgetting all else.

It was difficult at first, that concentration. Then in the whirl of light which followed the path of the jewel she saw something begin to form. There was no mistaking those hard features. Wittle! Yet the witch was not there, only a small semblance of her. Still Kelsie focused her full attention on that face and it seemed to her that Wittle was staring back as if she, too, could see them.

"Out!" Kelsie spoke the one word which meant the most to her now.

She watched Wittle's mouth open. If the witch spoke the girl did not hear her with her ears. However, into her mind flashed what might be an answer or even some mischief of the enemies. She stopped the whirl of the jewel with her other hand. The face of Wittle abruptly vanished.

But now she held the stone on her palm in spite of the heat it generated, which seemed enough to sear her flesh from her bones. Yet still she held and pointed a single shaft of light, governed by her tormented fingers, not at the stake before her where Yonan had made his attack but rather to its crown where the yellowish evil-smelling haze arose from some unsighted fire.

The point of that light thrust struck the haze, cut through it. She saw a bowl on the top of the shaft. It was that the light was attacking. She watched a blue spot appear on that side, grow not only in size but in brilliance. Then something dropped at their feet and the bowl showed a wide section shorn from it. Into that opening Kelsie beamed her light. But it was not enough. Into her mind spun that knowledge. She had not the full power she should have been able to summon—as a witch she was flawed by knowing far too little.

She spoke without turning her head. "Give to me the Quan iron. Lay it upon my wrist."

Kelsie might have asked him to supply a brand to burn her past all healing. She gnawed at her lower lip, determined not to cry out—to forget the pain of her body, to concentrate only on what she had done and would do.

For that strip of blue metal was like a second force, feeding into the hands she had cupped about the jewel. The raw pain of it she would have to bear but the pulsations of the light grew greater and closer together, firing up the jewel's azure beam.

Then—

There was a roar—had she heard that with her ears or sensed the final confrontation of force against force in her body? From the now shattered bowl at the top of the stake shot another flash of light momentarily as vivid as lightning across the sky so far above them now. The haze itself appeared to catch from that flame and billow out not yellow now, nor blue but forming a white glare which punished her eyes until she had to close them. Something struck her shoulder, another object grazed her hip. She heard Yonan cry out. A mailed arm closed about her waist in an ungentle grasp dragging her back against his body as he, too, retreated. Her arms wavered and fell though she did not drop the stone except to spin by the chain she still held.

Above their heads there wove back and forth ribbons of fire and these coiled about the stakes which made up the walls of their cage. They burned then, those stakes, crackling open as might flesh caught in a blast of flame. The heat ate in as the two now crouched in the midst of the circle. Above the crackling of that fire Kelsie was sure she heard voices shouting a guttural refrain, but she could see nothing now for she had shielded her eyes from that searing display with one forearm. She was not even aware whether the stone had finished its mad spinning or not.

The crackling and the stench became worse. She was gasping and felt the similar labor of Yonan's chest against her as they fought for breath amid the conflagration.

As yet the burning debris had fallen outward, she guessed, for the heat which struck at them was airborne, not from the gutted remnants of the stakes. Slowly that heat declined. At last Kelsie felt able to uncover her eyes and look about her. There were stubs of the stakes still showing ribs of spark producing fire. But outside that destruction there writhed and flailed those captor roots which had dragged them here. Now and then when one of the butt stumps blazed up the girl was certain she caught sight of some scurrying creature which in this light looked like a wadded pack of rootlets. It was possible that the owners of this trap were spinning another now, a more substantial cage for their captives.

Yonan moved from beside her, slowly, as if worn-out after a long day of tramping. While she was too tired to move at all. He tottered toward the nearest hole in the wall where the paling had burnt clear down to its root in the stone and with his sword he cut and stabbed at the small core of flame-eaten wood still showing above the surface. Then he held out his hand to her.

"Come!"

"Can't you see that is just what they want us to do—they are waiting there," she answered. She greatly doubted at that moment she could do more than crawl on her hands and knees, and so provide easy meat for those waiting beyond.

He came back to her in two quick strides, and, his hand under her armpit, pulled her up to her feet.

"They are confused," he said as he half led, half supported her to the exit he had contrived. "Whatever lord they serve—neither he nor his higher servants can be here now."

Kelsie could not see how he was so sure of that. But she was too tired to argue and she needed what strength and courage she had left not to waste in futile argument, but to be ready to face what lay beyond. That the breaking of the cage set them entirely free she doubted very much indeed.

They stepped over the narrow path fire that Yonan's sword had opened for them. In the failing light from the almost destroyed paling she could see that indeed roots crawled across the floor, the nearer ones heading for them.

Yonan made a quick thrust to his left, not using the point of his sword but bringing down the hilt sharply against the raised end of the nearest root length. The thing squirmed and drew back. On its surface where the iron must have touched there was an oval of light which spread swiftly as if power continued to eat into it.

It was then that Kelsie heard clearly a dull thud, a thud which was drumlike in its regularity but muffled. Also, there were other sounds in the rhythm of a chant.

As the seeking root writhed away from them, bearing its growing glow, a second one threw itself out, or was so thrown from some perch in the dark, whipping across the floor as if meant to sweep them from their feet. Kelsie lashed out the chain of the stone which was now a sullen shadow of itself. That also landed fair enough to send the root rope out of their way.

She tried to concentrate on the gem as she had in the pen but she could not summon up the same sure power she had known then. There was only a die-away spurt or two. Yet that appeared to be enough to keep the roots at bay. She wondered if Yonan knew where they were going. As far as she could judge he was heading on, straight into the dark. Again it was as if he could read her fatigue-deadened mind.

"There is an opening ahead. Taste the air—" She could see in the faint light from jewel and sword his tongue tip showing then between his lips as if he did in truth test so the fetid atmosphere. And she copied his gesture.

There *was* something! It was almost as if she had been offered a cup of water in the midst of all the fumes and heat of this dark place. The girl could see that her companion kept his tongue so as he urged her forward. Some of her strength seemed to return as she went until she could pull away from him and walk forward on her own.

The steady thunk-thunk of the distant drums and a hissing noise filled this place and she could hear voices rise and fall until it seemed that she could sort out the direction from which those came—to her right. The root ropes kept pace with them and now one or another, or sometimes two together would try once more to entangle their former captives. Though it appeared that Yonan need only show them the Quan on his sword hilt for them to flinch back.

Kelsie became aware that the stone under their feet was sloping upward and once she was sure she caught sight of a pale streak of light before them. Then came a sudden silence. The drums and the voices ceased, even the hissing of the root ropes faded away. She tongue-tried the air again—

The freshness was still there but in her nostrils was an ever growing taint of filth and damp and other odors she could not put name to. There might be an entrance somewhere ahead as Yonan believed but there was also a menace in between.

She gathered the stone swinging on its chain into the tender flesh of her hand and held it against her forehead. There was no reason that she could have told for that gesture, it simply seemed the right thing to be done.

Though her eyes were fastened upon the darkness ahead, there appeared in her mind another picture—that of a packed mass of the misshapen creatures she had only half glimpsed in the fire-lit ruin of the cage. To the fore were three who pounded with misshapen fists on the flat surface of bowl-like instruments they held between their knees. While the tooth-filled jaws of all showed as they sang no—called! Called upon what or whom? Kelsie shrank from knowing but she did not break the touch between her forehead and the jewel.

There was a swirl of reddish-yellow just before them drawing in upon itself, curdling into something far more sturdy than the mist from which it was born. Kelsie had expected a face, even a full figure, but what she saw was a sign which was a mixture of dots and lines, a pattern which reached outward for her own mind—offering more danger than the burning cage. She let the jewel fall forward but not before she gained a firm belief that that which had set the pattern had also been aware of her, and that they were far from being free from the hands of the servants—Thas—or perhaps even other and more powerful aides.

Only Yonan continued to walk steadily ahead and she saw that his attention was all for the Quan iron as if that could act as a scout and give them warning. Was the stone equal—

It flamed and the heat of that flare made her let it slide from out her fingers to dangle again. There were no roots this time to come slithering out of the dark. Rather she saw the light of her jewel mirrored in a mass of pairs of red points on the floor—eyes—?

"Rasti," Yonan broke the silence which had held between them.

Though there was a river of those eyes near the floor, it did not spread or try to engulf them as she had feared that it might. It would seem that these other dwellers in the dark were now as wary of them as the Thas had become. Yet, though they stopped their advance, they milled about, covering the rock between the two and what might be a door to the outer world. In experiment the girl swung out her jewel to the full length of its chain and noted that there was a wavering of the line in answer to that.

There sounded a shrill tittering call, rising sharply above the thumping of the bowl drums. The flood of the rasti parted, leaving a lane down which came something greater than the Thas, taller, stronger, and, Kelsie recognized by the instant repulsion in her, far more evil.

The yellowish light which had flowed from the stakes flared up once more spreading out from a rod that newcomer held. By its light the girl could see a figure as tall as Yonan, one which wore no armor, nor indeed any clothing at all, except patches of shaggy hair.

It pranced rather than strode, as if it were weaving a spell now by some unknown ritual. The crooked, hairy legs ended in hooves which were split for half their length. And those in turn kicked out at the rasti, striking home now and again against one of the animals to send it chittering and whirling off to thud against its fellows.

The rest of the figure was crooked of back as if it could not, because of its breadth and thickness of shoulder straighten to full height. Its belly protruded obscenely and altogether it was a daunting creature.

But above that crook-backed, flatulently-bellied body there was a head and that was as startling as if two separate creatures had been bound by some disgusting spell into a single form. For the head was perhaps neither male nor female, but it was that of great beauty with flawless features and masklike calm. While the hair which wreathed it was not the coarse stuff it grew elsewhere but a silken fall, brilliantly red in the light.

Strangest of all Kelsie discovered was the fact that it walked with closed eyes but not with the hesitation of something blinded, rather as if its body obeyed one set of rules which did not even reach behind the lowered eyelids.

She felt movement beside her. Then Yonan was facing the thing, with his shoulder before hers, as if to push her back and away from danger. The jewel was flaring up again and she could feel its drain on her own resources of spirit.

"Ah, Tolar that was—you have become over brave in these days. Or have you forgotten Varhum during your years of exile?" Those perfectly-formed lips moved extravagantly as the creature spoke and the lid-blinded eyes were clearly turned toward Kelsie's companion.

"Tolar is dead—long since," Yonan answered sullenly. "I do not remember."

"You mortals," the head shook a fraction and the voice was almost humorous. "Why do you so fear what is offered you? You were Tolar and perhaps the better for it, when last we met. That you must wait to be born again is the whim of the Great Power. But to refuse to remember, ah, Tolar, that is foolish. Varhum's walls were breached by—"

"Plasper forces," Yonan interrupted harshly. "And you are—"

"The eyes and mouth, and sometimes the weapon of one greater than you of the Light can even guess. Yet was I also once of your blood and kind."

There was a moment of silence, even the chittering of the rasti had stopped. Kelsie was aware of a shudder through her companion's body so close did they stand now.

"At Vock—?" It sounded like a question rather than the naming of a place.

Now the perfect lips curled in a small cruel smile. "Excellent! You see when you put yourself to it you can remember! Try no tricks to hide memory, Tolar. You know who I am in truth—Call my name if you dare after speaking of Plasper."

Again Kelsie felt Yonan's shudder. But what she could see of his face remained as unchangeably calm as did that other's.

"Lord Rhain."

"Yes. And there were other names they called me that day, were there not? Traitor, Betrayer, Dark One! In your sight I was all those, was I not? But you see I have grown in wisdom—though that was the beginning of such wisdom—when I realized that we were swords for the wrong side— when Kalrinkar had the strength of the future with him. And so—" those crooked shoulders shrugged and again the small smile was shaped by the lips alone, "I lived—"

"In such a guise!" burst out Yonan.

"Do I properly afright you, once comrade? If I wish—" from the mouth came a curl of smoke which grew longer and denser, curling around that misshapen figure to hide it from sight, though Kelsie was very certain that it was still there. There was a small puff of yellow-red and the smoke was gone. In place of the hairy, bloated body which had confronted them was a straight limbed, nearly majestic man whose frame now fitted well his fine head and handsome features. Kelsie had the idea that this was certainly all illusion. Yet he was as real seeming now as he had been moments earlier in the half-bestial disguise.

"You see," even his voice had a different lilt, one far more human, lacking the subtle contempt the other had held, "I am truly Rhain—"

However, Yonan shook his head slowly. "You *were* Rhain. Now what are you to the eyes of those who stand by the Light?"

On impulse Kelsie, though again she could not have said why she did it, swung out the Witch Jewel by its chain. The bluish beam which it had continued to emit now touched the tall, perfect body of he who confronted them. There was a fluttering in the air, almost as if some delicate glass had shattered and what she saw was the grotesque body come back into place while Yonan said loudly:

"Even our eyes you cannot bespell now, in spite of what you once were—"

But Rhain's attention had swung from the man he claimed as a former comrade to Kelsie and now there was as ugly a look on his face as to match his body.

"Witch!" he spat and a droplet of moisture hit the ground between them. "So you serve a female now, Tolar—you who were once your own man? Little do they repay those who march for them, being no true womenkind but only wills to rule. And you, witch, you shall find here that which you stake your life upon will have but little value. Long since Escore learned its secrets and powers which your kind may only have dreamed of dimly."

Power—into her from the jewel there was a warm flow—the draining she had felt so before was reversed. She began to walk slowly forward, edging around Yonan, then conscious that he had fallen in step with her. She raised her hands heart high at the breast and between steadied the jewel awkwardly, then more skillfully, as she sensed that what she was doing was right and meant to be. She fastened her will on the gem and once more reversed the flow, giving back to it what it had given her.

She heard dimly and then shut firmly out of her mind the chittering of the rasti who had milled around their master's feet, beyond that came the muffled sound of drumming where the Thas must have still lingered. But what held her mind and body was concentration on the jewel, rejoicing in the flaring up of its brilliance, in spite of the weakness it was leaving within her.

He who named himself Rhain, for all his brave words, fell back before her, each step of hers being equaled by one of his retreat. His handsome face twisted more and more into a scowling pattern and now he hunched his crooked shoulders and shuffled his hooved feet as he fell back.

He gave a cry and she was aware of surge of the rasti but she dared not drown the beam of the jewel. It was Yonan who swept forward with his sword, keeping clear the space before her. And Rhain cried out again, this time louder, more demanding.

Out of the dark came the living roots of the Thas—out to shrivel into nothingness as the gem light beat upon them.

"This is the best you can do, my lord?" Yonan's voice was both harsh and calm. "You who once commanded the Host? Your vermin are sadly less than that."

Rhain flung back his head and from his throat there came a roar as might be given by some great tormented cat. In Kelsie's hand the gem trembled and for the first time the steady beam of its radiance blinked.

9

There was a whirling in the air itself, a thickening of shadows. Still something within Kelsie held her to that advance and she kept her eyes on the man-beast before her. It seemed that he tried again and again to meet the flaming of the jewel squarely but could not hold his gaze. His hands raised as if to shut off the beam from his face, yet never did his lidded eyes open. While from his twisted mouth spilled grating sounds, as ugly in their way as his body.

The whirling of the air condensed into shadowy forms, manlike, yet she could glimpse them only from the corners of her eyes, for her gaze held on Rhain. Even as he chanted so did Yonan begin to answer with one oft repeated phrase.

One of Rhain's arms was held a-high as if he would urge on liege men into battle. She heard above his chant the rising squeals of the rasti. A wave of small dark forms rolled on, yet where the shine of the jewel was they appeared to shrivel into small black patches as if eaten up by fire.

Once more Rhain flung up his head and shouted—this time no rush of ritual words but what Kelsie guessed was a name. He might have called upon aid as a last resort.

The whirling shadows thickened, stood on the flooring of the cavern. Men, armed, battle-ready, each with weapon in hand and moving in with no care for the rasti whose bodies they spurned or overtrod.

There was the sweep of a mighty blow by axe at her head. She did not have time to twist or duck. Only the blade sheered away before it crashed against her. And to her right she heard a clash of metal against metal as Yonan at last found something solid he could attack. Yet still, moved by the will of the stone (for it seemed to her that that gem strove to make of her a servant, not tried to serve her) Kelsie advanced and Rhain withdrew step by unwilling step.

Then—

He was gone like a blink of eye, a shatter of lightning. With him vanished the shadow warriors. Only the rasti remained and from the dark behind came still the beat of the Thas bowl drums. But Kelsie knew as if it had been shouted aloud, that the strength of the attack had departed from them and way to escape was open—for the present. That Rhain or those who might control him had finished with them—that she did not believe. More than anything she wanted the fresh air of the surface, to be out in the open where there would be honest light of day or of moon and no more of this burrow. For with Rhain gone she was suddenly drained and stumbled, keeping her feet with an effort. Then she was aware of a strong arm behind her shoulder, the support of Yonan even though he needs must still swing sword to keep off the rasti.

So they wavered together up to a place where there had been a fall of stone and earth and from a hole above there shone the beams of the sun. In her hands the jewel glow died and was gone and she slung the chain back around her throat as she began to scrabble for a hold in that earth slide, to be out of this place of strange meetings and crawling fear.

It was Yonan's aid which brought her up and out and then they clung to one another as if, should they loose that grip, they would fall prey to the weakness in them. The man started to waver forward, dragging her with him, steering her around two great fallen stones spotted with an ugly orange-yellow fungus.

Then they were free and before them was a stand of brush by the roots of which flowed a trickle of water so clear that one could see the clustered stones on the sand of the runnel which contained it. She sank away from him, unable now to move one step before the next, and plunged her face into that water thrice over to wash away the remnants of the stench and the dust of the underground. She saw that Yonan had knelt beside her one hand cupping water to his lips, his other still on the sword lying bare now between them, his eyes sentry wise on all which lay about them.

Refreshed and somewhat more in command of herself, Kelsie looked back. The entrance to the underground world was centered in a scatter of fallen stone. Again her memory leaped to that similar ruin on the Scottish hillside. Had they come through another gate?

"Where are we?" she asked in a half whisper which seemed to be all she could voice at that moment.

She saw a trace of frown beneath his helm where it crossed above his brows. He arose and turned slowly, pivoting where he stood. Then he raised his sword and pointed to a way on her right.

"That is Mount Holweg. And this is to the north. We may have come farther than the Valley patrols have ridden. The shadow lies always north and east."

She sat where she was, considering him. Before this venture had begun he had been only one of the men who had been soldier sentries for the Valley. He was younger than Simon Tregarth and slighter. Yet she did not doubt that in his way he was as expert at this game of weapons and spells as the man she had first met—that other displaced from her own world. Only she wondered, now that she had time to think about his relationship to the monstrosity they had confronted in the tunnels below, about his past. At least he had been able to assure her of one thing—that they had not gone through another gate—back there among the fallen stones.

"He knew you—" she began abruptly, determined to make what sense she could of those words they had exchanged below.

To her surprise her companion shook his head.

"He knew Tolar." There was a straight line to his mouth, a slight forward jut of his chin as if he were fronting an enemy once more. "I am not Tolar—"

"Then why—?"

For the first time he stopped his roving survey of the world around them and spoke directly to her:

"It seems that a man can be born again even if he has passed the last gate of all. I have some proof that perhaps I was once one Tolar who fought the Dark in the long ago—and lost. If that be so then perhaps this life is a chance to right the swing of the scales and be another man. For, I swear it by my name giving, I am Yonan, and not he who went down to defeat then—"

"But you remember—" Kelsie dared not deny that anything was possible in this world. "You called that . . . that thing by name!"

"I remember . . . upon occasion," he agreed somberly, and then changed the subject with a swift question.

"Can you journey on, Lady? We are still too near to that!" He was reaching down one hand to pull her up to her feet, his bared sword still in his other so he used his chin to point to that unwholesome appearing tangle of fallen blocks through which they had come.

"Yes!" All at once she was remembering, too, not distant times but the rasti and the Thas. The one who named himself Rhain was gone with his shadow army, but surely the creatures he had left behind were just as deadly in their own way. However, could she go on? The gem had so drained strength out of her that she wondered if she could keep her feet to reach even the first tree of a small copse which lay in the direction they now faced.

She made it, accepting only now and then the grasp of his hand on her arm. Though the water of the stream had revived her in part she was aware now of a great hunger and her temples throbbed with the pain of a headache as if she had striven at some task which had been nearly at the limit of her strength.

"Where do we go?" she asked then. "I don't think I can go far."

His still bared sword pointed to some small plants growing in between the trees toward which he had been urging her.

"That is illbane. Even a power hunter of the Left Hand Way would avoid such as that. We can lay up in their protection until—" his voice trailed away and she asked more sharply:

"Until what? Do we head back toward the Valley with your mountain as a guide?"

"Can you go?"

His return question startled her and then she remembered the compulsion which had sent her in the beginning on this trail across an unknown country thick with danger. Deliberately she turned to face the distant mountain. There were the beginning banners of sunset forming to the west but she had no thought of starting out to retreat in the dark.

Kelsie took one step and then another, instantly aware of the movement of the gem which had begun a swing from right to left across her breast. Rising in her was still that need for pressing on, not backward to such safety as there might be in this country, but rather on in the opposite direction.

Reaching up she strove to take the chain into her fingers, to tear it away, throw it behind her. But her hands shook and she could not get grip which would serve. That chain might have been well greased the way it slipped away from her attempted hold.

"Can you go back?" Yonan had stopped at the edge of the copse to which he had guided her. He was behind her but no more than a sword length so. For that was all the space she had won.

"No!" Once again she tried to free herself from the chain, the gem of which was growing hotter so that she could feel its warmth through her clothing. A punishing warmth which would allow her no mercy.

"I can't. It won't let me!" Kelsie felt a rise of anger in her hot against the stone, against Yonan, against all this world which had so entrapped her.

"Then let us to such shelter as there may be," he sounded impatient and she turned again ready to burst forth with bitter words. He was already showing his back to her, intent upon advancing along the line of those plants he had named a most powerful weapon against the Dark which they knew. She had seen dried stalks of illbane, crushed leaves, kept carefully in the Valley—the greatest resource a healer could harvest.

It was Yonan who was harvesting the plants now. He had taken off his plain helm, shedding with it the under cap of mail with its swinging strips to be pulled across the face before battle. His hair, curled down upon his forehead, was dark with sweat, though he was much lighter of countenance than the other men she had seen. Now he grasped a handful of leaves, crushing them between palm and fingers and then raising the mass to smear across his forehead leaving traces of thick green behind its passing.

Not knowing what he was doing but that it might just relieve some of the pain of her aching head, the weariness of her body, Kelsie followed his example. The sharp clean scent of the bruised leaves did clear her head from the last remaining memory of the stench of the underworld and she felt more alert, firmer of purpose than she had when she had come out into the open.

Yonan carefully plucked two larger leaves from another plant and wrapped the wad of herb within those, putting it in the pouch at his belt. And Kelsie again followed his example.

The trees of the copse were not too close together as to refuse them a way, though they needs must twist and turn for opening wide enough that they might get through. But they broke out at last into a circle of open land around which the copse appeared to form a wall. Yonan had sheathed his sword and Kelsie wished for their packs which lay behind somewhere in the Thas burrows. Her hunger had grown and she could see not even any berries which would take the edge off that growing pain.

"What do we eat?" she asked Yonan. After all he was far more used to tramping the countryside. He took out not his sword but a long knife and went to the nearest of the walling trees on the trunk of which there was a growth of green-brown stuff as big as his hand. Carefully he hacked the parasite loose from its support and then divided it into halves, holding one out to her. She hesitated and heard him say:

"It is fogmot—and can be eaten. Men have lived on worse in these lands." As if to encourage her by deed as well as speech, he raised the half of the mass he held to his mouth and bit into it.

Kelsie was too hungry by now to deny his assertion. The thing had a hard rind, but once that was broken the inside was as crisp as a full-fleshed apple. It was tasteless, as if she chewed and swallowed a soft chunk of wood. But a very little, just the portion he had given her, appeared to satisfy her hunger. She wanted no more of it.

Yonan had finished his part of the supply first and was now prowling around the edge of the clearing into which they had come. He had resumed his helm and there was an air of a sentry about him. Kelsie licked the last fragment of the food stuff from her lip and asked:

"Do we camp here?"

She noted his actions more carefully and saw that he had advanced his sword a few inches out of its sheath and was pointing that toward the wood. She studied her gem. The faint glow showed that the power within it was still alive but it had not awakened as it did when there was some menace awaiting them.

"It is safe," he said as he took the last steps which had made the circuit of the tree wall complete. "In fact—" He strode to the center of that circle and swung his sword hilt around, arm's length above the grass of the turf. There was an answering gleam in the Quan inlay, and, as he thrust the sword point into the ground at that point, the blue flashed even higher. "This is a sanctuary," he said. "Try it with your jewel."

This time the chain did not resist her touch or slip through her fingers. She came close to where he stood and held the gem between her fingers. There was a noticeable gleam of life which came in answer.

"There are such places," he said more as if he were reassuring himself than explaining something to her. "And many exist near points of danger—though which came first—the blessed place or that of the Dark we do not know."

He dropped down to sit on his heels his sword once more in sheath. She confronted him settling cross-legged on the ground.

"So we are in a blessed place," she said challengingly. "But we cannot carry it with us and—"

What she would have added to that complaint was lost in a howl which arose to blanket hearing of anything but that long wavering cry. Kelsie clutched the stone to her and felt the heat of its full awakening. There was a second howl from a different quarter, answering the first eagerly.

She had heard their like before. That hound which had been set upon the gate place by the rider. Were they to be under siege again and this time so far from any help from the Valley as to be easily taken?

Yonan was plainly listening. It was near twilight now and shadows which had gathered under the trees were creeping out into the open where they were. A third howl and that from yet another direction! A pack of the creatures ringing around.

"Will . . . will they come here?"

"I think not," Yonan returned. "This is a blessed place, remember. Curses and blessings grow thin through the years but that which was set here answered to us. That we may be able to go forth again—that is another matter." His expression was set and grim and Kelsie shivered. To be pent in this place, no matter how safe it might be at its core was no way to stay. She watched Yonan, on his feet once more, sword out digging point into the tough rooted turf.

Soil and clods of grass flew. Was he trying to *dig* his way out? Kelsie shrank back and away, having no thought of landing below ground once again. Then she heard the sword point grate on a surface below and Yonan's efforts to clear what lay there speeded up. He was so intent that Kelsie thought he would not even hear her if she asked what he was doing.

He hacked and dug and then dropped on his knees, putting aside his sword and using his knife and his hands to continue. What he uncovered so was a star of white stone, large enough for a person to stand upon. Now Yonan was working more cautiously, shifting the soil away by handfuls, using knife point to dig out some stubborn clay which clung to depressions and cracks in the artifact.

"What is it?" Kelsie could contain her curiosity no longer. Why her companion thought it necessary to do this while the forces of the Dark gathered beyond the trees, and already evening shadows grew thicker and thicker, she did not understand.

There was a hole in the center of the star which he was clearing with care. Now he picked up his sword and dropped its point into that aperture. It was as if he had whirled a smoldering torch into life. From the Quan in the hilt streamed light which filled half the clearing with the brightness of day.

From overhead came a rasping sound and the rush of wings through the air. But nothing she could see cut the light of the sword. If the enemy had forces aloft they were not tempted to strike now.

"What was that?" Kelsie's question was now a demand.

Yonan looked at her across the flare of light. It seemed to her that his eyes blazed as had the hounds' when she had taken refuge in that other place of power—yet the sight did not revolt her as it had before.

"I have seen one other like this," he answered somewhat obliquely. "It is a gathering place for power. If we had the old knowledge we could take that," he waved toward the now blazing sword where up and down the blade ran runnels of light, "and win through any force which has been set against us here. But," he pounded his fist against his knee in open bafflement, "we know so little!"

It had brought his sword to life, what would it do for the Witch Jewel? On impulse the girl pulled the chain from about her neck and dangled the gem over the star. There was an explosion of light. Into her fingers, her arm, her shoulder, her whole body shot a flash of strength so powerful that she was hurled backward on the turf, thus involuntarily jerking the jewel out of line of the star. That inflow of energy stopped but the gem still blazed. Could this be the place Wittle had been seeking, where the old power could be summoned to enhance witch weapons?

Yonan's hand closed about her wrist, pulling back and down the hand which held the gem chain.

"Do not summon that!" his voice held the snap of an order. "You do not know what you may control or what may be beyond your knowledge of use."

He was right, of course, but she resented his interference. She had not spoken against his use of the sword.

"A key," it was as if he could read her mind. "The sword is the key. Now," he had not released his hold upon her but tightened it, setting his strength of body against hers before she could understand what he would do and resist having a part in it.

So did he draw her to her feet and forward also in a single movement so that she was treading upon the star stone itself. Quivers of energy vibrated in his body. She would have thrown herself back and away but not only Yonan held her there, this was part of the power they had aroused and it kept her motionless. Yonan reached out, his other hand gripped the sword firmly, and he called aloud in a shout which reached above the baying of the hounds.

"Ninutra!"

There was a hush as the echoes of his shout died away. The hounds howled no longer. Kelsie quivered with expectancy. What now had he summoned?

"Ninutra! Hilarion!" Now he had added a second name to the first.

There was a haze rising from the points of the star as if lamps or candles were sending forth a smoke which was of light not of dark. Each of those streams inclined inward and now they veiled the very center of the copse beyond the star. Yonan's grip on her had not loosened, instead it had tightened to a bruising ring of fingers leaving nail marks on her flesh. Under the shadow of his helm his eyes were closed, there was a strain on his features as if he dared now some deed beyond which he dared not even look.

"Ninutra!"

The sword blazed high, flames wrapped about his hand and arm but he did not loose his hold. The whirl of the mist tongues about them made Kelsie feel faint and ill. She closed her eyes. Then came a blast of cold, a feeling of such terror that she could not even voice a scream of protest. They were lost in some place where her kind was never meant to travel. Yet there was a power that whirled them on—and on—and on. She clung to that, fearing to be left alone in this place above all.

Then—dark—complete and terrible darkness—and still the power held them—

It was gone—they were lost in this—this—

"Kelsay! Kelsay!"

She was blind, she was sick, she was lost—

"Kelsay?"

She was so overcome by weariness and weakness that it required a major effort to raise her eyelids and see now that the dark was not complete. Yonan's face with the moon streaking across it was close to hers. She was in his arm still though she lay upon stone, his hold, rock steady, bringing her up against his chest.

"Kelsay—we are out!"

The words meant nothing for a long moment of time. Part of her seemed still caught and held by that nothingness which had been. Then behind his head she saw what was certainly not the tree wall of the grove but instead what could only be a wall of stone, dappled by the moonlight shifting through holes.

She drew a deep breath and then another. On her breast was a warm pulsing and she did not need to feel for it to know that it was the gem.

"Where—where are we?" Her voice was a weak whisper.

He drew her up higher against him so she could see more. Beside him lay the sword no longer a-ripple with power but still a small beacon of light. Kelsie could see now more walls and overhead the night of moon and stars. It was plain that wherever they were it was not the copse in which they had been besieged.

"Where are we?" He echoed her question. "I do not know—save that we are away from those who nosed so closely on our trail. This was once a mighty keep, I think." He was looking about, too, as if trying to see what had once stood complete and formidable.

"But how did we get here?" she asked quickly. It would be a long time before she would forget that passage through the Other Place where her kind went at great peril as she was now aware.

"We had a key; we used it—" His hand went out again to the hilt of his sword. "A year agone Uruk found such a path when the gray ones had him at their mercy, or so they thought. The old ones had their own ways of travel which are not ours except when the choice may be certain death behind."

10

Their new shelter had nothing of the stench of the Thas caverns, nor of the indescribable odor which had filled the copse from which they had been so strangely snatched. It was dark, save where the moon struck through rents in the walls, and very chill. So that the two of them huddled together for the sheer need of bodily warmth. Nor did they sleep, but dozed and awoke and dozed again until the gray of early morning showed them more clearly where they had come.

The walls of the place might have been laid by giants for there were great blocks fitted together with no sign of securing mortar—rather as if their weight alone, once they were in place, were enough to cement them for all time. These formidable barriers extended well up. Above was rubble less expertly laid, much of which had cascaded down into the great room where they were sheltering. By the revealing light of day Kelsie could see that they had spent the night in the center of another great star many times the width of that which Yonan had uncovered but fashioned in the same way. Between the points were symbols engraved on the pavement. One of those recalled a memory for Kelsie—of Wittle sketching a like pattern in the air.

Yonan was a-foot, first going to the nearest wall and jumping until his hands caught on the rougher stone above. Then by a feat of strength he was able to pull and work himself up, sending small cascades of ancient stones sliding down in a cloud of dust.

"Where are we?" Kelsie had turned around to survey the place of the star. That had been fashioned close to the wall, but there stretched out a large segment of space beyond. She could see no ground entrance to this room—only the walls about.

Yonan balanced, slowly turning his head from side to side, working his way around on the treacherous coating of the upper wall so that he could see at least three-quarters of what lay beyond.

"A keep . . . I think . . ." he was plainly uncertain. "But a very old and long since deserted one. There are such to be found, though usually we avoid them. But with that," he nodded at the star in which she still stood, "I do not think that this is any trap of the Dark. Look to your jewel—does it blaze in warning?" He held onto his perilous perch with one hand and with the other sought the hilt of his sword. There was a warmth in her stone but no fire and she reported as much.

He nodded. "The power is very old here—near exhausted and—" His head swung suddenly around and she could see his body tense.

"What is it?" She had moved now to the wall directly below his perch.

He made a silencing gesture with his hand. It was plain to Kelsie that he was listening, listening and staring beyond to seek the source of whatever it was he heard.

Now she concentrated on hearing, too. There was a distant bark—but it did not have the fierce threat of a hound's cry. Then, from the air, sounded a trilling which was far from the hoarse cries of the dark flying things which companied those of the Dark.

From Yonan's own lips came a whistle, close in pattern to the trill. Kelsie saw the flash of rainbow wings, the light body those carried. There hung in the air before her companion one of the flamen, the small humanoid body supported by the fast flutter of the wings. She had seen them often in the Valley and knew what was told of them, that they were capricious and short of memory—they might carry messages but could easily be turned from their task by something else new which caught their attention.

Now it landed near to Yonan, its wings only half folded, as if it would make off in an instant, peevish at being controlled even by so little as answering his signal. He whistled again, his face set in a mask of impatience.

Kelsie was as aware of the hostility of the flyer as much as if it had cried aloud denial of having to have anything to do with the two. There was a coaxing note in Yonan's whistle and then he spoke rapidly in a series of singsong words she could not recognize.

The flamen shook its head violently, gave an upward bound which carried it out into the air and almost instantly beyond Kelsie's range of sight. Yonan whistled twice more but it did not return.

"Not of the Valley," there was a disappointed note in his voice. "It is one of the unsworn. Which means—" He fell silent.

"Which means what?" she demanded, when he did not continue.

"That we have come far eastward—perhaps well beyond all the trails known to the Valley people."

"Can you still see your mountain?"

He shifted carefully about and searched the air so far above her. "That may be it. But . . . there are leagues now between—" He was facing at an angle to the room below.

She waited for that touch of buried compulsion which always in her answered any thought of returning to what safety this land could offer. Yes, it still rode with her even now. Without thinking she, too, turned to face in near the opposite direction from Yonan's stance. Whatever drew her lay still ahead in the unknown.

However, when she spoke it was of more immediately practical things.

"We need food and water—" Both hunger and thirst were making themselves known now.

"Come up!" He lowered himself to his belly and reached down his hands. She gave a jump and felt fingers catch one of her wrists while her other hand missed and scrabbled at the stone until he managed to seize it also. He was stronger than he looked, this warrior of the Valley, for somehow, with very little assistance from her, he brought Kelsie up beside him on the crumbling top of the wall.

What stretched for a distance before her and on every side were more walls marking rooms, or passageways, long unroofed. In addition the pile stood on a mound or small hill, and stretching out from that was a patchwork of fields each also partitioned by broken walls. There was an opening not far to their left which suggested a road had led here and that that maze of rock had been the entrance to this place. But nowhere was there any hint of water.

"That way—" Yonan pointed north and rose to his feet cautiously. His motion, as wary as it was, started a slip of loose stone down into the room of the star.

"There are no doors." Kelsie had noted that almost at once. These walls sealed in each room one from the other, and their only path to freedom appeared to be by the tops of those shaky divisions.

"That is the truth. Therefore we must take these upper ways and with full care. Follow me, and, if you can, place your feet where mine have been."

The sun was up and beginning to warm the rocks about them before they reached that point which once might have been a gate. Not only was Kelsie hungry and thirsty but she was also trembling from the tension of that journey. Twice they had had to make detours which had lost them much time because the wall tops were too unsteady to allow them footage.

Though she looked with hope into each room they passed she saw no way of going except by this dangerous path they had chosen. There were no doorways, no trace of any floor side opening from one space into the next. This amazed her.

"They might have had other means of entrance," Yonan commented when she spoke of this. "If they were winged for example."

"Flamen!" she burst out in denial. She could not think of the small airborne creatures as the architects of such massive walls.

"There may be—or were once—other flyers beside the flamen," he told her soberly. "It is well known that the adepts played with the very forces of life itself, creating new creatures for their own use or amusement. Such are the Krogan, the water people, and even the Thas. There were few of true blood left when the rest of the Old Ones thought to flee such unnatural dealings and went into Estcarp, laying upon themselves forgetfulness of their land lest they be tempted to so misuse the power again. But whoever set these stones together are now long gone. Ah, take this wall, and then that, and we shall be at outer bailey at last."

Perforce she followed him, though the footing was never safe and she tottered on the edge of slipping twice before they reached the point he indicated and could look down at the earth below.

Yonan selected a portion of the wall path which appeared to show the least of time's erosion and lay flat on it. Then he ordered Kelsie:

"Give me your hands and swing over. You will drop but I think that the space is not so much we cannot make it. We have no other choice."

There was a drop certainly and she hit ground, to roll over the edge of another small fall, coming to stop painfully against one of those broken field walls. There was a whir in her face which made her start and cry out as two birds took off out of a clump of grass before her, not ascending very high into the air but covering a goodly space before they alit and disappeared again into the tall cover of the field.

When Yonan joined her he was fumbling with his sword belt and produced a length of what looked like tough cord, a small weight fastened to either end.

"Circle," his command was delivered in a voice hardly above a whisper, and he motioned with his hand toward where the birds had taken again to cover. "Come at them from the south if you can, but get them up."

She obeyed in spite of her bruises, trying to walk as noiselessly as she could through the vegetation which was waist-high grass, giving support here and there to a loaded seed head as if it were some form of wild sown grain.

There was another whir and eruption of feathered bodies. Something whirled through the air and one of the birds fell, entangled foot to wing by Yonan's weighted cord. A moment later he passed her in a leap, knife in hand, and used that expertly to put an end to the wildly struggling bird.

Following the same method of hunt they added two more of the low-flying prey to their first capture. Then Yonan, swinging the birds by their feet, turned aside from the open into an ancient field where the stones at one corner into an ancient field where the stones at one corner had shifted forming a small half cave. He went to work at once, skinning and gutting the birds, saying:

"Get some dry wood." He jerked one hand toward where a straggle of trees stood. This once might have been an orchard, Kelsie decided, but only one or two of the trees showed any signs of life by ragged greenery. Some storm of the past had laid others low and she went among those breaking off branches and carrying an arm load to where Yonan was conducting his bloody business.

She watched him lay a fire of sticks hardly more than twigs and then light those with a stone from his belt pouch struck against his knife until sparks flew into a handful of grass in the center of his cave oven.

"This will break the smoke," he told her as he worked and she felt that he was deliberately sharing with her information which was the result of long training at living off the land, a land which had nearly as many perils as blades of grass in the field. He had pieces of the birds spitted on trimmed branches and already over the fire while others were hung well out of the flames but where the smoke, partially trapped under the stones, could reach them.

He was right as that smoke emerged in wisps which drifted in different directions at the will of the breeze. Kelsie having built up a goodly supply of wood inspected more fully the seed heads in the field growth. She rubbed some free of their stems and between the palms of her hands, blowing away the chaff and being rewarded with a handful of what was unmistakably some form of grain. She tasted it, finding it chewable and slightly sweet. Then she set about gathering enough of it still on the stem to make an arm load. Though as she went she watched carefully what lay around.

More of the birds were dislodged from their feeding and flew clumsily perhaps as far as the next field. She could smell now the odor of the cooking meat and it drew her, though she wanted most of all a drink of water to rinse away the dryness of the grain she had eaten.

She returned to their improvised fireplace to find Yonan, his attention divided between the roasting meat and something he held before his hands to saw at with his knife. It was yellow in color and shaped not unlike a gourd of her own world, though larger than she had ever seen. Having chopped off its top he was now turning the knife around and around in its interior, shaking free at short intervals pieces of woodlike flesh hung with black seeds.

Kelsie saw that two more of the odd vegetables, if that is what they were, rested beside his knee. She pulled loose the scarf that had covered her head when she had set out from the Valley and began to rub into it the grain she had harvested. Yonan looked closely at what she had found and then nodded.

"Pound that into flour," he commented, "and with drippings from those—" he indicated the birds, "you will have a kind of journey cake."

"What about water?"

He slapped the gourd he was working on. "There is a spring in that last opening beyond where we came down. Did you not see the water reeds?"

She had to admit that she had not, her full attention being on how she could zigzag along the walls without a slip. However, he did not wait for her answer as he set aside the first of his gourds and inspected the meat, turning the spits on which the chunks were impaled with the familiarity of an expert at such cookery.

The meat was done to his satisfaction and laid on the large leaves which he had harvested from the same plant as bore the gourds. Then he took the first of those and stood up, looking at her appraisingly.

"Can you give me a foot up. It is over the wall for our water."

She was willing enough, her dry throat and mouth sending her to stand braced against the outer wall while he got himself to her shoulders. His punishing weight only lasting there for a moment before he was up on the wall.

The sun was already well toward that rippling black line which marked the horizon as she stood there, pressed to the rough stone, wondering how they could find any safe shelter for the coming night. That memory of the howling hounds and the black rider were very clear in her mind. They might have come to this ruin through some knowledge of another race but that did not mean that they were free of pursuit, and she had an idea that the creature Yonan had called by the name of a once man—Rhain—would not so tamely accept defeat.

Kelsie was fingering the chain of the jewel when she heard a scrambling on the wall top and jumped back away from a clatter of some broken pieces which heralded Yonan's return. He lowered to her by the aid of the same cord which had entangled the birds a gourd slopping water. It was so full she had to exert all her self-command not to hold it to her mouth and drink long and full. Then he was over and down beside her and said:

"Take small sips—" he waved away the gourd when she would have given it back to him, "small sips first."

Obediently she sucked in a mouthful and held it for a long moment of sheer delight before she swallowed. Yonan had brought something else with him, a bundle of reeds, and as they went back toward their fire and the waiting food he picked up two of the fallen stones, each of which fitted snugly into his hand. With these he began to crush the reeds, turning them swiftly into strings of fiber which he twisted tightly one to another until he had a lengthline of rough cord.

Night was now fully upon them and their small cooking fire had been purposefully allowed to dwindle to a near dead ash, the sparks sheltered from sight by more stones. Yet Yonan bent over his task by that smallest gleam of light and continued to work. When he had a length of the coarse and, to Kelsie, not-to-be-trusted stuff, he set up two sticks and began to weave between them back and forth methodically, more by touch than sight.

She sat cross-legged at the other side of their palm-sized fire and at last curiosity won:

"What are you doing?"

"We need a bag for that," with a shadow of gesture he indicated the meat they had so haphazardly smoked, "also we need shoes—"

"Shoes?" Startled her hand actually went to the half boots she was wearing. They were scuffed and perhaps scratched past all polishing but they were still intact on her feet. To throw such away for a rough mass of the stuff Yonan was playing with was the act of a fool and she bit her tongue to keep from saying so.

"The gray ones," he was continuing, "hunt by sight and scent together but the night hounds by scent alone. We shall give them such scenting as will send them off our trail for a goodly time."

He had laid to one side part of his rough weaving and now he moved his foot into the faint glow of light. From the pouch at his belt he took out the mass of illbane which he had harvested and began to rub it vigorously along the length of rope. When he had done he laid aside the mass of leaves and began to wind the rope around one of his own feet, shaping it back and forth until he was sure by touch that the entire metal-enforced boot sole was completely covered.

"That will help?" Kelsie wanted assurance, though she had begun to grasp what he would do.

"We can wish it so—illbane has many services. Now we shall test one of these."

Thus when they settled for the night, one to watch for a space and the other to sleep, their feet were encased in stringy reed and small bits of torn vegetation. The clean, clear smell of illbane was in her nostrils as Kelsie took first watch, allowing the fire to die into ash. The moonlight gave her the only sighting of the pile of the ruin and the fields about.

She listened in a queer fashion which combined both mind and body. It was like testing the air for a strange scent—that loosing of thought waves to pick up the first alert against anything the shadows might hide. What she waited for tensely was the howling of the hounds that ran for and with the Black Hunter and his like.

There was life a-stir in the night rightly enough. She picked up rustling in the tall grain, once a screech which brought her scrambling to her feet until she realized it must be the voice of some aerial hunter. But there came no howl, none of that crawling of the skin which she associated with the hounds. How far they were from that copse in which they had been besieged she could not begin to assess. If Yonan knew—which she suspected he did not—he never said. Though his established sentry watches for the both of them certainly argued that he saw little safety in their present position.

Sleep pulled at her. She got to her feet once in that battle against drowsiness and walked over stones where there was no grass rustle to betray her to the outer wall of the roofless keep. There she stood trying to imagine what manner of intelligent creature had built this pile with such strength and yet had made no door to enter, no passage of inner walls to follow from one room to another. It was as silent and as much a part of long hidden and forgotten history as that broken circle back on Ben Blair.

Ben Blair—with a sudden shiver of new fear Kelsie realized that Ben Blair was now so far from her life as to be a distant dream. She had questioned Simon Tregarth about return. He had been evasive but when she had insisted he had told her that to return through the gate one had come through was unknown. One could find other gates in this land and make use of them to go still farther into strange times and places, but to return to one's own proper place—

Proper place. She remembered now that Simon had said that hesitantly, and at last had told her that most of those using the gates had done so for escape. Their "proper places" had come to be in this world, which many had deliberately sought.

Well, she had not! And she wanted—

Looking at the black bulk of the ruin only half displayed in the moonlight, she tried to think of a gate here. If she went through where would she find herself? With something better or something worse? She cupped the witch stone in one hand and felt its comforting warmth. Then her thoughts were swiftly served by an urgency and she held the stone away from her to stare into its heart where there was light flickering and growing stronger. She had taken one step back toward where she had left Yonan, aware that there had been a change. But not from in the land about.

The light emitted from the stone curdled about it until, though she could still feel the warming jewel in her hand, she could not see anything but a seething ball of light. Imprinted on that was a shadow which became darker and more distinct with every beat of her heart.

"Wittle!" She breathed that name aloud and at its saying the reflection steadied. Kelsie was looking straight into the witch's eyes as if they stood face to face, and she felt the compulsion which had always been with her since she had taken up the stone become more than she could control.

In the light the witch's mouth opened. But it was not words that reached Kelsie, rather a straight beam of sharp and compelling thought.

"Where?"

Kelsie answered with the truth. "I do not know."

"Fool! Look about you! Lend me your eyes if you cannot answer straightly."

The pressure of that order was such that Kelsie found herself pivoting slowly, facing first the ruin, and then the fields before, back once again to the ruin.

Now the mist face expressed exasperation and certain vindictiveness against which Kelsie stiffened.

"Is the man still with you?" The accent on the word "man" made an expletive out of it.

Kelsie pictured Yonan asleep as she had left him moments earlier.

"Go while he sleeps then! Follow the jewel's note—it seeks the great power."

Kelsie shook her head firmly. "I leave no one in this land asleep and open to attack." From that stubborn inner part of her which had always resented Wittle she drew the strength to say that—say it or think it.

She saw the witch's eyes in full light, trying to hold hers, to compel her. But instead she dropped the jewel out of her hand, let it swing back against her breast. The bubble which it had formed vanished. Wittle for all her knowledge had been vanquished—for now. Only Kelsie was left with the feeling that had they confronted each other in truth she would not have so easily come out the better of the two. The more she used the stone—was compelled to use it—the more that feeling of inner strength grew in her. But she had no wish to become a witch—one like Wittle. It would seem that she was in some way subservient to the stone but she was still herself, not of a sisterhood who had come to focus on their gems the whole of their lives.

She went swiftly back down from beside the ruin to their camp. There was no way of telling time but the shadows reached farther into the valley about and she was sure that she must awaken Yonan. He, at least, was not under Wittle's influence and— She hesitated a moment—must she tell him of that meeting through the gem's powers? He might from that gain good reason to distrust her and she was certain that only with Yonan beside her did she have a chance of survival. This far it had been largely his knowledge and training which had brought them through.

11

Kelsie need only touch Yonan's shoulder and he was instantly awake. His face turned toward hers and she realized that she would not tell of Wittle—since she had no intention of carrying out the witch's suggestion. Settling in his place on the mass of grass they had pulled for a bed she willed herself to sleep. But she had not willed herself to dream and she never knew whether it was the doing of the witch from Estcarp or her own imagination which straightway plunged her into one of the most realistic nightmares which had ever aroused her sleeping fears.

Kelsie was back in the room of the star into which they had entered so unceremoniously. But the walls were intact now and the star itself blazed on the floor as if drawn in lines of living fire. What crouched in the center of that field of protection was wholly alien. The thin gray-skinned body was hardly removed from a skeleton with skin and not flesh to cover the bones. Two leathery wings were half folded about that same body as a man or woman might pull a cloak.

However, it was the head and face of the creature which drew her full attention. The face was narrow, the nose more beak than just a nasal passageway and the chin retreated sharply. It was the eyes which dominated that sliver of countenance—huge and faceted as might be those of an insect, all seeing and—all knowing.

This was no servant of some adept who had pulled into this realm through his or her use of power. No, this was the adept! And that thing was aware of Kelsie for it swung swiftly around, the unreadable eyes turned on her.

In hands which were more like the talons of some bird of prey than palms with fingers, it held a slender rod topped with a point of Quan iron burning as blue as did the helm of Yonan's sword. This it also swung until it was leveled straight at her.

The small mouth under that beak of nose twisted, open and shut, as if the thing were chattering some speech, question, or bit of ritual. Yet Kelsie did not hear with either mind or ear. Then she traced a shadow of expression on the avianlike face. The spear-wand arose and gestured through the air, leaving trails of blue smoke after it. And that smoke outlined what could only be a face.

A face and yet not a face. There was rigidity to it which more nearly suggested a mask, yet one far more human in appearance than the countenance of the creature which had summoned it. The mask slipped down, fitted itself over its creator. Now the creature arose and fanned its wings outward. Those were no longer dull grayish skin but rather formed a nebula of light about a thoroughly human body and the creature was a woman.

Though the hands which held the rod might have changed, that weapon or trapping of power remained the same. Once more it traveled through the air and the curls of light which followed it straightened into a line moving out toward Kelsie.

Her wonder and beginning wariness was sharpening into fear. Though she was more than a little afraid of Wittle she could summon at least an outward stand against the witch. But this bird-woman was more than Wittle, Kelsie knew that instinctively. Whether she stood in the lines of the Dark or the Light there was no guessing for outward strangeness of body did not mean inward twisting of mind and belief.

Who—what—now claimed her?

There was warmth about her and Kelsie took heart from that for it seemed to her that with the evil always accompanied cold. Perhaps it was the jewel awakening to this other manifestation of the beyond-world.

"Far traveler—"

Into Kelsie's mind beat the words. It seemed part of a question. She was not aware of her physical body so she did not nod, only accepted the designation as the truth.

"Waker of the sleeping—"

"Not by my choice!" Out of her mind arose the answer.

"Back and back," continued that mind voice. "There was a choice and you were open to it—"

For a fraction out of time she stood again on Ben Blair and struck up the gun which was aimed at the already wounded wildcat. Was that the choice which had led to this?

"There was a choice," the winged one replied to her scrap of memory.

"There have been others and will be more. You have dared one of the ancient ways, you will dare another—and yet another—"

"Do you wish me ill?" Kelsie sent that thought impulsively into the dream.

"For me there is no well nor ill. But you have evoked the power in a place where once it dwelt. Thus you have loosed yet more of the stuff of struggle. That long asleep stirs, be careful at how you welcome it, woman of another world. Be very careful."

The wand dipped its point, the illumination which made the figure look human failed, she saw again the gray skeleton, its beelike eyes trained upon her. There was a remoteness which was raising a wall between them. If she had had any thought of appealing to this other one for aid to come that fast withered and was gone. Neither of the Light nor of the Dark, this was one removed by choice from the battle. But who else was now awakened to what passed in Escore through Kelsie's and Yonan's intrusion?

"What will you do?" She dared to ask that now of the alien thing once more crouched within the blazing star.

She had an impression of cold amusement. "Ah, but that choice is mine. And I do not choose—"

The inner room of the ruin, the winged one, all of that vivid dream was gone in an instant. Instead there was darkness and a freezing cold. In that darkness something moved, leaned forward to observe her, something aroused from a lethargy which had lasted for ages. It would seem that here were balances. This thing she now fronted so blindly was the obverse of the winged thing. It did not try to communicate, it was merely fastening her in its mind, homing in upon her as a link with the world.

This was danger! Do not let it read her—stand against it! Her only weapon was the jewel. Still she hesitated to use it here. She stood within the boundaries of a place which was wholly inimical to all of her kind, and that which languidly and lazily observed her was something which she could not see—only feel the slimy touch of its curiosity.

Think of the jewel—no! She believed that that was the last thing she must do here and now. Think of—Ben Blair standing tall on another world—the world of easy life which was her own. Grimly Kelsie clung to her mind picture of the mountain, strove to recall its scents, its very being.

Was the thing in the dark deceived? She had no way of telling but she was drawn away from that place quickly and awoke, to find Yonan on his knees beside her, his hand on her shoulder as if he had physically pulled her out of that place of foulness and threat.

"You dream—" there was a tone in his voice which was faintly accusatory.

"You broke it!" She was aware of warmth, perhaps not of the night around her—the true night—but rather that of companionship. Since Yonan had joined them on the trek she had many times realized that his skills were what might bring them to whatever goal the jewel had imposed upon her. But this waking was one of the things which was even more to her service.

"We have awakened something by our passage," she told him with eager haste, wanting to share with another human, to free herself from that fear and that sense of being now linked to what she did not understand.

In the moonlight she saw him frowning. He flicked a finger at the jewel she wore, not quite touching it.

"Such a symbol may indeed call—"

Her first warmth faded. After all was it not his sword which had provided the key that had opened this door?

"Yours the key," she returned.

There was a flush on his face which she could see even by moonlight. At first she thought he was not going to answer, then he said:

"Each time we use power we may be troubling the scale. And the result may not include only us." His hand was on the Quan iron in his sword hilt. "You dreamed—or did you answer some call of another?"

She told him then—of the winged creature and then of that which had stirred in the darkness. At her story of that his mouth straightened and she saw his sword hand tighten.

"We go— This," he waved to the ruin, "is a focus through which they reached you. If we go—" But he had already turned to bind up their now scanty possessions. The slightly smoked meat he stowed in the coarse bag he had woven while he urged upon her the foot covers, awkward and hard to fasten.

There was a grayness along the horizon when they had made their simple preparations to be on the trail again. Yonan pointed to that distant northern peak which he had indicated before.

"If we take that as a mark—"

"A mark for what and to lead us where?" she countered, still dealing with the mass of reed which made such untidy bundles for her feet. "Back to the Valley?"

His face was set. "The Valley has its own protections but no place is invincible. We could lead that which watched you straight into the heart of that which must be protected above all. You say that your jewel leads us—very well—follow—"

"To draw danger after us!" No question but a protest.

"If that is so, it is so."

She fired up at that. Who was this warrior who was willing to use her as bait to protect his own home? She had no need for loyalty to the Valley, her first thought should be her own peril. To wander through this cursed countryside was no choice of her own—but one she seemed to be forced into by ill luck, by being at the wrong place at a crucial time. All she wanted was to get back to Lormt. Lormt? To her mind she had never heard of that before. Yet she could close her eyes for a moment and see dim halls where ghostlike figures moved slowly as if bemused by their own surroundings.

Another dream or fragment of one—? Where was Lormt and why did she feel the need for reaching it again— Again? She had never been there!

No, but someone else had. Her lips shaped the name Roylane but she did not speak it aloud. By wearing the jewel did she also carry some frail remnant of the true owner with her now? Kelsie longed for someone she could trust enough to ask outright questions. Dahaun of the Valley might be such but they were far from the Valley and its co-ruler now.

"Where do you go?" she lengthened her stride to match step with Yonan. He answered her as curtly:

"It is more like where you go, Lady."

Her hand loosed on the jewel and it was warm. She pulled free its chain and allowed it to swing pendulumwise from her middle finger. There was a scrap of memory, gone so fleetingly that she could not pin it down. So she had stood once before—no, not she—but that other.

Through no urging of her own the jewel began to swing—not in a circle as it had before, but rather back and forth, pointing outward and then to her. And the way it took was east. As firm footed as if she had been given an order she could not gainsay, Kelsie turned in that direction and began to walk, knowing indeed that bound as she was, there was only the gem in real control of their path.

There were bright banners of dawn in the sky as they walked along what might have once been a road between the ancient fields. Berries clustered on thorny branches which hung over tumbling walls and she did as Yonan, swept up what she could garner, stuffing them into her mouth. They were tart and sweet at the same time and she found them refreshing, but too few to give her a feeling of having truly breakfasted.

The forgotten road transversed the open until they came again to where stands of wood broke up the fields and grew closer and closer together until they faced another wood. A small animal with a dusky red coat broke for cover, was gone before Yonan could free his throwing cord, if he wished to hunt. And there were birds—not in flight but sitting on branches to watch them pass, twittering and calling, to be answered by others ahead as if their coming was being heralded to some feathered overlord whose domain this was.

They still had a way which had narrowed to hardly more than a foot-path being overhung with brush and giving rooting to stubborn grass. Once Yonan flung out a hand to ward her from touching against a bush with singular ragged looking leaves and flowers of a dull green color which gave forth a thick and cloying scent.

"Farkill," he explained. "The odor is a sleep maker, to touch it raises ulcers on the skin, ones which even illbane finds hard to heal. And there," he pointed to a grim gray skeleton of a tree which set a little away from their path, "is also danger. Quick!" His arm fell about her shoulders so suddenly and heavily that she was swept from her feet as she heard a whishing in the air.

"Creep—on your belly," her companion ordered. "Do you want such as that in you?" he indicated a gray shaft which stuck, still quivering, in a bush at what might have been at the level of her shoulders had she still been on her feet.

It was in the shape of a thorn but as long as Kelsie's forearm and she gathered that it could have impaled her had it struck. In some manner it had been so shot by the dead-looking tree.

Creep indeed they did and she wrinkled her nose at the sour smell of the muck of long dead leaves which floored their path. Twice more they passed arrow trees until at last they came into the open once again, a glade such as the one in which Yonan had used his sword key. When they were in the midst of that he allowed them to stop and they ate the meat and drank from the gourds, but sparingly for they had not seen any source of water that day.

Kelsie was growing sleepy and longed to simply stretch out on the ground here and sleep away her weariness. Only Yonan made no sign of remaining where they were and her pride and stubborn desire to match him would not let her suggest a longer resting time.

Though she consulted the jewel now and then and was assured that they were following wherever that would lead them, she wanted more and more to drop it to this ground, let it be hidden by the tall grass, and return—Where?

In the day here Ben Blair seemed very far away in her mind, her whole life up to her coming through what Simon Tregarth had called a gate was more of a dream than her nightmare just past. She began to con-sider Yonan. He certainly was under no compulsion to travel so. Yet it was his knowledge which had saved them over and over again. He was not of the Valley by birth. That she knew. And he was even unlike most of the human kind who had gathered there. His hair was lighter and the eyes in his weather-browned face a startling blue. Who was Yonan? For the first time her mind wandered more from their present plight to ask a question. Dahaun apparently held him in repute having sent him after them for a guardian—or a guide. She had seen one of the other Tregarths—Kyllan—but there was nothing which appeared to make Yonan one of their out-breed stock. He usually companied with the huge axe-weaponed warrior Uruk. And there was that strange exchange which she had heard to suggest that he believed in reincarnation and had once been Tolar who had played some desperate game in this same land centuries ago.

"How far into this land have you been?" she suddenly asked.

He had paused to adjust the cord of his improvised shoulder bag and he did not look up as he answered:

"This land is new to me. Nor is it marked on any of the charts in the Valley."

"Yet you come with me—"

"I go with you," he returned, "since that is the duty laid upon me. When the witches out of Estcarp made contact with the Valley they bargained for guides. Nor did they understand that the influence of the Light flickers in many places and that there are powers upon powers which they have never heard of even within the records of Lormt."

Lormt! The place out of her half dream. Now she wanted straight answers. "What is Lormt?"

"A place in which ancient knowledge is stored. It was when Kemoc Tregarth went to Lormt that he learned of Escore—or at least that there was a country here to the east which had been forbidden to the Old Race who fled the adepts' war."

Now he arose and stood looking down at her. "What says your jewel? Which way?"

From her he had glanced at the wood about them. She had no desire to enter that darksome place of peril again but neither was there any sense in their remaining here in the open. So she dangled the gem hurriedly. It pointed again—more directly to the north Kelsie thought, though she was no forester or land dweller to guess aright at that signal.

The reed and illbane covering of their boots had shredded under travel and broken away so only bits of these remained. Also there were none of the herbs here and they could not renew that defense. Once more they entered the wood on the other side of the glade. There were no longer any faint traces of a trail and she noted that Yonan's pace had slowed. Now again he halted entirely, his head up as he sniffed the breeze, even as some animal advancing cautiously into unknown territory might test for some faint presence which was perilous to his kind.

There were still the arrow trees and the farkill so their advance was not straight because of these but took on a zigzag pattern. It was on one of their crawls to escape the arrow thorns that Kelsie set hand on what she thought was a round stone. Only to have it turn under her weight and grin evilly up at her—a skull! And, though there were differences in the wide ridges of bone above the eyes and the broadness of the whole, it approached that of a human. She uttered a little cry of disgust which brought Yonan's head around. But she had already noted two more of the grayish knobs a little before them and more—It was a pavement of skulls they had chanced upon!

Yonan shook his head when she asked what manner of creature had died here—here—and here—and there ahead—to form such a hideous track. But he kept to it even though she near refused to follow him. Then they came to the first of the monoliths.

The same grayish gleam of skull, of arrow tree, it stood out here in a half envelope of brush like a crooked giant finger pointing skyward—if there was indeed still an open sky above the ceiling of tangled tree branches.

The thing was taller than Yonan as he stood before it, and more bulky, but, though it was greened here and there with moss, it was easy to see that it had been purposely wrought into the form of a crouching image leaning forward a little—one massive arm raised and a great clawed hand or paw about to reach for some easily captured prey.

Kelsie sucked in her breath. She had seen many outré forms of life since she had so unwillingly begun this journey, but this was wholly malignant. The shoulders were bowed until it would appear that the creature it portrayed was humped. On those shoulders with a hardly visible neck perched a huge head, the bald cranium rising to a cone point. But it was the eyes which were the worst feature of that misshapen thing. They were as deep set as if they lay in pits. Yet they were not stone—or even inset gems—

She looked into them and gasped. Just like the hound that had appeared at the gate, these holes were filled with a yellowish flame. Stone and carven the monstrous thing might be. But—the eyes were alive! Was there some presence embedded in the stone—a prisoner without hope of freedom?

Without conscious thought she raised the Witch Jewel, not watching it as she did because she was entrapped by the fire in those stone-rimmed pits.

"No!" Yonan was upon her, his hand out to beat down the jewel. "No!"

She twisted in his hold, her fear grown a hundredfold. Only he had her arm so tightly pinned to her side that she could not break free to use what she had come to consider her only weapon.

"It is a watcher, let it not watch to any purpose," he added. Then thrust her away from him, so that meeting eye to eye with the thing was broken and she was free of what she now judged was indeed one of the more subtle dangers of this place.

Still holding onto her arm as if he feared she had not taken his warning to heart, Yonan pulled her along with him, their boots with the remnants of the illbane fastenings upon them slipping and sliding on the trail of skulls.

"It watched—was alive!"

"Not it but what watched through it," he countered. "If you had used the jewel you might have banished that watcher but you would have raised an alarm which—"

He stopped nearly in mid-word. There was another creature beside this noxious trail. It bore resemblance to the first but it was not graven stone—no, this was carved of wood. Some giant of a tree had been so used that the remnant of bark, now overgrown with leprous fungi, formed a skin, watched. There were the same pits of eyes—the same—after one fleeting glance she prevented her own sight with difficulty from meeting the eyes in the wood. They were also alive.

She pulled herself free of Yonan's grip and sped as well as she could down the skull road to avoid another meeting with that which so spied upon them. Now, as she went, she looked quickly from side to side to make sure there were no more of the watchers looming up before them.

No air stirred here under the trees, and there was a rising odor from the muck in which the skulls had been set which was putrid and sickening. There was a warmth here, too—not that protective one she knew when the jewel came to greater life, but rather a stifling sticky heat which eroded one's spirit as well as dragged at one's body.

However, the road led straight and she saw the ancient remains of trees which had been cut from their roots to clear a way for it. Here and there saplings had dared to reach up again, pushing aside the skulls which lay to grin at them. But they came across no more of the statues.

Not until they pushed through a last fence of brush and came to open country. The skull road had not stopped at their emergence into the open, though the bones here appeared to be more firmly planted.

"A road of the conquered," Yonan spoke for the first time since he had warned her in the wood. "It is very old that belief. To plant the heads of your enemies so that you tread ever upon them makes complete your victory." But Kelsie hardly heard him, she was looking ahead at the massive— thing—which had been erected there.

If she had believed the two she had seen in the wood were great and careful pieces of work, what could she call this?

For the road of skulls ran directly to a ponderous, outstretched belly of the thing squatting there—an artifact as large or nearly so as the ruin in which they had found themselves earlier. Both the hands were outspread and planted on the ground like giant pillars and those supported the huge form which was leaning forward as if to study whatever advanced toward it.

12

There was a dark hole where the curve of its pendulous belly touched the ground. So regularly shaped it was that it could be a door— A door into what? Kelsie dared a quick glance up into the eye pits. But there was no hellish fire burning there, they were only dark caverns.

A harsh noise brought a small cry from her. Surely the thing before her was not alive, had not delivered such a hail. No, that had come from the winged things circling about its head. They were brilliantly scarlet even in this early eventide except for their bills and their feet—which were the black of the orifice opening at the end of the skull road.

They were stringing out, away from that perfect circle they had made about the head of the squatting thing, coming toward them. Yonan gave a cry in turn, one which perhaps was meant to hearten himself as well as any who heard. He hurled about his head the weighted cord he had used for hunting. But it was nothing for the pot that he would bring down now. The cord flew out, so quickly she hardly saw it go and wrapped itself about the long neck of one of the flyers, bearing the thing to the ground where it flopped and fought.

Yonan was ready for it with sword and a single sweep of blade whipped off the darting head. But he had to whirl then to beat off another flyer which swooped, dagger bill ready, to attack. Then that one, too, was left to flop on the ground headless but somehow still living.

Kelsie shouted and tossed up the jewel as a third sped down the sky aiming straight for her. She had little hope of beating it off—the thing was fully half her size, its wing spread was beyond her reckoning.

The jewel flickered with life and the bird sheered off. Kelsie's eyes following its flight fearfully saw something else. From the broad nose which covered near a third of the face of the demonic monster there puffed two small clouds of reddish smoke, thin and without any flame to feed them but they spread forward in the air, not diffusing as she thought that they would, rather to form a distinct cloud or blot. It was already under the film of twilight but that smoke—or breath—was still distinguishable.

The birds had attacked Yonan again, seeming to look upon him as the enemy they could bring down the easiest. He called to Kelsie, panting a little as he countered with sword against bill to keep his feet and break the attack.

"Do not let them circle! Break up that—!"

She swung the jewel, with no hope of contacting any of the flyers but noting that they fled the sparks which flew in the air from her only weapon. Then she was back to back with Yonan.

"Back to the woods?" she got out that question.

"Not with night coming," he told her. And she could understand the wisdom of that. They might escape the birds when they gained the shadows of the trees but they also would be girt about by a place of the Dark. At least in the open they could see their attackers.

Three of the birds had fallen to Yonan's sword but still the others attempted to build up a circle in the air above the two of them. And it was Yonan's constant thrusts which kept them from forming it completely.

Why they just did not fly higher and out of his reach Kelsie could not understand. But whatever plan governed them meant that they must travel close to the ground and fairly close to the two they would take.

She drew a deep breath and coughed, her throat rasped, her eyes burning. That breath from the monster was settling on them. She swung the chain of the jewel vigorously. That might keep off the birds but it had no effect upon the puff of crimson air. She coughed again, near strangled by the breath which she had been forced to inhale. There was a wretched burning, in her nose, her throat. Her eyes were beginning to water so she could hardly see. But still she strove to keep her feet and ward off this new peril—only it did not answer the jewel. Had she come to depend too much on that because so far it had not failed her? To everything there was a limit and here they two might have reached that.

For Yonan was also coughing hard. He stepped back and his shoulders were now against Kelsie's so she could feel the racking shudders which shook him. The birds cried out again even as they had done at their first coming—harsh squawks but ones which held a measure of triumph in them.

She felt Yonan slump and turned just in time to swing the jewel out to stop a vicious bill which was aimed for him as he crumpled to the ground. There was blood on that part of his face she could see below his helm and the helm itself had been knocked askew. The bird which had launched a fight attack on him was on the ground, its long legs holding well above it but its head drawn back for a finishing stab at the feebly moving man who was trying to regain his feet.

"No—circle—" he gasped.

But it was too late. Kelsie was coughing with such pain and depth that she felt her very lungs would be brought up by her choking. She could only hunch over Yonan holding above the two of them the Witch Jewel. And that one of the fearsome flock who had been about to impale her companion drew back and sidestepped from the run which would have carried it to that action.

Moisture from her tortured nose dripped down on Yonan and she saw it form beads of blood on his mail. Her throat was rasped so raw that nothing mattered now save that she could find some refuge from this poisoned cloud.

Through her tearing eyes she could see an open space where the dancing red motes of the cloud made up the haze about them. On her knees, the gem in one hand, her other laced in Yonan's belt she strove to reach that promise of freedom.

She did not understand that she was being herded, not then. But she had a full moment of truth before the end came. The cloud lifted—she saw before her the black gap of an opening and only there was the promise of breath which had become a matter of life itself. One last effort— One effort and a momentary awakening to the danger—She had reached the ominous door in the monster's great belly and it was toward that she had crawled, dragging Yonan with her.

Kelsie strove to turn and the red haze settled. Coughing and tasting her own blood she fell forward into complete darkness in which she was lost.

Darkness again met her when she roused. For a moment she could not remember—and then the terror which had woven around her when she realized where they had been herded struck full force. She was not in that place of darkness where she had once been tossed, afraid and alone. No, she was truly awake and in a place of dark which was of this world. Her hands questing out on either side of her bruised and aching body were exploring over stone, rough and damp. Her fingers flinched away from a patch of slime.

She swallowed and her throat was sore burned by that last blast of the ruddy smoke. But this dark was so intense she was cold with another fear—that she was blind. She raised a hand feebly, for all her strength seemed drained and gone, rubbed across her closed eyes, opening them once more when she had done—upon thick dark.

Thick—for it seemed to have a quality of its own—smothering, holding her. Somehow she braced her hands on the floor and levered herself partway up, now depending upon her ears. There were no sounds—was hearing smothered and gone like her sight?

"Yonan!" There came no answer to her shout. Wherever she was trapped, she was alone.

Now she felt for that which had lain on her breast—upon which she had come to depend. Her fingers closed upon a cold stone; it could be any pebble she might have taken up. The life and warmth she had sensed in it from the very first were gone. It was dead—

Dead? Perhaps this was death and she had come from life into an eternal dark.

It was only when that last fear began to crowd all control from her mind that Kelsie first became aware of something which was not sound but rather a vibration, growing ever stronger and sinking into her own body. It followed a regular series of beats yet there was no extra rhythm in it as had been in the bowl drums of the Thas. This was more like the measured thud of a heart—a heart so powerful that it could echo outside the body which held it.

The black gate in the belly of the monster—had she entered a thing with a life of its own? Her thoughts squirmed away from that—even in this country of strangeness and hallucinations such a thing could not be true.

She sat fully up in the dark and with her hands explored her whole body. The last remnants of the illbane wrappings were gone from her feet, but at her belt, snug in its own sheath was the long-bladed knife which was a part of all the clothing of a Valley dweller. She edged that out of its covering now, afraid of dropping it in this thick dark and losing her only weapon since it seemed that the power of the stone had deserted her.

Kelsie did not try to stand up. Keeping the knife ready she used her hand as a sweep before her. Always at the back of her mind was the fear that she was in truth blind and that her movements might well be under observation by those who had arranged her capture. Yet she could not remain huddled where she was awaiting some unknown attack.

There was the faint grating sound as her knife swept across the stone and that broke somehow the pattern of the beating which seemed to grow stronger the more she moved. Suddenly her hand stubbed against an obstruction of some sort and she quickly felt a barrier of stone as high as she could reach and as far as her arms on either side could stretch.

Now she did pull herself to her feet, running fingers along that wall as she arose. Where the floor had been cold, slime-dotted and forbidding, this wall differed in that there was a warmth to the stone the higher she reached—and it extended far above her head even when she stood on tiptoe.

The vibration which had reached her through the floor was more apparent here and she thought that somehow her own heart responded in beat to match that rhythm.

Now she began to move cautiously to her right. Feeling outward with the toe of one boot before she took any step with her weight upon it, running her fingers as a guide along the wall. The steady inpush of the dark around her made her doubly unsure of herself and she tested again and again her blind impression of what lay around her.

Then her hand slipped from the stone into open space—a door? She turned slowly with as much caution as she could summon. The flooring seemed secure enough. With knife she probed to her right and both heard and felt the touch of the blade to another obstruction. So—a door. Yet there was still no light to give her any help and she would have to travel anyway ahead with the same caution she had used before. Perhaps it would be better to explore the rest of the room before she attempted to use this other opening which might lead only to worse entrapment.

She sidled past that open space and once more encountered a wall under her touch. Now she began to count and was still counting when she discovered a sharp corner and changed her way to skirt a new wall. Three paces farther on was another opening and from that came a puff of air. Not the clean, lung cleansing breeze one could find in the outer world—this was moist and carried in it the stench of decay. Clearly *NOT* a way to follow.

Kelsie soon established that she had awakened in a room which had openings in three of its four walls, the third one much like the first one she had discovered. And it was between those two which she must choose now.

She returned to the first and ventured into something which her sense of touch said was a passage. Though she shrank from using her hands, as those patches of slime which she had found on the floor were here more numerous and often joined with one another when her fingers swept over them. She tried hard in her mind to build up a picture of where she was but without sight her imagination was limited and she was forced to understand that there was nothing she could do save that which she was doing, blindly venture into the dark tangle of this way.

As in that air which had puffed from the second passage she could smell corruption and once her fingers penetrated, before she could jerk them back, a mass of something clinging to the wall which squirted liquid, to burn her flesh as she hurriedly wiped her hand down her breeches, the evil smell so being carried with her.

The vibration was growing stronger and—she blinked, and blinked again. No she could not be mistaken, somewhere very far ahead there must be a source of light for the darkness was now not so complete. She hurried her pace and gave a small sigh of relief as that grayness overcame the blindness of the complete dark. Now she could see the walls and need not fear a second contact with the patches of dull black stuff which seemed to grow there as moss had done on the statue in the wood.

Yonan! At the far back of her mind all along there had rested the picture of the Valley warrior as she had seen him last, choking and sick from the fog. At least her explorations in the cell in which she had awakened had shown that he had not shared it. Where was he?

The gray light was tinged now with a faintly reddish gleam and she feared another encounter with that smoke which had undone them both, yet she could not yet turn away from light and seek the full dark again. The red became brighter. Her hands looked almost as if their blood within her veins had been drawn to the surface. It was warmer, much warmer also. And while the stench had grown worse there was no hint as yet of the choking gas if that was what the monster had exhaled.

Ten strides farther on and she came to another opening. Dropping to her knees she looked out into space where the red light glowed. She crept out on what proved to be a balcony or upper walk around a deep chamber, most of which lay beneath her, and there she froze, belly pressed to the stone, striving to see without being seen. For she was not alone.

There were at least a half dozen of them, she could not be sure because they came and went and only three remained steadily at their post which was on a similar balcony to the one she occupied but on the opposite wall of this deep opening.

Below was what amazed her the most. For there were humanlike figures there but here was also a vast tub or basin as big as a good-sized pool. It was filled not quite to the brim with a mass of what looked like thick red slime and it bubbled continuously as if aboil on some gigantic stove. As each of the bubbles on the surface broke they released a reddish mist which floated like a cloud, thinning to a kind of dribbling moisture which poured down again into the basined stuff.

Those who watched and came and went—Kelsie drew a deep breath and strove to make herself still smaller and less visible. That black-clad rider who had urged on the hound outside the stones—here was his like over and over again. The Sarn—! Feared as they were, not even the records of the Valley had had much to say about them or their deeds—save that they were wholly given to darkness and despair. They wore thigh-length cloaks over tight black covering which appeared modeled to their bodies, these cloaks having hoods as tight fitting with only apertures for eye holes. Their gloved hands moved in stiff jerky gestures as if it were by this method they conversed.

Kelsie's hand reached for the Witch Jewel. However, even as it had been on her first waking here, so was the gem cold and dead. The power she had come to lean upon had deserted her.

Twice one of the masked Sarn Riders had glanced upward to where she crouched. So she flattened herself yet more but was not yet willing to withdraw from the chamber into the maze of dark passage behind her. There was a stirring below and she saw four other of the Riders come out of an opening to the side driving before them some captives. She had never seen the Thas in good light but there was no mistaking these creatures being hauled along by a rope knotted from one neck noose to the next, being pulled out into the dull red light of the ledge above that basin. They cowered and had to be dragged along. She was sure that over the ever hissing of the bursting bubbles she could hear thin, mewling, terror cries.

But the Thas were of the Dark—why had the Sarn taken prisoners from those on their own side? Or could it be that those of evil did not hang together by any desire save when such cooperation was demanded of them.

What she witnessed now shook her badly. Loosed from the first noose in that line the shaggy form of a Thas was thrust forward by the butt of a long pole held by two Riders. He—it—tottered for a frenzied second or two on the very edge of the ledge and then fell. This time it was easy to hear a grating scream as the creature was gone into the bowl of flame. The others in that line of sacrifice were tearing at the ropes about their own throats, pulling back on the ends the Sarn Riders held so firmly. As for their unfortunate fellow, he was swallowed up in the liquid fire and did not come to the surface once more.

Kelsie swallowed and swallowed again, again the raw sickness rising in her throat. If these Sarn Riders used one of their allies so—what death would they wish upon an enemy? She began to edge back inch by inch on the walkway which held her—though she had no wish to be hunted through the dark. There was another opening besides the one she had come through at the other end of the balcony and, after a moment of doubt and realization that to return to the cell where they had left her would avail her nothing, she chose to creep in that direction, keeping an eye on the Riders in the hopes of learning whether or not they watched her. However, they seemed completely intent on driving their captives to their doom one by one.

The girl gained that second doorway and crawled within it, finding that after a short distance it turned sharply to the right, seeming to run parallel to the chamber of the basin. Now it was dark. When she got well beyond the portal she got to her feet, for there were patches of growth along the walls which gave off a dull yellowish gleam, when her eyes adjusted to the dark. There were no side openings in those walls, and shortly she came to a flight of stairs leading down. Once more she hesitated and felt for the jewel. But it remained obstinately dead. She would have to rely on her own choices and powers. Where was Yonan? Kelsie was sickened by the thought that perhaps he had already been fed to the basin and that fiery thing which dwelt within it. Now that she was away from that actual chamber she was again aware of the steady beating vibration.

However, it was to go down or return and she knew that she had nothing to hope for in that direction. So she took the stairs step by step one hand feeling for any hold on the wall, for the patches of the yellow growth had in places swallowed a goodly portion of a step.

Kelsie counted again, trying to remember the position of the basin and guess whether this was carrying her below that or not. She had reached twenty when into her mind came that which for a moment wiped the memory of the Riders' hall from her.

"To the right—always the right—" She caught as a jog in the steps made her stumble and held on with both hands fearful for an instant at losing her step and plunging forward down this endless stair.

Yonan? Could that guiding have come from him? Somehow she could not tell. It was as if the mind voice which had sent it was hidden behind some distorting noise. Bait for a trap? She could not help but think of that. Yet if it *were* real and some other captive sought aid could she ignore it? There was always hope that the other would know more of this pile than she, and if she turned away she could be defeating the very purpose which had set her roving through the dark.

"Right—!"

The word faded and was gone. Kelsie took one step and the next with slow care, for here the yellow growth crossed the steps proving to be a jelly which gave forth a puff of foul decay. Then she had reached the level of another passage and sure enough it divided before her, right and left.

For the first time since she had awakened here she felt a faint warmth in the jewel and snatched it out. There was, in the very heart of it, a spark of light, far too small to aid her. But the very fact that it was able to project so much now heartened her. She turned right, one hand cupped tightly about the stone, following the direction given by that now silent voice. She made one attempt to use her own questing thought and then stopped that within almost the same instant. Among the terrors of this place there could also exist some method of picking up any mental communication and she did not have the use of the jewel strong enough to build up her call.

Again the way split and once more she tried the right-hand path. The eerie glow of the slime growths was augmented by a light from ahead—not the fearsome red of the basin chamber but more as if the flames of the leprous growths about her were increased a hundredfold. She was faced suddenly with a hole in the wall, but one which she must fall to her hands and knees to pass. Shrinking, sick from the odors which arose from the weird chamber before her instead of a passage.

There were growths here, also fungi perhaps, which had reached the height of small trees. Between them were smaller lumps of plants or mushroomlike things of different colors, as if in their misshapen bodies they aped flowers of the upper, clean world.

There was water also—or a liquid of some sort—which formed a small rivulet winding its way across the huge chamber. Its swollen looking waters were red and a haze arose above its length.

Through that she saw movement. Someone or something paced back and forth within the edge of the mist which spread out for a short space on either side of the stream.

Yonan! She dared not call his name, perhaps even think it. But she strode forward, trying to avoid contact with the smaller growth each of which when crushed added to the general foulness of the place.

13

There was no mail-protected fighting man across the mist-hung stream—though that other went clad in gray instead of in black as a Sarn Rider. There were rents in that long robe and hair hung in a tangle across the pacer's shoulders. Though she had lost the iron-bound neatness and sobriety of her garments there was no trouble in recognizing—Wittle!

The witch came to a stop as Kelsie approached the riverlet and now she stood with both hands cupping her own jewel with such intensity as to leave her knuckles hard knobs in her pallid skin.

"So it is you—" there was no trace of welcome in her voice and there was certainly no expression of it on her angular features.

"How did you come here?" Kelsie returned. Was Wittle able to use her jewel—if so how did she end in this noisome place of the Dark Force.

"There was a trail—it proved false." The witch replied shortly. "And how came you?"

"We were taken, outside." She believed that the door in the monster's belly had led her here. "Does your jewel aid you now?"

There was a flush up Wittle's spare cheeks which was not a reflection from the blood-red stream. For a space of two breaths Kelsie thought she was not going to answer. Then she said:

"Its power is greatly diminished but it is not dead. And what of the one you so falsely wear, outworlder?"

"It is still alive." Kelsie was sure of that spark of warmth which had arisen after she had left the cavern of the basin. "I cannot call it though."

"Well you cannot!" snapped Wittle. "Would you have these creatures of the Dark realize what they have taken? Come hither and join me, perhaps the gems, stone to stone, will give us true sight in spite of what lies around."

Kelsie had no intention of wading that steaming stream. She turned and walked along it to see if it narrowed enough for her to essay a leap to the other side. Within short space of time it did—though the rank growth on the other bank suggested no fair landing. But what Wittle had half promised was worth the try.

She drew back again and then approached the stream at a run vaulting over it and landing in the mass of fungous material which burst and broke under her weight, smearing her with a stench borne by viscid splotches. She kept herself from trying to brush the stuff from her for fear of some poison—for she could not believe that such a loathsome medley of stinking smears would not also prove poisonous. Wittle awaited her but bore back a step or two as the fetid smells grew worse at every move Kelsie made.

She pointed to a bare space where she had paced. There was a patch of loose gravel there and Kelsie gingerly scooped up some of that to brush the worst of the stuff from her body.

"The jewel!" Wittle did not leave her much time to try to cleanse herself. She advanced, her own stone lying across both of her palms, and Kelsie obediently did the same with the gem on her own neck chain. They touched and immediately there was a small flare and thereafter a core of light in each of them.

"So—they can be fed!" Wittle was exultant. "Let us see."

She settled down on the bare gravel, still careful that her torn robe did not touch Kelsie's beslobbered garments. With one hand still on her stone she laid it down and motioned for Kelsie to do likewise. The girl hesitated.

"And if we awake the Dark?" Kelsie asked. "You, yourself, have said that this could be so—"

"You would wait here for them to come? What profit for us in that? Already they know that they have a Witch of Estcarp." She drew herself up proudly. "They will expect no more than that I try my strength against theirs. That it be doubled now—well, that may be enough to penetrate some of their barriers."

Slowly Kelsie placed her own jewel beside that other one, taking care to have it touch Wittle's. The result was like a small fire, for the heart flame in each shot upward for an eye dazzling space and then died down into a steady double glow.

"The way out—" Wittle leaned forward her tongue caressing her lower lip as if she had just drunk deeply of some restoring drink.

But Kelsie was as quick with her own demand. "Yonan!"

The witch snarled and put out her hand as if to snatch away her jewel, but she did not quite break the connection between them.

"The way out!" She put her face forward, so close to Kelsie's that a small fleck of spittle hit the girl's cheek. "The man is useless—we must be on our way."

"Yonan," Kelsie repeated with stubborn determination. If she had to choose between traveling companions she already was certain which one she would take.

It would appear that Wittle did not feel strongly enough to gainsay her now for as Kelsie centered her gaze on the two glowing stones and built up in her mind her picture of Yonan as she had last seen him, the witch did not protest again. Though if she added her own focusing power to that search Kelsie had no way of telling.

There was a curdling of the light about the two stones. In that they themselves disappeared but there came a surface flat and shining like a mirror and on that formed a shadow which grew into a distinct picture. There was thick darkness there but a small gleam of light showed a hand gripping a sword hilt. Between fingers that light found its way and Kelsie knew or guessed that Yonan's scrap of the Quan iron was still alive. Black shadow moved against shadow and she believed, though the sighting was so bad, that the Valley warrior was moving through the same lightless kind of passage which she had dared upon her awakening here.

She leaned across and fairly hissed at the witch:

"Call! With me call if you ever wish my aid again!"

"Yonan!" she shaped the word in her own mind and suddenly felt an inflow of aid. She had managed to enlist Wittle after all. "Yonan!"

She saw that dark shadow halt and the fingers slip from the hilt to the blade beneath. The Quan took on a deeper gleam and the shadow which surely was Yonan swung to the right. Kelsie reached for the arm of the witch and felt her finger bite deeply into the other's spare flesh.

"Call!"

"Yonan," at each repetition of that name, aided by, she was sure, the picture she continued to hold in her mind, that shadow moved now more swiftly as if on the track of something which brushed the risks of chance from its passage.

There was light in the dark, dim and hard to see—the girl thought of the glimmer of the fungi along the walls. She saw the man with the sword. They had left him his mail along with his weapon. Perhaps it was the latter their captors had feared, not for its point (though she knew he had made good play with that) but for the talisman bound into its hilt. Just as they had not taken her jewel.

"Yonan!"

There came a faint answer. "I come!"

"Fool!" If Wittle had aided in that first call she was no longer doing so now. "What need have we for him? These," she touched her own jewel lightly, "are enough to win us out."

"I call one who is one of us—" Kelsie began, her temper rising in that inner heat which might lead to such recklessness as that which had brought her into this perilous land in the beginning. "He—"

"Is a man!" The witch interrupted her. "What power has he beside the power of fighting arm? We need no weapon—"

"Except these," Kelsie reminded her, pointing to the two stones between them.

Wittle grimaced. "The power is overlaid by this about us. We shall have to use it to the best of our ability to call. Were you one of the sisters—" her voice died away but there was still in her eyes the animosity which Kelsie had always seen there.

"I am not!" Kelsie was quick to deny. She did not know why the jewel had come alive in her hands but she refused to believe that some part of her was akin to this thin, bitter woman.

"Where are we?" she asked.

Wittle pursed her lips as if she doubted the need for Kelsie's question. Then she answered:

"This is a place of the Sarn Riders. Of them we know but little—"

"And none of it good," Kelsie finished when she hesitated. "Who are they, then?"

"They serve some great Dark One. Who they are and why they serve . . ." she shrugged. "Both Light and Dark draw together strange partners. In Estcarp we would know. Here," she made a small gesture with the hand which hovered over the jewel, "I cannot say. Those in the Valley hold by only one of the true adepts. There may be more of those left. Not all were eaten up by their enemies or withdrew into other worlds." For the first time she seemed to be under the urge to talk. Kelsie was very content to let her. The more she could learn the better, even though much of what Wittle said could be guesses only.

"These adepts—" she encouraged.

"They are the ones who would rule all. Some withdrew and were neither of the Light nor the Dark but followed paths of their own. Others struggled for power and there were wars, ah, such wars! Even the earth was wrung by the strengths they called upon. For the tissue of life itself can be changed if the will is great enough."

Kelsie thought of the stories she had heard in the Valley. "Did not those sisters of yours reach such powers? Did they not move mountains with their words of command, so that the enemy could not come upon them?"

"And so they died," replied the witch somberly. "For the power we called upon then burnt out many of the sisterhood. Thus—it is thus we must find that which will recharge our jewels to a greater holding than they have ever known."

"And this greater power, do you think that you will find it here?"

"It was pulling us—for like is pulled to like, and with the stones charged with the same energy we shall be led to the source of it. No, fool, it does not lie hereabout or none of this," again she made that small one-handed gesture, "would exist. Here," she reached behind her and pulled forward a travel-stained pack, much like the one Kelsie had lost in the burrow of the Thas. "Eat and drink—"

As if those two words had been a signal both her dry throat and her empty stomach made themselves known. The girl pulled out a metal flask and allowed herself a few sips of insipid and musty tasting water. This was followed by crumbs of a half-eaten round of journey bread. But the stench of the rank growth about her took much of her need for food. That smell rendered nauseating all she ate or drank.

Wittle leaned forward once again and was peering intently into the halo of dim light which circled about the two stones, springing from their point of touch. She began to intone in a voice hardly above a whisper, using her forefinger to sign in the air. Though there was no blue-lined answer to her now.

Kelsie crowded forward to see any picture which the stones might produce. But what she did perceive was instead lines of what might have been an unknown script. And she worried about the summoning of such in the very heart of one of the enemy strongholds.

Wittle was still repeating queer singsong uttered words in a murmur when Kelsie turned her head sharply and strove to look over her shoulder. The sense of being watched had come suddenly but it was so strong she was not surprised to see a figure dimmed by the fog of the red stream coming forward.

She had her knife and it was ready in her hand. At her hissed warning Wittle did not even look up or break her concentration upon the stones. But a moment later Kelsie was on her feet, moving through the haze, jerking from the ground the gem as she went to call to that shadow figure.

"Yonan! Here!"

Her call was near drowned out by a screech from Wittle as the stone against stone formation was broken. The witch sprang at Kelsie, clawing for the chain swinging from her hand. So that the girl had to turn and beat off her attack and did not see Yonan make the same spring which had brought her earlier to this sliver of ground free from the noisome vegetation.

"The stone—give it to me!" Wittle cried. "Almost I learned—stupid wench. Almost I had touched upon what rules here!"

"Be glad that you did not!" It was Yonan who answered that. There was a smear of dried blood, bits of it flaking off as he spoke, down the side of his face. He had one arm across his chest, the hand thrust into his sword belt and there were pain lines about his mouth. But he was gripping his sword by the blade close to the hilt and the Quan iron was fully revealed.

"This is Nexus—" he added as he came closer.

To Kelsie the word meant nothing and she thought that Wittle was similarly ignorant until suddenly a shadow crossed the witch's sharp features.

"That is legend—" she said in that same sour voice she had always used when she spoke to Yonan.

"Much in Escore is legend come to truth," he said. "How did you get here—did you not see the Fooger Beast—?"

"I slept for I was wearied; I awakened here," the witch returned. "The Fooger—!" It was as if she had bitten on something harsh and stinging.

"The Fooger. We are within it, Witch. And I do not think that any power of yours is going to get us out."

She pointed to the gem still swinging from Kelsie's hand. "There are two of these and," she gestured at his sword, "and what you carry."

"These against that which shaped the Fooger—" His lips quirked at the edges into something which was certainly not a smile but suggested derision.

"Small stones to bring down the enemy full armed and with weapons which we may not have known before. How come you here, Lady?" He swung so sharply to Kelsie that she stammered over the first word of her answer. But she told as swiftly as she could of her journey down the dark passages and her final emergence guided by the witch to this place.

His frown grew. "Thus I was brought also—by your calling on me. Have you thought that perhaps that which holds us wanted us together so that it might wait and see what we should do then, what power we can summon to break us out?"

Kelsie accepted the logical reasoning of that but Wittle shook her head vigorously. "Such as you envision, warrior, would not wish even the smallest of Light weapons to be used within its hold. Balanced always is the power and if that balance shifts but a trifle, the merest finger's breadth or less, then all within its range are affected. Why do you think they left us these?" she waved her jewel in Yonan's face. "Because they cannot handle what might be provoked into life should they meddle with them. Yes, it is true that they may have brought us together for some purpose of their own but also it may be as a test—to see if we dare to stand up to their might."

"You speak of 'they,'" Yonan said. "Who are these then? Sarn Riders and Thas? Their like we know. But the Fooger—"

"Is perhaps lying dead!" snapped Wittle. "What is death but a gate and we of the mysteries know many gates. Was not the adept Hilarion summoned back through the one he himself had opened when the Tregarth traitoress went a-meddling? So I speak of 'they' and you would know who and what they may be? Think upon your darkest nightmare and then count that light against what comes from the Dark, warrior."

"If they would test us, why bring us together?" he said musingly as if he asked that question of himself and not of Wittle. But Kelsie thought she could answer that.

She had settled down again on the sweep of clean gravel and was slipping the jewel from one hand to another.

"They would see what we can do when we try to defend ourselves— the three of us together—"

Wittle favored her with a grimace. "Have I not already said it? And have we not already given them a showing of banner in that we *HAVE* come together?"

Yonan stood looking about the cavern. It was perhaps larger than the one which held the basin of fire, but the most of it was choked by the growth. And the constant stench of that made Kelsie nauseous so that she was like to lose the small mouthfuls she had taken. It was Yonan who moved first. Without a word to Wittle he used the Point of his ensorceled weapon and drew about the three of them a five-pointed star, digging deep in the sand and gravel to keep the line intact. Wittle watched him and for the first time Kelsie saw a shade of astonishment on the witch's face.

"What would you do?" she demanded. He neither answered nor looked to her but out of his belt pouch he took a mass wrapped in a withered leaf. Kelsie caught the unforgettable aroma of illbane. At each point of the star he faced outward and, spearing a bit of the crushed herb on his sword point, he planted it in the ground.

"Fool!" Wittle came to life and moved as if to erase the marking nearest her. He swung around and in a quick movement slashed downward before her the sword as if so locking her in.

"They will come," she screeched at him, both her hands cupping her jewel. "To set up a place of power within their own holding—you are a madman."

"I am one," he returned, "who wants to see his opponent. Fighting blind here will avail us nothing. Do you," now he spoke directly to Kelsie, "take your jewel and," he turned a fraction toward Wittle, "you know the signs—use them and let her follow. We are now locked within this hold, better that we learn what will come of us—"

For a long moment Kelsie thought Wittle would refuse. Then stiffly as if each gesture she made was forced out of her, she knelt and reached out one long stick-thin arm so that she might use the point of her jewel to draw in the slipping ground a line here, a circle there—and more intricate symbol somewhere else. When she had done in the first of the points Yonan gestured to Kelsie so that the girl squatted on her heels and tried to copy the signs—though she doubted much her ability to match them, so loose was the soil. Around the inner part of the star the two of them crept, Kelsie duplicating as best she could all that Wittle did.

She had more than half expected that the witch would utterly defy Yonan's orders, yet she tamely obeyed him. Perhaps within her she thought that what they did might establish—for a space—an island of safety.

Only it was not meant to work that way. For when she had done and arose, Kelsie behind her, she favored Yonan with a display of yellowish teeth which surely was no smile.

"SO—the bait awaits, warrior. What do you expect to bring into being by defying the balance here?"

"What you wish to see as well as I," he replied. "I do not fight blind when there is a chance of seeing openly."

"You shall see," she cackled. "Oh, yes, you shall see!"

Kelsie swung about where she stood and began carefully to examine the vegetation on each side, turning slowly. So grotesque was that growth and in such tangle anything might be creeping upon them now unseen until it reached the very edge of the open space. That they were now bait she firmly believed.

But as the minutes passed, her heart beat slowly. She could see nothing moving and the growth remained the same. Nor did anything come out of the river. Wittle spoke first.

"They know how helpless we are," she said grimly, "why trouble themselves with us?"

"Balance," Yonan said firmly. "Balance. In the heart of their own holding there is this." With his sword he pointed to the star about them. It seemed to Kelsie that she could smell the fragrant freshness of the illbane combating the stench of the growth.

A tendril of haze snaked out from that murk which clothed the stream. It was almost like the weighted line Yonan had used to bring down the birds in his hunting, but this was aimed at them. It curled like the lash of a whip through the air. But when it reached the star it snapped back.

Wittle again made that harsh sound which was her laughter. "Do you think that is all they have to send against us?" she demanded.

Yonan did not answer. He had stooped and picked up one of the small stones which studded the sand at his feet. Now he blew upon it and then spat, rubbing the moisture into it with his thumb. Having done so he rubbed the stone three times against the Quad iron of his sword hilt and called upon a name Kelsie had heard him summon before.

"Ninutra!"

Out toward the questing tongue of haze he hurled the stone. It passed through that arm of mist and that lifted for a moment so that Kelsie saw the stone fall into the red river. The liquid there roiled, churned, droplets arose to sprinkle the vegetation which straightway fell into a black liquid rot. And the mist snapped back toward its source.

"Child's play!" Wittle said. "And who is Ninutra? Some Old One long since gone?"

"If she has gone," he replied, "then she has left certain strengths behind her. I serve a Lady who is her chosen voice in the here and now. And—"

"Look!" Kelsie interrupted him.

From out of the river where the stone had fallen there arose something which chilled and sickened her. Perhaps once it had had life—it must have had—but this was the worst of death's decay incarnate. Half-skeleton, half-boiled and seared flesh, it was tossed ashore as if the river itself had so sent one of its slaves to dispute with them. Was it a man—or had it been a man? Kelsie wanted to close her eyes, to refuse to look upon it but she could not.

Slowly, clumsily it got to its feet and for the first time turned the blob of its head in their direction. Kelsie cried out. Those swollen, bloated features were ones she knew—Yonan's!

She heard him whisper from beside her. "Uruk—NO!" While Wittle seized upon her jewel and cried out "Makeease!"

The half-eaten away features of the thing writhed and changed—now the girl saw Dahaun wasted and blasted, and after her Simon Tregarth. While from her companions, she heard other names given to that nightmare.

It tottered on legs which were bare bone, heading for the star. Kelsie gripped the jewel and in her mind refused any belief—this could not be true. It was not true! Even as the thing became Yonan once more she cried out:

"No—it is not true!"

Yonan—that was no longer Yonan, nor Dahaun, nor the eldest of the Tregarths. It was her own blasted face which crowned the shambling figure.

14

It wavered to and fro on its bony feet as it continued to advance and Kelsie cowered back, though Wittle's hand shot out and caught at her before she stepped outside the star.

"Illusion!" croaked the witch, though Kelsie saw her straight mouth twitch as if she barely stifled some cry of her own. "They play with illusion!" She held out her hand, pointing her gem toward the thing from the rivulet.

There was no bright sword thrust of power as there had been on other occasions, only a small diffusion of a bluish haze clinging around the stone itself. And still the horror came ahead. Yonan raised his sword to ready. But the thing had reached the edge of the star and shifted from one foot to another as if it were faced by an impassable barrier.

"Ah—" the sound came from Wittle like a long drawn out sigh of relief. "By so much the old knowledge holds—by so much!"

The shambling figure turned first right and then left as if trying for a free path to reach its prey. It seemed to Kelsie that it grew more solid and real every moment. It was still her own face that it half wore, though she believed now that it showed another countenance to each of the two with her. There was a wavering, the thing swayed back and forth and then plunged forward as if some giant hand aimed at its back had sent it so to confront them. It fell across one of the points of the star and there was a blast of light which left Kelsie blinded, then with blurred sight.

Where the figure had fallen there was a stinking mass of stuff which still moved feebly as if the force which had given it pseudo life still urged it on. Then it crumpled away to black ash. But it had been the key to unlock the fort Yonan had erected and Kelsie felt the chill of the utter dark through which she had once passed sweep in over that break point.

Though she could see nothing, that cold clung to her, wrapping her in and she felt a viscid stuff netting her prisoner. Wittle's arm with the hand which held her jewel beat at the air and Yonan slammed out with his sword hilt, the blade gripped with his fingers. All to no purpose.

Kelsie was motionless. That invisible web had her entirely in its power now, she could not even move a finger across the surface of her own jewel. She saw Wittle's arm fall to her side as if struck down by some heavy blow, Yonan's reversed sword play fail. They were all caught by what had won through the boundaries of the star. Then, against her will and by no action of her own, the hand which held the chain of her jewel began to quiver and shake. However, her fingers locked on the links did not move. Back and forth, more and more wildly shook her hand, the gem swung but it did not fall, nor did it part company with her flesh. She had a sudden mind picture of the jewel flying out to land in the red rivulet and being overwhelmed, that if she would save her life this is what must happen. Then over that slid another picture, the young witch who had died on the hillside, her lips shaping her own forbidden name as she gave that to Kelsie. With her was another head also, that of the wildcat, its lips drawn back in a full snarl, daring McAdams, ready to spend its life for its kits and freedom.

Around and around whirled her arm and the pain of those wild swings which pulled at her muscles grew more intense. There was also a twisting now, a pulling. And still the chain clung to her as if it were a part of her own flesh and nothing would take it from her unless the enemy, whoever or whatever that might be, would scrape that from her bones. Twice she cried out against sudden shocks of pain, in spite of her promise to herself that she could and would endure.

She could see both Wittle and Yonan. They stood statue stiff and neither of them appeared under attack. Did what assailed them believe that she was the weakest of their company, the one most likely to give way? Somewhere under the fear which had held her since that creature had come out of the mist anger stirred. That emotion grew as the assault upon her doubled in its fury.

Deliberately now she summoned up the picture of the young witch who had died. She could not call upon Wittle—perhaps she was held now against a similar attack—but she was trained, one with her stone as Kelsie did not feel herself to be. As the cat had faced McAdams so did she snarl and stand trying to wrest from that other power the control over her own body.

She had a sense of anger and frustration—not her own but coming from somewhere beyond. Then she was struck a sudden buffet between her shoulders, driving her to her knees, and was enveloped in that sharp stench which was the mark of the evil.

Something cried out in a high squalling voice and now came a blow on the back of her head, sending her flat with a weight on her back. Gravel gritted against her cheek and her body rocked under blows. Her arm was seized and drawn backward at a painful angle. Once more her wrist snapped to and fro under vigorous shaking. The chain remained as much a part of her as the fingers curved about the links. She tried to throw off the weight upon her and managed to shift her face around to see one of those which bestrode her—shaggy, rootlike covering—Thas.

The servant of the Sarns grabbed at her hand. She felt the sharp pain of teeth in her flesh and then there was a convulsive jerking to the body perched on hers and the Thas rolled off to lie beside her, its rootlike fingers, its thin arms, threading wildly in the air. She caught a glimpse of red eyes in the ill-fashioned face and then those eyes clouded. The limbs fell to the gravel limply and there was no more struggle out of it.

Yonan—had he won to freedom and used his sword? Wittle she could see, still standing, still staring not at the struggle on the ground at her very feet, but at the haze which masked the rivulet as if she expected some further attack out of that.

Kelsie tried to draw up one foot, get to her knees. The cold shell still held a part of her but the attack of the Thas appeared to have broken through it and now it was as if pieces of net tore and fell away.

She dragged her arm around and saw the tooth marks on her wrist slowly welling with blood which striped both the chain and the stone it supported. Her body ached from the attack but slowly she won to her knees, her hurt wrist nursed against her body.

Yonan stood even as Wittle faced outward. But she could see his features, not set as those of the witch, but his eyes striving to catch hers. His mouth open as if he shouted some war cry she could not hear.

On impulse she reached out with the hand dripping blood and set it to his mail-clad thigh which was nearest her. A shudder ran through his body and he turned his head fully to look at her. A moment later he had stooped to support her, draw her up to her feet leaning against him, the dead Thas kicked aside that he might come closer. If Wittle was still bound it was plain that he had been freed.

He reached out to take her bitten arm and then his fingers snapped back as if they had been beaten off. Whatever had kept chain and stone with her during that attack was still in force. Now Yonan brought his sword around, cautiously advancing the hilt so that it was in touching distance of that invincible chain.

The Quan iron slid easily through and over, caught at a loop of the chain, drawing that away from the wound which was bleeding steadily.

Kelsie felt her other arm and hand tingle as if recovering from some paralyzing force. She put out her finger and touched the chain. At her touch they loosened and she was able to take jewel and chain into her other hand.

She sat at last, the throbbing in her wrist not unlike that beat of the vibration around them, her injured wrist resting on her knee where Yonan had placed it after binding it with a strip of her own shirt and some of the dust of the illbane he had managed to shake out of his bag. Wittle had blinked and then turned her head to look at the two of them, as if just awaking from a dream. Yonan had booted the body of the Thas out of the star but, though he redrew it with sword point, he had not enough of the herbs left for its guarding points.

"You have not won—" Wittle broke the silence which had held them all from the moment of the Thas attack. "This was merely a feint to learn what powers we held."

And it picked me, Kelsie thought, though she did not speak her guess aloud, as the weakest point in our defenses. Yonan might have guessed her belief for he said:

"They sent the Thas. They would not have used such force if they had believed they could take us by will and power alone. They—"

Kelsie slipped the chain of the jewel about her neck again and it rested on her breast just above where she cradled her bitten wrist against her body. "Who are *they?*" As she had tried to learn earlier from Wittle so she asked him now.

"Old ones—perhaps even an adept tied somehow to this land. Only he caught, with his force, something which he can neither digest nor subdue." Yonan was again at the star redrawing the lines. "In the heart of his own place he has . . . us!"

Wittle turned her head. Her face was expressionless but her eyes glittered. When she spoke it was directly to Kelsie, ignoring the warrior:

"What have you, outlander, which stands so against the Dark? What is the power that you control?"

Kelsie shook her head. "No power that I know of. They will be back?" Once she had stood up to the battle, a second one she was not sure she could face.

"As he said," Wittle pointed with her chin to where Yonan stood, feet slightly apart as if about to engage in combat, all his attention now for the haze about the stream, "we are within territory where the lord here, whoever or whatever he may be, would destroy us—or have us forth. Warrior!" she raised her grating voice a fraction. "Look to your sword. We have yet to face the worst they can send. What does one do to a piece of grit within one's boot—one shakes it out. It may well be that he or it—or she—cannot use full strength here lest the defenses of this place be damaged. Therefore—it will shake us forth—"

As if her words had been the recital of a spell there came a sudden change to that ribbon of fog about the river. It split and peeled away on either side revealing the narrow part of that shore, which Kelsie had earlier leaped to come here, and held so—clearly an invitation to leave.

Leave so that they could be easily hunted down in some one of the passageways which ran from this cavern? Kelsie's wrist throbbed and her other hand cupped over the jewel could have held only dull stone for all its response to that invitation.

Slowly Yonan worked his way out to the place where the noisome thing from the stream had essayed its attack. He carefully skirted the shriveled mass on the sand and stood now at the very edge of the rivulet. Reaching forward he put out the hilt of his sword toward the nearest clump of the fungilike growth.

It moved, actually pulling away from the Quan iron. Wittle, as if not to be left behind, had swung out her jewel and the misty emanation from that, nebulous as it was, had the same effect on another of the bulbous plants. Under Kelsie's hand her own stone moved and grew a little warmer.

"Can you foresee?" Yonan rounded on the witch. "Is that gem of yours a compass for our going?"

She shrugged. "Who knows. But if we remain here we shall never know, shall we?"

Kelsie bit her lip. To go out of this small haven of safety broken though it was now—she could not raise a voice to say yes. The pain in her wrist had spread up her arm, was slowly fighting a way into the rest of her body. She was not even sure she could get once more to her feet and go now. Yet the witch, as if to show the strength of her own charm and power, had passed Yonan, taking the lead and swinging the stone from side to side as she went until she kilted up the stained skirt of her robe and sprang across the stream. Yonan turned to Kelsie holding out his free hand and once more pulling her up beside him.

"She is right," he said, "To remain here self chained and wait for what more they can send against us—that is folly."

She allowed him to lead her to the stream bank, wanting to close her eyes lest some new horror arise from there to take them as they crossed. But cross they did and without any interference from what dwelt here. But to get out—that was a different matter and in her innermost mind Kelsie never believed they could or would make it. They would wander through the warren of passages until hunger and thirst weakened them to be easy for the taking, or some other servants of the Dark would run them down. She remembered very well the hounds of the Sarn and those grim Riders themselves.

Wittle stalked ahead and was entering one of the passage openings before they had caught up with her. The pain which had earlier been like fire in her veins now left Kelsie's wrist and arm limp and numb. She staggered now and then but Yonan's hand was always ready to support her.

Back in the passage it was dark, only the scattered patches of growth gave them thin light and those grew further and further apart as they passed. Kelsie listened as she went, sure that she would hear soon sounds of pursuit, yet those did not come. Perhaps they were in some manner being herded toward a place where they would be easier to handle. Why Wittle moved so unceasingly, seeming to find choice between passages so easy to make, the witch did not explain.

Now there was light ahead—not a red glare, nor the sickly glimmers thrown off by a multitude of fungous vegetation—rather a gray gleam rounded a corner and was gone. Yonan led Kelsie after and they came out suddenly into an opening which drew a cry from Kelsie as she pulled backward two or three steps which might have ended in a ghastly fall.

The three of them were crowded on a space which could hardly support them. And they were high in the air above red stone. Kelsie held with her good hand to the edge of the door from which they had just emerged. But Yonan edged forward to look down into the space which surrounded them.

In a moment he was back. Wittle had seemed to drop once more into one of her possessed times when nothing about her could matter.

"We are on the monster's head," the warrior reported. "We must climb down."

Kelsie nursed her numb hand and arm and remembered only too well how the monstrous carving or building had towered above the skull road they had followed. She had no hope of daring to descend the outer surface of that. No wonder they had passed so unchallenged through the last ways. She did not doubt that the enemy knew exactly where they were and had a good method of handling them in this exposed position. Why, an eruption of Thas from the mouth where she now rested could send them out into space. To say nothing of what the Sarn Riders could do with their fiery bolts.

"There is no way down," she said dully.

He was standing over her again and now he pulled her to her feet with less gentleness than he had used before.

"There is a way!" His voice was an imperative as if he had shouted in her ear.

"Look!" he pointed out a moment later.

There was an overhang beneath where they stood and the flare-out of a rounded ledge. All was pitted by time's erosion with holes for fingers and feet. Were it not for her wrist pulsating with dull pain she conceded she might be able to climb down. But one handed she could not begin to try. However, it seemed that Yonan had taken that also into consideration.

He was working at the clasp of his sword belt and had that free before she could protest. Now he reached for her again.

"Your belt!" he demanded. One handedly she tried to obey, only to have him push aside her hand and open the clasp himself. Then he buckled two ends together, testing them over his bent knee. He set together the end of her own belt in a sling which he motioned her to put over her good shoulder and drew her to the lip of the drop.

"Down!"

Because she inwardly shrank from that action she set her teeth and made herself crawl over, dangling in a sickening fashion out into space, refusing to look at anything but the pitted stone before her until her boots did thud home on the bubble of the cheek of that hideous visage and she looked perforce into one of the eye holes. She flinched away and pulled herself as far from that as she could get. For in its depth either memory played her false or she had seen the reflection of the flames which had danced in the bowl of that chamber of death she had spied upon.

Yonan had said nothing to Wittle but apparently the witch had decided on her own that escape was possible and she came down from one handhold to the next. However, Yonan won there before her and then busied with Kelsie lowering her farther—to the thing's puffy shoulder.

She was wet with sweat when a last swing brought her to the ground after a time she had no desire to remember. Twice she had knocked the elbow of her wounded hand and the pain of that nearly made her sick so that it had been hard to even think what she was about until she made a last descent from the monster's folded knee and felt dry earth under her weak and shaking legs. Then Yonan was beside her and she saw through eyes dimmed with tears of pain the back of the witch who was striding away from them as if she no longer chose to be one of their company.

Yonan got Kelsie to her own feet and steered her in the direction of the witch, keeping a close hand on the belt which still hung from her shoulder. Every moment when she could think at all beyond the pain of her arm Kelsie expected to hear from behind the hoarse bellowing of a hound, perhaps the shout of a Sarn Rider urging on a hunt. But there was nothing.

She turned to the warrior who was half supporting her. "They will not let us go—" she got out that protest.

"Have they in truth?" he returned. "They seek what that one," he nodded to the witch now well ahead of them, "came here to find. Why not give her an illusion of freedom and let her lead them to what they would have also. Do you think that they have put aside all interest in why we roam where those of the Light have not ventured much before?"

"Then—you believe that it was all play with us?" she faltered. Three mice and a sleepy-eyed cat that let its prey run a little and then brought down a paw to end the game.

"Some of it was testing, I think. But I also believe that had they not wished it we would never have come alive out of that place."

She tried to push aside his grim reply but the logic of it was too sound. They were mice, allowed to run. And there were those or *THAT* which would watch them well from now on.

However, if Yonan believed in what he said he acted as if their escape had been a true one, keeping a good pace and helping Kelsie to equal it. She purposely did not look back, for, in her mind, was a picture of the squatting monster rising leisurely and setting out in their wake ready to bring stamping foot or clutching hand upon them when and if it wished.

They had come to a tangle of growth—not the fleshy fungi of the inner ways but rather rank stuff with good-sized thorns, and it seemed to be so matted and grown together there was no way to get through it.

Only Wittle still in advance swung out her jewel which flashed as it never had in the inner ways and sparks from it fell into the mass from which arose small twists of smoke and a backaway shriveling of the growing stuff.

If the witch believed also that they were allowed to run free just to bring their search to an end, she showed no sign of that, nor did she do anything to cover her trail. But the brush flaked swiftly into ash and parted before her and the other two followed where she led. Kelsie wondered how much longer she could keep her feet to stumble on. The pain had risen to her shoulder and was now moving over across her breast so that she could hardly draw a full breath. She wanted nothing so much as to lie down, close her eyes, and fall into a black nothingness.

Nor was she aware when the brush about them ceased to be an entwined matting of thorns and became fresh and well growing bushes, some with flowers enough to give forth scent. Save that she was free at last of the stench of the burrows Kelsie was indifferent to everything but the claims of her own hurt body and she roused only when Yonan's grip, which had grown more and more compelling, lightened and she was lowered to the ground.

From somewhere came the sound of running water—water or fire? She strove to struggle up again to make sure she was not back in the cavern. Wittle, bending over her, pushed her back and the other's touch on her body brought with it such a thrust of pain that she dropped back into darkness at last.

There was a time when a fire did burn not too far away. And she was aware that the belt held now not her hurt arm but her good one. There was a punishing weight on her hurt arm and shoulder, so that she cried out and through tears saw Yonan waveringly turn from the fire, his sword in hand.

The blade plunged down on her wrist. But what followed was not searing torment but cold, icy cold as if she lay in a bank of snow near frozen. And the cold spread from that touch up her arm into her body. She was awake inside the envelope of that flesh and bone but it would not obey her, nor could she even give tongue to ease the torture of the cold.

It withdrew and she felt the return of the fire, all the worse now because of the cold which had produced it. She heard words but they did not mean anything.

"The poison spreads—she will die—" Was that Yonan? Did it matter? Dead—maybe she was already dead or so near that gateway that she was done with struggle.

"Where is your jewel, Lady—?"

"It is not for such a purpose."

"No? You would let her die when you know that she means much to your search?"

"I can search alone—"

"Was that what your council asked of you?"

"You are a man—what do you know of power?"

"Enough to judge that you can use it for more than one thing, Lady. And I say—use it here—and now!"

Once more the cold—the aching numbness returned—she fell down the monster's length—perhaps—but it was all darkness at the bottom.

15

Kelsie was walking, though it was no more than a weak stumble upheld by the strength of another. When she strove to focus her eyes what she saw just ahead was the swing of a gray robe. Or was it that? Fur? The upheld banner of a cat's tail as that animal, grown to panther size, stalked ahead of her. Cat—there was a cat—and a gate—and after that a wild range of action which one part of her had never accepted as reality. She raised her hand in a gesture which demanded a mighty effort. There was no chain embedded in the flesh about its wrist—but there were scars there which certainly she had never borne before.

"Lady—" from some distance came that call. Kelsie tried to refuse to hear it. Just as she tried to command her legs to halt, to let her rest.

"Lady!"

More strident, demanding. Somehow she made the very great effort to turn her head and look to a face half masked by a war helm. The gray robe tail before her twitched and swirled as its wearer halted and turned to look at her.

"Girl!" there was no concern in that, only demand. "Look to the jewel!"

From somewhere, a third of the way down her weakened body, there came a glow. She dropped her head a little and saw that there was a spot of twirling light on her breast. She moved her scarred hand up to clasp it. Fire! Immediately she dropped her hand—there had been blasting fire before, she wanted none of that again.

"We are followed," those words were spoken over her and meant nothing.

"Can you aid then? What of the jewel, will it not sustain one who wears it?"

"One who wears it rightfully, who does not come to it by the left hand as this one does—perhaps—" Was it the cat who answered? Kelsie really did not care. If they would only leave her alone!

"Let—me—go—" she got out those words with great effort.

She swayed back and forth in the hands of the one who had been leading her, while the cat stood and watched and would have nothing to do with the matter.

"Come—Lady—wake! They sniff behind us and we cannot let them catch up with us."

Her hand batting blindly before her, closed now upon the jewel on her own breast. Then—

She stood in a place where there were many pillars though few of them still supported any remains of roof. The black marks of ancient fires sooted paths up the outer ones. But she had not come here to see the remaining disaster—she had come because she must. There was that which drove on her weakened body. Again in the very far distance she heard voices which had no real meaning:

"Where does she go?"

"Loose her, fool. The drawing of the stone is on her where she goes—that is our road."

There were the pillars and she passed them, but, still, though the outer ones stood behind her there were ranks upon ranks of others reaching to the far distance so she could see no end to the way between them. Once her path tightened to a double line of the stone trees and she saw behind them great chairs of state. Each of those was occupied by a weaving and wreathing of smoke as if what sat there was or could not be wholly fixed in this world. If those shadows of shadows meant her ill they did not move to stop her, nor turn her from the way. On she passed with the burning jewel in her hand and there was nothing left for her but to seek what had been lost and must be found again.

How many miles did that pillar path run? She might have been walking an hour, or a day, and still there was no end. Now there crouched strange and grotesque beasts between the upright columns of stone but none laid paw nor tooth upon her as she slipped on. For she did not seem to be walking any longer, instead she was—

Awake! That waking was sharp, she might have been brought out of sleep by a blow. She knew who she was—who wore that gray robe and now marched to her left, who matched step with her to the right and upheld her body. It was night and the moon, just beginning to wane, brought sharp light and shadow to the ground around her.

They were no longer in a wood but on an open plain where they must be clearly visible to any who followed them and she turned her head to ask of him who so guided her what they did here—

Only she already knew. She must follow where the jewel led. Although she no longer held it cradled in her hand, rather it was stretched forward on its chain, away from her body, she could even feel the fret of the chain against her neck as if it would be free of all anchorage, free to seize its own road and speed to reach what called it so.

There was another bright glow. The other gem, the one worn by Wittle, was also alive but it did not pull against its chain and Kelsie believed its glow was not as great as the one she wore.

"Where are we?" she managed that question and her voice came out more strongly than she had felt it would.

Wittle answered almost breathlessly:

"This is the path you have chosen, yours the answer. Where are we? We have walked through a day and when we rested it was necessary to curb you like a restless horse. We have walked through much of the night. And those who hunt, hunt—yet they bring not their hunt to take us—not yet. You were never wedded to the stone, so how comes it that that jewel takes life as I have never seen before? What do you with it, outlander?"

"I do nothing. It is the stone—"

"They have always told us," Wittle continued as if Kelsie had not spoken at all, "that when a witch dies, so does the power of her stone. Yet Makeease is dead and you who have no right to it are governed by it. This is a thing beyond the bounds of what must be."

Kelsie longed to raise her hand and drag the thing from about her throat, hurl it out into the ocean of tall grass through which they now strode.

"It is no choice of mine—" she said dully.

"This is a thing which—"

"Why keep you on that rack of speech?" Yonan broke in. "You have said it far too many times. It should not be but it is. Therefore accept it."

The witch turned her head and the look which flashed past Kelsie to the warrior was one of pure and blazing anger.

"Be quiet, man. What do your kind know of the mysteries?"

Kelsie had a flash of memory but it was vague as if she watched it happen to another. Of the Quan iron hilt being pressed to the wound in her wrist and then lips sucking—then the cold of a jewel following upon that.

"He won me life," she said out of that memory. "Of what good your spells were then, Wittle? And I think," she was frowning a little, "that we come upon something which is stronger than a jewel." Her head was being bent forward and now the jewel she wore was tugging as if to free itself entirely from her body. Yet she understood in part that were it to vanish along the path it had found for itself she would lose all trace of it.

Even the witch's own jewel grew brighter, lifted a little from the gray robe.

The sea of grass tall enough to switch about their knees had been broken by what lay ahead—some shadows which might be heights, save there was no range of mountains—only a soft rolling as for hills. They were headed directly for that shadowed land.

Twice birds swooped and soared over them—black and red feathers showing up plainly even in the dull light. And, while they made no move toward attack, Kelsie was certain that these were of the Dark, perhaps scouts for the Sarn Riders or those like them. Yet the three of them made no effort toward concealment but headed straight for the hills across the open plain.

Wittle was repeating some words, by the sound of them the same ones over and over. Yonan marched without any comment, but always at her side, close enough to reach out and touch her should some necessity for that arise.

The moon made sharp divisions between light and dark. Here and there a bush grew above the green of the plain and she eyed each of those with apprehension for it seemed to her that the shadows those bushes threw were not like in outline to the shrubs at all but had a curious shifting as if something invisible but still answering the power of the moonlight lurked therein.

A first pale streak of dawn was in the sky when their footing changed. They were not walking over a pavement of half-buried skulls but the grass became thin clumps edging up between blocks of white stone which had undoubtedly once formed a road. And as they fell into step on that rough surface where many of the blocks were uptilted Kelsie became aware of something else. She could not hear nor see, she could only feel it—that greater compulsion, the sense that what must be done must be accomplished quickly, filled her and she began to trot. Wittle and Yonan, after a moment matching her stride for stride.

The road led through a gap in the first line of hills and on either side as they entered that open space there were stone pillars, rough hewn, licked by time into uneven surfaces so that only fragments of what might be designs or patterns remained.

As she passed between these, a little ahead of her two companions, something very far within her stirred. This was certainly not of her own memory but she raised both hands in a salute to the east and to the west. Excitement flashed into life within her.

On ran the road, in better condition here where there was less growth of grass to impinge upon the surface. From the pillars there continued a line of hummocks or small rounded stones, perhaps never meant as walls but to mark more clearly the path. Twice they turned with the road, once right, once left. Then their way was blocked by the rise of a larger hillock straight across its surface. To this Kelsie went, the stone tugging at her as if she were on a leash. Then she found herself spread-eagled against the very side of the earth, the gem a small fire between her breast and the soil against which she involuntarily pressed her body, as if her strength alone could draw her into the earth to seek what the Witch Jewel sought.

She turned her head and looked to Wittle. Her jewel also was now standing away from her body, on a direct line with the hill.

"Within—or beyond," the witch said.

Kelsie found herself digging with crooked fingers at the turf and soil, trying to burrow within as might an animal seeking a den. She saw Wittle's fingers reach out to copy her. Then they were both pulled away and Yonan took their place, hacking with his sword at the covering of the tough-rooted grass. The Quan iron in his hilt was ablaze as Kelsie had not seen it before.

He pried and pulled and there came loose a large slab of soil mixed with roots. Under that, plain to see in the dawn light was stone, streaked and earth stained. He attacked again and again until there was a slab as big as a doorway facing them.

Kelsie gave an involuntary cry. She was pulled forward as her stone fitted itself against that doorway, being thrown to her knees so that the bursting fire of the jewel came where normally there might be a latch. Against that stone, though she tried to tug it away with her hands, or to protect her face from coming in contact with the rough rock, the jewel began to turn, slowly and steadily to the right, twisting its chain and shutting off her breath as if she were being garroted by the silver lengths. She got her hands between her throat and that twisted loop but she could not break its hold upon her, nor free the jewel again from the stone to which it clung.

She cried out in a choking croak for aid and Yonan was beside her, his dagger beating down against the chain. She was gasping for breath when his assault was successful and the chain broke suddenly as she fell gasping, rubbing her throat and drawing in deep lungfuls of air. Then she saw that Wittle had fallen on her knees to take her place. As Kelsie's stone had circled right so did the witch's now plant itself beside the other and turn left.

But, warned by Kelsie's experience, the witch had withdrawn the chain from her throat and now she kept hold but was not prisoner of a choking line of links. Right from top to bottom passed one gem like a hand on a clock face, and on the left the other followed the same pattern. They glowed with a fierce fire so that Kelsie shaded her eyes unable to look upon them.

There was a sucking sound, and then a dull grating. Yonan's hands on her shoulders pulled her back quickly so that, still on her knees, she came up against his legs and now she dared peer between her fingers. There was an opening. The stone slab stood ajar, not open all the way, and somehow in spite of the light in this valley there was utter dark beyond.

"They seek that which there is to be found!" Wittle also on her knees crowded closer. "We have come to what was lost and is now found!"

She held out her hand, passing it through the glow of the two stones and that which was hers loosed itself from its anchorage and fell into her grasp. Reluctantly Kelsie followed her action and once more held the gem, dangling from its broken chain.

If the slit was meant to be a door time had cemented it nearly closed and all three of them tugging together could not bring it open but a fraction more. Wittle at last scraped her way through between the edge of that slab and the frame on which it was set. Once more Kelsie's stone had lifted outward and was in a straight line pointing to the same slit. Nor, she was sure, would it allow her now to step aside. Her body, her feet, moved by another will and, though she longed to hold to that door and allow the chain to go from her with its perilous burden, she again had no chance, her fingers would not unhook from the links.

In Wittle's wake she edged through and, hearing the scrape of metal against stone, knew that Yonan was following. Ahead she saw the sparkling motes and with them the edge of the witch's gray robe but whither they walked she could not tell. Save that there was more of the icy chill she had long ago come to associate with the Dark and the places it haunted.

She smelled earth and stone and there was something else—a feeling that the three of them were not alone—that there was a thing which watched them, not with menace, nor welcome, good will nor ill, but in a kind of dulled awakening.

Wittle's figure suddenly arose and then Kelsie came to the first of a rough-hewn stairs and followed. Though both the jewels were alight, their outer expansion of radiance appeared confined by the dark showing nothing of the walls of this passage or what lay ahead. They came into another passage twin to the one on the level below but at its far end was the gleam of light which was not born of the gems but of the day itself.

They came out on a broad ledge to look down upon a stretch of country which had the appearance of utter desolation. At first Kelsie thought they were above a forest where the trees had been denuded of branches and leaves and only the upstanding trunks left like rows of shattered teeth. Then she realized that these were instead pillars of pitted stone, though there were no signs of what kind of a roof they had once supported—just the gray-white line of rounded columns.

From the ledge a long stairway of badly eroded steps formed an unprotected descent against the side of the cliff and Wittle was already on the first steps of that, headed confidently downward. Kelsie had no recourse but to follow, for the gem in her hand turned and pointed in the direction of the strange ruin below.

That filled completely a valley of some size and triangular shape. They were in the narrow end of the triangle. Kelsie could guess that what had once been erected here was of great importance in its day—temple, palace, fortress, whatever it had been.

They passed from the steps directly onto a pavement in which the columns were rooted. It was not the universal gray of the pillars but a blue which was nearly green—so at a distance one might even believe that it was a stretch of turf. This in turn was patterned in a brighter blue with signs or symbols which formed intricate arabesques under their feet, though here and there wind-driven patches of soil had blown in to cover the lines. There were no marks in such dust, no sign that any had been here before them through long quiet years.

Again Kelsie found no trace of that Dark which chilled body and spirit. Nor in fact anything but the vague impression that something very deeply asleep was waking at their coming, and, had she had the power of controlling her own body, she would have raced back up those stairs and out through the passage to a world more normal than this.

If she had suspicions, Wittle did not share them. Instead the witch marched forward with a rapt expression of expectation on her face. Thus they paraded down one of the aisles between columns, Wittle in advance, Kelsie on her heels, Yonan bringing up the rear. He kept his sword unsheathed and ready—either because he had come to depend upon the Quan iron in the hilt or because he actually feared that they would meet active opposition sooner or later.

Between the columns they could see the walls of the valley gradually opening out wider and wider, the pillars arranged so that one could be sure that this erection had covered the whole of the valley floor at one time. Unlike the building in which the monster dwelled there was no vibration, no sense of any life save their own. Not until they were well away from the place where they had entered the forest of stone trees.

One of the drifts of soil which had entered here and there to carpet over the blue stone lay across their path. Wittle showed no intention of halting but Yonan pushed beside Kelsie and actually caught at the wide

sleeve of the witch's robe, bringing her to a sudden stop. With his sword
the warrior pointed to that stretch of earth.

Pressed deeply into its surface were tracks. Kelsie was sure that the
most clear, which overlaid others mingled before, were those of a bare
foot that looked human. Wittle tried to free herself from Yonan's hold
with a sharp pull. Her mask of expectancy cracked and it was with fiery
anger she looked to him.

"What do you?" Her harsh voice scaled up and awoke echoes as if
behind a myriad of those columns stood other Wittles to add their
demands to hers.

"Look!" Again he indicated the tracks. "These are fresh—see where
the soil yet crumbles into the impression. We are not alone here, Lady.
Would you march to a meeting and take no heed of what may await us
ahead?"

She gestured to the aisle before her. "Do you see aught to dispute us
here, warrior? I say again—try not to deal with what no man may
understand!"

"Perhaps we understand more than you would allow us, Witch," he
said with a spark of anger in his reply. "Did you not agree that we may
have been allowed to escape so that we might be traced to that which you
revere so mightily—a source of the true power? If some trap has been laid
ahead we shall be the better for suspecting it."

She had cupped her stone in her two hands and now held it up to
breathe upon it. Her lips moved but they could not hear what she said—a
ritual, Kelsie suspected. The gem flared higher and then its radiance,
which had been growing as they marched forward, disappeared. It looked
to the girl as if instead of a jewel Wittle held a palm full of water and was
brooding over it.

There was change in her own stone also and she hastened to examine
it. Though the beam it had given off so far had been white with a tinge of
blue now it became fully blue—as clear and welcome as a fair day in
midsummer, cloudless and promising a fine day. Then a shadow crossed it
and she saw as plainly as if she stood before them the form of the wildcat,
her two kittens, and the snow cubling she had adopted. They lay in the
warm sun on a rock, the cat nursing all three of her family, her eyes half
closed in her own contentment. But, even as Kelsie watched those eyes
opened and were raised, as if the animal saw her in this place and time.
Then the picture shivered and was gone.

Cat? What had the wildcat to do with her here and now. She remembered that the stone she held had not been a direct gift from the dying
witch but had come through the cat. And—she looked down at that foot-
printed reach of soil on the floor. Yes! Now that she looked carefully she

could see those other tracks—the sign of one of the feline family cross-ing beneath the barefooted prints. Cat—she had never seen any in this valley save the one who had brought this whole adventure on her. Famil-iars—the old stories from her own world of how cats had consorted with those deemed witches in the past. What had cats to do with this place here and now?

Wittle looked up from her own jewel. "There is no trace of the Dark here!" she exclaimed.

"And of the Light?" Yonan persisted.

The witch hesitated as if she weighed truth against falsehood in order to gain her own ends. Then she admitted reluctantly:

"Nor of that either."

"But of power?" he persisted. She gave him a look of true hatred.

"There is power—power can exist without Dark or Light." Kelsie thought Wittle spoke as if to reassure herself. "Many were the adepts who drew upon neither but strove for pure knowledge alone. Our records speak of such. We may now be approachng a place where such neutral power can be tapped. If we reach there," her eyes glistened and there was a small bubble of saliva at one corner of her thin-lipped mouth, "then we can claim it for the Light. If the Dark reaches it first then—"

"Then you would say all is lost? But have you any thought as to what has already sought it according to this trail?" For the second time he pointed his sword to the tracks.

She leaned over that stretch of soil and deliberately allowed her jewel to swing low, nearly touching the disturbed earth. There was no change in its color now, and it halted on the outward swing, still pointing to what-ever lay ahead of them.

She favored Yonan with a malicious smile. "Do you mark this, war-rior? There is no harm."

He did not sheath his sword but met her eye to eye. "I do not question any power, Witch—yours or those of the Dark we have left behind. But mark this, you may be intruding upon something which even all the learn-ing in Lormt does not now hold. It is best to go wary—"

"Do you go wary!" she snapped. "What man can know unless he is shown—as you will be shown when the time comes!"

And she deliberately stepped on the barefooted track as she started on.

16

The rows of columns stopped abruptly. Though on the other side of the deep gap now facing them, Kelsie saw more continuing for stiff, endless miles. However, there was no bridge. Wittle, who had been so intent on their journey that she had watched her jewel far more than she had watched her footing, teetered on the brink of a drop until Yonan swept her back.

They stood together then looking down into another world, or was it the same they had known and they had soared above it? Were they now so mighty of body, so long of sight that they were giants who could cross a land with three or four crushing strides? For what they saw below was a miniature landscape, and a second later Yonan was on his knees hanging over the edge.

"The Valley!" he cried out, "and the mountains of the west— Estcarp . . . Escore!"

The witch swung her stone or it was being swung for her. Her eyes were piercingly bright in her narrow face. "Lormt . . . Es—"

It was indeed a country in miniature. There were mountains raised herein which, seen this way, equaled peaks, there were flowing rivers, and lakes, and the bold stand of keeps and villages, a city or two—forests and glades, plains and highlands. There were circles of upstanding stones and other markings raised by the power of men—or more than men. Yet all of this seemed to center about one huge building in the center of the miniature landscape, a building which was roofless, open to the sky and which might be the one they stood within. Therein was another hollow and in it another miniature world yet smaller, and in that another columned place and a third road.

Kelsie shook her head to cure her dizziness. All this was like one of those confusing paintings in which there was a second painting and inside of that another and so on until there was a final dot too small to distinguish clearly. Thinking that, she looked up into the light of early day to see if there *were* walls about them and if they were, in turn, part of a larger world.

Both Wittle's jewel and her own had swung out over that small world and now jerked against the hold kept upon them. They might live and move by a purpose beyond human reckoning. Kelsie loosed hers. It sped out across the miniature world until it hung above that second columned temple, over the second miniature world, and up toward it lanced a gleam of light from the center of that world. The jewel became like a sun burning with such brilliance that Kelsie was forced to shade her eyes. Wittle, through carelessness or desire, had loosed her stone also and it was winging its way toward the same place. There was a shattering, a brilliant light which appeared, not in the miniature of their world, but over their own heads. Then fell a rain of slivered crystal, each piece rainbow bright about them. Though none fell on them or did them harm.

Yet there was also a ringing, a trilling, as of crystal bits set swinging against each other in the breeze. It was a singing which began in high joyfulness but which declined, as Kelsie listened raptly to the music, to more somber notes. Also now there were patches of shadow which flowed across the small world. Here and there it was dark where there had been light and the dark grew wider and thicker. Until perhaps a third of the small world was enshadowed. While more and more somber grew the crystal music.

Kelsie found herself stretching forth her hands as if to sweep away the nearest of those shadows, to awaken once more the brilliant light. She discovered that she could not distinguish her crystal from that which had come from Wittle's hold, for they spun together in a ball, fighting the shadows with the sparkling light they threw. Their light completely held that second miniature world free of the dark, though Kelsie knew as well as if she could see it that the shadows attempted to override that world also.

Wittle was on her knees and from her lips poured words in rhythm which could only be a spell or a song. While Kelsie found herself also singing in notes which fitted the tinkling of the crystal:

> "Light to Dark,
> Dark to light
> After Day comes the night
> After night the morning clear
> Hope rises always from all fear!"

She saw Wittle hold out her hands to summon back her jewel but it did not come. Tears she had never expected to see the witch shed ran from her eyes down to soak the bosom of her gray robe.

Kelsie also knew a sense of loss so great that it darkened for her all the wonder which she watched. Her singing dwindled to a sob and then another. But she did not reach for that which she had never wanted but which had become a part of her.

Now that battlefield between Light and Dark became more vividly defined, more broken, cutting one side of the country below from another. The darker bits grew darker. Yet the jewels which formed the light of that world continued to spin. Where their sparks fell the Dark retreated. Though, as they spun also, villages were deserted and fell into ruin, the very shape of the country changed. Mountains danced to the somber sounds of the crystal and were raised and twisted. Only here and there did the light hold bright and clear.

Kelsie knew that what she looked upon had happened and this had been the fate of this land. But though it changed she saw no people—only the growth and the ebb of the jewel light. Now that light was growing again as if the faster it whirled the more power it was drawing toward it.

She took heart as she saw one shadow fade, another break suddenly into bits as if it were tangible and could be so handled.

Then—

Out from the columns on the other side of this world-in-the-small came a beam of fierce red to strike full upon the whirling crystals of the jewels. Their clear light clouded—what was white and gold became red and darkened. The shadows on the surface of the world took heart, gathered, spread, ate up more and more of the land. Kelsie cried out wretchedly for she knew that in loosing her gem here she had given an opening to the Dark which was avidly seizing upon it.

She leaned perilously over the edge of the miniature country and tried now to reach some part of her jewel, one of the flying ends of chain if that were possible. Only it was far beyond her touch. She heard Wittle give a great cry and saw her crumple up and lie, one arm swinging down to brush the top of one of the mountains below.

"To me!" Did Kelsie cry that aloud or only shape the call with her whole body? As she had done before, she willed her strength to the spinning jewel. It was not hers, it had never been hers by right, but it had served her before and now she was determined it should not vanish into darkness and defeat.

Into it she aimed her thought, all her will. She saw it spin as it had, she would hold to that picture in her mind no matter what happened. Spin it must—for if it faltered it would be gone, all the power within it to feed the Dark which would grow a hundredfold from such a feasting. She willed—and willed—

A hand dropped upon her shoulder and from that touch she greedily drew more strength. She only half saw, so intent was she upon the battle in the pit, that Yonan was between her and Wittle, that his right hand rested on her, his left was on the witch. She drew and from him came the energy and she willed—oh, how she willed. Yet one part of her, small and far withdrawn, wondered at what she did and how she knew what was to be done.

The red was an angry fire and more and more the clear light of the jewels was swallowed up. Yonan's hand was gone from her shoulder, she was no longer a part of that linkage which had given her the energy to go on fighting. She saw the warrior running, skirting the rim of that pit which held the miniature world. He was heading for the source of the red beam. That musical tinkling which had been a part of the meeting of the jewels was drowned out by a thumping which reminded her of the vibration in the mountainous monster, of the drums of the Thas. Still she struggled to hold alive her jewel, to feed it with her will.

Wittle stirred, levered herself up with her hands. Her face was drawn and she looked as if dozens of years had racked her during the space while she had lain there. But once more her lips were moving soundlessly and Kelsie believed that she was reciting the ritual which was a part of her witch training.

There came a distant shouting, the clashing of arms. Yonan—he must have won to the enemy! Though Kelsie thought there was little he could do there. Then a shout which overran the drum sound—

"Glydys—Ninutra!"

While Wittle, now on her knees, cried out:

"By the will of Langue, by the power of Thresees, by the memory of Janderoth!"

Those they called upon or evoked had no meaning for Kelsie—she had only that determination not to yield. Again that small part of her wondered why it was so important that she win. What was this world to her? Yet the rest of her quivered and shrank as she watched the shadow spread.

But was it spreading? She was sure that a finger of the dark which had been aimed across one corner to reach a cape stretching out into a strange sea was withdrawing. From that cape itself, there roused a spark of fire which burned blue. There was another blue fire burning also, closer to her, and its flame was clear. The twin suns which were the jewels spun on and the blood-red haze about them was fading a little.

Kelsie concentrated on that and tried to put out of her mind those sounds of battle which came from the other side of the world basin. These people called upon their gods, their forms of power. What had she to call upon save what was in her?

She snarled without knowing that her lips shaped that sound, there was anger deep within her, an anger she did not understand but which heated her as had that first flash of protest which had led to her coming through the gate. Just as she would not witness the death of an animal, so now she refused to witness the death of a world. For the miniature land beneath had become as real to her now as what lay outside the columns of stone.

NO! She did not shout any petition of gods nor battle cries, she just poured in her will. Perhaps Wittle did that also, for now the gems spun so fast that they formed a single ball of fire. The red beam lapped around it but it could not cut off that burst of radiance, subdue it.

The shouting came from her right now. Yonan might be forced back by a superior force. Yet the red beam began to pulsate, its strength interrupted and broken from time to time. There—when it died next—will—use the will! And so she did.

That red beam no longer struck at the jewels, it strove to aim straight down at the miniature world—its force seeking out that spark of blue which was on the sea—and the other on the land. The jewels whirled into dazzling brilliance and sparks flowed and sprang from their action. This patterned out across the world, and where they struck new blue flames arose. The shadows flinched back from those, and began to dart here and there striving to douse each spark before it started a new fire burning.

A clashing of swords. Kelsie, torn from her concentration, looked to her right. Yonan was being forced back right enough. Engaging him were two manlike figures and a creature which might have been out of a nightmare. Yet he parried and thrust as if he had erected such a wall of steel many times before.

"The jewel—hold—the jewel!" Wittle had broken her chant and was close to the girl, raking painfully down Kelsie's arm with crooked fingers.

Yes—the jewel. She looked back to the battle over the basin world. And her folly brought a gasp from her. For one of the gems was spinning slower and slower, there were no more sparks cast off to start those alternate fires on the ground below. The red beam of light no longer strove to battle the jewels and their sparks, instead it raised, struck straight at Wittle, at her.

It was like being caught within a wave of liquid filth. All that was cruel, wrong, seedlings of evil in her own nature answered that red beam. Now Kelsie had to fight—not that—but what lay within herself. All the small meannesses which she had ever been capable of and had yielded to arose in her memory, all her failures and self-doubts near overwhelmed her. What was she doing here risking her life and perhaps more than mere physical life, in this battle? She had no reason to defend a world into which she was not born, with which she had no ties. No, that jewel she had cherished belonged to a dead woman, a woman who had suffered the same penalty for her foolhardiness that Kelsie was about to have visited on her.

She had no powers such as Wittle and all the rest had prated of ever since she had arrived here. What was she trying to do?

That small part of her which had doubted and scoffed throughout all the days and nights she had traveled thrust aside barriers in her mind and came to her. She need only rise, let go her tenuous tie with the jewel, and she could walk out of here in freedom—no, in more than freedom, for those of the other side offered gifts—

Their gifts! Perhaps they might have won her but they went too far and showed her their bribes. If she did nothing here which was to their harm why should they offer more than to let her withdraw from the field? She shook her head against their mind pictures, no longer subtle—no longer dealing with her own thoughts and fears. She saw images slipping by so fast she could hardly seize upon any of the individual pictures. Did she want to rule—be sure there would be a throne for her. Did she want treasures—a wavery picture of such floated there. Did she want revenge— cruel and bloody pictures flashed by. Did she want this world before her to play with, to change to her fancy, to hold its whole destiny—to—

Her will arose again and fastened upon the slower spinning jewel. She was no witch, this power had been lent her second-hand. But neither did she want what had been offered her. Will it—will the end of that other—that which was the red flame now ringing her about, its heat reaching for the seeds of her anger and striving to turn them toward its own goal.

She did not know if similar temptations had been thrown at Wittle, though she was sure that she had seen the other jewel also falter for an instant or two. But the witch had been long lessoned in what she did. Per- haps those who spun that web had built it for the people of this world, and the very fact that Kelsie was not born of it was not a weakness but a strength.

The gems spun on as the red beam closed around both women. It was more than a mind goad now; heat came from it searing her flesh as if she were thrust into a fire. And that pain was the final key which set Kelsie free of any temptation which might have moved her. She set her teeth and held to the jewel, concentrating upon it with all her might. Power as Wit- tle understood it she might not have. But perhaps that which she had brought with her was as solid and steadfast in its own way.

The spin no longer faltered but grew swifter and the sparks it once more flung off were brighter. Down in the basin world shadows retreated. Here and there a fresh blue glow answered from newly-freed land. She felt the concentration of the red fire building up and knew that while it still tried to disrupt the power of the jewels it was now also being bent toward her in a last frenzy of battle. She could have screamed under the lash of that heated beam but she did not—to her own growing wonder she held. Kelsie saw Wittle begin to lever herself up from the stone, her gaunt face turned toward the spinning gems.

Suddenly, instead of trying only to hold to her own, Kelsie tried to fight back—to actually aim those sparks of cleansing light to the portions of the basin where the darkest of the shadows clung in a noisome and threatening mist. The blue glows elsewhere grew stronger, spread. There! Exultation filled her—she had actually placed a spark where she willed and, though it was dimmed by the dark, it was not forced into oblivion. It remained. There came another not far away.

"Ninutra!" Through the concentration which held her she held her control though Yonan was being forced back toward them. There were crumpled forms, both human and monstrous, marking the path of his retreat, and blood dripped from sheared mail on his own side. But still he was buying them time. Time for what? How long could they hold their jewels and defeat the semblance of the dark? No—any doubt weakened her control—she must concentrate on what spun out there above the basin land.

The red haze thickened. Yonan was hidden from her; even Wittle was only a shadow within the bloody fog. But that could not hide the flash of the jewels nor the fact that the shadows were in retreat from that light.

"Die then!"

The threat may only have touched her mind, spun out of the fog, but it was like a shout to awaken echoes from her very bones. In an instant the red beam loosened its struggle with the jewels, was shot straight to where she and Wittle carried on their part of this strange duel.

"Die!"

She was gasping for clean air, her lungs filled instead with thick flaming gas. Yet that was not true, another part of her proclaimed. This was the last weapon of the shadow—and where was her weapon—out there!

She held to her thought of the jewel, unable to see it now that the thick haze wrapped her round. Hold—only hold—

Past her will there worked another order which she could not contain and defeat. Fight! Aim the jewel not toward the land she had guarded but down the beam of the red curtain—strike so a blow of her own. The gem answered to that impulse. No longer did it spin and weave its own kind of protection above the world in miniature—instead it wavered on its axes and then settled into a sharp pattern of its own, speeding down the ray of red which formed a guide. It hurled its way as she might have thrown a stone full force. From it came a whining note, rising ever higher and higher, until she could no longer hear it, only feel it throughout her body.

But Wittle's jewel held in place though it threw off no more of the life inducing sparks and the shadows began to gather once again. On sped the star which was Kelsie's borrowed stone. There was no sight of it by eye anymore; only in her mind could she follow its furious pace. Around her the fierce lash of the heat was beginning to fail—whoever had raised that was indrawing all strengths, preparing for a final battle. She felt no lack of confidence. Instead a fierce pride and exultation. As if by carrying battle to the enemy she had doomed her own cause.

"Ninutra!" Again came Yonan's war cry out of the ruddy dusk, seeming farther away. Kelsie crouched, her whole sense of will and strength concentrated on the disappearing jewel.

She had a vision which dazzled even her open eyes, causing her to blink. There was a single figure on the other side of the basin. She could not see it clearly, but she had a mind picture of a gleaming white body twisting and turning as if in some strange formal dance. From each footfall on the stone there came a new puff of red to fit itself into the stream of the beam. But the jewel had reached there and come to hang over the dancer's head.

Kelsie threw forth in that moment all her strength of will. The jewel steadied, began to spin as it had above the land in the basin. Now she could mind see it, now she could not as another blast of red fumes arose. But she sensed something else—that the dancer had not expected this, that it must take time to recall the strength of the beam in self-defense. That time must not be allowed. As she had struck sparks by will from the star in the basin, so Kelsie now tried to gain the same from the spin of the jewel in that place the Shadow's servant believed safe. Round—so! Round again!

She felt as if the beam were searing her to her very bones yet there was that in her which would not recall the miniature sun which now fought her battle beyond the reach of eyesight. Turn—spark—spark! There!

A first speck of light broke from that encircling brilliance about the jewel. The flying feet of the dancer were fashioning a new pattern, one which must not be allowed to become a form. There—another spark and the dancer faltered for a single instant, less than a breath out of time. But faltered it had! Now!

With all the strength she could summon up Kelsie aimed her second blow. And perhaps her last. She was so wrapped up in the haze that she felt she was completely encased from the real world, entrapped in this torment. Perhaps the mind picture she held to was also an illusion and she was being tricked.

There was a tremor down the beam which closed her in so. And then a second one. She could breathe without those torturing rasps for throat and lungs. Her spirit arose. Yes! The dancer was not so sure of the pattern now—there were sparks—not as great as those which the jewel had flung into the basin world but enough to cut through the web the other wove, to loosen here and there some portion of the intended design. Now!

Kelsie threw herself to the left, rolled over the rock until her body thudded against that of Wittle. One hand lashed out and tightened about the witch's bony shoulder.

"Give me power!" Kelsie may not have shouted that cry but it rang through her body. Perhaps the very suddenness of it made Wittle obey. Through her hand upon the other came a surge of strength and in the girl's mind the jewel began a wider swing, following the dancer in and out, emitting a shower of sparks which struck downward.

Kelsie felt as if she were swelling through her own body—that what she gathered in from Wittle was too great to be held or she herself would be consumed—and she fought to channel it in her mind—aim it toward that other world weapon she could not see.

The red curtain enclosing the two of them began to diffuse; she could see the witch now—though Wittle had not turned her head nor made any gesture to suggest that she saw Kelsie. Wittle's gaze strained instead out over the basin. There, very dim in the red of the slowly disrupting beam was her own jewel—still suspended in the air but no longer spinning so swiftly, rather wobbling as if what supported it was nearly gone.

But Kelsie had no mind for that—the battle moved across and they must defeat the dancer not the again growing shadows over the smaller world.

"Release—send!" demanded the girl. "Give strength—"

She could still feel the inflow from her hold upon the witch but it was lessening. Her mind picture of the dancer grew hazier and hazier until she could not be sure that that other existed at all, that she had not been drawn into a trap which had finished both the jewels and left the basin world open to the Dark.

17

There was dark, a fume filled, suffocating darkness and in that still moved the dancer though the lightsome patter of feet had become a desperate shuffle. Then—nothing—

Kelsie opened her eyes. She lay by the edge of the basin and near her was a heap of travel-stained gray which would only be Wittle. From far overhead came the faint crystalline music she had first heard when the jewels had been loosed over the miniature world. With an effort she turned her head, edged toward the verge of the basin. The red wave was gone and afar there twisted and turned a single jewel—Wittle's, she thought. Her hand sought her own breast somehow hoping that she had not lost what had seemed to be a burden she had never asked to carry but which had become a part of her.

"Yonan?" she called in a voice which sounded cracked from the ordeal of the heat. There was no answer. She got to her knee then and started to search toward where she had had the single sight of him during the battle. There were bodies there—two of them—one in mail.

Somehow she got to her feet and lurched in that direction. There was an emptiness about her as if something had withdrawn or been banished from that world within a world. Not only her jewel, she thought.

Past those bodies she tottered, stooping to make sure that he in the mail was not the Valley warrior. But it was a dark, cruel face which met her gaze. She skirted well by the monster having no desire to see it the closer.

There were splashes of blood on the stones and she kept to that trail. Where her jewel had gone, that was where she must go also. Though she already knew that she had no talisman, no weapon she could now claim.

A third body mail clad, lying face down. She made herself stoop and lift the head, turn it to look upon more strange features. Where was Yonan? She lifted her voice and called aloud his name which came in echoes back from the world of the basin. On she plodded, now working her way from the support of one pillar to that of the next. More blood, a hacked body of a monster thing all hair and talons. Then she could see a little ahead.

Someone sat, back to a column, head fallen forward on his breast.

"Yonan!" she pushed away from the pillar she had just embraced and stumbled on. There was blackened stone here, and the stench of fire-seared flesh. Yet she was sure she had seen a movement in the one who was seated. She had almost reached his side when she saw that other. Crumpled as if all strength of body had been withdrawn in a single instant lay a child!

Nausea arose in Kelsie. Among the bodies, half seared, half flame eaten, those white limbs were intact with no sign of the fire which must have exploded here.

The man by the pillar turned his head slowly. Yonan! She had found him in truth. His sword, the blade snapped off raggedly a handsbreadth from the point, lay beside his empty hand. In the hilt the Quan iron was dulled, spotted black like a fruit in decay.

He raised his head a little to look at her. For the first time she saw a slow smile move his lips, striking years from his somber face.

"You are hurt?" She stood over him uncertainly, knowing nothing of the healing arts for men, only those which she had used with animals. But now she knelt and strove to free him from the blood-stained mail to get at the wound in his side.

With fumbling fingers he tried to help her. Then she uncovered a gaping slit in his flesh which bled sluggishly. From her shift she tore a strip and bandaged him as best she could, using the very last of the powdered illbane which had clung to the inner seams of his own belt wallet to spread upon the stout cloth before she wound it about him.

He lay passive under her hands now, his eyes closed, that curious youth which had touched him earlier all the more plain, so that she could no longer see him as the self-contained scout who had led and protected them, but only a young man who had fought with raw courage to advance a quest which had only been half-possible from the first.

When she had made him as comfortable as she could, curiosity, a fearful and half-ashamed curiosity, brought her to the white figure who lay so still. A fair body of a very young girl, dark hair streaming to conceal her face. Her bare feet so small—surely matching the track they had seen before. Still there was something about her— Was this the dancer who had sought to make an end to the jewels—to them?

Though she shrank from it she made herself uncover the face of the dead, lifting away a heavy strand of the hair. Beauty, yes, and yet with a subtle marking of evil, though Kelsie did not know how or why she judged that. There was the tinkle of crystal and, peering more closely, she saw that on the arm, on the white skin of the dead, was a shifting of small bits of crystal—one or two still alight with a faint bluish glow. The jewel! Again Kelsie knew a pain of loss. Never hers, yet she had borne it and dared to use it. And it had been her final burst of will which had killed this child, brought an end to a battle and—what else had it done?

She went to the rim of the basin and looked down.

Wittle's jewel still spun, slowly, but from it emitted sparks of blue which fell to the world and she saw that the shadows had not altogether been banished but had withdrawn into somber pools of dark here and there and seemed fewer and smaller.

Wittle had come to find power. In a manner it had found her and made use of her—as well as of Kelsie. What they had accomplished here the girl could not understand—maybe it would take an adept such as the people so often spoke of to measure what had been done and whether for good or ill.

"It was an eftan." Yonan spoke for the first time as she turned away from the inner world. "They had suborned an eftan to their purposes."

"An eftan?"

"An air elemental," he explained. "They who can dance up a storm if they wish. And this one danced on the pattern set there—" He pointed to the pavement which was so blackened and scarred around which lay the bodies of the dead save for her who rested inside.

Rested inside?

There was a faint line or two still to be seen on the stone. But— Kelsie put both her hands to her mouth and held back a scream. The white body—it was dissolving—tendrils of whitish smoke from a fire were curling from beneath it. Now she saw the dark disappear, a blast of chill—as from the edge of a mountain snowfield spread outward as the smoke gathered into a long finger. She shrank back a step or two waiting for that ice to thrust at her—to freeze her where the others had burnt from the fire.

But around the white there was a tinge of blue and the smoke arose straight up into the sky above the roofless columns, streaking outward like a thing suddenly released from captivity. Then it was gone and all that lay there was the tiny shreds of crystal.

"What—?" she found it hard to frame proper words. Surely the dancer had died.

"Back to its own place," Yonan said and grimaced, his hand going to his side. "Maybe it was spell-held to what it did here and is now free. Those of its kind seldom mix in the affairs of men—or of demons—" And he glanced at one of the fire-scorched bodies which lay near him.

"Will it come back?" she demanded. "The jewel—it is broken."

"I do not think we shall see that weapon again," he replied, "which does not mean that they will not try other ways." And his grimace grew as he reached for his broken sword, looking from the break to the discolored Quan iron. "We seem to be singularly weaponless now, my lady."

"There is Wittle's jewel—"

"If it still answers her; if she wishes it so—" he did not sound very confident.

"Can you walk?" Her own question sounded harsh and demanding. But she did not want to leave the witch alone. To have their mismatched party all together was her object for the present.

"I am not to be counted out yet, Lady," he made answer and struggled to get arms under him to lever himself up. She was quick to aid. At his gesture she sheathed what was left of his sword and slung the battered coat of mail over her shoulder, placed her arm about him so that they made a slow journey back around the edge of the basin, moving from one pillar to the next and halting many times when she saw the drops of sweat on his forehead, the set of his mouth, as if the last thing he would ask was a slower pace or perhaps a longer rest.

Before they reached her Kelsie heard Wittle's voice. The witch was singing, hoarsely and with a crack in the rhythm of her words. She sat, they could see, on the very edge of the basin, not looking down at the land beneath her but rather out at the slow spinning jewel. And as she so sang she reached out her hands as if to cup it again and hold it unharmed against all comers. There was an avid hunger in her face, the eyes which watched the distant jewel were as deep sunken in her head as if she had been fever-ill for a long time. She paused in her song now and then to rub her forehead with her hands, pressing her fingers on her eyes as if to clear away some film to enable her to see what she wanted to see—that which was a part of her winging its way back into her hold.

Yet the jewel did not pause in its turning, nor change a fraction of its stance. It was playing a strange new sun to the basin world, one seemingly as fixed as might be an actual fire globe in Escore's own sky, the warmth of which reached them now between the pillars.

"Wittle," Kelsie released Yonan against the nearest column and went to put her hands on the witch's bent shoulders. "Wittle!"

She might have been calling now upon the wind or upon that tongue of frosty air which had formed the dancer who had so nearly put an end not only to them but also the world in the basin.

"Wittle!"

The witch swept out one arm, catching Kelsie at thigh height nearly spilling her into the basin. Looking down and out over the miniature world Kelsie could see that there was still a fleeing of shadow, a rain of sparks sending that into nothingness here and there.

"She is one with her jewel," Yonan's voice behind her sounded as if from a distance. "She will be one with it to the end."

"But I—that other jewel—" protested Kelsie.

"You are no witch, at least not one of Estcarp where the power is one with the person. If she recalls her jewel, then she is safe. But if it comes not to her urging—"

"We must get away!" Kelsie had thrown off most of the spell which had been woven about her. With the gem she had carried now nothing but splinters, she felt oddly naked, weaponless, prey to be easily hunted down. And she could not believe that they had indeed defeated that which had striven to destroy not only them but all that lay in the basin.

Now she looked and saw the Valley—of that she was sure. And there were other places where the blue of the Light promised comfort and safety. She began to study the miniature land carefully to see where was the nearest of those islands of true safety. The place of columns as it was in the basin seemed unduly large in comparison with the rest of the countryside. And to the north of that was one of the darkest blots of shadow—though that had been driven back in upon itself she was sure. Originally it had reached out to touch upon the place of pillars. But if she could not rouse Wittle from her trance, nor support Yonan for long, then how could she—

"Get away?" her own earlier words repeated back to her. "Think you we are now meant to get away?" Yonan's voice was low and very tired. She glanced at him quickly. He had slumped farther down against the pillar and now lay there, all color faded from his face so that his weather tan looked gray and dulling.

Kelsie's chin came up and she looked at him straightly. "So far we have won—"

"One battle in a war," he answered her slowly and closed his eyes. Wittle, meanwhile, regarded nothing but the spinning jewel to which her hands still stretched, her crooning now reduced to a hoarse whisper. Kelsie looked out over the bowl. Her stubbornness would not allow her to accept the defeat which seemed to have fallen on Yonan, the entranced state of the witch. She settled down on the rim of the basin and began a survey threaded from the place of columns back toward the Valley. That they would come again to any great source of power such as Wittle sought she did not believe. The compulsion which had carried her on and on to this very place was gone with her—or Roylane's jewel. There was retreat which could save them. If they left the columns here and went so—a little farther west—there was a river and she could trace there to within a short distance of the Valley. Surely once they were back into patrolled territory they would be found, taken back.

"Wittle," she moved along until she knelt by the witch again and now she took her by the shoulders and shook her so hard the woman's head flopped back and forth on her shoulders— "Wittle!"

The dark eyes stared through her as if she were as bodiless as smoke. Nothing she could do would rouse the witch from her need and longing for the jewel. But Kelsie was not through. Now she slapped that lean face hard, on one cheek and then the other so that the print of her hand began to show in reddened patches.

This time there was a flicker in the eyes, the straight stare was broken.

"Wittle!" Under her hands the witch's body twisted as the woman attempted to see beyond Kelsie to the spinning jewel. Now the sparks from that had become fewer and fewer, only a handful were spilled to hunt the shadows out of the corners in which they lay.

"Wittle, they will be hunting us. We must go."

"By Hofer and Tem, by the ten lights, and the nine cups, the six faggots and the three fires—" Her words were understandable but they made no sense to the girl. Wittle raised a hand and drove it finger straight for Kelsie's face, aiming at her eyes. The girl ducked and lost her hold on the witch.

Wittle arose then, the strength of her body such that she had no trouble in tearing away from Kelsie. She took two steps forward, over the edge of the basin.

Kelsie screamed, Wittle was gone. She might have stepped through a door when she had taken that stride forward. There was no sign of her body crashing on the mountains of that other world. At the same time the jewel picked up speed where it hung in the air, whirled twice as fast, threw off a greater volume of sparks. It might have been that Wittle's act had revived it.

"She—she's gone!" Kelsie swept her hand forward where moments earlier the witch had stood. Nothing but air, not even the traces of something such as the eftan had given off in its going.

"Her power was her—" Yonan said, in a tired, fading voice. "When it would not come to her, then she went to it. She has found what she came for—the final consuming power."

As if in answer to his comment the jewel was indeed ablaze—almost as bright as it had been when Kelsie's jewel had joined with it in splendor. The shadows—they were fleeing, racing back to certain dark places.

Even those, one after another, were vanishing to become spaces bare of the blots of evil which had held some of them for so long.

A source of greater power—that was what the witches of Estcarp had sought and that was what Wittle had found.

Kelsie turned to Yonan. That whirling ball of light out there was frightening. If her own jewel had endured would she, too, have been so drawn into it? Could she be influenced now by Wittle's?

She edged back from the basin.

"You were not sealed," Yonan's words meant little to her. She wanted nothing as much as to run down an aisle of those columns, to get out of this place. "You are not a witch out of Estcarp. The jewel came to you as a gift, not a weapon—"

"A gift," she repeated. Such a gift as no one would welcome— "Who would want such as that?" She gestured to the miniature sun the gem had become.

"Many," he returned shortly. There was a shadow across his face, not a reflection of evil but rather one of loss. "To each there are given gifts. Those which we cherish grow." His hand sought his sword belt, closed about the hilt of that broken blade. "I knew another who was offered much and claimed it. She walks now other roads, nor does she remember much of what was before, except as something which is far off and has no longer any connection with her. Glydys," his voice lingered over that name as if he would call its wearer to appear to them now.

But Kelsie was not interested in things of the past. She had retreated so that the rise of a pillar was between her and the whirling sun-stone. For she could not rid herself of the belief that if she remained directly in its light it could also draw her who had so long carried and used its fellow.

"Let us go!" she demanded of Yonan.

His smile was crooked. "Go indeed, Lady. Though I do not think that evil will hunt now. For me," he raised his hand in a small gesture which indicated his sprawling body, "I need two legs which will carry me."

He was right. For him to rise and retreat down that long way between columns would be perhaps impossible. If they went together they would continue to be exposed to what was here for a long time—maybe too long a time. Yet Kelsie could not take the first step which would take her away to leave him there alone.

"What shall we do?" he asked the question which hung in her own mind but which she would not allow herself to voice. "Why, it is simple, Lady. You go for help, I remain—"

"To face that again?" she waved toward the opposite side of the basin and the scorched dead which lay there. He might have been cut to pieces there had not her own jewel played a hand in the final battle. Final battle?

How could she judge that that had already passed? She thought of the hounds, the Sarn Riders, the dead monsters she had seen.

Nor could she believe that the single sun-gem would expend itself beyond the place where it now hung to protect either of them now.

"They have failed," Yonan answered. "Whatever they would have done here is ended. As long as that blazes they are driven back. For I think that this world below us is the mirror image of what surrounds us, and what Wittle has set in motion is for good instead of ill. No, get you gone, Lady—and bring help—"

Instead of answering him she deliberately made herself approach the rim of the basin once more and there stand to trace out what she was sure was the reflection of the Valley, noting the distances between that and the place of columns. With a horse they might have done it—but any horses hereabouts would be those fell beasts of the Riders. It might take her days and she had no surety of keeping to any road when she left here— especially one which led by the keep of the squatting monster.

The Valley. Yes, she could trace it from where she stood. It was . . . right there!

Out of it now arose something which was almost like the mist of the fleeing eftan. She fell back, her hands going uselessly to her breast where there was no longer a jewel to save or strike. There was a small sound of explosion as if the air itself had burst open and then a fierce snarling.

She was looking at the wildcat, the animal which had led her into the whole of this venture. Its lips were curled back showing its sharp fangs, its fur stood erect, and its curved tail was a stiff brush.

"You . . . come—"

Two words in her mind, quavering as if the animal labored mightily to make her understand. It padded back and forth between her and the basin rim. She understood well enough; it wanted her to follow Wittle, to leap out—or in—aiming her body at the mountains below. She rubbed her eyes sure that this was an illusion, that surely the wildcat was not here, that it was part of her memory playing tricks on her.

"So—that is the way of it?" Yonan's voice startled her so that she started and nearly touched the rim. He was crawling like a sadly wounded beast toward the opening in the floor. She tried to reach him, to grasp his body and hold him back, for it was plain that he was about to do just what the cat wished.

Only, as she took a step toward him, the cat flew at her, one paw up, the talons extended to their farthest limit. Those hit her thighs and she stumbled back. It was too late. Yonan had reached the ridge of the basin, with both hands gripping there he pulled himself forward, leaving a small trail of blood on the stone. Over he dragged himself and was gone!

She looked to the gem, awaiting another flare of energy. But that did not come. Instead she felt again the rake of claws as the cat sprang at her for the second time. She gave way—stumbled back and to her terror felt herself go over.

There was no interval of dark, no feeling of falling that she could ever afterward remember. She opened her eyes and above her was the brilliant tapestry of the roof of feathers. Back in the Valley! Had it been a dream—her journey? Or was this the dream—a nightmare brought on by her fall?

Paws landed on her breast. There were large eyes turned upon her. The wildcat! And above her was Dahaun's face, her eyes also large and mirroring concern.

"This," Kelsie got one elbow bent, had lifted herself so far from the low mat bed on which she lay, "this is the Valley—"

She had not made a question of that but it would seem that Dahaun took it so, for she nodded.

"This is the Valley."

What was the truth then? Was there a second Estcarp and Escore in a basin within a forgotten temple, if temple that was, or merely the appearance of it strong enough to draw those attuned to its home?

"Perhaps," Dahaun was thought reading again, and Kelsie did not resent it.

"Wittle—the jewel—" she said.

As Yonan before her the Lady of Green Silences answered that. "She has what she sought—power unlimited, though not as she expected to choose it. But already the Dark is withdrawing—in that she does what she dreamed to do."

"And I? Or what is your dream—think upon that, sister." Dahaun arose and was gone. Only the purring cat kneading the front of her faded and soiled jerkin remained.

"For you," Kelsie said, "it is easy—you want only safe shelter for you and your family. For me—what do I want?"

By the light it was early evening, she had come out of the Valley and none had spoken to her. It seemed that she was to be left alone until she decided—decided what? She was not even sure of that.

She found herself going arrow straight to the stones—those blue, shining stones. There were no hounds, no Rider now. She had had enough confidence in Dahaun's words not to fear this night and she walked briskly until the stones stood before her.

Kelsie stepped forward until she could lay one hand on either side of that gate she could not see, which might never open again.

"Is it back?"

Startled she looked over her shoulder. Simon Tregarth stood there. For the first time she saw him out of armor, wearing the green dress of the Valley, his head bare of any helm.

"Can it be?" she asked.

He shrugged. "I never tried. I have heard it said, no. But of that I have had no proof. Do you want to try it?"

She looked back at the gate and thought of what might lie beyond it. There was none to have worried about her, grieved for her, and none she grieved for either.

"I am no witch—the jewel is broken," she said slowly.

"True enough. But that all power is bound to a gem, in that belief, too, there is error. You might be more than you expect—here."

"Here." She turned her back to the gate and looked about her. There was a yowl and the cat sprang from the bushes beyond and made a hunter's flying leap upon something small which ran in the grass.

"I think," Kelsie said, "that it is here." She took one step and then two and then began to run back to the Valley.